# JONATHAN D. LAMBERT

# OF GEMS AND STONE

## BORNE BY BLOOD

### BOOK ONE

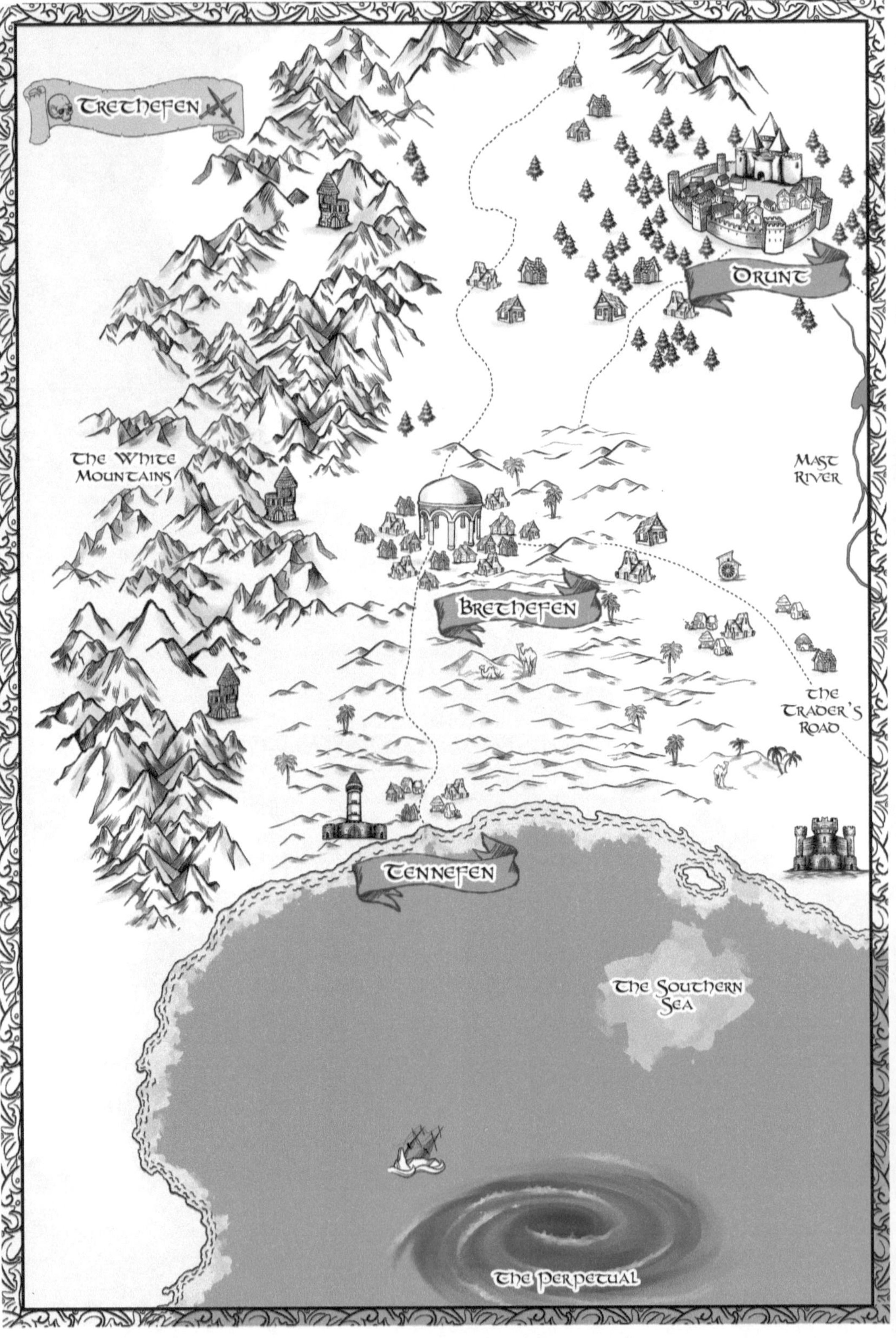

TRETHEFEN
DRUNT
THE WHITE MOUNTAINS
MAST RIVER
BRETHEFEN
THE TRADER'S ROAD
TENNEFEN
THE SOUTHERN SEA
THE PERPETUAL

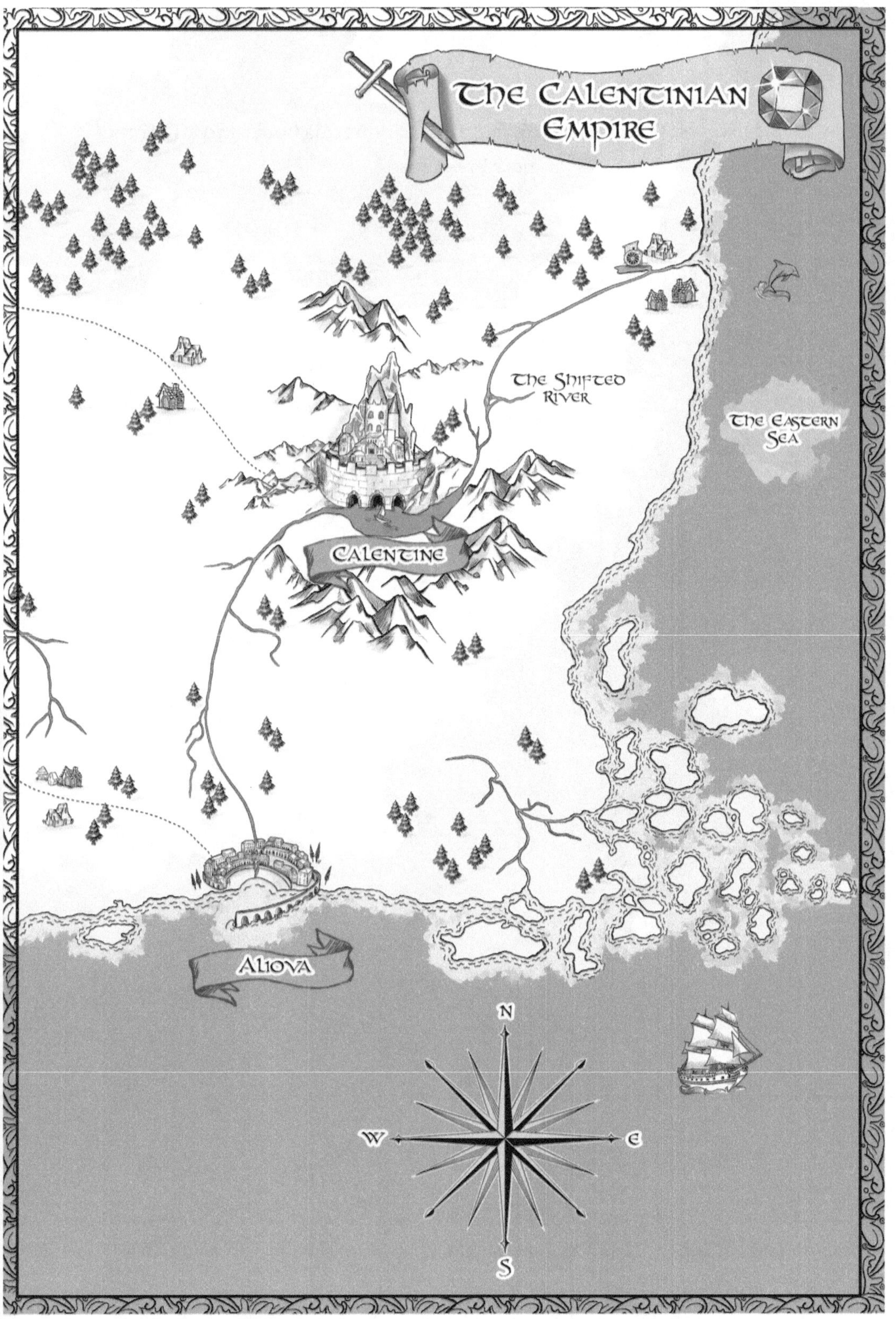

THE CALENTINIAN EMPIRE
THE SHIFTED RIVER
THE EASTERN SEA
CALENTINE
ALIOVA
N
W E
S

To Marlee,
who has listened to my ceaseless ramblings about this book, and still somehow loves me.

And to Jared,
who lent an ear whenever I was stuck, and whose immense imagination
sparks my own.

# PROLOGUE

Vestiges of the evening sun sailed behind the mountainous horizon on a breeze that cut with a chill. Protorus stood on the polished stone, the barren landscape surrounding him a reminder of what had been lost in this once lush plain. Even decay seemed wary of this hallowed site, splintered and charred trees lay scattered and unblemished from their many years in the elements. Not a fleck of green nor trickle of water suffused the ground's morbid gray.

Perhaps, one day, life would return here.

Or, perhaps, this land would remember the carnage wrought over the very spot Protorus now stood, and forever remain the desolate mausoleum that stretched into the distance. The distinct mixture of smoke, blood, and rage still burned his nostrils.

He was early, though as the agreed upon hour arrived, he was not surprised by the tardiness of the others. He himself had wavered on whether he could follow through with these orders, the last treatise of the decimating war that had claimed more than any generation since the Greats themselves.

As dusk saturated the land in red, another figure stepped to the rim of the wide stone circle. It was large enough that Protorus couldn't make out the features of the new arrival from where he stood, but there was little question as to who it was.

The fractal pattern of cadentite set into the enormous dais projected its steady glow up onto the newly arrived mage, casting odd shadows in the evening light. Stepping across the mosaic of candescent purple lines set into pitch black, the man with well decorated travel clothes and long hair that hung with a slight curl approached Protorus carrying a sense of gloom that was incongruous to his normally cheerful nature.

As he stepped up, Protorus almost wished the man would refrain from opening his mouth, if only to save him from the crass atrocities that often followed. He stayed patient—and quiet—however, as despite the man's tendencies, he was always there in Protorus's times of need.

"Protorus!" He could smell liquor on the man's breath. "I'd say good to see ya', but, frankly, I don't want to be here."

"Neither do I, Masini," Protorus replied quietly, standing tall before the shorter, more relaxed man.

"So, do you, uh, think any of the others are going to show?"

"It's their duty as much as it is ours."

"Pfft, 'duty.' These taint-nuzzlers only care that this is their last chance to take some vidut, where else are you going to get it in this damned wasteland? Place is drier than your grandmother in a whorehouse," Masini said, tapping his foot against a line of glowing stone. "I'm still willing to bet that some of them are going to try and go back."

"They would be executed. You, myself, and the others are all well aware the gate is being watched and guarded from the other side. We cannot disobey our directive."

"Yeah, I'd be watching it too, after all of this," Masini said with a wave. "Doesn't mean they won't try. Not seeing home again could be a powerful motivator in doing something incomprehensibly stupid."

"I'd agree, except that we couldn't activate the gate even if we wanted to. The key is missing."

The key, the guiding core of the gate upon which they stood that attuned it to a matched dais back home, had not been present at the center of the device when he'd arrived.

Masini spun his head, hair trailing behind it, as he looked towards the empty slot in the center of the circle. "What? How... You think it was stolen, don't you?"

"Possible." It was hard to deny. Keys were difficult to create, and were undoubtedly the most critical part of a gate. "It could have been hidden under orders; we will have to ask Reedjin once he arrives." He could feel the doubt in his own words.

"We both know that's not what happened. This was his charge, only thing he's ever been adequate at is looking out for himself. Probably took it for his own gain, whatever that might be."

"Even still, once we are done, there isn't enough cadentite in the entirety of this realm to recreate the gate. The key will be, essentially, useless."

"None that's accessible, anyway..." corrected Masini.

They stood, waiting in the crisp air of twilight, as the other remaining mages began to arrive, their reluctance emanating as plainly from their faces as the warm glow of purple light radiating from beneath their feet. Eleven of them gathered near the center, their disquiet mirroring the dead landscape. Several asked about the key, but none were able to supply an answer.

*Only one missing,* thought Protorus.

Some shifted uncomfortably, others maintained an eerie stillness to their demeanor that came with too many battles seen. A few stood resolute, though Protorus wondered if they shared the same sentiments he did regarding their task. To Masini's point, several warranted a cautious eye—one he tried to hold without appearing distrustful. Now was not the time to argue.

They couldn't begin without their final member. Their orders were clear: Acquittal would come only from their sacrifice—an acknowledgment of what they'd done here. Their superiors would be watching from afar to ensure, in the ways of old, that the ritual would be performed with all present. A sort of self-inflicted punishment, akin to removing a limb to save the body.

Finally, a few hours after night had taken hold and stars filled the sky, the last member arrived. The plump mage walked slowly to the circle's center, his bald head held high, displaying no signs that he cared about making them wait on him.

"About time," said an annoyed Masini.

"Masini," the new arrival said, "I assumed we'd be waiting for you to drunkenly stumble your way from the nearest brothel. Imagine my surprise to find you here before me."

"I'd offer to bring you along Reedjin, but I hear they're a little old for your tastes."

"Quiet your tongue before I cut it out, you—"

"Enough!" cut in Protorus. "Let us be done with this. Do you know where the key is?" he asked the fuming Reedjin.

"Taken to one of the sites, I was not informed which one," claimed the portly man.

Protorus doubted his words. And by the glances from some of the others, they did as well. What he'd said to Masini earlier had been true, however, and while it may remain a large reservoir of vidut for whomever held it, it would be otherwise useless. He was mentally and physically exhausted from the war, and was ready to be gone from this haunted place.

"We are the last," said Protorus. "The task assigned to us: less final than some of our brethren, but in some ways more difficult. Here we shall re-main—"

"No one is here for a damned speech," interrupted Reedjin, "let's be done with it and on our way." He spread his arms to the side, palms facing down as spiraling patterns of purple light coalesced beneath them. Protorus stifled a sigh and imitated the motion, as did all the others around him.

The entire enormity of the pattern beneath them began to dim as the essence—the vidut—of the glowing stone was drawn into each of them. Huge reserves of it flooded him and the others as they took it for themselves, drain-ing everything from the gate. It was power incarnate, a wealth they hadn't had access to in what felt like an age.

It was intoxicating.

And it would damn them to this place.

Faster than any would've liked, the well ran dry, and the once glowing pattern vanished as its very soul was absorbed by the group. Light from the stars struggled to outshine the gentle hue that now pushed through the fabric of some of their clothing. With few words they began to disperse across the pure-black rock. They all knew as well as him what they'd done. Their way home was closed.

Forever.

# PART 1
## SECRETS

# Chapter One

*What is time to the one who sails along its cosmic tides? Open ocean lay before him in endless directions, an infinite array of possibilities, safe harbor hidden beyond the distant horizon. He has sailed this sea and glimpsed land, a journey so great that it's impossible to know whether it shall be a welcoming port or enemy stronghold. But hope still drives him, and his course is set...*

Spoken during a moment of brief lucidity,
Fortieth Day of Autumn, Fiftieth Year of the Seventh Epoch

These people made her skin crawl.

A fine, silk dress and a bit of face powder went a long way towards blending in with the pompous class of the appropriately named Upper Tier. Making one's way up the spiraling stone towers that dotted the wall separating the elevated plateau from the common citizens below was one thing. Not standing out as a said commoner was another.

Desnia let a grin creep onto her face as she looked down from the stone railing at the edge of the lush green park into the bustling streets below. There was a certain gratification that came with being where one didn't belong, those around her none the wiser. And someone such as herself blending into the apex of propriety, well, that was a satisfaction that was difficult to match.

The Merchants' Quarter below was dense with swarms of those seeking the luxurious and extravagant. Most bazaars were a cacophony of shouts and attention-grabbing colors, every street vendor vying for the attention of each passer-by. Not so in the Upper Tier. Up here not a street vendor could be found in the noxiously thin air. Just neat lines of warehouses and storefronts that quietly glowed in the soft evening light that warmed the pink granite stone from which they were constructed. The reputation of their name hanging from iron rods above the door was all that was needed to attract the hordes of aristocrats, nobles, and dignitaries who sat atop great mounds of lucre in need of spending.

Desnia despised them for the fortune of not only the gold they possessed, but of the ease of their upbringing. The hard times of the folk living—surviving—in the Lower Valley would never be known to these people. Their only struggles in life were the likes of decisions such as which color carpet would best suit the entry room of their lavish estate, or where to dispose of the food left over from their great feasts. *While people down below beg for scraps.*

She tried to refocus her thoughts on the task at hand. But it was hard to not become distracted while waiting hours for the sun to hide behind the imposing mountain that the great city of Calentine was set into. She looked back to a building on the street below. *The same people are coming and going, no one left outside, and no one heading anywhere but home or out for lunch. Nothing new. As if they think themselves untouchable. The owner didn't even show up until an hour ago, fat prick.*

Her eyes wandered again, watching as the peak's shadow cut across the breadth of the city like a knife, plunging the Upper Tier and Lower Valley into darkness alike, cloaking indiscriminately. The resplendent sky above fluoresced in spectrums of vivid yellows and oranges as the sun scraped across the clouds.

The metropolis, carved into the mountain by mines—which operated ceaselessly—sat entrenched deep into the heart of the mountain's granite core. Meticulously cut walls of stone reached high into the sky on Desnia's either side, their precipices displaying where the slope's grade had once existed, long since eroded away by the toils of those employed to incessantly seek the King's riches.

The city splayed out into the distance, the workings of centuries of laborious digging beheld from her carefully picked vantage point. She could see the outer walls, stretching in an arc at the excavated fringes of the Lower Valley with its towers looming down to the slums behind it. A relic of times long since passed, or so she'd been told. *Now it's just another means of control over those of us already squeezed to our limit,* she thought, flicking a pebble off the wide railing.

She glanced at the Shifted River flowing like a moat beyond the outer walls. The enormous estuary swelled pregnantly in the center, creating the Calentine port, which appeared a mere nook from this distance. She sneered at it, and then her attention drifted further, to the distant pastures of green and their bordering forests. To Desnia, they were near enough to dream of, a sweet escape from the city and its tugging play strings ever tickling the back of her mind. The reality, however, was always at the forefront. Reminding her, in a way that did anything but placate, that the world beyond the outer walls wouldn't be known to her. Not unless—

"Hello," said a diminutive and feminine voice from behind her.

Desnia spun with a start, her fists clenched in defensive aggression. She'd let her mind wander a little *too* far. It had been a long time since someone had snuck up on her.

The small woman who'd spoken took a step back with a flash of fright, and Desnia quickly had to mask the expression that had come from years of fending for oneself in the unforgiving streets.

"I'm sorry." Desnia hastily straightened her posture, pulling her head back straight to look slightly down her nose. A look she was all too familiar receiving. "You surprised me," she said with the poshest accent she could manage. "I seem to have drifted off and wasn't expecting to see anyone in the park at this hour."

It was only once Desnia had composed herself that she noticed the woman was pregnant, and nearing the end of it by the size of her protruding belly. The young woman lowered arms that had been drawn to her chest and stomach upon being startled by Desnia and donned a polite smile, then took a few cautious steps closer. A chill ran down Desnia's spine, her instincts telling her to squirm away. She couldn't allow anyone a chance to recognize or identify her. She knew, however, that the best way to remain hidden was to do so in plain sight. Strange acts and blatant parrying of conversation would only raise suspicion.

"It's quite alright," the woman replied. "I should've been more careful not to sneak up on you. My husband always says that I'm being too quiet when I move about."

*Shocking,* Desnia thought.

"I saw you," the woman continued, "from my window just across the park. These past few weeks have been rather vacant of conversation, what with my husband working so many hours. And I fear I have just about chatted my servants' ears off in that time." The woman shyly blushed and turned her head away before continuing. "I saw you here by yourself and, well, you've been here so often this week all alone that I thought, maybe, I would come and introduce myself. I hope that doesn't seem too improper. My name is Winter ce Brun, by the way. It's a pleasure to meet you," she said, with a small curtsey.

*Great,* thought Desnia. *So much for quiet discretion.* She was going to need to think of an excuse for her presence, and quickly. She would need to talk enough to appease this woman, but not so much that she left an impression.

"Yes, well, the view here is spectacular," she said in a half truth, curt-seying back to Winter. There was also the small bonus of being surrounded by actual grass. "And no, not improper at all. Are you hoping for a boy or a girl?" she asked. The Uppers loved to talk about themselves. Made it easy to steer a conversation.

"Oh, well my husband wants a boy. Says that he would join the military and lead battles in his own footsteps. Someone to bring glory to our house and draw the favor of the King. He says that a son would be able to compete in the contests of honor, 'Swords unsheathed' and all that. He does have a strong lineage to maintain, of course, and keeping the family name going is his responsibility. He doesn't have many siblings, and they're all sisters, so it's really a great deal of pressure to continue the ce Brun name. But me? I want those things too, of course. I would never wish to deny the wants of my husband," she rattled.

*Of course not. Gods forbid,* thought Desnia.

"But, well," Winter continued, "I think—and please don't tell my husband this—it would just be fun to have a little girl. Someone to chat with and dress for balls and play with dolls..." Her thoughts seemed to drift as she gazed down at her stomach with a small, loving smile on her face. Her hand rubbed the top of it, and it was then that Desnia recognized the bulge of something solid underneath the woman's dress.

Desnia shivered. She'd heard of the exposure process, but rarely had an opportunity to see it firsthand. There would be a sapphire—blazing a deep, azure blue, and half the size of a fist—tied to a thin chain either around the midsection or neck, pressed to the womb day and night. Only those with too much money and not enough conscience could afford the absurd price the King set on the gems. And what it would do to that child...

It made her sick to think about.

Her nausea soon bubbled to anger and her concentration became focused on suppressing her temper. If she had an outburst now it could ruin everything.

As Winter opened her mouth to undoubtedly prattle on further, chimes from the bells of the King's Tower began to peal through the air and Desnia let out a sigh of relief. Other, lesser, bell towers began to ring in unison in the distance. None compared to the clarity and volume of the tolls coming from the magnificent structure behind Desnia though.

Set against the most inner escarpment of the mountain's hollowed core, the tower's base began at the rear of the Upper Tier, then climbed over five hundred feet above the city, like the trunk of a mighty tree growing against the cliff face. Its grandiose point nearly scratched the top of the cliff high above them. It stood as a monument to signify the heart of the mountain, the seat of the church, and the residence of the King.

Carved from the mountainside itself, black streaks of inanite, which striped the granite cliffside like strokes from an artist's brush, ran through the seamless facade. The tower was covered with ornate statues, blue and orange-stained windows, and stepped levels to allow the exclusive members of the wealthiest of Calentinian society to look down upon the subjects of the realm.

Most people considered it one of the greatest buildings ever constructed.

Desnia just thought of it as the ostentatious home of a tyrant.

In this rare case, however, she was happy for it, for it allowed her to excuse herself from the current conversation.

"Oh!" said Winter as Desnia was about to turn away. "Are you going to the evening speak? I could join you! I haven't made it to one all week on account of my husband's—"

"I apologize," interrupted Desnia, "but I must be getting to my own husband. I'm afraid spending so much time here has kept me from my, uh, own duties." A vile disdain filled her mouth at forcing out the words. "He will be *mighty* upset with me if I don't get them done before he arrives home. I will just go to the speak tomorrow morning."

"Well, if you're here again, I will keep an eye out and join you!" Winter replied, a hint of desperation in her voice.

"Of course!" replied Desnia with a false smile as she backed away towards the stone steps behind her. Without giving more opportunity to the woman to continue her begging, she began to hurry down the stairs, Winter calling out behind her, "King and His grace upon you!"

"And you!" replied Desnia with a final wave as she reached the bottom of the stairs and filtered into the crowded street below.

The chaotic bustle had surged into a flood as the levees of shop doors broke open; the merchants closing their stores for the day and their employees rushing to the street. No doubt a significant portion of them would make their way to the nearest sanctum, some even to the King's Tower, to pray their guilt away and listen to some priest perform a speak and rant about the glory of their immortal God King.

*Idiots.*

Desnia refused to ascribe to the idea that the gods ever came down and chose Him to be their messiah. Their undying prodigy. How was she to believe that He'd been alive for as long as the priests claimed? After all, in all her years she'd never even glimpsed the man, how could she know if He was the same ruler as her previous generations'?

The gods had never done her such a favor. They hadn't saved her from a life of turmoil, nor recused her of the curse they placed upon her and others alike. The poor, the hungry, the sick, all left to rot. No, she hardly saw reason enough to put faith that such deities existed, let alone created a new one among the people.

*He's no different than the rest of the aristocracy. Worse, actually. At least they have rules they pretend to follow.*

She refocused, maneuvering through the crowd with the lithe of experience. The time had arrived. It was the night to execute what two weeks of planning, stalking, and investigating had cumulated to.

She slipped from the crowd down an alley and made her way to a shadowed veranda at the rear of an unoccupied shop. The shop's owner—conveniently away on business—enjoyed the privacy afforded by a tall fence. A fence which, despite its height and the annoying ruffage of her long dress, Desnia was able to deftly scale.

With the sky blocked by the roof above, and there only being a small gap between it and the fence, the veranda took on an oddly eerie and darkened tone. Most merchants had rooms such as this. Private sanctuaries where nefarious and scandalous deals could be brokered. The evasion of taxes, movement of goods, people, coin, the true workings of the gears that turned the behemoth of a government, took place in rooms like this one. With people the likes of which she was all too familiar.

For now, however, it offered her a secluded place to prepare.

Pulling forth her hidden stash, she began changing, eagerly stripping off the stuffy dress to exchange it for the contents of the bag. Boots, trousers that fit loose enough to move easily—but tight enough that they would not rustle—and a cotton wrap which she tightly spun around her chest, were donned first. After that, a loose-fitting shirt and a dark leather jacket with a hood. She pulled her short, blonde hair tightly under a cloth bandana, and then wiped the makeup from her face.

The ensemble gave the distinct impression of that of a man—or at least a younger one, given her thin frame and insubstantial height. There was a certain advantage that came with being dressed as the opposite sex; especially as the hours grew darker, and the cravings of men along with them.

She'd begun dressing as a boy at a young age. Too many times had she seen the untamed desires of men take advantage of people she knew, other girls who struggled to survive. Their only provocation being the unfortunate proximity to the bastards. As if their existence was for nothing but the whims of men with false smiles. And it didn't matter whether these assaulters, rapists, or sickened scum were clothed in linen and drunk from ale, or robed in silk and quenched by wine. Once the propriety of the day's sun was gone, and the night's malevolence took hold, they all looked at you with the same intent.

So it was that she hid herself away. Not in a static, dark corner. Those who didn't keep moving on the streets were always the first to disappear. Instead, she threw herself into the camouflaging throngs of the city, always alert, the guise of a young boy keeping away the majority of predators that ever prowled for an opportunity.

There was one thing that made Desnia stand out though. One talent above the others that brought her unwanted attention. And it was the reason she was here tonight.

But before she got to that she had to finish preparing, and then wait. She drew a belt around her waist; a long, thin dagger hanging from its side. Most wouldn't see it as anything special, but as one of her few possessions, she prized it. It had gotten her out of trouble more than once, and the pure utilitarianism of its simple design was a constant need.

Being armed in Calentine wasn't illegal. In fact, the majority of citizens—men and women alike—carried some form of weaponry, even if most didn't know how to use it. Many "proper" ladies would turn their nose down at such an act, though Desnia knew that the slyer ones merely hid their blades in clever ways. Most of the other Uppers just wore it for show.

She stuffed the dress away—she'd come back for it later. Then she sat down and waited for the hours to pass. It was only once the night had reached its apex, and the locals were either well into sleep or a pitcher at the tavern, that it would be safe for her to emerge and make her way to her target.

The fully risen moon reflected a dull gray hue, the feeble luminosity of its black face offering little more than to outline the roofs of buildings as Desnia walked down the alley behind Merchants' Row. Her only real guides were the intermittent oil streetlamps, which served little purpose, other than highlighting the rear entrances of the stately shops, as they hardly pierced the vast darkness between each other.

She'd waited under the veranda until a patrol of guards had passed. Based on her observations from previous nights, she expected a full hour before their rotation brought them back here again. As long as there wasn't a random patrol of Blues, she should have plenty of time.

Hopefully.

She arrived behind the spice merchant's shop, cautiously observing the ends of the alley before pulling herself up the nearby lamp post and smothering the flame within. Her surroundings were suddenly consumed by darkness, and she intentionally avoided glancing at the lamps to either side to allow her vision to adjust to the inky night.

Her breath began to quicken, her body tensing slightly, prepping for what came next. She'd confirmed the information acquired from careful bribes and clandestine eavesdropping. The owner of this shop—a wealthy man by even noble standards—had recently come down with a case of gout. Normally she'd wish him to lose a foot, smiling at what befell the old glutton. But, as it so happened, this particular owner tended to be rather untrusting of his employees. His home was also much closer to the shop than the nearest bank. Several blocks closer, in fact.

This combination of seemingly arbitrary information presented a profitable opportunity for Desnia. One that others might not be intuitive enough to discover. For the affluent merchant, not able to walk the distance to the bank with any regularity, and unwilling to trust any of his funds with his self-proclaimed "untrustworthy" employees, had taken to storing weeks' worth of trade profits in a newly installed safe.

She'd watched for the entire week, confirming that no one—the merchant *or* his staff—had traveled to the bank after departing the shop. No couriers or armed guards had provided escort. Nothing. Meaning that there was, at minimum, a week's worth of profit from one of the wealthiest merchants in the most opulent part of the city, sitting inside.

And it was going to be hers.

Well, *partially* hers.

Desnia's years of experience afforded her an apparent demeanor of calm, despite the mild tension she was feeling in her mind. The rear wall of the shop—which stood three stories tall—was constructed of smooth granite, contrasting streaks of black inanite becoming more visible as her eyes continued adjusting. A heavy steel door that lacked a visible keyhole and iron bars set into the window frames safeguarded the structure as though a fortress. Her plan, however, was aimed a bit higher.

She pulled a small metallic tool from her bag and clipped it to her belt before tightening the shoulder straps to prevent jostling. She approached the building's polished stone wall and found its finite mortar grooves with a touch. Even her small fingers had a difficult time finding purchase in such a narrow gap, but it would suffice.

With the vast majority of buildings in Calentine being constructed of the excavated granite that was endlessly hauled from the mines, the Masons' Guild here had, naturally, become the most renown and skilled on the continent. And the buildings of the Upper Tier were crafted by only the most talented among them. Desnia appreciated this, for it meant that they were nothing if not consistent.

Each mortar line, minute though it was, tended to be nearly identical. So, when she lifted her boot and put the nearly imperceptible notch cut into the sole's toe against one of these gaps, it locked in perfectly. The sliver of metal that was hammered into the toe of the thick sole acted as support—and also made for a handy defense, as a swift kick to someone's shin would drop them to their knees faster than a stone.

Desnia began to climb, her body holding tightly to the wall, her fingertips white with chalk to aid in the ascent. She rose above the first story, and then the second. It was a cautious climb, but not a slow one. She couldn't afford to waste time, though too hasty an ascent could end in her demise. She moved methodically, taking each finger hold anew, and being sure of her boot's lock in a seam before progressing.

Eventually she reached the highest floor. Windows here were sparser, but it did have one important feature the others did not: a pair of loft doors framed into the stone wall. A crane arm extended out from above them, meant for hauling goods into the attic space. The sturdy oak doors were devoid of orifices or seams, excluding the thin gap between the imposing pair. Keys were not a thought for an entry so inaccessible from the exterior, and most hardly considered access through such an obscure location possible.

Which is what made them a favorite of Desnia's.

She carefully shimmied her way onto the bottom lip of the doors' frame, her feet thankful for the few inches of support. Her body pressed tightly to the oiled timbers, one hand with a firm grip to the frame's cornerstones, while the other unclipped the oddly shaped metallic tool from her waist.

Wide and flat, with a strange hook at the end that pointed back at the user, the unique device was a creation of her own design. Some of these loft doors were held shut with nothing but a crossbar of wood or metal, easily popped out of place with a quick upward jerk of her dagger between the doors. The more security conscious, however, liked giving her a challenge.

Holding the tool's handle, she slid the hooked end between the center gap, lifting until it contacted the locked crossbar within. Desnia then pulled the device towards her, the hook pressing into a keyhole on the inside of the door. There were only a select few locksmiths that made the mechanism that held loft doors together. The ones used by most in this district had a fatal flaw—pressure applied into the bottom of the keyhole would release the latch. It was meant to occur when the key turned an internal depressor, but the effect could be mimicked with, say, the pointed end of a strange looking hook...

She tilted the handle down and yanked, bracing for the doors to release.

They stood fast.

There wasn't even a budge from the oak behemoths. Frustrated—and cursing under her breath—Desnia yanked again.

And again, nothing happened.

*Please don't tell me this gimp bastard didn't install a Mothly,* she thought. She'd spent too much of her coin—and time allotted to her—getting this far. Failure was not an option.

With an anger brewing inside of her like a pot simmering on the verge of a boil, she gave the hooked tool a vicious jerk. Maybe this would be enough to—

There was a click from within and the doors simultaneously swung open, aided by the force Desnia had applied. Distracted by her frustration, the momentum of the door's heft knocked her off balance, her precarious footing losing ground and her arm—tool still in hand—swinging wildly to avoid the thirty-foot fall to the cobbled street below.

Desnia let her instincts take over, and as her body pulled away from the building, she did the only thing that she could—she leaped with all the strength she could muster. She flew through the air, the uninviting stone pavers of the dim alley watching patiently below. She reached up, and with her palms scarcely above the top of the wooden cantilever, grasped onto the crane arm jutting out from above the loft. The metal tool made an all-too-loud *clank* as it struck the beam, the sound making her wince.

As she swung, hanging from her fingertips, her pounding heart began to slow to a point that it no longer tried to burst from her chest. She took a few deep breaths and—with one hand holding her to the crane—reattached the hooked tool to her waist. She reoriented herself towards the now-ajar doors and moved hand over hand until she reached the entry. Back and forth she swung, releasing her grip at the right moment and landing softly into a crouch inside.

Desnia took a moment to appreciate the solidity of the flooring beneath her, a mild amount of adrenaline still running through her veins. She pulled the doors shut with trembling hands, leaving them unlocked to exit through later.

The loft was packed to the rafters with baskets, jars, and other various containers. Desnia maneuvered through a narrow path that wended sporadically through the towering stacks in near blackness until she found herself on the second floor, with windows affording additional light from the streetlamps outside. She passed an opening in the center of the floor of the spacious back room, likely for moving items down to the main showing area, more crates and goods stacked near its protective railing.

She didn't expect to find anyone within the building, but still she tested the floorboards for creaks as she crept forward all the same, the habit of silence ingrained in her.

As she reached and carefully swung the door for the front corner office open, she felt a sense of relief that her informant had been correct. Rich couches adorned the space, thick rugs matted the floor, and in the center of the room stood an ornately carved desk, its finery and polish clear even in the faintly lit chambers.

The owner's office.

After closing the door, she slowly drew the heavy curtains closed, tucking them tightly into the window's frame. Only then did she dare to light a single candle, bringing the sumptuous quarters into clear view. The walls were ordained with a variety of paintings and mounts, but there was only one that drew her attention.

Desnia approached the portrait, its gold frame reflecting the candlelight. It depicted the merchant that owned the shop, standing several inches taller than his true height, also looking slimmer—and healthier—than he'd likely ever been. She guessed that it must have cost a fortune, as it was rather skillfully painted, somehow managing to look absolutely *nothing* like the overweight monger, yet was still—amazingly—recognizable as the same man.

She set down the candle and carefully lifted the painting from its mount, setting it to the side. Behind the narcissistic fantasy was what she'd been seeking—a solid, darksteel lockbox, set and mortared into the stone wall. Desnia raised an eyebrow, the first modicum of respect for the merchant coming over her as she stared at the blackened metal with a single keyhole in the center. Apparently the man was willing to spend as much on his security as he did his paintings.

She didn't have time to dally and admire the *true* work of art before her, unfortunately. Quickly removing the bag from her back, she pulled out her collection of lockpicks. Sifting through them one-by-one, she procured the select few needed for this style of lock and got to work.

Sliding the pronged slivers of metal into the keyhole that was set into a Merchants' Guild symbol, she masterfully began to poke and prod, each movement direct and intentional. Every pin was tested, the pressure of its spring evaluated and then understood. She counted as the tool—which acted as though an extension of her own hand—felt its way further and further back into the cylinder, picturing it in her mind and looking for false pins. A touch to one of these—set in the back where the key would not reach—would seize the lock. The only way to access the strongbox afterwards being an intense amount of extremely loud hammering and hand-drilling. A safety feature against lesser thieves who would fumble and assume each pin was part of the lock mechanism.

Lesser, Desnia most certainly was not.

Minutes passed as she hyper-focused on the task. Soon a quarter hour. Then half. Nearly three quarters of an hour passed until she heard the gratifying click of the final pin falling into place, and the light pressure on the cylinder releasing as it started to rotate.

Desnia allowed a small smile to grace her lips as she turned the lock enough to hear the interior door-bolts retract, and then slowly pulled the door open.

Bumps raised on her skin and a chill slithered down her back as the door swung wide. The interior was lined with muted inanite, its stark white contrasting the dark exterior. The bottom shelf held neatly bound stacks of coins, mostly silver moons and a few golden suns. On the shelf above were small, velvet-lined boxes abundant with rubies and emeralds glistening expensively. Lacking in carats, they were supplemented by quantity, sparkling like clusters of stars in the night sky.

In the center of the shelf, however, was something that filled Desnia's heart with dread and tightly bound her stomach.

An enormous sapphire, nearly as large as her palm, reflected its burning luster into Desnia's eyes as she stared into the blue depths which seemed to plunge endlessly within itself. In a way that felt as though she were entranced, it pulled invitingly at her, almost as though it wanted to be taken from its improper home. For a second, she debated taking the accursed stone. But no, she did not crave death.

And death would've been a preferable option to the punishment for being caught with one of these rare sapphires. The stones were the property of the King, and among all his riches, they were the most precious. Those few that dared to steal one were hunted and caught—almost without fail. The perpetrators were not given the luxury of the gallows, or the quick gratification of the block. No, these insolent criminals were made examples of.

She'd seen them, placed in the center of the common squares, publicly tortured in ways meant to inflict pain, but allow the recipient to survive. Their screams deafened all within earshot as bits of skin were peeled away, burns applied to their body, and small, near-bloodless cuts were given and then scrubbed with salt. The longer the person lived—and the intention was for them to live as long as possible—the more creative the torture became, many surviving weeks while cursing and pleading for death. The point was clear—no one was to steal a sapphire from the crown.

No one.

The merchant, as far as Desnia was aware, had no children, was unwed, and most certainly wasn't a Blue. He shouldn't have one of the gems in his possession. Yet here it was.

As she rummaged through the safe and stashed its contents away within her bag, she avoided touching the polished stone, treating it as though it were a pestilence incarnate.

Finally, she reached into the rear of the box and—after finding the small release latch—removed the false back, revealing the item that was the true origin of her presence here tonight.

A small, glowing stone, perhaps the size of her fingernail, sat within, purple light emanating from it in a soft hue. Its gentle luminance warmly basked her face in its ample glow, the shadows seeming to darken around her. Desnia recalled miners talking about the mythical mineral, cadentite, those that believed it existed, anyway. The rare few that had encountered it—typically the ones with more white hair than dark—claimed it was only found in the most substantial lodes of inanite and was scarcely larger than minute specs of glowing sand. They believed it was a bad omen and were eager to avoid it. There were, however, an exceptional few that were aware of its properties, and they sought it with fervor.

This is what had brought Desnia to this merchant. A rumor that he'd purchased one of the largest specimens of cadentite seen in years. A rumor that led to her strict instructions of securing and removing it from his possession.

She picked it up, the sensation of it in her fingers strange and foreign. She wondered if it was a trick of her mind, but she felt as though the light were penetrating through her fingers, coursing its radiance into her veins.

She shook the feeling and quickly slipped it into her jacket pocket, ensuring it stayed close. If she ran into trouble and lost her bag of loot, at least this—the critical component of her night's thievery—would remain with her.

She closed the thick steel door and turned the lock mechanism back into place. For a moment she thought she felt a pang of guilt. But why? This was a man who hoarded wealth, who put himself before all others, and used his power and influence to oppress all he saw as "beneath him." Guilt should not have even been a consideration of Desnia's. She rehung the portrait and upon seeing its twisted idealism again, whatever emotion had stirred within her quickly evaporated.

She put out the candle and made her way back from whence she'd come. The hallway was dark, her eyes having adjusted to the candlelight while working. As she blindly extended foot after foot forward in the darkness, she had the misfortune of her toe nudging a small table. The ornate candle holder atop it rocked, and then toppled to the floor, the blanket of night making her unable to see or react to the teetering silver stem.

With a *clang* that might as well have been a hammer to a bell, it collided with the flood. Desnia held her breath, cringing at the sound as it resonated off the reflective wooden walls.

*Fuck,* she thought. *Please, please, please don't let anyone hear that.*

She listened carefully, air still held in her lungs. No shouts from outside, no torches moving around and casting light within the storehouse, nothing seemed to be happening.

She allowed herself to exhale. But then, as she took another step forward, a rustle came from behind her.

The door adjacent to the office from which she'd just left was slightly ajar. There was movement from within, and the door creaked open. A growl, deep and guttural, came from inside, and the faint light offered by a window within the room cast enough light to see the outline of a beastly dog, causing her stomach to tighten and turn, eyes growing wide.

It stood taller than her waist, and upon its back the hair stood on end. The white of its teeth reflected the dim light and it snarled in aggression at the intruder to its home. With a loud bark it bounded towards Desnia, and she in turn sprinted down the hall as fast as her legs would carry her. It was on her heels, its breath hot against her legs. She turned a corner leading back towards the loading area and as she did the hound lunged at her. It took aim at her arm and moved with a speed that defied its mass. Her eyes went wider, the white of teeth from foaming jowls about to clamp on her arm all that was clear to see in the blackness.

Then, nothing. To her amazement and relief, it missed her arm, biting down into nothing but shadow and its full weight ramming against the wall. The error gave her the briefest of windows to place a gap between her and the pursuer. After rounding the next corner, she sprinted, not caring for anything that got in her way, hearing the dog start to bark again and running towards her. She fled to the back room, the balcony overlooking the main storeroom below, and ran towards it. Without a second thought—there was no time to think, let alone plan—she flung herself over the railing and down to the floor below.

She soared through the air, the scant shadows only suggesting what she might land on. Her arms stretched out for balance, while a lump in her throat reminded her that it would likely make little difference.

With reckless calamity, she crashed into a stack of baskets and pottery, billowing clouds of varying spices filling the room. Cinnamon and other odors assaulted her olfactory, sending her into a coughing fit as the fine powders and dried herbs dusted her entirely. It burned her eyes and stung her lungs, overpowering the pain of the crash.

The dog barked from above, and its alarm reminded her to ignore the pain and pull herself up, lest it find the nearest stairs and attack her again.

She stumbled to the backdoor, rubbing her burning eyes. The lack of an exterior key made it a poor entry point, but it was still a decent enough exit. As she gripped the latch to unlock the door, pain shot through her forearm, and she looked down to see a gash dripping blood in a trail behind her. Panic flashed through her, frantic thoughts swimming in her mind, but the howling guard that was making its way to what she could only assume was a flight of stairs left her with little choice.

She flung open the door and slammed it behind her as she burst back into the alley. Guards—or worse—would be on their way if they weren't already. She gripped her arm tightly and delved into the night, seeking the refuge of the Lower Valley, leaving the ravings of the beast in the distance behind her.

# Chapter Two

*My kin, desecrated and scattered, his blood siphoned in ignorance.*
Heard by member of the night shift while patient slept.
Sixty-seventh Day of Winter, Sixth Year of the Seventh Epoch

The rays of sun that streaked brightly through Delvan's barracks chambers were accompanied by the crisp sound of a trumpet's tune, its blare a painful reminder of how little sleep he'd gotten during the night. He rolled over in the thick, comfortable mattress and pressed a spare pillow to his head in an attempt to drown out the morning summons. He could probably afford to sleep a little more, where was the harm in that?

As the brass reveille died away, Delvan relaxed and felt the sweet escape of sleep start to come back over him, a kind reprieve from the pulsating pain in his head. Just a few more minutes was all—

The door to his private quarters burst open and the iron handle struck against the stone wall with a ringing *clash* that caused Delvan to jerk upright. His reddened eyes struggled to see through his disheveled hair, the brown locks hanging over his face. With a brush of his hand he was able to see Hilbrun standing at the door, already dressed in his armor and holding a goblet in his hand.

Delvan groaned and flopped back into bed before grunting a few words through his pillow. "Just a few more minutes, I'll find you after roll call, I swear."

"We're not going to roll call," replied Hilbrun. He walked over to Delvan and ripped the silk sheet from his grip to expose him and the large sapphire hanging from his neck to the brisk morning air before extending the goblet towards him. "Here, drink this, it'll help. We need to get going and I can't have you looking hungover when we arrive. We've got a special assignment, so stop lounging and wasting time. When did you sneak back in last night anyway? You look terrible."

*A special assignment?* Delvan had never been sent on a special assignment before. Although, he had just graduated from the Academy a few months ago. Hilbrun was a few years older and had probably been on several. He supposed it made sense to send him *and* Delvan, being his paired first year.

"Who says that I snuck out?" replied Delvan as he took the goblet and smelled the contents. He turned his head with a repulsive grimace, the smell alone pungent enough to rouse him.

"The fact that it smells like a tavern in here is a pretty good indicator," said Hilbrun. "Now drink up. I know it smells horrid, but the apothecary says it's the best way to sober up quickly. Let's go, Del!"

With a feeling of disgust, Delvan held his breath as he drank the foul liquid as quickly as he could, not wanting to taste it for a second longer than necessary. He handed the goblet back to Hilbrun and felt his stomach turn into a sickening knot. He dove for the chamber pot in the corner and wretched so powerfully that he thought his stomach might come along with its contents as they gushed from him.

"Yeah," said Hilbrun, "she did say that would happen. Probably should have mentioned that. Anyway, that should get most of it out of your system. Drink some water and get dressed. We need to double-time it."

*Asshole,* thought Delvan.

As much as he wanted to chide Hilbrun, the Senior was still his superior officer. Delvan's insubordinations wouldn't be tolerated by most, and Hilbrun ignoring them—to a certain extent—was enough to earn him some of Delvan's respect. He pulled himself up, quickly washed his face and began to get dressed.

His armor, identical to that of Hilbrun's, was crafted of thick leather and dyed blue with sapphire dust. Darksteel back and chest plates covered the top half of his torso, with the blue gem sitting underneath the armor against his breast. Similar steel ran down his off-hand arm, with a metal shoulder pad on the opposite. The leather and steel alike were masterfully filigreed, the superb craftsmanship matching their station. Blues were, after all, a class above.

He looked himself up and down in the embellished mirror as he drew his short sword around his waist, its white scabbard and ornate handle reflecting brightly in the morning light.

He *did* look terrible.

Delvan checked the pouch to his side and confirmed the handful of inanite blocks were still contained within. He quickly laced his boots and was out the door in a blur, Hilbrun prodding him to hurry all the while.

They marched past the assembly of soldiers and then Blues in the barrack's courtyard, orders being shouted out for the day shift and reports coming in from the night patrols. Once out onto the street, he struggled to keep up with Hilbrun's quickened pace, his body aching from dehydration as they approached the stables.

Part of him wondered what this special assignment was, the rest of him mostly focused on his still-turning stomach and pounding head. They made their way through the city streets on horseback, working their way across the Upper Tier. Few people were out at this early hour. Some trekked towards the chapels for morning speaks, the others—likely shop owners—were running errands and walking at quickened paces.

As they reached the Merchants' Quarter, Hilbrun finally slowed the pace, approaching a large shop with what appeared to be two armed mercenaries standing outside at the door. They both shifted uncomfortably as the pair approached. Most people were uncomfortable around Blues.

"Where's the owner?" Hilbrun asked, dismounting his horse. "He sent for us."

"Inside, my Lords. He was in the back room last we saw. He's expecting you," the shorter of the two guards replied, opening the door and beckoning them in.

The scent of the store hit Delvan like a cudgel to the face as he walked inside. The pain in his stomach and head flared as he struggled to breathe. Their boots left prints in the spices that dusted the floor like sand as they reached the back of the shop's elegant interior. The further back they went, the louder someone's angry screams became.

"CLEARLY NOT!!" cried the raspy voice. "One of them *must* have left the front or backdoor open! Gather them all and question them until you get a confession. Do you realize what this has cost me! Losing their job will be the least of their—"

The portly man's voice cut off as he saw Delvan and Hilbrun enter. He dismissed the store worker in front of him with a wave of his hand as he limped over as hurriedly as his cane could carry him.

"King and His grace—" started Hilbrun.

"What took you so long?" the man wheezed directly to Hilbrun, angry eyes sunk into his face above dark circles. "I sent for you nearly an hour ago."

"Apologies," replied Hilbrun with a quick glance to Delvan. "We got here as fast as we could. I had to get to the barracks and grab my first—"

"Yes, yes," he said with a wave of his hand, seeming to accept the reasoning before hearing it. "I need you to hurry, we must catch the thieves. They must be discovered!"

Delvan watched the conversation with feigned interest, slightly disappointed their "special assignment" was little more than a common theft. Investigating robberies wasn't necessarily outside of their duties, but it also wasn't common. This richly dressed merchant must have some powerful connections to pull a pair of Blues to investigate. He did wonder why Hilbrun had been in such a rush to get here though, as the thief was likely long gone and would be difficult to track down. Seemed like a waste of their effort. There were much easier assignments they could have taken, not to mention more interesting.

"Can you start by explaining what you know?" asked Hilbrun. "I was given only a few details before coming here."

"Yes, yes," replied the merchant in a flurry of hand gestures. "One of my employees must have left the rear door unlocked. They deny it, but the loft doors were *also* unlocked! What do I even pay them for?! Useless. If they forgot to lock one, they must have forgotten to lock the other. *But,* I have another idea of what must have happened.

"When I arrived this morning—early mind you, as I'm expecting some other important members of the guild today and my assistant has decided to disappear on some escapade or something, kids these days—I unlocked the front door and came in to find this mess!" he said with a wave of his arm towards a pile of destroyed containers that were now a mound of powders and ruin. "I thought maybe something crashed from the ceiling, some idiot leaving something too close to the railing and rolling off. But once some of my employees arrived for their shift I went to my office and found my lock box had been emptied! Emptied!" Delvan noticed the man's face contort slightly into a flash of anxious fear.

*What has him so worried?* he wondered.

"You understand the importance of what I say! What am I to tell my clients? When the Guild hears of this...

"I locked that safe myself last night. I tell you, one of my employees must have stolen a key from me and made a copy! That safe is the finest money can buy! It is neigh uncrackable! And there wasn't a scratch on it, it was not cut or drilled into. Not that you likely could, as it's *true* darksteel, not that knockoff garbage. A key must have been used, there is no other explanation. So, I've brought all my employees in, and my own private guard is outside and at the back entrance to keep them from leaving. I need you to interrogate them. All of them! One of them must be the guilty party!

"I found blood by the back door. I believe that the thief—or his accomplice—must have felt like hurting me more than just the damage of stealing from my purse and destroyed some of my stock before leaving. Well, it looks like they wounded themselves while doing so. Serves them right! I was considering having my guards force the workers to strip to see if any have any such hidden injury. I thought they'd dislike the idea, but with a pair of Blues here, they won't dare say a word. Come, you must help me round them up."

"Um," said Hilbrun quickly, "how about first you show me this safe you mentioned. We can take inventory of what was taken. We'll address who the culprit may be afterwards."

"Yes, yes. I suppose they can wait a moment; they're not going anywhere. Come, follow me," the merchant said.

Delvan had been absently looking around at the scene. The merchant's story seemed probable enough, but something wasn't sitting right with him. A feeling he couldn't quite put his finger on, though his pounding head didn't help. Or maybe that was the issue, since none of this seemed worth their time. Did he really have to get up early for this?

"Del," said Hilbrun, snapping him out of his half-trance, "stay here and look around, see what you can find. I'm going to go look at the safe."

With that, Delvan watched them walk to a small loading platform, the merchant shouting at his employees to raise them up. Two men began to turn a large wheel adjacent to the platform and elevated it to the balcony above, locking into place as Hilbrun and the merchant disembarked. They walked out of sight, speaking in tones too hushed for Delvan to hear, the merchant's cane beating loudly against the floorboards with each hobbled step.

*I wonder if he's used that platform since before or after his limp started.*

He dismissed the thought and turned back to the scene before him, his mind's haze seeming to fade slightly. He began his task with hands in his pockets, feet shuffling along the floor. He was doubtful of anything coming from an investigation, it wasn't their job to question people, that was for inquisitors. Was he going to need to spend half the day listening to the rantings of some merchant?

*What a waste of time,* he thought. *Do I really have to do four more years of this?* He'd already spent six at the Academy, now he was required to play city guard and investigate the slights of whining dignitaries and oafs. *Just knight us and send us on to tasks more deserving of our station already and be done with it. This old tradition is ridiculous.*

With slumped shoulders he decided that he might as well get on with it, otherwise Hilbrun was going to spend the second half of the day reprimanding him. That actually seemed worse than looking into this mess, but it was a close call. With a sigh and dragging feet, he first looked at the shattered clay pots and scraps of shredded baskets that melded with the mound of powdered spices, sifting through it with the handle end of a broom he found nearby. It kicked up dust, causing him to lean back so as to not inhale any of the nose-stinging blend. There were indeed a few scraps with blood on them, but his rummaging was dusting up a cloud. After a short while he moved on, not wanting to get covered in the intense fragrances. Who knew how long it would take for his gear to get scrubbed clean of that smell.

From there he turned and walked to the guarded rear door, seeing a blood trail start to appear after a few steps in the same direction. Dried drips turned into splattered globs, the dark spots apparent against the lighter stone, covered in the same dust as everything else.

The back door did in fact have a large smear of blood across the lock lever, and he opened it so that he could look closer in the sunlight. The blood had dried, and in the daylight the steel handle of the thick, wrought door almost seemed to change the hue of the blackish-red tone to something else. Perhaps it was just the metal deceiving his eyes, they weren't exactly fresh at the moment.

Back inside, he sauntered around the first floor of the storeroom. It was mostly spices, imported in all sorts of different vessels, but some other random objects were strewn about. Small statues, carvings of varying deities, tubes with parchment likely rolled inside, and other valuables blended with the rest of the merchandise.

A sudden, incessant barking as Delvan rounded a corner made his heart jump and washed away some of his grogginess. He leaped backward as a massive, black coated dog jumped forward at him, its snarling jowls flaring to expose its angry teeth. The chain tied to its collar snapped tight as it came an arm's length beyond Delvan's outstretched hand.

"Sorry 'bout her, m'Lord," said a voice from his side. A man came forward and scolded the dog, commanding it to sit. "She doesn't much like strangers," the man continued as the dog closed its jaws and became quiet. "One of the neighbors came by this mornin' and asked about the commotion last night. Seems ol Sugar here frightened off whoever it was that broke into the place. And before you ask, no, they didn't see much of nothin', unfortunately."

Delvan relaxed his stance and looked at the worker as his arm lowered to his side. He was dressed well enough for a commoner, likely a requirement of being employed in an establishment like this. Though the clothes were clean, he could clearly see they were well worn, probably a few seasons beyond the point they should've been replaced.

"Sugar?" Delvan asked, looking back at the dog who now sat and stared at him, drool hanging from its jowls.

"Aye, but she's anything but sweet," the man replied with a half chuckle. "Listens to me well enough, and some of the boys here. But we mostly keep her locked up in the spare room upstairs. Can't have her yappin' at every person who walks through the door. Owner thought she'd make for a good guard dog, but the bitch must have slept through most of it last night if they managed to clean out the boss like that."

Delvan took another look at the dog, the man wiping its muzzle with a piece of linen to clean the saliva hanging nearly to the waxed floor.

"Thanks for the info," said Delvan as he backed away from the beast, now apparently tamed.

"No problem," the worker said.

Back in the storeroom he looked about at what he'd seen. Things didn't seem right to him. Something was off about the owner's original guess of what happened. He had felt detached and indifferent about the robbery when they'd first arrived, but now he began to wonder. What could have actually—

There was a sudden rhythmic clatter that burst loudly from the front entrance. Several soldiers clad in full armor marched in and fell into rank and file in the storeroom. Striding in behind them was a Blue that Delvan didn't recognize. Gray hairs streaked through his temples, the rank on the side of his shoulder marking him as a knight commander. He had thin but hardened features, with a narrow, pointed jaw. His posture and cadence indicated him to be a man of serious disposition, the glare of authority in his eyes was enough alone to scatter anyone from his path. Had the influence of the merchant really been enough to pull such a high-ranking officer to investigate a simple crime?

Delvan may have been laxer than most soldiers—even many Blues—but the better part of a decade's worth of military training was still ingrained deeply into him. He clicked his heels together and stood at firm attention as the superior officer entered the room.

The knight commander walked up to Delvan and glanced at the red markings on his shoulder. "Pupil, huh? Name, cadet," he ordered.

"Delvan ce Saffstar, sir," said Delvan with cold rigidity. The captain, who carried himself in a way that seemed to raise his stature, stood a few inches shorter than Delvan in actuality. Yet he still somehow managed to stare down his nose at him, not acknowledging his name in any way.

"Where's your Senior, Pupil?", the commander asked. "I need to speak with him, and since you clearly didn't drag your own ass here based on the foul state of your breath, I'm assuming he must be accompanying you. By the fucking gods, what are they allowing pupils to get away with these days? Well? Where is he? I want to know what two cadets are doing at my crime scene, unsupervised no less."

The berating reminded him of the taste that clung to his mouth from Hilbrun's concoction that morning, turning his face a shade of green.

Before he had a chance to answer, Hilbrun and the merchant's heads appeared above the balcony railing. The merchant had a look of concern upon his face, and Hilbrun looked... angry?

"There he is," said the commander, looking up. "Both of you, present yourselves."

The two stepped onto the platform, the merchant struggling on his cane, and workers lowered it back to the first floor with loud rattles and creaks from the turning gears. Hilbrun walked forward and snapped to attention, the merchant hobbling behind him, sweating and panting from the short walk.

"What is the meaning of these soldiers, my Lord?" asked the merchant with a wave of his arm. "I appreciate you coming, Commander, but I believe these two Blues should be—"

"I will get to you in a minute," interrupted the commander. "Cadet, what is your name? And what barracks are you stationed in?"

"Hilbrun al Portaine, sir. Third quadrant barracks, sir," he replied.

"Al? Of course you're a fucking southerner," the commander said with disdain. "I don't know what they teach you lazy burnt-skins in between your mid-morning swims and afternoon wine about protocol and command structure, but when reports of a crime come in, you're to immediately notify your commanding officer. So, tell me, why is a senior cadet from a different quadrant investigating a crime in my command's jurisdiction without at least sending a messenger or pigeon? What in the gods' names even makes you think you're qualified to be here?

"And you," he said, turning to the merchant, "why am I not hearing of this theft from a messenger of your own? I came here, instead, based on a report from the residents nearby, yet I come to find you've brought in cadets from another quadrant?"

"I am the victim here!" exclaimed the merchant. "Don't interrogate me as though I'm the thief. I'm the one who has lost everything! These young men came because I sent a messenger this morning and told them to get to the nearest barracks and bring Blues to help catch this vandal. I will settle for no mere city guard or black bag inquisitor in this matter. My messenger must have clearly thought that their barracks was closer, Commander, and he brought them right away as I asked.

"I do believe we have the situation well in hand though, and this troop of soldiers you've barged in here is completely unnecessary. I'm sure that these cadets will file the necessary documents with you once they finish here with me."

"You're right, it is well in hand," said the commander coolly, "because I will be taking over from here. Cadets, you're dismissed. Return to your barracks for new assignments. Soldiers, search the whole building, report to me once you've combed through everything."

"This is ridiculous!" said the exasperated merchant with a flamboyant bobble of his hands. "Why do you need to rummage through my wares? I have customers that I need to deliver to, and these soldiers are going to destroy my organization system! What is your name, Commander? I will be speaking to my contacts about this!"

"Knight Commander Ferrand ce Lione. You'll come to know it well, since we are about to spend most of the day going through every detail of the night's events and your stolen goods together. The King takes crimes among His high citizens seriously, and we are here to make sure that every clue to the events of last night is discovered. These soldiers are an extension of myself and should be treated as such. Feel free to speak with whomever you need, but first, you are going to show me what was stolen from you.

"As for you two," he continued, looking at Delvan and Hilbrun, "I said *dismissed*. Now get out." He pointed towards the back door with finality, and they both gave a salute and marched out into the alley.

A soldier slammed the door closed behind them and Delvan stood in silent confusion, dumbstruck by what had just happened. Hilbrun paced back and forth, his olive skin blazing red with anger.

"That bastard!" screamed Hilbrun. Delvan anxiously glanced at the door to the shop, hoping it and the stone were thick enough to deaden the sound of Hilbrun's outburst. "How dare he!" Hilbrun continued, yelling at the ground in front of him. "Who does he think he is? That indignant prick!"

He suddenly stopped in his tracks and then began walking away—in the opposite direction of their barracks.

"Come on," Hilbrun said to Delvan, who still hadn't moved.

"Where are you going?" Delvan asked.

"There's a blood trail on the ground here. We're going to follow it."

"What? But what about what the commander just said?"

Hilbrun spun on his heel and faced Delvan, hushing his tone, "I don't care what he said. Look, I've heard of Commander Ferrand before, and let's just say he doesn't have the most *upstanding* reputation. I don't trust him. This might technically be his quadrant, but it's out on the edge of it. Our barracks is half the distance away as his. No, he's clearly up to something here. Plus, all those soldiers he brought in? Why does he need to search the whole building? I don't think he's here on anyone's behalf but his own. We need to be wary of him. Trust me on this, Del. Now come on, let's go."

He turned back to following the speckled dots of dried blood on the granite pavers, easily contrasted against the gentle pink hue of the stone. Delvan tracked close behind as Hilbrun followed the trail, backtracking on occasion when he couldn't find another spattered droplet or going down several different paths to see where the next sign was. Some were already worn away by trampling feet of the now busy day, others hidden in cracks of the neat stone, making the task difficult at times.

As they wound through the narrow passages—the thief appearing to have cautiously kept to back alleys—Hilbrun began to calm, and asked Delvan, "What did you find while I was with the merchant?"

"Well," said Delvan, thinking about it. What *had* he seen, and more importantly, what among it was important? He rubbed his eyes as he tried to force the haze from them and his mind. "Most of what he said seemed true, at first anyway. But..."

"But?"

"His assumptions just don't add up to me. I mean, if someone wanted to destroy his stockpile, there were easy enough ways to do so that wouldn't have ended with the person injuring themselves, especially on the first stack they happen to go at. And then there's the dog."

"Dog?" asked Hilbrun. "What dog?"

"They have a guard dog. Thing nearly bit me just for getting too close. But it listens to the employees, or at least leaves them alone. Apparently, some people heard it barking like crazy in the middle of the night. So, I guess I have to wonder: why would it have barked if it knew the person breaking in? It doesn't make sense. So that makes me doubt the merchant's assumption that it was one of his own people."

Delvan was becoming invigorated by the thought process, each piece of what he'd seen earlier clicking into place for him as he described it to Hilbrun. His aloof mannerisms faded, and he became enamored with his deductions.

"And *then* there's the blood on the door's lock lever," he continued. "Why would the thief need to unlock the door *after* they'd smashed the spices? If the merchant is right, and the rear door had been left unlocked, why lock it again once you're inside the building? Seems unnecessary to me. If it had been one of the workers, and they'd somehow managed to copy the key for the safe, why not copy the key for the front door while you're at it?"

"They could've come in from the front, like you say, then left through the back because it was more secluded," Hilbrun retorted.

"Maybe," said Delvan. "I'm not saying it wasn't an employee, *but* there are just too many other things to consider to say it was for certain. My instincts are telling me it wasn't one of them."

Hilbrun turned and looked at Delvan, a half-surprised smile on his face.

"What?" asked Delvan.

"I always knew that you were smarter than you let on," Hilbrun said, smugly. "This might be the most excited I've ever seen you about anything that wasn't inside of a tavern."

"Well, I mean," he said, clamoring for words to say, "it just seems odd. Plus, a knight commander shows up to a theft? They're normally looking into murders, or escorting nobles, or busy overseeing entire companies of soldiers and quadrants of people. Why did he *personally* come to a robbery at a spice shop? I get that the owner's probably a high-ranking member of the Merchants' Guild, but still, we were already there, wasn't that enough?"

Hilbrun gave him a hearty slap on the back, smiling at him. "You know, if you put half as much effort into your duties as you did sneaking out for a night on the town, you'd likely be knighted early. And I agree with you," Hilbrun said, his tone turning more serious. "This wasn't an ordinary robbery, but I do think that our merchant friend knows who robbed him."

"You think it was a worker? But—"

"No, I don't. And, deep down, I don't think the merchant does either, but that would be a much easier solution for him. And one that would have gotten him out of the mess he's in. I think he desperately wants it to be one of them, but after talking to him in his office, I think it was someone else entirely.

"There was a wealth of emeralds and rubies stolen from his lock box, along with a few hundred moons and some suns. But he confided with me that he had something much, much more valuable in there. Something worth as much as his entire shop, if not more." Hilbrun quieted his voice. "A piece of cadentite. A massive one. And it being taken, well, let's just say that it's a very serious problem."

"Cadentite?" said Delvan, surprised. "As in the glowing pebbles? Why would that make you so confident that it was someone else who robbed him?"

The fleeing thief must have managed to bandage the wound in some makeshift way while meandering the alleys, as the drops had become intermittent and much further apart, eventually fading away completely. It didn't matter much now anyway, as Delvan and Hilbrun found themselves standing before the entrance of a wide, spiraling ramp of a wall tower leading to the Lower Valley.

"Well," said Hilbrun, "this is going to make things more difficult. Looks like they went down below." He turned to Delvan and asked, "How much do you know about what cadentite is used for?"

"Uhh," Delvan wondered if it was a trick question, "I've seen it as a tiny display piece in a few estates. My father always thought it was nothing more than a dumb trinket and never allowed it onto the grounds; said he didn't like the way it felt. Other than that, I've heard it's traded at a high value because it's rare. Why?"

"It has other uses," said Hilbrun, grimly. "Including a rather despicable one. Come on, I have an idea as to where to go next."

Delvan trailed behind him as they began the descent into the densely packed Lower Valley. Questions plagued his mind, a need for answers taking root deeply into it. Something about this mystery had grabbed his attention; so, he supposed, he might as well try to get to the bottom of it. As long as it stayed interesting, at least.

# CHAPTER THREE

*The heart gives life, binds the soul to its bearer. Tragically, the one who carries it is but a husk of his previous magnificence. A shadow that can only outline the former glory of its caster.*
Spoken during a session,
Sixty-second Day of Spring, Fifty-third Year of the Seventh Epoch

Desnia flitted through the currents of the crowded street as she made her way towards the port. The structures of the Lower Valley surrounding her were shorter in stature and less refined than their Upper Tier counterparts. They sprawled and stacked atop one another across the cavernous basin like the leaves of a tree at the end of autumn, the Upper Tier and King's Tower rising above like the sturdy trunk, the mountain its crown, always visible in the distance.

Some of the buildings she passed were little more than wooden shacks crammed in the gap of two stone buildings, their granite facades chipping and crumbling at the corners. Others were deteriorating shadows of their former glory, their masonry looking more like stones hauled from a river than the neat squares they might have once been. All around newer buildings used old as foundations, as many times the only place to build in the valley was up. Glass panes were broken in many of them, at least in the ones that had once been wealthy enough to afford glass. Grime from chimneys and time laid a thick film over the once polished stones, now no more than blackish-pink remnants of what was once a shine that could rival the Upper Tier. There were a few neighborhoods that managed to clean and maintain that sheen which spoke to their arrogant affluence, but for the most part, buildings like the half-dilapidated church she now walked by were the more familiar sort.

It had been nearly daybreak by the time she'd gotten home and found a barber to stitch the wound on her arm. After sleeping through the morning—and a good portion of the afternoon—she'd timed her departure during the shift change of a nearby mine, the dense flow of workers an adequate form of cover. She was to deliver her haul from the previous night today, and her employer wasn't known for his extended patience.

With fatigue still weighing heavily on her, eyes straining, arm aching, and the smell of cinnamon permanently hovering about her, she instinctually maneuvered through the throng. There was a certain balance of comfort and paranoia that came with a crowd. It was easier to blend and go unnoticed, people unable to single out the boyishly dressed Desnia. Empty streets led to more attention from their occupants, attention she wished to avoid. Instead, she opted for the heavy stream of people, judging its dangers to be less than the alternative.

Desnia weaved through the crowd, her eyes shifting rapidly. Was anyone holding her gaze? What was in that person's hand, hidden away in their pocket? Was that the first time she'd noticed that person behind her? Or were they following her?

These instincts were ingrained in her, a part of her subconscious and always active, regardless of her exhausted state. The streets did not forgive those that didn't heed them caution, and a lapse in concentration could quickly end in her demise as it did so many others.

As she passed through the massive gates of the city's imposing exterior wall and onto the docks of the port, her senses remained heightened, but changed focus. The docks were a host of ships of all shapes and sizes, magnificent masts rising high into the air while others waited in the harbor for an opportunity to berth. Yesterday they'd seemed like ants in the distance, now she would need to crane her neck to fully appreciate the immensity of them. Traders from far lands and nearby towns alike swarmed to the commercial wealth of the hub, grander than any in the kingdom—or so she'd heard, anyway. She couldn't care less about places she'd likely never see, and the harbor held none of the romance for her that others seemed to preach. It smelled like disgusting, rotting fish and was host to the parasite that leached from her. Nothing would make her happier than never having to see this corrupt jungle of masts, crates, and rope again.

The people here moved with purpose and urgency. Time was money and the longer you were docked, the higher your fees. A seldom few sauntered about, watching the people and ships intently, eyes shifting like Desnia's. Except that theirs had a gaze of authority, in contrast to Desnia's defensive paranoia.

She watched these men and counted them as she went, paying attention to the distance between them and how long they hovered about each vessel. These were the local enforcers, and she'd made it a point to track them and their habits each time she'd been forced to come down here. Knowing a danger before it became one was another lesson she'd learned young.

She reached the harbor master's pier and walked under the iron-mounted sign into the entrance of the warehouse-like structure. Before her was a wall covered in an assortment of scrolls, filed away into the cabinet that covered its entire length. In front of it was a man scribbling away with his quill, on a desk no longer visible under the organized piles of parchment. He did not even grace her with a glance as the bell above the door rang as she entered.

"He's available to see you," the studious man said to her, continuing to scrawl, eyes holding to his documents.

Desnia walked past him indifferently and down the nearby hall. After working her way through a maze of doors and corridors—long since memorized—she came to an entryway guarded by two large men. They stood with crossed arms and scarred faces, doing their best to look intimidating. Between both of their boulder shaped heads, she estimated them to have the combined mental capacity of a squirrel.

Perhaps that was a little harsh on squirrels...

She attempted to ignore them and went to enter the door between their hulking frames. They took a step towards each other, blocking her path, smiling down at her menacingly.

"And what do you think you're doing, street rat?" asked the first doorstop.

"Yeah," the second said, "you know the rules. No weapons in the boss's office." He pointed to the dagger at her side and gestured to hand it to him.

With a reluctant sigh she removed the dagger from her waist and handed it over, holding an unwavering glare at the brute.

"What's in the bag?" the first one asked.

She gripped the straps strung over her shoulder. "That's for Mixton to know, and if it were any of your damn business you'd actually be used as more than a barricade," she chided coldly.

"Ohh, she's feeling feisty today," said the second guard with a chuckle. "You know, Werv, we should check her for more weapons. You never know with this one."

"You're right," Werv replied. "She might be hidin' something' under them baggy clothes. I'd certainly like a, hmm, *closer* look. How about you take a few layers off and give us a twirl, love?"

"Yeah," said the second with a malevolent laugh and eager eyes. "A twirl to start, that'd be nice."

"Try and make me, you overgrown river slug," hissed Desnia through gritted teeth.

The smiles on the two guards turned to spiteful frowns, and Werv's monstrous hand grabbed ahold of the scruff of Desnia's jacket.

"Oh, that can be arranged, it can," he said. "I tried asking all nice-like, but I guess now we will just need to hold you down while we check you, and I plan to be thorough."

A high-pitched voice called through the wooden door before Desnia had a chance to respond in kind to Werv's violent gesture. "Let her in already! I don't have all day!" yelled the person from the other side.

Werv let her go with a look of annoyed disappointment, he and his partner taking a reluctant step back from the door. Desnia barged past them wearing a scowl and slammed the door behind her.

"Could you not break my door, Des?" asked the short, corpulent man sitting behind the desk at the center of the room which was permeated by the stink of cigar.

"I don't know, Mixton. Could you hire muscle that thinks with something aside from its dick?" Desnia retorted as she sat down in the leather chair opposite the desk, discretely shortened legs forcing her to look up at the bulbous man in front of her.

"Ha! Well, if you could find me some then I would consider it," he said, leaning forward, his bald head glistening in the light from the window, deep bags under his beady eyes. *I wouldn't be able to sleep if I were you either.* "Now, come, let's see what you've got for me, you've kept me waiting most of the day as it is. I trust you didn't have too much trouble last night?"

"Depends on how you define trouble," she said. "But no, not in any way that involves someone seeing me," she quickly added at a concerned glance from Mixton.

"You know, I could get here a lot sooner if your office was actually in the city." She took off the bag she was carrying and unloaded its contents onto the desk. Heaps of moons, suns, and small emeralds and rubies littered its surface.

"I'm the harbormaster, Des, that's why I work in a *harbor*," he said, eyeing the glistening valuables, his pebbly eyes almost crossing. *You're a harbormaster as much as I'm a noble, you fucking goon.* "Besides, it's too crowded in the city. A million people, all stacked on top of each other like crates in a warehouse. How you all live cramped together like that is beyond me."

She rolled her eyes, and from her pocket pulled out the black cloth that was wrapped around the cadentite and placed it on the center of the pile. She pulled the fabric away to reveal a glow, its purple light refracting through the gems and scattering its captivating shine across the leather desktop like coalescing stars. It seemed dimmer to her now, in the daylight, but still vibrant.

"Now that," Mixton said with no small amount of awe, "is the largest specimen of cadentite I have ever seen. Even more rare than sapphires! If you can believe it. Those at least come in a steady supply, even if it's only from the mines here. This, on the other hand, well a stone this size comes by once in a lifetime." *I wonder if he's this fascinated by it because of how much money it will make him? Maybe he's got some weird thing about rocks.* "And look—wait, what happened to your arm?!" he said, looking at the torn, bloody sleeve of her jacket. It was almost as if he actually cared. Almost.

"I fell," Desnia said, flatly. "After running into something... unexpected."

"Oh, you mean the guard dog, I assume? I heard that people could hear it barking from five streets away. It must have been impressive!"

"You knew about the fucking dog?!" Desnia exclaimed, a rage bursting from inside her.

"Of course not!" he said with a reassuring smile. It would be just like him to hide things from her as a challenge, for no other reason than his own amusement. "I hope it's not what did that to your arm?"

"No," said Desnia, leaning back in the chair. She rubbed her forearm thoughtfully, remembering the dog's fangs flashing in the night. "No, but it did lead to it."

"Well, maybe next time you should check to find out if the shop has a guard dog, yeah?" said Mixton. "Now, where's the rest of it?"

"What do you mean?" she asked, trying to suppress her anxiety. Mixton was well informed; after all, he was the one who knew where to find this piece of cadentite. He couldn't know the *exact* amount of money the merchant had on hand though, could he? She knew he'd physically rip apart her home looking for anything that he deemed his, not that there was much to find. The fractions that she skimmed and hid elsewhere in secret couldn't—shouldn't—be noticeable at a glance.

"You think I didn't know there was something else in the safe? Something else of incredible value?" he asked with an inquisitive and hard expression.

*The sapphire*, she thought. *Of course he knew about the damn sapphire.*

Desnia didn't care, no amount of threats or money could sway her to touch one of those. "This is everything, Mixton," she lied. "I completely emptied that safe. Even the hidden compartment in the back, where your precious cadentite was. Which, by the way, no one else you would've sent would be able to find, let alone access." She crossed her arms and held her eyes to Mixton's narrowed gaze.

She had to hold to the lie. He wouldn't dispose of her; she was too valuable to him. It was the skills that she possessed which had gotten her into his indebted servitude, after all. He knew her talents well, as he'd once been the target of them.

Worst mistake of her life.

"Hmm," said Mixton after a moment. "My sources did tell me that the safe was empty this morning, and the place got torn apart without anything else being found. I'd assumed you had... Well, I suppose the merchant must have moved it then. I'll have to have a discussion with my informants. Let's get this counted, shall we?"

He then began meticulously stacking the silver moon coins into even heights, along with the gold suns and noted their sums. Setting the cadentite aside, he took the rubies and emeralds and inspected them diligently with a loupe. He placed them into a box hopped down from his chair, his diminutive legs waddled him to the other side of the room. Desnia watched as his vest's buttons—strangled by the effort of holding the fabric together—threatened to pop off and become projectiles with each wheezing step.

Desnia tapped her finger as she waited, hoping that he would either move faster so she could leave or for one of the buttons to rocket off and do something interesting.

He produced a scale and weighed the jewels, taking additional notes. Sitting back in his chair he silently marked a ledger while Desnia watched, the scratching of the quill the only sound. Disappointingly slow and uneventful.

"Hmm," he finally said. "With the estimated value of the gems, and the added coinage, the sum total of this haul comes to four thousand two hundred and sixty-five moons. Well, Des, that might be a new record for you, impressive! *But* my informant told me the merchant claimed to have lost a few hundred more than this, but he must be lying, because you wouldn't dare steal from me, would you, Des?"

"The only thing I stole is what's in front of you, Mixton," she said, heart suddenly racing. "The merchant probably lied, looking for a higher insurance pay out. You can't trust any of them."

"Indeed," he said, seeming to believe her. "It's actually impressive that the sum you have here is as close in value as what he claimed. Perhaps he was trying to avoid attention, you know how *unsavory* the people seeking cadentite can be. Who knows who might have come to his door if they discovered he had any in his possession. Theft might become the least of his concerns."

"How much is the cadentite worth?" she asked, noticing its exclusion from the original sum.

"That's for me to know, and you not to ask about. Understand?" he asked rhetorically.

She shut her mouth and slouched sullenly in the chair.

"Now then," Mixton said, "with your take at ten percent, your cut is—well, I'll be generous and round up—four hundred and twenty-seven moons. Then, subtracting fifty percent for your debt, you will be paid two hundred and thirteen moons."

He pulled four suns from the pile and counted out thirteen moons before putting the handful of coins into a small bag and extending it towards Desnia.

As she sat up and reached for it, however, he jerked it back with a jingle, looking as though he were pondering a thought.

"Wait," he said, "what happened to the dress that I loaned you? The silk one you said you needed so desperately. I must admit, I have a difficult time imagining you wearing anything besides that loose men's ware."

She clenched her jaw, and answered, "I... I don't have it. But I swear I'm going to get it back for you! I couldn't go back for it, they've probably tripled the guard in the Merchants' Quarter. But once they get back to normal patrols, I can go get it, I promise."

"Hmm. I believe you, Des," he said, with an empathetic nod. "But, until you get it back for me, I'm going to be forced to withhold some of your pay. You understand. Once you get it back to me, I will repay you, minus the interest, of course. It was a rather expensive gown, and I can't let people think that I will just hand out such things without the expectation of having them returned, can I?"

He reached into the pouch and withdrew three of the gold suns, handing it back to Desnia considerably lighter.

She snatched it out of his hands, attempting to temper her contempt. She stood up to leave, but before she could, Mixton spoke.

"Now hold on, Des," he said in his squeaky, nasally tone. "I have some other things to discuss with you. Please, sit." She sat back down and folded her arms. "I need you to deliver this cadentite to its rightful owner. Are you aware of the den on Dust Street? Good. Bring it there and tell them that I sent you. Go straight from here, these are *not* people you want to keep waiting. Don't expect any payment from them either, they've already paid. Fantastic customer.

"After that, I have something else for you. Another job. A big one."

Desnia tried feigning a smile, but even she could tell it fell far short of being convincing. "What is it?" she asked.

"I don't want to ruin the surprise," he said with a greasy smile. "Go to this address tomorrow night and knock three times, then five, then one on the back door. You'll get the details from there." He quickly wrote a note on a slip of parchment and handed it to Des. "Gods, am I glad you can read. Do you know what it's like trying to explain directions to the likes of the boys out there? Torture."

"I think I'd rather stab my own hand," said Desnia.

"I'm sure," he said with a chuckle. "But listen, Des," he said, again becoming serious, "this job, it's not like anything you've ever worked before."

She doubted that. Mixton gave all the high-stakes jobs to her, a high success rate and her debt to him made her a known—and reliable—quantity.

"You've had me rob a prison before, Mix. I can't see how it could be much worse than that," she said, suppressing a roll of her eyes.

"Des, the people that reached out to me about this job... They're after something *big*. Just thinking about it, it makes me..." He shuddered. "It's hard for me to not just blabber all about it in my excitement. They'll talk about it for decades. You'll be infamous, Des, there won't be a person on the streets who doesn't know your name." *That's the last thing I want, you selfish weasel.* "You do this for me, and I'll consider your debt paid. *That's* how important this is. I'll even forfeit the interest."

Desnia sat upright. "Are you being serious?" she asked with a reserved desperation. What was the angle? The catch?

"I thought that might get your attention," Mixton said with a slimy smile.

"Who am I stealing from that could have enough to cover a three thousand sun debt *and* get you your profit?" she asked, potential targets scrolling in her mind. Who could have a hundred-thousand-plus moons in reserve? Only the richest and most powerful could have that kind of liquid wealth, but there were reasons that people didn't succumb to the temptation of robbing them. She knew the consequences could be severe, but did it matter if it freed her from Mixton's choke hold?

"I know you have questions," Mixton said, seeing the confusion and shock on her face, "but I assure you, this offer is real. We both may very well be able to retire after this. One small thing, though."

*Of course,* she thought, *here it comes. This snake always has a catch.*

"You'll need to work with a team," he concluded.

"What?" Surely he was joking. "I don't work with other people, Mixton. They can't be relied on, they fail, and frankly are all awful at their jobs. Just tell me what you need, and I'll take care of it."

Other people couldn't be trusted. They were either unprepared, overconfident, under qualified, or—more often than not—a combination of all three.

Jobs *never* went well when she had to work with other people. She seethed at the thought.

"I would, Des, truly. But I'm not the one organizing this job, and the person managing it already has the team working on it. They just need your expertise. If you want out of your debt, you're going to have to deal with it, like it or not."

She sat and thought it over for a moment. Not that she had much to mull about. Declining Mixton wasn't really an option, and if this was as lucrative as he implied, then he was likely to force her into doing the job anyway. Or he would tie stones to her and drop her in the harbor with his other protestors.

"Fine," she finally said. "I'll do it."

"Great! I knew I could count on you, Des. Here, take this and you can get going. I have other appointments today, you know. And please, don't forget that it's worth a fortune." He handed her the piece of cadentite and waved her away.

As she reached the door, he called out, "Don't let me down, Des."

*Wouldn't dream of it, you despicable fucking sewer rat,* she thought before opening the door and leaving silently. A small ember of hope smoldered inside of her. She tried to ignore it, a lifetime of disappointment and betrayals had taught her better. Yet, there it was. Maybe this was it.

Maybe this was her chance to finally be free.

Partially, anyway.

# CHAPTER FOUR

*Their fall must come! Their fall will come! Eternity will feel as though a fleeting moment for those who thought to avoid the inevitable...*
Episode during sleep,
Third Day of Summer, Twentieth Year of the Seventh Epoch

The first thing that Delvan noticed was the smell.

There was a certain aroma woven into the fabric of the streets in the Lower Valley. It hung like a cloud over everything in the basin. More *refined* areas were a tolerable state; others, like the homeless slum that was only two streets away, created a toxic odor so foul that Delvan could not decide between inhaling through his nose and gagging at the smell, or withstanding the taste of the air passing over his tongue as he breathed through his mouth.

*How do these people live like this?*

He and Hilbrun were standing in front of an empty merchant's cart in what was supposedly a "better" area, but it looked much the same to Delvan as all the other streets had. Beggars sitting at corners, dirty faces looking at them from the corner of dark eyes, and people sifting through garbage smelling scraps of food just a few of the nose turning sights nearby.

"Where is he?" muttered an annoyed looking Hilbrun.

"Who exactly are we looking for?" asked Delvan, still debating how to breathe.

"The merchant who owns this stall," said Hilbrun. "He's given me information before, for a price." *Unsurprising*, Delvan thought. Members of the

Merchants' Guild rarely gave anything away for free. "I've never not seen him here before though. It's strange."

"Why a merchant? Why *this* merchant? What are we looking for anyway? There has to be someone else we can ask." Despite the odor, Delvan's curiosity was piqued, but he wouldn't mind if their investigation took them somewhere more civilized.

"This merchant because I've helped him out in the past and he gives me information for a discount, which is more than I can say about half the others I'd have to haggle with around here. We're Blues, Del; our wealth and social standing is implied. Most merchants wouldn't think twice about charging you half a sun to tell you where the best food stand is," Hilbrun said in an instructional tone, "even though we could arrest any one of them for any reason. Or worse, if you're anything like Commander Ferrand.

"You'll spend your life going through first encounters where most people will have an upper hand on the conversation just because they immediately know something about you, and you might not know anything about them. All because you wear a Blue uniform. Don't let them take advantage of you."

"Spoken like the true son of a merchant."

Delvan agreed with the concept of what Hilbrun was saying, but who would dare challenge a Blue? They were the knights of the King's Sapphiric Court. And the fact that they were highborn should make these people *more* likely to give them information, as was their duty. Not charge a fee. But, Hilbrun had spent more time in the Lower Valley than he had, and if Hilbrun was saying it, there was probably a reason.

"He's not humble enough for the title of 'merchant.' Magnate is more appropriate. Alright, follow me," Hilbrun said, turning and walking towards a storefront further down the street. "To answer your first question," said Hilbrun, walking with determination, "we're asking merchants, specifically ones in this area, because it's near one of the slums. When the homeless find the money—likely stolen—they come to the nearest stores to purchase whatever they might need. Usually alcohol and food. In that order. These people, they talk. And when they talk, the merchants hear. So, unless you want to go through the slums trying to speak with any homeless that don't immediately run or hide from us, this is going to be the easiest way to get the information we're looking for."

Hilbrun then reached the door of a small liquor store. Most alcohol was sold in taverns, but there were some private vendors that sold by the bottle for consumption elsewhere. This one was far more ragged than any Delvan had ever been in, however. Paint flaked from the door, the granite walls caked in the same filth that pervaded the rest of the buildings along the street. The sign above the door was hardly legible, horribly faded from the sun.

They entered the equally unkempt interior. A thin, middle-aged man behind the counter looked up from the box he was unpacking, giving a smile without flinching. "My Lords," he said, "how might I be able to serve two knights of the Court, such as yourselves? I am sure that I could rummage through my supply and find some rather good vintages for you, if you'd like?"

"No, thank you," said Hilbrun. "I was actually wondering if you could tell me if you've seen Reltand recently? From the booth up the street, has a red birthmark on his jaw."

"Ah," said the merchant, his smile wavering. "No, I haven't seen him in a few days. Not that I am complaining, the man is always undercutting me. Trying to make up for his lack of supply in comparison to mine, which I assure you is extensive, even into the cellars. I'd be happy to give you a tour."

*The man is nothing if not persistent,* Delvan thought.

"Have you checked with the guild about it?" asked Hilbrun, looking concerned.

"Gods, no," replied the man, "he's only been gone a few days. And he certainly doesn't include me when discussing his travel plans. We may be members of the guild, but that doesn't make him any less my competition. Perhaps *I* could help you with something."

"Perhaps," said Hilbrun. "I assume that you get some of the homeless here, from the slums?"

"Indeed, yes. Filthy vermin, I have to fan out the smell after they leave each time. *But* if they have the coin to pay... I have been known to make a few transactions with them, yes."

"Have any of them ever discussed local iguan dens?" ask Hilbrun. *Is that what he wants to look into?* thought Delvan. "Might have been as simple as them talking about where they've been recently, or where they wanted to go. Any list of places to start would be helpful."

"Hmm, well I seem to recall a few things, but the specifics are hazy to me," said the merchant with feigned concentration. "Perhaps a purchase from your good self would shake the memory free, hmm?"

"If, and only *if*, your information turns up anything, I'll come back and purchase a bottle of something, how about that?" haggled Hilbrun.

"My Lord, I would only want to provide you with the selection from my most prestigious reserves. I have a bottle of liquor fermented from berries that grow in the grasslands, picked after the first frost of the year and made in a secret way. The bottles from last year's harvest came in a few weeks ago and I think it would be quite suitable for you. I'd even be willing to give you a discount: fifty-two moons, and it's yours. Though I would need payment up-front. You understand, of course, my business cannot function as a pawn shop."

He was clearly smart enough to not ask directly for a bribe from a member of the military—an imprisonable offense—but he certainly wasn't being subtle about it.

"Market value on ice gin right now is thirteen moons," said Hilbrun confidently, holding the man's gaze. "Mostly because last autumn's harvest was entirely lost to a hailstorm. That bottle you're sitting on is over a year old at this point, and I am well aware of how it sours with age. If you have something worth *actually* buying, I'll consider it. And I will come back and pay you *after* I've confirmed the information you provide. A courtesy I'm sure you're willing to provide to lords, such as ourselves."

The merchant let out a nervous laugh, "Ah, yes, how could I have forgotten how long I've had those bottles. Yes, I'd be happy to hold a bottle of Drunt whiskey for you, fifteen years barrel aged. Forty moons, just for you, Sire."

Hilbrun gave him a nod.

"I'll get a list for you," said the merchant as he pulled out a quill and parchment.

The sun had begun to set, the gloom of dusk masking the filth of the streets and replacing it with a sense of the unknown. Delvan noticed that Hilbrun cautiously turned his head towards dark alleys, his hand remaining near the hilt of his sword. *Why so cautious? Not like anyone would dare try to assault two Blues.*

They had just finished looking into the third dead-end lead on their list—another seven remaining—and Hilbrun was clearly agitated, scratching at his head and grumbling through a tight jaw.

"Gods-damn it!" Hilbrun shouted, turning the heads of some nearby people walking by, giving the pair a wide berth.

*Why's he so frustrated?* Was it because he wanted to retaliate against the knight commander who insulted him? Did he have some sort of relation to the spice merchant that he hadn't disclosed to Delvan? Maybe he was passionate about solving this crime? In the months Delvan had worked with him, he had never seen Hilbrun become so irate.

"Maybe we should come back tomorrow," suggested Delvan, "there's no way we can get through the rest of the list tonight."

"Why?" asked Hilbrun angrily. "Do you have drinking buddies that you need to get back to? A dress to chase? Why don't you do something useful for once and actually *help*."

Delvan's jaw went slack, and he felt a pang of anger and shock in his chest. Why was Hilbrun acting like this? Delvan wasn't doing anything wrong by going out. Hell, half the people he met at the tavern with were other Blues. This wasn't *his* fault.

"I've been helping all day!" he said. "Going to door after door with you, dealing with the smell of this place... I feel like my armor is going to reek like a horse stall for weeks. Maybe if you actually told me *anything* about what we're doing, I would be able to help! Why are we looking for iguan dens anyway? What does some plant that these commoners like to smoke have anything to do with stolen cadentite?!"

"Keep your voice down," said Hilbrun in a hushed, but angry tone. "Come here." He pulled Delvan into a quiet alley away from the herds of people in the street. "Look, what do you know about iguan? Huh?"

"I don't know," said Delvan, feeling pressured by the question. "It's a drug, people down in the Valley like to smoke it. I had an instructor at the academy that said the weak willed sought it for an escape, that it made these people feel better about their miserable lives."

Hilbrun shook his head and said, "They tell you that at the Academy because they don't want you to touch it, it has weird effects on Blues when grown a certain way and they figure it's better to make you detest the people that use it, rather than to tell you not to. What did you do the last time anyone told you *not* to do something?"

"Um," Delvan said with a shrug, "I did it anyway?"

"Exactly. Also, Del, I know being raised in a noble house—yours especially—can lead to a twisted view of the world. But these people, the ones down here in the Valley, they're not as different from you and I as you might think. I've grown up around people of all types making deals with my father, some of them poor with meager items to sell, others wealthy, looking to negotiate shipping lanes. I've seen paupers with negotiating skills that rivaled my father's best men, and wealthy nobles looking to undercut and steal whenever they can. Stop looking down at these people from the Upper wall as though they are a necessary nuisance and start trying to remember they are people trying to survive.

"Anyway," Hilbrun continued, "iguan—when grown in normal soil—causes mild optical illusions if ingested. People might see colors a different way or think stationary objects are moving. It's hardly much different than having a few too many drinks."

*Doesn't sound half bad.*

"But, when you take a small amount of cadentite dust and add it to the soil it's grown in, well it becomes something much different. People disassociate, think they've been transported to clouds in the sky or the lands of the dead below. You see people and shadows that aren't there. It's also *highly* addictive. That's why it's illegal, but cadentite is so rare there aren't many places you can find it laced into iguan. A small amount of the dust will last for years, and it makes cadentite worth a fortune on the black market. Assuming you can even find any.

"There was a Blue in my pupil group that tried it and got hooked. After a few months he was about as sane as a Seer. They shipped him off and I haven't heard anything since."

"Is that why you want to find this so badly?" asked Delvan. "Because you knew this other pupil?"

"I suppose that's part of it," said Hilbrun, looking into the distance retrospectively. "That stolen cadentite is going to end up in an iguan den, Del, I'm sure of it. It's also just that... Never mind, it's not important."

Delvan furrowed his brow, "What?" he asked, wondering what it was that Hilbrun wasn't sharing with him. He shared his entire life with Hilbrun, something he was never able to do with anyone else. Growing up in a long line of Blues had been more systematic than it was nurturing. Expectations were laid on him by his parents, his older siblings, all of these people who he hardly even knew because he'd spent his life in boarding schools, or with them away on behalf of the King. There was a certain expectation of service for Blues, a demanding loyalty that superseded all.

"I just," said Hilbrun with a heavy sigh, "I want to do this because it's what *I* want, you know? Not some order from a barracks captain who's on a power trip or is just trying to appease the annoyed rantings of another noble. There are things we can do to make a *real* difference, and if we find this cadentite and get it to the right people, away from the hands of those that want to keep power for themselves, then we could make a difference in the world."

"I mean, isn't that what we do anyway?" asked Delvan. Blues served the King, first as law enforcement in the capital, a way to gain experience and have a presence in his shadow while waiting to be knighted. Then, they would lead armies, be the right hands of city lords or lords themselves, oversee crops and farms of sprawling duchies. The list went on and on, but they served the King and His kingdom for the better of society.

"Is it?" asked Hilbrun. "We didn't choose this life, Del. Our parents made us what we are, disregarding our consent. They lease these gems from the King to turn us into his sword, and we are swung with no regard to our own wants and desires. We're brought up so that the only life we know is this sapphire around our neck, our future laid out for us like some map.

"Every Blue does what you do, Del, at some point in their life. They rebel, go out and try to experience some taste of freedom. Everyone lets us do as we please because they know, in the end, that we will succumb to the will of the King. The fight will be bled from us, and we'll follow orders as we were taught and indoctrinated to do."

*That's a little dramatic,* Delvan thought. How could Hilbrun just reduce his desire for some fun into something so rudimentary? He was more than some rebellious child going through a phase.

"I know you feel the same thing I do," said Hilbrun. "I know that there is a spark in you, hidden behind the person who pretends to not care about anything. You've been excited about this investigation since we defied orders and came here, rather than heading back to the barracks like Commander Ferrand instructed. You want more, and maybe there's a way you can have it. I know it sounds ridiculous, but if we can find this cadentite, we take a step towards a life that is *our own.*

"Just think about it. If what you want is to appease parents who care more about their own image than your free will, then don't come with me tomorrow. But if you want an opportunity for more, well I could really use your help."

Delvan wasn't sure what to say. He was interested in this case because of the mystery, wasn't he? He had wanted to help Hilbrun with finding the thieves since their arrival at the spice shop. Or was it when he started putting the questions together, looking at the evidence? When had that been? Questions spun in his mind like a vortex, and he was unable to find words to respond.

The sun had vanished behind the horizon now, and lamplighters were diligently walking down the street, illuminating the stone pavers to guide people in the late hours. As one was lit next to them, Hilbrun finally seemed to consider the hour.

"Let's go back to the barracks," Hilbrun said, folding the parchment list into his pocket. "We can't get through all of these tonight, and it would be too hard to search for something so well hidden at night."

Delvan trailed behind as they returned, head hung in thought. Being a Blue was his destiny. His purpose. Everything that he'd ever known. Sure, it wasn't something he had chosen, but it was still his calling. His life was his own.

Wasn't it?

# Chapter Five



*Eyes, not my own, stare out and search. Ever wanting for means...*
*Anguish, pain, and resentment. Grief. So much grief...*
Spoken during lamentations after letter from family,
Twenty-ninth Day of Winter, Tenth Year of the Seventh
Epoch

Desnia worked her way through the maze of streets and stairs as though she were following an invisible line guiding her path. People said that the city was too immense to ever be able to commit to memory. She never saw it that way. She saw the alley where she ran after picking the pocket of a miner, smelled the stew-pies of her favorite tavern, and felt the rough texture of the crushed granite stones that covered a patched sidewalk. The streets were part of her mind, each turn a memory, and every sight an association. Maybe she didn't know every street, but few could claim to know more.

Her payment was strapped tightly to the inside of her shirt, not wanting to risk the telltale sound of coins bouncing around in a pouch. She might as well throw the money in the street now if she were to do that.

She thought of the money as she passed several taverns, the sounds of patrons already becoming boisterous. It didn't matter the time of day, there was always a tavern to be found with warm food and tapped ale. The mines never ceased, and the crews of each shift sought taverns like flies to a horse after their day was done. Desnia desperately wished to join them. She hadn't eaten much in the past few days, and her stomach ached in protest as she passed the scent of yet another warm meal.

She couldn't go. Not yet. She had to deliver the cadentite. She was willing to take risks, but losing cadentite worth more than most of the buildings on this block was not one of them.

She fiddled with the small stone in her pocket, feeling it through the black fabric she had it wrapped in. The thought of stealing it for herself had occurred to her, of course. But others had considered the same. None of them had lived long enough to reap the rewards.

No, she had enough to worry about as it was. And apparently a way out of her current debt with Mixton. Assuming he was telling the truth.

She reached a nondescript building, a beggar sitting beside a pile of garbage out front. Stone steps led up to the center of the large structure. The lack of windows on the first floor indicated that it was likely a storehouse. Flanking the side of the main stairs, a flight went down and turned into a dark basement door.

This was the location of one of the largest iguan dens in the eastern Lower Valley. Desnia knew the apparent homeless man to truly be a guard and lookout, with others like him lining the street, prepared to give signals and have the people inside flee at the first sign of trouble.

She walked down the steps and entered the unlocked door. Inside was a small anteroom, and she stood, waiting, staring at the door into the main basement. Someone inside would see her and open it. Knocking was a sure sign that you were *not* supposed to be here.

The door silently swung open, the windowless room beyond its burly guard was dimly lit by candles with red shrouds, dulling any harsh light and giving the room a pinkish glow. Just beyond the entry was a small desk, an attractive woman with long, black hair that flowed over a contrasting white robe sitting behind it.

She looked up at Desnia with a smile as she entered. Desnia did her best to crack a semblance of one back, her face contorting awkwardly.

"Hello," said the woman in a polite manner, "will you be needing a room today?" She gestured with her hand to the rows of paper-paneled screens filling the enormity of the basement behind her. They stood just taller than Desnia, and if she stood on the tips of her toes, she could see all the way to the back wall of the cavernous space. Each created a makeshift room for customers to lay down and smoke iguan, giving the room a haze that burnt her eyes.

"No," she replied. "Mixton sent me."

"Ah," said the woman with a knowing nod. "Please, head to the door in the back. Knock lightly before entering."

Desnia again tried to smile as she walked away, shaking her head as she crossed the basement at how awkward it felt. Why was it so hard for her to even *pretend* to smile? And what was so good about these other people's lives that they were able to draw one on command? Maybe they were all just better liars than she was.

She noticed that most of the screen doors were closed, only a few rooms left unoccupied. She could hear mild coughs and rustling from behind them as she walked down the corridor, the people likely lost in their high.

She shuddered at the thought and quickened her pace.

Set into the black, inanite walls at the rear of the basement was the heavy wooden door she was looking for. She knocked lightly and then entered, finding herself in yet another antechamber. Ahead of her was a heavy steel door, the guard beside it sitting there patiently with an axe leaning against the wall at his side. He looked at her and then pointed at the closed door to her right.

Desnia knocked lightly again and cautiously entered the small room. The interior was lit with a few candles, providing a familiar yellow light opposed to the strange glow in the main room. Bookcases and tables lined the wall, covered in strange-looking equipment and texts, leaving little to none of the surfaces bare. More cluttered tables in the center made the room cramped. There was a man wearing a black robe sitting at one of the tables writing, his profile facing Desnia. His eyes looked weary but sharp, set deeply into a gaunt face with boney features, she thought that she could see the bumps of his spine under his robe.

As she quietly closed the door behind her, the glint of a small ring on the table next to her caught her eye. Wide and of polished silver, it had a beautiful recurring pattern covering the entire surface, the black lines set delicately into the metal. A bit of temptation fluttered through her as its luster pulled at her provocatively.

*Nope,* she thought, *that's a terrible fucking idea. Let's leave everything* exactly *where I found it.* The people that operated this den were not the type to forgive. And they were not the type to punish quickly. She forcibly kept her hands in her pockets, though she couldn't help staring at the seductive jewelry as she walked forward, her fingers craving freedom as they burned with an itch to snag it.

"You may leave the cadentite on the table there," said the robed man, pointing with a boney finger to the table beside him, his eyes staying on his parchment.

Desnia pulled the cloth from her pocket and put the cadentite inside of it onto the table, its purple glow streaking across the cluttered tabletop in all directions. It still felt strange to her, as though it were projecting more than just light, penetrating into her chest.

She didn't know all the details regarding cadentite use in iguan production. Her instincts told her that this was likely enough of the mineral to provide iguan for decades—if not longer—for an operation the size of this one.

The man looked over at the glowing stone with a stoic expression. Desnia put her hands behind her back and stepped away from the cadentite, fidgeting with the cloth in her hand. She didn't dare say anything unless spoken to, and waited for an indication from the man that she could leave.

"Is that all of it?" he asked, as though he expected there to be more.

"Yes," she said with a nod, not daring to question his inquiry.

"Thank you," he said, with what sounded like a hint of disappointment. "You may leave."

She bowed her head slightly and backed up, her backside and hands bumping into the table behind her. The contents quivered slightly, the sound of glass and metal chiming against one another stabbing her in the gut like a blade. Her fingers fiddled and felt at something with a mind not her own before she shoved them in her pockets as the man quickly turned his head at the disturbance.

How had she been so clumsy?

"Sorry," she said, bowing again—more carefully this time—and hastily exiting the room.

She closed the door behind her, still cringing at her carelessness. What had happened there? She was never so unaware of her surroundings in a lit room that she would unintentionally bump into something. Maybe it was the lack of food, or perhaps sleep. She rubbed her eyes, her bandaged, aching arm throbbing with pain as she moved her fingers. Walking away, she noticed again how hungry she was, maybe she should've ventured into a tavern on her way—

Desnia stopped mid stride as she put her hand in her pocket. She'd grabbed the small bit of cloth within and felt... something hard, circular, and small? *Oh no.* She realized with sudden terror what she'd done. When she collided with the table she must have instinctually swiped the ring from it, wrapping it in the cloth and shoving it in her pocket.

How tired was she? How could she have done something so monumentally stupid? A lift like that *was* instinct for her, without a doubt, but she would never unconsciously steal after adamantly deciding *not to*, would she? And from someone so dangerous?

The guard was now looking at her with growing interest. She could either turn around and return the ring, admitting that she'd stolen it and facing what was—in her mind—an unquestionable wrath. Or she could keep walking and hope that he assumed it was misplaced, or that it was taken by someone else. Both options seemed terrible, but she had to decide quickly.

She stepped forward into the main basement, exhaling the breath she seemed to have forgotten about. What was she doing? Was delaying the ire of the cloaked man a wise decision?

She paced anxiously, fiddling with the cloth-wrapped ring in her pocket for a moment before pulling her hand out and making her way to the den's entrance. She was deaf to the sounds of the room, her eyes focused on the tiled floor and her mind racing with a hundred thoughts. She only lifted her eyes upon reaching the desk and seeing the woman behind it smile at her in a calmingly genuine way.

How did she do that?

"Is there anything I can interest you in before you leave? Our first session is free for new customers," said the woman with a gentle tone.

Desnia shook her head out of her trance and said, "Uh, no, I don't partake. Thanks though?" *Why did that come out as a question?* "But you don't have any muted inanite, do you?" she said, quickly changing the subject.

"Why yes, actually," the woman said, still somehow holding that damned smile, "a Jack left some here on his last visit." She reached into a drawer of the desk and produced a small, perfectly cut block of pure white stone.

"How much?" asked Desnia.

"For you, this one is free," said the radiant woman, "just come back and see us again for the next one. We don't have much use for it anyway, it just gets sold to some different guilds on occasion. We don't really have it in the quantity that they want though, so it mostly just piles up in the drawer here."

"Thanks," said Desnia, finding it impossible to attempt a smile with anxiety over the ring still coursing through her. She took the block and put it into an empty pocket, looking back at the curled lips and big eyes. *Does she look different than when I got here? Gods, I really need sleep.* She had no intention of returning and exposing herself to the victim of her theft, presenting herself like a rat in a snake's burrow. She felt a twinge of sadness about that, for some reason.

"Are you sure I can't interest you in a free session? I can give you one of our private suites," the woman said.

"I'm good, really," said Desnia.

"Well, if you change your mind, you know where to find us. And you look familiar, have I seen you around here before? Maybe somewhere nearby?"

"The Hillview Tavern, maybe?" said Desnia, absently, enamored by the gentle smile. "I'm there pretty often."

"Hmm, maybe, I've been there once or—"

Before she could continue, a man stumbled out from one of the many aisles. He meandered around, looking lost, and immediately caught the attention of the woman behind the desk. From the shadows along the wall, a strong looking man appeared and grabbed the confused and inebriated patron.

"Please, excuse me for a moment," the woman said as she stood and walked over to the customer, her robe flowing gracefully. "I'm sorry," she said to the man, his eyes low and sunken, unable to look directly at her, "but you cannot leave until you're sober. Can't risk having a Blue notice you, now can we? Gor here will walk you back to your booth, and in an hour or so you'll be free to leave."

"I-I don't wanna leave," he muttered. "I just need one more hit, that's all. I swear I'm good for it. One-just one more, please..."

"I'm afraid your ledger is already rather red, mister Aubron. If you come back with some form of payment, then we can see about getting some more for you. Gor, please escort our guest back to his accommodations."

"No! P-Please! I need-I need to see it again. That beautiful land beyond the sky and stars...I need it!" cried the gaunt looking man as the guard's oversized hands gripped his shoulders and guided him back down the aisle that he emerged from.

*She has the patience of a priest. How's she deal with ruffians like that and stay so calm?* she wondered while the woman stood with her back to Desnia, watching as the man was guided back to his booth. *Have I seen her at the tavern before? There's so many, what're the chances she goes to the one near me? She doesn't seem the type to come around to my neighborhood, she's far too put together to come by that slum—*

She felt the stab of anxiety twist in her chest like an animal unleashed from its cage, tearing her thoughts apart with claw and fang. Why was she still here, while the stolen ring weighed down her pocket with worry? She had spent too long here as it was. And had she just told the attendant her favorite tavern?

Before she could allow herself to commit any additional and atrocious lapses in judgment, she turned and left hurriedly, heading back onto the street. A goodbye wasn't needed to someone she would never see again. Though a small pang of guilt struck her as the door thudded shut behind her.

She needed a meal, *several* pints of ale, and a long night's rest. Maybe that would put her head back on straight. Hopefully.

# Chapter Six

*Upon my arrival discord shall be sown and minds will be sickened with the disease of distrust. I will watch as they turn against each other. And then we may have vengeance.*
Ravings after accidental exposure,
Fifty-second Day of Spring, Fifty-fifth Year of the Seventh Epoch

The early morning fog hung around Delvan as though imitating the one in his mind.

A night of questions had led to doubts, and doubts had led to more questions. The cyclical conundrum had trapped him, like a pool in the current, and no matter how hard he tried, he couldn't escape its pull. Who *was* he, really? The disappointing son of a great house, pretending to rebel against the guided path that had been laid out for him? Or was he going to be his own man? Was that even a possibility, given his circumstances?

He tried to shake the thoughts. This wasn't something that he was going to answer in a night. For now, he had decided to help Hilbrun recover the stolen cadentite. Maybe it would help him understand who he *could* be, like Hilbrun had said, though he wasn't sure on how exactly that was going to happen. Or maybe it would just cause him to realize and accept that he was trapped in this life. He didn't know. But this would at least buy him time to think.

He trusted Hilbrun, and he didn't have anyone else. Not anyone that he could share these types of dilemmas with anyway. If Hilbrun said this was something that could help him become his own man, then it was at least worth trying.

"I'm glad you came," said Hilbrun, the morning mist dewing on his armor, a contented smile on his face. He came and stood by Delvan at the wall's parapet, nothing but a gray mist before them, hiding the hundred feet of wall face that plummet straight down into the Lower Valley below.

"Yeah, well, you'd be lost out there without me," said Delvan, sarcastically.

"Ha! True, very true. How would I make it through the day without you? You're not going to regret this, Del; you're doing the right thing."

"Even if it's disregarding direct orders?" asked Delvan. He was committed to helping Hilbrun, and not following orders wasn't particularly unnerving for him. But upsetting a knight commander? That was a dangerous game, even for them.

"We'll be fine. I requested Lower Valley duty for us last night, told the captain that I had some leads on iguan dens. It's pretty low priority for him, but there wasn't much else on the docket for today anyway. If any of Ferrand's sycophants run into us, we have official orders," said Hilbrun, looking out into the silvery fog, leaning against the stone.

"We should head out," he continued after a moment, standing up straight. He stood a few inches taller than Delvan, but sometimes it felt like he was a full head above him with his commanding posture. "There's a lot of places left on this list, and they're scattered throughout the Valley."

Hilbrun led the way and Delvan followed, resigning to the commitment of aiding him in the investigation. The pair mounted and trotted their horses down the Upper Tier tower and into the shrouded streets below, and Delvan tried to put his questions out of his mind.

The midday sun had burnt away the morning vapor and was now beating down on them, sweat building under the thick leather of Delvan's armor. Businesses were operating in full swing, and the streets had come alive with the activity of daily life. People gave them a wide berth as they stood in the street, refusing to look them in the eye. Even after all these years, it still felt odd to be feared in such a way, despite their prestige.

Hilbrun crossed another line off the list with a bit of charcoal and sighed in frustration. "That leaves three more to check," he said. "The next one is on the east side of town. The merchant wrote that some beggar named Rockin' Mari was in his shop and ranting like she'd recently been on iguan."

"I don't know, Hil," said Delvan. "I'm beginning to think this merchant is sending us to mine an empty lode. We haven't seen the *slightest* indication of an iguan den, and half the people he put on this list don't seem to exist."

He was frustrated, and tired. Existential crises and sleep were not a conducive combination for rest, as it turns out. The heavy, humid air didn't help either.

"He wants to get paid, so there has to be *some* validity to this list. No one's going to just hand this to us, Del. We have to put in the work. Come on."

Delvan rolled his eyes in silent protest, but followed Hilbrun as they mounted their horses and led them down the street, mainly following the larger, more highly trafficked roads. These at least had an occasional signpost, and tended to travel in straight, predictable paths. Delvan had already almost been turned around more than once today.

They arrived at the intersection that Hilbrun had been searching for. He turned to Delvan and said, "Alright, this one is going to be more difficult with all the alleys and side streets around here. I think there's a guard outpost nearby. I'm going to see if they have a few soldiers they can spare to lend us a hand searching to help this go faster. In the meantime, why don't you start taking a look around. I'll only be gone a few minutes."

"Works for me," Delvan said. He wasn't optimistic about finding this beggar—most seemed to scatter before he and Hilbrun arrived, like they knew they were coming. The ones that did remain did little talking and weren't the most forthcoming with what information they would provide.

Regardless, he tied off his horse and walked down the street looking for any beggars to talk to. Trash littered the cobbles, the areas around some of the rudimentary shelters of the local homeless surprisingly being the cleanest part of the street. Most of these people burrowed their way into the piles of stacked, wooden crates and tattered fabric that looked like organized garbage as he approached, hiding like mice from a hawk. Walking through a nearby alley he found a man sitting on a crate that—finally—didn't flee.

"You, sir, can—" Delvan stopped and took a step back as a wall of stench hit him, burning his nostrils and making his throat gag as he struggled to breathe. He covered his mouth—lips pulling down with revulsion—with his hand as he realized that the dirt-covered vagrant had been sitting on this crate to defecate, a regular occurrence based on the buzzing abundance of flies he had to swat away.

Delvan rushed past the man who seemed ignorant of his presence and went further down the alley. Hilbrun had said that he needed to view everyone down here as people, the same as either of them. But he was having a hard time dealing with just how *disgusting* some of them were.

He came back into sunlight and—thankfully—fresher air. He was on the adjacent street now from where he started. Looking around, it appeared much like the previous one. As well as the one before that. And all the others they had visited today.

He supposed they *were* specifically looking for homeless people to talk to, though he imagined there had to be *some* other way to get information on where these dens were. *We could see if we could get a Truthsayer, maybe? Probably wouldn't matter if we can't find anyone to talk to, I guess.* It was hard to imagine living in a filthy, stench-filled place like this.

Wiping sweat from his brow, hair sticking to his skin, Delvan caught sight of someone diagonally across the street. The loner wore a strange collection of tattered men's and women's clothes, with frizzled black and gray hair standing nearly on end. She sat on an overturned bucket—and he hoped to the gods that's all she was doing—and was gently swaying side to side.

She hadn't run away, which was uncommon, and Delvan slowly made his way towards her, hesitantly sniffing the air as he walked. As he approached, she began to sway more and more aggressively, muttering words under her breath. He slowed and crept closer, keeping his eyes on her, and moving with caution as her ramblings became louder.

"The First will be reborn!" she said. "The Eighth has shown me. Yes, shown me. Not before. No, not before the return. Later, much later. Trust that those that trust will be misguided, and that those that mistrust will come to be trusted. The one that wants will know, they have seen. They have seen..."

The woman rocked back and forth, the movement becoming a near jerking motion with each step that he took closer. She stared off into the distance, as though looking to the other side of the mountain itself, clutching a small carved idol. It was some pagan figure of a god of the Ones Before, but he didn't know enough to say which one. This woman had to be Rockin' Mari, or at least it would be a fitting name if she wasn't.

"Ma'am, hello, ma'am," Delvan said, "are you Rockin' Mari?"

"Me? Unimportant compared to you and your friends. Only eyes and ears now. You feel… you feel like you're lost. Ups and downs, back and forth you go. Very lost, like a storm. Mouthing hard, doesn't speak words correctly. Yes, yes. A storm approaches, why are you wearing wings and not a cloak?"

"A… what? There isn't a cloud—" he cut himself off as he thought about how ludicrous it sounded trying to have a conversation with the ravings of a mad woman. "I'm looking for local iguan dens, it's very important that I find them. I understand you might be able to help me. I could buy you some food in exchange for information?" he said slowly, punctuating each word.

*I can't believe I have to bribe these people. They should just give me this information, as their duty to the King. Instead, I have to waste time trying to barter with someone who probably doesn't understand a word I'm saying,* he thought.

"Food. Fuel for my mind, but my mind is not mine. Have you seen it? At night? Blind faith will blind you in the night and grant sight of the unseen. Soul will become shadow with the mindsight of the Eighth. Light and transformation await. You, you are the two ends of life, drenched in blood. You are destruction, and you are mending. Life, and death."

Delvan slowly reached into his pocket and procured a chunk of dried fruit from it, meant to be his snack for later. He held it out cautiously with his left hand, while his right rested on the white, muted inanite handle of his sword. Mari spryly snatched the fruit from him and held it tightly to her chest.

"It burns like fire. Forgotten what this felt like. What it's like to see. Take it back, maybe. Maybe. Maybe…" she sputtered.

*How in the gods' names is this woman supposed to help us find an iguan den? All she does is ramble about nonsense.* Delvan wondered how someone like her could survive out here, lucidity vacant from her eyes. He relaxed and stood up straight with a sigh. This woman wasn't a threat, and he doubted she was going to be able to help them. He was going to have to tell Hilbrun that this was another dead end.

He looked down at her, moving back and forth as though being pulled by invisible rope, and felt pity. She reminded him of someone he knew when he was younger, a Blue that was... one of the unfortunate ones. Actually, now that he thought about—

Mari's head suddenly snapped to him, her eyes locked with his, and said in a chilling tone, "They are coming, and I must have it. Must be prepared. It is *MINE!*"

There was a flash of silvery metal as she suddenly jumped to her feet. A dagger plunged down towards Delvan's throat, and all he could manage was raising his plated arm in front of him. It wouldn't be enough, she had caught him off guard. A careless mistake on his part, one that made his eyes flash with surprise and adrenaline pump through his veins. All he could do now was hope to deflect the blade towards his armor.

He braced as he backstepped, instincts and training taking over as his other hand reached for his sword. Everything was a blur, his eyes trying to focus as he took another step back, his muscles tensely waiting for impact.

But it never came.

He backpedaled further from the shockingly agile mad woman. Sword now drawn, free arm extended forward with palm open, with ample space between him and Mari, now revealed how he'd avoided the point of her blade. Frozen in place, her face contorted into an expression of anger and desire, she hovered there, still as a statue, the fresh breeze wafting through her clothes like wind over grass plains.

Delvan spun his head from side to side, looking to see—

There was Hilbrun, walking towards them, his arm stretched forward, and fist clenched in a ball, short sword drawn, face tight and stern. *Is he actually exerting effort?* Hilbrun was the most skilled Reacher that Delvan had ever met, a single person shouldn't have him sweating.

Two soldiers in full armor ran past Hilbrun, the steel plating clinking together rhythmically. They seized Rockin' Mari and Hilbrun released his gripped fist. Mari's body regained its mobility, and she began wailing, thrashing around in a feeble attempt to resist the soldiers' strength.

"Take her to the holding cell at the outpost," said Hilbrun to the soldiers. "We'll be behind shortly."

"Yes, my Lord," they replied as they towed her between them down the streets, the sound of her screams slowly dying in the distance.

"What in the gods' name was that?" asked Hilbrun with a concerned expression and elevated voice.

"What? I had that situation under my *complete* control. Wasn't that obvious?" said Delvan sardonically, trying to cover his chagrin. He hated that Hilbrun had witnessed his poor judgment. He was capable of taking care of himself, but now Hilbrun was probably going to assume he needed to be watched over constantly. *Gods-damn it,* he thought.

"You were about to get skewered," said Hilbrun, unamused.

"But I *didn't*, that's the important part. I knew you were coming, I timed it *perfectly*."

Hilbrun shook his head, undoubtedly about to give Delvan a lecture. But as he went to speak, Delvan felt something small touch against his skin. A welcomed cool, wet sensation. More came, speckling across his face. A burst of rain soon sprayed across them, a small cloud venturing over the mountain's skyline and loosing its contents upon the Valley.

"Uh," gapped Delvan, thinking back to what Mari had said in her ravings, "Hil, I think that Rockin' Mari may be more than we thought. I think that she's a—"

"A Seer?" Hilbrun interjected while reaching into the pouch on his belt.

"Yeah," said Delvan, "How'd you guess?"

Hilbrun pulled one of the inanite blocks from his own pouch and showed it to Delvan. It had been completely muted, the pitch-black stone turned into a stark, snowy white.

"I drained an entire square holding her. She put up a hell of a fight, definitely not a normal commoner. Doesn't leave a lot of options." He tossed the muted square to the ground, *clicking* as it bounced off the stone cobbles. It would be useless to him at this point. "Come on," he said, "let's get out of this rain and find out what a Seer is doing wandering the streets. And I thought the Tempests weren't planning on bringing rain today? Wish I had brought a cloak now."

"Looks like Almedia had other plans," replied Delvan. *And at least one person knew about them.*

Steam rose from Delvan's armor, the short downpour having drenched him and Hilbrun while returning to the nearby outpost. Hilbrun stood in front of a fire they'd lit in the hearth upon arriving in an attempt to remove the chill, though Delvan couldn't see how he could possibly be cold.

The outpost was small, by military standards. Well over a hundred similar to this were scattered throughout the city as local policing stations, with the larger barracks housing large concentrations of troops being far fewer in number.

A few weapons racks lined the walls, desks and tables for the officers stationed here filled the center of the room, and against the back wall opposite them were a handful of stone cells with iron barred doors. The incoherent screams of Rockin' Mari blared from one of them, the frustrated soldiers scowling as they tried to read through their reports and tune her out.

"How do you think she ended up on the streets?" asked Delvan, walking over to Hilbrun.

"Not sure," replied Hilbrun with a shrug. "I've heard rumors, but never put any stock in them."

"What were they?" asked Delvan, curious. "I've only ever known of one Blue that was one."

"Someone told me once that when they're being transported to wherever it is that they take them, they manage to escape sometimes. Who knows how. He said that it didn't matter which direction they ran, they always ended up coming back here, to Calentine. No one knows why, but you can't expect insane people to make decisions that make sense, I suppose."

Delvan thought about that for a moment. Something about Hilbrun's logic didn't make sense to him. If they *were* insane, why would they all make the conscious decision to come back to the same place?

"I think they're trying to get their sapphires back," said Delvan after a moment.

Hilbrun looked at him and seemed to give the idea some thought. "Makes sense, I guess. What shit luck to have *that* be your gift, if you can even call it that. Spend your childhood training and being told what great power you're going to hold, only to have that same power turn you into a raving lunatic just as you get into your teens. Your gem gets taken from you, and you're taken away to gods'-know-where to spend the rest of your life screaming at the walls.

"To your idea's credit, if someone were to take *my* sapphire, you can bet I would do everything in my power to get it back. If you're going to find one anywhere, it'd be here."

"Probably why she seemed to get worse and worse as I approached her," said Delvan, thinking out loud, "the closer I got the more she could draw from mine. Assuming she actually is a Seer."

"Oh, I bet you she bleeds violet like you or me. No normal person takes that much inanite to hold."

"She did predict the storm," he said thoughtfully.

"They're about as good at predicting the future as you or I, Del. Half of what they say is gibberish, the other half is vague nonsense that you could say means just about anything. If they say it's going to rain, and it doesn't rain until three days later, you could say that, yes, they predicted it, but I could also say the same thing. Of course it's going to rain eventually. The sun will also set at night. The river will rise in the spring and lower in the summer.

"Don't buy into it. We need to figure out what she knows about iguan dens, that's all. Then we'll let the Court deal with her."

"She must have been on the streets here for *years*," said Delvan, looking over at the cell. "They send Seers away when they're young, and her hair is turning gray. She must have been living out there for decades."

He felt a well of pity forming for her. Losing your identity, having the world forget about you, it wasn't something this woman had ever asked for. Who would he be if his sapphire was taken? *Who am I with it?*

"We'll have to question her from a distance," said Hilbrun. "Even from this far she seems to be incoherent. Hopefully that isn't her normal state..."

Hilbrun was probably right, everything she said had been deranged. He couldn't help but feel perturbed by the rain appearing so soon after she mentioned it, the thought gnawing away at him as his armor finally began to dry.

They walked as close as they could towards the cell without Mari starting to scream, a soldier standing by her barred door to repeat anything they said if necessary. She sat on the cold floor in the center of the cell, her swaying more like a tree in a calm breeze, opposed to the violent quake she'd reached earlier.

"What do you know about local iguan dens?" asked Hilbrun in a loud, clear voice.

"Sights and sounds," she muttered, barely audible to Delvan at this distance. "So many places, voices, plans. Yes, plans. She wants it. She wants us. You too. Craves it. People like us, but different. Soldiers from the High place. Coming back here."

Did she mean Delvan and Hilbrun? Coming from the Upper Tier? Maybe he shouldn't be trying to interpret everything she said. Though Hilbrun seemed to have become intensely focused.

"Dust. Dust and smoke. I've been there before, to the place of freedom. Together they bring us to the place beyond. Beyond..."

She went quiet, mumbling in a whisper that even the soldier by her door appeared to struggle with hearing.

"What else?" said Hilbrun. "Tell me what else!" he said, his voice raising nearly to a shout. He took several steps forward and Mari released a high-pitched scream, lunging at the door, her arm reaching through in an attempt to extend the impossible distance to Hilbrun.

"Hil," said Delvan, grabbing Hilbrun's arm and pulling him back, "I don't think we're going to get anything else from her. Not with our sapphires here. Let's leave a list of questions with the lieutenant here and have him ask for us once she's away from our influence. He can have the scribe record what she says."

Hilbrun took a breath and nodded. "It's getting late, anyway," he said. "I think we can get to one more place on the list if we leave soon." He still seemed agitated. This was the closest they had come to getting anywhere with their list, and he seemed desperate to get *something* out of her. Nonetheless, Delvan could tell that he agreed that it would be better to come back later, since it was unlikely that she would be lucid while the two of them remained.

Delvan waited while Hilbrun sat with the outpost scribe. Rockin' Mari laid still and quiet on the floor now, looking defeated by her imprisonment. Delvan wondered about some of the things she had said. A part of him tried to dismiss her ramblings as just that. But his inquisitive mind kept spinning the words in his head. *Everything she said, is there truth to any of it? How could she have known some of those things? Why does everyone have to keep putting these questions about myself into my own mind? She's as bad as Hil.*

He was left, yet again, with more questions than answers.

# CHAPTER SEVEN

*To hear, and never be heard. The great irony of their solitude. Their will trickles forth, blocked and restrained, slowly filling the world with their influence as they search for the one who can swim.*
Overheard as new patient arrived,
Seventeenth Day of Summer, Eighth Year of the Seventh Epoch


Desnia pulled her hood over her head as she walked down the dark street, a faint hint of mist forming from her breath. The depths of the night enveloped her in a protective embrace, the only guardian she'd ever known. She found a certain comfort in the shadows, a welcoming feeling that was always there, unbiased and undemanding.

Behind her the sounds of the rowdy tavern faded in the distance, its humble offerings still fresh on her lips. A hot meal and much needed ale helped to strip away the weight that seemed to always hang from her neck. She felt as though she were walking on a cloud as she trekked home, the inebriation propelling her like a breeze through the sky. Only a few lanterns from inside uncovered windows illuminated her path. This wasn't a part of town that afforded luxuries such as streetlamps.

Which was exactly why she had chosen it.

After some amount of ale—she'd lost count after a while—she could almost feel relaxed, or what she assumed relaxed must feel like. She still watched the shadows for waiting predators, eyed people as they walked by, hand on her dagger's hilt, and maintained a certain air of precaution. These were instincts that were a part of her, they occurred without thought.

The conscious majority of her mind—the portion that seeded her with doubt, worry, fear, animosity, and anger, the concoction of emotions that so often felt as though they defined who she was—had been smothered under a lake of ale. Drowned to provide her with a brief but pleasant respite.

She didn't have far to travel. She turned a corner down an alley that was darker than even the street, its narrow length hardly wide enough for even her thin frame. Shoulders rubbing against the stone walls, she twisted and shuffled through the narrow passage. She emerged onto a small side street—she never approached home from a main road—and looked around the near-black strip, the multiple stories of buildings to either side blocking all but a narrow line of stars in the sky above. The faint smell of garbage floated through the air, piles of it mounding near some doors of the unkempt street.

She walked across the lane and lithely made her way up a set of iron treads set into a stone wall, which didn't so much as creak under the weight of her steps. Reaching the door at the top of the stairs, Desnia squatted low and checked that the strand of hair that she'd lodged between the door and its jam was still in its place.

*Exactly where I left you,* she thought, finding the golden filament was still in its home. She unlocked it and entered into the cramped space, resetting the lock and throwing another bolt as she closed the door behind her.

The room wasn't much, but it was enough for her. A small bed of straw on the floor, a rough-looking desk with some tools strewn across it, and a beat-up chair were all that could manage to fit within the unpainted wood walls close to her either side. Desnia checked the hair strands placed in the rear door and window, confirming again that no one had intruded upon her small room.

She'd chosen this apartment for a few reasons. It offered multiple exits, all with branching routes beyond them. It was near the tavern, so she didn't have far to travel on the nights she could actually afford to go. And it was cheap. The landlord downstairs wasn't either awake or sober enough to identify her comings and goings. He only cared that he got paid, assuming he remembered. He'd drink through his collection of growlers and come asking for rent soon enough, she was sure. But at least for tonight she wouldn't need to worry.

Desnia took off her jacket and hung it on a nearby hook, pulling the small block of muted inanite from its pocket. She remembered the robed woman at the den as she felt the white stone between her fingers, its smooth sides and granular structure reminding her of a sugar cube, almost soft to the touch. Although this was much easier and cheaper to find than sweets.

She still wasn't sure what had come over her earlier. Sharing information about yourself was dangerous. She was alone. She *needed* to be alone. Other people were unreliable, at best. They only cared about themselves, and for her to survive she needed to do the same. Though part of her wondered if maybe, once this next job was done, she could... No. She refused to hope, to ponder the possibility of the future. Hope led to heartbreak, and she wasn't sure how much of a heart she had left.

She sat down at the desk and used a hammer to break off a small corner of the stone, then put it into a small mortar and pestle on the desk and began to grind the white rock into a powder. A bit of the chalky dust touched her tongue as it rose in the air, robbing her mouth of moisture.

A distant voice caught her attention. It sounded like someone outside was yelling, but it was too muffled to hear clearly. *Is the landlord hounding someone for rent? He should be passed out drunk at this hour.* She felt at the pouch under her shirt, noticeably lighter after the night at the tavern. She'd finally be able to pay him for the last two months. Most of it, anyway. That could wait until morning though, assuming he didn't come barging up here.

A bit of that missing weight pressed back down on her. What money she had wouldn't last long, not unless she dipped into her stashes. A question forced its way to the surface of her mind: Could this new job from Mixton actually be a way out from under his thumb?

What could be so valuable that he'd be willing to forgive her debt? She was still suspicious that he was going to come up with *some* caveat, a loophole to his promise that he'd conveniently forgotten to mention. Still, he'd never flat out promised her a way out before. It was something.

Once the muted inanite was a fine powder, she took a small spoon, roughly half the size of her fingertip, scooped a bit of the powder onto it, and snorted it.

She crawled onto the bed, looking forward to a long night of dreamless sleep with a full stomach. A rare event. It even seemed that the landlord had stopped yelling and the alley had grown quiet once again. She closed her eyes and drifted off into the sweet abyss of darkness, basking in the pure, unadulterated, peace.

# Chapter Eight

*Used, twisted, betrayed. BETRAYED!*
Words shouted before a riot,
Eightieth Day of Summer, Thirty-ninth Year of the Seventh
Epoch

The walk down the tower's spiraling stone ramps into the Lower Valley's domain was starting to become a familiar experience for Delvan. This morning was less misty than the previous, and the shadow of the sun could be seen casually sliding down the basin's outer walls in the distance towards the buildings within.

The day before had ended much in the same way as their first: empty-handed. After discussing it, they'd agreed that Mari would be worth a visit in the morning, uncertain as to how long the hangover effect of their sapphires would last on her. It had been another quiet night for Delvan, fatigue of the day preventing him from even having the thought of leaving the comfort of his bed during the night. Not that it had done him any good.

He knew that Hilbrun was trying to stay optimistic about what information they might glean from the ramblings of the Seer. Delvan had lower expectations. Maybe she could say something useful, but everything the day before had been random jumbles of incoherent sentences. Gods knew he'd thought about it enough last night. Hilbrun wasn't putting *all* his faith into the Seer, however, and they discussed the last locations on the list while en route.

Hilbrun seemed tired. It looked like more than a mild morning grogginess, as though he'd also been up half the night. Unshakeable thoughts still plagued Delvan, and he had little interest in sneaking out for a few pints while he considered who he wanted to be, who he wanted to fight for, and what—if anything—he could do about it. And it, yet again, left him exhausted.

They reached the outpost where they had left Mari the previous day, with only a few officers currently at their stations getting ready for distributing the day's assignments. They worked quietly, the lieutenant looking up as the pair entered.

"King and His grace upon you," said Hilbrun.

"And you, my Lords," greeted the lieutenant, his face painted with a confused expression.

"Do you have that report for me on the prisoner? The responses to our questions?" Hilbrun asked the man.

*Is she sleeping?* Yesterday Mari was still sputtering uncontrollably when he and Hilbrun had been in the room. The level of silence was strange.

"What do you mean, my Lord?" the lieutenant replied.

"What... Do I have to spell it out for you? The prisoner, Rockin' Mari, who we left in your care, and you were to question. Where is your report on the interrogation, Lieutenant?" said Hilbrun, frustrated.

"Sir," said the lieutenant, now both confused *and* worried, "we released her into the care of the Knight Commander this morning. We thought... We thought you were aware? He came down himself. Took all of the notes and thanked us for helping you apprehend a loose Seer."

*Well,* thought Delvan, *that would explain the quiet.*

"What!?" ejected Hilbrun. "And he took all of your notes? Tell me you have a copy here!" His face was turning red, and the nervous lieutenant was struggling to speak.

"I-I'm sorry, m-my Lord, but he took every copy. Said the Sapphiric Court wanted to keep a missing Seer quiet and that we weren't to speak further of it."

"Which knight commander was it?" said Hilbrun through gritted teeth.

"Ferrand, sir. Knight Commander Ferrand."

*How did the commander find out about Mari? We didn't share our discovery with anyone. Unless...*

Some sycophant looking for a promotion likely overheard their conversation about her being a Seer and thought that being the first to report it would gain them favor. For all Delvan knew, it was the lieutenant himself that had sent a pigeon to the Court.

Hilbrun pinched the bridge of his nose in his hand as his eyes squeezed shut in utter frustration. He cursed under his breath and took a deep breath before speaking. "You're going to tell me *everything* that she said to you. Every word, every incoherent rant, you're even going to tell me the fucking tempo that she was rocking, do you understand?" said Hilbrun, ice in his voice.

"Sire, we tried talking to her more, but she wouldn't say much of anything. None of it made any sense and, to be honest, the notes were short. She hardly produced more than a mumble all night. I'm sorry, my Lord, but she didn't say much of anything worth writing." The lieutenant was now visibly sweating in terror, a fiery rage building in the Blue before him.

The lieutenant became eerily still, his face lacking so much as a blink or twitch. Delvan looked down to see Hilbrun's hand clenched, the horror on the lieutenant's face captured in place.

"Hil," he whispered from behind him, trying to ease him off his ledge.

Hilbrun let out a growl that turned into a hateful scream, finally waving his hand. The lieutenant flew back a distance, as though suddenly pulled by an unseen horse, and landed on the floor on the other side of the room. He groaned in pain, but Hilbrun had let him off easily, incurring the wrath of a Blue was not something everyone escaped from unscathed.

*Still, was that really necessary?*

Hilbrun stormed out of the outpost and into the street, putting a distance between him and the source of his vexation. He finally slowed and began pacing back and forth in the street, rubbing his brow. Delvan had never seen him this angry before and hesitated to say anything, wondering what he even could say. He wasn't worried about Hilbrun turning his anger towards him, he would never consider such a thing, but that didn't leave him in a much less delicate situation.

"That bastard! He *does* know about the cadentite. He realized what we were doing and is trying to cut us off at the knees. Gods-damn it, I was hoping that we could stay ahead of him," said Hilbrun, talking to himself more than he was addressing Delvan.

"Wait, why wouldn't he know that cadentite had been stolen?" asked Delvan, confused. "As long as you're not growing iguan with it, it's not illegal to own. The spice merchant must have told him about it."

"No, you don't—" Hilbrun cut himself off and struggled for a moment. "Look, just trust me, the merchant wouldn't have willingly told Ferrand that he had cadentite. He had to have been coerced or Ferrand already knew."

"That makes absolutely no sense," replied Delvan. "If the cadentite is supposedly worth as much as his entire business, *why* wouldn't he claim it and try to collect a reimbursement from the crown?" *And why assume that the commander would force the information out, or somehow already knew about it?*

"Because, Del, he wants to—" Hilbrun struggled for words again. What was he hiding? "Alright, listen, I'm going to tell you something, but I need you to swear to me that you won't repeat it. This could land us both in prison, or worse. Understand?"

He doubted it could be *that* bad, but it did seem to have Hilbrun scared, or at least gravely concerned. "I swear it," he said. His honor would have to be enough for Hilbrun, he wasn't sure what more he could offer to convince him.

Hilbrun looked around and then pulled him to the side of the street, away from any prying ears. "This wasn't the first piece of cadentite stolen," he said in a hushed voice, "this is just the latest in a string of thefts. The spice merchant sent for me because of my ties to the guild through my father. Cadentite has been disappearing and no one can prove who is responsible. What we do know is that almost *all* the thefts were in Commander Ferrand's district, and he's *personally* overseen each of the investigations.

"Not only that, but like our break in, he shows up *before* the merchants have even stated what was stolen. The guild, well they can maybe see a knight commander looking into highly valuable goods stolen on his watch, but to arrive at crime scenes before he even knows what was taken? You have to admit it's extremely suspicious."

"So, you think... You think that he's involved?" Could a knight be behind the thefts, like Hilbrun claimed? "What if he's just showing up to high profile robberies?" he asked.

"We thought the same, but it's been stolen from low profile locations too, and then he just appears, despite no notifications being sent to him.

"Other high-profile robberies with no cadentite? Doesn't even show his face. No, the only explanation is that he is involved. I think he might have something to do with the robberies and he's there to make sure no one discovers the truth, or he's trying to recover the cadentite for himself. We think that someone from inside the guild might be giving him information, as disgusting to think about as that is.

"The fact that the arrogant bastard has only shown up to *those* robberies... He's taunting us. He's in too powerful a position for anyone to do anything about. The man only reports to generals, the Court, and the King. I swear his ego is bigger than the King's Tower."

All of the Sapphiric Court was made up of retired Blues, Delvan knew all too well, and most generals were also gem-bearers. It made sense that none of them would want to believe that Ferrand had anything to do with the thefts. And convincing the King, well, you'd need an audience first, which was a rare accommodation.

"The guild has collectively agreed to not discuss cadentite with him," continued Hilbrun, "or any other Blues for that matter, except for a select few. The amount that's disappeared recently could buy you a duchy, and this was the largest piece yet. No, if he knows about it it's not because the merchant told him willingly."

"Why take Mari then?" asked Delvan. "If he's involved, wouldn't he know where it was? It's not like he needs to question her." Then it struck him, as he was speaking the questions and talking the problem out, he realized why Ferrand would need to take Mari away. "It's because she knows something," Delvan said, his eyes wide with the realization. "She must know something about the cadentite, where it's been, where it's going, *something.*"

"Yes!" cried Hilbrun. "He's covering his tracks. He heard that we found a Seer to question—this one specifically—and maybe thought that she could reveal something, then had her removed. Maybe he knows she's a regular at the iguan dens, or has lived near them. I don't know for certain.

"We have to be careful, Del. He knows how difficult it would be to remove us from looking into this, so he took away our best lead. If we get too close, and he finds out? Who knows what he'd be willing to do."

Delvan had a hard time fathoming that the commander—or any Blue—would be willing to go to the extent that Hilbrun was implying. They were practically kin, bonded by something even more powerful than blood. Turning against a fellow Blue was unheard of, and not a light accusation. No wonder Hilbrun was so concerned about this.

"But we now know that she was dangerous enough for us to talk to that he is sending her off to never be seen again. What did she say to you yesterday, was there anything that could help us?" asked Hilbrun.

Delvan racked his brain. "A bunch of stuff about trust? That a storm was coming, and something about faith, I think? It all seemed like random babbling." Could any of it have meaning? His mind raced trying to make any sense from it once again.

Hilbrun shook his head dismissively, his face tortured with anguish. Was there something else that they had missed? Delvan wanted so badly to have an answer for him, to show him that he was worthy of the confidence that Hilbrun had put in him, sharing the weight of his burdens. But he was coming up disappointingly short.

Hilbrun pulled the list from his pocket and examined the last few locations, his face transforming into one of deep thought. "What was it that Mari said yesterday, in the outpost? Something about dust?"

"Uh," thought Delvan frantically, "'Dust and smoke bring us to the place beyond', or something along those lines, I think."

"Look at this," said Hilbrun, excitedly pointing to the list, "the next location is on Dust Street. Maybe that's what she meant? Smoking iguan is what gives you the high and going to places beyond is about the hallucinations they see. It's too much of a coincidence. This *has* to be it."

Delvan thought it was a bit of a stretch, but clearly Hilbrun was desperate. He'd been the one to tell Delvan not to believe in the ramblings of Seers, and now here he was, finding connections that reached farther than the ocean's shores.

Still, he found himself chagrined that he hadn't made the connection himself, even if it was a bit hyperbolic. But he was glad to see Hilbrun's face so relieved, as though he had the answers now. Who knows, maybe he was right about this?

Hilbrun scurried away, Delvan following closely behind. They marched across the district, stopping along the way at the barracks nearest to Dust

Street. Hilbrun commandeered over a dozen off-duty soldiers after explaining to the captain he needed support in pursuit of a high-profile thief.

It was more of an explanation than he needed to provide. When a Blue made a request—within reason—you followed it. Aside from being high-born nobles and aristocrats, they were the right hand of the King. Their authority was that of the crown, almost no one—outside of other Blues—ranked above them.

Being cadets and not fully knighted Blues yet, Delvan and Hilbrun were *technically* under the command of their assigned barracks commander—Blue or not—but it was more a formality than a strictly enforced code. Most officers didn't want to deal with the politics of distinguishing between a cadet and knight, and they generally treated all Blues as commanding officers.

Hilbrun and Delvan now walked down Dust Street, fourteen fully armored soldiers marching in a rhythmic cadence behind them. The street became eerily vacant upon their arrival. If there were any vagrants along the road's stone sidewalks, they vanished in a near-instant, the sight of a squad of soldiers driving them into hiding.

*Subtly is out of the question, clearly,* thought Delvan.

Bits of debris danced across the granite pavers in the breeze, the sun above providing a comforting warmth to the desolate street. The neatness of the stone facades couldn't hide the broken windows, shabby doors, and rusted iron fixtures. The silence made it feel tense, or maybe that was the anticipation building inside of him. He hoped that this was the right place, for Hilbrun's sake.

"Lieutenant," said Hilbrun to the officer behind him. "Take two men and go into the alley behind the west buildings, make sure that no one sneaks out through the back doors. Spread out and cover as much area as you can as we make our way down the street. Del, you take the alley behind the east buildings with two others.

"The rest of you, start kicking down doors. Spread out and get through as many buildings as you can. Check lofts, basements, storage buildings, everything. We're looking for an iguan den. If you don't find it, move on. The more time we waste the longer they have to find a way out. And they're definitely going to know we're coming."

The soldiers wasted no time. If there wasn't an answer after a few hard pounds against the shaky doors, then steel met wood as they kicked their way in. Delvan led two soldiers to the alley, looking for back exits from the structures lining the street.

He drew his short sword, its decorated, white hilt and scabbard a juxtaposition from the reflective black of the blade's darksteel. Rockin' Mari had got the jump on him, and he wasn't about to disappoint Hilbrun by letting that happen again.

The three of them spread out and slowly walked through the alley, keeping attentive eyes on windows and doors, searching for any movement within. He could hear the soldiers shouting from the street, demanding access. They were going to get inside whether the occupants wanted it or not. Allow them in, let them search and be on their way, or resist, and make matters *much* worse for yourself.

Delvan turned his head as he heard some screams from the street, which went silent with a sudden abruptness. Hilbrun had likely taken care of—

A door to the basement of a nearby storehouse creaked open near him, a hooded man in a black robe emerging, looking cautiously around as he crept up the stairs.

From under his hood, he locked eyes with Delvan, freezing for a split second, but looking stern and unafraid with his hollow eyes. Then he ran, bolting with a speed that surprised Delvan. He took off in pursuit, but as he passed the basement stairs from which the man had emerged, someone flew up them with a burst of speed, shouting as he lifted an axe towards Delvan.

Instincts, drilled into his muscles until they acted as though under a mind of their own, took over. His entire life, from the time he could hold a sword, had been filled with day after day of training, sparring, tactics, and stances. Not a day had gone by in his youth, his entire life for that matter, where hours weren't spent forcing him to learn the art of the sword, other weapons, and his gift.

Life as a Blue in one of the oldest houses in Calentine meant tutors, specialists, and studying. Classes on history, writing, and politics had consumed what time didn't go into combat training. He had never been sure what a real childhood for other nobles—ones too poor to afford sapphires—was like, but he envied them, sometimes. He spent his youth surrounded by people, yet entirely alone. Parents always away, siblings long since sent off to the Academy or knighted themselves, and surrounded by servants that dared to only speak when commanded, had made his world absently hollow.

He might still be questioning what it was that he wanted in life, and much of what Hilbrun had said to him still weighed heavily in his mind, but there was one thing that he had been correct about.

He was a sword.

A quick sidestep and a parry of the axe with his sword guided the man's wild swing easily to the ground. With an upward slice, the tip of Delvan's blade expertly slashed across the man's neck in a fast and fluid motion. Blood sprayed out before the assaulter dropped the axe and grabbed his throat in a feeble attempt to staunch the bleeding, falling to his knees as blood flowed through his fingers.

Delvan ignored him, spinning to look for a glimpse of the robed man. There was nothing in sight. He took off in a sprint down the side alley that branched perpendicular to the street, where he'd seen the man initially run.

He burst into an intersection, skidding to a halt. The narrow street split into different directions around him, each a cluttered mess of garbage and junk. He concentrated intensely, listening and looking for signs of movement.

A flutter of black turning a corner in the distance to his left had him sprinting once more. Armor *clinked* to the beat of his pounding soles, wind whipping his hair as he flew down the alley. He ran to the corner, grabbing the wooden post of an awning to help him swing around it at full speed.

He nearly slipped on the smooth stone as he came to a sudden stop. The man he'd pursued stood before him, as though waiting. He was taller than Delvan had realized, and his commanding figure seemed to darken the entire narrow lane, the black robe like an abyss in the middle of the sunny passage. He appeared unarmed, but Delvan approached cautiously nonetheless, sword at the ready, knees bent, and arm extended.

"I'm going to need you to—" Delvan started to say.

The man's hand violently lashed upward at him, a strange flash of light emitting from it and streaking towards Delvan. He turned and shielded himself with his guard-arm, but the strange projectile hit him in the side of his abdomen, below the shoulder.

It felt like he'd been punched by a Jack, the air evacuating his lungs in an instant. He gasped as he fell to a knee, his back arching as he tried to draw breath into his empty lungs. Straining, he thought he saw a strange glow from under his foot, the color nearly matching the pink tinge of the granite. Maybe it was just from the stars in his vision?

After a second—which his old instructors would've said was a second too long—he regained enough sense to keep his sword pointed toward the enemy, who—

Who wasn't there?

The man had vanished in the moment it had taken Delvan to recover. He forced himself back up, still struggling to regulate his breathing. He needed to chase after this man. Was he a Blue? What had he cast at Delvan? It had been unlike anything he'd seen before, like a Feeder, but more concentrated.

He went to run, but nearly tripped as he realized his foot was... stuck? It felt as though his boot were melded to the stone, refusing to so much as budge from where it touched the granite. It stood flat on the rock, not caught on anything, but the sole and stone had become one. No matter how hard he pulled, kicked, or pushed it wouldn't release itself from its impossible adhesion.

Finally, after minutes of struggling, the boot released itself from its hold, sending Delvan tumbling backward. His back came to rest on a nearby wall after impacting it, trying again to catch his breath. He lifted his foot and inspected his boot.

*Looks like... A normal boot,* he thought, thoroughly perplexed. *What was that?*

He looked at his side where the strange ball of light had struck the blue leather. There was a scorch mark about the size and shape of his thumb, but the leather looked to be intact. The sapphire dust dye had done its job.

He let out a long sigh and felt a sharp pain in his side. Likely a fractured rib, if not more than one. That was about two weeks of healing time to fully recover. It wasn't anything he hadn't dealt with before.

That didn't mean he was happy about it.

How was he going to explain this to Hilbrun? Twice in as many days he'd been bested, embarrassing himself to the one person he cared to impress. The hooded man's casting abilities were too much of a strange coincidence to *not* be related to their investigation. And because of his brash actions the man had gotten away. He'd been taken by surprise *again*.

He could already feel the shame of disappointment as he held his side and began walking back towards where he'd left the other troops. Hopefully Hilbrun had had better luck.

# CHAPTER NINE

*When you bury me, let it be not in stone. Turn me to ashes, so I do
not have to spend another eon surrounded by the cold, silent rock.
Set me to the wind, so I may hear the call of birds, and be carried
over the trees once more.*
Final request,
Forty-fifth Day of Spring, Sixteenth Year of the Seventh Epoch

Desnia tried to walk the pain away. It—along with the other remedies she'd tried—didn't do much to improve her malady.

She'd slept through the few remaining hours of last night after getting home from the tavern, and then proceeded to sleep through most of the day as well. What few hours of daylight had remained passed with crippling agony as she laid in bed and reaped the consequences of the outing the night before. She hadn't dared leave while the sun still blazed its ingloriously bright rays upon the city, the cool dark of her room a lavish comfort by comparison.

But now the sun had set, and she had a meeting to attend. She made her way towards the port district, her hood pulled low not for anonymity, but so the lights of lamps and braziers didn't compound the throbbing in her head. *This should have passed hours ago, how much did I have last night?*

It prodded at her already agitated state. She hated working with a team. She'd had a few mild successes on jobs with others, but generally she was left burned, broke, and on the run. Working alone afforded her control over the situation. She could choose the method, the time, and the escape. She had back up plans, routes, and bribed the right guards. How could she expect anyone else to be so thorough? To attentively comb through the details that others would miss?

Desnia knew nothing about what this job was, who the crew members were, or even what they were stealing. She also didn't trust Mixton to let her off his leash. She hoped for it, sure, but planned for it? No. She needed a backup plan. Something she could do to get away from him forever. She just... hadn't the slightest idea how to do that. Yet.

The building in front of her would offer some of those answers. It was the rear door of the address that Mixton had given her, an old cobbler's shop that appeared vacant through dark windows. The port district, particularly the thoroughfare that this shop sat on, was second only to the Upper Tier in its density of wealth. Proximity to the port allowed for first selection from imported goods, and travelers had to pass through here to access the remainder of the city. Grand, cathedral-like buildings lined the street, serving as storehouses, meeting locations, guild houses, master tradesmen, and more; all booming from the economic monolith that was the Calentine port. *And these rich assholes probably don't even realize people are starving three blocks away.*

Walking to the backdoor she noticed that the nearby streetlamp was extinguished, and partitions to either side separating the building's rear exits obscured the entrance rather suitably.

*Maybe these ones aren't* complete *idiots.*

She knocked on the back door in the order that Mixton had indicated. Three times, pause. Five times, pause. And then once. She eyed her surroundings as she waited. Some sounds came from the street at the store's front, its light cutting through a nearby alley. The windows dotting the masterful stonework looked down on her like the many eyed monster of a beast of legend, watching in the night. All of them were dormant, their occupants having gone home in the earlier hours.

She continued waiting, but still nothing. Minutes went by as she stood, tucked inside of the door's deep frame, obscuring her body's outline from any who may wander this way.

*This is what I get for relying on other people,* she thought with a sigh. She went to knock again. Three knocks, pause. Five—

The door latch released from inside and then swung inward without so much as a creak. *They oiled the hinges. Impressive.*

It opened enough for her to slide through, and then hastily closed behind her as she entered the dimly lit space. The smell of leather potently filled the air, the room clearly storage for unfinished shoes and materials. The only illumination was the glow through a nearby door, the lamps outside the storefront casting their radiance through the glass window display beyond.

Turning from the door was a man who stood tall and appeared well dressed, based on the dark jacket with custom stitching and polished shoes. His hair was slicked back, a dark shade of black that was more jet than even his wardrobe. He wore a rapier at his side, and gave Desnia a well-executed bow and a supercilious smile.

The flattery might work to con others, but Desnia could already see what kind of man this was. One who saw himself as a peer to nobles—or at least tried to be—and looked down upon the thieves of the city's recessed corners. He would work with you but would detest every moment of it.

"King and His grace upon you," he said in polite fashion.

"Fuck the King," said Desnia, folding her arms.

"Dangerous words," he replied, maintaining the haughty smile.

"Well, you can turn me in to the guard or we can get to work. Your choice."

"Hmm, a woman after my own heart, I see. I'm Magnar, organizer of this endeavor. You must be Desnia."

"Just call me Des."

"Of course. Pleasure to meet you, Des. If you'll follow me, I'll introduce you to the others," Magnar said. He even seemed to have the Upper accent correct, though she noticed him slipping on some of the minor inflections.

He didn't light a candle as they walked, which was a relief to see. Anyone walking on the street would be likely to notice. He guided her through the dark passages and rooms of the shop, mentioning in a hushed voice to look out for boxes and a few benches along the way.

She rolled her eyes and shook her head as he described obstacles while walking ahead of her. Did he really think that she couldn't make it through a dark room without colliding with something? She had a reputation, one that was not bestowed to clumsy pretenders and had been built over years of effort. Yet here was this man, patronizing her.

There *had* been that issue with the dog the other night… But no, it had been much darker. That didn't count.

She made it through the shop—flawlessly, of course—and crossed under a curtain draped in the hallway. Beyond it was a door with a faint light pooling on the floor from the gap underneath. Magnar opened it and the light from candles and lanterns from a basement below filled the room with a warm glow. She tried not to show the pain the sudden change in light caused her pounding head.

He waved for her to head down the stairs, but she didn't move. "You first," she said.

He looked at her with a knowing grin, seeming to appreciate her caution. He descended down the steps, turning and saying, "Make sure you close the door."

*How dense does he think I am?* she thought as she closed the door behind her.

She walked down the worn stone steps to a landing but caught the railing as she turned. Her hand covered her mouth and nose as her nostrils were assaulted by an abhorrent stench. The putrid scent thickened the air, a noxious gas that clung to you like a wet shirt. The taste lingered in her mouth, it crawled up her nose and down her throat, and it was everything she could do not to heave. Dried mud caked the floor that was framed by disorganized shelves stacked to the ceiling. One storage shelf in the back of the basement had been removed, a heavy cloth hanging on the wall in its place.

"I apologize for the smell," said Magnar, "but it's an unfortunate byproduct of a necessity for our plan."

In the center of the room was a small table where three men sat playing a card game. Each was covered from head to toe in grime and dirt, their boots heavily laden with the same mud that coated the floor. In the brighter light Desnia could now see that Magnar's clothes were immaculate, not even a speck of dust tarnishing his shoe's perfect polish.

"Des," said Magnar as she stepped down the last few stairs, "these three are Grunner, Sanco, and Ox."

The three men had paused their game to look at her. The one he called Ox was befitting the name; well over six feet tall and fairly heavyset, he was built in a way that made her believe he could pull a fully loaded wagon. Sanco was smaller—shorter than her, even. His hair was wily despite being coated in layers of filth, and he had a scar covering his cheek from his nose to his jaw. Grunner was modestly average. His most distinguishing feature was his shaved head, which had streaks cutting through the dirt where the sweat had streamed down it. And he had linen wrapped tightly around his hands, whether for, or to prevent, an injury she couldn't tell.

Grunner eyed her with a cold, ravenous glare. It wasn't a familiar craving or desire in his eyes, but something more sinister. He wanted something, but she couldn't quite figure out what. She returned a hard stare in kind.

"Gentleman," continued Magnar, "this is Des, who has come to us highly recommended. My understanding is that she's the best lockpick in the city." He gave her a wink as though he had done her a favor. *Typical.*

The men sat silently, whether they were waiting for her to speak or for Magnar, she couldn't tell.

"So," she said, breaking the silence, "is anyone going to tell me why I'm here?"

Magnar looked at her with that damned, fraudulent smile again. That was going to get annoying.

"You, my dear Des, are here because we are in desperate need of someone with your skills. Someone who can circumvent the most complex locks in the city, and has an aptitude for discretion," said Magnar.

Ox leaned over to Sanco and said, in a horribly failed whisper, "What does 'cir-circum...' that word mean?"

Sanco turned his head, looking annoyed. "Shut up, Ox," he said in an equally exaggerated whisper.

"In short, Des," continued Magnar, "you're here because you're the best. And I was informed you have experience with the specific type of lock that we want to penetrate. Are you interested in participating in one of the most lucrative heists that has ever occurred in the city? Possibly even the kingdom? This could become legend, you the hero of the story. Does that sound appealing to you?"

*This guy* really *likes the sound of his own voice.* "Would you just tell me who in the name of the gods we're stealing from already?" she asked, already tired of this con artist.

Magnar smiled and replied, "Yes, straight to the point. I've been told about your candidness. We, my dear Des, are going to break into the vault of the Merchants' Guild."

Despite the horrid taste in the air, Desnia's jaw loosened and mouth gaped. The Merchants' Guild was one of the wealthiest and most influential organizations in the kingdom. They—under the guiding hand of the crown—controlled the trade routes, set prices for all the other guilds' goods, and had become an amorphous entity that could be considered a kingdom in its own right. They were also *extremely* protective of their leveraged spoils.

"Are you insane?" asked Desnia with a wave of her hands. "It would be easier to rob a bank!" She was generally open to an opportunity, but she lived in a world where ambition could get you killed. She preferred to keep herself grounded in mediocre realism, rather than suffocate in the clouds of elevated optimism.

"Des," said Magnar confidently, "just hear what the plan is and what you could reap as a reward. This is worth the risk, which, given the beautiful simplicity of this plan, I promise is very low."

She eyed him with an unconvinced stare, but folded her arms and waited.

"In case you haven't realized from the smell," he continued, "our entry will be via the sewers." He walked over to the heavy cloth on the wall and drew it back like a curtain. A wave of amplified stench washed over her. She could clearly see the tall arch of a brick sewer beyond as her nose cringed. "Approximately two hundred yards down this sewer, based on the information that we have, is the vault room of the Merchants' Guild headquarters. All we have to do is finish removing the wall between the sewer and the vault room, and we'll be able to walk in during the night, open the vault, and take whatever we want."

Guilds were notoriously close-knit and secretive. Information on something this valuable was incredibly rare and difficult to come by, otherwise this would have likely been attempted before. "Where did the information on the vault room come from? I'm assuming there will be guards to deal with inside?" she asked, still circumspect.

"There is in fact one guard posted every night in the vault's anteroom. With others posted throughout the floors above. We have learned, however, that the guard posted here has some, let's call them regular, habits. He likes to frequent a certain damsel before starting his shift. She has agreed to slip him something that will put him out cold the night we break in, giving us the room until the following morning."

"You're hinging this entire plan on a *prostitute?*"

"*Professional*, Des, a professional," he said charismatically. "They're very business minded individuals. Offer them a large enough payment for certain services, regardless of what they are, and they can be quite accommodating."

"Do you have a backup plan? What if it's a different guard? What if the drugs aren't effective?"

"We do have a backup plan, though I don't think it's going to come to that."

The vague lack of substance to the answer told her that the backup plan involved violence. It wasn't uncommon in jobs like this, but it made things messy. She preferred to avoid it whenever possible.

"I assure you that all the information is accurate. I—we—are betting our lives on it," Magnar continued.

*Because believing it* definitely *makes it true...*

"Inside the vault we estimate there to be a sum potentially above fifty thousand suns, jewels larger than a man's fist, and writs of land and debts that are worth more than any of us could fathom. This isn't just a meager take that keeps you alive until the next job. This is the type of treasure that creates *generational* wealth. Every one of us will become rich enough to buy ourselves a retirement filled with servants and leisure, along with the land and title that comes with it."

"I want to know where this information is coming from. I'm not going to risk going into a building that houses a private army based on the ramblings of a drunkard or self-proclaimed clairvoyant," she said sternly.

"I can say that it is someone within the guild itself. Nothing more though," he said with finality. "The only thing we are missing is someone to get through the vault's lock. We needed the best, and here you are."

She clenched her jaw as she pondered the scheme. Was she actually considering this? With a sum totaling what Magnar described she might *actually* be able to see Mixton releasing her debt. This would be enough for him to retire, surely. He was likely to take the majority of her cut, but she'd been skimming into her stash for a while now. There was a nice little sum tucked away for her, even if she didn't get to keep a vast majority of the stolen gold. The thought of what she most desired became a little more tangible.

"What kind of lock are we talking about? And why don't you just break through the wall that's *inside* the vault?" she asked, prodding the plan for pitfalls.

"The vault is, unfortunately, not adjacent to the sewer, just its anteroom," replied Magnar. "As for the lock, my information tells us that it's a Diamond."

Desnia's stomach twisted into a knot. A Diamond? Of course that's what it would be. Its creator, arguably the best lock craftsman in the city, had arrogantly named it to boast it as uncrackable, a not-so-subtle promotion of his own work. She'd tried to disprove that claim once before, but after six wearisome hours she'd been forced to abandon the endeavor empty-handed. And resentful.

"Do you understand how enormous of an undertaking it is to try and get through a Diamond?" she asked.

Ox leaned over to Sanco again. "What's 'enor-enormous' mean?" he asked in his audible half whisper.

Sanco, not even bothering to whisper this time, responded, "You, Ox. You're enormous. Now, shut it."

She ignored them and continued. "I want this to happen," she admitted, "but a Diamond takes hours to get through. The last time I attempted one it took me five hours just to complete the first set of *three* tumblers, even if the others went faster, I still don't know if I could have finished in one night."

Grunner spoke for the first time, half muttering under his breath, "I told you we couldn't trust a woman on a job this big."

Desnia shot daggers at him with her eyes, piercing like cold steel, while she rested her hand on the hilt of the blade at her waist. He looked at her with an empty stare that seemed to both not care about her obvious rage, and also begged her to try something.

Magnar quickly stepped between the two of them, and put his hand on Desnia's shoulder. She jerked away and turned her fury towards him, stabbing with eyes of pure ire. Magnar raised both of his hands into the air and gave her one of his smiles.

"Des, I apologize for Grunner, he sometimes is a bit closed minded. And don't worry, you won't have to hear him speak again, will she, Grunner?" he said, giving him a look that flashed malignance in a way that unnerved

Desnia, as though she'd seen a glimpse of a monster that hid behind the handsome smiles of the well put together man.

Grunner sneered, his face coated with cold incense. He nodded begrudgingly and hung his head down uncontested.

As quickly as the expression had come, it disappeared from Magnar's face, replaced with his impeccable smile as he looked back at Des.

"Now, I understand your concern," said Magnar as though nothing had happened, "and I was aware of your previous attempt at the Diamond. We knew it wasn't going to be easy to get through, and whoever we hired to crack it was going to need practice. So, our employer procured this."

He drew back a cloth that had been placed over a bulky object sitting on a nearby shelf and revealed a block of steel approximately one foot square, a wide, singular dial in its center. The sides were exposed, as though the contraption had been cut directly from a safe door, with gears and other components exposed.

Desnia studied it with interest. Wearing a thoughtful expression, she walked over and ran her fingers along the steel, admiring the complex precision of the mechanism that was so simply and beautifully stated by the single turn style in the center of the exterior plate.

"This," said Magnar proudly, "is an old lock prototype built by the Diamond's creator himself. It's a bit dated, I admit, but I understand it cost our employer a fortune and was extremely difficult to acquire. Apparently, the man is rather secretive about his lock designs, who would've guessed? I hope that this will be able to sufficiently provide you with the knowledge you need to break into the actual Diamond in less time?"

"This isn't a Diamond prototype," affirmed Desnia. "And this design isn't just older—it's practically *ancient*. It doesn't even have an integrated key lock." It had to be older than she was. The man had been building locks for a *long* time. Though, she'd never been able to get a glimpse of his internal mechanism design before. Could this help? Or was it going to lead her to make incorrect assumptions?

"This *might* fill in some gaps. I had wondered about a few of the mechanism transitions..." She caught herself falling into the beauty of the mechanics as she spoke. Despite its age, the level of craftsmanship and skill was still apparent—from polished cogs to perfectly matched gears, and cylinders that seemed to be turned with impossible precision. An awe of respect brewed within her. Just as she'd attempted to become a master of her own trade, she could respect someone who had clearly mastered theirs.

She often pictured the interior mechanisms as she worked, but so much of the Diamond had been a mystery to her. Guesswork and experience had gotten her decently far last time, but she could already start to guess which things she'd been incorrect about.

"Des," said Magnar, "I'm confident that if anyone can glean information from this, it's you. This is not a Diamond, I admit. But think about what this *is*. The same mind that built this later created the greatest lock ever known. But, at one point, I would guarantee you that *this* was the standard, the bar that all others tried to reach. And then, someone like you—though undoubtedly less talented—came along and beat it. Proved that it was as fallible as any other design. With this, my dear Des, I am sure that you can learn enough about his mind to be able to do the same for the Diamond. Think about how far you got last time, no one else has ever accomplished even the small amount you did. Trust me, I've asked around. *A lot.* You are the person to do this, I'm sure of it."

"Maybe," she said, still staring at the reflective metal devices, ignoring his pandering, "but it's still going to be incredibly difficult. It could take me most of the night to get through. And this could honestly be completely different from the Diamond design. Hopefully not, but still..." She pulled herself from her infatuation and the reality that this might be possible began to set in. It would still be a difficult task, without question, but perhaps it *was* feasible. "When do you plan to pull this all off?" she asked.

"Three days," said Magnar.

Her eyebrows raised. Three days might be enough time. *Maybe.* Without digging through the lock, she wasn't sure if she would need more or less than that, but it would have to do. "How long is the owner of this place gone for?" she asked.

"Don't worry about him," replied Magnar. She didn't dare ask what that meant. Sometimes it was better to remain ignorant, even if she was only pretending to be. "Even still, we don't want to overextend our stay here. There are some other factors in play as well that I don't wish to go into detail about, but you should know that they could also limit our timetable. Three days is as long as we dare wait."

"How exactly do you intend to move all of the money once we're in?" she asked.

"Right back through here," he said. "The boys here are going to bring everything back here over the course of several trips, and we've got a carriage that our employer has arranged to wait behind the building, where you entered. We're going to load it up, then it and us will go straight to the docks where your good friend Mixton has already arranged passage aboard a vessel. If all goes to plan, then we will have set sail before anyone even realizes that the money has been stolen."

"That's a big *if*," said Desnia.

"Not at all! With you here, we're sure to succeed."

It was a solid plan. Loading the gold onto the carriage was a little less tidy than she preferred, but it wasn't a *bad* option, as long as it was still dark when they did it. The docks were close enough that they weren't likely to run into problems on their way. And Ox looked like he could carry twice his weight if he needed to, even if it was the only thing he *was* able to do. Overall, it was a satisfactory plan. She hadn't expected that.

"I'm going to need a quiet place to work with this," she said, pointing to the lock, "preferably somewhere that doesn't smell like shit."

"Ox," said Magnar authoritatively, "carry this lock up to the third floor. And be *careful*. We can't afford to damage it."

"There are a few rooms up there without windows, you can work by candlelight. And please try to limit your comings and goings to night hours. We don't want anyone asking questions."

*Condescending asshole.*

She followed Ox as he capably hauled the heavy device up the stairs, lost in thought.

Three days. It wasn't much, but most of the planning had already been taken care of. Her only task was to get through the Diamond. It sounded simple, in theory, but it would likely be the most difficult accomplishment of her life. Assuming she succeeded. Thinking about that, three days didn't seem so long.

It would have to be enough.

# Chapter Ten



Delvan grimaced as he walked down the alley, his side aching with each breath. He was going to need to find an herbalist to get yertwood root tea for the pain. That could wait though; years of sparring and training had taught him to work through the physical pain, to put it out of your mind and fight through.

Didn't stop it from hurting like a demon's fang.

As he approached the building where he'd slain the axe-wielding man, he saw that two soldiers were now posted at the rear entrance, clearly acting as guards.

"Lord Hilbrun is waiting inside for you, my Lord," said one of them as he approached. He nodded while his hand pressed against the side of his ribs. This was going to make for a *long* day.

He stepped over the body that he'd left and walked down the stairs into the basement. A few torches brought flickering life to the stone walls, skipping across the streaks of inanite striating the granite foundation. A trace of pungent smoke hung in the air, slowly ventilating through the open stairwell.

To one side, several soldiers were attempting to use a table as a makeshift battering ram to break down a reinforced door. The table had begun splintering and was failing terribly compared to the unflinching mass of iron. They were going to have to go back to the barracks for more effective measures soon enough.

He walked past the struggling soldiers and into the main basement, their loud banging following behind him. The high ceiling made clear just how enormous the room was as he gazed past the top of the thin screens into the hazy distance. How many people could fit down here?

Soldiers were walking around and removing red shades from lanterns that were littered throughout the vast space, bringing a more natural color to the previously tinted air. He felt a strange sensation that he couldn't describe, as though he was swimming through a pool of water and had found himself suddenly in a glob of oil.

He walked down an aisle, the center panels of the paper rooms having been pulled back to reveal individuals laying on small mats on the floor, completely oblivious to their surroundings as they stared off into the beyond.

A stale smell masked the mustiness of the basement, and Delvan could see sunlight coming from a portal in the wall ahead. Hilbrun must have vented the room once he entered. He wondered how thick the smoke must have been when they'd first arrived.

He could hear Hilbrun shouting orders from the basement's end, near where the sunlight shone like a beacon in the distance. As he walked beyond the rows and into the foyer framed by them, he found two soldiers standing around what he assumed were the only coherent people in the room. Three brutish looking men and a woman of surprising beauty wearing a silk robe were kneeling together, their hands tied behind their backs.

"Del, there you are," said Hilbrun. "Where did you go? The soldiers out back said you handled someone at the rear exit and then took off running."

"I was chasing after someone," he said, flinching at the pain of speaking, "man in a black robe. Tall, thin, with a hollowed face. Hil, it... it was strange. *He* was strange." He shifted his voice down into a hushed whisper and moved closer to Hilbrun. "He cast something at me, it was like-like a bolt, or an arrow of energy. A concentrated, focused shot unlike anything I've ever seen. Like a ball of light. Hit me in the side, but it didn't get through my armor. I think it fractured a few of my ribs though." He removed his hand to show the scorched patch to Hilbrun, who was listening intently. "And then... I don't know how to explain it, but *something* stuck my foot to the ground. A hundred men couldn't have moved it, Hil, I swear. I-I tried to go after him, but my foot was stuck there for minutes, until it finally released somehow. I'm sorry."

He tried not to sound dejected. He knew that Hilbrun was going to be disappointed, and it made him feel sick. Hilbrun expected him to be better than this, and all he'd done was let him down.

Hilbrun looked at the armor and then at Delvan, his brow furrowed in what Delvan could only assume was complete dissatisfaction. He rubbed his face as it cringed, and he was silent for a period. He'd entrusted Delvan to guard the back door, and he'd utterly failed.

"It's not your fault, Del," Hilbrun finally said, putting a hand on his shoulder, letting out a sigh.

*What?*

Of all the scenarios that Delvan had played through his mind on the walk back here, this had not been one of them.

"I will explain what I can later, but for right now I think you should count yourself lucky. If that was who I suspect, not many have fought him and lived to tell about it," said Hilbrun, softly enough that the soldiers nearby were unlikely to hear. "For now, keep what you saw to yourself, and help me interrogate some of these people." He drew back and started projecting orders again.

Once the soldiers had been assigned their tasks, Hilbrun motioned for him to join him by the kneeling prisoners.

"I am looking for something," started Hilbrun, speaking down to the prisoners, "something valuable and very important to me. So important, in fact, that I would be willing to offer amnesty to the first person that offers information that leads me to what I want."

"We're not helpin' you," said one of the burly men, spitting at Hilbrun.

Hilbrun reached out a hand into the air, grabbing at the immaterial space as though it were fabric, and jerked it with the motion of a downward pull. The man—several feet away—pivoted forward on his knees, his face being thrown into the stone floor with a loud *crack*. As he groaned on the ground, Hilbrun continued, the other men looking at their associate with glimmers of fear in their eyes, the woman turning away.

"A large amount of cadentite was recently stolen from a spice merchant in the Upper Tier. I'm looking for information on where it could have gone. We haven't found any growing rooms here yet, but rest assured, if there are any, we *will* find them. If it was delivered or sold to this establishment—or if you know of any other locations that may have been potential buyers—now would be the time to tell me, and buy your freedom."

Delvan heard banging in the distance along with shouting. It sounded like soldiers were trying to get into other sealed areas of the basement.

"We-we don't see much of nothin'," said one of the remaining men. "People, they come and—"

"Shut yer mouth, Gor," hissed the other man.

Hilbrun extended his arm and in the same motion brought the second man's face to the floor, as though he'd ripped him down with an invisible rope. Two men now lay on the cold tile, bleeding and groaning in pain. Delvan had never been part of an interrogation like this before. He tried to remain stern and imposing, but wondered if this level of violence was necessary. Was this the best way to obtain the information they sought? *A Truthsayer would make quick work of this,* Delvan thought. *Why not call for one?*

"Gor," said Hilbrun calmly, "please, continue."

"People, they come in and all go through Mal," he said, tilting his head towards the woman in white. "We just stand around and make sure no one goes and wanders off."

The woman, Mal, gave Gor a look of anger drowned beneath pure terror. He turned his head away in shame.

"Thank you, Gor," said Hilbrun, turning to Mal. "Mal, do you know if the cadentite that I am looking for is here? If you tell me where and save all these soldiers the trouble of searching, I would be deeply grateful."

She shook her head, a tear forming at the corner of her eye. She refused to look at either of them. "I don't know," she said in a whimper, "I just send people to the back that aren't customers. I don't see anything that happens back there."

"I believe you, Mal," said Hilbrun coolly. "I need to know if anyone has come in here that *wasn't* a customer. A messenger, courier, anyone not looking for a fix. This would have been in the last two days. This is very important."

Her lips trembled as tears now streaked down her face. She shook her head and finally managed to speak. "I-I can't. I can't. They'll do things. You don't understand who they are, who you're asking me to betray."

"What I understand is that they are out there, a threat for your future self. But *I* am here, right *now.*" Hil reached to his side and repeated the yanking motion, Gor's surprise-stricken face implanting into the ground with the other guards a few feet away. "You can deal with me, gain amnesty, and worry about 'them' while you hop on the next ship to the southern continent, or you can accept the same fate—or worse—as your friends here."

Delvan was becoming uncomfortable as the woman started to tremble, the silk robe shimmering in the light of the nearby candles. She may just be a commoner, but she hadn't hurt anyone, had she? Were these measures necessary?

"My Lords," exclaimed a soldier as he came running over, out of breath, "I'm sorry to interrupt, but we weren't... You should come quickly and see for yourself."

Hilbrun gave him an annoyed glare, but Delvan was glad for the interruption. He wasn't sure how far Hilbrun had been willing to go.

He knew that the cadentite was valuable, and that Hilbrun's family relationships gave this investigation a personal connection, but he seemed... overly committed to finding this cadentite. What was driving him to the edge like this?

They followed the soldier as he marched to the room's edge at the side wall. As they moved past the rows of paneled rooms and the full wall came into view, Delvan could see a long row of heavy wooden doors set into pink stone before him. The private rooms.

Some of the doors were already broken open, and Delvan quickly understood the source of the noise from earlier as soldiers continued to kick and knock down the remaining closed doors.

"We found him in one of these rooms, Sire. He's just like the others in this place, I'm afraid. We tried to rouse him, but we only dared get so close," said the soldier as they briskly walked to one of the busted doors.

Delvan felt a pit form in his gut as he and Hilbrun finally arrived at the room's entrance and saw its occupant. On the floor, surrounded by a hazy smoke, eyes closed and mouth agape, was a Blue cadet. Scrawny with a sunken face, Delvan didn't recognize him, and he wasn't sure if Hilbrun did either, but it still stung like finding a brother for both of them.

Delvan stepped forward, looking to Hilbrun to make sure he was ready, just in case. He had no idea how someone reacted under the influence of iguan, and a Blue who suddenly felt threatened and wasn't able to make clear headed decisions would be dangerous. Hilbrun gave him a nod, and Delvan stepped into the room, cautiously kneeling next to the young cadet. He lifted the chain around his neck ever so slightly, finding the clasp and seeing that was shaped like a bear's head. There was only one Blue sect that used the visage of Ursorner as their crest.

*Fuck*, the thought with a grimace. He stood up and took a few steps back.

"He's a Jack," he said to Hilbrun. The look on Hilbrun's face turned to mimic Delvan's.

"We need him to sober up so we can get him out of here," said Hilbrun in a concerned voice. "This is already going to spark rumors in the barracks, and I've sent for more soldiers to help search this place. If they all see him there won't be anything we can do to keep it quiet. We can't have people talking about this."

"How do we sober him up?" asked Delvan.

"Well, there's only really one way that I know of," said Hilbrun. "We need him to channel."

"You're joking..."

"Unfortunately, no. He doesn't have his inanite pouch on him, and I don't see it around here, so you're going to need to give him one of your blocks. I'm going to need all of mine to hold him. Put it in his hand or pocket or something and then shake him until he wakes up and tries to attack you. Once he starts channeling then most of his high *should* go away."

"*Should*?!" said Delvan. "Do you think I have a death wish? Do you think you can even hold him once he starts channeling?"

Hilbrun gave him a look and a shrug that said: *Maybe?*

"Even a single block is a lot for a Jack," said Delvan, running his fingers through his hair, lips pulling back in a thin line. "There's a ton of inanite in the walls here, let him draw from that instead. He might be easier to hold then."

"But far less sober by the end of it," said Hilbrun. "Besides, you see the walls over here? No inanite, just clean granite. I bet the bastards who run this place made these rooms specifically for Blues. Can't risk having one lose control while on a trip."

Delvan felt a flash of panic as he paced in the small room. He didn't like the idea of being in an enclosed space with a hallucinating Jack. Still, they couldn't leave him here. He was just going to have to trust Hilbrun to hold him.

He pulled a single inanite block from his pouch and slipped it into the Jack's trouser pocket. He looked to Hilbrun one more time to confirm he was ready, and then began shaking the Blue by his shoulders. His head bobbed to the sides, his eyes barely more than slits as drool dribbled down the side of his mouth.

He needed to do more.

Delvan then reached towards the cadet's neck. There was one thing that all Blues would notice: someone touching their sapphire. They were a part of them, as conjoined with their essence and soul as the hair on their head or the eyes that captured the world. Removing it was akin to losing a limb.

He grabbed the chain and pulled the sapphire from under the uniform that the Blue was wearing. The opulent gem, facets glittering and amplifying even the faint light of the dark basement, slid out and into Delvan's hand. Any time now something—

The cadet's hands clenched, and his eyes opened and locked with Delvan's.

*This is not going to end well,* he thought with a bit of terror lumping in his throat.

The young man screamed and jumped to his feet, a wild look in his eye. Delvan stepped back as the Blue began trudging towards him. He moved with an exaggerated, struggling motion, as though he were attempting to wade through thick molasses. Delvan turned to see Hilbrun's arm extended, his fist clenched and arm shaking. Blood trickled from his nose, his teeth gritted together, and strain was accentuated over the whole of his body as he struggled to slow the Blue. His abilities weren't nearly as effective on other Blues as the general populace, and Jacks were difficult for him well beyond even the norm for Blues.

Delvan backed out of the room as the cadet pursued him. The Jack grabbed the door as though trying to use it to pull himself forward against Hilbrun's Reach. He pulled, and Delvan heard the wood creak, then crack, under the strength of his bearing. There were popping noises as the hinges bent and then snapped, bits of iron falling to the floor. The door then fully released from the jam, the Jack casually holding it at his side as though the solid oaken panel were made of the paper walls throughout the rest of the basement. He flung it to the side, a burst of splinters spraying through the room as the shambles crumbled to the floor like hay from a bale. Slivers of wood bounced off the cadet's face that Delvan was sure should have stabbed into his skin. He kept stepping forward. Foot slowly fell before foot, stomping into the ground as though he carried the weight of a mountain atop his back. The fear at the back of Delvan's mind seemed to twist and feel strange, fluctuating like the muscles on the Jack's face.

The Jack began to reach for his sword, but as he did Delvan thought he could see a realization befall the man's eyes. Clarity came to him as though a veil had been lifted, and he looked at the pair of fellow Blues before him with a strange confusion, immediately followed by fear.

"What-what are you... Who... Oh no..." the cadet said, falling to his knees looking humiliated. He still appeared to be somewhat incoherent, but the majority of the drug seemed to have worn off. He reached his hand into his pocket, staring at the block of stone before dropping it to the floor. The once black inanite clattered on the tile, now a bright white cube, completely muted.

Hilbrun slowly opened his quivering hands and wiped the blood from his nose, nearly teetering over. He put his hand on Delvan's shoulder for support, looking exhausted and sweating profusely.

Delvan felt anger and betrayal as he looked to the sullen shell of a man that wore the same sapphire as him. Each of them represented the Sapphiric Court, coming to a place like this pointed a dirty light on the entirety of their image. And why a place like this would even consider allowing a cadet to patronize their establishment was even more distasteful than the business itself.

"Del," said Hilbrun through heavy breaths, "I'm going to need a few minutes after that. Was like trying to hold a charging bull." He found a nearby chair and sat down, sweat soaking his black hair.

Delvan wanted to help, but he was aware of the fatigue that Hilbrun felt. Short of some rest and a large meal, there wasn't much he could do about it.

"I want to go talk to that woman," Delvan said, his mouth vocalizing the first thing that came to his mind as he thought of ways to assist that didn't involve standing around.

Hilbrun eyed him with a questioning expression. "If you think you're up to it, go ahead. I don't know how much she was going to tell me anyway. Maybe you'll have better luck with her than I did. If we don't find the cadentite here, then she's our only lead left. Probably shouldn't have played my whole hand back there with her.

"If you don't have any luck then I'll be back over there in a bit. I want to keep an eye on our friend here while I send one of the men to get another Blue to take him somewhere quiet to recover."

Delvan nodded and made his way over to where the prisoners were being kept. The three men still laid on the floor, dark red blood pooling around one of the men's heads.

Delvan stood over Mal, still on her knees with guards to either side.

"You mind telling me what that Jack is doing here?" he asked her, his profile domineering her diminutive, huddled figure.

She turned her head away. Anger roiled inside of him. He wanted answers. He wanted accountability.

"Why is there a Blue here!" he shouted. "Did you hook him somehow? Lure him here? Explain!" He wanted to believe that maybe someone else had been responsible. That perhaps the Jack was a victim of circumstance.

"No different," she murmured.

"What?" he said, drawing closer.

"You're no different!" she said, raising her trembling voice for the first time since he'd met her. "You Blues think that you're so superior, like you're elevated above us somehow. You're not the King. You're not gods. You're *human*, just like the rest of us. Each of you is as susceptible to desires as a random person on the street. We didn't trick him into coming here. Another *Blue* brought him in here. So, you see, you and I, we aren't so different. Stop treating us like we're beneath you."

Delvan took a step back. Her accusations about the other Blue must be false. A fabrication to get her out of her situation. But he saw no deception in her, and what reason did she have to lie? Everything she'd just said was enough to put her in prison, and given her associates on the floor, she might have even assumed that those would be her last words.

What was he doing? She wasn't responsible for the failings of the other Blue. He could at least admit that to himself. And Ferrand was enough of an example to prove to him that the conclave of Blues might not be the impenetrable fortress of bonded knights that he had always pictured. He didn't need to approach this with the same desperation that Hilbrun had. He wanted to help, true, but there were other ways that he could achieve that. Afterall, he needed to decide who he was going to be. Who he *wanted* to be.

He knelt down on the floor, putting himself eye level with the woman, who was now turning her head as far as possible. She probably thought that this would be her last breath.

"I'm not going to hurt you," said Delvan with a sigh. What was he supposed to say? "You," he said to one of the guards, "go grab us a couple chairs." He pulled a small knife from his belt and walked behind Mal, who was fidgeting at the sight of the glinting steel. "Stay still," he said.

He cut her bonds free and helped her into a chair as it was brought over. He took the other and sat across from her. He then ordered the guards to go help the others search the building, leaving just him and the cowering Mal.

"Mal, my name is Delvan. Delvan ce Saffstar. Is Mal your full name?" he asked.

She rubbed her wrists and spoke after a moment, still not looking at him. "Malanai. My name is Malanai," she said quietly.

"Pretty," he said. "Look, Malanai, I have no desire to hurt you. My friend, Hil, he... well he really needs to find this cadentite. And I think that maybe the pressure he feels he's under is putting him in a certain... mood.

"I can see you're scared." He leaned forward in the chair. "I know what you said earlier, but can you tell me who it is you're scared of? The man that I chased he, uh, certainly left his mark," he said, rubbing the scar on the side of his armor with a wince. "Is he who you're worried about if you talk to us? Can you tell me who he is?"

She shook her head. "No," she said, "I won't. I can't. Even if I wanted to help you, tell you about him, I couldn't. Please, don't ask me to."

That was disappointing. Delvan hoped that she might shed some light on the mysterious caster, his curiosity burning with questions.

"Alright," he said, not wanting to put her under more duress. "Can you tell me anything else instead? If we find the cadentite here and you don't tell me anything, it won't matter. But I am guessing it's not here, is it?"

She shook her head.

*Figures.*

"Can you tell me who brought it here? A courier? Someone else?" he asked, still hopeful for answers.

She paused for a moment, biting her bottom lip as if to stop herself from talking. Finally, she said, "There was a woman here, two days ago. She came in and saw the man in the back, she stopped and talked to me for a minute, but I turned my back for a moment, and she vanished. She's the only one who hasn't been a customer in the past few days to come through here." She hung her head with shame, tears still streaming down her face.

"Can you tell me about her? Who she is? What she looks like? Where she might be from?" he asked.

"She had blonde hair," the woman said, failing to hold herself back from crying, "and she was not much older than you. She wore loose men's clothing and said she frequented the Hillview Tavern. She took some muted inanite. That's all I know. I swear."

Delvan leaned back in his chair. Maybe this was enough information to help them. If nothing else, it was a lead they hadn't had before.

"Please," she said after a minute of silence, "you have to help me. They'll kill me just for telling you that. They... They can do other things. Horrible, horrible things to someone. I'm in terrible danger. Can you help me?"

Could he help her? The hooded man in the alley was capable of things he'd never seen nor heard of. If these people were capable of more than that—which he was inclined to believe—what good would amnesty do for this poor girl? Could he—

Before he had a chance to answer, a soldier came running down the aisle.

"My Lord," he said, "Lord Hilbrun requests that you head to the rear exit. He is still recovering, and we've broken through the door in the back room. He'd like you to oversee the search, sir."

Delvan looked at the woman, quietly sobbing with her head hung deject-edly, and then gave the soldier a nod. "Stay here with her," he said. "I'll be back."

He would talk with Hilbrun later about sending her off with amnesty. The information that she had shared seemed to take every bit of her willpower to muster, and given how terrified she was, he doubted they would be able to get much more information from her.

He went to the rear exit, finding the door to the anteroom closed. He walked through it and found the space choked with a billowing, black smoke. The iron door to the locked room was ajar, dents and scars covering its face, with thick smog pluming out from within.

A few soldiers were coughing while attempting to fan the dark cloud through the rear exit, up the stairs he'd originally entered through. Inside the room he could see the charred remains of the space's contents in heaps of smoldering coals.

He took a cloth from one of the soldiers to wrap around his face and helped fan the remaining smoke from the anteroom. After a few minutes the smoke cleared through the staircase like a chimney, making the air somewhat breathable once more.

Most of what was left in the room were glowing embers on the floor, heating the room and the antechamber. He walked in, ignorant to the searing heat, and looked around, few of the scorched remnants still intact. A tapestry hung on the wall, blackened by the fire, depicting the continent. The writing seemed strange to him, and while there were one or two locations he recognized, some of the cities were in places he'd never known to have a population beyond a small village, if anything at all.

Remnants of the spines of tomes littered the floor, the bindings appearing ancient. Perhaps some of it would be legible, but he doubted it would contain anything useful. The bulk of the fire had started with a pile of fuel in the center of the room, made clear by the ashy mound that sat there, scars burnt on the stone spreading outward from its original blaze. He pulled a metal plate from the pile of ash; cracked in half and carved with a strange pattern. He wasn't sure what to make of it, and placed it back down on the floor.

He knew all too well how flames could spread, the paths they followed, the destruction they reaped. The fire had probably gone out when the enclosed space ran out of air, leaving a precious few items relatively untouched.

He attempted to pull a text from one of the remaining shelves, but the heat had damaged it too badly, and it fell apart and scattered on the floor as he tried to open it.

He sighed. Hilbrun was undoubtedly going to want to check the room for himself, but Delvan felt the hollowness of disappointment as he looked around. Nothing in here was going to be of use. Maybe Hilbrun would see something he didn't, but his optimism was waning.

It seemed that the only lead they had now was this courier that Malanai had described. He left to go and talk to Hilbrun. There was more to do today.

# Chapter Eleven

*Perhaps this is the one. After so many failed attempts, it begins to make one wonder if success is possible, if the dreams of today can become the reality of tomorrow. Insight can only get you so far...*
Reference forgotten,
Second Day of Autumn, Forty-ninth Year of the Seventh Epoch

The late afternoon sun sifted between the rustling leaves of a nearby tree, glimpses of light shining through the shade that covered the bench Delvan and Hilbrun sat on. The park was quiet and poorly groomed. Plants and weeds grew as though wild, as if emphasizing the poor condition of the neighborhood. Pavers all around were cracked and broken, and the small squares of soil that held a few half-dead trees were dry and wasting.

The smell of smoke had adhered itself to Delvan's armor like moss to a stone. The odor, however, proved insufficient in masking the pungent spices of the second of Hilbrun's three meat-wraps. He watched as Hilbrun took another voracious bite of the marinated brown meat held together by a tightly wrapped flatbread, his mouth a disgusted sneer.

"How can you eat that?" he asked, the scent burning his olfactory. "It smells terrible."

"It's amazing," said Hilbrun, his mouth full. "You should try it."

"It looks disgusting. I can't believe you're eating some mystery meat from a street vendor in the Lower Valley. For all you know it could be rat that you're eating."

Hilbrun took another large bite. "You should try some new things, Del. You might be surprised at what you find you enjoy. Our port back home was always full of different foods from around the continent, even some from across the southern sea. This spicy 'rat' is delicious. Here, try some."

He held it up towards Delvan, and he pulled his head back in disgust. Did the people down here really eat food like this?

"No, thanks," he said, holding up his hand.

Hilbrun gave him a shrug and continued eating.

He knew that Hilbrun needed to recover from their encounter with the Jack earlier that morning—Blues had a certain reputation as to the amount of food they could consume—but he seemed to legitimately be enjoying the mushy mixture. Delvan just shook his head as they waited.

As he'd suspected, Hilbrun had wanted to sort through the fire's debris, and spent several hours picking through the refuse. He hadn't stated whether or not he'd found anything useful, but based on his frustrated demeanor Delvan was guessing that it was unlikely. After telling him the information he'd learned from Malanai, his mood had seemed to improve, going as far as to praise Delvan's work.

They'd spent several more hours at the iguan den, Hilbrun explaining that he didn't trust Commander Ferrand to not come and take any evidence or clues to the cadentite's location if they left. Delvan guessed it was likely enough for Ferrand to find out about their discovery, but had been frustrated staying there for most of the day to find nothing of any use or value. He needed to know who the man he'd chased had been. How he had done... what he'd done. He became even more aggravated as they sat here waiting, again, while he had to endure the wretched stench of Hilbrun's recovery meal.

"What do you know about the man I chased?" asked Delvan, keenly aware of the pain in his side.

"In truth, not much," said Hilbrun between swallows. "He's more a myth than anything else. He supposedly runs all of the major iguan dens in the city, but almost no one has met him and lived, or so they say. Been the ring-leader for a *long* time, which is a feat in and of itself. The call him Protorus."

It sounded a little like urban legend to Delvan. A story propagated to reinforce fear of his reign. But the pain in his side reminded him that perhaps there was some validity to it.

"Why is that such a feat?" Delvan asked.

"We used to have some similar issues in the port with smugglers. These cartels all have the same problem. Ambition. Someone kills or inherits his way to the top, takes over the business, and gains all the power he's ever dreamed of. Problem is there are always others just like him—ambitious, amoral, and willing to do whatever it takes—to take his place, claim the power for themselves.

"Some of these ring leaders last a few months. A few will make it a couple years. The ones that you have to be wary of are the ones that have been there for a lifetime. They're cunning, ruthless, and smart enough to eliminate any competition. They rule through fear and a death grip on their control of power. You might be only one of a handful who even know what this man looks like."

"How did he cast though?" asked Delvan, annoyed at the nebulous information. "He wasn't wearing a gem, Hil. I would have sensed it. It's not possible without a sapphire, it just isn't. If he'd struck me in the head with that blast... I'd probably be joining the other group of unfortunates who've crossed his path. And my foot... Hil, I swear the ground beneath my foot glowed. It was faint, but I *know* I saw it. It was like my boot had been nailed to the stone. What he did was *impossible*."

Hilbrun sat quietly while he started eating his third wrap, staring off into the distance.

"If we can find this courier," he finally said, "maybe you can get some of those answers. Not much we can do until then."

Delvan crossed his arms sulkily. Hilbrun had said he could explain. Instead, he was stringing him along with vague answers and misdirection. Why did he insist on asking him to aid in his endeavors but still treat him like a child? He thought he'd been taken along as a partner, not just a Pupil.

"Maybe we should go up there ourselves," Delvan said. "We might have better luck finding this courier than that street vendor you paid to ask around the tavern."

Hilbrun shook his head. "We're not going to risk scaring off our only remaining lead because you want a few pints."

More demeaning assumptions. Couldn't Hilbrun tell that he genuinely wanted to help?

"If we went in there," continued Hilbrun as he finished his meal, "half the building would scatter, and our courier would likely hear of us long before coming in. The vendor—aside from selling delicious meat wraps—is better known around here. Familiar faces are more welcomed, more likely to get people talking and answering questions, like when a certain young blonde girl might come in, or where she might live.

"I'm paying him more than he likely makes in a month, we'll get some answers. We just have to wait."

Delvan felt a tension building within him, one that felt like it was going to rip him in two. He had no answers from Hilbrun as to who that man had been. No *real* answers anyway. He had to sit and wait while he felt a stabbing pain in his side with every inhalation, and Hilbrun was clearly still withholding information, despite everything over the past few days.

His thoughts turned to Malanai. How scared she had been, the dangerous situation she was now in.

"What do you think is going to happen to Malanai?" he asked.

Hilbrun didn't even bother to look over and notice Delvan's annoyance as he wiped his face. "What do you mean?"

"She seemed to think these people, like the man I chased, that run the dens were going to come for her. Where can she run so that she'll be safe?"

Hilbrun looked at him, puzzled. "Run? She's not running anywhere. What are you talking about?"

"You said you'd give her amnesty," said Delvan.

"Yes, *if* she had information that led to the cadentite. Which I hope to the gods this does. Just because she's pretty and looked at you with puffy eyes doesn't mean she was telling the truth. And if this leads to another dead end then she's the only thing we have that can give us another trail to follow. I'm not risking letting her go until I am holding that cadentite or this courier gives us a promising lead."

"Hil, they'll kill her! What about Ferrand? What if he finds out about her and whisks her away the same as he did with Mari?"

"Relax, I had her guards bring her to people I trust. She's perfectly safe. I don't think even the Knight Commander could get to her."

Delvan wasn't sure how much he trusted that statement, but there wasn't much he could do about it now. Perhaps he would try and find out where she had been taken later.

He watched their horses chew on the overgrown weeds as the hours passed. After a while he could see Hilbrun becoming almost as impatient as he was. Delvan was trying to avoid suggesting going to the tavern themselves again, hoping that Hilbrun would propose it this time instead, giving him the satisfaction of being right.

No such suggestion came though, and as Delvan was about to give in and risk getting belittled for his ideas once more, the shop vendor appeared and approached them in the park.

"Took you long enough," said Hilbrun, standing. "I was about to go there myself and start looking."

*Not such a bad idea, was it?* thought Delvan.

"Gravest apologies, my Lord," said the overly tanned man in oil-stained clothes, "but this is not an establishment where you simply ask about some-one. The crowd there is rough, and bluntness can land you on the sharp edge of a blade."

"At least tell us you found something," said Hilbrun.

"Aye, I did, sir. Took a while to find someone willing to talk, and it didn't come at a cheap price, hmm." The man held out his hand and rubbed his thumb against his first two fingers, clearly looking for reimbursement. Hilbrun looked at him in an irritated but deliberating way. With a roll of his eyes, he pulled ten moons from his purse and handed them to the shrewd man.

"Ah yes, that should cover it," he said, slipping the coins into his own purse. "There is only one woman who was as you described that people knew of. Sounds like she's a regular. I heard that her landlord is also a frequenter of this establishment, as he was ranting to the bartender recently about her having not paid her rent in the past two months."

"Did you happen to find out where this landlord lives?"

"Aye, that I did. That I did."

Delvan stood in the dingy street as Hilbrun pounded against the locked door of the landlord's residence. They had tried knocking more discreetly but hadn't been able to get the man's attention. He just hoped that none of the neighbors were going to run and tell the courier—assuming she hadn't already heard them and run off.

"Agh! I can literally hear the bastard snoring in there!" said Hilbrun furiously. Delvan tried to keep a watchful eye on the surrounding buildings and alleys, looking for any sign of their target.

Hilbrun had said he would get answers from this courier, but what could she know? From what Malanai had said, she had met with the man that he'd encountered, but that didn't mean she knew him. It didn't even sound like she'd been to that den before. He felt like he was chasing a phantom, inferable through effects upon its surroundings, yet noncorporeal and ever evasive.

With a few additional and forceful pounds, the snoring ceased with a sudden jerk, and Delvan could hear the man cursing through the door.

"I swear, I'm gonna beat yer ass if you keep—" Delvan heard the man say, his gravelly voice muffled through the door. The door swung open, and the man's face flashed from rage to wide-eyed panic. "Um, my Lords, I beg yer forgiveness. I didn't realize... well I thought it was someone else."

"I'll exchange an apology for information," said Hilbrun. "We understand you have a tenant, a woman, about our age, wears men's clothing and frequently visits the tavern down the street."

"Yeah," he said, nodding his ruddy face, "the wench still owes me two months' rent."

"Do you know her name? Which room is she in? Is she here now?" asked Hilbrun expeditiously.

"Name's Nia, but people round these parts aren't really known for givin' out their real names, so who knows." Delvan could smell the alcohol on his breath from the base of the stairs behind Hilbrun. "She's in the loft above here, but I don't know if she's there now. Didn't get a response when I went knockin' this mornin'. She always comes in all quiet like, hardly even tell when she's here. If she sees you two, she's bound to take off runnin'. That girl gets up to no good, I tell ya."

"We need the key to the loft," said Hilbrun. Delvan could see that his face was contorted from the assault of the man's vile breath. "And *don't* tell her we've been here. If I find out you've so much as mentioned it, a lack of rent will be the least of your concerns."

"Ya don't have to worry 'bout me none," the man said as he pulled a key off a large ring at his side. "Here ya go, my Lord. Before you take her off, I'd appreciate it if ya could get the eighty moons she owes me, if ya could."

"I'll see what we can do," said Hilbrun as he took the key.

The man receded back into the dwelling, its rank musk blending with the rest of the alley. *How do people live with this smell?*

They walked up the squeaking stairs to the loft door, entering with the key from the landlord. Delvan shut the door behind him, noticing the simple bolt that was mounted to it. Unkeyed from the outside, this bolt could only be locked in place if you were inside the room. Whoever this girl was, she was cautious.

Or paranoid.

The first thing that he noticed was how *small* the room was. He wasn't even sure it could be called a room. It felt more like a closet, the entire space feeling cramped with just the two of them inside.

Delvan took the two steps over to the table against the wall that consumed a third of the floor space and inspected its contents.

Strange steel tools, mostly thin with strange hooks and bumps at the end of them, laid strewn about it. A broken, muted inanite block sat among the other objects, a cap of snow on a gray mountain, noticeable in its contrast.

*What ever does she have this for?* he thought.

Hilbrun was checking under the thin mattress and testing the floorboards for any that may be loose. His fingers clawed and pried at each board, the nails creaking and resisting him. The search turned out to be frivolous, nothing beyond the meager contents of the scattered tools on the tabletop contained within the room.

Part of him hoped that they would find the cadentite and this would be over. But another part—the louder majority—desperately wanted to find answers to his questions. This woman could be another step towards those answers, or she could be what the rest of the past few days had been: a lesson in how little he truly seemed to know about the world.

Hilbrun was now inspecting the sheathing of the walls, looking for any hidden compartments, rapping the walls with his knuckles.

"Do you think you're going to find anything?" asked Delvan.

"No," said Hilbrun, sounding resigned, "but I had hoped. Doesn't hurt to look. You'd be surprised how often I've searched a residence and found something hidden away in an obvious place. A lot of these people aren't what you would call 'intelligent'.

"Given that the landlord has a key to the apartment, the smart thing to do would be to store it somewhere else. Somewhere more secure. Looks like our girl might be one of the smart ones. What did you find on the table?"

"A bunch of strange tools, I think. I've never seen anything like them before. And muted inanite."

"Why does she have that? Do you think she's building something with it?" Hilbrun took the three steps to Delvan's side and wondered at the miscellaneous items.

"No, it looks like she's grinding it up. No idea why she would do that though."

"Who knows... Alright, I don't think there's anything here, but we need to find this girl. Hope you didn't have any plans tonight, because we might be here a while. I want you to find a hiding place in the alley outside and keep an eye open for this *Nia*. I'm going to wait here. Hopefully she walks right in, and I can grab her. Not sure I'd be able to Reach far enough if I'm out in the alley."

Delvan nodded and internalized a sigh. He'd spent most of the day already standing around and waiting, now he had to do more of it?

He went to the alley and found a stack of crates to settle between, reeking of rotting vegetables. *Wonder if this is what went into Hil's meal,* he thought. He sat down and leaned his back against the crates, still wincing at the pain in his side. Hopefully this would be a short wait.

# Chapter Twelve

*Revenge is indulgence. There are those that abstain and move on, abandoning prejudice. Then there are the hedonists, gorging themselves till they burst. Which do you think they shall be?*
Spoken during a spring storm,
Seventy-third Day of Winter, Forty-sixth Year of the Seventh Epoch

Desnia savored the frothy ale as she pulled the ceramic mug from her lips, the babbling of the tavern echoing around her. She'd dedicated most of the previous night to tinkering with the antiquated lock that Magnar had provided. A few hours of sleep on the dusty floor of the cobbler's spare room had been all she'd managed, the design of the complex device deconstructing itself in her mind. She'd tried closing her eyes—the muted inanite barely effective a day later—but her brain just continued to visualize the contrivance's pieces and movements, overriding her necessity for rest.

Having given up on respite, she toiled away through the entirety of the day. Magnar had made it clear that leaving during daylight hours was too much of a risk—a point she vehemently agreed with—and she used the time she had in the abandoned shop as well as she could.

She had managed to learn more than expected from the archaic prototype, although her confidence that the designer's methods were still the same came with a strong sense of doubt. Still, what she'd been able to derive filled in some missing pieces from her previous experience with the humble leviathan that was the Diamond. Maybe she had a shot at this.

The sun had set, however, and the thought of spending another night in the same building as those men made her stomach turn. She'd locked the door and wedged a chair beneath the handle while she worked, but she knew as well as any that would only deter a motivated individual for so long.

So, she'd left, as soon as the hour turned dark. Her eyes felt heavy, her body weary, and even the obsessive analysis by her mind of the locks inner workings were not going to be enough to keep her awake tonight.

Best to make sure, though, and calm her mind to match the fatigue of her body.

Hence, she found herself sitting at a corner table of the Hillview, her back to a wall and exits within view, a tall pour of the local brew in her hands. She had no intention of reaching a similar level of intoxication as the other night—she kept her drinking to a minimum when working a job—but an ale or two was hardly going to affect her ability to work.

She observed the people around her. Some were having quiet conversations in the secluded corners, their eyes as shadowy as the tables they sat at. Their whispers were shrouded by the raucous groups at tables that were as exposed as the opinions the men shouted at one another. Then there were the ones lonesomely eating meals, fork in one hand and a knife in the other, held in a way that was meant to stab anything but their food, eyes shifting and scanning while they choked down the meal as quickly as possible.

Something itched at Desnia's neck. Not like a fly or spider, but like her hair had stood up, defying its natural position. The sound of a distant voice seemed to be unaccounted for, was there a conversation nearby that she couldn't see? The itch compelled her to scan the lips and eyes of everyone in the room fervently. Was there someone watching her? Or was this a figment of her enervation? Something about it bothered her.

She wasn't in the habit of ignoring her instincts. Finishing her drink with a single lift of the cup, she left her table with lissome ease and exited the tavern via the nearby door. She walked down the street, trying to casually catch a glimpse of anyone that might be behind her.

She quickly turned left down an alley that went the opposite direction as her home, then another quick left, and then another. She was now facing the street she'd been walking and, sitting in the enveloping shadows, she watched.

Desnia rubbed her neck in an attempt to wipe away the sensation that hovered there. Despite its lingering she saw no one out of the norm, and wondered what it was that could have her on edge. The tavern was still faint but distinct in its boisterous chatter, one voice particularly blaring above the others.

She darted across the street, still unconvinced that there was no one following her, and made her way down the alley towards her apartment.

The narrow street appeared empty. She shook her head as she made her way to the base of the stairs to her room, trying to shed the odd sensation that had her out of sorts.

She could hear her landlord snoring loudly—as he was wont to do—and sighed. She hadn't been able to find him to give him the rent she owed yet, having slept through most of the previous day as a result of her liberal libations. She would have to pay him soon, but she just wanted a few hours of sleep first, hopefully—

A chill ran down her spine as she silently climbed the stairs and approached her door. Something was wrong. She crouched low, her senses heightened, as she inspected her door.

The hair was missing.

Someone had been inside her loft. Someone had *violated* her home. This place was hers, one of the few things to her name. She internally berated herself but then forced the feelings down and buried them. Now was not the time.

Who had it been? Mixton? Was he trying to see if she'd skimmed from the last job? Was it Magnar? She wouldn't put it past the smug imposter to go out and research his newest crew member, though she doubted he'd do it himself. Or was it someone else? A competitor maybe?

Ignoring her instincts was the mistake of an amateur. Someone *must* have been following her earlier. Maybe they had come to wait here after she ditched them back on the other street? She couldn't hesitate. She had to run.

The tools inside didn't matter, she had most of the ones she needed at the cobbler's. She almost paused as she flew down the stairs at the thought of the muted inanite, but no, it was cheap, and she could find more. There was only one priority now.

Escape.

As she reached the bottom of the stairs she turned toward the end of the street, wanting to flee in a different direction than where she'd come from. She flew into a sprint, but before she made it more than a few steps someone cut her off, a figure emerging from behind some crates and yelling for her to stop.

She skidded to a halt, her heart beating nearly out of her chest. She spun frantically and started sprinting instead towards the other end of the short road, another escape route awaiting her. Her legs were swift and pounded with the urgency that only a fear of death could provide. Soon she was halfway down the street, then further, until the alley of her escape was only a few feet away, panting as she ran.

The door to her loft slammed open and she suddenly felt *heavy*. It was like a hill of snow had been dropped on her and she had to force her way through its crushing mass, instantly dragging her from a sprint to a crawl.

She heard boots rapidly descending the iron stairs leading to her loft. Another pair approached swiftly from the same direction, calling out to her. Her face went pale and eyes wide as the realization of her situation struck her like lightning from the sky.

These were Blues.

What she felt as she slowly propelled herself forward, her legs screaming as they carried a burden of unseen weight, couldn't be natural. There was no other explanation.

A redoubled sense of panic jolted through her. She managed to reach the gap between buildings—scant wide enough for even her—with the Blues a dozen yards behind her, the one still clamoring to the bottom of the stairs. She felt the weight shed off of her as she shimmied between the structures, rough stone tearing at her jacket with each shuffle. She emerged on the other side as the two Blues shadowed the gap on the opposite end like phantoms in the night.

That weight... it gripped her again, wanted to suffocate her, tried to push her down, but it failed. All of her will, her determination, her strength, went into moving away from the Blues. The bulk of Calentine Mountain itself pressed down on her shoulders, and with each step a stone was chipped away. An elder with the aid of a cane could have moved faster than she did in those fleeting moments. Yet she took step after step, separating herself from the influence of the Blue's distant grip.

She heard screaming from them. They wouldn't be able to fit through like she had. They would have to go to the end of the street and loop around. If she could just gain some more distance...

Her hobbled gait became a slow walk, and with each step she propelled herself further, faster. Her pace became brisk, and after a few yards she lurched forward as though the invisible leash choking her had snapped.

She caught herself from falling forward, taking enormous breaths in rapid succession. Her face was drained to a pale white and her body felt as though it were shaking uncontrollably. She didn't have time to catch her breath. She needed to run.

And with knees still wobbling, she flew.

Twists and turns as familiar to her as her own hands flew past in a blur of blackness. How far did she have to go to be safe? For them not to be able to find her? She started making her way to the port district, legs burning and feet aching with each pound against stone.

No. She couldn't lead a pair of Blues directly to the cobbler's shop. That could risk everything. She had to make sure they hadn't been able to follow her first.

She made her way, instead, towards a nearby mine. Even in back alleys a single figure stood out, distinguishable and noticeable against a background of vacancy. She needed a crowd. A calm flow of the masses in which to float with the current and disappear.

Desnia stopped near an intersection, a new shift of laborers making their way towards the mine. She pulled her jacket's hood low over her brow and faded into the crowd, allowing the flow to guide her and becoming another head in the throng.

She mingled and walked, her gait matching that of the others around her. She became one with the herd of people, always keeping herself surrounded, her head low, and allowing herself to be led wherever the crowd moved. People paid her no mind, and she paid none to them, except as guides to her eventual destination.

Before she was eventually carried all the way to the mine's entrance, she broke off from the crowd, and again maneuvered her way through side streets and back alleys. She eventually pulled herself underneath a set of wooden stairs—in place while the stone ones were being constructed—after checking to make sure she was alone.

She huddled with her back against a wooden beam, the confined space pressed close all around her. She took deep breaths, her fingers woven through her hair and pressed to her scalp. Her heart was jumping into her throat, her body still shaking. How had they managed to find her? How much did they know?

As her breathing steadied and her heart slowed, she realized she knew the answer: the girl at the iguan den. Mixton wouldn't risk the heist and Magnar had likely already done his research into her if he was half as competent as he seemed. No one else knew enough about her to identify where she lived or which tavern she liked to visit. It couldn't have been anyone else.

*So STUPID,* she thought, smacking her head. What had caused that simple, yet catastrophic, lapse in judgment?

Desnia put her hands in her jacket pockets to help fight the night chill. She couldn't go back to her place. Jeopardizing the job with Magnar would be imprudent and carried its own dangers. She'd have to stay here, hidden for a while, if not most of the night, before she dared go back there.

Her fingers touched the stolen ring through the cloth it was wrapped in, tingling from the fading adrenaline. What was she doing? Stealing this ring, lowering her guard around the woman in the white robe. She'd spent her life avoiding mistakes like this, then she makes two within the span of a few minutes?

As she dwelt on these thoughts her ears stayed attentive. She needed to stay alert. Her head nodded and jerked upright. She had to resist. Had to stay focused and awake. Her eyes strained in the dark, their lids weighted like lead. Maybe she could just lean her head against the post. Listening. Ever listening...

Desnia hovered in a sea of fog, an expanse of snowy white that shimmered like silk. Overhead, a faint but gentle ambiance of purple stretched outward above the white, so dim it was almost indistinguishable from the colorless abyss. She was standing, yet nothing of substance lay beneath her feet. The void around her reached to the end of the world itself, its unknown limits seeming both close and distant.

There was no sound, yet the volume was overbearing. Pressing on her from all sides, a force engulfed her, held her, and evaluated her. Its lens searched within her, weighing her soul as though issuing judgment.

She was motionless, paralyzed and incapable of resistance. She inherently knew that it was an impossibility. Escape from here was as feasible as resisting the eventual pull of sleep.

*CHILD,* she heard in a voice that reverberated into her soul. A haunting, deep sound, one that unnerved and made you feel as though you were a grain of sand staring up at a monumental peak. It came from within her. The voice of dreams. *His* voice.

*YOUR ABSENCE IS MISGUIDED AND AVOIDANCE OF MY ADMONITIONS NOW VERGE ON DISASTER. THOSE WHO SEEK RECLAMATION SHALL ATTEMPT IT SOON, THEIR GOALS NEARING REALIZATION. THE GATE CANNOT BE REOPENED, ELSE YOUR WORLD TOO SHALL FALL.*

*Why do you do this to me?* she thought, her voice a ripple among waves, her mind feeling as though it were splitting in two. There was a familiarity to all, an excruciating repetition.

*KNOW YOUR PLACE. ACCEPT THIS FATE AND HELP CREATE WHAT THEY FEAR MOST. SEEK THE GATE AND DESTROY IT, FOR ONLY THEN IS YOUR AND THE POPULACE'S SALVATION POSSIBLE. TRUST THE CHILD OF THE FIRST, FOR HE IS TO BE OUR DELIVERANCE. YOUR TRIALS WILL BE LEGION, BUT YOU MUST PERSEVERE, FOR THE FUTURE OF ALL OF US REST ON YOUR SHOULDERS.*

*Please,* she thought, *stop. Make the pain stop.*

Her mind seared with a hot flame. She felt tears stream down her face, though it remained dry. Her body was still, and yet trembled with pain. She felt herself breaking under the omnipresent voice, her mind nearing its capacity for bearing, another crack in the foundation. In this place she was but an image, her being harbored on another plane.

*WE MUST BEAR THE PAIN OF BURDEN TO BE FREE OF ITS WEIGHT. THIS QUEST IS YOUR IMPERATIVE. THESE SCANT WORDS ARE AN ABUNDANCE,*

*FOR LITTLE MORE CAN PASS BETWEEN US, AS I DARE NOT RISK FRACTUR-ING YOUR MIND FURTHER.*

*What have I done to deserve this?* she thought. *Why do you torture me again and again? And* why *do you think I would help* you?

*BECAUSE YOU CAN LISTEN AND STAY WHOLE. THE STONE THAT HAS NOT SHATTERED, YET HAS BEGUN TO CRUMBLE DESPITE YOUR EFFORTS. I HAVE WAITED COUNTLESS LIFETIMES FOR YOU, CHILD. AND I CAN OF-FER WHAT YOU SEEK MOST. FREEDOM, SAFETY, AND THAT WHICH YOU GUARD SO POSSESSIVELY. YOUR SANITY.*

She wanted to rebel, to discard his words and run. He spoke of freedom, yet claimed she must accept her fate. She thought of those that pulled the strings of her life, like she was a marionette who existed only to be controlled by greedy men with too much power. Mixton, with his debt and subtle threats. Her landlord, drunkenly extorting her because he knew she had nowhere else to go. And *him*. The lord of her nightmares. The ruler of her dreaming dominion.

How *dare* they claim such command over her? Her life was her own. She was not a dog to be set upon who or whatever they chose.

Yet, there was no escape. She delayed his ravaging of her dreams, trans-forming them into terrors, but eventually he found her again. Was there a way to be free of it? Did she *have* any other choice than to do as instructed? Or would she eventually break like the others always did?

Her mind was whole, but fractured. Could he offer a cure to this unseen ailment? Or would she bury it in white powder hoping to avoid the fate that always befell those like her?

A sound came in the distance. *Clink.*

*LISTEN TO YOUR GUIDE.*

*Clink.*

*HEED MY INSTRUCTIONS.*

*Clink.*

*FIND ME.*

*Clink.*

Desnia's eyes sprang open, pain drilling into them from the bright light outside her hideaway. Her whole body was drenched in sweat. Her head pounded as if an axe were wedged in it, the intense pain rendering even the light unbearable. Her hands shook and tears welled in her eyes.

*Clink.*

The sound pierced like clapped thunder. What was that noise?

She groaned as she held herself in agony. Her body felt wrung out, as though she'd tumbled through a stony, torrenting river. Aches plagued her and her neck was stiff to the point that she struggled to turn her head.

Wait. There was *light* outside of the staircase. Daylight. How long had she slept?

*Clink.*

She dragged herself towards the opening at the side of the stairwell. She emerged, the sun's intensity amplified by the pain in her head and making the surrounding stone seem to glow. She struggled and blinked as she saw a group of masons working stone, striking their chisels with heavy hammers.

*Clink.*

One of the masons stopped and looked up, seeing Desnia emerging from the secluded cubby under the wooden treads.

"Hey!" he shouted with a voice that hit her harder than his hammer did the chisel. "What are you doing there? Get out of here you vagrant!"

She pulled herself to her feet and stumbled away, shielding her eyes from the onslaught of the sun's light from above. The masons seemed satisfied with her hasty escape, and she could hear them cursing about the homeless in the distance as she hobbled away.

She rounded a corner and vomited, her back arching as her stomach constricted so tightly it ached. With quivering legs, she found a bench to sit on, the cold stone draining what little heat she had left in her body and causing her to shiver despite the day's warmth. She didn't care, her legs couldn't support her right now.

She needed time to recover. Time awake.

*This will pass. It always does. A few hours and a hot meal, I should be fine,* she thought.

She couldn't always remember her dreams. The ones she did she didn't understand, just like this one. Random, meaningless words accompanied with hours of torturous, waking pain. The ominous warnings and commandments seemed to vary. But they always ended the same.

*FIND ME.*

# Chapter Thirteen

*I hear you, conversing your plans with those who long abandoned you...*
Notably spoken by deaf patient,
Twelfth Day of Summer, Fifty-first Year of the Seventh Epoch

Empty.

Delvan gasped for breath after sprinting as fast as his legs would carry him. The street was dark, desolate, and absent of the woman they'd been chasing. The lack of streetlamps caused the few illuminated windows in the nearby buildings to cast long shadows in the street. The veil of glimmering stars above a bright contrast to their surroundings.

She had somehow escaped. How had she known they were there?

From his vantage point on the street, he'd watched her stop at the top of the stairs, and then suddenly bolt and flee. Had she heard Hilbrun inside? Had she seen him behind the crates? He felt the pangs of chagrin as he watched Hilbrun glance down the nearby alleys. Another question came to Delvan's mind.

"Gods-damn it!" Hilbrun cried as he kicked an empty crate. "She's gone! She could be anywhere. Our *one* lead and she's vanished!"

"How did she escape your Reach?" asked Delvan.

"She was too far and—" Hilbrun opened his inanite pouch and pulled out a handful of pure white blocks, throwing them to the ground in anger. They scattered, glistening in the faint light like a mirror to the stars above.

"I must have used almost all of them on that Jack," Hilbrun said, burying his face in his hand. "How did she know we were there? Did she see you? You must have done something to tip her off."

Delvan looked at him, eyes glaring and face turning hot at the accusation. "Why are you assuming she saw *me*? She didn't even look in my direction! If she saw or heard anyone, it was you!"

"That's horse shit!" shouted Hilbrun. "I didn't make a sound! You've lost our last lead, Del!"

"How is this my fault?!" he asked. He'd done everything he could to help so far. Now Hilbrun had the gall to accuse him of tipping off the courier? A feeling hit him, as though he'd been punched in the gut, the lack of Hilbrun's trust a sickening betrayal.

"First you lose the man from the den, now you lose the courier. Whose side are you on, Del? Huh? Are you intentionally trying to undermine me? Are you trying to hinder this investigation? Did they put you up to this? I *trusted* you, Del."

Delvan stood there, frozen and perplexed. The nauseated feeling was replaced with a hollowness, as though his heart had plunged and joined the muted inanite on the street's pavers. His insides were carved away, replaced with the angry words of Hilbrun's condemnation.

"You-You said the man from the den wasn't my fault. How is that… I've been trying to help you…" he stuttered.

"Well, Del, it *was* your fault. We both know that if you had wanted that man dead, you're more than capable. But gods forbid I injured your fragile ego! So, I told you what you needed to hear, because I couldn't have you wallowing in a corner.

"Did he make you an offer? Huh? Did you take it in exchange for fucking me over?! I honestly hope that was the case, because the only other explanation is that you are *grossly* incompetent. You call yourself a Blue? You're a waste of a sapphire.

"*Why* did I even drag you along in the first place? All you've done is make things worse!"

Hilbrun stormed by him and walked into the distance. Delvan didn't follow. He stood there, motionless, as if the slightest movement would cause him to fall apart. His insides were a bottomless chasm, leaving him an empty shell. Sparks of anger kindled within him, but they were doused by the torrent of emptiness.

He wasn't sure how long he stood there. Time was an afterthought. Or—more accurately—not a thought at all. His mind felt as blank as muted inanite, refusing to process or acknowledge what had just happened.

How could Hilbrun accuse him like that? If anything, the woman escaping was *his* fault. Not carrying enough inanite was careless, he shouldn't blame Delvan for his own shortcomings. And to say that he let that hooded man escape... He wasn't there! He hadn't seen what happened. Delvan had put his all into helping Hilbrun the past few days, and this was the thanks that he got?

Well, if Hilbrun wanted to do this on his own, then fine. Delvan would leave him to it. If he truly didn't need Delvan's help, then he could try to do this without him. Maybe after a few days he would realize the mistake he'd made.

He finally broke his statuesque stance and began walking. Not towards the stables. No, Hilbrun was likely there, and he wished to avoid him with every fiber of his being. Instead, he made his way towards the tavern nearby.

He hadn't been out for a drink since this whole ordeal had started, a drive within him had wanted to keep his mind sharp, to be the best he could. Apparently, that was for nothing. It wasn't likely that the courier was coming back, so what did it matter if he went to the tavern now? Hilbrun wasn't there to tell him otherwise anyway.

When he walked through the front door of the Hillview it was as though a wolf had entered the coop. Activity halted, voices dulled, and all eyes turned to him. Some looked afraid, others curious, a few angry, but all of them cut through a thick air of trepidation. A hundred eyes fixed on him in suspended silence, waiting with tense anticipation as to what was coming next in the shadowy light of the sparse lanterns. Most here thought they were probably about to be arrested or killed.

They weren't worth his time.

He walked to the bar, his boots sounding thunderous amid the breathless quiet. His armor clanged together as he leaned his arm on the counter and settled into a seat. He pulled a single golden sun from his pocket and laid it on the stained wood of the bar in front of its tender, who stared at him with cautious intrigue.

"Ale," he said to the short man, "and if it gets low, refill it. I don't want it empty as long as I'm here."

He found that he didn't care that the place smelled like stale beer, or that the floor clung to his soles with tacky adherence. He knew that everyone in there was staring at him, a few even slipping out the nearest exit, but it didn't matter. None of it mattered. They would leave him alone. He was a lord, and they were nothing more than commoners.

"Aye, my Lord. I can do that," said the barkeep as he took the sun off the beaten-up counter. He placed an ale in front of Delvan. In one long draft, he finished it and put the mug back on the bar top, wiping the dribble from his face.

The bartender was true to his word, and the golden liquid once again filled his cup.

The rest of the patrons seemed to relax, at least as much as they could with a noble—a Blue no less—sitting inside their humble refuge. Chatter picked up, and Delvan finished another draft. And then another.

The hours passed, not that Delvan noticed much. The only thing he was counting was how many ales he'd finished, but even that was half-hearted. He hadn't even noticed how quiet it'd become, the other patrons having slowly filtered out as the night crawled closer and closer to the hour of the rising sun.

*Hil thinks he can ditch me? He thinks he's better off without me? He wouldn't have even known about that girl if I hadn't gotten the information from Malanai, and now he throws it back in my face? He thinks he's so infallible. Damn him, let him go out and realize how much help I was.*

Delvan's head bobbled from side to side. His eyes struggled to focus, and his limbs felt disconnected, able to muster only temporary control over them at best. He finished off another draft, slamming the mug onto the countertop with a spray of stale beer.

"An-Another," he slurred to the bartender.

"My Lord, the sun will be up in a few hours. It's well past closin'. Everyone else, they've all gone home, sir."

He looked around and noticed for the first time that he was indeed the only one left in the tavern's hall, the lanterns flickering as they ran low on oil.

"Don't care," he said. "Another." The words came out sounding hollow, just like him.

The bartender poured another with a look of exhaustive annoyance. Delvan drank it. Time was measured by the rings of foam inching down his mug. He drank until he went numb. The world spun around him, and he finally stumbled his way out of the tavern. The street welcomed him with a ceiling of the early morning sun's distant glow, draping the stillness with a thin light.

He made his way to the stables. His horse would get him back to the barracks. What did that matter though? It's not like he had *chosen* to join the military, to wear this gem, to follow this guided path of life that was mapped for him. What if he did make a choice? One to not go back?

He found his horse, a gray-blue mare, and looked for someone to order her saddled. The stables were empty, however, and he didn't have the wherewithal to go searching for its attendant. He felt tired. He walked around, swaying like a top that had spun too long, and found a mound of hay.

*Well, that looks comfortable.*

He dropped himself into it, the bales feeling like pillows of the softest down, and fell asleep.

# Chapter Fourteen

*They killed her! They agreed to go, to be hidden away. And once bound... they... WHY?!*
Cried out during the night,
Nineteenth Day of Autumn, Eleventh Year of the Seventh Epoch

Clouds rolled across the sky and saturated it with a deep gray, providing Desnia with a blissful reprieve. The cold stone of the bench that thirsted for her body heat found itself wanting, a shiver spreading bumps over her skin.

In the hours she'd sat there, little color had returned to her face, but the pain that had spread through her bones and mind was now reduced to a mild headache. Her muscles felt heavy, her breathing deep and slow; a recovery from the extreme fatigue that one of the dreams invariably left. She was awake, yet on the edge of sleep, like an overloaded ship, water threatening to lap upon the deck and consume it into the depths below.

Sleep would have to wait. Her dreams rarely came twice in a row, but just thinking about closing her eyes made her heart quicken and chest tighten. Not that her waking moments were much more relaxing. The memory of the Blues from last night still haunted her, hovering over her like the clouds above.

Her hands burrowed in her pockets hoping for warmth but found nothing except the few items contained within. She remembered the ring as her finger touched against it. What had compelled her to keep it for so long?

Desnia pulled the cloth from her pocket, which now was a light gray for some reason, feeling the ring wrapped inside of it. She held it in her palm and peeled away the layers of the wrinkled fabric to reveal the circular jewelry within. It was silvery in color, with a repetitive hatch pattern encircling the inside and out, the black, inanite lines a contrast to the reflective polish. Its design was unique, and unfamiliar to Desnia, but it was clearly crafted with expert—

*FINALLY!* she heard a man's voice shout with ecstatic relief.

She jumped, suddenly alert, spinning her head in search of the voice. She thought she had been alone on the street. How had someone managed to sneak up on her?

*By the Greats, is that cloth dyed with inanite? Felt like I was being suffocated in there,* she heard the voice say.

She now stood up, looking around feverishly. *Where is that voice coming from?* she thought. *There must be someone nearby, there* must *be.* Her dream couldn't be overlapping into her waking moments, could it? That had never occurred before. Had she finally gone over the edge?

*Hello,* the voice said, *down here. It's me, the ring. I'm the one talking to you. Please, just listen before you—*

She briefly looked down as her mind processed the words, then let out a small yelp as her hand jerked away, the ring falling to the stone pavers and rolling a few feet from her. She could hear the voice fading in the distance.

*Wait! No, just listen to me...* the voice said as it became merely a distant, uninterpretable mumble.

She found her hands trembling again. A lump formed in her throat and her eyes went unnaturally wide. Her heart raced and stomach fluttered wildly. She wasn't hearing voices. No. That couldn't be it. She wasn't like them.

The indistinguishable rantings of the voice in the distance continued, sounding like a man attempting to shout from a hilltop to the people below. Audible, yet unintelligible.

Desnia wanted to run. She wanted to escape. But, like her dreams, she felt paralyzed. She had the freedom of flight but couldn't manage to take it. Instead, she stared at the shining ring on the ground.

She had to know. Was she truly hearing voices? Was this the point where the strands of her mind finally snapped?

She stood and took a step closer to the ring, the voice becoming louder.

Another step. It became distinct.

One more step, and the voice rang with the clarity of the bells from the King's Tower.

*Wait*, it said, *don't run off! You're NOT crazy.*

*I'm not so sure about that*, she thought.

*I repeat, you're* not *crazy*, the voice claimed. *Although it's understandable if you think so, since I probably just look like a talking ring to you. But I'm most definitely a person. A person inside of a ring. Which I realize sounds crazy. But you're not! So please get me off this filthy ground, it's disgusting down here.*

*This is a part of the dream*, she thought, her mind racing for an explanation to calm her frayed nerves. *They're just changing, making me think I'm awake. Is this how it's going to be? Am I never going to know if I'm awake or asleep? If the gods do exist, which one of the cruel fucks put this curse on me?*

*Hey*, she heard, *just so you know, you might be able to hear my thoughts, but it's kind of a one-way street, given your, uh, condition. So, if you could just pick me up, I can explain everything. Well, mostly everything. Actually, just some things. It's a long story. But if you could get me off the ground before I end up on a brown river expedition through the tunnel of a stray dog's intestinal tract, I'd appreciate it.*

"This isn't real. This isn't real..." she muttered.

*Real as bird shit falling from the sky and into the mouth of someone trying to catch the rain*, said the voice.

"Prove it," she said snappily, suddenly looking around to make sure no one saw the homeless girl talking to the ground.

*How, exactly, do you suggest I do that?* the voice asked.

"I don't know, but if you don't think of something then I'm throwing you down a drain and leaving with my sanity."

*Okay, let's not do anything reckless now, like make the life of the guy trapped in an inanimate object any worse than it already is...*

"Now!" Desnia hissed.

*Wait! Wait. Uh, you took me from the desk, in the iguan den. You probably did some emotional and stupid things afterward. I'm not sure what, exactly, as you basically hid me in a solitary prison cell and have left me there since. By the Greats, it's so nice to hear a voice after days of—*

"What do you mean, did something emotional and stupid?" she said, her attention caught.

*Pick me up off this gross, horse shit-covered stone, and I will tell you.*

She stood there, looking down at the polished ring. Why was she entertaining the thought of picking it up? Would the voice go away if she left? Or would it choose another object to project from. *Is it just my own memories playing tricks on me?* she thought. *Does it* actually *know that I made mistakes? Or is it just manipulating the thoughts that have plagued me over the past few days?*

After standing there for several minutes—the voice apparently waiting patiently, or perhaps apprehensive—she gave in. A feeling had pervaded through her, something reassuring, calming her nerves. It fought the instinct to kick the ring away, strong as it was, and with chattering teeth she resigned to acquiescing. With a still-shaking hand, she reached down and went to grab the small ring, using the gray cloth as a barrier. Whatever that was worth.

*Woah! Please keep that away from me. How would you like it if I threw you in a small dark chamber with no windows and no one to talk to for days, huh? Pick me up with your bare hands or get* any *other fabric. I don't bite. Or do I? No, no I don't, no teeth.*

Was that...

"Are you making jokes?" she said, confused.

*Apparently not,* the voice said dryly, *because if it were a joke then* someone *would laugh. Instead, I get left sitting in filth. Greats, you're as bad as...as...damn it! Him. Anyway, are you going to pick me up? I did say please.*

She put the cloth away and slowly reached out her hand with a mild tremble, her senses heightened and eyes wide. Would something happen when she touched it? Him? That was disgusting to think about.

She pinched the ring between her fingers and felt... nothing. She rested it on her open palm and stared at it, looking for changes or movement, but even as she began to hear the voice again, the band remained perfectly still and unchanged.

*Thank you! See, that wasn't so hard,* the voice said. She thought she felt some mild tingling in her hand, but perhaps that was the nerves.

"Tell me," she said. "Tell me how you knew that I did something stupid." She waited eagerly. Maybe this hadn't been entirely her fault. Maybe there wasn't some lapse in judgment from her and there was some other explanation. Or perhaps her mind had finally, truly broken, as she *was* asking questions of a ring...

*...I actually can't.*

What? Not only did this… thing have a terrible sense of humor, but it lied to her as well?

What was she doing?… Was she really entertaining the idea that a piece of jewelry could talk to her? She needed to end this; it had already gone too far.

She closed her hand in a fist and drew back her arm. She would throw the ring as far as she could and then try to forget this day ever happened. She'd done it with her dreams, why not a simple little silver band?

*WAIT! Waitwaitwait! I meant to say I can't tell you* everything. *The man that you dropped the c-c-c-gah! The glowing rock off to, he did something to you, he also did something to me—aside from the obvious, you know, putting my soul into a ring, thing.*

She lowered her arm slowly, contemplating the words, a part of her desperately wanting to accept that what it said was true. That she had been affected by *something*, whatever that meant.

"Explain," she said, a strange concoction of emotions flowing through her.

*Alright, how can I say this… When you walked into that room, Pro-Pro-Pro-ugh… that man did something to you. He basically made it so that you would be more… open. More susceptible and apt to act on your own desires. Like drinking a brewed aphrodisiac. He knew you were a thief, and I'm magnificently shiny, so he gave you a nudge that encouraged you to take me home. Although the suffocation thing is a weird kink.*

"Gross," she said with a sneer.

*Anyway, the… thing has a tendency to last a certain period before wearing off. It was very mild, but I'm sure you must have done* something *at least minorly stupid while under its influence. I may or may not be speaking from personal experience.*

"Why didn't he just give you to me? Talk to me about it? Anything?"

*Oh, a smart one. I like it. Well, two things. First, consider what he did a test of sorts. He then paid attention to the results—we wanted to make sure you were what we thought. You passed by the way.*

*Second, when under the influence of this… thing, you tend to become more attached to the objects or people you're drawn to. That's why it's called a love sp-sp-sp-damn it!*

The voice fluxed with frustration.

*If he just gave you a random ring as payment, what would you have done? Sold it? Kept it? And if he told you that he wanted you to take a talking ring? You wouldn't have thought him crazy and then run out of the building when you heard my glorious eloquence?*

*Besides, our enemies have eyes and ears everywhere. If he said more than a word to you it would have painted you red, and we couldn't risk it. I can talk to you more discreetly. Some of our enemies could hear me if they wanted but would need to be doing something specific. Like, crossing-three-fingers-and-sitting-with-two-toes-crossed-while-in-a-receiving-position kind of specific. Even dropping off the glowy rock was a risk. But this way you were also more likely to keep me around and give me time to properly introduce myself, winning you over with my compelling charm. Though instead you basically buried me alive...*

"How could you have known I was going to steal you?" she asked, questioning its logic.

*Ah, well, we have quite a bit of experience in this sort of thing. There was a chance you didn't, but then I'd have gotten to you another way. We thought this would make for the lowest chance of you throwing me in a gutter, which it appears you are wont to do. Also, why does your jacket reek of cinnamon?*

"How... You can smell?"

*It's complicated.*

She shook her head, then sighed a small, but noticeable, weight off of her. Her shoulders released some of their tension, and her mind slowed. She hadn't made a mistake. It had been something else. Something hadn't been wrong with her. *Well,* she thought, *aside from the fact I am talking to jewelry. Or is it a person? Not sure if this is an improvement from a slip of the tongue.*

"How'd you end up in a ring, then?" she asked, the question directed at him as much as her own sanity.

*Excellent question! You have a lot of those,* he said in his chipper tone. *Yes, so I was running from this... man, and then he, um, let's say he threw something at me. I dodged it, being the skilled and smooth ma-ma-ma-fuck! The smooth guy that I am. We fought, and I nearly had him! Our battle was epic I tell you, full of my valor and his malevolence, exchanging blow after explosive blow, it was truly a sight to behold. But he tricked me, and snared me in a trap. Oh, but I still got him good. Nearly took his leg off,* the voice said, sounding proud.

*Wasn't good enough, though.* He turned morose as he continued. *He still beat me. Pulled away most of my... let's call it energy, soul, whatever. Slowly, over days and days. Partially because it's hard to remove from a person, and also because he's a twisted fuck. Then the bastard stabbed me in the chest and watched as I finally bled out. He likes to watch his prey die. He's like a cat—the most evil of creatures—cold and heartless.*

*He left when he thought I was dead. Greats, even I thought I was dead. Until our friend from the den of pleasures—he hates when I call it that by the way, it's hilarious—came and found me. He, um, well he did things, and saved my immortal soul by putting it into this ring. I think he had it set aside for himself, to be honest.*

"That story is about as crazy as me hearing the voice of a *ring* in my head," said Desnia. Was it too late for her to still put this unnatural event behind her? Maybe she could test if the voice came back if she threw the ring into the river.

*I can see how it could seem that way to you, yes,* he said. *But I assure you that you're* not *insane. In fact, that's why we chose you. Because of how mostly sane you were!*

Mostly?

"The fuck do you mean, 'mostly'?"

*Well,* he said with a nervous chuckle, *I mean, c'mon. I wouldn't be here with you if there wasn't something special about you. What's the nickname they have for the ones like you? Canary, right?*

Her stomach twisted back into a knot. Tension suddenly snapped within her muscles, and a scowl wrinkled her face.

"You shut your fucking mouth!" she hissed. She looked around again. How loudly had she been talking? Could anyone else have heard that?

The street was thankfully empty, save for the two of them.

*Uh, right. Noted. Don't bring up mention of bird monikers. But look, you have certain talents and capabilities that we need. Some bad people, like the feline-esque bastard who stabbed me, are trying to do some very evil things.*

"Why should I care? Evil people do evil things every day, there's nothing that any of us can do to stop that," she said. She slumped back down onto the stone bench, her mind overcast with memories of times past, acquaintances—she didn't have friends—lost, and how numb the acts of evil men could make someone. It was an inherent trait which merely slid along a spectrum for all of them, in her experience.

*Well,* he said in a more serious tone, *there's evil, and then there's villainous-with-the-intent-to-enslave-all evil. What I'm referring to is the latter. If they open the g-g-g-damn it! Agh, that's annoying. Anyway, if they open the... door? Ha!*

*That worked. Yes, if they open the door then plan to be enslaved and likely tortured and experimented on, given your nature.*

"What *is* that?" Desnia asked. Now that she was, mostly, over the initial shock of what was likely her mind irreparably shattering like glass, the constant stuttering and vague word choice was beginning to irk her.

*What is what?* he asked. *The door? Villain? Well, she—*

"No," she interrupted, "the stuttering, why can't you say things correctly?"

*Wow, way to mock someone with a speech impediment. Really big of you,* he said sardonically.

"What? No, I-I meant the—"

*Ha! Nah, I'm just messing with you,* he said, back to his cheery demeanor. *Remember how I said that my friend did something to me too? Apparently—although I have absolutely no idea what would lead him to believe such things—he worried that I talked too much. And I also happen to know a great many secrets. Not a great combination for a group that values their privacy.*

*He worried that I would fall into the wrong hands—a pun that I did not appreciate, let me tell you—and so he scribbled these, uh, markings all over my shiny new body. He did some other stuff and it basically made it so I can't talk at all about who we are, where we come from, or really anything that people of this... place might not be aware of in the grand cosmic scheme of things.*

*Which is why, every time I try to say his name, or talk about the impending doom coming from our home, my mouth—wait... mouth? Is that right? Eh, whatever—I can't say what I want. I've started discovering loopholes though. Still working on the nuances of them.*

"I thought you said that this man was your friend? Why would he do that to you?" she said, the workings of a close relationship foreign to her. Trust was dangerous. And confusingly contradictory, it would seem.

*When you've known someone as long as we've known each other, you can start to get on each other's nerves. I trust him with my life—we've saved each other's more times than I can count—but the old scraggly bastard has less of a sense of humor than a boulder. As you can imagine, my comedic genius was lost upon him, and he spent most of our time together in a rather foul mood. I think that him putting this... restraint upon me is the closest thing to a joke he's ever pulled, actually. I'm almost proud, but mostly irritated.*

"He made you unable to talk because he found you annoying?" Desnia asked.

*It's complicated.*

She leaned back and released a deep sigh. This conversation was draining her already dwindling reserves of energy. Couldn't she just be normal? *I'm cursed*, she thought, *it's the only explanation.*

*What's your name?* he asked. *I'm I-I-I...nope. I'm L-L-L... oh c'mon! Mas-Masini. Ha! You can call me Masini.*

"You can't say your own name?"

*Well, it's not like I introduce myself very often. The seldom few that can hear me think they're hearing voices or going crazy. Can make for an extremely entertaining prank though. And I haven't been in this 'body' for all that long. It takes some getting used to.*

She was reluctant to tell him. Sharing information about herself was not something she did lightly. She'd never been able to escape the dreams or voice that accompanied them, and it made her wonder if it mattered? Perhaps it already knew her name and was just testing her?

"Desnia," she finally said, wondering if it had been a good decision.

*Desnia,* repeated Masini, *old name. Ancient even, by your standards, been an age since I've heard it. Do you know what it means? It's—*

Footsteps approached. She gripped the ring tightly in her hand and made herself small on the bench. A stranger walked down the street, dressed in the clothing of a miner.

"Shh!" she hushed.

*Fine, don't listen to a history lesson from someone who's lived it. Youth these days. If I had eyes, I'd be rolling them.*

"Quiet!" Desnia said in an exaggerated whisper.

*Why? That guy? He can't hear me. Well, he probably can't hear me. Unless he also happens to be an oddly specific child of circumstance, which I doubt.*

She sat there, huddled and her muscles tight. Her hand cautiously sat on the hilt of her dagger, and she watched the man casually saunter by, ignorant of her strange conversation.

"You *do* talk too much," she said as the man fell out of sight.

*Rude,* he said tersely.

"So, no one else can hear you?"

*Like I said, others like my friend and I under certain conditions, and a rare few Blues can, yes,* Masini said, *but generally, no.*

"Lucky them."

*Again, rude.*

"Sorry, Masini, but I don't think I can help you. You're going to need to find yourself another 'specific child of circumstance'," said Desnia. She could hardly help herself right now, let alone someone else. *Homeless, indebted, terrorized in my sleep... Yeah, I don't intend to add helping a talking ring to my list of problems,* she thought.

*I assure you, there isn't one,* said Masini solemnly. *I need you to help me find...someone. There are people who are looking to open a door, and if they succeed then tens or even hundreds of thousands of them could march here and enslave you all. We need to find this someone. They could help us and stop the door from opening.*

"Why do you care?" she asked. She knew that there was always a motive. People didn't do heroic deeds from the good of their hearts. They did it for some kind of gain.

*Because I don't want to see a kingdom enslaved?*

"What's in it for you? Revenge? Money? Power? An *actual* body? You're not doing this as an act of charity."

*You're a jaded one, aren't you?*

"Am I wrong?"

Silence. The longest she'd had since pulling the ring from her pocket. The wind whispered in her ears, the scent of rain carried on its whisps.

*No,* Masini finally said. *No, you're not.*

*I made a promise a long, long time ago, to protect my home. As strange as it sounds, I need to stop the people from my home from coming through the g-g-g-agh! The DOOR, in order to do that.*

"That doesn't make any sense," Desnia said.

*It's—*

"Complicated. Yeah, I got that," she said with an exasperated sigh. "Who is this man you're looking for anyway?"

*Not a man. You don't really have a word for them anymore, we were rather thorough in the cleans—* Masini stumbled for a moment. *Uh, let's just say it's not part of the common vernacular anymore. You'd probably just call them a god, which is not a perfect word, but it makes a point.*

"That's ridiculous, you can't honestly be serious. I doubt there even is such a—"

Words pealed in the back of her mind. An all too fresh memory. She could hear it, and whispered it in repetition, "...the gate cannot be reopened. Else your world too, shall fall."

*That's the word! Wait... where did you hear that? Ohhh, have they been talking to you?! Please tell me they have. You have no idea how much time that could save. We didn't even think it would be possible until you were close to them, this is amazing! Maybe there's something wrong with their enclosure—*

Desnia shoved the ring—Masini—back into the cloth and then deep into her pocket. Her hands gripped her upper arms as she held herself tightly. She trembled, but not from a chill. *It can't be real,* she thought. *They're just dreams. It's just in my mind. None of this is real.*

*It's just in my mind.*

# Chapter Fifteen

*I cannot find them... Where are they hidden? What was their fate...*
Recollection of a Hand,
Sixty-seventh Day of Winter, Twenty-fifth Year of the Seventh
Epoch

Delvan groaned as his eyes cracked open. The air carried a dusty haze accompanied by the sounds of horses as they were being tended to. His head throbbed as even the dim light of the overcast sky blared with stunning brightness through slats on the walls and the distant stable door.

He pulled himself upright, immediately turning to his side and vomiting. The knot of his stomach and pain of it lurching pulsated through his body. His rib screamed with a pain so intense that he thought it might cause him to pass out. He leaned back, holding his side, taking shallow breaths until the pain subsided.

*What time is it?* he wondered.

He stood up and shuffled into the main hall of the stable. Pens lined the walls, and Delvan spotted his horse's head sticking out from its stall, a narrowed eye giving him a judging glare.

"Don't give me that look," he said, wiping his face, "you slept here too."

The horse snorted and shook her head, as if to state its silent disappointment.

"M'Lord!" exclaimed an all too loud voice of the nearby stable master. He was an older man, with more white than gray in the stubble on his chin. His clothes were worn and dirty, and Delvan worried for a moment that his horse was cared for in the same manner as the man's clothes. But he found that his horse's pen was well cleaned, and her blueish thundercloud of a coat emitted a pristine shine. "M'Lord, we, um, didn't want ta wake ya. Hope everytin's alright. Yer mare 'ere is a mighty fine animal. We brushed 'er for ya, and she's well fed and watered."

He seemed nervous, just like everyone always did. Delvan had become accustomed to It over the years, but this morning he could hardly pay it any mind as his focus was directed to the pounding in his skull. He pulled a sun from his pocket and handed it to the man, whose eyes became wider than the golden coin in his palm.

"For taking care of her," Delvan said groggily, "and for the, uh, mess." He turned his head and avoided eye contact, attempting to hide the flash of shame.

"Thank ya, m'Lord, thank ya deeply. The King an' His grace upon ya, sir," said the man with multiple bows of his head. "We'll get 'er saddled up for ya, right away m'Lord."

Delvan waited with the distracted patience that the pain of his previous night's sins afforded him. As the stable master and one of his hands prepped his horse he remembered to ask, "Do either of you know the time?"

"We don't 'ear the tower bells so easily here, m'Lord, but my guess put it around midafternoon, sir," said the stable master as he tightened the saddle straps.

Delvan's ears perked up, his back straightened, and his stomach sank. *It's after midday?* he thought. *I've missed role call... again. Oh, the captain is going to be furious. And Hilbrun...*

The thought of Hilbrun was a sobering one. His worry about missing role call was erased by the animosity that raged like an inferno within him. It inhibited his pain, stealing his focus. Hilbrun's words still stabbed at him, like tips of arrows lodged deeply into his chest; hurtful, sharp, and freshly bloody.

Delvan wanted to avoid him forever, to bury the broken trust deep in the darkest pits, never to be seen again. He wiped his clammy forehead with his hand and squeezed his eyes closed. He knew that he couldn't avoid Hilbrun forever. He was his assigned Senior. They always had to pair together.

That didn't mean he couldn't prolong their reunion for a few days though.

Once she was saddled, he led his horse from the stable and, with great effort, pulled himself into the leather seat. He looked around at the road he was on and realized that he actually wasn't entirely sure where he was. The peak of the city's namesake could be seen thrusting into the sky over the buildings, its snowcapped crest a landmark that helped guide all, pointing his way home.

*I'm already too late for roll call, and Hil might be getting to the barracks by the time I show up,* he thought. *Maybe I can delay for a while.*

He let his horse guide him through the streets, occasionally giving her a nudge one way or the other. It was easier to let his and her instincts choose their path than think about it himself. With the hangover he wasn't capable of much thinking at the moment anyway.

He had never wandered through the Lower Valley on his own, his life having been isolated to the Upper Tier. The only time that he had come through here was to travel to the port for some excursion, like a hunt. His parents—his father specifically—always put a heavy emphasis on his Blue training but would tell him that occasional outings were a good political environment to meet potential suitors, as well as members of the other noble houses.

He had no interest In marrying. Not yet anyway. Besides, he had time—more than most, in fact. One of the many benefits of a sapphire, for all the crises it currently plagued him with. Hopefully the other benefits would start working soon; the fact that after an hour he was still hungover gave him an idea of how drunk he must've been the night before.

His daydreaming distracted him from his surroundings. His horse trotted along, the people parting like water over a bow to allow him through. The ambling pace of his mare carried him through various streets and districts. He found that even with a heightened sensitivity to smell from the lingering aftereffects of last night, he had still become somewhat nose-blind to the stench that had originally suffocated him. The smell of a baker, the smoke of hearths' fires, fish from the piers, all created a concoction that he realized gave this place a life of its own. Not one he'd ever want to live in, of course, but maybe it wasn't quite the slum he'd originally thought.

Or maybe he was just hungry.

The sound of someone shouting in a way that reached out and grabbed one's attention snapped him out of his daze. Pushing his way through the crowd was a man, waving wildly and yelling towards Delvan, a look of shock and fear in his eyes.

*Great, just what I need right now,* he thought.

The man approached his horse, and Delvan pulled on her reins to bring her to a halt. "My Lord," panted the man, "please, you need to come at once. We've found something, down past the docks. The others sent me to find the city guard."

Delvan leaned forward, his forearms resting on the saddle's horn. *Do I really need to worry about some problem at the docks?* he thought. *Maybe I should just tell him to go to the nearest barracks or outpost, tell him I have other matters to attend to.*

There weren't any other matters, he well knew, and with an aloof sigh he asked the dock worker, "What is this problem, exactly?"

"Murder, my Lord. Two dead men washed ashore, beat up something awful, their throats... Well, sir, you should see for yourself."

*Murder?* he thought, sitting up. Perhaps this wasn't something he could pass off. If nothing else, it would serve as a sufficient distraction.

"Lead the way," he said to the man.

As Delvan walked along the wooden pier a cool breeze wove through his disheveled brown hair. The churning depths of grays in the clouds above forebode incoming rain, reinforced by a rapid dip in temperature. The smell here was more nauseating than what he'd encountered earlier, the river only able to wash away so much of the stench of rotting fish and molded cargo.

Making their way past the vast collection of ships in the mercantile hub, Delvan was led towards a gathering of onlookers, craning necks trying to catch a glimpse of something at the cluster's center. He and the dock worker forced their way through the crowd, most taking a reactive step back upon seeing Delvan's uniform.

They emerged through the inner lip of the throng into a central opening like the eye of a storm, a large cloth draped over what Delvan assumed were two bodies. A few burly men—dressed in dock workers garbs—were the only barrier between the amassing crowd and the cramped space surrounding the all-too-still pall. They gave him a cautious glance from the corner of their eyes, but remained in place, only one shifting to the side to allow Delvan through.

*Strange,* he thought, *why aren't there any soldiers? Shouldn't the guard have an outpost here?*

"Who found them?" Delvan asked the worker who had led him here as he knelt and pulled back the covering, which appeared to be a small sail. A childhood preparing him for his service to the crown as a Blue had made him well acquainted with the deceased. He remembered back to one of his weapons masters taking him to a morgue, stating he needed to know what it felt like to cut into a man's flesh. The sensation of tiny vibrations traveling through his sword and into his childhood hand as steel scraped bone that first time still echoed in his palm.

"A fisherman, my Lord. Saw them washed up on the bank 'bout a hundred yards from the end of the pier. He docked and told the harbormaster, who sent some of the boys here to check it out. They brought the bodies back here and sent me to get some guards, sir."

"Why did he go to the harbormaster? Why not straight to the city guards?" Delvan asked, confused.

The man suddenly looked tense, his eyes shifting from side to side. Delvan noticed that he was looking at the men holding back the crowd. They pretended to not pay attention, but he could tell that they were intensely focused on their conversation.

"Probably just who he knew best, my Lord," he said shakily. "I was the first one who was free to go get the city guard, so I went lookin' as fast as I could. Hard to find people to spare around the docks, my Lord."

*What a terrible liar,* Delvan thought. Still, the dead men weren't going anywhere, he supposed. *Doubt anything about them changed in the time it took him to speak with the harbormaster. Seems odd though.*

The corpses were swollen and slightly discolored, with the evidence of the brutal beatings the two men must have endured overly apparent. Bruised and heavily swollen faces disfigured each in a unique way, and many of the teeth looked like they'd been knocked out. A large gash ran across each of their necks, a sharp blade the obvious culprit.

They each wore simple, but costly, white shirts bearing blackened scorch marks, highlighting severe burns on their skin scattered about. Caked soil and a pinkish stain covered the fronts of each—their blood dying the garments, washed by the river. They wore shoes which were too expensive to be dock worker's, but not quite the exquisite quality Delvan expected from nobles.

The inside forearm of one had a compass rose tattooed on it. The four points surrounded a single-lined, repetitive flower pattern blossoming within. It marked him as a member of the Merchants' Guild, which fit with the clothes.

"I don't suppose anyone knew either of these men?" Delvan asked.

"No, my Lord," the man said. "We've asked around, but no one seems to know them. Lots of people come through here though, might be able to find someone eventually."

How was he supposed to determine who had killed these men? He was trained to be the one leaving the bodies, not hunting down others that did the same. He reached into the pockets and began rummaging, looking for any hints as to who the men might have been.

Some people in the crowd shifted uncomfortably, and murmurings spread around him like wildfire. The superstitiously pious believed that stealing from a body was disgraceful and robbed that person of money needed for the afterlife.

"Leave the dead for Strigi's owls!" someone from the crowd cried.

Delvan wasn't surprised by the outburst, but the carryover of his darkened mood from the night prior had still not withdrawn, and he found himself irritated at the protest. *Superstition has overridden nobility now, has it?* he wondered.

"Who said that?" he said as he stood up, projecting his voice. The crowd fell silent, the whispers sailing away with the wind.

*Thought so.*

"Get these people out of here," he said, directing the order to the men containing the crowd. He needed a quieter space to investigate, not misguided objections in defense of piety.

Delvan, like virtually all other nobles, had been raised a strict Cordist, though he found many of the superstitions to be a bit dramatic. He found himself skipping speaks on what his parents would consider a too regular basis, but that didn't mean his faith had necessarily waivered. He just had... other, more pertinent interests. He could be reverent in a tavern, communing with the divinities through the eyes of a beautiful girl, couldn't he?

The people began to disperse, giving Delvan space to work without the assault of a hundred reverent eyes upon him.

His search of the men's pockets ended up being for naught, however, as whoever had dumped the bodies seemed to have already emptied them. Something caught a glint of cloudy sunlight. He turned the stiff head and saw a golden stud earring, its unblemished features reflecting the overcast sky above.

*Poor attempt at a robbery if you're leaving that there,* he thought.

Something else caught his eye, and a memory itched in his mind. Across the same man's chin was a large red mark. Delvan could tell it wasn't a bruise, the edge of it was far too distinct. Something Hilbrun had said a few days ago: "...Reltand recently? From the booth up the street, has a red birthmark on his jaw."

Delvan became remarkably still, and his eyes went wide at the realization. This was Hilbrun's missing merchant. The one that he went to for information. Given the burns and beatings, Delvan wondered if they had been tortured to learn of locations of cadentite. Is that how the thief had known to rob the spice merchant? Because other merchants were being tortured for information?

Another realization struck him, tying his insides together. "Have you told anyone else about these bodies?" he asked the dock worker who'd led him here. If Commander Ferrand *was* involved, then he wouldn't be happy to learn that these two men had washed ashore so quickly.

"Nay, my Lord, just you so far. I can send for someone to get you some more soldiers, if you'd like," the man replied.

"No!" said Delvan in a far too quick response. He had wanted to avoid this, to just enjoy some blissful silence for a brief period. He wasn't ready to talk to him again, but two men were dead, and who knew if more were to follow. There could be another robbery being planned at this moment. He had to put aside his resentment. For now.

"I need you to go to the dock's carrier station," Delvan said, "and send a pigeon to the third quadrant's barracks in the Upper Tier addressed for Cadet Hilbrun al Portaine. Tell him Delvan found his merchant and to hurry here. Got it?"

"Aye, my Lord," the man said.

"Good. Is there a secluded place we can take these bodies? Somewhere I can wait with them?"

"Aye, I'll ask some of the boys to help ya, and I'll get that message sent for you right away, my Lord."

Delvan felt sick. He had hoped to put this meeting off for a while. To let things cool down. But torture and murder took precedent, despite the squeezing sensation in his stomach that extended into his throat. It seemed the moment of their reunion had been chosen for him.

# Chapter Sixteen

*I was born for a purpose, though people always assume that of divinity. Molded, twisted, used, like horses to charge into battle upon. I thought it grand, until I looked into the distance, tumultuous with emotion. Something was there, a possibility I chose to ignore in my ignorant youth.*

Unclear who was being described, may be unimportant, Thirty-sixth Day of Winter, Twenty-eighth Year of the Seventh Epoch

Desnia walked with hunched shoulders, her head pulled into the depths of her hood. People passed by, her attentiveness to them a flickering half thought, her mind distracted. Questions itched at her, like the scabbing wound on her arm, festering there like an untreated infection.

The polished stone walls of the buildings around her reflected the shimmering glow of the streetlamps, the sun having fully settled into its nightly bed beyond the horizon. She was making her way to the cobbler's, considering what her explanation about the previous night's absence would be upon her return. But first, she needed to remove a malignant burden.

She walked over the small, arched bridge that crossed the canal. It was one of a multitude of tributaries reaching like tendrils within the city walls, leading out to the port and its estuary through small gates in the city walls. She stopped in its center and walked to the thick railing, looking down at the still water below, the black sheet darkened like a bottomless ravine. Clouds covered the stars, and the depths of the empty sheet stared back at her, her mind believing that if she were to dive from the bridge, she would fall endlessly into the unknown pits of the underworld below.

It reminded her of the other emptiness. One capped by a thin purple veneer stretching from horizon to horizon. A voice reaching out to her and resonating within.

Desnia reached into her pocket and pulled the gray cloth from it, her fearful eyes covered in shadow. She didn't unwrap it, no, that risked destroying the mask of sanity she'd been working to reconstruct. Gripping the tightly bundled ring, she extended her arm over the ominous chasm, her lips in a tight line and brow furrowed.

She couldn't allow herself to become like one of them. Her life, her mind, was her own, and she intended to keep it that way. She refused to accept that the voice she'd heard, this *Masini*, had been real. He was a figment of her night terrors, and nothing more. But... he had spoken of the voice, familiar with it somehow. Was Masini just a waking concoction of her mind's tricks? Would he return even if she abandoned this tangible figment here and now?

*None of it was real,* she thought pensively, *I imagined it all. The dreams, they're just dreams. Perhaps I'm still sleeping now? Can I even tell anymore?*

Her solution was the same as always: ignorance. Acceptance—true acceptance—was like a distant land: an object of imagination and tales, sitting beyond her reach. Part of her psyche, the survivor instincts which helped her fight for her life on the streets, sought desperately to avoid risks. Discard anything which may bring harm, and focus on tomorrow, plan for what you could and adapt when you couldn't. Anything else was folly. Another, minuscule part, the one struggling for breath as it was drowned in the panic of survival, tried to say she *was* strong enough, that she needed this.

She'd made a choice. One that was based on all the instincts that had kept her alive. A choice to actively avoid the voices in her head, to mute them, and remove whatever she could from her life to give her the divine clarity of peace.

A choice to survive.

She turned her hand over and watched the ball of cloth fall, striking the water's surface, it and the ring it contained sinking below the black sheet. The tiny ripples presented the truth of the chasm's mysteries, its illusion broken. The sound of water lightly lapping the canal's edge gave it a tangible presence, shattering the endless abyss that had stared at her ominously.

She let out a sigh and her shoulders relaxed. The relief, however, was fleeting. Something began clawing away at her insides, digging with the fury only a trapped animal could know. It screamed that what she'd done was wrong, that it was a mistake.

Desnia forced it back into its cage, then turned and finished traversing the bridge, her footfalls silent upon the stone. The Merchants' Guild entrance was visible beyond the intersection, framed between two buildings a block ahead of her. It stared at her in challenge, inviting her to enter its guarded halls.

*Soon enough,* she thought. *Soon enough.*

Desnia knocked on the rear of the cobbler's shop in the designated beat and waited. Her nerves felt frayed, her eyes wide and alert despite her tired muscles. She looked nervously at the windows around her and took a step away from the rear door. She didn't trust what was behind them anymore.

The sound of a lock clicking into place drew her eye, and her legs tensed to flee in the opposite direction. The door gradually opened until she saw the distinct outline of Magnar silhouetted in the timid darkness.

He waved her in, and she silently flowed through the door, hearing it latch behind her. The faint light drew long shadows on Magnar's hard features as he turned and faced her, holding his nose high in his air of false nobility.

"Where were you last night?" he asked in a hushed whisper, his brow furrowing with concern. "When you didn't return, we thought that perhaps something had befallen you."

She wasn't sure how much she wanted to recall, but the entire heist could be in jeopardy. Not telling him could be reckless.

"We have a problem," she said emphatically, trying to remove any wavering from her voice. "When I got home last night, I was jumped by two Blues waiting for me. I barely managed to escape, then I spent the night hiding so I wouldn't draw the bastards here."

She could see creases of concern break through the calm smile that he wore so well. *Is he going to blame me for this?* she thought. *Be outraged that I possibly endangered the job? Or will he ask how the Blues managed to find me and wonder if they know my involvement in his plans?* His true skills as a crew leader were going to become apparent in short order.

"Were you followed? Do you know how they found you? Or what you might've done to draw their attention?"

*Was I followed? Who does he think I am?*

"I'm not a fucking amateur. No one followed me last night, and no one followed me tonight, they already knew where I lived." *Someone at the tavern probably sold me out, pricks.* "As to how they found me... Not entirely sure," she said in a half truth. "Could be related to a job I did a few days ago, but I didn't stick around to ask. I'm lucky to have gotten away as it was."

"Lucky indeed," he said, as his head listed to the side in thought, the shadows over his face becoming longer and darkening its features. She tensed again, considering possible exits from the store, and which paths she could take to reach them. For someone who had been so readable to her before, he stood now like a carved bust, his face fixed in stone.

"Come with me," he finally said, "we're going to need to act fast."

She followed him to the basement where Sanco, Grunner, and Ox were all getting dressed for what she assumed was another night's work. She recoiled from the stench, but tried to push through it, holding back a gag.

"Gentlemen," Magnar said with a clap of his hands, "there's been a change of plans." They looked from Magnar to Desnia with glares of consternation. "The Lady Desnia here had the unfortunate pleasure of finding two Blues waiting for her at her home last night. We can't confirm why they were there, and there is the obvious possibility that they are following her due to the discovery of our machinations."

*Obvious?* Desnia thought. *What part of 'I wasn't followed' did he not understand?*

"If that is the case," Magnar continued, "then I assume that they don't know where we are yet, as there would undoubtedly be a few dozen soldiers raiding the building at present. Still, we can't take the risk of this location being discovered. Our labors here cannot have been for naught. Failure in this endeavor is *not* an option.

"So, we're moving our timeline. Rather than breaking into the vault tomorrow, we go in *tonight.*"

Desnia lifted an eyebrow at the aggressive move. She didn't like rushing into things, too many opportunities for something to go wrong, but given the circumstances she agreed that it might be the most prudent option.

Sanco opened his mouth to object, but Magnar silenced him with the quick raise of a finger. Grunner was staring Desnia down with eyes that felt as though they cut through her. There was something about them that didn't betray anger so much as conniving, like a predator stalking its prey.

"I know this isn't what we planned for, but if we hurry, we can prevail. It's still early enough for the plan to move forward, but it will be close," said Magnar with confidence. "Sanco, you're going to hie over to our lady compatriot about the guard's drink. He isn't set to be on duty for another two hours, hopefully you beat him there. If not, get one of the other girls to help you. Then come back here, *immediately.* You can indulge when you're rich.

"Grunner, Ox, we've got two hours to make sure we're able to get through that wall. Can you finish getting us through by then?"

Grunner turned his attention from Desnia and looked at Magnar. He thought for a moment and then said, "We can make a small hole, gonna be cramped getting in, but we can work to make it larger while the thief works on the vault."

*He says 'thief' like he isn't one himself. What does this creep think we're doing?*

"It will have to do and—" Magnar broke off. "Sanco! What are you still doing here? Go! Now!" Sanco hectically started shedding his work attire and was running up the stairs while tying his boots, trying to avoid incurring further wrath from Magnar.

"I will go and talk to our carriage driver. I should be back within an hour. Des, you have two hours to prepare, and then we commence."

While the others moved with haste to complete their assigned tasks, Desnia made her way up to her room with the lock and her tools. She didn't need more time with it. She'd extracted as much as she could from the ancient device. A brief urge, flashing like a firefly, crossed her mind. One that begged her to consider sleeping the next two hours.

She shivered.

No, she would use the time to practice instead. Even if it wasn't necessary, it was better than the alternatives.

Two hours. All that remained between her and the cost of freedom.

# Chapter Seventeen

*The paradox of expanding one's mind to the futures is that your patience is both eternal, yet fleeting.*
Lucid discussion,
Sixth Day of Summer, Forty-first Year of the Seventh Epoch

D elvan waited.

And waited.

Then continued waiting until long after the sun had extinguished itself for the day. He presumed it was still closer to midnight than it was dawn, but only by a narrow margin. It was difficult to gauge, as the port's bells didn't toll during the late hours. If he were out on the docks themselves, he would be able to see the lit clock tower—time was money in the Port of Calentine, and even at this late hour he could still hear people moving about beyond the warehouse doors—but he didn't dare leave the secluded structure for fear of attracting unwanted attention.

The scent of musty crates enveloped him like a blanket, and the flickering light of his draining lamp made the enormous space feel cramped. He sat with his back to a heavy crate, its worn timbers scratching against his armor, his arms resting on knees that tucked toward his chest. He found himself questioning whether the pitter-patter of footsteps were the people working the docks outside, or rats that scavenged the building's stock.

He also couldn't tell what stank worse, him or the corpses.

They had moved the bodies in here at Delvan's request. He didn't want to increase the already elevated chances that Commander Ferrand would hear of the murders and swoop in to make the evidence disappear. Again.

Hiding in a half empty warehouse wasn't a foolproof plan. If a knight commander came marching into the port and demanded information, it would take an act of a god to stop him. This way, at least, there would be fewer eyes to wonder and mouths to whisper.

Delvan had spent the time, at first, trying to determine if there were any additional clues on the bodies he may have missed. He'd done what he could to reason through what details may or may not be important, but after a few hours he'd resigned himself to accepting that there was little else he could learn from the cadavers. Perhaps he needed another set of eyes.

Which brought him to the other matter that consumed his thoughts. Hilbrun. What was he going to say when he arrived? Different scenarios played through his mind, like a show at the theater. In some he demanded an apology from Hilbrun, refusing to share what he'd learned without such an admission. In others, he avoided the topic completely, and tried to make things go back to exactly how they had been. Those left him revolted and full of angst, however.

What should he say? Should he say anything? Hilbrun *should* be the one to apologize, not him. He'd been blamed for something that wasn't his fault. All he'd wanted to do was help, and that's what he'd been doing, until Hilbrun had exploded in a tantrum and brought the burden of blame all down upon Delvan's back.

What had caused Hilbrun to become so irate? What about this cadentite made him so quick to anger? Was it his familial ties to the Merchants' Guild? That stood to reason, but he still shouldn't have been so harsh on Delvan. Sapphires trumped all. Hilbrun was a fellow Blue, bonded by a power greater than anything besides the King's jewel itself. That came first. Not family, not guild obligations, not some glowing rock that was used to grow drugs. Blue before all.

So it was that Delvan sat on the floor, his back to a crate, mind racing too quickly for him to even consider sleeping. Scenario after scenario ran their course through his head, the prolonged wait only amplifying his trepidation.

Finally, he heard a door open. His stomach tightened and face went cold as he saw Hilbrun walk in, the lamp in his hand throwing a tall, looming shadow on the wall behind him. Delvan felt small, sitting there on the floor. He pulled himself up, taking his own lamp which was beginning to fade in the late hours.

Hilbrun looked at him, his face hard and accentuated by the raking light. What was he going to say? Was he going to apologize?

"You said you found the merchant's body? Reltand? Show me," Hilbrun said tersely.

*What?* Delvan thought. *That's it? Straight to the point, like nothing even happened?*

The scenarios that he'd thought so long about flushed from his mind, as though the dialog he'd recited was suddenly forgotten. He pointed to an obfuscated mound to his side, the bodies and the crates they laid on covered in the small sail. His shoulders slumped and chest collapsed as he stood there, completely chagrined.

Hilbrun walked over and hung his lantern on a nearby post before pulling the sheet back and inspecting the bodies. He didn't speak. He just scanned the corpses and began investigating them closely, without so much as a glance at Delvan.

Delvan felt frozen, but deep inside he felt a flame. It was fueled by the silent tension in the air and fanned by the complete lack of acknowledgement. Its embers grew wild, and his frozen posture began to melt.

*No,* Delvan thought, *I can't let him just ignore what he did. What he said. I have to say* something. *I need to hear him acknowledge that he was in the wrong.*

"Hil," he started to say.

"Who found them?" Hilbrun interjected without looking at him. "Where were they? And did you find anything on the bodies when you arrived?"

*He doesn't even want to discuss it,* he thought. *He doesn't even want to talk about what he did to me.*

"Hil," he said, a quiver resonating in his voice. "I need to... Last night..."

"We need to talk about these murders," Hilbrun said curtly. "No need to bring up last night."

That was it. The inferno within him exploded in a cloud of steam and fury.

"No!" he shouted, his face red, lips tight. "We DO need to talk about last night!" The people working the docks outside could probably hear his near hysteria, but he didn't care. "What happened wasn't *my* fault. All I've done this entire time is help you, but you don't tell me half of what you know, and when something goes wrong that was completely on you, you blame me! I defied—gods, AM defying—the direct orders of a *knight commander* for you, Hil, and this is the fucking repayment I get?!"

Hilbrun stood there silently, eyes forward as though staring off to an unseen horizon. Delvan breathed heavily, his eyes blurred from tears that he valiantly fought back, waiting for a response.

"You don't understand," said Hilbrun quietly, the terseness of his voice having vanished, "the pressure I'm under to find this cadentite. The people who are watching my every move. I have to succeed, Del. I have to."

"Then help me understand!" Delvan screamed. "How am I supposed to help you if you don't tell me anything? If you don't share critical information? What is so gods-damn important that you can't tell me, huh? Who are these people? What are you hiding from me?!"

The words flew out of him like missiles from a bastion. His voice was becoming hoarse, and he could feel his face sting with tension. Hours of pent-up animosity sprang from him in a flurry of ire.

"I can't—" Hilbrun stuttered as he finally turned to face him. "Del, I can't tell you. These people, they... All you need to know is that they do not tolerate failure. The stakes here are so much greater than you could possibly imagine."

"Then help me to understand!" he repeated. His voice cracked under the pressure of the words forcing their way out of him like a striking hammer. "Tell me, Hil. Tell me or I'm *done*."

Hilbrun craned his head towards the ceiling, his lips pursed tightly. The struggle on his face was apparent, and Delvan waited while a crashing wall of fatigue landed on him, his anger having been the foundation of his wakefulness.

"You realize what you're asking of me, don't you?" Hilbrun asked after what felt like an eternity, "The guild has a lot of secrets Del, and this is among its biggest. Telling you what I know would risk everything, not just for me, but my family, our businesses, the guild, all of it. Can't you trust that I'm trying to do the right thing here? Isn't that enough?"

The weight of Hilbrun's words made him pause. Hilbrun actually seemed *nervous*, not just reserved, and in all his time with him, Delvan had never witnessed that expression cross his Senior's face.

But he had to know.

"Secrets? Every family has secrets, Hil, mine is no exception. But I'm not going to get towed around half the city and berated by you because of some piece of cadentite that you are treating like it's worth a hundred times more than it is! It's not like you need the money! And don't tell me it's because you're against iguan or some other excuse. Give me *something*," he said, exhaustion wavering in his voice.

Hilbrun sighed and looked at him with a hint of reservation. He still looked as though he didn't want to speak, holding his mouth closed between thin lips.

"The cadentite is just one part of it," Hilbrun finally said. "Have you ever given much thought to the Ones Before?"

*That's what this is about?* he thought. *A bunch of crumbling stones littering the continent and some pagan beliefs?*

He recalled seeing some of the ancient statues and mounds of once square blocks while on hunts, deep in the forest. The worn columns and oddly shaped nubs of stone covered in moss, roots, and vines were the only indications that anything had once existed there other than the forest itself. He'd heard that such fragments of the kingdom of the Ones Before could be found throughout the empire, even beyond the southern sea.

"Old ruins and stories of specters that haunt them that parents tell their children," said Delvan, wondering why he had to explain this. "It's a bunch of peasant folklore. *How* is this relevant?"

"Have you ever wondered where they went, Del? We still build half our cities on their ruins, how advanced must they have been to lay foundations we can still use centuries, millennia, who knows how many, years later."

Delvan looked at him scrupulously. "We don't even know if they *existed*, Hil. Don't tell me you buy into all of that? They're an old fable! If you have me running around the Valley looking for some pagan nonsense, I swear..."

"I'm not talking about the myths the elders like to tell their grandchildren, Del," Hilbrun said, sounding offended. "The truth, the reality that is excluded from the texts, that was scoured from the libraries, and purged from all but the ones who dared whisper it in the darkest nights, is unlike anything you can fathom.

"There was a power, Del, a power that they wielded—"

"*We* wield a power, Hil. It hangs around our necks," Delvan said incredulously, tapping his chest.

"No," Hilbrun said, sighing and digging his forehead into his palm. "It was like our sapphires, but even more potent. A power that could rival the *King*."

"*What*?!" Delvan's brow scrunched together as his jaw hung open. *He's completely delusional.* "That's impossible, Hil, and you know it."

"It's not!" Hilbrun retorted, his own brow digging deeply into his nose, the lamp at his side casting cavernous shadows across his face. "And they used it to build an apex civilization, and then it disappeared along with them."

"Of course it did. Seems awfully convenient." Delvan waved his hands to the side. *How does he believe any of this?*

"Just listen to me for a gods-damn second, Del! Can you imagine something that powerful? What if we could harness that? Think of what..." Hilbrun's voice trailed as he got quiet and looked around. Then he turned his voice to a whisper. "You and I, the others, we could be free. No more bending to the King's every whim. No more having our lives chosen for us. We could be free to make our own choices... We could free ourselves of the King's grip. I *know* that's what you want, as badly as I do."

Delvan mulled over the words, trying to understand what it was that Hilbrun was saying, what he was implying. Is that what he wanted? The past few days had impregnated his mind with the question, but he was yet to determine an answer. Now more questions poured over him like falling rain.

"That's..." said Delvan, still processing the information. "You think the Ones Before had some wildly magnificent power and, what, you're trying to rediscover it somehow? That's ridiculous! Where did it go? Why is there no record of it, except what you claim to know, and who says *that's* accurate? Who told you all of this? And how is this connected to these murders and stolen cadentite?!"

Had Hilbrun even stopped to consider these questions? Was he just moving forward on blind, indoctrinated faith because it's what his family or the guild had told him?

"The cadentite is the key, Del," exclaimed Hilbrun. "We've been trying to collect it—the Merchants' Guild, along with a few select others—because we know what happened to that power, and we need the cadentite to bring it back."

*He can't be serious, can he?* "This sounds like a bunch of heretical fallacies. I know I'm not the most devout, but this all sounds insane, even to me." This entire, unbelievable conversation was taxing his already exhausted body and mind. He would've yawned had his jaw not been clenched so tightly.

"I know how it must sound," said Hilbrun, turning to face him, his expression as serious as Delvan had ever seen it. "But I assure you, we've been going at this since before the first chunk of rock was carved from Calentine Mountain. And now finally, after all that time, we are *this* close to being ready."

"Ready for *what*? I asked for answers, Hil, not vague responses that don't tell me a damn thing."

"To bring it back!" Hilbrun said with a wave of curled fingers. "The power they held, it was *stolen*, Del. Taken from the people and hidden away. We've been passing down knowledge over the centuries because we want it back. We want back our freedom, and with this last piece of cadentite, we can have it."

Delvan was becoming too tired to want to keep arguing, but the thought of Hilbrun actually believing this myth born of old wives' tales kept him moving forward. He took a deep breath, trying to calm his anger and decided to approach this a different way.

"Let's say, for a second, that I believe *any* of this," said Delvan. "You're saying you want the cadentite because you can, what, bring back some power greater than our sapphires? Which, by the way, the only one who wields *that* kind of power is the King, and I don't see him giving it up at any point soon. That doesn't explain what happened to it, or even what happened to the Ones Before, assuming they even existed."

"It vanished for a *reason*." Hilbrun was leaning into the words, like a priest giving a speak. "A schism broke apart the Ones Before; I don't know exactly what it was, but it was catastrophic, and it desolated the continent and all other lands. Almost everything was lost, including nearly all of this power.

"The ones watching me, the people that have entrusted me to find this cadentite, they're descendants of the loyalists who were dedicated to giving their power to the people. But we need cadentite, it's the only way to bring the power back to where it belongs. Here, with us."

Delvan leaned his back against a crate, the smell making him think the vegetables within were beginning to rot. He was too tired to care. He rubbed his face with his hands as his head pressed against the rough timber. "None of this explains why people are stealing the cadentite from you."

"Because." Hilbrun gave a harsh sigh, as though he were annoyed with having to explain this. *Let him be.* "There are scant others, like us, that remember those times. They want the power for themselves, Del. And through murder, guile, manipulation, and subtle thievery they've tried to ensure we can't collect enough to triumph."

"For something so secret, sure does seem like a lot of people know about it." Delvan's frustration was discarding any filter his mind had for the words his mouth produced. Combined with his exhaustion, his comments were beginning to take an intentional tone of malice.

"This is serious, Del!" Hilbrun's jaw was now the one tight. "They're trying to stop us, to keep the power from those who deserve it and solely with them! And worse, they've been succeeding! We almost have enough cadentite, Del, we're so close. The piece stolen from the spice merchant was the largest we've found in decades; with it, we finally have enough."

Delvan processed what he was hearing with a dose of incredulity. Talk of the Ones Before was for pagans and children, not nobility and members of the Sapphiric Court. But Hilbrun's eyes spoke louder than his words ever could. They wrinkled with disdain at the mention of those who would oppose him and his, pleaded with hopeful lust at the words of power to escape the King, and burned with a zealous intensity as he raved about reclamation. Now they focused on him, waiting, hopeful.

Almost begging.

Whether or not any of what he'd said was true, it was clear that Hilbrun believed every word.

"Hil," Delvan said in a tone that erred toward skeptical belief, rather than indignation, "I can see the Merchants' Guild fighting over the cadentite. Even that others have been stealing it from you. It doesn't surprise me that the guild has kept this quiet, the thefts must be costing them a fortune. The secrecy makes *sense*.

"But to believe there is some ancient power that suddenly vanished? It sounds ridiculous to even say out loud! You talk about these people like they were gods that walked among us! *This* is what you had me running around for?"

"You of all people should believe me, Del," said Hilbrun, looking unsurprised at his maintained skepticism. At least he seemed to understand Delvan's doubt. "You've seen the power for yourself. Outside of the iguan den."

"I... do you mean... the hooded man? But..." Delvan trailed off as he recalled the encounter, his head leaning forward from the crate and eyes narrowing as they darted in recollection. The strange force cast at him, his foot affixed to the ground. It *hadn't* been like anything he'd even seen or heard of before. The man hadn't been a Blue and he'd cast. Something Delvan had always intrinsically understood to be impossible.

*Could there be some truth to what he's saying?* Delvan thought, hesitantly.

"You're saying that the man I chased, this *Protorus*, could wield this power, and that's what he attacked me with?" He rubbed his hand against the black scar on his armor, the pain in his rib still stinging.

"Yes," replied Hilbrun. "I meant it when I said you were lucky to be alive. He's not known for leaving witnesses, not even Blues. He must be weaker than we'd even thought."

*That was him, weakened?* thought Delvan. "How does he use this 'power'? Didn't you just claim it was gone?"

"There are a handful that can still use it, but it's diluted and whatever they know they hide with jealous greed. If we truly want it back, in full force, we need this cadentite."

"And..." said Hilbrun with a pause, "I shouldn't have blamed you." His head turned to the side, as though ashamed. His hands balled up, and his face became hard. Delvan could see the excruciating effort it had taken to say the words. "This whole thing has me on edge, they've been one step ahead of us this entire time. I took it out on you when I shouldn't have," he said with a cracking voice.

Upon hearing the apology, the tension inside of Delvan released. He exhaled slowly, as though he'd been holding his breath since the night before.

He was still unsure about everything that Hilbrun had said, but it was clear that belief in it had put enormous pressure on his Senior. What he'd seen and felt outside the den in that alley couldn't be denied. But taking all of this on faith, even from Hilbrun, was asking a great deal. He turned it all over in his head, thinking on Hilbrun's words. Then another thought struck him.

"So, wait," he said, scratching his head, "if Commander Ferrand has appeared at all of these cadentite thefts, do you think he's working with these people that are trying to supposedly stop you?"

"There's nothing 'supposed' about it," Hilbrun said sternly. "But as hard as it was for me to accept at first," he said with gravity, "we do. I don't know how to explain it otherwise, and him interfering with us the past few days has just proven it to me. I'm not sure how those bastards got him on their side, but it's become a serious obstacle."

"Accusing a knight commander is no small thing," said Delvan. "Has the guild brought formal charges against him with the Court?"

"Are you crazy?" *I'm not the one talking about ancient powers and clandestine plots.* "We can't bring this into the light. We've kept it secret this long for a reason. Besides, we don't need to. He hasn't been able to take away all of our leads. I spent most of the day interrogating the woman from the iguan den—not that she seems to know anything. And now we have these two," he said, gesturing towards the two corpses.

"Wait," said Delvan, "you're still holding Malanai? She doesn't know anything, Hil! She knows less than I do, why are you still holding her?"

"She's with *them,* Del," Hilbrun said, his voice grating against contempt, "she can't be trusted."

"You promised her amnesty, Hil. Would you break that oath to her?"

Hilbrun's lips turned to a thin line, his fist clenching. "If we find the cadentite, I'll release her. Alright? It's a terrible idea, but if we get the cadentite it won't matter anyway. Satisfied?"

*Enough that I won't argue it further,* he thought. *I'll have to check with him later about her.*

"Now," said Hilbrun, focusing on the two bodies, "what did you learn from these two? Anything on them?"

"Not really," said Delvan. He recounted the words for Hilbrun from the dock hand about how they were found. "The one you called Reltand still has a gold earring in, so I assumed it wasn't a robbery. All of these scars and the beaten faces makes me think that they were tortured. I couldn't say why though. No one seems to know who the second person is, but I suspect he's also a merchant, or at least someone fairly affluent from his clothing."

"I think you're right. It's too much of a coincidence that my regular informant disappeared around the same time as the cadentite. This stinks of our enemies but they're normally more subtle than this. It's been a while since they took such violent action against us. Their forces have been eroded significantly and they lack resources, which is why they started setting up the iguan dens a few years ago: to gain capital.

"They must have been tortured for information. I suppose that Reltand could've known about the cadentite in the spice shop, he was a regular courier. But that robbery felt like it was done by a professional; there was an exactness to it, and almost seemed like a key was used to get into the safe, it was picked so cleanly. It must have taken days or weeks of planning and scouting. He's only been missing a few days. There could be enough overlap, but it seems off..."

Delvan held his hand to his chin in thought. Hilbrun's assessment was sound and logical, and he agreed that not everything was lining up. What else could these men have been tortured for? Maybe there was something else—

"Hil," said Delvan with a strike of clarity, "you said the guild had more cadentite, that you were collecting it? *Where*, exactly, are you keeping it all?"

Hilbrun's eyes lit up, his eyebrows lifting with the realization of Delvan's implications. "We need to go. Now." Hilbrun grabbed the lantern from the nearby post in a rush.

"Where?" asked Delvan, taking his own dwindling lantern.

"The guild's headquarters, near the docks," said Hilbrun. "We need to tell someone there that our cadentite stores' locations might have been compromised. I hope we're wrong, but what you're saying makes sense. They must have an idea about how much cadentite we have, and they could be getting desperate. We need to hurry and hope that we can find someone there at this hour to warn. I just hope we're not too late."

# Chapter Eighteen

*His final form shall be born of anguish and pain, but will be our salvation. Is it worth the cost, having endured the same? My life shall be spent contemplating this question.*
Screamed during sleep,
Thirteenth Day of Autumn, Fifth Year of the Seventh Epoch

The vile aroma of the fetid underground canal permeated the entirety of the arch-shaped brick tunnel. Desnia walked behind the others as they hunched low beneath the arch's curve and stepped along the elevated walkway that ran alongside the river of sludge, grateful that she could keep her feet dry.

Despite the thick cloth that she wore over her face, she still felt as though every breath was thick with moist particulates and suppressed a gag reflex more than once on the short walk. Ahead of her Magnar carried a small lamp, outlining his figure in dark shadow, eclipsing the others behind him in obscurity. She could hear rats squabbling in the distance, fighting over whatever morsels of sustenance this rancid hellscape offered.

Time seemed to drag at a pace slower than the churning flow beside her feet as she bated her breath, dreadfully regretting each inhalation. The air seemed to cling to her as if to drown her in its foulness, and her body drew into itself as though to safeguard from the pungence that curled her lip.

After the longest, short walk of her life, they arrived at an opening in the arch's wall, the brick broken and jagged, similar to the tunnel carved into the cobbler's basement. It began wide and tall, with a few wooden beams to support the wall of the tunnel, but rapidly tapered inward to a narrow, short shaft, ending at a flat piece of stone.

"Sanco, Grunner," whispered Magnar through his mask. He tilted his head to the side with a flick, indicating for them to proceed.

Sanco unstrapped a crossbow from his back and stood behind Grunner as he crawled forward. Desnia's heart raced, and her mouth drew into a line as she watched the crossbow get loaded. Magnar had promised a lack of violence, and part of her knew that this was a precaution, but she still looked on with nervous eyes.

Grunner crawled to the smooth face of the carved stone at the breach's end, and with a pointed metal instrument, carefully removed chunks of thin stone in a too-perfect straight line. Desnia realized that this must be a wall tile of the vault's anteroom and the chunks falling to the ground were its grout line.

*The care they must have taken to not alert the guard while digging... Maybe this Grunner isn't entirely useless, even if he is a creepy bastard,* she thought, watching intently.

Grunner pulled out a small hammer, and then turned to Sanco who nodded and brought the tip of the crossbow's bolt beside Grunner's head. Grunner expertly tapped the corner of the tile and it fell inward, leaving a triangular hole only a few inches wide on the side. He ducked his head while Sanco brought his weapon up to the orifice and aimed along its length. Desnia held her breath, disregarding the disgusting air that filled her lungs.

No shot came, however, and Sanco withdrew from the hole, giving a nod to Magnar. "Guard's down," Sanco said, "looks like our lady friend was able to come through."

"Nice work, Sanco," said Magnar, maintaining a hushed tone. "See, Des, *professionals.*"

She rolled her eyes.

With a few carefully placed taps, Grunner was able to quietly remove the remaining sections of tile with skill that spoke to him being a Calentinian mason. *What led you to this life?* she thought. The ice in his eyes made her think it wasn't for the money.

There was soon a hole large enough for her and Magnar to crawl through. He went in first, and she followed close behind. Once through, a large duffel of fabric was pushed into the hole, and she could hear the faint, muffled sound of stone chipping away on the opposite side.

She found herself in a modestly sized room, perhaps fifteen feet wide and twice as long, which was strangely bare, aside from a few hanging banners and torches on the walls. A stone-balustrade stairwell sloped up and out of sight along the wall to her side. The walls, floor and ceiling were covered in highly polished, pink granite tiles, inanite veins spider webbing through them, connecting in an endless array.

The wall opposite the stairs held the true splendor, however, along with the unconscious guard, collapsed on the floor.

Encased in the finery of masterful stonework was the largest safe door Desnia had ever seen. The pair ambled over and stood before it, Desnia in awe of its ominous simplicity. Easily eight feet wide and equally tall, the darksteel slab was devoid of markings, handles, or even hinges, the tinted metal running flush along the stone that encased it. In the center, just above waist height, was a single keyhole and numbered dial, the Merchants' Guild compass rose insignia etched into the dial's center.

It was the single most impressive piece of craftsmanship she'd ever seen.

Magnar broke the appreciative silence, removing the cloth covering his lower face and whispering, "The others will continue their labors while you set to work on this. We have maybe seven hours before this lad's replacement comes in." He pointed to the man asleep on the floor. "I'm going to confirm the door at the top of the stairs is locked and return presently. I don't suspect that we need worry over other guards, the door above leads to a sub-basement that only has one entrance, and that is what is guarded. I would recommend quiet prudence, however. No need to take unnecessary risks. How long do you expect this to take you?"

"A while," she said curtly.

"How long, may I inquire, is 'a while'," he asked.

"Longer every time you fucking ask it." She didn't bother looking at him as she slipped off her pack and began rummaging through the tools within. Magnar must have found it a suitable response—or perhaps he'd taken the not-so-subtle hint—and left her to work, tiptoeing up the stairs and out of her sight.

Desnia knelt down so that she was eye level with the two lock mechanisms, an elegant mask for the reticent juggernaut before her. She turned all of her focus onto it as she tested the dial, the smooth turning action hardly giving away the perfectly intervaled clicks from within as the tumblers spun. She used a narrow, bump-ended pick to slide into the key slot and test the pins, looking for any that may be false and primed to lock her out. She tried to picture the complex arrangement of gears, mechanisms, and wheels in her mind, tuning out all other external inputs.

She knew that she had a time limit but ignored it. Rushing resulted in mistakes.

She began working on the key slot first. Correct application of pressure in a twist against the cylinder, gentle prodding of the pins to test where they might need to sit to allow a key to turn beneath them. The near perfect machining of the slots made finding such a position a delicate task, one that her highly experienced fingers were struggling with. The slipping of the pins over the miniscule gap of the internal parts was nearly imperceptible.

Nonetheless, one by one she slotted them into the correct locations, her mind utterly fixated on the task, the world around her non-existent. That was the one benefit of a team, they could handle the boring work while she gave the lock her unwavering attention.

She didn't know how much time had passed. An hour? Maybe two? She tried to force it out of her mind as she continued to work, her gentle and precise touch working through the lock with unmatched mastery. With a *click* she felt the sweet release of the key cylinder. She exhaled as she turned it into the unlocked position, the overly tight muscles in her neck relaxing as she stretched them side to side.

There was movement to her side, and she suddenly became acutely aware that the others were all in the room with her. She noticed that the hole they crawled through was now closer to four feet tall, with a heavy cloth draped over it.

*How long did that take?* she wondered. *They're already done?*

She needed to confirm how much time she had left.

"Is that it?" asked Grunner, even his stoic face showing a glimmer of excitement. The others turned to her, their shifting bodies and movements to stand from the cool floor betraying their eagerness.

"No," she replied, putting the picks back into her pack. "Now I have to get past this turn dial. *Then* the door will unlock."

Grunner's eyes became intense, a flare of anger coming over him as he asked, "How long's that gonna take?"

"Longer than my patience will last if you keep asking stupid fucking questions," she said tersely, failing to not expose her annoyance at his urgency.

"You bitch, I—" started Grunner before Magnar stepped between the two and raised his hand. Grunner clenched his jaw so tightly that Desnia could hear his teeth grinding.

"Grunner, we must let Lady Desnia work," Magnar said. "She's clearly skilled enough to have bypassed the key lock, so let's please let her continue. In *silence*." The word was emphasized in such a way that Desnia knew Magnar could keep the dog on a leash, but she did wonder for how long. Did Magnar have something over Grunner? Or was Grunner scared of him?

Either option painted a malevolent image of the smiling noble-pretender. *I'll have to be careful of that one,* she thought.

"Des," said Magnar in his polite, smile-tuned way, "Three hours have already passed. If we are to have any chance of getting out of here with the untold riches behind this door, we need to breach the vault in even less time."

She could hear the pressing urgency he tried to hide. She was feeling it as well, she knew that she had to get through the dial's tumblers quickly. Her future depended on this, too.

*Three hours,* she thought, *that's less time than what it took me when I tried this before. Maybe the tumblers will go faster as well.*

She thought back to her previous attempt at the Diamond. Four hours to bypass the lock, another one to get the first of three tumblers in the correct position. Then the sound of pounding on the door as the guards had attempted to break it down, cutting her efforts short. She had taken her last resort escape route: a high jump onto a tiled roof, a slide down to its edge, and a tumble down into a canal below. She'd rolled her ankle and had been bedridden for over a week after.

Compared to that, she was ahead of schedule.

The practice with the old prototype lock provided by Magnar had been a necessary advantage. Not that she would ever admit that to the man. But she found that the insight, even if discretely different, was enough to get her past the obstacles that had hindered her previously.

She took a deep breath and shook her arms loosely at her sides. She could do this. She *had* to do this.

She put the eyes staring at her out of her mind as she pressed her ear to cold metal and listened for cues while she turned the dial with a feathery touch. Her heartbeat thumped in her ear canal, partially obfuscating the sound of gears spinning behind the thick steel.

She found the first number and used a piece of chalk from her bag to write it on the door. She spun the wheel, waiting to hear when all went silent. That was the trick that most got wrong. The *lack* of sound was just as important as the sound itself. It could tell you, for instance, when a wheel that ever so slightly rubbed against the bar meant to set into it no longer ground against the metal, and indicated where a slot was.

Time passed. It felt both distant as she pushed it from her mind and also near, like an owl hovering over her shoulder, ready to take her when the time came. She wasn't sure how long it had been, but the restless shifting of the others crowding the room gave her a rough idea.

Too long.

She noticed herself moving faster, adjusting the image in her mind, trying to connect what she was hearing to her experience and the prototype she'd practiced on. She could almost *hear* the stares of the others, burrowing anxiously into her as their clothes rustled in annoying rasps upon the stone floor.

The second number clicked into place. How long had she been at this? *I have to stay focused,* she thought. But it was hard to fixate on the problem at hand when another loomed so menacingly overhead. What if she couldn't solve it in time? What if she did, would Mixton free her from her debt, as promised? Even if he did, there were other things that haunted her, things she never seemed able to escape...

"How much longer?" she heard Sanco ask, an edge to his voice. "We're running out of time."

"Almost there," she whispered to avoid her voice resonating through the metal she was so intently listening to.

"You said that an hour ago," Sanco retorted, throwing his arms to the side. "Magnar, how do we know she can even do this? Maybe she's lied and fucked us all."

She pulled her ear from the door, looked at him and snapped, "You're welcome to do it your-fucking-self."

She looked to Magnar, who lacked his patented smile, notably not interjecting. "We have barely over an hour left, Des," he said. "Are you *actually* almost done?"

"Yes," she hissed, "I have just one more tumbler. I just need a little more time. I can do this."

Her brow furrowed as she glanced between the doubtful faces of the men around her.

*This is* not *going to beat me again,* she thought. She was tired, at the end of her wits, the residual headache from the night before a suppressed reminder of what her mind had created to torture her.

Her fingers fiddled with more urgency, spinning the dial in less of a graceful dance and more of a panicked tumble. She listened to the now familiar signs of the first two numbers' positioning, scanning, listening for another one. It had to be there. She was almost out of time. Any longer and this might all have been—

There it was.

Her fingers stopped abruptly, and she pulled her head back, jaw slightly agape. She spun the wheel, reset the tumblers and turned the dial to each of the digits, spinning it one direction and then another. At long last, she stopped it on the last integer and stood up, her knees aching from the prolonged meditative work.

The others now stood, curious expressions on each of them, walking cautiously towards her, as though they were worried that if they approached too quickly, they would somehow undo all of her work.

"Is it done?" asked Magnar, a glimmer of hope in his voice, his eyes wide.

"Yes," said Desnia as she ran her fingers through her hair, the tension leaving her with a long breath. "That was the final tumbler. It's unlocked."

"But how do we open it? I don't see a handle anywhere," said Magnar as he began looking the large slate of steel up and down.

As she scanned the door herself, she realized that she had no idea. "I'm... not sure," she said. "The last Diamond I attempted this on had one."

The relief that had begun filling the room vanished like a mouse through a hole, and they—being the pursuing cat—began frantically trying to find a solution.

Grunner tried checking the stone surround for possible latches, and Desnia and Magnar were running their hands across the steel's surface, hoping that something was hidden with the tight tolerance of the master craftsman who had created the door. Nothing appeared, and Desnia's heart began to race as a deep sense of worry began to set in.

A voice resounded through the air. "What if we have to push it?" said Ox from behind them. She had almost forgotten the mountain of a man was still there.

"That," said Magnar with a quizzical look to Ox and then back at the door, "might be the smartest thing you've ever said, Ox."

They heaved on the door, all five of them pressing against it with all the strength they could muster.

It defiantly refused to so much as flinch.

The others took a step back. Desnia stood there and pressed her head to the unforgiving metal. She stared down at the dial and keyhole before her. She didn't have it wrong. There had to be something else, another explanation.

*I can't have failed,* she thought, *I did everything perfectly.*

She thought back to her last attempt at the Diamond. The scramble and injury in her evasion. She thought back to the spice shop, her forearm still bandaged around the future scar. Her debt with Mixton. The endless desires of others to control her life. She remembered the haunting, booming voice splitting her skull, the hallucinations earlier that day.

A simmer of frustration soon raged into a boiling anger and came to over-flow as she let out a guttural scream. She slammed her open palm against the door, a *smack* of skin and dull *thud* of metal ringing in the room. It hurt; the door was unforgiving in more ways than one.

But then she hit it again, pain reverberating from her palm through her forearm.

Then again, and again. She struck it in a wild flurry, her palm smudging the polished steel. She had been so close, nearly within reach—

Her hand smacked against the center of the turn dial, its edge leaving a deep pain throbbing in her hand. As she retracted and clenched her fist, she heard a loud *click*.

The dial had pressed inward and locked into place.

She stared at it while she held her hand. Had it been that simple?

Magnar must have noticed this too, and as he pushed with an effort that required scarce more than the force of a finger, the entire door swung, pivoting around a point about one-third along its length.

The door had now truly unlocked.

Desnia let out a small laugh, a smile broaching her face as the door swung open with an elegant ease. She'd done it. She'd cracked the unbreakable Diamond. Fuck everyone who doubted her, looked down on her because of her gender, her age, or any other bullshit they could make up to make themselves less insecure. This was a victory that couldn't be—

A familiar chill ran down her spine, like a cold breeze on a wet back, and her hair stood on end. Then there was something else. A sensation which drew from the same senses but felt *different*. Her smile melted from her face.

The door fully swung to the side, and a sight that few ever witnessed now befell her eyes. Rows upon rows of stacked suns lined the wall on neatly organized shelving, their lustrous shine reflecting the dim light within. There had to be tens of thousands of them. Walls of cabinets holding deeds to properties and investments ran down the side opposite. In the back was a glass case, and resting upon velveted pillows within were at least six sapphires, obvious even in the dim light inside. Their magnificent size and the grandeur of a perfectly faceted sheen of a Blue's stone unmistakable even from this distance. Adjacent to them, shining like a lone lamp in a dark forest, was a square tile of cadentite, nearly three inches wide and just as tall, with strange markings patterned across its face. It cast a mild, purple luminance through the nearby sapphires and sprinkling dots of light across the room like stars. Its nebulous glow seemed to shift as you gazed upon it, a living energy swimming in a void of purple light.

Desnia's jaw fell loose, her eyes went wide, and her head withdrew as she looked at the contents in shocked horror, unable to move. *They must have known,* she thought, *they must have known about the gems. They're insane.*

She needed to run. The Merchants' Guild was willing to hide stolen sapphires from the crown, who could say what atrocities they would commit against the ones who stole from them? And the size of that cadentite! It could purchase a kingdom. Her mind screamed, but her muscles refused to respond. She needed—

An arm wrapped around her chest from behind and the cold edge of a blade pressed against her throat. "I guess you could do it, after all," whispered Grunner in her ear, sounding gratified and annoyed simultaneously, "too bad you won't be able to reap the rewards."

Magnar stepped in front of her, another smile on his face. This one was different though, it had a deviousness about it, his eyes cold and dark. He looked at her in a way that made Grunner's predatory glares seem timid, and she knew then that Magnar held nothing over Grunner's head. He had never been the danger, just a student in the presence of a master. She looked into his eyes and saw a darkness within, a deeper black than the darksteel door behind him, and she knew what he was.

He had not flown in as an owl with talons, sharp claws grasping to carry her away with wings beating gusts of darkness upon her to the afterlife. No, he came instead in a way she'd never expected.

Death had come with a smile.

# Chapter Nineteen

*Grief! I have felt his, and I know that in the pain of his darkness he*
*would burn the world to bring light back to it for but a moment.*
Spoken through tears in the middle of a session.
Eighty-first Day of Summer, Ninth Year of the Seventh Epoch

Rain began to mist down upon Delvan and Hilbrun as they hastily reached the Merchants' Guild headquarters. The covered lanterns along the thoroughfare they walked cast orbs of light, the limits of their luminance defined by the refraction through falling droplets. One nearby extinguished as water dripped through a crack and doused its oily flame.

Two guards stood adjacent to the tall iron gate affixed to the matching fence which encircled the building's perimeter, the gothic edifice rising high into the night above the sharpened points of the fence's ridge. They stood in statuesque repose, the rain having no apparent effect on the commitment to their station.

Hilbrun walked up to one of them and was addressed. "Good evening, my Lord."

"We need to speak with one of the Guild Masters, if there are any inside," Hilbrun said, his voice full of emphatic command.

"Sire," replied the guard in a stern tone, "allow one of us to go inside and fetch a guild member, you should have an escort while on the premises."

Delvan raised an eyebrow at the request. One did not refuse a Blue—knight or not—entry. But he was also aware of the delicate political situations surrounding the guilds. Similar to the noble houses, such as his own, the larger, more predominant guilds held such a sway on the economy that any slight against them could result in tariffs, price gouging, and other passive methods of hurting the purse of either a single person, or an entire region. The Merchants' Guild was one of the richest in the empire, and they were afforded an extreme amount of leeway by the crown and Court.

Hilbrun shook his head and grunted as he rolled up the sleeve on his right arm. "I don't have time for this," he said as he turned his inner forearm towards the guards, exposing the guild's compass rose to them, his beady eyes portraying his impatience. Delvan glimpsed the fringes of another tattoo just below the edge of the sleeve at Hilbrun's elbow, its thin black lines evenly spaced.

"Apologies, my Lord," said the man. He nodded to the other guard and opened the gate with a groaning creak and grind while Hilbrun pulled down his sleeve and walked through, Delvan close behind.

They entered the building through imposing wooden doors that soared high above them, their intricate carvings only a sample of the extravagant interior. Thick carpets lined the stone halls, murals and tapestries hung along the corridors, and furniture with rich and polished finishes could be found wherever one's eyes glanced.

Many of the rooms were dark—dawn still having not arrived—with guards at intermittent posts throughout. Delvan followed Hilbrun, who seemed somewhat familiar with the maze of halls, but noticed that he kept turning them around, spinning his head to gain bearing of where they were on several occasions.

Finally, a light from an office at the end of a hall drew their attention. They strode towards it, a spring of haste in Hilbrun's step. With a knock from Hilbrun they entered the spacious office.

The bald head of an older man lifted from the documents which piled his desk in undulating mounts of parchment. Delvan could smell the fresh ink from across the room. He looked at them over spectacles that sat low on his nose, his neatly trimmed white hair and beard shining in the glow of the room's lamps.

"King and His grace upon you, my Lords," he said with his head still tilted low, puzzlement on his face, "what brings you to my office at such an hour?" The words were spoken as both a question and demand.

"I apologize for the intrusion," said Hilbrun with a humility that surprised Delvan, "my name is Hilbrun al Portaine, and I come with dire warning that I must share with a Guild Master."

The old man tilted his head back and squinted. "Al Portaine, you say? Hmm, yes, I can see the resemblance to your father. Quite the merchant, that one, rather excellent businessman. I had the pleasure of meeting him about ten years ago in Aliova. I suppose you must have already been sent off to the Academy at the time, but he spoke highly of you."

"Thank you, sir," said Hilbrun with a modest bow. "I will be sure to write to him of your praises, Master?..."

"Master Rwendal," the man said. "Now, tell me, my Lords, what can I help you with at this late, or early, I suppose, hour."

"Sire," said Hilbrun as he shut the door to the office. It was a simple term, but Delvan narrowed his eyes and his brow shifted down slightly at hearing it. Blues did not address anyone aside from other members of the Sapphiric Court or the highest-ranking leaders of the military as such. There were few exceptions, and this man was not one of them. "My partner and I have reason to believe that the locations of our cadentite stores have been compromised. I suggest we move them as expeditiously as possible."

The man leaned forward and lowered his brow until it sank just above his eyes, looking from Hilbrun to Delvan.

"I've... informed my partner of some minor details," said Hilbrun, holding his hands tightly together behind his back.

The man's eyes, live and vibrant despite the hour and his age, flitted between them as he sat in silence. After a moment, he spoke, "We shall discuss such transgressions later. Tell me, what makes you so certain of this exposure of such carefully guarded information?"

With a loud swallow, Hilbrun recounted the theft at the spice shop, the details of their investigation, and the two bodies that had been found in the river. The man listened intently, his face unreadable as Hilbrun recalled every step of their previous days.

"Hmm," said the man after Hilbrun had finished. "The knight commander has been a nuisance, but I didn't think he would be so bold as to turn to murdering guild members. I've met Reltand, it's a shame to hear about.

"This other body, I fear I may know who it is. The young associate of our spice merchant acquaintance has been missing for some time. He often worked late hours here on his master's behalf and was known to the guards. We have not been able to find him at home or anywhere else in the city, and frankly myself and a few others had assumed him a spy. Seems we were terribly mistaken."

He leaned back in the opulent leather chair, his face wrinkling with the deep crevasses of age as he thought.

"Sire," said Hilbrun, "if he was familiar with this building, anything stored here might be at risk. Perhaps he was a spy, and was no longer of any use? We should confirm everything is secure and increase the guard, at least until we can transport the cadentite elsewhere."

*There's that title again,* thought Delvan. *He said that he worked with this group, but he can't actually presume them to hold title over him, can he?* The possibility was a foreign one.

"I will check it, personally, young Master Hilbrun, although I assure you that there is no place more secure than our vault. It is rather impenetrable. I will also discuss what you have told me with the others in the morning and we shall determine a way to move forward. We'll also discuss your... inclusion of your Pupil in our designs. You are otherwise dismissed," Rwendal said with a wave of his boney hand.

Delvan's eyes glared. Who was this man to assume to dismiss two Blues? He looked to Hilbrun, who showed not even a hint of being perturbed by the command.

"Sire," Hilbrun said, standing firm, "given the attack on Delvan and the evasion of an enemy agent, I believe the risk too high to ignore. Coming after Blues in the open is bold. I'm concerned about their desperation, and therefore the security of this building. I'd like for the two of us to accompany you to check the vault, and then remain here to guard it until reinforcements can be requested."

"I appreciate your prudence, young man," said Rwendal, "but I assure you that there is no more secure building in the Lower Valley than this one. Although... I do suppose that having a pair of Blues here wouldn't be of harm. I think I'd like some time to discuss certain matters with you and your Pupil here anyway. What is your name, my Lord?"

*At least he remembered* my *title,* he thought.

"Delvan ce Saffstar," he said, omitting Hilbrun's title usage for the man.

"Saffstar…" Rwendal looked at Hilbrun with narrowed eyes. "Yes, it is well you stay. And if you insist on being this persistent, then I will check on the vault's integrity more immediately. Come, you may accompany me to the sub-basement, but I cannot allow you into the vault room. I am familiar with its contents enough to inspect for missing items. Once we confirm everything is in its proper place, we can discuss other matters."

With a spryness that surprised Delvan, Rwendal lifted from his chair and made his way past them and through the door, apparently expecting them to follow.

Delvan found himself striding to nearly the pace of a jog to keep up. They wound through a series of halls until they were led down a wide, short set of stairs, two guards adjacent to a filigreed darksteel door at its base.

Rwendal turned to them, pulling a ring of keys from under his heavy, velveted jacket. "My Lords will need to wait here a time," he said, "while I go inspect the vault. There is a sitting room across the hall if it would please you."

Delvan thought he heard something through the door, a distant echo drowned by the mass of stone and steel.

*Was that a scream?* he thought.

He looked at Hilbrun, who seemed to not have heard the cry. Was he imagining things? His eyes *were* burning with exhaustion. It *was* nearly dawn, and the emotional thrashing—like a ship lost in a storm—he'd experienced over the past few days had left him feeling tattered and ragged.

An unmistakable warmth suddenly pervaded through him, a sensation that all Blues knew, a bonded feeling of something that was fused with their entire being.

Sapphires.

He felt the glow through the door, and he and Hilbrun now exchanged glances.

"Is there another entrance into this basement? To the vault?" Delvan interrupted, the man still sorting for the correct key.

"What?" asked Rwendal. "No, this door leads to a storage room for less valuable items, and the vault is in a lower basement through a door beyond. Why?"

"You're certain?" he asked.

"Yes," he said, annoyed at the questioning of his veracity. "The storage room is built of stone walls and no windows, I assure you, this is the *only* entrance."

*Then how did several Blues just appear beyond that room?* he wondered, his forehead creasing in deep thought. He looked to Hilbrun, who fidgeted nervously, lacking the same concern for their brethren that Delvan held. *He can feel it too,* Delvan knew, *so why is he not expressing the same concern? Unless...*

"You have sapphires in your vault..." Delvan said, his eyes wide and jaw low in astonishment. Hilbrun knew. He *knew*.

"Absurd!" blurted Rwendal emphatically. "We would never consider such—"

"Stop!" Delvan commanded. Hilbrun might not be willing to act upon his given authority with this man, but Delvan held no such reservations. "You have Sapphires here, somewhere. I can feel them, so can Hil, so don't even try to deny it. They're in the vault, aren't they?"

He looked at Rwendal, whose eyes had become narrow with anger, and saw a bead of nervous sweat betray his stern demeanor. He hadn't sensed the gems when they'd first arrived, which meant that they'd been insulated in muted inanite. *Smart,* he thought, *wouldn't want some random Blue to realize what you had here.* But that would have to mean that the insulation had been removed. Something was happening with the sapphires!

"Is there anyone else in there? In the vault room? Anyone that is allowed access?" Delvan demanded.

"The only other person beyond these doors is the single guard posted at the vault," Rwendal said, his voice steady but hesitant as he carefully chose his words. "Guard," Rwendal turned to the armed sentinel at his left, "has anyone else entered the vault room this night?"

"No, Sire," said the guard.

"If the gems are in the vault, then it's been breached somehow. We need to get in there. Now!" Delvan said, extending hand to demand the keys from the old man.

"Certainly it has not!" Rwendal said, retracting his hand holding the keys in a defensive posture. "And you shall have no such access! Master Hilbrun,

I would suggest restraining your Pupil from coming in here making such demands and accusations!"

Hilbrun's lips tightened, and he glanced between Rwendal and Delvan.

Delvan held his breath. Hilbrun was going to defend him, wasn't he? A sinking feeling dragged through him as he waited for Hilbrun to speak, the seconds extending like an eternity. Could he rely on Hilbrun to support him? Was he going to betray his trust, again?

*He knows I'm right,* thought Delvan. *He* has *to know I'm right.*

"Sire," Hilbrun finally said, a precarious caution in his voice, "Delvan is right. Someone is moving sapphires in there. Your guard might be a traitor, and given what we've seen the past few days... I think we both know who is responsible. You need to give us the keys and go gather as many guards as you can find. Them as well," he said, pointing to the two guards, "get back here as fast as you can. We'll investigate. We have to assume the worst, and Delvan and I stand the best chance of fighting anything we may encounter down there."

Delvan exhaled, a reignited, warm sense of reassured faith helping him to stand tall. His eyes wrinkled with the smile that his mouth didn't betray, for it needed to hold its rigidity in front of the stubbornness of Rwendal.

Rwendal fumed, and the keys rattled in his hand as it shook. He glared for a moment before finally extending the keys and placing them in Hilbrun's hands. "No one is to be taken from the premises, understand! *If* the guard or anyone else is down there stealing from us, they shall be dealt with internally. After this ordeal is through, the three of us shall be having a long discourse. You two, with me!" He pointed to the two guards and stormed off.

Delvan looked to Hilbrun and nodded, a motion that held a conversation in and of itself. Hilbrun gave him a smile which was tempered by concern. Delvan realized that Hilbrun had been forced to betray a different trust to maintain their own. It was a decision which held consequences no matter the choice, and Delvan felt a sudden sense of pity for his friend.

*What has he risked by exposing me to all of this?* he wondered.

"Let's go in quietly," said Hilbrun as he found the correct key. "We need to assess what we can before we barge in. If I give you a nod, then prepare to jump in and take any that I can't hold. And Del," he said, grabbing Delvan's shoulder, "remember the man in the alley. You got lucky once, don't push it. I want to have someone to interrogate, but you can't trust anyone still standing. If you even *think* they can do you harm, drop them."

Hilbrun turned the key and Delvan followed him into the room, a wealth of art, furniture, and rich linens stacked nearly to the ceiling making the large space feel cramped. He closed the door behind them, leaving it unlocked. They shuffled silently as they wove through the labyrinth of piled merchandise, careful not to bump into anything and risk alerting anyone present. A single lamp on a distant wall provided the only light in the space, casting long shadows in the windowless room. Presently they reached another darksteel door, mounted firmly in the stone wall.

Hilbrun found the correct key, carefully testing several from the cluttered ring. Delvan thought he could hear voices from inside the vault, but they were muffled by the thick, steel barrier. They both crouched in preparation as Hilbrun turned the key with a slow, gradual progression, not wanting to alert anyone beyond the threshold with the telltale sound of a ringing *clank* as the door unlocked. The key fell into place, and Hilbrun warily opened the door just enough so that they could squeeze through.

Delvan led, passing from Hilbrun's shadow cast by the light on the wall and heading down the stairs with quiet trepidation. The balustrade's near-solid baluster blocked them from view below as they crouched. Small, ornamental openings allowed them to peer through the stone and into the room below. The voice Delvan had heard became clear, and as the pair crept down the stone treads, they gained a clear vantage of the happenings below.

"—promised you to Grunner for his fun after this, though you must believe that I feel it a terrible waste of your talents. My employers had asked that you be spared, and I had considered, but you have two Blues pursuing you, my dear Des. You've become too great a liability. Grunner, restrain her and bring her to the carriage. Once we're loaded onto the ship, she is yours, but please do let me know before you've finished. I'd like my turn prior to you completely extinguishing the fight from her. They are so much more pleasant while still warm."

Delvan looked through the flower-shaped hole and saw a man in black, rapier at his side, standing before a woman. Her blonde hair obscured the face of another man—bald with dirty clothing—that appeared to be holding her from behind at knife point, their backs to Delvan and Hilbrun. The guard looked dead or unconscious, slumped against the wall. He could hear other commotion from somewhere, but couldn't see anyone else.

Behind the man in black, framed in the wall opposite from them, was the open vault door.

*I knew it,* thought Delvan.

He could feel the radiating warmth of sapphires, a comforting cradle that was as natural to him as the heart beating in his chest.

*Who are these merchants to think themselves above the King and His Court? What is Hil caught up in?*

But there was something else, an unfamiliar sensation that felt *different*, but his body somehow recognized. It flowed through him, and he was given the sense that an unknown cavity in his soul had been filled. A part of his body had been missing, like he'd spent his whole life with one lung, and now he suddenly knew what it was to truly breathe.

He looked to Hilbrun, who met his gaze, and with a quick glance into the room below, nodded the signal to attack.

Delvan sprang up and rushed down the stairs, while Hilbrun stood and extended both hands, each gripping tightly to freeze the two men holding the hostage. With a clatter from his armor as he jumped down the last few steps, Delvan drew his sword, its black depth emerging from the brilliantly white scabbard. He inched forward, his knees bent and sword held up in a defensive posture while Hilbrun began slowly descending the stairs behind him. He'd rushed into the encounter in the alley before, and it was not a mistake he intended to repeat.

Checking to his side, the vault appeared empty, but its dark interior disguised sharp details, creating an unknown void with a strange purple glow at its rear. Beyond the people in the center of the room was a heavy fabric over what appeared to be a hole in the wall. Was that how they'd gained entry? He needed to dispatch the two held by Hilbrun to free him for other potential encounters first, so he cautiously made his way towards them.

He came within an arm's reach of the bald man holding the knife, the whites of the woman's eyes in his grasp fully surrounding the iris as she looked at Delvan in horror. She was writhing, trying to force away the arm that held her, her legs twisting and kicking while her captor held her in place, a statue that would hold firm as the finest marble. The grip of a Reacher holding the man was beyond the abilities of nearly any to move, save a select few. He saw the blade against her throat scratch and draw a hint of blood, the small trickle running down her neck.

The lighting and tenseness of the situation must have been playing tricks on his eyes. Was that—

"Look out!" the woman shrilled.

A motion from his side. He turned to see the raging charge of a man who was built with proportions meant for tales of divinities and the ogres that guarded their realms. Shoulders wide as a door stampeded towards him, a loud bellow coming from the immense man. Delvan didn't have time to react, not seeing the man until it was too late. The hidden depths of the vault's unlit bowels must have obscured him from sight.

A boulder rolling down a mountainside would have hit Delvan with less force. He grunted with pain as he was launched from his feet and thrown backward, slamming into the wall beneath the stairs. His vision blurred and spun. His sword clattered to the floor, and he heard a crack that seemed to emanate from inside of him. He grunted as he crumpled into a slouch on the floor, gasping for breath as his diaphragm struggled to draw air.

Delvan saw through wavering vision that Hilbrun had made it to the bottom of the stairs and was nearby. Delvan blindly reached his arm to his side, searching for the hilt of his sword. His hand slid along polished granite as he rolled slightly, his body screaming in an ache which became more acute by the second.

He knew the rib that had been cracked by the strange casting the other day was the origin, his side wailing in a piercing pain. He had little doubt it was fully broken now. He tried to force himself to a knee, his hand reaching down for support, all while the shadow of the giant of a man that struck him slowly approached. His arm couldn't hold, the tightening muscles in his chest wrenched in an agony that threatened to rive him.

Muddled noises became clear as his vision regained equilibrium. Screams of the woman, still fighting to pull the fixed blade from her throat, pealed through the air. He saw she now had her own dagger in her hand and plunged it deep into the leg of the man holding her, stabbing again and again into the unmoving statue. He heard the orders from Hilbrun for him to get to his feet, to fight.

And in the back of it all, a *crack* sounded.

A resonating sound that was familiar to Delvan. The sound of a crossbow firing, which drew his focus back in like a magnet. His head spun, looking for the weapons wielder. To his right he saw the hole in the wall, a short man kneeling at its opening. He held a crossbow in hand, the drawstring loose and aiming past Delvan.

He spun his head and the pain vanished as adrenaline flooded him. His eyes lurched open, and with a drowning agony that ripped through his chest—a pain that suffocated that of his broken rib—he saw Hilbrun's hands loosen, a blank stare on his face. An arrow shaft protruded from his chest, piercing the dyed leather just below the lip of the darksteel plate. Hilbrun looked down at the fletched bolt and touched it with a confounded brush of his finger, then fell to his knees, staring at Delvan, his mouth open and eyes distant in shock.

Delvan felt the pain of flesh leave him as the torture of grief took its place.

"*NO!*" The word started as a low, guttural growl and shifted octaves to a chilling cry. A battle scream that would have petrified even the most tested of warriors. His face stung with rage and his chest filled with the boiling pressure of fury as he watched his friend slump to the ground.

As Hilbrun's grip fully released the two men—formerly effigies within the soul-clench of the fallen Reacher—found themselves free to move. The grimy, bald one screamed in horrific pain, able to finally react to the stab wounds the woman had inflicted into his upper leg. He fell to the floor, gripping the gashes in an attempt to slow the profuse bleeding, releasing his captive in the process. The man in black that had been talking fled behind the girth of the bull that had struck and now loomed above Delvan.

Delvan, still on the floor with his back to the wall, raised an outstretched arm and glared at the man who'd rammed him with darkened eyes. Only a mere two steps away, the man hesitated, his head tilting with a confused expression as he looked down upon Delvan's collapsed figure.

He did not realize, in his ignorance, what a danger it was to be in Delvan's proximity. He did not realize, in his stupidity, the wild power that brewed inside of the crumpled form before him. He did not realize that he was standing in an unequivocal radius of death.

Delvan released a blood curdling scream, and before his palm flared a light, one that exploded into a torrent of yellow and orange as a spinning vortex of immolation spewed outward. A heat flooded the room as he cast flame and ire at the oversized man, the licking flames tasting flesh and devouring the behemoth as the fire swallowed him entirely.

The screams as he burned alive etched themselves into the stone walls. He flailed his arms for not but a moment before he was incinerated, a pile of scorched skin and muscle collapsing into a heap on the floor at Delvan's feet.

Delvan pulled himself up, the pain in his side an abstract thought, hidden behind a wall of wrath. He held his hand to the side, palm upward while he glowered at the filth responsible for Hilbrun's demise. The high brow and sneer of the man's weasel-like face depicted pure horror at the charred remains of his companion. The impulse struck the man to try and reload his crossbow, perhaps to make an attempt to take down Delvan.

It was a fatal mistake. He should have run.

A ball of flame began to coalesce above Delvan's palm, the spectrum of oranges swirling and twisting inward upon themselves, expanding continuously. The sphere grew larger than his outstretched hand before the crossbow could even be drawn, and with all his might, Delvan flung the orb of searing death at the assailer.

It struck directly in his rotten chest. A cry echoed in the chamber as the diminutive man dropped his weapon and fled down the tunnel, running frantically as he tried without success to extinguish the flames that quickly engulfed his face and hair. Delvan heard the sound of a splash in the distance, and the screams ceased with satisfying finality.

He picked up his sword and walked past the groaning bald man on the floor. He was grunting as he attempted to further himself from Delvan, gripping his blood-soaked leg, his head sweating. Delvan would leave him for later, perhaps they could get him to talk before he bled out. Either way, Delvan preferred the idea of him suffering on the floor instead of the quick, singeing death he could offer. He marched toward the vault door, there was a remaining threat that needed to be removed.

*Where is he?!* his mind raged, as he looked for the man in black. He wouldn't leave one of them standing. They would meet their end through him. He would avenge Hilbrun.

Another scream. This one from behind.

He turned around, finding the man with the bleeding leg hobbling and somehow upright. His arm was raised, dagger in hand, set to plunge down upon Delvan like a wolf's fangs into the neck of its prey. Delvan took a step back and nearly lost his balance as the blade's edge brushed past him, glancing off his chest plate.

He realized it wasn't this attacker who'd cried out, however. Someone else, with a higher pitch, released a lengthy cry in the background.

There was a flash of gold and a blur of motion as the woman jumped on the man's back and drove her own dagger directly into the chest of Delvan's would-be assassin. The bald man howled as he dropped his knife to the stone floor then grabbed the woman and flung her from his back. Delvan heard a loud crack as her head smacked against the floor, her eyes closing and body going still.

Delvan raised his hand as the last flicker of life in the man's eyes looked back at him with a cold hollowness. Delvan was going to have the grim satisfaction of taking that last moment from him, of having him endure the excruciating pain only otherwise experienced on the burning pyre. He cascaded a river of flames over the man, those sunken eyes turning a deep black as the fire flowed over them, his figure curling inward upon itself as he dropped to the floor and smoldered.

The smell of burnt flesh engulfed the room, its pungence only offset by the smoke that was billowing as the banners on the walls roared in a blaze. The tiles mounted on the ceiling were falling and shattering on the floor, the wooden beams becoming exposed and starting to flicker with the glow of fingers of fire that wrapped around them.

Delvan felt a push from his back, having turned it to the vault door to address his previous attacker. He stumbled two steps forward but held his footing and spun to see a dark streak across the room. The man in black was fleeing towards the tunnel, his outline a contrast to the fires' intense power.

Delvan grew another sphere of fire above his hand and drew his hand back to throw. But before the ball even exceeded the size of his fist it sputtered, and with a puff, was no greater than a candle's tip.

His inanite was drained. The filaments of the ebony mineral that striated the stone around his feet were blanched, and he knew the blocks in his pouch were completely muted to a brilliant white.

*No! He CANNOT escape!* he screamed in his mind as the man reached the tunnel's entrance.

He put his left hand against the cold, darksteel vault door and pointed his other forward. A concentrated stream of flame spouted from his palm, driving through the air like water from a spigot. It illuminated the tunnel in a wash of light, and in the distance, beyond the narrow escape's end, he caught a glimpse of the flames' tendrils finding their target. But in a flash the coward was gone, turning down the main sewer beyond. Around Delvan's hand the blackened steel had begun to turn a milky white, the discoloration radiating out like the glow of the rising sun.

Delvan took two steps forward and stopped. He wanted to chase the thief and turn him to ash as he watched the life fade from his eyes. Slowly. Painfully. He wanted him to answer for what had happened to Hilbrun. But he looked back at the room, thick with smoggy smoke, Hilbrun's body on the floor alongside the woman who had risked her life to save him rather than running to her own freedom. He couldn't leave. He couldn't abandon Hilbrun, or anyone else he owed his life to.

Delvan ran over to his fallen friend, the life drained from his pale face. He dropped to his knees and held him, ignoring the flames that threatened to collapse the ceiling down on them. He needed to do something. He needed to help them but found himself unable to move. He cried out Hilbrun's name as an anguish ran wild inside his heart, trampling every thought within his mind and pulverizing his soul. The only thing he could do was kneel there and pray for his friend back, to beg with Strigifious that his owl had claimed the wrong man. If he could have exchanged places at that moment, there would have been no hesitation. This was the person who had taken him under his wing, who had trusted him with his life... and he'd failed him.

The door above burst open. Delvan looked up through reddened eyes and saw Rwendal standing there, several guards at his back. The old man's eyes went wide with terror, then he began to shout commands in a frenzy, screaming to save the items in the vault and to remove Hilbrun.

Soldiers filed down, scrambling into the scorching furnace that the vault and anteroom had become. A guard pulled him free of Hilbrun, two others lifting and rushing his limp figure up the stairs. The rest of the group sprinted into the vault, attempting to salvage all that they could in the fleeting moments available.

They ignored the bodies on the floor, two instead running to the hole in the wall and disappearing into its shadows. A guard frantically asked if he was injured. Delvan shook his head as he knelt there in a stupor, his eyes distant and fixed. His world spun around and was collapsing into him, everything feeling heavy, like he was molded from lead.

He looked around, unphased by the furious panic surrounding him. He looked at the girl on the floor, her chest moving slightly with shallow breaths, her eyes shut, and the back of her head bleeding. The guards flowed past her like ants around a twig, she was an obstacle to them. An enemy.

*I can't...* he couldn't think beyond those words. The crack of a wood beam above him triggered something in his mind, a switch that began to wake him from his trance. An ember of urgency kindled within him and grew into a flame.

He walked over to the girl—ignoring the pain in his side—and lifted her from the ground, pulling her over his shoulder. The awkward motion sent pain reeling through him, but he couldn't allow himself to fail anyone else. He had to save one who'd done the same for him.

He hiked up the stairs, his feet landing with the weight of loss. Coughing soldiers bounded around him, carrying whatever they could from the vault. The coughing, raspy voice of Rwendal shouted the order to seal the vault, and the men slammed the massive door shut with a weighty thud. Perhaps they thought that would save the contents? Delvan knew it was unlikely.

Fire did not forgive.

He could hear Rwendal choking as he screamed to evacuate the building and call the fire brigade. He stepped past the man, his white hair flaked with ash, and into the room he and Hilbrun had passed through earlier. Flames had burst through the floor from below and were beginning to consume the fueling contents of the space, leaving black scars across the ceiling as they climbed the mountains of merchandise.

Delvan followed the trail of guards who didn't even seem to notice him in the frenzy, their priority the desperate attempt to save what they could. Their panicked scurrying led him to the building's front entrance, piling what they could on the front lawn where the grass grew from imported soil, an uncommon sight in a city of stone. It was being soaked by the rain which now came down in a deluge, black clouds above slightly grayed by the unseen sunrise in the distant east.

Beyond the mounds of hoarded valuables was the body of Hilbrun, a guard standing above him. Delvan heaved himself forward, taking step after despondent step. He rested the girl on the grass beside his fallen comrade, the rain washing soot from her stilled face.

Rain soaked through him as he fell to his knees and cradled Hilbrun's fallen body in his arms. It was merely a sprinkle compared to the downpour running from his eyes as he wept. Flames burst out of the windows behind him, the fire spreading destruction indiscriminately, cleansing the guild headquarters with its unforgiving heat. He didn't care.

Nothing mattered now.

He was alone.

# Chapter Twenty

*One, two, three, four, five, six, seven, eight, nine, ten, eleven... One, two, three, four, five, six, seven, eight, nine, ten, eleven... One, two, three, four, five, six, seven, eight, nine, ten, eleven... One, two, three, four, five, six, seven, eight, nine, ten, eleven... Twelve?*
Recited for endless hours,
Fourth Day of Spring, Fifty-fifth Year of the Seventh Epoch

*WAKE, CHILD.*

The voice was less thunderous than in Desnia's previous dreams, more a whipping storm upon the sea than a seismic shift within her mind. She had not been carried to some distant plane, the ominous haze she was so accustomed to absent from the horizon. The world around her was palpable, there at the edge of her mind, but separated by the membrane of consciousness.

*YOU MUST RECOVER THE MAGE, PULL HIS INCARCERATED SOUL FROM THE DEPTHS. THEN FLEE.*

It carried the faintest hint of urgency. She'd never heard it fluctuate from anything other than its commanding overture before. It came as though talking *to* her, rather than talking *at* her.

She could feel her body, her soul connected to it with tangible sensations abound. There was a wet chill upon her skin, a burnt feeling in her throat, and her head swam in pain. Not the crushing vice she'd always associated with his voice—instead it radiated from the back of her head, pulsating with every heartbeat.

*Where am I?* she wondered.

She remembered fire.

Memories flashed into her mind in rapid succession. Breaking into the vault, Magnar's betrayal, the arrival of Blues, stabbing Grunner in the chest.

Then, nothing.

Desnia's heart raced, exacerbating the pounding in her skull, and she felt her muscles tense as she called out in a panicked fright. She thought for a moment that she might be dead, that this tortured darkness was how her soul would spend eternity. She was afraid, stricken with anguish at the thought that the voice might follow her to the beyond, that she would never escape her eternal tormentor.

No. This had to be a dream. He would not have called to her to wake if she'd been taken by winged talons. Her consciousness screamed to be released from the smothering disconnect. The curtain needed to be drawn back, the light of the waking world her only thought.

*Let. Me. OUT!* she demanded in her mind.

Her eyes snapped open.

Her back lay flat on oddly soft ground. The storm above poured rain upon her face, its turbulent rumblings only matched by the chaotic inferno that had once been the Merchants' Guild headquarters—now a pyre that soared into the sky and touched the clouds themselves, fighting a battle in an eternal war. Around her people were running frantically, their desperate shouts merely fanning the flames and furthering the pandemonium.

Splitting pain shot through the back of her head as she tried to turn it, causing her to wince and bring her hand to her skull. She gingerly pressed her fingers to the source, unknowing how severe the wound was, her hair soaked from the rain. She pulled her hand before her face, finding rain-diluted blood painted onto her fingertips.

Desnia tilted her head in a slower, more gradual manner. Her body was stiff, unmoving while her overstimulated mind tried to assess the damage to her head. To her right was the gated iron fence, a crowd gathering outside its barbed limits as the early morning onlookers stared at the flame in a reverent awe, a somber astonishment infecting them all in the heat of the flames.

She tilted her head to her left, her body finally deigning to move her other arm and bend a knee as it tested her mobility. The flames burned with an intensity that dwarfed the hottest summer sun, its oppressing heat beating against her. Outlined in the center of the blaze not but a few feet from her, like a shade born from its heart, was the Blue who had ignited the destructive force.

He knelt, holding his dead partner in his arms. His features became clearer as she stared at him, fixed in place. The initial panic of awakening to the havoc all around faded and was replaced with a deep, endless void of grief, a vacuum that pulled and threatened to collapse her inward. Tears welled in her eyes as they met his. Looking into them, she knew that she was not just witnessing his emotions—the blood-shot eyes sunken in ash-covered skin, the hunch of his back, the trembling gasps of breath—she was sharing them.

So much sorrow. So much despair.

Desnia began to extend her arm towards him. The excruciating connection of empathy tore through her, wanting to reach out and ease his internal strife. Their eyes locked in shared suffering, the world whirling around them while time stopped in their bubble of misery.

A pain shot through her skull like lightning. She squeezed her eyes closed and clutched her head as it ricocheted through her brain and rang in her ears. From deep inside herself she heard the resonating voice, one which had never before bellowed during a waking moment.

*RUN!*

She hoarsely cried out as the agony rooted itself and dug its fingers into her head.

*You're not real,* she thought desperately, *you're only in my dreams.*

*I AM AS VERITABLE AS THE RAIN ON YOUR FACE OR THE LOSS IN THE KNIGHT'S HEART. HE CANNOT YET AID YOU, YOU MUST FLY. SALVAGE THE MAGE. I WILL GUIDE FOR AS LONG AS I AM ABLE. GO.*

Desnia didn't just hear but *felt* the urgency in its tone. She knew that her life depended on this moment, the truth of that knowledge imprinted upon her with indisputable clarity. There was something underlying the message, she noticed. An almost imperceptible emotion that betrayed a truth about the master of her dreams.

Fear.

It was afraid. Of what she couldn't be certain. Was it worried about her endangerment? Was it concerned for its own safety for some reason? It was minuscule, nearly entirely hidden from her, but it was there. As assuredly as her life was in danger at this moment, it was there, hidden behind a deafening, regal superiority.

The ache faded and Desnia opened her eyes. A force that coursed through her entire body brought her to her knees, planting one foot solidly in the trampled grass and forcing her up with a thrust of her leg. Her back straightened as she stood and took one last look at the grieving Blue, his eyes still lost in mourning as he watched Desnia pull herself up.

A nearby guard, previously distracted by the roaring fire, noticed Desnia clamoring to her feet and shouted. The bonded, anguishing grief the Blue held for his fallen friend was flushed from her in an instant as adrenaline pumped through her body. She spared the Blue one last glance and then turned and ran, a foot partially slipping on the grass. She caught herself with an outreached hand and regained her balance despite her dizziness as her legs carried her forward.

The guard's hand landed on her shoulder with a fierce grip. She spun and landed a kick of her boot-tip directly on the man's shin. He dropped his spear with a wail of pain and fell to the ground as he clutched the damaged bone. With a wobbly spin Desnia was running back towards the gate.

The cacophony of cries and yelling blending with the omnipresent static of the burning building drowned out the injured guard's commands to seize Desnia while she was sprinting past the floundering guards and guildsmen. Before anyone could realize who she was or that she was attempting to escape, she reached the gates—opened for the fire brigade—and forced herself into the throng of spectators.

With the lithe and grace associated with a lifetime of practice, she maneuvered through the mass of people. A correctly angled, slight push, then a twist and slide between someone's back and another's chest, and a duck below the adjacent shoulders of two taller men were all a part of the dance. Like a fish swimming against the current, she carefully made her way through, every motion a natural instinct. Meanwhile, a guard screamed futile orders to the bystanders and attempted to brutishly force his way through the front of the crowd, making little headway as Desnia reached the thinning rear.

She saw a clear line through the remaining people, their figures casting long shadows on the wet cobbles as though pointing her towards safety and took off in a run. She wobbled as her legs propelled her forward, vomiting mid-stride as she tried to maintain her balance despite her disorientation, refusing to stop for anything.

A compass within her directed each step, keeping her on the correct path with an unquestionable certainty. This was the route she must take, the one that led to freedom.

The realization of the full scope of her plight came together in her mind as her boots splashed through the puddles collecting along the street that led away from the guild. She had been at the scene of a crime, one which included stolen sapphires, a murdered Blue, and the destruction of a building and the immeasurable value of its contents—its proprietors being some of the most powerful men in the kingdom.

*They'll hang me without a second thought,* she knew. *Or something much, much worse.* She shuddered at the thought of being displayed in a square for weeks on end, begging for quick death while being tortured in ways that would prolong her life for as long as miserably possible.

A plan that she had forged over the years, one which she never dared enact, was now her only option. She needed to get to her stash, where what she'd skimmed from her jobs with Mixton was hidden. Then she could—

She skidded to a halt. A vacant street lay ahead of her, and the guards, still in pursuit, were far enough behind that she didn't have to worry—yet. Why had she stopped? Her body had followed an instruction, but had it come from her?

The compass that had been guiding her forward now redirected her immediately to the left, and Desnia realized that she was standing on the exact bridge she'd dropped the ring from the previous night.

*Oh no,* she thought. *No. That wasn't... Please!*

She tried to fight, but she knew what she needed to do. There was no commanding voice to compel the instruction. Instead, she felt a magnetic pull, urging her in that specific direction, filling her with a comforting reassurance. It spoke without words, conveying what must be done through a calming of her fear, and an ease of anxiety.

With the screams of a winded guard fast approaching, Desnia climbed onto the balustrade and dove head-first into the water below. She plunged into the water, delving nearly to the bottom of the canal. Her arm reached forward, like a moth to a candle it was drawn to a point. In that moment and the time after she could not have said why, but it extended with a mind of its own and from the silty floor of the murky water it clutched a small bundle, slipping it into Desnia's pocket.

As though back from a dream, her arm was her own again. Holding her breath, she swam under the water's surface which was being pitted by the torrential rain above. Her lungs burned and her head throbbed, but she was encouraged to swim onward until she reached a set of loading stairs that stepped down into the canal for dock deliveries. She broke the water's surface around the corner of this stairwell with a desperate gasp of air, out of sight of the guards on the bridge behind her.

Desnia crawled up the steps, a few of the earliest rising workers looking at her in confusion as she battled to catch her breath, drenched and dripping water. She pulled herself up, the tug of the internal compass was beginning to fade, but she knew where she needed to go. This was her realm, the streets as familiar as the sound of rain that fell all around.

With a small stumble she righted herself and increased her pace to a full-on sprint. She wouldn't have much time. She made her way towards the port, the instinctual need to flee the city having stayed strong, even as the guiding pull within had retracted.

Desnia, years ago, had concocted a dream—one of her own design, a waking goal rather than a slumbering nightmare. It sought to escape the chain of her newfound warden—Mixton—and go wherever his oppressive arm could not extend. She had begun to stash what she could skim from her thefts—a few moons here, an emerald or two there, even a couple suns on the last job—away in locations throughout the city. She couldn't trust leaving it in her own home of course, Mixton could have searched it whenever he pleased, and he was known to be as thorough as he was shrewd.

Her grand design had faded after witnessing the result of a few people attempting the same scheme. Some had been careless, practically begging to be caught, but others, including a few that she even held a scant amount of respect for, all experienced the same fate. A slow death and a wet grave. She kept skimming money as a defiant act of hope, but she never thought she'd *actually* follow through with the idea.

She was left with little choice, however, and knew she had to take the risk.

One of her hidden caches was near the port. She had needed to make sure it would be accessible if she were to be forced to leave the others, and there was the slight amount of devious pleasure she got from hiding money stolen from Mixton so close to his operations.

She forced herself to slow her pace to a walk. Desnia knew—being well beyond the reach of the guild's guards at this point—her best chance of escape was to blend with a crowd. The rain kept the street mostly empty, aside from the few people going to their shops for opening preparations, and it had the advantage of stopping people from wondering how she had become soaked to the core after her swim.

With her hood low and path kept to the street's edge, she made her way through the granite arteries of the city. Branches and turns brought her to where she needed to go—avoiding the heavily guarded square near an outpost, holding to one street because a small gang controlled the one adjacent. These bits of knowledge helped her flow to her destination, unhindered by obstructions.

Finally, Desnia reached the stone staircase she was looking for. Its fluted railing curled outward at the base, a small alcove carved into each of the two sides containing a small figurine of Amenesol. The nearby buildings, presumably built after the staircase, were so cramped that they nearly abutted the edges of the staircase's base, making the idols nearly inaccessible.

After scanning for curious eyes, Desnia hopped into one of these crannies and reached into a small cavity, hidden behind a loose stone on the backside of the carving. She slid out a leather pouch, the telltale jingle of coinage coming from within as she gripped it in her hand. She sighed a small breath of relief.

There wasn't much money here, Desnia's full collection of her stashed coinage hadn't been enough for a carefree life by any means. But it could buy her passage, once she was out of the city. If she could get out of the city.

Which brought her to the more difficult part of her plan.

She tucked the money away and continued down the street, reaching the main gate to the port after restraining herself to a walking pace. She checked constantly over her shoulder, expecting at any moment for guards from the Merchants' Guild or royal soldiers to come running up behind her to drag her away. Desnia ducked behind a stack of crates and cautiously peered past the blind's edge.

Above the nearby roofs an orange glow could be seen casting a beacon of light onto the clouds above it, billowing smoke visible even through the rain as it rose and blended with the dark clouds above. The docks had come to a rare standstill, crowds gathering to gawk and point at the fiery destruction in the distance.

She searched for dock workers—the ones in Mixton's employ, painfully obvious to the trained eye—and began counting. There were always three to a pier, and she slowly accounted for all of them on the one directly ahead of her, and each adjacent. They, like everyone else, were completely enthralled with the radiant inferno.

*Never going to get a better opportunity than this,* she thought.

She passed through the open gate without a second glance from any of its guards, all equally engrossed in the distant fire's glow. Walking along the docks was still too risky, even with the distraction she could draw attention. Rather, she slunk off the side of the causeway into the reedy muck below and carefully made her way to the boardwalk's edge, holding tight to the pile supports of the wooden decking, the splashing of rain masking her motions as she waded through reeking water that became deeper with every step.

She reached the boardwalk's edge, now swimming, and stroked forward as quietly as she could, the planks of the thick wooden dock shielding her from above. She swam out under the pier and along its length, water lapping against the hulls of ships to either side.

Desnia did her best to judge the ships from their hulls. She sought one that would be smaller, hoping that they wouldn't be able to afford the docking fees for an extended period and would be gone a few hours from now. But it also needed to be large enough that she could stow away without being noticed.

Not that she had much time to be picky.

At the end of the pier—her arms barely able to push through the water, legs screaming with fire in her muscles—she found a ship that met her criteria. As best it could, anyway. She swam to its side and tried to pull herself up the small ledges the sailors considered rungs. It was all she could do not to cry out as her arm struggled to drag her bodyweight from the buoyant water. Her fingers held tight as she refused to let go, years of climbing giving her the endurance to hold on despite her fatigue. She slowly made her way up the several rungs with excruciating effort, her face grimacing all the while.

Peeking over the hull's lip onto the deck she found it was empty, save for one deckhand standing at the bow in awe of the distant fire. Desnia dragged herself onto the deck, trying to relax her breathing as her lungs attempted to gasp for air, the now torrential rain helping to muffle her movements. She couldn't afford to alert anyone now.

She sidled over to the entrance of the hold and climbed down its ladder as stealthily as she could manage. It was nearly empty save for a few crates near the bow marked "Aliova". She climbed behind one and shrunk herself into a corner. The foreign presence that had guided her faded, abandoning her to the pain in her quivering body.

The memory of the shared, crippling grief experienced by the Blue sunk deep into her chest. Tears squeezed from her eyes and over a shaking lip. Trying to quietly steady her breathing, she wished to be numb, to push down the emotions with deadened weight, or even anger. She should be angry at this all—the betrayal by Magnar that she should have foreseen, the death of the Blue that she would surely be held at fault for, the destruction of property, and more.

Instead, the anger was replaced with something else. A driving insecurity as to her future, a voyage into the unfamiliar, and lack of a plan bred a wild uncertainty. It paralyzed her, a maelstrom of doubts ravenously consuming her. The utter exhaustion of the night's events was the only anchor that held her from slipping. That, and the driving instinct of survival that was so deeply ingrained.

Fear meant death, yet death struck fear. Surviving was to walk the rope between.

Desnia wondered how long she could balance.

**END PART 1**

# PART 2
## DESTINATION

# Chapter
# Twenty-One

*This land, barren as it is, flourishes with life. How this has come to pass is contrary to all facts that are now clearly not but incorrect assumptions. Even with our abilities becoming diminutive from the prevailing scarcity of vidut, the locals revere us as gods. Their submissive nature will make harvesting an easy task.*

The arid morning breeze rippled across Nerio's robes as he walked along the colorful street. The white attire was a contrast to his dark skin, a single red ring around the cuffs of his sleeve the only splash of color on his humble priestly robes.

Brazen rays of the desert sun were cresting over the eaves of the stout adobe buildings surrounding him, warming the mud-brick pavers beneath his sandals. It brought life and vibrancy to the bright pastel shades of the densely packed structures, their colors as varietal as a rainbow after a spring rain.

Nerio had once thought it to be a divisive way to express one's piety, painting your home to identify to which god you were the most devout. But spending the majority of his, albeit young, life in the service of the church had shown him that Cordism did not place one god above another. Each served an important function, sharing an equal stature among their peers. That the farmer should pray to Almedia for rain, and the hunter to Ursorner for blessings, bore less ill-will than Nerio had once considered. Their deific voices were heard and relayed by the King, and through Him the priests spread their words. Though he felt less like a messenger and more a studious listener of late.

Nerio approached his destination, a broad white building with narrow slits for windows, a royal guard standing in the shade of a small awning, resolute in his station. White paint in Brethefen marked the building as one belonging to the church, the neutral color an equal devotion to all, though in the case of this structure it served a dual purpose.

He strolled past the guard and through the door. White poured into the interior, and the thick mud walls still clutched the night's chill, cooling the space. Nerio walked to the attendant who sat at a desk in the anteroom, waiting to sign in for the day as the man jotted notes in a thick ledger.

"King and His grace upon you, Brother Nerio," the robed man greeted. Several rings of differing colors climbed from his cuff to his elbow, the white of his robe matching the hair on his face and head. "I hope all is well this morning. When you get inside, can you please find Brother Algus and make him aware of your arrival? He is the only person left from the night shift and may want to head home, t'was a long night."

"Loud?" asked Nerio.

"Indeed," the priest said with a nod, "one of them received another disavowal letter from their family yesterday. Took it rather poorly, and the melancholy spread through the place like a virus. I swear some of these houses do it just to stop paying their board, caring more about their own coffers than those of the church. When did nobility stop acting nobly?...

"Anyway, perhaps they will sleep through the day for you; not sure any of them got much of it last night."

The aloof nature of his tone panged Nerio with sadness nearly as deeply as the thought of someone's family patriarch casting their own child aside for the simple reason of being born different. These people needed support, not dismissal.

With tightly pressed lips he nodded to the attendant and walked through the door behind him, leading to a small sitting chamber where dust covered chairs and benches lined the walls, a preparatory room and kitchen through the door beyond.

He collected a large jug of medicine and several cups from the kitchen before making his way down the nearby corridor. White pervaded throughout: muted inanite tiles for the floors; walls, ceilings and doors coated in the same pure white paint as the exterior, dyed heavily with muted inanite.

The hallway was lined with doors, the heavy wood framing a small, barred window in the center of each. A single guard sat in the center of one of the long hallways, nodding off even as Nerio made his way past him.

He opened the door at the far end of the corridor where he heard muttering from inside, unlocking it with one of the many keys hanging from the white sash around his waist. The patient inside was one of the few currently awake on this floor and should have his treatment administered now so that he could rest, likely having been up all night. He would find Brother Algus—probably on the second floor—later.

Inside was a middle-aged man wearing simple white trousers and shirt, huddled in a corner. His eyes were soaked with red, staring off to a distant location beyond the cell's walls.

"Good morning, Lord Grundan," Nerio said in a placating manner, "would you like some medicine? You look like you could use some sleep."

"Y-Yes," said the man shakily. "Couldn't sleep last night, everyone screaming about our old lives, how *his* voice was calling. Thought it best to avoid sleep for a while, let him try to visit the others instead."

Nerio pulled the cork from the jug and poured the murky mixture into a ceramic cup, handing it to the man then sitting in the chair by the bed. Grundan would drink it in his own time, and Nerio was not in a rush. He found that they were more likely to drink the concoction while he was in the room, and he got a certain gratification from giving them a reprieve from the loneliness of their caged lives.

Lord Grundan sipped on the drink, cringing slightly with each mouthful. They flavored it with tea, but it did little to mask the chalky flavor. He visibly began to calm and looked toward Nerio with weary eyes. "Some days it all seems so overwhelming, you know?" he said with vague lucidity. Nerio wondered if Grundan were really addressing him, or speaking to himself, his gaze still distant. "I can't decide if my thoughts are my own, whether you are truly real or merely a figment of my forced imagination. I wonder why the gods chose such a life for us. All of us."

*Why indeed,* Nerio thought poignantly, turning to stare out the thin slit of a window. The gods must be testing them—all of them—and he wondered at the varying degrees of harshness. There was a reason, he was certain of that, but it did not mean that it hurt any less. Perhaps that was the point...

After a few moments he helped Lord Grundan into bed, a sleepless night making for a quick passage into the land of quiet dreams. Nerio left and locked the door. He had many more patients to see today, and he wasn't sure how many other brothers and sisters of the clergy would be here to help.

While duties *could* be forcefully assigned by the clergy—some of the critical roles always retained a minimum, non-rotating staff—many were at-will. And, even though there were many peaceful moments such as this, events like the ones reported the previous night were somewhat common here.

It made for a rather unpopular assignment.

Nerio gained a sense of satisfaction from it, a cooling oasis in the parched desert, but he could understand why others so often found it unappealing. Before he got to more patients, Nerio found Brother Algus and encouraged him to head home for rest, or to at least find a vacant room and lay his head down for a time. Several of the residents were sleeping off their nightly outburst, so Nerio started his round on the second floor, where the afflicted who were... quieter resided.

He reached the first door and looked in to find a young woman, perhaps in her mid-twenties, in a gown standing motionless, staring out the thin portal to the outside world. He could only see her back, and if not for the color of skin on the hands to her side, he'd have assumed her to be carved from stone.

He stood quietly himself, a mirrored image of empathy. Her pain resonated within him, the hollow grief of a life lost, tormented to live within a cell of emotion, the white walls a physical representation of the caged mind. It chiseled away at his core, the mined pit threatening to break through the skin and sink him into an abyss.

*'Illness of the mind shall corrupt the body, and in doing so, trap the soul,'* he quoted in his mind, the passage of scripture an incongruous adage.

He heard an unsteady shuffle of feet, breaking him from his trance of sympathy. He looked to his side and saw a Hand at the end of the hall, carrying a bucket but obviously quite lost. It was a frequent occurrence.

He waved and then beckoned her over with a thin smile. She moved to him with a more assured beat, leaning to counter the weight of the bucket in her hand, a sloshing sound coming from it as specks of water spilled over the sides and splashed onto her robes.

"Yes, Brother?" she asked. She was maybe a year older than Nerio, her robe white with a white ring around each cuff. She also had dark skin, hair long and in thick locks, her face one of confusion. She was probably a newer member of the Holy Hands and had been given this assignment without knowing what it entailed.

"Are you new here?" he asked politely.

"Is it tha' obvious?" she said with a sigh and brush of her hair. Her street accent was especially heavy. "I was jus' assigned here this mornin', buh nobody's been able to tell me nothin' abow whas I'm suppose' to do here. I grabbed this wash buck here and have been tryin' to find mah way around like a lost street dog.

"And whas with everyone in this place? They has abow as much goin' on behind their eyes as my gran before she died. Freakish. Givin' me the creeps, it is. And you're the firs' priest I've seen since I arrived."

Nerio felt his heart sink at her assessment, one shared by so many that came and left through here. He would have to see if he could convert her to a different perspective.

"Hmm," he said with a nod. "Not a popular assignment, this one, so we tend to be a little short staffed, as this post isn't ordained as 'critical'. I understand your feelings, though I think perhaps it's a little misguided? Some of us are here to help these trapped souls and, gods willing, make them comfortable until their owl eventually comes for them. They require help as much as any in need, whether that be you or I. Would you mind helping me with this woman here?" he asked as he unlocked the door.

The Hand shrugged, clearly having little else to do. They walked in and Nerio set down a cup and began to pour a copious dose of medicine for the woman, who seemed oblivious to their presence.

*Did I forget the cup in Lord Grungan's chambers?* he wondered as he noticed he had fewer than when he'd started. *I'll have to go get it later.*

"Whas wrong with her?" the Hand asked as she cautiously walked to the motionless woman's side, staring at her eyes with a curious look.

"Some patients are more acutely afflicted than others," he said, placing the cork back in the bottle. "Despite all of our treatments, their visions persist and mental fortitude falters. We're forced to perform a procedure, one which can make their life more... comfortable." The word sickened him as he said it, a repetition of his superiors which he had no choice but to obey. How he wished there was another way.

"You make 'em dumb?" she asked, an ignorant innocence to her question.

"We take away the voices," Nerio said.

*I hope, anyway,* he prayed, his faith telling him that in the life after they could be made whole once again.

"Whah kinda thing does *tha'* to a person," she asked, a contorted expression on her face.

"It's called a lobotomy," Nerio answered as he walked over. "Now please, help me just rotate her—yes, just like that—and guide her to the chair..."

They maneuvered the woman—her expression blank and eyes fixed on the distant horizon—to a sitting position on the bed. He just needed to grab the cup for her, and she should be able to—

A flit of the woman's eyes caught his attention. Never had he seen one who'd undergone the procedure move their eyes in such a rapid way. They became focused on the chest of the Hand, who still leaned over as to adjust the woman's sitting posture. Nerio now noticed a small necklace dangling there, the true fixation of the patient. He hadn't seen it earlier, the dark string and carved black block blending with the Hand's skin tone.

With a surprising and impossible quickness, the woman's hand sprang from her side and clenched the medallion, her eyes piercing into the Hand's. A voice rumbled from her, a depth to it that sounded unnatural from the dainty woman, "Free me! Release me from these chains of imprisonment and set me back upon the world!"

The Hand's eyes went wide as she jerked back and screamed, snapping the necklace free. Nerio quickly grabbed the thin strings and pulled it from the patient's tight grip as she resisted with both hands, her strength surprising.

He stumbled backward as he pulled the jewelry free, and as the woman regained her own balance, she lunged forward in an attempt to take it back from Nerio, a piercing scream coming from her sneered face. He extended his arm backward beyond her reach, his free arm struggling to hold the woman back as she flailed like a wild animal. The Hand, rather than assisting him, fled from the room in fright.

With as strong a push as his thin arms could manage, he flung the woman back at the bed, taking the brief escape to scramble from the room and slam the door behind him. There would be nothing he could do until the woman's symptoms passed. Trying to make her take any medicine during an episode would be like trying to feed a rabid dog.

He looked at the black necklace then to the Hand, who was trembling with her back against a wall.

"Didn't anyone tell you that you can't bring inanite in here?" he asked as he caught his breath, holding up the necklace as the woman screamed from within the cell, pounding her fists against the doors.

"Nobody told me nothin' abow that," she said, raising her voice in self-defense. Sweat dripped from her brow as she panted for breath. "These people, they cursed. A demon's possessed tha' woman, it ain' natural."

It wasn't the first time he'd heard the statement. This Hand's words carried less vitriol than some of the others, maybe he could convince her to stay. He gave her the same explanation that had been provided to him.

"I assure you, there are no demons, or haunts, or souls that possess these people. The principles have all agreed that these people simply have symptoms of an illness of the mind and have a hard time differentiating what is imagined and what is real. The gods chose this role for them for reasons we cannot begin to understand, and they are afflicted as such to test our virtues as much as their own. It is our duty to help them and try to make their lives comfortable.

"But that cannot be done if you bring inanite anywhere near them. You need to make sure you check the rules at the front office with the high priest, understand?"

The other patients along the hall were now becoming riled at the sounds of the high-pitched screams coming from the cell behind Nerio. The cacophony perturbed the Hand even further, her glances rapid and hands pulled tightly to her chest.

He held out the necklace and she took it back with a shaking hand. "Go, ask Sister Gruthga to send another Hand or two and take the day to calm yourself. When you return, be sure to leave the necklace and any other inanite with the attendant downstairs or in your quarters."

She nodded and scurried away, trying to keep a distance from each cell door she weaved through the hall. Nerio knew she wouldn't be back. Too many carried the same superstitions of the Ones Before, despite the religious foundation of Cordism that saturated the city. The most holy of cities outside of Calentine itself somehow still was an intermingled mixing pot of beliefs. The principles said that each of the citizens found their way to Cordism in the end. Pagan rituals and reverence were forbidden, but the blasphemies persisted. Too many of the city's eldest generation remembered the ways of Trethefen across the White Mountains from before the civil war a century ago, taught to them by their parents or grandparents, and such heritage was difficult to root out.

Assuaged moans were emanating from the cell as the effects of the inanite exposure began to wear off. Nerio looked through the viewing hole on the door and watched as the erratic motions of the woman inside slowed and faded into stillness like dust settling after a windstorm. He made a mental note of her comments to mark in the ledger, wondering at the recurring theme of these rantings.

To most, the ramblings seemed just that, innocuous words of the deranged. Many never worked in the Asylum long enough to hear the repeated phrases, spoken by people who had never once met, and could not be found in any literature that Nerio had yet to find. It itched at him, a curiosity drowned in pity. And then there was the question of why Principle Jerdine had ordained that their words be recorded, the logs sent away once filled to never be seen again.

The principles vehemently insisted that their patients were not a group possessed. But the voice that cut through the halls so often—a deep, unnatural tone—spoke to a singular mind. Perhaps it was that they all suffered a disease of identical origin. The strangeness of it irked him. Was it possible that a god, maybe even the great Amenesol himself, spoke through these men and women? Had he attempted to make them his messiahs, and they'd reacted by locking them away?

The thought gave Nerio hope, even if it was a dim flicker in the night. Regardless, there was an unspeakable torment in the eyes of those instituted here, a pain that clawed away at their insides, slowly killing their souls. Lack of visibility and vocalization did not exclude its existence, and Nerio committed himself to helping save what remained of them.

He didn't know if he could speak on their behalf, but he could listen to the silent pleads, even if no one else would. Perhaps that would be enough.

# Chapter Twenty-Two

*Seeds of dissidence have been sown through the populace. They've begun to question the missing, as though they have the right. Not only here in the major center, but across the greater continent. We must take corrective action. Though it will pose challenges not commonly encountered, we cannot afford to let slip this great wealth we've discovered...*

A mixture of snow and mud sloshed under Kolden's boots as he made his way towards the city's walls. Winter had been creeping upon Drunt for several weeks now, and the air was just warm enough to give the night's snowfall a slight melt, turning the thoroughfare into a sloppy disaster.

The scent of fires from the nearby hearths made him think of the forge, an annoying reminder of where he would rather be as opposed to running this stupid errand. As he walked past the timber-framed homes, holding the bag over his uniformed shoulder tightly as he nearly slipped on a buried patch of ice, he thought about the unfinished projects back at the shop. Not the likes of the trivial tools in his pack now, but the exciting projects, the ones that innovated and challenged. Instead, he was tasked with delivering a bunch of flat steel with a sharpened edge, all because the shop's owner was too cheap to hire a delivery boy.

The city walls grew from a speck at the end of the road to a dominating upheaval of black as Kolden reached the structure which encircled the town. Made of solid inanite, the original foundation built by the Ones Before was masterfully crafted—something Kolden could appreciate—but over however long it had been since its construction, some of the black stones had begun to fade to gray or white. The muted inanite wore and crumbled in the harsh northern weather of Drunt, leaving a jagged and aged feel to the once great barrier.

A team of masons worked to repair it, slowly restoring it back to a sheet of darkened luster. They were currently toiling away at the eastern gate when Kolden arrived, a large chunk of wall removed from the upper reaches, exposing the compacted fill between the two faces of stone. He paused to watch as a group of masons fitted a new block near the top of the gate's arch. The fit looked sloppy, even from this distance, the angle abutting the neighboring block inconsistent and leaving a wedged gap.

*These lazy idiots actually seem satisfied with that garbage fit,* Kolden thought as the masons began hauling mortar up the scaffolding to set the stone in place.

The foreman—apparently the only competent craftsman among the large group—began berating the crew, shouting for them to bring the block down and cut it correctly. With reluctant sighs and heads that drew back in annoyance, the workers began pulling out the stone, marking it for more adjustments with chalk.

The foreman then turned his attention to Kolden, who stood in the center of their designated workspace. "You need somethin' soldier?" the burly bald man asked.

"Quite the crew you got there," Kolden said with a raised brow, unimpressed.

"Aye, they wouldn't last a day at the guild in Calentine, lazy shits," he said with a shake of his head. "If the new lord woulda just paid to get my entire crew here, rather than just shillin' out for me, he'd have this wall fixed in four months. Instead, he thought to give me the local talent to save money, but it'll cost him in the end. Be lucky if we're done in a year. Gods, I can't imagine having to spend that long in this frozen forest, the people here are simple in the head. No offense, of course," he said as Kolden gave him a side eye.

"None taken. Any time spent here is too much time," Kolden said with a hint of disdain.

"You here for guard duty or somethin'?" the foreman asked.

"No," replied Kolden. *Though it's certainly as mundane.* "The smith sent me," he continued, sliding the bag off his shoulder and handing it to the foreman.

The foreman opened the bag, and his eyes went wide, his lips curling into a smile. He pulled out a darksteel chisel—one of several in the bag—and admired it against the dull gray of the cloud cover.

"Now this here is an absolute treat!" the foreman said with a slack jaw. "I thought I'd have to send an order to Calentine for more of these, wouldn't have seen them for months. This inanite is tougher than my mother-in-law on King's Day, and these brainless rats have gone through half my tools already. Tell the mastersmith I'll be by later with his payment. Still can't believe I found one out in the middle of bum-fuck who can forge darksteel."

Kolden gritted his teeth and clenched his fist as he tried to calm himself. He happened to agree with the foreman's opinion about Drunt as a whole, but giving credit to that sloth of a smith drove him mad. *This is the way it needs to be*, he told himself, *I'm going to have to accept that for the time being*. Once he managed to finally get out of this place, then that might be able to change. At least the foreman genuinely appreciated the quality, which was something.

"I'll tell him you'll be by," replied Kolden. *If I can wake him from his drunken stupor*, he thought.

Kolden's eyes were drawn beyond the open gate, the shifting shadows beneath the untamed forest's towering canopy an ominous mirror to the edifice beside him. Like a drip of black oil, someone emerged from the hidden depths of the eastern road, his black clothing and dark horse like the hidden spirits incarnate. The hood over his head hid much of his face, and Kolden was filled with a strange sense of irregularity. It was said strange beasts lived in the deep forests, and for all the shadows surrounding the man, he seemed as though he could fit among their number.

Merchants and travelers passed through Drunt constantly; it was, after all, on a primary trade route, its forests supplying much of the timber for the royal navy. But to see a singular traveler with little gear and no wagon was a strange sight, and it itched at Kolden's curiosity more than it normally would.

The foreman continued inspecting the tools as Kolden watched with narrowed eyes as the traveler spoke with the guard posted outside the gate. He must have had valid enough credentials as the guard ushered him through, his horse steady as it passed below the scaffolding which clamored with masons, the ringing of hammers to chisels all around.

"Anything else?" The foreman's voice pulled him out of his focused stare.

"Uh, yeah, actually," said Kolden. "Do you have any inanite powder? I'm-uh, we're nearly out."

"Oh, we have loads of the stuff," said the foreman with a shrug and a wave of his hand. "We use it for the mortar, and gods know these lads fuck up enough of the blocks to have excess. How much you need?"

The traveler was passing the pair, and this seemed to catch his attention, his head turning enough for Kolden to glimpse under his cowl. A large scar climbed up the side of his face, a freshly healed wound that looked to be a terrible burn. Kolden would have thought him to have been wounded in battle, but he carried himself like a noble, not a soldier.

The stranger caught Kolden's gaze and quickly turned his head away, his horse trotting through the slush as he continued into the town. Kolden stared at the man as he made his way down the street, apparently indifferent to his surroundings.

"How much do you need?" repeated the foreman.

"Hmm? Oh, a five- or ten-pound bag should be more than enough," he said, refocusing on the conversation. Something about the stranger bothered him, an instinct that he couldn't explain.

The foreman traded him a hefty bag of inanite powder for a few moons and he was away, back towards the forge and his waiting projects, a chilled breeze of the foreboding winter on his face. He brushed away the thought of the stranger, trying to focus on the next steps of his project rather than some random traveler. He had ideas for a new sword, one that made him laugh as he pictured its future wielder being annoyed in its use, angered by its impracticality, but stubborn enough that he would still attempt to master it.

Yes, a sword would do nicely.

# Chapter Twenty-Three

*...She's managed to create something beyond what any of us expected. Power. Power to fold the rebellious into our pocket of subservience. Unquestionable rule of this land has returned to its rightful deities. Even the air feels different now that gripping fear has soaked it.*

The sun was especially torrid today, the heat of the red sunrise already raising sweat through the hair cut close to Nerio's scalp. He made his way through the spectrum of colors that were a hallmark of Brethefen streets, and as bells rang in the distance the devotion of the city's residents became tangible in the flow of people leaving their homes to join Nerio in his walk to the Devapuram.

There was a sense of distant bondage to those around him. To an extent he could understand and know everyone migrating with him at this moment, the shared veneration forming a web of connection. It still felt as though he were separated from them all, however, like he was sailing a ship in the sea, other sails visible on the horizon but steering their own path.

He wished for a closeness, to anyone really, as he strolled with the throng. The rapport of religion was powerful, but unlike the majority of others within the clergy, or even among the devout, he was left with a vacant hollow—a missing part that he knew should exist but was absent. This was not to say he was apostatizing; he was still devoted and faithful, but he longed for a more *human* connection. Someone in whom he could confide and would provide less ambiguous responses than the gods often did. It seemed a selfish want, but that did not force it from his heart.

As he and the crowd flowed along, the crest of the Devapuram came into view, its radiant white roof softly reflecting the crimson of the sunrise. The scale of the monumental sanctum became apparent the closer Nerio drew to the pillar-supported shrine. Several concentric rings of the white columns carried the five-hundred-foot-wide dome, which shimmered like the grains of finest sand against the grazing morning light. Nerio walked up the deep, stone steps that led to the first ring of pillars, each several times wider than he was tall, soaring to an impossibly high ceiling.

Nerio listened to a nearby priest reciting to those who wished to hear the scripture carved vertically into the tall column at his back. "...and the light he gives to you a piece of himself, that which is necessary for life. Through his altruism all may be fecund! His givings lessen himself for our betterment, and for that we pray thanks." He reflected on the meaning of the prayer, trying to find the underlying interpretations beyond the plain farming reference.

*Maybe that's all it needs to be,* he thought. *Who am I to judge its meaning for others?*

From his vantage he could see out over the flat roofs of the low buildings, the metropolis sprawling out before him towards the horizon. Undulating plains of golden barley fields and fig orchards lay beyond, a contrast to the wall of snowcapped mountains to his back which were painted like a canvas in the crimson sunrise. The city was a manifestation of the gods' favor; one of the largest cities in the empire thriving here, in a desert, against the inhospitable odds.

An immense populace densely compressed within the city limits, the quiet of isolation an impossibility, yet Nerio was left feeling as though he were the only resident.

He turned and walked towards the core of the sanctum, passing people leaving food and gifts as offerings to the gods before different columns and the priests before them. He made his way towards the center of the immense structure, the only enclosed space beneath the dome's circumference. He wound through the forest of pillars until a wide, cylindrical room stood before him, two priests to either side of the ornate doors set in magnificently carved stone greeting people as they entered. They nodded to Nerio, orange sashes around their waists, rings laddering their sleeves past the elbows.

The air inside of the room carried a haze of smoke, the incense burning strongly and overpowering his nostrils. Taking a small bundle of fragrant herbs from a golden bin to the side of the entrance, Nerio lit it against a candle as he walked into the room.

The holiest site in the entire western half of the kingdom had earned itself the reputation of a great marvel, and inspired awe. The masterfully crafted stone interior was indeed a spectacle to behold, and Nerio was made to feel diminutive and simple within its walls. A hole in the center of the dome's peak above allowed light to cascade in, reflecting off the beautiful perfection of the curved white walls. In the middle of the room stood five statues, carved of the finest marble and smoothed to the polish of glass. Four of the idols stood in a circle, facing inward at a kneeling figure, each a domineering thirty feet tall and the true focal point of the space.

Ursorner's principle, dressed in a deep green robe with bands that rose up his sleeves to his shoulders, was beginning a speak for the earliest arrivals. "The King's deification," he said, his voice resonating clearly throughout the room, waving at the statues behind him. "A story you know well but brings new meanings to our lives each day. Amenesol, King of the gods, performing the greatest act of selflessness known. To cut out a piece of his own heart, a sliver of the sun itself, and bestow it upon our eternal King. Weakened by this sacrifice and needing to rest often, his daily slumber departs the sun from us, and night is wrought. It has left us a better world, and in our own sacrifices, we too can improve the world and people around us. Let us pray." Nerio thought on that history as he looked at the figure of golden-crowned Amenesol extending an orange gem to the outstretched hands of the kneeling statue, a destiny fulfilled.

*By what divine prescience do the gods decide our destiny?* he wondered. He knew it was more than he could hope to know, but with the thought of those that suffered in the world he couldn't escape the tantalizing question.

Nerio placed his small bundle on the black stone alter at the feet of Ursorner's effigy, which lay covered in the ash of smoldered incense despite the early hour.

He hung his head low and closed his eyes. The god of the hunt's depiction was large and muscular compared to the three others, a source of strength and fortitude for all those who may need it. A stern face peered out from beneath a bear-headed cowl, fiercer than the fangs which adorned the carved head like a crown. Nerio asked for that strength now, enough for him to help those that needed it, as well as himself. He regularly reached the end of each day exhausted—both mentally and physically—and the perpetual fatigue was taking its toll. But he *was* making it through the day. It seemed selfish to ask for more. But sometimes the pain could be... overwhelming.

His contemplation was disturbed by a few hushed gasps nearby. He cracked an eyelid with a slight turn of his head to reveal a small group of women—foreign based on their fair, unburnt skin—covering their mouths with eyes wide as they looked at the statues. He could hear whispers about "depravity" and "improperness."

He never understood why so many pilgrims were shocked by the effigies. Statues in the nude could be found throughout the western kingdom, he couldn't see what was different about these, or why some foreigners looked upon them with sneers of disgust. The lithe, feminine grace of Almedia, her wings spread wide, the wisdom of Amenesol's bearded face, the lean physique of Strigifious with an owl perched on his shoulder, and the might of Ursorner were captured in a way that came as close to heavenly as could be managed with human hands. To consider it prude was blasphemy.

He ignored the gossip with a shake of his head and finished his prayer before leaving the inner sanctum. He was already going to be late to the morning shift at the Asylum, the Devapuram being well out of his way. He worshipped regularly at other, smaller churches dotted throughout the city, but he liked to make it to the Devapuram at least once a week. On certain days, anyway...

The sun had risen higher, and its heat beat down on Nerio as though he were in a kiln, his mouth becoming parched and the sweat evaporating from his skin as soon as it was produced, the dry air robbing him of his moisture. A nearby clock tower told him he was almost an hour late for his shift. Hopefully the posted guards and Hands could deal with anything in the short window between the last shift's departure and his arrival.

He rounded the last corner and the Asylum appeared before him, its flecking paint noticeable in the higher sunlight, exposing the hardened mud beneath. The same attending priest in the anteroom greeted him and ushering him through.

"Don't worry," the gauntly thin priest said, seeing Nerio nearly out of breath from the trek, "Brother Algus left not twenty minutes ago. I think he figured you were long at the morning speak. They should be fine if you want to catch your breath for a minute."

"Thanks," Nerio replied. He sighed a breath of relief and relaxed his tense shoulders. It took him and the other healers—on the rare occasion it was more than one of them on duty—nearly an hour to do rounds and check-ins between the two floors. A twenty-minute gap was little to fret over.

He collected the medicine as he always did and made his way down the hall, the guard fast asleep in his chair, head rolled down.

*So much for relying on them in my absence,* he thought with a disappointed inward sigh. Hopefully there was a Hand or two on staff today, he would be needing the help. He thought about his morning prayers, wondering what he could offer to the gods for their favor. He lived a simple, meager life, one filled with piety and devotion. Yet, no matter his offerings, his prayers, his begging, he was left to deal with the harsh realities and cruelty of life on his own. What was their plan for him?

The possibilities chipped away even further at his insides, a chasm that almost extended beyond his own limbs. He rubbed his face and changed focus, he needed to tend to the people here first and foremost.

He looked through the barred openings in the doors at the slumbering patients, their rest appearing tranquil. *They have it so much worse than I do,* he thought, a stab of guilt piercing his gut. How could he look at his own life and think it so despondent? Here was a group tortured by their own minds, fated to live their entire lives within a painted cell, their families disowning them and choosing to ignore their very existence.

The abandonment struck a chord within him, and he thought back to his own childhood, his parents leaving him with the church to live a life spreading the gods' wills. They couldn't afford a child, and he'd been consigned to doctrine in exchange for removing his needs from those of his parents. As he wondered at what his life would have been, he saw these unfortunate souls undergoing trials set by the gods, the likes of which he hoped never to endure. Perhaps this was his test of strength, their continued existence a boast to the fortitude he aspired to have.

He checked window after window, the group must have been awake late into the night for so many to still be sleeping. It wasn't uncommon, but he was thankful that he hadn't been on the nightshift.

*I shouldn't take such relief from the avoidance of duties and helping these people,* he thought, his body shrinking in shame. No, that was simply not—

He stopped abruptly in the hall. Something dark on the floor catching his attention: a curtain of violet fanning out from under Lord Grundan's door, reflecting like glass. His chest went tight, and his grip faltered, dropping the jug of medicine to the floor, shattering the ceramic container on the tiles.

The guard jerked awake at the crash and jumped to his feet with a start, spinning his head in confusion. Nerio quickly refocused, shouting to him to go find a Hand or a priest and to bring them immediately. He hoped that he was wrong, that what he expected on the other side of the cell door would be different than the image in his mind.

He knew better but prayed regardless.

Nerio pulled a medical kit from the nearby wall and ran to the door. He nearly slipped on the slick floor as he feverishly searched for the key to unlock it, his heart pounding and a cold sweat upon his brow. The small bits of metal *clinked* against one another as he fumbled through them with shaking hands.

He found the key and swung the door open, his feet tracking through the slick blood. The full view of Lord Grundan—laying on his back, his wrists cut, a chunk of broken ceramic in his hand—revealing itself. The hemorrhaging covered half the floor, and Nerio steeled himself against the heinous sight. On the white tiles beyond the pool of blood were three words written in the semi-dried liquid, a finger the clear writing instrument. They simply said, in smeared letters, "FIND NIGHT DAUGHTER."

Nerio dropped to his knees and tightly wrapped the lacerated wrists in bandages as quickly as he could. He moved Grundan's hands on top of his stomach, then pressed his own fingers to the neck, trying to detect a heartbeat. He held them, feeling nothing. Tears began to blur his vision, but still he held his fingers to skin.

Nothing.

He gripped his hands together and pounded on the man's chest, hoping to beat life back into it. He whispered under his breath, begging for aid, pleading with Strigifious to hold his owl back just a little longer, to let the man live a little bit more of his life.

*What kind of life was he living?* It was a dark thought, there was a *wrongness* to it. Nerio couldn't help but ask it all the same. Such an act would damn you to the labors of hell's prisons. Would Grundan, perhaps, be made whole again in that pit of damnation? Was that worth eternity as a slave?

The tears now flowed freely down Nerio's cheeks. He rested his hands on his legs as he leaned back, unphased by the stained floor he knelt on, his knees wet with blood. He looked at the chunk of ceramic on the floor that had laid by Grundan's hand. It had broken, sharp edges all around, the terracotta orange now a deep, wet brown. The memory of the other day struck him, when he had wondered at whether he'd left a cup in the room.

*I was distracted by the other patient's outburst, I never came back to check.*

His face went pale, his lip trembling as he reached out a hand and picked up the makeshift blade. He inspected its blood coated sides, the shape of subtle curvature. There was no doubt. This was part of the cup he'd forgotten, shattered and turned into a weapon of deliverance.

*This is all my fault,* he thought, his throat tight. He should have been more careful. *How could I have been so thoughtless as to leave this here? I'm here to help these people, not hurt them!*

There was a hustled trample of feet from the hallway as the guard and a Hand appeared at the door. The Hand's face—an older man with a large scar along his jaw—became hard at the sight in the quarters, and the guard turned and held his face in his elbow in morbid shock.

Nerio tucked the ceramic away in his sash, the weight of embarrassment duplicative to his guilt. The older Hand—a war veteran judging by the way he held himself—looked to the weeping Nerio with an empathetic stare. His eyes spoke of understanding, this was someone who had lost friends on the battlefield, who knew the pain of helplessness.

"I-I-I..." Nerio started to say, his blood covered hands at his side.

"It's alright. Why don't you leave this to us, son," said the man in a stern but comforting tone, taking a step in the room and seeing the attempted treatment. "There was nothin' you coulda done for him, it was valiant of you to try. Now c'mon, we'll deal with him."

Nerio looked at him and nodded. He wanted someone else to handle this, to remove his responsibility and let him force it from his mind.

*How selfish of me.*

Slowly standing—the front of his robe dripping in blood and soaked a deep violet hue—his shaking knees carried him from the room. He walked a few yards down the hall before he simply couldn't carry on, his body slumping against a wall, the density of his guilt dragging him to the floor. He held his knees to his chest with his back to the wall, silently shrinking himself, hiding from the world around him.

"He said he wanted to see him," said an unexpected voice from behind the door to Nerio's side. He turned to see hands gripping the bars in the window, the patient speaking to him through it. "The dreams, they shook the night. But the medicine—the medicine makes it hard to hear. Sounds muffled, distant. He wanted to know, to see behind the veil and know if it would make him whole again, escape into the astral lands. So he went into the deepest sleep, the last one."

Nerio couldn't even think of a response to the strange claims, his mouth hanging agape. This "escape" went against his religious upbringing, something that was deemed selfish and sinful. Was there a chance that in doing this, Lord Grundan had found himself again, become who he was meant to be? Was that worth his eternal punishment?

His thoughts turned to the writing on the floor, the dying wish of the lord to find this *Night Daughter*. Nerio had no idea what that meant; he knew of no one who went by such a name, nor any groups. He was at a loss. Not only had he failed the man in life, but now in death as well.

He wasn't sure how long he sat there on the cool floor. His legs had long since become numb, his mind unable to process a thought as his emotions submerged him in disquiet, his face blank and his stare distant. People moved around him through a fog, a still figure before him eventually making him crane his head from its stare at the floor.

The Hand from earlier stood above him with military rigidity. Nerio heard his voice, but it came to him as sounds dissociated from meaning. His head nodded, a subconscious part of him filtering language from the sounds. Another priest had been called on duty for the day, and they were asking him to head home. *That's what it was*, he recognized, his brain finally catching up with the jumbled noises.

He stood in a trance and went to the storage room, finding a clean robe and changing into it. He went to the wash basin and scrubbed his hands with vigor. He washed them repeatedly, the abrasion of the pumice stone grinding at his skin. But he found himself unsatisfied, as though the blood had seeped into his flesh and could not be removed.

He dumped the water, refilled the basin and with newly added soap he scrubbed again. His skin began to burn, the palms turning red from abrasion and fingers pruning. His own hands began bleeding and staining the water red, and the sight of additional gore put a twisting grip on his stomach, the nausea preventing him from washing further.

Nerio left, no words of departure spoken to the front attendant or anyone else he passed. The blazing heat of midday felt like a punishment from Amenesol, and rather than seeking shade he basked in its fire.

He deemed it insufficient.

He wandered through the streets, not wanting to go home—there was nothing for him there. Instead, he decided to make his way towards the library.

Perhaps he could find something relevant in the texts to Lord Grundan's final words. He owed the man that much, at least. If nothing else it would serve as a distraction, for now.

# Chapter Twenty-Four

*Why am I maintained at this station? I feel crippled by the want for that which makes me whole. Like an archer who has lost an arm, or a fish trapped on land...*

Kolden snapped his eyes open, his heart racing, a cold sweat on his brow despite the chill in the dark forge. The dream that had pulled him from sleep was already forgotten, lost in the transition to consciousness like the leaves of autumn taken by a windswept rain, forever torn from the trees.

He rubbed his eyes and tilted his head with a painful creak, the stiff muscles threatening to break with too quick a motion. With a groan he sat himself up straight, the wooden chair having numbed everything pressed to it, making him shift awkwardly.

He looked to the dead fires of the forge beside him with a sigh, his fresh darksteel billet on the anvil beside it. Buried at its very heart he thought he saw the faint glow of an ember alone among the ash, but it vanished to black under his gaze.

*How long was I asleep?* he wondered.

He had told Orne he would meet him at the tavern tonight, but he had no idea how much of *tonight* was left. He stood up and made his way through the shadow-strewn shop. A streetlamp outside was the only source of light, its yellow glow raking against the anvils and benches through the distant window. The old bastard of an owner must have put out the lamps when he left, leaving Kolden in the dark.

Again.

He donned his coat and walked outside into the frozen street, the mixture of mud and snow crunching beneath his feet in the icy night. The moon was near its apex, its drab, silvery light dully reflecting off the snow. The sight made Kolden's face cringe.

*Orne is going to be* pissed, he thought, wondering if the tavern was going to be open much longer.

He had a long trek ahead of him, needing to climb the hill upon which the lord's castle stood and the barracks was situated, a popular tavern for soldiers nearby. Kolden debated sleeping the rest of the night on the floor of the shop—it wouldn't be the first time. He weighed the idea in his mind but with a reluctant sigh decided against it. This would be easier than dealing with the fallout of missing another roll call, not to mention Orne's annoyance.

With soot-covered hands burrowed into his pockets and head tucked deeply into his shoulders, he began walking. His route overlapped the one he'd taken earlier in the day, heading towards the city wall and then turning north to the castle. The late hour had left the street completely barren, the crunching of newly formed ice crystals beneath his boots the only sound.

The noise was a reminder that two years of being stationed in this frozen tundra had left him bitter, with sharp edges like those of the icy shards under his feet. It was a ridiculous waste of talent, forcing him to work under the jealousy of the town's supposed "mastersmith." The man was a lard. Soldiers weren't allowed to join a guild while serving though, and the arrangement was the best he could manage.

If they could actually achieve their goal of getting an assignment somewhere else, he stood a chance at having his work noticed, appreciated. The years of study at the military boarding school combined with countless hours of trials and experiments might still bring him the accolades he deserved. If nothing else, it would get them out of this backwoods shithole.

Alas, his transfer requests were dismissed, a stamp of denial from the general himself imprinted on each one, building the angst that brewed inside of him. Reasons cited included "previous infractions" and "lack of conduct befitting his station."

*What a pile of shit,* he thought with a shake of his head.

Kolden's eyes felt heavy as he fought off the grogginess inflicted by the late hour. Each step was slow, carefully placed to avoid slipping on freshly formed sheets of ice. As he came upon the intersection near the eastern gate, he looked over curiously.

*I wonder if that block the masons had been trying to fit before was corrected and joined properly?* he thought.

An impulse drove him to go inspect it, but his curiosity could wait until tomorrow; he'd walk back past here in the morning, and he was already late. Although, something about the gate *did* seem out of the ordinary.

*The lamps are out,* he realized.

The tall steel gate was shut, that was clear from this distance even in the dim moonlight. But there weren't any torches, braziers, or lamps burning for the guards on night shift duty.

He looked to his left at the road that led up the hill towards the barracks, then back to his right at the gate steeped in darkness. He drew his lips into a line, struggling to make a decision.

*I could just leave it, the gate's shut. Any bandits would be spotted from another outpost, and there's a whole garrison here besides. Then again, what if it was sabotage from inside?* he argued in his mind.

Kolden hung his head and drooped his shoulders with a sigh. The soldier in him wouldn't allow him to just keep walking, he wasn't even sure why he bothered to debate the decision. He turned toward the wall, the dark gloom fully enveloping him as he approached with a cautious gait, holding to the edge of the street to avoid outlining himself to anyone who may be present.

He reached the building's corner nearest the wall and looked out across the twenty yards of open space from his hideaway to the gate. He struggled to see anything, the waning moon making even shapes difficult to distinguish. He listened, staying in the building's shadow, for anything unexpected. Wind-rustled trees beyond could be heard through the thin, cold air, and was a background wash of sound. But there was something else, more distinct—a pattern of rumbling, then silence, repeated.

*Is that… snoring?* He rolled his eyes at the realization and stood straighter, no longer deciding to hide in the shadow. The guard must have fallen asleep and let the torches go out. Kolden shook his head and decided to go wake the man, hopefully saving him from reprimand in the morning hours. That was assuming—

A blurred shift of motion caught Kolden's eye as he was about to step from his secluded corner. In the middle of the masons work area he saw movement, nothing more than shadows and blended shapes, but motion all the same. He heard sounds, like metal scraping on wood, accompanying the shadowed activity.

Was someone attempting to steal the masons' tools? They didn't leave anything valuable out overnight, but that wouldn't stop vagrants from coming to claim a bucket or rope for themselves. He couldn't just let someone walk off with the masons' equipment. He gripped the overly long dagger at his side and prepared to walk over. He just wished he had more light. Perhaps he could shout and hope to wake the guard on the wall.

As he was about to step out, something peculiar happened: a purple light, just a sliver of it, burst into existence in the workspace. It was enough to illuminate the vicinity around the man who Kolden could now clearly see, but not much further. He hunched down all the same, staring with awed intrigue at the glow that beamed with impossible continuity.

*What the hell could be producing such a perfect and unwavering light?* Kolden wondered.

He could see a hooded figure now—his face blocked from view—standing over a small bucket, mixing the contents together. The purple luminescence seemed to emanate from within the figure's pocket, the radiance bleeding through the fabric. Kolden watched as the man poured inanite powder into the bucket, continuing to mix the contents.

Kolden was still frozen with curiosity as the man stood up with the pail and a small shovel in hand, his face briefly exposed to Kolden in the purple glow. By the burn present on his visage alone, Kolden recognized him as the stranger who'd arrived earlier that day. *I knew there was something suspicious about that fucker!* The stranger turned and climbed the scaffolding near the gate, reaching the level where the most recent block had been laid earlier that day.

By the faintly illuminated outline Kolden watched as the scarred stranger dug into the soil and stone fill behind the outer block layer, listening as the shovel cut away debris with a ringing repetition. The sound stopped, the shovel rested against the scaffolding. For not but a blink the wall became drenched in purple light, sparkles thrown against the black stone like sparks from a hammer striking hot steel.

As quickly as it appeared, it was gone.

*What in the gods' names was that? Did he just bury it?* he thought.

With a heavy sloshing sound, the mysterious man dumped the contents of the bucket into the hole he'd dug, the captivating glow vanishing. Kolden heard the repetitive shoveling as the remains of the hole were filled in. His eyes suddenly went wide as he came to a realization.

*He's encased it in mortar!* It was the most logical answer. But why? In a few days this entire portion of wall would be reconstructed, and whatever it was that cast the fluorescent glow would be buried—permanently. Or, well, that's probably what the stranger thought anyway.

He probably didn't realize that Kolden was going to steal it.

Actually, *steal* was a rather negative term, and it wasn't one Kolden was fond of, as he wasn't a thief. But clearly this person didn't want whatever he was burying. Sealing it behind a wall for perpetuity was a good indicator that he no longer desired to be in possession of said object, and therefore Kolden was merely... reclaiming it.

With the light gone, visibility was reduced back to naught. Kolden listened and let his eyes readjust to the darkness, the stranger clearly taking the time to clean up any evidence of his presence. By the sounds heard and the shifting of shadows, Kolden was fairly certain he'd even cleaned the bucket and returned it to its original home.

After a few minutes of straining to watch for movement like he was following wraiths in the night, Kolden finally heard footsteps trailing off into the distance. The illusive man was seemingly satisfied that his mischief would go unnoticed. Obviously he wasn't familiar with the clowns working this wall, as leaving the site *too clean* might actually make them more suspicious than making a mess.

Kolden waited, the footsteps long since fading in the distance, the muffled snoring of the guard the only sound. He didn't want to risk the chance that the person who buried the unknown object was watching as a precaution, but if he waited too long the mortar would set and he'd have to chisel it out from its embedment.

Minutes passed, then a quarter hour. Kolden decided that he couldn't wait any longer, the mortar likely setting soon despite the cold weather. He crept as silently as he could, finding the shovel with a fumbling hand as he went through the masons' work area with outstretched arms, feeling his way around as much as he was seeing.

Tool in hand, he made his way to the scaffolding, his eyes having readjusted enough for him to make out the ladder rungs and climb his way up. He cringed slightly with the mild creaks resonating from the wooden ladder as he stepped on each rung, finally making it to the level where he'd seen the burned man bury the light. As he walked across the heavy planks several stories in the air, he couldn't help but notice the stone from earlier now fit snugly into place, a nearly perfect cut angle allowing it to sit flush against the adjoining stone. Kolden's brow raised up as he inspected the masonry with a slight nod, impressed with the adjustments the foreman had forced his lackeys to make.

He ran his hand over the compacted earth that sat behind the interlocking blocks. Most of the wall's core was semi frozen from exposure to the night's air, so it didn't take long for his hands to find the loose soil that had been so carefully put back into place. He used the shovel to remove the recently excavated gravel and sand mixture, finding the mortar below already taking on a thick, plaster-like consistency. He grabbed a small wooden shim from nearby and began carefully scraping back the thick slurry, not wanting to damage the radiant treasure within.

After a few strokes with the wooden spade a dim light began to filter through the sieve of mortar, its purple glow more entrancing in his nearness. With bare fingers he scooped away the last remnants of mortar to expose the gorgeous brilliance of the luminous source.

A stone, whose clouded translucence rolled inside of its expertly carved facets like an explosion of fire, burned a light into existence from its entirety. It reflected a steady flood of light off his mesmerized eyes, plunging his face in splendor.

It was the most incredible thing he'd ever seen.

A few inches square and maybe half as deep, it had strange, repetitive patterns carved into its face. The artistry of the perfection in each facet and curved line in the design was not lost unto him, and Kolden was awed by the exacting beauty. He only knew—well, had read vaguely about—one substance that was capable of producing such a glow: cadentite.

*I always thought the glowing was a work of fiction, the play of light in the sun,* he thought, clearly in the wrong.

If this indeed was a sample of the rare mineral, it was larger than any he'd ever read of being discovered. And the care and skill that had gone into carving it in such an ornate way! This singular stone was likely worth more than the entirety of Drunt, which begged the question of why someone would go through the effort of burying it inside of a wall, likely to never be seen again.

*How did that stranger get this? And* why *in the gods' names was he hiding it here? He clearly never intended for this to be found, so why? WHY?*

There were too many unknowns to answer his questions, but something this valuable was bound to attract the most dangerous of villainy. He quickly ripped off a bit of his undershirt and wrapped it around the stone, letting the fabric absorb what little inanite-blended liquid still remained in the mortar. From what he understood about cadentite—assuming any of what he knew was even correct—Blues could sense the rare mineral somehow. The way those knights used powers was mysterious enough on its own, so he didn't bother trying to understand the science of it in his mind. But he did remember that even they couldn't sense cadentite hidden deep in the lodes of inanite where it was found, something about the black mineral preventing them from sensing it.

Fortunately, there weren't any Blues stationed in Drunt. After all, what self-respecting nobility would *want* to live in this place. Even the new lord had claimed the title after the heirless death of the previous duke. He spent a substantial amount of money attempting to improve the city, Kolden would give him credit there, but he doubted it would ever change his opinion on the isolated hellhole.

Better to not take any chances, regardless.

His hands dripping in icy liquid, chilling them to the bone, he shoved the tightly wrapped treasure into his pocket, checking to make sure no light pierced the now-black fabric. He hurriedly filled back in the hole, taking less care than the burned man had, and rushed back down the scaffolding. His hands were shaking as he reached the bottom of the ladder and began sneaking away. He couldn't decide if it was an effect of the cold, or his body's response to the peril he now carried in his pocket.

The wealth that the dense stone represented would challenge the morals of almost anyone, he knew. No one could be trusted with the knowledge of its existence—well, almost no one... he wasn't sure if that was a good idea or not—and he swore that it began to sink more deeply in his pocket as he weighed the idea of it in his mind.

He had no intention of selling it, wealth wasn't what interested him and he had money enough for the tools and learning that he required. No, this was an intellectual curiosity, a need of understanding that drove him now. No one had any idea how the mineral worked, not in any written capacity. There were the rumors that spread about its use in the drug trade, but soldiers gossiped, and gossip was not an adequate platform for truth.

He didn't bother to consider options as he reached the illuminated intersection. He was consumed with the allure of the unanswered questions of the stone in his pocket. Orne could wait, and roll call was a waste of his time. He turned left down the street, checking over his shoulder constantly, and made his way back towards the blacksmith shop.

He'd slept enough for tonight, he had work to do.

# Chapter Twenty-Five

*The masses look upon them with dread. Almost as though we've been forgotten, despite our clutch upon their hilt. Their purpose is still served, however, and our reign continues unblemished.*

The odor of leather and musty parchment deluged over Nerio as he passed through the tall, arched doors and into the grandeur of the library's vaulted ceilings. Like the Devapuram, the endless rows of organized texts inspired awe, but there was a comfort here that Nerio could find nowhere else. He felt a sense of belonging, the static words capable of moving cities and swaths of people alike. The tomes were similar to religion in that way, an offering of answers and insight to those who sought it.

The building was laid out as a long hall, a second story balcony wrapping around the central study with additional rows of texts and scrolls visible beyond the railings. Those shelves reached to the arch of the ceiling which peaked high in the center of the cathedral-like space. Stained glass windows sifted colored light between the shelving, rainbowing the hall as it stretched to the distance.

It was a welcoming beauty, one that Nerio wished he could indulge in more often.

He approached an older priest sitting behind a desk facing the door. The head librarian wore low spectacles, his patchy, curly white hair accompanying wrinkled and ancient features. He looked at Nerio with a thin, crease-covered smile.

"Young Brother Nerio, King and His grace upon you," the man said in a frail voice.

"And you," Nerio replied. "Were you able to find any texts related to what I asked about?"

His voice refrained from including hope. For months now he'd been coming here regularly, at least a few days a week, searching for information pertaining to this unknown "Night Daughter." His free time was spent roaming the rows of books, no subject precluded from his investigations. Maps, histories, tales of heroes new and old all were thoroughly studied under his questing focus. He'd found nothing in page after page. Sources on botany revealed no discovered plant with the name in any language he knew, nor stars in the night sky in any terminology of sailors that was available. The library of Brethefen was one of the most complete in the kingdom, the answers he sought must be hidden here *somewhere*.

"One, in fact," the elderly man said with a nod. He stood from his chair with a crooked lean and ran his hands along the spines of several books piled high on the desk behind him. He muttered to himself as he sighted down his nose through the spectacles until Nerio heard the utterance of an, "Aha," of discovery.

"Here it is," said the man, sliding out an ancient looking tome from the stack, the heft of it threatening to topple him from his equally aged posture. He set the book down on the table in front of Nerio with a *thud* that kicked dust from its pages, sitting back down to catch his breath. He almost sneezed from the dust, the familiar scent of old parchment assaulting his senses.

Nerio looked at the tattered cover and frayed edges, delicately grabbing the fore edge and tilting it up, noticing how much thinner it was than the bindings at the spine. He opened it and began carefully flipping through the thin pages, each threatening to tear with the slightest tug.

"That is one of the few writings we possess regarding the Ones Before. Most of the others merely reference them, you see, but this was claimed to have been written by their hand. I do suspect that it's a copy of the original, given the binding materials, but it is well over a millennia old, yes," the old librarian said with an assured nod.

The text was written entirely in old trethish, which wasn't a surprise given its age. What was a surprise came with the turn of a page: a thick line of paper running along the spine where many pages had obviously been ripped out.

"What's this?" asked Nerio, running his fingers along the rough tears. "Why was this tome defaced in such a way?"

"Yes, well, that's not too uncommon with these older books. The Ones Before were pagans after all, much of this text was probably heresy, mhm. Once the King ascended the clergy spread His wisdom through the empire, and the supposed pagan 'gods' were purged from the records; few followers of the religion still existed at that point besides. That even this one survived is an act of the gods themselves. I don't wish to judge their wisdom in allowing its longevity, but I understand it to be mostly meaningless accounts of some noble or another at the time, not much to learn from it I dare say. What is your curiosity in such ramblings, young Brother?"

Nerio had hoped that perhaps there was some reference that could possibly give him a direction of where to look. He was digging holes in the sand looking for water, never finding an indication of the moisture he sought. He was lost and blind with few avenues left to pursue, looking into the Ones Before was just another hole dug searching for an oasis.

"Scholarly interest," he simply replied. He didn't think, "Following the words of a dead man," would elicit the most understanding of responses.

"Mhm, yes. Well, you always were one to delve into these books with fervor. Pity that you chose healing as your specialty, so few even more aged than I mastered old trethish the way you have. And at such a young age! You're one of a handful that can even read this text, young brother, you realize this?

"Mental acuity such as yours is wasted nursing the sick, you could easily take my position with a mere few years of training. I'll extend my offer for you to work here again, perhaps one of these days you'll take my request into consideration, hmm? Add some yellow bands to your arm and put the red of healing into the past?" The old man looked at him with the crooked eyebrow of persistence, looking to persuade Nerio once again.

Nerio gave him a polite smile. As a youth he had poured himself into the texts of the library—there was security, a non-threatening comfort in them. They did not abandon you the way his own blood had to him, and the knowledge among their pages did not vanish into the recesses of his mind in the way the forgotten identity of his original family had.

He knew they had been poor, he remembered hungry nights and sickly days, but there was little else. They had unburdened themselves of him by placing him in the tutelage of the clergy. Whether they wished to be freed of the needs of a child, or they hoped to place him into a home of better care, he couldn't say. How little they knew...

"I help those who cannot help themselves, Brother," Nerio said. "The only one I help in spending all my time here is myself."

"Bah," said the old man with a dismissive wave, "I sometimes forget about the naive idealism of youth. Leave the simple tasks to ones of simple mind. Someday you will come to realize that this is the place for you, mhm. I just hope I am still alive to see it."

"Thank you for finding this for me," Nerio said to the incorrigible librarian as he picked up the heavy tome.

The elderly man raised a finger from his heavily ringed sleeve and said, "You know, young Nerio, there may be some other scrolls or texts regarding the Ones Before that I could find for you. They're not here, but instead in the personal libraries of some of the principles. They don't normally make them available for viewing, but under their supervision and with a suggestion from me I may—"

"No!" blurted Nerio. "No, I appreciate it, Brother, but this is quite enough. Like I said, this is merely a curiosity on my part, no need to impose such a request. Especially on my behalf."

"Mhm, I still think you're far too humble, young Brother, but fine. The offer shall stand as long as you are interested," he said with thinly slit eyes.

"Thank you again, Brother," bid Nerio as he left the librarian and walked along the great expanse of a hall to an empty desk. It was basked in violet light from a nearby window, circular eyes of a horned owl staring down at him from the center of the pane. Spread out around him were a few other priests—they and nobility members of the few sects allowed into the divine study—the quiet turning of pages and scrawling of quills the only sounds in the great hall, aside from the occasional cough or sneeze.

He opened the bulky book on an angled stand, sitting to read and study the pages. Translating old trethish was a slow process, and what he could ascertain from skimming the volume was that this was a catalog of sorts. It spoke of land acquisitions and donations to a dozen *Ra-Ghans*, which roughly translated to someone of great wealth or power, likely kings or warlords across the empire at the time.

Each of the few remaining pages detailed out traded supplies and goods used for purchases. A hundred head of cattle to one, a small fleet of ships to another, land rights to a mountain valley and so on.

*This is futile,* he thought as he leaned back in the chair and rubbed his eyes. Despite his best efforts, he'd dared to hope that this relic of a tome would hold the answers—or at least a direction—to his question. Instead, it was merely the accounting records of some ancient nobility.

He'd left the Asylum early today to spend additional time on this research, and now that he'd wasted hours delving into its pages, he was left with guilt of abandoning his station for this fruitless endeavor. Why had he thought today would be different from any other?

With an extended sigh Nerio closed the book. The lowering sun was reaching through the stained windows with a final breath of effort, and Nerio had other duties that required his presence. He returned the book to the head librarian, who had dozed off in his chair and breathed lightly. He shuffled out into the streets, making his way to the bell tower a few blocks away.

He felt his heart in his feet as they carried him along the pavers which still shimmered with the heat of the desert sun. Months of searching and to what end? Why did he cling to this frivolous mission? It was not as though an answer would bring Lord Grundan back from the dead, nor would it absolve him of the errors he'd committed leading to his death. He fiddled with the piece of ceramic that he now kept with him, thinking about the day he'd found the body. He'd told himself that he was doing this as a last right for the passed lord. That a dying wish was sacred. The reality was that he wished to cleanse himself of the guilt which consumed him, one of many stones which dragged him deep into a dismal abyss.

*I'm so selfish,* he thought.

He reached the tower, only the top half of the tall stone building still bathed in sunlight as night began to drag itself over the city. He climbed the wooden steps and ladders of the tower's interior. The wood was yellowed and polished in spots from the countless feet and hands that had performed this daily ritual. Near the spire's apex, he brought himself into a small room, a single rope hanging from above in its center.

Through a small window he looked to the distance at another clock tower, distracting himself with the intense focus. The distant hand struck the top of the new hour, an end to the day and a time for evening worship. He pulled down on the thick rope, his toes lifting off the floor a touch as it gave way and steadily succumbed downward. A bell above him pealed through the air, and in the distance a symphony of synchronized tolls rang throughout the city.

After a few additional pulls, Nerio released the rope, his final daily responsibility complete. He would make it to prayers eventually, but for now he climbed one final, small ladder to the platform above. The bell still swayed a foot above the platform, its ringing fading but still crisp. The open balcony provided an unparalleled view of the city, the pattern of the roads below clear from this vantage—the repetitious curves all twisting inward to the Devapuram at the center, like a spinning storm with a great white eye.

Nerio sat on the platform's edge, his feet dangling above the road a hundred feet below as the dry desert air began to rapidly cool. His mind was again back to the lack of results in his search. Could it be that he was chasing the ravings of a mad man, and that this was his goad from the afterlife? Had he blamed Nerio for his complacence, knowing his own lack of self-control, and written the words as a punishment meant to send him chasing after something which did not exist? Or was the answer on the tip of his tongue, as he had felt it was these past months?

He came to a decision sitting there in the vestiges of vanishing daylight, one that had been eating away at him for weeks now. He'd tried to avoid it, to ignore it as though it were a festering wound that he'd hoped would heal itself.

He would no longer continue his search for whatever or whoever this "Night Daughter" was.

Nerio felt the choice in his chest, as though a piece of his heart had been cut off and fallen into the empty pit of his bowels. He'd failed. Not only had he failed Lord Grundan in life, but now in death.

He needed to focus his time on those who still lived inside the Asylum's walls. But what if he made another fatal mistake? Could he bear *two* souls haunting him?

His eyes focused on the street between his dangling feet, his head hanging low. Again, he was left with emptiness as a thought repeated in his head like the ringing of the bell at his back, the resonating sound filling his mind.

*I'm a failure.*

# Chapter Twenty-Six

*I have become concerned with recent tell of altered children. The validity is yet to be confirmed, but I must see that this news does not reach the council. I cannot allow false rumors to hinder my reintegration into High society. Else this despondent pasture will have my sanity before long.*

Kolden pumped his foot against the pedal, turning the steel grinding stone. His fingers pressed the edge of the cadentite to the spinning wheel, removing the layer of black, inanite paint that he'd coated the radiant mineral in and exposing a fraction of its lustrous glow. The narrow slit of streaking light illuminated the interior of the makeshift tent Kolden had set up in the shop, the black fabric creating a sweltering environment in the already scalding blacksmith's forge.

He tasted the salt of sweat mixed with metal as the cadentite refused to grind. It was nearly as hard as inanite, and he wished he could use the black grinding wheel instead of this steel one. He couldn't afford to mix inanite powder with the shavings he sought, however. The properties of the precious stone could be negated by too much of the black dust in the process he was attempting, and he couldn't risk ruining all this effort.

The wheel spun through a water basin, any cadentite dust ground away collecting and settling in the pool. Once he had enough of the fines accumulated, he'd place the basin by the forge to evaporate the water, leaving nothing but cadentite dust on the bottom.

That was the idea, anyway. It wasn't currently going to plan.

For every speck of cadentite that shimmered in the basin, ten flecks of steel accompanied it. The wheel was beginning to form a divot in its center, and after three hours of grinding he still only had a small percentage of what he would need for even a small billet.

*This is taking FOREVER*, he thought with impatience, his fingers beginning to cramp. Kolden had spent weeks experimenting, debating, and hypothesizing in the late or slow work hours which he was free of shop aides or the awareness of the owner. He'd decided to try copying the process which secured his place in the shop—despite the owners stewing annoyance at his necessity. He didn't know what the results would be, but that's what made it *exciting*. His mind raced with possibilities. Perhaps next he would—

The sound of the front door to the shop opening and then slamming closed caught his attention, the gush of a wintery breeze rippling the fabric walls around him. He couldn't risk being caught with the glowing mass of cadentite. If word spread, then any number of people could come looking for it, including the burned man who'd hidden it in the first place. He heard what sounded like shouting as he shoved the stone into an inanite dyed bag and slipped it into a hidden sleeve he'd nailed to the bottom of his stool, a tightness forming a lump in his throat.

He emerged from his haphazardly pitched tent into the relative brightness of the shop, his eyes straining as they adjusted to the snow-reflected light streaking through the windows. He walked away from his nook in the back corner, tucked away and out of sight courtesy of the shop's proprietor. As he turned the corner he found the owner—swaying with the unbalanced grace that came from perpetual drunkenness—arguing loudly with a soldier who towered over him, his head taller than the doorframe he'd entered through. His thick neck was bulging below a vitriol spewing face as shoulders wider than the door swung hulking arms that pointed and prodded at the swaying drunk before him.

Kolden sighed a breath of relief, his muscles relaxing as he watched the behemoth of a man berate the owner.

"—and if you think I'm leaving my armor with your sorry ass to be repaired, you have another thing coming! Now, where's Kolden?" the overly muscled man asked with pointed intensity.

"You can't-You can't jus' come in *my* shop and talk to me like tha'," the blacksmith said, his enormous gut attempting to topple him with the slightest tilt. "You'll give it 'ere an-and pay me your due!"

"How about you go fuck off to whatever latrine trench you crawled out of you fat piece of shit. The only person who touches my armor is Kolden, now where is—" The bulky man cut off, the white of his eyes raging coals in the fiery red of his face above his beard. He'd caught sight of Kolden, who was watching from a distance, a smug smirk on his face.

"There you are!" the tall man said. "Get out of my way, asshole. Go find a bottle to drown in."

"Hey!" the owner sputtered. "Get back 'ere! I won't sta-stand for insults from the likes of you. This 'ere is *my* shop. An you!" he said, pointing a pudgy finger at Kolden. "You need to keep the likes of him outta my shop. If you don' the-then I'm gonna report you to the guild, just you watch."

Kolden shook his head. He and the smith knew he wasn't going to say anything to the guild, but Kolden still needed the bastard, as much as he hated to admit it. Some passive aggression from the man was one thing, but to leave him irate was another. He was going to need to smooth things over, though the thought of doing so put a sour taste in his mouth.

Before he had a chance to speak, however, the enormous brute of a man turned around and took two long strides towards the drunk, looking down on him from his broad shoulders.

"The only reason you aren't working as a farrier's apprentice, you shit eating swine, is because Kolden knows how to make darksteel and you don't. Go ahead and report him to the guild, but you better dig a big hole to bury him in, because if the guild doesn't throw you in there for lying about your skill set, then I sure as fuck will. Now why don't you do something useful for once and go get us some food. I've worked up an appetite out there protecting your sorry ass," the tall soldier said with derision.

*Gods, I wish he hadn't done that,* thought Kolden as he rubbed his brow. While he appreciated the support—and certainly enjoyed watching the smith get a dose of humility—he wished that Orne could show just the *slightest* amount of impulse control. The cadentite hidden in the back made angering the smith an even bigger risk, and his chest felt tight at the idea of guild inspectors showing up at the owners beckoning.

The sloth of a man growled as his face turned red with contempt. He didn't speak for a moment as he tried to angrily stare down Orne, doubtfully unaware of the soldier's angry stubbornness. Eventually he let out an angry huff, pointing to both of them and shouting, "Fuck you both! You insolent pricks! Go hide in yer stupid fucking tent."

The smith stormed over to the door and slung his coat over his shoulders as he walked out into the cold, slamming it closed behind him.

"You know he *already* hates me, right?" said Kolden with a look that said: *Really?*

"Eh, fuck 'em," replied Orne with a wave of his hand. "Asshole had it coming."

Orne walked over to Kolden and looked down at him, the top of Kolden's head barely reaching his chest.

"You get shorter or something?" Orne asked, only revealing a hint of a smile.

"Fuck off, you overgrown tree trunk," replied Kolden. He tried not to express his annoyance at the remark, but his brother always knew exactly what to say to get under his skin. "What do you need anyway?"

"Why don't you start by telling me why you haven't shown up to roll call in over a fucking week? I'm getting sick of covering for your ass."

"I've been working on something," Kolden replied, warily eyeing the door. He didn't want to risk someone overhearing the conversation.

"Could you maybe elaborate a little? I was beginning to wonder if you were dead."

"And lose opportunities to annoy you? Never. Did you really just come here to check on me? Gods, you're worse than mother."

"Oh piss off," Orne said with a corner of his mouth pulling back in resentment. "We had a run in with a bandit group on the western road this morning. One of the little shits caught a spear under my shoulder pad and broke the links, I need you to fix it."

Orne grabbed at his left shoulder plate and jostled it, showing how it had disconnected from the rest of the darksteel ensemble. Kolden inspected it from his low vantage, seeing where the hinge and link had sheared and disconnected. It looked like the layer of mail underneath had done its job in protecting him though. His brother was always volunteering for patrols, and

Kolden's custom designed armor draped him in the best protection he could manufacture. Despite his design improvements, the ogre always managed to break *something*.

"Take it off, I can probably fix it now if you can hang around here for an hour or two."

"Fine, but first you're going to tell me what the fuck you've been doing down here for the entire week. Army smiths are still a part of the *army*, in case you've forgotten."

Kolden glanced at the door again. Wanting to avoid an intrusion or prying ears, he walked over to the window and checked to see if anyone was outside, his brother watching him with a confused look. Once he was certain that there was no one else around, he bolted the door shut and motioned for Orne to follow him to the back of the shop.

"What the hell is this?" asked Orne, looking at the makeshift tent. His eyes wandered to the cot Kolden had set up in the opposite corner, and he glared at him with an expression that spoke more clearly than words. One of the benefits of growing up with a close sibling was the ability to eloquently communicate non-verbally, the poetic expression of Orne verily stating: *What the fuck is wrong with you?*

"Just listen to me for a fucking minute before you start to diatribe," said Kolden. He pulled a large black curtain closed across the opening to the cranny of the shop, sealing them in the small enclosure. He wasn't sure if the inanite-soaked curtain was enough, but it was the best that he could manage given the circumstances.

He could tell that Orne's head was about to burst with questions. He pulled the stool out from his makeshift tent and withdrew the cadentite from its hiding place, exposing the purple glow to Orne for a moment before synching the top of the bag closed again.

"What is *that*?" asked Orne with a furrowed brow, his eyes wide.

"It's cadentite," replied Kolden in a hushed tone.

"Cadentite? What's that? And where'd you get it?" boomed Orne. Kolden swore the man was incapable of subtly.

"Would you keep your voice down!?" exclaimed Kolden in a loud whisper. He then proceeded to explain what he knew about the rare stone, and how he had come into possession of it.

"It's worth *how much*?" asked Orne with a slack jaw. "Kol, you need to tell the army guard about this! Whoever this person is, we can't just let him roam around Drunt. People who need to hide something like this are nothing but trouble," he stated as though it were a matter of fact.

"I *am* telling the guard—by telling you. Also, I need you to swear that you won't tell anyone about this."

Orne looked at him, his mouth contorting in differing ways as he struggled to decide what to say next. Kolden knew that he could trust Orne—once he convinced him. For that he had a plan. But first he had to break through the barrier of stubbornness that was his brother's hallmark. Then he had to make sure he didn't slip and say something stupid later.

"No. No, I'm not doing it," said Orne with a wave of his finger. "I can see that look in your eye, Kolden. I won't be involved in another one of your damned experiments, that's what landed us here in the first place!"

"Hey, that design is still valid! One small issue—that can easily be rectified, mind you—and the army throws out something that could completely change warfare as we know it! All because it went up in smoke *one time*."

"Oh, it went up alright. Up, sideways, down, and in every other direction," said Orne with a sardonic chuckle.

"It wasn't *that* bad."

"You destroyed half the fucking barracks…"

"Yeah, but no one was injured! If it could do that to a barracks imagine what it could do on the battlefield! Gods, why is everyone's point of view so focused on what happened instead of the *potential*?"

"Whatever, Kolden. It was fucking stupid and got us sent back to this ice block, that's all that matters. I've finally started to impress the captain here and I think that with a few more months I may be able to convince him to grant us a transfer order. Don't fuck up what I'm doing for some glowing rock!"

Kolden buried his face in his hands and ground his teeth. Sometimes he wondered if his brother did the opposite of what he wanted to get under his skin. And how could he consider something as stunning, mesmerizing, and rare as cadentite to be nothing more than a stupid rock? How dense could he be?

"Look, Orne, for one thing it's more than just a simple 'glowing rock.' Second, a transfer order isn't coming from some captain in the middle of nowhere. We both know who we need to convince for that.

"And aside from its value, cadentite has never been known to do anything more harmful than glow... and maybe be used to grow some drugs. *BUT* I don't intend on doing anything like that. I just wanted to test a few things. It's completely benign, I promise."

Orne looked at him with a mixture of expressions that told him he was considering Kolden's request. Had he finally worn through his thick head? If he could get him to agree he had something that would distract Orne enough to make him forget about his cadentite concerns for a while. His brother did tend to worry excessively; it made him a fantastic soldier, but a frustrating sibling—at times.

"Fine," stated Orne, "but if anything strange or dangerous comes up you tell me. Immediately."

"Yes, yes, of course," said Kolden with an overenthusiastic nod.

"Mhm," grunted Orne with a suspicious squint of his eyes. "What are you planning on doing with it anyway?"

Kolden let out a sigh of frustration, reminded of how little progress he'd made thus far. "If I can ever get enough of it to grind off, I was intending to make a steel in the same process as darksteel. Except instead of adding mostly inanite powder with a little muted inanite powder to the molten metal, I'm going to add what I can grind off the cadentite. Maybe just a little inanite powder to balance the mixture out. Although I'm not sure if the same ratios used for inanite in darksteel can be utilized. It's three and a half percent by weight of inanite powder to produce darksteel when heated to just shy of white hot. Not to mention the chemical changes undergone during forging and special quenching. And then there's the tempering process, which—"

Kolden cut off as he saw his brother's eyes glaze over, his stare becoming distant. *Can't this man pay attention to something that doesn't involve swinging a weapon for more than ten seconds?* He knew better than to expect that from Orne, but he felt a fractious annoyance whenever his brother's thoughts wavered from their conversations.

"A knife, Orne, I'm making a knife with it," he stated bluntly.

"Ohh, well why didn't you just fucking say that?" said Orne as though it should've been the obvious way to communicate his plans.

Kolden brushed off the comment. "It's taking forever, though. I won't be able to produce something more than *maybe* five inches of blade length, depending how long I can stand to sit at this grinder. I might make a jig that or something to help, I don't know."

"A blade of any length can kill a man," said Orne confidently. Kolden knew this wasn't a snide remark, but an honest assessment. His brother might not have the focus for science, but there was no one more lethal with a blade. There was an assurance that even a small blade in Orne's massive hands—which were weapons in and of themselves—would be enough to attract a parliament of owls.

"Funny you should say that," said Kolden with a sly smile. "I've been working on something else for you, just finished it up before you got here."

Ornes eyes perked with interest as Kolden walked to the corner of the room and grabbed the sheathed sword that leaned against the corner. At nearly six feet long from pommel to tip, it was considerably taller than he was, the handle and sheath having required almost his entire stock of muted inanite-dyed leather. He handed it to Orne who now looked at Kolden with his head tilted in confusion.

"Is this a joke?" asked Orne as he drew the darksteel blade from the sheath, the lines of layered metal waving through its length like water lapping on a beach. A long fuller lightened the two-handed weapon, the balance of which Orne was testing with puzzled intrigue. Despite the ridiculous length—which had been a challenge, but watching his brother struggle to master it later would make it worth the effort—it *almost* seemed to fit with Orne's enormous girth.

"I know how much you love your halberd," said Kolden as he watched his brother step out of his small corner of the shop and into the larger workspace to take some practice swings. The blade whistled through the air, Orne's skill apparent in the way he rapidly familiarized himself with the weapon's length, missing the ceiling posts with the sword's tip by only inches as it sliced through the sweat and ash filled air. "But I thought: you know, what if Orne has to fight people who wield man-sized swords one day? He'd be at a complete loss! Besides, this was a fuck of a lot more interesting to make than those damned chisels."

"If this is man-sized," said Orne as he swung forward, then back stepped into a defensive position, "what does that make you?"

"Ha-ha," said Kolden sarcastically.

*Asshole.*

"This thing is obnoxious, Kolden. What the hell would you even use it for?" asked Orne.

"I have faith in your talents, Orne," said Kolden with a curl in his lip that turned to a smile. His brother was already locked into his bull-headed persistence. He'd probably practice with the thing for weeks. He'd go back to his halberd eventually, but Kolden would get to watch him stumble with the disproportionate sword for a while.

As Kolden was watching his brother move with the flowing grace of a mastered form—an act that shocked people on account of Orne's size—there was a sound at the door, followed by a heavy pounding.

*Here I was thinking that the old drunk had stumbled his way to a tavern,* thought Kolden. He sighed with disappointment and walked over to the door, lifting the locked latch and cracking it open to glimpse whoever was hammering at it.

As he did, a hand unexpectedly shoved the wooden panel into his face, smacking hard against his eye and forcing him to step back and permit entry to the forcible shove. He squinted through his uninjured eye, the other covered by his hand to massage the pain, and saw four young men, hardly old enough for the roundness of their childhood features to have faded, saunter haughtily into the shop. They were adorned in the finery afforded only by nobility, the silk garments and cloaks of rare furs a boast of their station.

"Why is your door locked in the middle of the day?" the one who'd slammed the door in Kolden's face asked. "Were you two perhaps in need of alone time?" The comment came with the devilish grin of superiority, the man-child's sycophants letting out a forced laugh. Kolden would have loved to wipe the smile off his entitled face, but this was the son of the new Duke of Drunt, and Kolden knew that this was—unfortunately—not someone he should bother to disrespect. Recovering from that would be more annoying than Orne.

He just hoped his brother would know the same.

In case he needed to prevent him from saying or doing something disastrously stupid, he backed away and stood next to Orne. They couldn't chance attracting the ire of the local lord, not with the cadentite in his possession.

"Wow, the ogre found a sword that's as large and stupid as he is! Do you fiddle with that massive thing because you can't find your dick to play with?" chided the boy, looking to his friends for laughs of affirmation for his terrible joke. Kolden could feel his own face turning red in a rage, the self-control that Orne was exhibiting was nothing short of miraculous.

Orne's face was wrinkled with a scowl. Kolden put his hand on his brother's arm, a prescient feeling telling him Orne was about to do or say something profoundly foolish.

"What do you want?" ask Kolden, hand still over his stinging eye.

"Where's your master?" asked the boy, as if he were annoyed at having to speak to Kolden. "My father promised that the man was crafting for me the finest sword in all of Drunt as a birthday present. It was to be delivered yesterday but I still have yet to receive it. Where is it? This delay is unacceptable."

*Oh shit,* thought Kolden. *I forgot about that order.* He'd been so enamored with the cadentite and forging Orne's sword he'd forgotten about the lord's purchase. He was going to have to workday and night to get it done now.

"It's not ready," said Kolden. "The mastersmith says that quality takes time, and this sword will take a little longer. A few days and you should have it."

"No, I want it now! It was promised to me yesterday and I have already waited a day beyond that," the boy said petulantly.

If his eye didn't hurt so much Kolden would've rolled it. He didn't want to take risks, but his patience was wearing thin.

"Look, it'll be done in a few days, it's not like *you* have any duels to attend. I think I have another here that you can use in the—"

"You shall address me as 'my Lord', as is proper for one of lowly title such as yourself, smith. Or else I will see you hanged from the ramparts." The arrogance of the statement bothered Kolden more than the threat. He could hear Orne's teeth grinding.

"My name is *Lord* Kolden du Traskor, and I don't have to address a witless infant like you with title as your peer. You'll have your fucking sword in a few days, whining about it won't hasten the process."

He despised using his title, it was a dominating shadow that he wanted to escape from. He and Orne actively avoided mentions of their full name, hoping to build a reputation of their own rather than be carried along by the legend of their parentage. For a moment he almost regretted saying it, but the brief silence from the boy and the confused look of his companions made it seem worthwhile.

"You're not lords. No self-respecting noble would be a simple blacksmith's assistant or a... whatever you are," the self-assured boy said with a dismissive glance at Orne.

"Go ask one of your father's advisors," said Kolden with a condescending tone. "Until then your sword won't craft itself, so leave so I can get to work."

He could see the confidence of the youth waning, but it was being replaced with a clear frustration. Impersonating a lord was a capital offense—not that Kolden was lying—and the boy was probably thinking that he could have Kolden punished later. *But* he couldn't risk much more than he already had if Kolden was telling the truth. The child knew there would be other ways to exact his petty revenge. The impatience of spoiled youth, however, demanded more rapid gratification.

"When I find the mastersmith, I shall tell him that you need to stop making such a mess of his shop," said the boy with a devilish grin.

Kolden looked at him in confusion. *What the hell is he talking about?*

Before Kolden could act, the boy walked over to a tall and narrow barrel, filled to the brim with oil for quenching, and with a push that strained his frail arms he tipped it over, spilling its expensive, viscous contents all over the shop floor.

With a boisterous laugh from him and his sycophants, the boys left through the way they'd come, leaving Orne and Kolden with a slick mess soaking the rough, wooden floorboards.

"I'm gonna rip that kid's fucking arms off one day..." said Orne through gritted teeth.

"He's gonna try to make our lives a living hell now," said Kolden with a shake of his head. The boy was as petty as he was peevish. He was going to have to be extra careful about concealing the cadentite now.

"If I get sent on night shifts for the next month, I'm blaming you," said Orne vengefully. "You should have just kept your fucking mouth shut."

"Me?! You were the one about to go punch him! And besides, he knocked me right in the eye with that door, probably going to be swollen up like a plum later."

"Quit being a pussy," said Orne.

"Fuck you. Give me your armor and clean this up while I fix it."

"I'm not fucking cleaning this!"

Kolden clenched his free fist and shook his head. The obstinateness of his brother boiled his blood sometimes.

"Fine, then leave the sword and get someone else to fix your armor, you ungrateful oaf."

Orne pulled the sword closer to him possessively, taking an instinctual step back to keep it from his brother's reach. He stood and looked between Kolden, the sword, and the oil on the floor for a moment.

"Fine!" he finally contended. "But ales are on you next time!"

Kolden just rolled his eyes with a wince. While his brother removed the armor, he thought about the cadentite, and the new risks that he'd stupidly brought upon himself.

He was going to need to be careful.

# CHAPTER TWENTY-SEVEN

*...they've refused me! It is beyond their place, and yet they do not bend to my commands! I've appealed to her about it, but she's unable to persuade them. My vanguard cannot manage this growing blight...*

The cold, humid air inside of Delvan's tent clung to him, the moisture on the verge of dewing upon his armor on the stand nearby. He could hear the rest of the caravan beginning their morning routine—squires preparing breakfast, horses being hitched to wagons, aides breaking down tents, all while trudging through the knee-deep snow that had hindered their progress these past weeks.

By the amount of weighty sagging in the top of his modestly sized tent, he judged it had snowed again last night, which meant they were in for another long day of traveling through the northern forests. None of that concerned him at the moment, however, as he lay on his cot, staring at the canvas above him in the dim light provided by a small gap in the tent flap.

His eyes burned with fatigue. There had been little sleeping for him in the weeks since Hilbrun's death, each night bringing on a dread of closing his eyes in the angst that he might have to relive that night in the terrors of sleep. The days were therefore a haze of exhaustion, a flow of motions that could distract him from the thoughts of stillness.

A rustle at the entrance brought a flash of white into the tent, his squire standing in the blinding glow.

"The commander sent me, my Lord, he says that you should come assist the caravan," the young man said. Delvan had never met this squire prior to his departure from Calentine. He was someone that worked for his family's house, one of the few courtesies that his father had afforded him. After weeks together he still struggled to remember the boy's name.

"Those were his exact words?" Delvan asked apathetically, still staring at the roof of his tent.

"Well, no, my Lord, but I dare say his words should not be repeated in polite company," the squire said nervously.

*Assumed as much,* he thought. He could feel the veins in his neck start to throb, a pain shooting through his jaw at just the mention of their caravan's leader.

"I'll be out in a few minutes," he managed to say as his breath became shallow and fast. His muscles tightened, pain like lightning shooting through his arm, and he dared not move for fear of making the onslaught worse. The pain crawled from his arm to his chest. It became impossible to breathe, as if his lungs were drowning, desperately struggling for air. In the midst of all this, he found himself praying to Strigifious to let him remain in this life.

Delvan felt as though he were a living contradiction. Here he was, terrified of the talons of death's wardens, yet he wanted nothing more than to cease existing and rid himself of this submergible torment. It was as though the hidden hand of an apparition were randomly reaching from the ground and gripping his heart, spreading icy agony through him, its touch lingering for hours after release.

And he was helpless to stop it.

After several of the deepest breaths he could shakily manage, the touch receded, leaving him jittery and racked. His body felt as though he'd been thrown from his horse, and his mind spun into a deeper fatigue of unmanageable thoughts. Still, he donned his armor and thick cloak knowing that too much delay would bring the wrath of his angry commanding officer.

As he walked out into the stark, bright reflection of the morning sun off the freshly fallen blanket of white, which clung to the leafless branches of the trees like cotton, he thought back to the day he was sent on this assignment. It had only been a few days after Hilbrun's death, and he had been called before the Court.

"Pupil Delvan ce Saffstar," the elderly, but strong looking man had formerly stated from the high podium which curled around Delvan, other members of the Sapphiric Court spread evenly around its arc. "After hearing the testimonies of the events surrounding the destruction of the Merchants' Guild headquarters and the death of Cadet Hilbrun al Portaine, we have voted to allow your continuance as a cadet of this Court."

The words had come from the man's hard face with even pontification. Delvan could hear the familiar disdain in his voice. He'd always looked at Delvan as a waste of a gift, a cliff dive short of his potential. The rarity of Pyromancers carried a mountain of expectations which the orator had time and time again deemed Delvan to fall short of. If the man had spent more time with his youngest son, perhaps Delvan would resent him less.

"However," his father had continued, "the reckless negligence of your actions cannot be ignored. The gifts granted to us by the King's grace and will of the gods are not frivolous endowments to be abused with reckless abandon! Your lack of self-control and disregard for proper procedure directly led to the destruction of property which will cost the kingdom the equivalent value of an entire noble house.

"The traditional system of cadet understudy is clearly not suited for one of your... nature. Therefore, with the regal seal as authorization, I've submitted an executive order to place you under the tutelage of a fully anointed knight. They will be responsible for reporting your progression to this Court, and only with their recommendation will you be permitted to apply for knighthood before us."

Delvan had continued to stare off into the distance, his face blank and unmoving as he avoided eye contact with his father, his voice echoing in the baroque, stone-walled chamber.

"Furthermore," his father said, an edge to his voice, "you will be sent on assignment with your newly selected mentor, with a task that is of the utmost importance to this Court and the King. I would like to note that I was originally against giving you responsibilities to this degree but was convinced by my peers due to the utmost respect we hold for the knight whom you shall report to and his long history of fealty. I pray it is enough to offset your own shortcomings.

"You will be delivering sapphires to several lords who have been graced with the King's approval to sire children who will bear gems in his name. They are in duchies across the kingdom, from here to Brethefen, where your new mentor has requested *permanent* transfer, and which will serve as your outpost for the foreseeable future."

For the first time since he'd entered the Court chambers, he looked up at his father, his eyes wide and jaw lowering to the floor.

"You're *banishing* me?" he'd asked with disbelief. Calentine was his home, the only one he'd ever known. None of this had been *his* fault, why was he being ostracized? Was his father just using this misfortune as an opportunity to rid himself of Delvan? Rage flared inside of him, a focused outlet for his storming emotions. "The guild was hiding sapphires, and instead of charging them with treason you're reimbursing them? And then you have the gall to punish *me*?! How can you justify this?!"

"No evidence of sapphires was found in the wreckage you left behind," his father stated coldly, his eyes fixed and stern. "The guild has stated that you forced your way in and demanded entry to their vault. They have even gone so far as to claim that you were conspiring with the thieves who—"

"LIES!" Delvan had screamed with clenched fists. *How* dare *they*.

"Witnesses claimed you were seen carrying one of their members from the fire, a story you yourself corroborated." There'd been a condescension to his tone, barely veiled to the others present but glaring to Delvan.

"She's not the one you should be looking for, and I already told you, she saved my life! She should be absolved, not persecuted and hunted! You're wasting time and resources when the people you should be out there hunting are—"

"Enough!" his father had bellowed. "We will hear no more of this. Our decision is final. Your belongings are being packed and added to the royal caravan as we speak, you leave tomorrow at dawn. This hearing is adjourned."

The words were spoken as though carved in stone, an indefinite permanence to them. As the members of the court had filed out of the chambers with indifference to his presence, Delvan had felt the grip of the shadowy, ghoulish hand around his heart for the first time. He'd tried to breathe with lungs that seemed filled with liquid so icy it burned, and cold sweat beaded on his paled brow. He'd stumbled out of the chambers and into a corner of the grand hall outside, shaking as he struggled and gasped, his heart threatening to burst from his chest and body shooting with pain.

It was a betrayal not easily forgotten. The first of two.

Delvan shook the memory from his mind, the mere thought of it enough to make his heart race uncontrollably. He instead hiked through the tall snow to his horse, checking on her as she was being saddled. The mare snorted lightly as he petted her neck, something about the animal's tranquility was able to ease the pain in his chest, and he found himself coming to her often. She nudged him as he stood there, and a faint smile shone from his face, one of the few he had these days.

"I'm alright," he said in a quiet voice as the squires worked to saddle her.

A shout rent the air and wiped away his smile as quickly as it had come, the sound as grotesque to him as bile. "And where the *fuck* have you been?" the second of his father's betrayals asked.

Delvan turned to see Knight Commander Ferrand kicking his feet through heavy, knee-deep snow as though it were dust on the floor, his perpetual scowl carved deep in his face. Of all the knights in the kingdom who were possible candidates for Delvan's mentorship, the Court—his father—had chosen this one. His father was not a man to make decisions out of hand, nor at random. It left him wondering what the meaning of this assignment was, but more than anything it filled him with a disgusted resentment for both his father and the commander, the man who'd acted against him and Hilbrun at every turn.

"Well, don't just stand there looking stupid," Ferrand said. "Get out there and start clearing some of this damn snow! Fucking useless as a Pyromancer, I swear. What good are you if you can't make a path for us? Huh? Get a gods-damn shovel and get to work."

The man's face was narrow and hard, eyes seething with rage as he glared at Delvan. He could feel his heart racing, the fingers of shadow touching him on the shoulder as a delicate warning of its cruel intent. Something leashed its grip—a caged fury inside of him. It was a fiery hatred, a demon which grew every day as its enclosure shrank around it.

This man, this supposed knight and brother in bond, was responsible for the thefts of cadentite in Calentine. This was fact to Delvan now, the evidence Hilbrun had shared with him and the man's constant interference with their investigation ample proof. Over the past several weeks of travel, through his haze of grief, a question had blossomed in Delvan's mind, one that screamed at him every time he saw the commander's face: Was Ferrand somehow involved in the theft that led to Hilbrun's death?

It had festered in his thoughts, infecting him with a need to know. The Blue in him resisted the idea, wanting to believe that there was no possibility another gem-bearer could commit such a treachery. But the logic behind it was counterbalancing the deep-seeded loyalty. There had been a large specimen of cadentite in the vault; Delvan had seen it, *felt* it, there could be no other explanation for the glow he'd witnessed. It stood to reason that the commander, involved in so many of the other thefts, would be complicit in this one as well.

Delvan's face tightened and his mouth flashed a sneer of contempt as he thought about Ferrand's possible responsibility for his friend's murder. He needed proof, but what he *wanted* was to watch the man suffer a slow and painful death atop a pyre of his own fashion. He would find evidence proving the commander was complicit, even if he had to pry it from his lips while they were touched by flame. His heart pounded now in a different way, a fierce rhythm of wrath.

"You going to say anything? Did you go deaf as well as dumb? Your insub—" the commander cut off his berating as he turned to the sounds of struggle from one of the carriages. Four horses of the royal stable, well-muscled and premier examples of equine beauty, attempted to pull the carriage of the royal ambassador to no avail. The gloss of the exterior intensified the orange paint with blue trim, and its finely carved details sat delicately upon the curves of the frame, a shape that could only be achieved with mastery of craft. Its stunning opulence exemplified its grand stature, stating without words it was an extension of the King and Court.

It was also extraordinarily heavy.

The central carriage of their caravan was constantly getting stuck in an unseen rut or deep in the snow and had been slowing them down immensely. Even with six other carriages full of royal staff and supplies specifically for this journey, their party was frequently stopping to get this particular carriage free of one obstacle or another. They were supposed to have arrived in Drunt weeks ago, and their delay was becoming exacerbated with each of the increasingly frequent heavy snowfalls.

Commander Ferrand muttered under his breath and yet again seemed to dismiss Delvan's presence from his mind. He walked over to the rear of the carriage while shouting at the driver to make sure the horses would start moving once the carriage did. With feet locked and knees bent in the snow, the older Blue pressed both hands against the cart and shoved.

The wheels, which had been locked in a deep, frozen rut, turned as the cart lurched forward. The driver whipped the horses into motion, and the vehicle pulled itself forward several feet, now free of the constraining divot.

As though it had barely cost him any exertion, the knight commander was back to screaming at everyone a few seconds later, driving the party to get moving. Delvan glared at the man from a distance, his chest dueling between the steady beat of hatred and the painful, uncontrollable beat of the unseen hand's clutch.

He took a deep breath and left his horse to the squires, instead going to his tent to help his aide pack up some of his lighter gear. The thought of going to the front of the caravan and casting fire nearly set his brain into a frenzy. He didn't want to attribute anything that the commander had stated to being true, seeing only lies and venom spewed from his mouth. But the comment about wasting his gift...

Delvan had not cast since the night at the guild, and the commander's words had struck an exposed nerve.

He had tried, but before even congealing a spark of flame, his heart had threatened to beat out of his chest. He'd collapsed to the floor, his face cold and chest so tight he thought he'd been stabbed. No Blue in recorded history which he was aware of had lost their ability to cast while still carrying their sapphire. Yet here he was, again exemplifying their entire order and continuing to be the disappointment his father always claimed him to be.

*Why did the gods choose this for me?* he thought.

He avoided the commander whenever possible, trying to stay invisible in the lengthy caravan. That, however, seemed to just increasingly draw the man's attention. The only thought that kept him moving forward was the need to find answers, for Hilbrun's sake. But even as that grief-fueled anger sparked inside of him, he felt the torment of his mind as the commander's voice tore in the distance.

# Chapter Twenty-Eight

*I've had another approach me with a possible solution to my circumstance. It carries risk, but it avoids my own destruction. My agreement carries with it an indebtment, but I can foresee no alternatives.*

The black sword flourished in a figure-eight pattern, whistling through the gray air of another overcast winter day in Drunt. Orne held the handle of the oversized sword with one hand near the cross guard and the other at the pommel—nearly a foot and a half apart from one another—as it was the only way he found he could maneuver the weapon's bulk in a controllable fashion.

He was annoyed with his brother for creating such a monstrosity and had spent much of the past few days trying to conceive of uses for the elongated blade—which Kolden had clearly not considered, instead forging it out of an amused curiosity. As much as he hated to admit it, the more he contemplated it, the more practical applications he could think of. The length, combined with the strength and flexibility only offered by darksteel, could be effective against calvary, or perhaps soldiers armed with pikes in a phalanx.

*Damn it.* He'd wished to tell Kolden he was an idiot for creating this blade—he still thought his brother stupid, but for a variety of other reasons. Now it seemed he was going to have to do the opposite. He'd have to be careful not to include a compliment when he gave his assessment, lest it boost his brother's already impossibly vaunted ego.

He remembered when Kolden had completed his Halberd for him—a weapon he cared for as though it were his own offspring—and he'd praised his brother's crafting skills. It was the moment his brother had shed any remaining sense of humility, and now he had to listen to Kolden's constant superiority complex.

*Never again,* he thought.

Orne switched to a defensive stance, pulling the blade's hilt in by his side and keeping the point forward and up. He'd modified several common forms to accommodate for the sword's unprecedented length, adjusting constantly to find something that wouldn't end with a motion that pulled the sword away uncontrollably after a swing.

A thrust, followed by a quick shift to a more offensive posture, allowed him a follow up strike which slashed, the momentum of which he then fed into a full rotation of the blade around his head. The move could clear anyone within the tip's radius to a similar degree as his halberd, and crowd control was invaluable in battle. The sword, which still only weighed a few pounds but was heavy by normal standards, gained enough speed in the overhead spin that it sliced through the dowel supporting the practice mannequin before him, removing the straw-stuffed head.

*Maybe I should purchase a cleaned hog from the butcher, see what it's like against bone and flesh,* he thought, wanting to give the sword a more realistic test. The last time he'd done that, however, the company's cook had been rather frustrated by the oddly sized and thoroughly cleaved sections of pork he was forced to work with afterward. *At least he got a free meal out of it, so who cares,* he decided.

"Is that a sword a spear, Orne?" a voice from behind him called over the sounds of other soldiers' weapons clashing and ringing against practice dummies such as his.

He turned to see the company's medic, Nalhen, approaching from the other side of the barrack's training yard over snow compacted by hundreds of marching feet, the duke's castle rising into the gloomy sky behind him. He was a taller man—shorter than Orne, but most people were. His blonde hair and naturally tan skin gave away his southern heritage. The winters of Drunt were brutal for him, but he was acclimating well enough.

*He's wasted as a medic.*

"It's something Kolden built," said Orne, looking the blade up and down.

"Obviously," Nalhen replied. "You do any sparring with it yet?"

"Well, you're the only one who ever wants to fucking spar with me anymore, so what do you think?"

"I think that you need to challenge something that can fight back," he said, pointing at the dismembered head of stuffed straw on the ground.

"You looking to get your ass kicked again? Do you even have anything left to wager that you haven't lost to me?"

Nalhen was nothing if not persistent. Soldiers often made casual wagers on sparring sessions—rounds of drafts, small amounts of money, coffee rations—and most of the company were deeply indebted to Orne already, none as much as Nalhen, however. Orne had to give the man credit, he was the best fighter in the company aside from himself, and he challenged Orne relentlessly in an attempt to finally claim a win.

Nalhen's lips drew back, and he waved his hand in dismissal, "You can't keep winning forever. C'mon, let's give that Orne-sized piece of steel a test. You pick the wager."

"Fine," Orne said in his deep, reserved sounding voice. He was actually eager to test the sword in combat, but he tried to hide that from Nalhen. "Whoever loses has to buy a hog carcass for the other."

"You'd lose *and* buy me dinner? I'm amazed at your selflessness, Orne," Nalhen said with a grin.

"Shut up and get yourself ready," Orne stated as though an order.

He pressed thick, tanned leather specifically for sparring to the blade's edges, then tied the banding tightly to the sword with leather string. The additional weight threw the sword slightly off balance, but it was manageable and safe to wield in a practice setting against a fellow soldier.

Nalhen chose a blunted spear from the weapons rack nearby. It was what he was most proficient with, though Orne knew the man to have aptitude for several other tools of war. He was pleased with Nalhen's choice though—it was the exact scenario he thought this new sword best for, and now he'd be able to test the theory.

Each postured in front of the other in a readiness to fight, Nalhen starting the contest with the traditional statement, "Swords unsheathed." Orne gripped the leather wrapped hilt tightly, taking a deep breath of the cold air. He pushed thoughts from his mind and focused on the fight before him. The previous fights he'd won against Nalhen mattered little to him, despite the boasting he did. Every encounter presented a chance for failure, just as it did in battle, and he focused his mind as though his life depended on this crossing of steel. This could come down to luck as easily as skill.

He replied, "Blood drawn," to state his acceptance of the duel.

Nalhen started without hesitation by feinting a few rapid, forward thrusts, testing Orne. The sword's length allowed him to deflect the prods early, compensating for the slower, bulkier movements of the weapon. But even with two hands the momentum of the blade's length strained his wrists to control and bring it back into position. He adjusted his left hand near the pommel, trying to use that hand as a lever and guide, with his front as a pivot.

Orne went on the offensive, thrusting forward, but Nalhen's spear was able to easily deflect the strike with the dense, wooden shaft with a dull *clunk*. Orne used the momentum of the blocked attack to flourish in front of him, deflecting an attack from Nalhen's spear that looked to take advantage of the opportunity Orne had presented after his thwarted thrust.

He pulled himself back into a defensive stance. He wasn't yet able to swing the sword adeptly enough for an offensive encounter, the spear more agile than the lumbering blade. Instead, he would have to wait for Nalhen's eventual strike. Their feet shifted in a mirrored dance as they circled each other, each fixing their eyes intently on the other as they watched for the slightest flinch, any indication of what the other was planning.

It was not a long wait, Nalhen reaching the spear towards Orne's armored chest with perfect form as he thought he saw an opening. With a small step to his left, Orne deflected the spear to his right, the sword's tip going near the ground and slightly behind him. He stepped closer to Nalhen, who'd also planted his foot closer to Orne to add power to his strike, and brought the sword's pommel in front of him, the darksteel blade now pointed fully backward. With a powerful joust he jabbed the handle's end into Nalhen's chest—rather than his face as he would in combat—and knocked the air from his lungs.

Nalhen gasped for air, and for good measure Orne swept his leg at Nalhen's feet, laying him out on his back with a swift and smooth motion. Orne brought the blade's guarded point to Nalhen's neck and waited.

"Y-yield," said Nalhen through gasping wheezes.

Orne extended an arm and helped him up from the icy ground. "Not bad, not bad," he said mockingly.

"I nearly had you," said Nalhen through ragged breaths. "That damned sword is almost as annoying as your halberd."

"The fuck you did," said Orne with a disconcerting look. "Lunging head on like that, instead of taking advantage of your spear's agility over my sword's. That was stupid, even for you."

"You're such a prick," said Nalhen as he bent over and rubbed his chest with a wince.

"Well, this prick is hungry, so why don't you run on down to the butcher and see about that hog. I've got some field tests I want to perform next."

"Uhh," said Nalhen hesitantly, "about that... You wanna just add it to my tab? Not sure I can afford a hog until we get our next monthly allowance."

*Then why accept the wager?* he thought with a tightened jaw. He didn't lack for money and could buy the hog himself but found the blatant lack of honorable accountability distasteful. Nalhen, however, *was* the only one willing to spar with him, and he gave him a certain amount of slack on his wagers. *Fine, if he's not going to pay up on his bet, then he will spend the next couple hours helping me train with this sword.*

As he was about to inform Nalhen of this commitment, Orne spotted the captain, who was the current highest-ranking officer in Drunt, walking at the edge of the yard towards the barracks, having come from the castle's grounds.

"Wait here," he said to Nalhen, who was just barely starting to breathe normally.

He strode with the gait that only legs as long as his could achieve, catching the captain as he neared the barracks entrance.

"Captain," Orne called out. "A moment, sir?"

"Yes, Sergeant, what is it?" the older, grizzly man said with a sigh.

"Sir, I was wondering if you'd heard anything from my most recent transfer request?"

"No, Sergeant, I haven't heard anything."

"But, sir, that was nearly two weeks ago, surely a carrier must have come—"

"I haven't received one because I never sent it," the captain interrupted.

Orne's brow furrowed as the shock of the statement processed in his mind. After a brief pause, his face shifted from an open mouth and bewildered eyes to teeth clenched and face steaming.

"What do you mean you never sent it?!" Orne demanded, his military training forcing out a last, unconscious word, "Sir."

"We both know what the response is going to be, Orne. The same as the last dozen requests that I've submitted: *Denied*. I'm not wasting any more of my or others' time just to appease your delusions. The general isn't going to approve your request, not if it comes from me. Try writing him yourself."

The problem was that Orne *had* tried writing to the man—many times. On the rare occasions his aides had time to respond for him, they always had similar answers for Orne's requests. He'd hoped that recommendations from his superior officer would encourage a transfer, but it made little to no difference.

The captain dismissed Orne and turned to walk to the barracks, leaving him standing by himself looking angry and bitter. How was he supposed to get out of this place and fight in real battles against enemy armies, rather than roadside bandits? While he blamed his brother for getting them this station in the snow-covered wasteland, the truth was that their previous outpost had been eagerly meek and similarly *safe*. He yearned to earn his own name among songs of valor, rather than being a footnote of his father's greatness.

Orne wanted more, and was desperate to get it.

His fists were still clenched long after the barracks door closed behind the captain. Burning oil pumped through his veins and a tension built in his muscles. He turned to see Nalhen still in the practice area walking off the pain of Orne's previous blow.

"Pick up that spear," he shouted to the man as he stormed towards him.

He had some frustration to work out.

# Chapter Twenty-Nine

*Naught has gone according to my new master's plan. I'd antic-
ipated subterfuge, the sly cunning of their repute well known.
We've one success, true, but the remaining arsenal now turn
their sharpened edges toward us. A possibility which our own
hubris never allowed us to consider before it was too late.*

The White Mountains glowed like a collection of snow caps in the
distance behind Nerio, the midday sun reflecting off the white stone
slopes that struck upwards like great upheavals which blocked a portion
of sky from view. From his vantage atop the bell tower, he looked out to
the east, across the rolling hills of crops to the barren browns of the desert
beyond. The land in the distance had grown dark, a shade as deep as night
drawn over it by clouds that rose like a turbulent wall and now charged
towards the contrasting mountains.

The clash of a raging storm against the stalwart peaks meant rain in
torrents for Brethefen, the dry soil's inability to absorb water creating
flash flooding and danger for the residents. He and his fellow bell tollers
had struck brass at midday to send everyone home early in warning. Most
would be safe indoors, the flooding well controlled by the streets which
all sloped downward towards the city walls, away from the elevated
Devapuram at the city's heart.

Lightning flashed and illuminated the distant contours of the clouds,
the sounds of thunder rumbling as though the gods themselves clashed
with demons in the storm.

*What has upset Almedia so that she spreads her wings and delivers this deluge upon us?*

He could see the people hurrying to their homes below, tiny specks that scurried through the streets. Their urgency was palpable, a looming rain not taken lightly.

This storm would bring water they desperately needed, but at what cost? What was this twisted irony that the goddess of the sky would send unto them? Whatever divine logic enforced her will, Nerio could not guess.

He left his perch on the bell tower balcony down to the street below and began walking towards the city center. People all around him clamored up the brick steps that led into each home, the doors all elevated above the road to stop flood waters from forcing their way inside. The bright colors of the homes took on a dun tone as the clouds began their descent upon the city, the racing desert storm carried on a chariot drawn by the howling winds.

He neared the Devapuram, mist now pelting his face and robe, and turned away from the pillared hall to a nearby structure. Stout and long, the communal bathhouse was constructed of the same ornately carved stone as many other religious buildings and was richly decorated in carved images of holy visages. This was the closest of Brethefen's bathhouses to the clergy house where a majority of the priests—including Nerio—resided, and its high elevation in the city's center meant that it was generally safe from flooding.

Nerio walked up the few steps to the iron-clad doors of the front entry, several people leaving and making their way to their residences. During periods of inclement weather most stayed home, and the bathhouse would be sparsely populated with other members of the clergy whose duties for the day had been suspended.

He walked through the anteroom and into a tiled space full of low benches. Shelving and hooks for storing and hanging clothing and personal items lined the walls, with more freestanding in the room like rows of bookshelves. The large room was humid, which was always a strange feeling environment after coming from the parched desert air. Nerio began to disrobe, sweat already starting to bead on his skin.

While he neatly arranged his few personal items on a shelf, several bathers entered from the door at the room's opposite end, looking to leave the bath house to avoid the storm's fury. The men and women, still nude and drenched from the communal baths, each grabbed a towel and began to dry themselves as they walked to where their own clothing hung from the wall.

One woman walked to Nerio and stopped beside him, grabbing her Holy Hand's robe from the wall and dressing. He looked her in the eye and gave a small but polite smile before walking towards the door she had entered from, now fully disrobed himself.

The bathhouse, immense with its low, ridged ceiling, could comfortably fit one of the city's side streets within its linear hall. Large copper tubs—illuminated by torches and braziers to compensate for the lack of sun through the skylights above—were arranged along either wall and were each capacious enough to fit ten people. Fires burning beneath some of them were enclosed by brick and vented outside, bringing many to a temperature that forced copious amounts of steam into the grand hall. The moisture filled air vented through an open but covered ridge above, which was currently allowing the sounds of drumming rain to enter the vast room. No other bathhouse in Brethefen compared to this one's grandeur.

To be clean was an act considered as devout as daily worship. This and other bath houses provided the space to perform the holy ritual for the masses.

On the wall was a dial gauge connected to a nearby bath pump, showing the current levels of water available in the deep, underground cisterns the city was built atop of. Very rarely was water allotment for the bath houses denied, and close attention was paid to the water level in every part of the city. From what Nerio understood they were approaching extreme lows since their last Tempest had been required to relocate to another city, and the incoming rain was much needed.

*The flooding will still affect so many. Crops and fields washed out, those on the outskirts seeing the highest levels of water, all potentially harmful,* he thought as he walked past several of the tubs. With each gift came a cost, and Nerio found himself guiltily upset about this simple concept of life. *'That which is placed in thine hand has come from another's,'* the scripture stated. It was a simple verse, but Nerio found that his own interpretation and feelings paralleled the potential cost this rain would incur.

He walked along the long array of baths, some occupied with small groups, others by a single man or woman, until he arrived at one that was unoccupied and with dying coals beneath. The water, hardly lukewarm, was a comfortable reprieve from the heat of the desert, even with cold air being blasted at the city by the approaching storm front.

He listened to the wind whistling through the vented ridge above him, the dull gray light of its opening already less luminous than the torches mounted to the walls. He sat down on the bench that was molded into the tub, the water up to his chest. He leaned back and closed his eyes as he listened to the soft mutterings of the other bathers, shifting of water, and the variable gusts outside.

Relaxation should have spread through him, but instead his muscles remained tense and his mind raced as it flashed thoughts across the back of his eyelids like a turning page. He'd failed in what seemed like a repetitious cycle and had come to the point where he dared not attempt anything new for fear of that inevitable disappointment. Each day his body shifted through practiced motions, nothing new ever occurring.

He still helped people, a person in need was one thing he still could not bear to witness. In the months since Lord Grundan's death, two more residents of the Asylum had attempted to send themselves to prisons of the underworld. Nerio hadn't been able to save one of them, and he now felt like that man's tortured soul connected to Nerio via an invisible thread, weaving a fabric among others which tugged at him and woke him in the night.

*Why wasn't I better? Perhaps then I could have saved them.*

The sound of water being disturbed in his tub pulled him from his introspection, the splash rippling over his chest. Someone had stepped in to join him, it would seem. He'd come a distance from the entrances to have some private respite, and wondered who could have decided to get in the same bath.

He opened his eyes to a sight which chilled him to his core and made him unable to speak or think, the only desire of his body to flee. Instead, it paralyzed itself and trapped him within the domain of this... creature which walked into the water.

The man stepping into his tub was older, his gray hair trimmed short with much of it receding back and enlarging his forehead, wearing only his black locket around his neck. His stomach protruded outward as though engorged and ready to burst, his face equally round and rotund. Thin, hairline scars covered much of his skin, so faded that they would be unnoticeable at most distances, but Nerio was all too familiar with them, and could see them hatching the silver hair on the man's body.

This was Principle Jerdine, the head priest of Brethefen. A man that Nerio spent a significant amount of effort trying to avoid.

"Brother Nerio," said Jerdine as he sat next to him, shifting so that their thighs touched under the water's surface. His muscles constricted, like chains had bound his insides so tightly that he ceased breathing, his eyes focused on a point far in the distance, beyond the walls of the bath house. "Why has it been so long since I've seen you at one of my speaks?"

*Can you not leave me be?* he thought.

"I-I volunteer at the other end of the city," he managed to say in a low mumble, "I get to the Devapuram when my schedule allows."

*Where did Jerdine even come from?* he thought. *I didn't see his robe when I came in and with the storm coming, he should be deep in prayer, not bathing.*

"Ah yes, at the Asylum, so I've heard. Your talents truly are wasted there, Nerio, think of all you could do if you were to rejoin my disciples. You could even take the position that the old librarian has been trying to convince you to take for years. You'd be closer to the library, the Devapuram, the clergy house, all of it."

*And you,* Nerio thought with a shiver and twist of his insides.

Jerdine wrapped his arm around Nerio and caressed his shoulder. It was the putrid arm of a cursed disease, spreading an infection of discontent and sickening revulsion through his body and soul. He felt his mind trembling while his body remained fixed and still.

"I am needed to help people, and those in the Asylum need it most. They are forgotten and uncared for by society," he said in defense of his avoidance.

"Bah, that's what the Hands are for. You can't help them any more than they can help themselves. I've missed you, my boy, I know I've given you less attention over the past few years, but I shouldn't be so remiss. In fact, in this dim light, that face of yours still holds such... youthful features. Mhm..." The man trailed off in thought, and Nerio could feel his eyes fixed with hooks upon his face. He remained looking forward, not daring to meet the man's gaze.

"Take the morning off tomorrow, they can manage without you for a period, I'm certain," continued Jerdine after he regained focus. "Come to my speak at the Devapuram, I'd like to catch up with you in my chambers after. It's been so long since we last had time to ourselves, after all.

"I'd offer for you to accompany me this afternoon but, alas, I must go speak to Almedia about this storm. Her idea of gifts can so often be full of brutality. I look forward to seeing you tomorrow," Jerdine said as he removed his arm and stood to leave. Nerio's shoulders and neck shuddered, the man's touch refusing to be forgotten by his skin.

Nerio remained staring straight ahead, wanting to implode into the smallest possible form of existence. His body pulled itself inward like a turtle into its shell as Jerdine stepped out of the bath and walked away, a despicable smile drawn on his face. As air finally came back into Nerio's lungs his body began to tremble, a delayed reflection of the shaking in his soul. How could he have allowed this encounter to happen, what mistake had he made? He was always so diligent in his caution, yet it had been insufficient.

He would have to find an excuse for avoiding the Devapuram tomorrow, possibly for the next several weeks. *I must do something, anything to avoid him further. Perhaps I can take residence in a clergy house nearer to the Asylum,* he thought. As a priest he did not have many personal items aside from basic necessities, and moving from the primary clergy house to a smaller one in the city wouldn't be difficult. But he knew that if Jerdine wanted to find Nerio, little would stop him.

Another thought crossed his mind. It was brief, a quick flash of light no brighter than a single star in the night sky, but it was born of his own thoughts and that disgusted him almost as much as Jerdine's touch had.

*If I can avoid him long enough, he will become distracted by someone else. Someone new.*

How could he wish for someone else to suffer in his stead? What type of monster would wish for such things? Was he no better than Jerdine himself? Guilt from the idea flooded him and broke the seals of his eyes, trickles of it running down his cheek. His throat tightened and each breath shook his lean frame.

He'd lived with the weight of fake ignorance of Jerdine's actions for years. Each day he did not have to see the man's face or feel his touch was a day survived, but it was one perhaps lost to another. Many of Jerdine's favored disciples did, one day or another, leave. Fleeing the city or going into hiding.

Nerio had friends that had managed to escape from Jerdine's overarching prowess, friends he longed to see once more. He'd done his best to imitate them, removing himself as a disciple and instead taking the white sash of equitability, then taking positions as far as possible from the principal's favored locations.

It had worked—for a while.

He'd considered trying to flee to another city—many travelers and merchants would take a priest into their company or caravan for little to no fee—but something kept him trapped here. It could be said to be fear, or perhaps it was that this was all he knew. He didn't know the answer, he just understood that this is where he would remain.

Sitting there, trembling in the cooling water, he shoved down the thoughts of what Jerdine would do without him present, and while the idea might have been silenced, it took on a twisted form of blackness, a voracious pit of guilt that devoured and chewed at his soul. An animalistic creature that only desired to grow and spread.

It was nothing new. In fact, its familiarity was perhaps the closest thing he had to a kindred relationship. His one constant companion.

# Chapter Thirty

*The most catastrophic weapons to have ever existed in all the realms now turn their ferocity against us. There is no victory in sight. I hide, for they guard the gate. The home I long wished to return to seems an even more impossible distance.*

Steel clashed against wood as Orne's halberd swung through the air, dropping down onto the shield of the practice dummy in the training yard. Another layer of snow had fallen last night, but he'd already flattened and cleared the area around his training space with the practiced movements and forms mastered through the years.

He shifted the weapon's shaft to his side, making semicircular motions around the shield's exterior. He brought the axe-head to the legs, then the spear point to the neck, and then repeated the arcing attack. Switching, he then spun the weapon around his head, a whirring sound cutting through the cold air as the seven-foot-long polearm rotated around him. The side opposite the axe-head had a long-headed hammer, rather than the traditional spike, and it was a favored feature of Orne's. Not much wider than a carpenter's hammer's head, the blunted protrusion took some practice to get accustomed to, but it was mortally effective when used correctly.

He used the full momentum of the spin to connect the hammer to the helmet affixed to the mannequin, the speed and force deeply indenting the steel helm and crushing the straw head beneath. The halberd, forged of darksteel and mounted to an ash pole, fit his height well and with it he had deftly defeated every opponent he'd fought against.

*And I'm stuck here using it on mannequins and bandits.*

"Hey Orne," he heard Nalhen call out from behind him, "you hear about the caravan that arrived last night?"

"No," he replied dismissively. "Why should I care about another caravan?"

"'Cause, this one was a *royal* caravan. Almost all military, protecting some emissary or something."

A pit formed in Orne's stomach. If there was ever a party to join that could not only lead him out of Drunt, but onto greater things, a royal guard would be it. Not that the captain would ever sign off on the transfer.

"Great," he grumbled. He squeezed his halberd tighter, the sound of the handle's leather grip-wrap creaking audibly against wood.

"Yeah, and here's the best part," Nalhen said with a gleam in his eye, "they had a couple *Blues* with 'em."

Orne turned and looked at Nalhen with an eyebrow raised. He'd only ever briefly met a few knights, despite him and Kolden attending one of the best military academies in the kingdom—Blues attended their own, special school. None resided in Drunt, not that he could blame them.

*What are a bunch of Blues doing here in Drunt? Who would* willingly *come—*

"Oh look, the ogre is trying to think!" a pubescent voice said with derision. Orne turned to see the duke's son and his entourage standing a few yards away on the path that led to the castle, snickering arrogantly. He gripped the shaft of his polearm so tightly that it threatened to splinter.

"What, did you forget how to talk, Lord Ass-wipe?" the boy mocked as Orne glared at him.

"Just ignore them," Nalhen said quietly, unable himself to speak down to a lord. "C'mon, I'll grab a spear and we can spar."

"Fine," forced out Orne through clenched teeth and narrow eyes. He turned and took a step before the haughty child spat out another statement.

"Yeah, that's right, walk away. You probably can't even swing that oversized stick worth a damn anyway."

Orne stopped dead in his tracks, his face turning a deep red and his eye quivering.

"Ohh," said Nalhen, taking a step back, "don't do it Orne. It's not worth pissing off a lord, just let it go."

Orne had no intention of "letting it go."

He spun and pointed the halberd at the child across the yard and shouted with a deep voice that carried his wrath, "Come here and duel me, then! Let's see how your skills stand up!"

The boy's face went pale as his hand grabbed the white hilt of the ornate sword at his side. The rest of the grounds went quiet as soldiers stopped and stared, their faces turning almost as white as the lord's snowy visage. Most were not aware of Orne's title, and probably thought he'd signed his own death sentence by challenging someone of a higher station.

*But the brat knows,* Orne thought, *and he knows his options are either to accept and be humiliated, or decline and face quiet, widespread ridicule.*

Challenging someone so young was distasteful, and most skilled warriors—outside of official games or contests—were noble enough to not challenge people so unmatched. But Orne didn't care about bullshit propriety, he was done taking abuse from someone who weighed as much as his leg. It was time to put the arrogant teen in his place.

"I-I, uhh..." the boy stuttered.

"I'll fight in his stead," came a projected and commanding voice from Orne's side. In the heat of his anger, Orne had not noticed the man approaching from the castle. His gray-speckled hair and stiff features marked him as an experienced military man, but what concerned Orne the most was the armor he bore: darksteel mixed with blue-dyed leather and patches of mail.

A knight.

Orne immediately stood at attention in the presence of the superior officer, as did the other soldiers in the yard.

"Ha!" the boy excitedly exclaimed. "Now you're done for, you—"

"Shut up, dipshit," the Blue said, cutting him off, "before I throw you over the wall. What do you say, soldier? You got the skill to back up that brawn? I haven't had a good duel in ages."

Orne couldn't help but crack a smile at the aghast expression on the boy's face. But he'd never fought a Blue before, and questions mixed with concerns rampaging through his mind. There were stories about what Blues could do, rumors spread among the men that made them sound like they had the power of the gods themselves. He wasn't sure if he believed it all, but even if *some* of it were true, it could result in a disastrously unbalanced duel.

Still, he wasn't one to turn down a challenge.

"I'm not a caster," the Blue said as though he could read Orne's thoughts by his hesitation. "Traditional dual rules and you don't need to worry about being turned to ash or stone, how's that sound?"

Orne eyed the short man up and down, noting the diminutive sword at his side and the expensive—but battle scarred—armor adorning him, his shoulder pad marking him as a knight commander. There was no doubt the man was battle hardened, a level of experience that couldn't be taught in any training.

After a moment he nodded with a grunt in acceptance.

"Great. Name's Lord Ferrand ce Lione, and you are?" the knight commander said.

"Orne," he replied. It had not been a formal name and rank request, a loophole he often used to avoid his full title.

"Well, Orne, tell me: how does a sergeant afford such pricey equipment? Darksteel armor *and* weapon... Ten sergeants combined couldn't pool enough money to buy anything that exquisite with a year's salary. You bounty hunt on the side or something?"

*That's actually not a bad idea,* he realized, annoyed he hadn't thought of it himself.

"Mastersmith made it for me," he said bluntly, constantly wary of Kolden's delicate situation, even if his conceited brother assumed otherwise.

"Man of many words, I see," said Ferrand. "I'll have to go see this mastersmith about some equipment myself before I leave, might make stopping in this frozen ice-block worth it." Ferrand's eyes drifted to the side and suddenly went wide with excitement. "What is *that*?!" he said with awe.

He walked over to the covered weapons rack and grabbed the elongated sword Kolden had forged for Orne. The commander drew it from the white leather sheath and stared at it with a gaped jaw, his eyes inspecting every inch.

"It's one of mine, sir," Orne said to him, maintaining his military stoicism.

"It's *magnificent...*" the commander said in a long draw. "Your same mastersmith made this?"

"Yes, sir."

"You'll need to tell me how you've gotten so much darksteel, Orne," the commander said as he turned his attention to him and narrowed his eyes. "I'll find out what it is, eventually, but for now I'll spar with this. No wager this round, just whatever pride that waste of a sword over there might have," he said with a nod to the young noble who was still pale and dejected.

Orne wasn't going to deny a knight commander use of his sword, not that it sounded like the man was giving him an option. It could possibly work in his favor; it had taken weeks for him to gain even a semblance of mastery with the oversized weapon. He'd actually grown fond of it, for certain scenarios anyway, but it was still more difficult to nimbly maneuver than he'd like. He was curious to see how this knight, who was shorter than the sword's length, would deal with—

A burst of perfect figure-eight flourishes from Ferrand immediately dispelled any advantages Orne thought he had. More impressive still was how he swung the enormous blade—with a single-handed grip.

*That's damn near impossible,* Orne thought, becoming increasingly more cautious about this duel and his assumptions. Was this Blue using his abilities? He'd promised not to cast, but did his power work some other way?

*I swear, if he tries to play me for a fool...*

"Perfect balance too. I have to say, I didn't think I'd find anything so impressive in this gods-forsaken town. Alright, you ready?" the commander asked as he took a wide stance with his feet, his right foot digging into the snow behind him.

"Shouldn't we bind the blades, sir?" asked Orne, looking at the reflection of sharpened steel in Ferrand's hands.

"I much prefer a more realistic feel, don't you?" he said. "You seem capable enough, and I won't maim you, don't worry."

Orne grew even more cautious. Almost any sparring session could have a misstep, a minute error that led to contact of blade to flesh. More than one noble had died in official contests, but again, Orne sensed that the commander was making less of a request and more of a demand.

He slowly planted his feet firmly into the compacted snow in a defensive stance, his halberd pointing straight into the gray morning air. He kept himself a distance away from the knight, not wanting to be in the lunging range of the blade's enormous reach.

"Swords unsheathed," Orne said to state his readiness.

"Blood drawn," replied Ferrand.

The moment the words left Ferrand's lips Orne's left foot stepped forward and he dropped down the axe-head of his polearm. Its extreme reach was difficult to gauge by opponents, and he looked to gain an advantage early, taking care to aim the uncovered blade at armor rather than the commander's head.

The commander was quick—unnaturally so—and raised the sword above his head to block the incoming blow. He stood fast, not even sidestepping to glance the blow away. Instead, with a one-handed grip, he allowed the sword to take the full brunt of Orne's downward strike. Without even a bend in the knight's wrist, the halberd struck the blade as though it had collided with a stone wall, stopping abruptly in place with the ringing of steel against steel.

There was a low gasp from the growing crowd of soldiers who had stopped what they were doing to watch. None of them, Orne included, could have stopped the falling polearm in such a rigid fashion.

*What is this?* thought Orne with eyes wide. *He is using his powers, he has to be. That should have snapped his wrist.*

A surge of boiling blood flowed through his veins. This was meant to be an even fight. *So much for the honor of nobility,* he thought. If Ferrand didn't want to fight fairly, then fine, fair fights didn't exist in battle, and Orne was more than willing to pull out some tricks of his own.

With an upward shove, Ferrand pushed away the halberd. Orne harnessed the momentum instead of fighting it to pull it back into an upright position and take an immediate backstep. In the same motion as the push, Ferrand brought the sword down in an aggressive strike, taking a step forward for extended reach.

The blade's tip whistled through the frigid air as it sliced downward, missing Orne's arm by a mere few inches, thanks only to his backstep. Ferrand quickly stepped back, his eyes flicking to the head of the polearm high in the air, wary of its reach.

Orne feinted a few chopping motions, Ferrand smacking away the polearm with a defensive blow from the side. Orne needed to goad him into a harder deflection. He chopped downward once, then twice, the commander repeating the deflection to the side each time. With a third, full force motion, Orne brought the ax-head down again, making a showing of the effort he put into the blow.

The commander followed through with another deflection, this one continuing in an arc all the way to the ground, planting the axe-head in the snow just behind his left foot.

Exactly where Orne had wanted it.

He had to be fast. With his halberd in the snow and pointed downward, the sword on top of it could easily strike out at him with a twist of Ferrand's body. Normally a sword wouldn't have the reach for that sort of attack, but the oversized blade was perfect for such a lengthy slash.

As Ferrand began to twist with his uncanny quickness, Orne rotated the halberd's shaft, the hammer head now pointed at the commander, and he pulled with all his strength. The hammer caught the back of Ferrand's ankle like a hook and pulled it out from under him, floundering his slashing attack and causing him to lose his balance. The loss of footing, combined with the twisting of his body, sent Ferrand to the ground, the sword narrowly missing Orne's abdomen yet again.

Orne brought the spear point of the halberd to Ferrand's throat, angling it downward in a striking pose. He waited while the commander caught his breath, his muscles tight and heart racing as he waited to hear the word.

"Yield!" said Ferrand with a growl in his voice, smacking the spear tip aside with his hand. Orne proffered a hand to help him up, but the commander ignored it and pulled himself to his feet.

There were murmurs from the still-growing audience. Orne had just beaten a knight in single combat, a feat accomplished by very few, by men who lived mainly in legends. He lifted his head, standing taller as his chest swelled with pride. This was a victory that couldn't be taken from him, one that would bring glory to *his* name, not that of his father's.

"Seems I underestimated you," said Ferrand as he brushed snow from his armor. "What in Ursorner's-fucking-name is someone like you doing in this shithole?"

"Long story, sir," Orne replied.

"I'm sure it is," replied Ferrand looking at Orne with a glint of curious respect in his eyes. "I don't intend to go easy a second time, what do you say to another bout?"

Orne looked at the commander with a stern face. The Blue's words made him wonder if he hadn't put forth his best effort, and he felt his glowing sense of accomplishment dim slightly. While Orne had been taught by the best sword masters that could be found within any of the adjacent duchies, it was well known that the weapons training at the Blue's Academy was the most proficient in the kingdom.

*Was he truly not taking the fight seriously? Was I wrong about him using his power in the fight? No, can't be, he's just saying that to save face...*

He intended to accept the challenge, but as he was about to speak, an idea sprouted in his mind.

"Alright," said Orne, "but I'd like to make a wager."

Ferrand smiled and then shrugged, "I'd be willing to do that, what do you propose?"

This was possibly the only opportunity Orne would get to try something so bold. A knight commander greatly outranked his captain and was one of the few stations high enough to challenge the commands of a general. Maybe this was their chance.

"If I win, my brother and I join your caravan and get placed under your command."

"You mean there are two of you fuckers?" Ferrand said, astonished. He was clearly unaware that he and Kolden were opposites in almost every way, but Orne wasn't about to mention that. "I'd have to talk to your captain about that," he said after he got over his initial shock. "I served with him in the southern war and owe him at least the courtesy of asking to take his two best soldiers."

Orne chuckled on the inside. Kolden was a capable enough fighter, but far from the *best*. Nalhen could best him three times out of four.

*He seems young to have served in the southern war,* Orne thought. Then his jaw tightened as he had a realization. *I can't let him talk to the captain, if he does, he might find out about the general's denials.*

"However," Ferrand continued. "I always appreciate talent, and I can't see the captain needing two of you to protect this place. I'll take you—and only you—if you win. But my wager is going to be equally steep. If I win, I claim this sword."

Orne's grip on the ash handle of his halberd tightened, his muscles flexing. He didn't want to leave Kolden, they had been together their entire lives. He was an annoyance and source of constant strife, true, but he had never once envisioned them separating. But this was an opportunity that he couldn't throw to the wayside. Maybe he could prove himself enough to convince the knight to bring Kolden under his command structure later?

An invisible cage of iron clamped around his chest. It bound a weight surrounded by a flurry of turmoil building inside of him as he struggled to make a decision. How would Kolden react? What would he do with Orne gone?

*I can't ignore an opportunity like this.*

"So, what's it going to be?" Ferrand asked.

"Agreed," Orne said, the thorned words cutting his throat as he forced them out. He'd figure out how to tell Kolden later.

"Excellent!" said Ferrand with a spin of the overly long blade, getting himself into position and taking a more defensive stance.

Orne postured himself a distance away that would keep him out of the sword's extended reach, pointing the spear-tip of his halberd high in the air. As he dug his feet into the snow, the cold penetrating through the soles of his boots, he became overly conscious of the palpable silence that had fallen upon the crowd of soldiers—it seemed most of the company had gathered to watch the duel.

"Swords unsheathed," Orne started.

"Blood drawn," replied Ferrand, who threw himself forward and thrusted the sword at Orne's chest. The defensive stance had been a feint, but Orne managed to sidestep and deflect the point of the sword with the shaft of his polearm, the *thud* of metal against wood echoing in the quiet courtyard.

Ferrand took two quick steps backward as Orne dropped his halberd's axe. The commander deflected the blow with a more controlled and shorter arc of the sword. Orne noticed that he now held the hilt with two hands, an indication that he was taking this bout more seriously.

*Maybe he wasn't giving it his all last time,* he thought nervously.

Orne pulled the halberd close to his side, pointing it forward and just above his opponent's head. Ferrand kept his sword's tip next to its spearpoint, a full eight feet between them as they danced a duet of prodding tests, circling around each other with taps of the deadly blades. If Orne stepped forward, Ferrand glided back, avoiding the same hook that had brought him down previously. When Ferrand batted the polearm to the side, Orne used the momentum to arc downward and sweep at the knight's legs, keeping him at bay.

Tension was carved in the air with each testing cut and prod. The sounds of icy snow crunching and compacting beneath their boots were only broken by their misted breaths and the crossing of steel. All else was quiet, the onlookers watching with the silence of anticipation. Every clash of metal reflected off the stone walls of the nearby castle, creating an illusion of battle echoing around them.

Ferrand put extra power into a parry, forcing the halberd far to Orne's right, while sidestepping to his left. The commander was attentive to the threat to his legs, but with separation between himself and the polearm's end, he lunged forward at Orne, driving the sword point-first at his chest.

Orne danced back and to his right, the blade scraping across his darksteel chest plate. Ferrand pulled the sword's hilt back close to him, but he now found himself within reach of the polearm. Orne raised the head of the halberd and forced it downward with all the strength he could muster. Ferrand would have to deflect it to the side, he couldn't stop it midair—as he had earlier—in his current stance. Once that happened, Orne could try hooking him with the hammer head again.

As expected, Ferrand stepped to the side, cutting the sword through the air with an arcing slash above his head. The blackened steel moved in a blur, humming as it cleaved the cold air with inhuman speed.

Orne had never seen steel move with such fluid power.

As it connected with the smooth ash of his polearm, he felt a vibration that threatened to shatter the bones in his hands, and a loud crack resounded through the courtyard.

The head of his polearm stabbed into the ground beside Ferrand, a short, splintered stub of shaft sticking into the air. The sword had snapped it a foot above Orne's hand, and he now held nothing but a shortened wooden stave. The sword appeared to have taken no damage, the darksteel holding true to its reputation of indestructibility.

*What was THAT?* Orne thought in a rage. Ferrand *was* using some kind of power. *He promised not to use his abilities, but no human could have snapped my halberd in two like that.*

Orne didn't have time to act. Instincts screamed for him to step back, but Ferrand could now get close with little worry. The commander grabbed the end of the broken staff and pulled himself in towards Orne with the weight of a boulder, bringing the edge of his blade to Orne's neck.

Orne stood tall, unflinching despite the blade pressed against his throat. He knew he'd been beaten, but nothing about this contest had been on even terms. There was a sanctity to duels, a test of skill that could balance the peasant with nobility. But the scales were unjustly balanced here, the abilities of Blues a counterweight to talent.

"Yield," he said through barred teeth and a burning face that verged on steaming in the chilled air.

The commander stepped back with a smug smile. "Well fought, Sergeant," he praised. "I'd dare say you're one of the best I've had the pleasure of challenging. Almost had me there, perhaps I'll talk to the captain on your behalf yet. Thank you for this," he said, admiring the sword before sheathing it.

Orne didn't respond, standing in the yard with his hands trembling as he restrained himself from lashing out. The commander smiled and walked away without any further acknowledgement.

*He cheated. That bastard, he had to cheat to win.*

Orne now hoped that the captain would turn down Ferrand's request—if he made it—to take Orne under his command. He hoped to never see the man again, unless it was to challenge him on even grounds.

The sooner he left Drunt without him, the better.

# Chapter Thirty-One

*...losses beyond measure. Our armies, decimated. Our strongest, defeated. For not more than a stalemate. One which will require more sacrifice.*

The crisp, dry air of winter's onset turned Protorus's breath into a burst of fog before him. The sound of his horse's hooves compacting the fresh layer of snow was all that he could hear in the otherwise deadened forest, its voice muted by the large flakes of heavy snow that fell all around.

After the incident at the Merchants' Guild, he'd fled the city. He'd never intended for such an affront to occur—not such an obvious one, at any rate. He'd been promised subtly, the advantage of a head start. Instead, he was provided a blazing beacon visible to the entire realm. He now had not only the Magridi to fret over, but the royal army as well.

*Why is competency so elusive in this day in age,* he thought.

His spy network indicated they believed his plan had been successful, though their confidence was fickle. The guild had become secretive to the extreme about the extent of their losses in the ashes of their headquarters, let alone what remained of their vault. The report of casualties—including a Blue—had been confirmed prior to his departure. Had any of those he'd sent in survived?

The answers would be discovered by his agent at the rendezvous location he'd provided the crew, west of Calentine. He couldn't risk going, for even now he found himself looking over his shoulder, wondering when retribution might find him.

He instead made his way northeast, parallel to the coast a hundred miles away, in hopes that he might lure his pursuers away from the final destination of his agents. He would be their primary target, after all.

He listened to the peaceful silence that permeated the forest. The black trunks of trees silhouetted against the white background surrounded him like the gravestones of friends lost. The quiet sublime became a haunting wake, and his head hung in reverence.

There was a sound—a whistling through the air from behind him—which wavered through the silence. Protorus instinctually projected a barrier behind him, a purple glow from the glass-like sheet of the shield dancing off the falling snow. His body shook as the protection shattered with a burst of light from a projectile piercing it. It punctured his shoulder like a strike from a hammer as he grunted loudly at the sharp pain.

He whipped the reins of his horse urging it forward, but at the sound of another whistle it released a whining scream and bucked, throwing him backward and to the ground. As he fell into the blanket of snow, he saw a bolt dug firmly into the horse's hind leg, blood dripping as it kicked and flailed as though to rid itself of some predator digging in its claws. After a few wild motions it ran into the forest, abandoning Protorus on the forest floor.

He pulled himself up and scrambled behind a tree, trying to keep himself from the sight of the unseen bowman. He folded and bit down on the leather strap of the bag to his side before reaching over his shoulder and jerking the arrow from it in an agonizing motion. His teeth dug deeply into the strap, his gaunt face wincing at the burning pain radiating from the wound.

He looked at the arrow's head—a solid chunk of sharpened inanite. This was specifically designed for him, the most effective way to break through his protections.

The Magridi had found him.

*Who is it they have sent after me?* he wondered, though he knew the likely answer. There was only one that they would trust to send. The one who had so successfully tracked and murdered the other members of the Sraddhana with a sick sense of pleasure, methodically reducing their number until Protorus remained the only original conspirator that still drew breath. He no longer went by his given High name. That had long since been abandoned, despite the Magridi's desire to return home. Now he was only known by a single title.

The Hunter.

He reached into his pocket and withdrew the small chunk of cadentite—stolen by the girl from the spice shop—which flickered and dimmed slightly as the bleeding from his shoulder stopped. It would take weeks to heal, even at this accelerated rate. Not that it mattered, it was unlikely that he would live through this ordeal.

*I am so tired of running,* he thought as he gripped the purple mineral in his hand. He needed to distract them, to lead them along the wrong paths to buy time. Perhaps it was best this way; with him gone and his plans set in motion, how would they know where to follow?

He wouldn't go passively. No, he would make The Hunter work for his kill. If luck played into his favor, he may even escape this pursuit.

He stood, keeping his back to the tree, and drew from the cadentite to produce the shadow of an image before him: an outline of wispy, translucent black. It mirrored his shape and moved as he would. Many from this realm would assume it an apparition from up close, but at a distance it could trick even the trained eyes of his pursuer—he hoped.

With a flick of his wrist the ghastly semblance moved from out behind the tree, as though running for unknown shelter. Protorus peeked from around the tree's edge into the sparse underbrush, waiting. Following a distant snap like the breaking of a branch, an arrow drove through the falling snow and cut through the illusion like it were mist, bursting it out of existence like a breath of fog.

Protorus followed the angle of the shot back to a cluster of trees, catching the faintest hint of motion from behind them. He looked at the cadentite in his hand. It was a flood in comparison to the drought he was accustomed to on this barren plane, but still not enough for some of the more demanding conjurings. He would need to be creative, as he'd learned over the many centuries spent here.

He pulled inward from the purple stone, feeling its strength fade, struggling to warm like the winter sun hidden behind the clouds above. Purple lines formed around his fingers in a pattern, a bright light glowing at the center. He spun from around the tree's trunk and threw forth a ball of energy from his fractal encircled hand, flashing through the air in a blink. He didn't aim at where he'd seen movement, instead directing the blast at the tree trunk his assailer hid behind.

It struck the tree's bark and shattered the wood into flying fragments and splinters, the yellow heart of the tree a splash of color among the dulled tones of white and gray. The explosion of wooden shrapnel went out in all directions, and the tree toppled with a crash that shook the earth beneath his feet.

The snow kept falling, unphased by his burst of destruction.

He crept toward the smoking stump, moving between trees to keep protection—what little they could offer—between him and the bowman. Such a blast had used more of the cadentite's vidut than he'd have liked, years of dealing with its scarcity making him overly conscious of each use. But should he fall it was better he bled it black and leave the Magridi with one piece, rather than two.

It felt good to cast with such strength again. It felt so minute in comparison to times of old, but still, there was a certain thrill of power associated with the use of High magic. It had been so long since the last time he'd cast that powerfully, he'd almost forgotten what it felt like.

He reached the tree's fallen remains, the stump sitting like a smoldering tombstone in the snow. Behind it lay what remained of a man, chunks of blood-stained wood jutting from all over his still body, his crossbow in the snow a few feet away.

The blood was red. The crimson of someone lowly born. Unchanged.

This was not The Hunter.

Protorus spun his head, searching for whoever had laid this trap, as it was clearly meant to draw him in.

*I should have known,* he thought, *this would never be so easy.*

He turned to run, but nearly fell forward as he realized his feet were stuck to the ground. He swept away the snow around his boots with frantic heaves, and found a faint glowing circle around them, the telltale fractals bound within, and his feet firmly adhered to the soil.

There were ways to counter or break the spell, rather than waiting out however long the person who cast it had charged it for. He cursed himself for leaving his darksteel blade on his horse and abandoning the arrow that had dug into his back. He began to focus and channel the cadentite's vidut, feeling the resistance of the skillfully cast trap, when he heard a voice from behind him.

He immediately disregarded the counter spell and threw up a shield that encapsulated his entire person, hoping there wasn't another inanite tipped arrow pointing at him.

"Protorus, Protorus…" the voice said in a long draw as it moved around his side. "I hadn't expected to catch you in something so simple. You, always the ever careful one, hiding from us for so long, with such great success on your part in hunting some of my own brethren. Or, I suppose I should say *our* brethren."

As he came into view, Protorus saw the man speaking. The young face with unexpected, salted hair, simple leather armor dyed black with inanite—designed more as winter gear than protection—and the dead eyes that seemed to contrast the disappointed expression on the man's face.

"I had so looked forward to this encounter, Protorus. And now here you are, a mouse in a trap. Put down this shield, man, and speak with me. We both know you don't have the cadentite to hold it for long anyway, it's far too large."

Protorus glared at the man, this… Hunter. He recalled his former name, it had been one of vile repute long before he had become so willing to kill his own kind. It was associated with the pleasure of watching others die. He was not one who hunted from necessity, but for sport.

Unfortunately, he was right—Protorus couldn't hold the shield long. Perhaps there was something else he could do, something that would come at The Hunter in an unexpected way…

He lowered the shield, The Hunter standing a few feet beyond the trap-ring's limits.

"I knew you'd be willing to have a civil conversation," The Hunter said. "No need to go on wasting cadentite like that. I've waited a long time for you, Protorus, I'd have no issue waiting a little longer while that cadentite expired.

"How have you been, old friend? I feel as though it has been ages since we last spoke. I've tried finding you several times, but you always seem to change your address."

Protorus wanted to shout at him to get to his point, stop this foolish toying. The man acted like a cat playing with its prey. *If he keeps talking long enough, however, perhaps I can set him in a trap of my own,* he thought.

"I love what you did with that plant, by the way," continued The Hunter. "Iguan, right? Must have been a nice cash flow for you, though I still think you'd have been better off with one of the guilds."

"The dens are yours," Protorus said, his voice low.

"Really?" said the Hunter with a false gratitude. "How kind. I would consider taking you up on the offer, but I don't think that it will matter much soon. Our work is nearly complete, my old friend. Which brings me to the point of this encounter. Well, aside from the obvious, of course."

As he dribbled on, Protorus watched where the Hunter stepped. He waited, focused. He'd no idea how much cadentite the Hunter carried, and in a true test of skill between them, Protorus suspected it would come down to whoever carried more. He would need to do something... unexpected.

The Hunter's face took on a quizzical expression, his eyes holding that widened height so accurately associated with the crazed and deranged. "Do you have it on you? The key for the gate? Don't try to tell me that the Merchants' Guild wasn't your doing, Protorus, this theft has your signature about it."

*So, they did manage to steal it.* Protorus couldn't help but allow a smile to tug at the corner of his mouth. *Perhaps my original plan may yet come to fruition. I must stop him from finding the key, if he obtains it then too much will lay with Masini and the others.*

The Hunter didn't get angry at Protorus's outward signs of pleasure, instead continuing his leveled questioning.

"I would never have assumed you so careless as to keep it on your person," the Hunter said, "but given your lack of caution today, I must say I am beginning to doubt your once-great prowess, Protorus." His voice sounded as though every emotion, from the disappointment to praise, were forced, false. "I will find your horse and see if it is there, but if you have it on you, you should hand it over. I will lessen the pain. I may even consider a swift death, given our history."

*Thousands of years to practice, and the man still cannot lie worth a damn,* thought Protorus. If a death came to him swiftly, it would most certainly not be at the hands of this creature.

"I don't have it," said Protorus. "I drained it and cast it in a river after that night."

The Hunter looked at him, unflinching, cocking his head as he debated Protorus's words. A smile—the first true emotion that Protorus has seen from the mask of a face—crawled across his wide mouth.

"Ahhh, so you *are* going to make this fun. Thank you, old friend," the Hunter said, his fingers tapping the small blade at his side. "I've been following you for several weeks now, and if you had drained such a volume of cadentite, I, *we*, would've noticed. No, you sent it off somewhere, didn't you? You sly... Well, forgive me for doubting you, you clearly haven't lost all of your wits. Tell me, who did you have help you? Surely you weren't there in person, seems unlike you."

He pulled the narrow blade from his side, the steel gleaming even in the dull gray air. Protorus found his feet still firmly held in place, the binding spell a protracted one. He didn't know if he'd hold up under the torture of this fiend, experience told him well that everyone broke eventually, guilty or not. There was something else he could do, something more... final.

He squeezed his hand tightly around the cadentite pebble, fully drawing its power into his chest like a gasp of air. His left hand, hidden behind his flank, drew a binding and a draining spell in thin, patterned lines around his fingers, casting them below the foot of the Hunter—who had realized that Protorus was channeling, and tried to move on him with a flash of steel.

Protorus was faster, however, the spells being small, weak, and therefore more easily cast. Creating both a binding and draining spell at the same time was a rare talent, even for the most senior among them, but it was a defense that Protorus had mastered after countless years of practice. Neither would hold more than a few seconds, their haste a downfall, but a few seconds was all he would need. The Hunter looked down at his affixed foot, then back at Protorus, his head tilted to the side with that half-crooked smile on his face.

Protorus drew on everything that was within the cadentite, the power of life, a taste of water in the sere desert, and then drew from other places inside and out of him. He wanted to drain it all, down to the deepest, irreversible black. He drew and drew, pulling it inward until he felt his own life fade away.

A purple glow began to shimmer from beneath the folds of his robe, his face turning beet red as he focused all he had into this one spell. A ring of purple lines filled the air around his waist, crawling out like vines as they formed a patterned disc with him at its center.

The eyes of the Hunter somehow went even wider, the smile mixing with a gaped jaw as he looked on at Protorus in an awed wonder. He let out a wild laugh. "You wouldn't! Oh, I knew this was going to be interesting. Thank you, old friend!"

With a defiant cry, a sphere of energy burst from Protorus, emanating outward with the force of a meteor strike. The ground around him was blasted barren, the circle of soil a strange defect in the perfect white of the land. With the sole of his foot held in place flat on the ground, The Hunter was laid out on his back, his bone having snapped above the ankle as he'd been punched with the force of the blast. His garments were shredded, and his flesh burnt nearly to the bone in various places.

Despite the wounds, his laugh cut through the cold air. Nothing but scarred earth remained where Protorus had once stood, a small chunk of inanite beside the faintest, flickering glow of a similarly sized piece of faceted cadentite laying on the ground in his place.

Flakes of snow continued to drift through the air, their descent a quiet inevitability.

# Chapter Thirty-Two

*The enemy deactivated the gate in an attempt to stop reinforcements. It may be irreparable, but we must proceed regardless. We will have time to find the key later. They can never be allotted the opportunity to be unleashed again.*

Daylight outside the shop's windows had long been replaced by the yellow light of streetlamps and a lone lantern near his bench as Kolden put the final touches on Orne's repaired halberd. His brother had barged in earlier to complain about his broken polearm, waiting to tell him the *important* information in his bull-headed ignorance.

"What happened to this?" Kolden had asked, examining the broken shaft of the halberd.

"This *asshole* cheated during a duel and snapped it. Bastard! He knew he couldn't win in an even match, and he broke the terms of the fight!" Orne had cried, pounding his fist into his palm.

"How the hell did he manage to snap it? Did he cheat by pulling a fucking bear out of his pocket?"

"What?" Orne asked, wrenching himself from a distant thought which had caused him to clench his jaw tightly. "Oh, no he was a Blue, a knight commander. Said he wouldn't use magic, next thing I know he uses *my sword* to snap my halberd in two. No way he didn't use some kind of power."

Kolden's face felt numb as it turned white as snow. "Orne, there's a Blue in Drunt and you're just telling me *now*?!"

"Yeah," Orne had said, a curious but disinterested look on his face, "why are *you* getting angry? Look what he did to my halberd!"

"Orne you du—" Kolden had looked to the shop's corner where the smith was snoring, an empty bottle hanging loosely from his hand. He then pulled himself in closer to Orne and attempted to whisper, "Because, dumbass, I have a *massive* piece of cadentite here! Did you forget how I found it or about the knife I made?" He gripped the short dagger at his waist, the sheath, handle, and fittings all constructed of materials dyed or imbued with inanite.

*If the Blue hasn't come looking yet, maybe the inanite is shielding it. Or maybe Blues can't actually sense the cadentite. What if he can and finds me and asks questions?* Kolden had thought, having felt nauseated by the possibility of his "reclaiming" being discovered.

"Sounds like a you problem," Orne had replied, the full weight of Kolden's predicament lost on him. The world always seemed to revolve around Orne when he was upset. "Now fix my halberd."

"Fuck you," replied Kolden. "Fix it yourself, seems like it's a *you* problem, after all."

"Fine," Orne had said with a dramatic roll of his eyes. "I'm *sorry* I didn't come tell you about the Blue. Now, fix my fucking halberd!"

"Alright," replied Kolden reluctantly, "but while I work, you're telling me what happened."

Now, as he tied the last knot on the leather grip, he thought about the story that Orne had told.

*I can't believe he lost that sword in a wager! Idiot...*

Part of him wondered if Orne had even been honest about beating the knight in the first bout, but he was certain that the other soldiers at the tavern would regale the story when he met up with his brother shortly.

He'd hidden the dagger and cadentite in a box lined with inanite he'd scavenged from the masons. That, combined with a thorough cleaning of the shop, would hopefully be enough to hide the glowing stone from whatever senses the Blue possessed.

*All this effort to hide it, and for what?* he thought.

The results of his experiments had been disappointing. The blade he'd produced a few weeks ago from the ground-off corner of the cadentite did have a slight luminance to it, humming with a tinged purple glow, but was otherwise similar to darksteel. Aside from the seductive depth of its purple hue, he'd failed to discover anything unique about the mineral.

He'd taken an enormous risk for something which, for all intents and purposes, appeared to be little more than a pretty rock...

As he leaned Orne's repaired halberd against the wall and closed up the shop, he was tempted to go back to the city wall and rebury the stone. It was a notion quickly dismissed, holding out hope that he was missing something, that there was *some* attribute worth finding about the cadentite. Something inside of him nudged the drive to pursue his testing further, despite the disheartening lack of results.

*Having a Blue in Drunt will make that difficult. I wonder how long he plans to stay?*

The cold air frosted his lungs as he stepped outside and locked the door to the shop, sporadic flakes of snow falling around him like stars falling from the sky. The hour was getting late, the district the shop was in nearly empty at this hour with all the businesses closed; most people would be at home or making their way to a tavern.

*Then who was that I just saw ducking into an alley?*

Kolden had seen the shadowy figure from the corner of his eye and wondered if the snowfall had tricked him. He looked to where he'd seen the wraith vanish, then back along the opposite direction—towards Orne and the tavern.

He craned his neck back and slipped out a puff of foggy air with a sigh, his finger tapping his leg.

*It's probably nothing... Then again, what if it's someone looking for the cadentite?*

Unless someone physically tore apart the stone forge they wouldn't find the hidden stash, but did he dare leave that to chance?

With another exaggerated sigh, he turned and walked towards the alley, careful not to step on any ice that may crunch under his boots. He approached the building slowly, cautiously peering around the edge to see the tail of a black cloak slide around another corner. He crept down the dark alley, quietly placing each foot in the tracks of the person he was following.

As he reached another turn, he slowly craned his head so that only a sliver of his face was beyond the building's wooden corner post, a hand on the stucco wall balancing him. The dim outline of a person standing in the center of the haunting darkness was visible, and he continued to watch as the figure remained motionless.

*What is he doing?* Kolden wondered.

A few minutes passed, the cloaked man unmoving. Was he trying to sense the cadentite? Or was this just a strange man lost in the night? Despite the chill seeping into his legs, Kolden remained as fixed and motionless as the man ahead. Being lost did not preclude you from malintent.

As he began to wonder if perhaps the man had frozen to death, a light began to glow and sway from the alley's opposite end, silhouetting the figure as a black demon against its flame. The bearer of the torch appeared from around the corner, and with a shift of the man in black, Kolden was able to view the oncoming wanderer.

His eyes went wide, and his legs felt weak as Kolden took in the sight of the short, middle-aged man with silver speckled hair, blue-dyed leather armor, and an unmistakable, six-foot sword on his back.

*That has to be the Blue Orne dueled!*

As he approached with a stride that landed with confidence, the cloaked man drew back his hood and glanced backward towards Kolden. He pulled his face quickly to the side, but before he did, he'd caught sight of the man's face. The predominant scarring, dark hair, grim depth to his eyes—it was a visage he recognized, one that he'd not seen in many months.

The stranger who had buried the cadentite in the wall.

He held his breath as he listened, trying to hear what the two could be discussing in such a clandestine meeting. He inched his head back around the corner, hoping that he hadn't been spotted. The two men were facing each other now, the torch barely penetrating the pitch black of the windowless alley, and seemed unaware of his presence as the Blue began speaking.

"You sure you weren't followed?" the knight with the scowled face asked.

"Of course," the scarred man replied. "What took you so long to arrive? I expected you here two months past."

"*You* don't have the privilege of having expectations of *me*," the Blue said with a malicious tone. "What the fuck happened back in Calentine, Magnar? A Blue is *dead* and the entire Merchants' Guild burned to the ground?! You were supposed to be discreet, they shouldn't have even known you were ever there!"

"*You* were supposed to keep those Blues off our trail, instead they ambushed our safecracker at her home and then somehow found us right as we opened the damned vault. How did that happen? And besides, he was Magridi, what do you care that he's dead?"

Kolden saw the knight's fist clench at his side, his eyes darkening.

"We don't have the resources to have an all-out war with the Magridi, and a dead Blue draws too much attention. The gate's supposedly nearly ready and you botched this whole thing! What the hell were you thinking?!" The knight rubbed his face and recomposed himself with a deep breath. "What about the key? All your pigeon said was that you'd managed to acquire it, but what have you done with it?"

"Don't worry, it's safe," the scarred man said with a reassuring tone, his original stoic posture deteriorating slightly.

"*Where?*" the Blue asked.

"I buried it in the city wall near the east gate, covered it in inanite mortar, and it's been sealed behind inanite blocks. No one—Blue or otherwise—is going to know it's there. If *you* didn't notice it upon your arrival, then that means that it's sealed away for the next several hundred years, at least."

*So, inanite* does *hide it from Blues,* Kolden thought with relief. But what was this about it being a key?

"Well, at least you managed not to fuck that up… Should fuck them over pretty hard," the Blue said, his shoulders loosening and his voice carrying less venom. "About the girl though—I thought we explicitly told you she wasn't to be harmed? The account of the other cadet stated that you were preparing to kill her when they arrived, is there something about your self-absorbed brain that doesn't allow you to follow *simple orders*?"

"She was a liability, when she saw the contents of the vault she lost her mind, threatened to report us and save her own skin."

The knight stared at him for a tense moment before finally giving the man a terse response, "Well, this is the one thing I'm *glad* you fucked up, because my reports are that she survived and is on the run. Your insolence has cost us more than you can imagine, Magnar. I've been trying for weeks to figure out a way to salvage this and am still at a loss."

"They can't do anything without the key. What about Protorus, doesn't he have some plan? And what about the other cadet?"

"Don't concern yourself about Protorus, the only reason you even met him was of unfortunate necessity. And the kid's an idiot, I'm not even convinced he knew what his partner was doing."

"So, there's hope for him yet?"

"I doubt it, he's useless since you killed his partner. Does anyone else know about where you hid the cadentite?"

"No, just you."

"Did all the others die in the fight?"

"Yes. Your 'useless' Blue slaughtered them, I barely managed to escape with my life. He cut through them like a boat through water, the fact that we even were able to shoot the other was a matter of gods-given luck."

"Mhm," the knight said through tight lips. His relaxed posture seemed to rub off Magnar, who lowered his arms to his side and began—

The Blue threw a sudden punch, hooking and landing squarely on Magnar's cheek. Kolden's throat went tight, preventing him from gasping as the man's scarred face spun and abruptly stopped between his shoulder blades, staring back towards Kolden while his body faced the knight. It had turned like a child spinning a doll's head, as though his spine had been malleable and unobstructive.

*All from a punch.*

It was difficult to tell in the shadow of the lantern, but Kolden thought he saw Magnar blink before falling to the ground, a dead heap of black in the white snow. Kolden couldn't take his eyes away from the scene, watching as the knight looked down on the corpse.

"If you hadn't killed a Blue, I might have actually felt bad about having to do that. Can't be having anyone know about where you hid the key though."

Kolden backed away as quietly as he could, though it was difficult to tell if he were being noisy over the pounding of his heart in his ears. His hands shook and chest heaved as he stepped in the compressed footfalls he followed earlier, trying to get away as expeditiously as possible. He heard noises coming from the alley—the knight was doing something to the body, but he refused to find out what it was. Even his curiosity had limits.

He made it back to the street and moved as fast as he was able over the icy sidewalk towards the tavern. He had to find Orne, he was the only other person who knew about the cadentite and he couldn't afford for him to say something stupid, or else they might both face a similar fate.

# CHAPTER
# THIRTY-THREE

*Those few of us that remain are either to commit the great sacrifice for entrapment, or are seeking the calves of the herd for cleansing. All in the name of High duty. We do not stand strong enough to control the populace of the realm, and I fear that we may need to slip into shadow for a time, if not by necessity, then by orders.*

K olden burst through the tavern doors, drawing the attention of a few nearby patrons. He composed himself as he looked around the crowded space, trying to find his brother among the packed tables. The lanterns and hearth gave the post-and-beam interior a flickering yellow glow where shadows glanced out from under tables and in corners. A warm chatter filled the air, and the smell of stale ale enveloped the room. He finally spotted the hulking Orne, brooding by himself at a table near the wall, his back leaning against it.

Kolden wound his way through the maze of chairs and chattering soldiers mixed with a few locals and sat himself across from his brother. Orne didn't bother to acknowledge him as he tilted his head back to finish off an ale, the pitcher before him nearly empty on the stained wood table.

*I wonder how many of those he's had?*

"Orne," Kolden said in a hushed whisper, "I need to talk to you about something." He glanced around to see if anyone was nearby or discreetly trying to listen in on his conversation.

"Can't you see that I'm busy?" asked Orne as he poured the last of the pitcher into his mug.

"Oh get over yourself," Kolden said. "You lost one fight, who cares? I saw something that—"

"Who cares?!" expelled Orne, who somehow seemed sober, but angrier. Was the ale just fueling his rage? "He *cheated*, Kolden. He cheated and stole my honor, the bastard."

"Orne, SHUT UP!" Kolden almost screamed. "Listen to me for one fucking second!"

Orne grumbled but became quiet, eyes still on the table.

"I was just coming back from the shop and—"

"Is my halberd fixed?" Orne asked, looking up with his brow fixed in a position that dug it into his nose.

"Would you just... Yes! It's fixed. Now listen. I was coming back from the shop and saw the same man that hid the you-know-what in the city wall. I followed him to some meeting in the alley and then your fucking Blue shows up! They talked for a minute and then he punched him so hard that he snapped the guy's neck. Orne, they were talking about the *you-know-what*." Kolden had whispered as quietly as he could, his brother leaning in and listening with the same permanent expression.

"Wait, what? What do you mean, 'you-know-what'?"

"Would you keep your damn voice down?!" cursed Kolden. "The fucking *cadentite*, Orne. It sounded like the two worked together to steal it, and then the commander killed the man who hid it. Now I have it. A *knight commander* committed murder to keep this quiet, Orne. You need to make sure you don't say *anything* about it to anyone. Ever."

Orne's eyes went wide with realization. "Kolden, you need to get rid of that shit. Now! That bastard killed someone to keep his secret... I knew he was no better than bear shit. We need to turn him in, he needs to be court-martialed."

"Are you *insane*?!" exclaimed Kolden, calming himself with a deep breath before continuing. "It'd be my word against his. I don't even know if there's a body to prove what he did. And even if we had the body, no one's going to believe me over a fucking knight commander. No. No, we keep this quiet and wait until his caravan leaves, then think of what to do with it. The stone is hidden so that even he can't find it, we need to wait this out. Just keep your mouth shut until he leaves, got it?"

"That's fucking stupid, Kolden," said Orne with a harsh rasp, "we can't just let him get away with this! If you don't talk to the captain, then I will."

"Don't you fucking DARE!" said Kolden. "What is the captain going to do, huh? The Blue outranks him, hell I don't even know if the *duke* could do anything about it. The only people that will end up being hanged are the two of us! I'm telling you this so that you keep quiet, not so that you can get revenge for him beating you in a damn fight!"

The muscles around Orne's jaw flexed, his grip on his mug threatening to shatter the ceramic. Kolden could tell that he was considering his words—his brother could be persuaded, it just took a significant amount of arguing.

As Orne opened his mouth to say something a quiet hush drew over the tavern, a silence matched only by a heavy snowfall on a winter's day. Kolden turned to see that none other than the knight commander himself had just walked through the door, the cross of his sword's hilt above his head like a banner. His insides suddenly became vacant, and blood drained from his limbs and face.

*Has he come here after me?* Kolden thought. *Did he see me in the alley?*

"As you were!" the knight shouted. He sauntered over to a nearby table, a lengthy top which held a congregation of soldiers that Kolden didn't recognize, probably from the royal caravan. As he went to sit down, he looked over to Kolden with a quick smirk and a nod. Kolden thought that his heart was about to drop through him to the floor when he realized that the commander had given the nod to Orne, who Kolden turned to see was turning a faint shade of red.

The Blue sat down, and chatter regained its place in the background of the room as a companion to the smell of the hearth's fire and kitchen out back. Kolden turned to face his brother once more, sweat dripping over his temples. As he was about to speak to Orne, who was looking as though he could explode, something caught the corner of his eye.

He turned and saw someone a few tables over sitting by himself. The uniform gave the man—more of an older boy, to Kolden's eyes—away as being a Blue, though Kolden didn't recognize the rank insignia on his shoulder. He again felt his heart drop as he turned an angry glare to Orne.

"There's another fucking Blue over there!" he whispered with a tilt of his head.

"What?" said Orne, pulling his death stare from the distant table. He turned his head and looked at the Blue sitting a few tables away. "Oh, yeah he's been sitting there for hours. None of the other caravan soldiers have even spoken to him. Everyone else seems too skittish to go over and talk to him. Fucking Blue bastard."

"Are you... Why didn't... FUCK, ORNE!" Kolden grabbed the edge of the table and squeezed with all his strength, imagining that he was strangling his brother. "Did you not think to mention that when I started telling you what happened?!"

"What? It's not like he can hear you," replied Orne dismissively.

*How can this giant bastard master a hundred different ways to kill someone, but not have the common sense to tell me important information?!*

"You don't know that! What if that's his ability or something? What do you know about Blues?"

"I know they cheat," Orne said with conviction.

Kolden rolled his eyes so hard it almost hurt. How could the man be so dense? He looked back at the Blue, his curiosity digging at him. The young Blue stared across the room, directly at the commander, with a glare that rivaled Orne's.

Why was *he* so angry with the commander? Wasn't he traveling with him? He looked like he'd been cast out like a pariah, sitting by himself. *Did I misjudge what he was doing over here, thinking he was trying to spy on our conversation?*

The questions ate at Kolden. He *hated* unanswered questions. A small part of his mind thought to leave the matter, to not worry about this other Blue and let him leave with the rest of the caravan. But he also couldn't help but wonder if there was something to learn from the reclusive knight.

*Maybe I could learn something that would ease my mind about the commander? I could at least find out when they're leaving.* He didn't know enough about Blues to know if the commander had some trick up his sleeve to find the cadentite. Maybe, with the right questions, he could find out more about Blues if he talked to this one.

He stood up and went to the bar, placing two moons on it in exchange for a fresh pitcher of ale. He walked back to his brother and said, "Come with me."

"What?" asked Orne. "Why? Just sit down and pour me another glass. We still need to discuss what you're going to do with your stupid glowing rock, which apparently people are willing to kill over."

"That's what we're doing, come with me."

"Where?"

"You'll see."

"No, fuck that, just sit down, Kolden. I want another drink and I'm not playing your games."

Kolden sighed. This was going to take a little extra incentive. "Come with me and I'll pay for drinks the rest of the night."

Orne looked at him with an expression that asked: *Are you serious?* Kolden, in turn, gave him one that confirmed his commitment to his promise. An entire conversation passing within a short second.

Orne begrudgingly stood up with cup in hand and followed Kolden, who walked directly to the circular table that the lone Blue sat at. He heard hesitation in Orne's footsteps behind him, a grumble of remorse coming from his brother. He knew Orne would sit, even if he didn't like it—the man was too cheap to ever turn down free ale.

Kolden stopped at the edge of the table, Orne looming over his shoulder, and asked, "Mind if we join you? I brought ale." He placed the pitcher on the beat-up table, not waiting for a response.

The young Blue looked to him, and then his brother, with hollow, sunken eyes. He shrugged, then waved a hand at the seats in front of him.

Kolden sat down, his brother following suit, twisting a chair so that he could still face the rest of the tavern. Kolden poured a fresh glass for the Blue, then his brother, and finally himself while saying, "Name's Kolden, and this walking, talking tree trunk is my brother Orne."

Orne grunted and didn't look at the Blue, who simply responded, "Delvan."

"Nice to meet you, Delvan," said Kolden as both of them took a sip of their ales. "You a member of that royal caravan that showed up last night?"

The young knight nodded.

"Right, thought so," said Kolden, taking on a more lighthearted demeanor. He tried to push the memory of a man's neck spinning like a top from his mind. "Well, maybe you can clear something up for Orne and I. You see, my brother here had the pleasure of meeting the knight commander over there earlier today in the training yard. One thing led to another and, as he normally does, my brother ended up in a duel with the commander. Fought him twice, in fact."

This managed to draw a raised eyebrow from Delvan, who looked to Orne. His brother still obstinately refused to meet Delvan's gaze.

"Apparently," Kolden continued, "my brother *won* the first bout."

Delvan's face flashed with surprise, it was the most animated gesture Kolden had seen from the Blue thus far.

"There's nothing 'apparent' about it," Orne grumbled. "I won that fight, don't be spreading doubts otherwise."

"Fine, fine," said Kolden. "So, anyway, they fight again for a wager, I'm not sure what my brother bet as he refuses to talk about it, but the commander over there wagered the sword on his back—Orne's sword. So, I'm guessing you can figure out how that went.

"But he apparently—sorry, definitely—used the thing to snap my brother's precious halberd in half. Now, that sword is a fine piece of weaponry, but I don't know of anyone that can swing a sword and snap the better part of two inches of ash in two. My brother is convinced that the commander used some sort of ability or magic to win the fight but has no way to prove it. I'm hoping that you, in exchange for copious amounts of ale, would be willing to enlighten us as to whether or not he did anything... nefarious during the fight."

"He cheated," Orne stated with confidence.

This was the time to test Delvan's relationship with his Blue companion. Kolden waited for a response, hoping that it could help him determine if this young knight was an ally of the commander's, or the outcast that he appeared. Kolden hoped for the latter.

"Sounds like he used his gift," Delvan replied, his speech carrying melancholy. "I wouldn't put it past him, he's never been one to fight fair."

Orne slammed a fist on the table. "I knew it!" he growled. "That bastard, I should go over there and demand my sword back."

"I wouldn't recommend it," replied Delvan, unphased by Orne's outburst. "He doesn't care about you, or anyone else for that matter. He always gets what he wants."

*Maybe there's hope to learn more from this kid yet,* thought Kolden. Maybe he knew more about who the commander murdered in the street? *I can't risk asking him yet, though. Maybe I can find other questions to prod at him?*

"How?" Kolden asked. "What did he do to best my brother?"

Orne finally looked at Delvan, now interested in what the Blue had to say. If this young knight was truly a rival of the commander's, then Orne may actually take a liking to him.

"Strength," Delvan said passively, "that's his gift. Sounds like he used it to break your halberd."

"What do you mean, 'strength'?" asked Orne, now deeply intrigued. "He's smaller than even Kolden, he can't be that strong."

Kolden ignored his brother's jab at his height and waited for a response.

"Jacks are always small," Delvan replied. "Their muscles are already incredibly strong, so they don't build muscle from exercise like you or I do—unless they stopped channeling inanite, which they almost never do. I saw him push a fully loaded carriage that two horses couldn't move in thick snow on more than one occasion. Trust me, the fact that you beat him even once is an amazing feat."

*That would explain how he spun that man's head around with a single strike.*

Orne chugged another full cup of ale and slammed it on the table with a force that almost shattered it. Orne did *not* like to lose, though on the occasions he did, he often contained his anger and looked to learn from the person who'd bested him. It was one of the few things that Kolden could praise the mountainous man for. But to lose to someone who had cheated? This was a grudge that Orne would likely take to his grave.

"Well, what else can he do?" asked Kolden.

"That's it. Blues only have one gift, and his is the strength of half a score of men," Delvan replied, his voice slow and pained.

"Do you get to pick?" asked Kolden. He'd never beens able to ask a Blue questions like this, most of them were like the commander—aloof and arrogant. But this Delvan seemed willing to answer all of his questions.

"No, it's random, though certain families tend to have more of one type over another."

"*Interesting,*" said Kolden, not meaning to utter the word aloud. "So, could you say, kick down a tree, or punch a hole through a wall? Anything else you can do?"

*Was that too obvious?* he thought.

Delvan shook his head as he drew another long pull of ale from his cup. "If I were a Jack, then yeah," he said, wiping his face, "but I'm a Pyromancer. The only strength we get is what we can build naturally."

"What the hell is a 'Pyromancer'?" his brother asked, now seemingly fully invested in the conversation.

"I can create fire," Delvan said, his words trailing off and growing quiet.

"Really?" asked Kolden with excitement. He was envious, thinking of how he could utilize such a power in the forge. "Can we see?"

Delvan's eyes seemed to drift off into the distance, and he grew quiet and stiff. Kolden waited in the silence for a moment before asking again, "Well, can you—"

"Shut up, Kolden," Orne said with an aggressive glance. He used that expression to try and state that he was being serious, but since he used it all the time, Kolden always struggled to know if the situation was truly dire, or if his brother was overreacting. Delvan was still staring into the unseeable horizon, and Kolden decided to listen to his brother and stop talking.

"Hey," said Orne in a surprisingly calm manner, "you don't need to worry about that, have a swig of ale and tell us about something else. Where'd you come from and what are you doing in Drunt? No one ever comes willingly to this shithole."

Orne *never* talked that much to people he'd just met.

It took a moment, but eventually Delvan seemed to regain his senses, taking a few shaky breaths. Kolden wasn't sure what he'd said to make the Blue react in such a way, but he'd have to be more careful with his questions.

"We're, uh," started Delvan, "coming from Calentine, traveling to Brethefen, and making some stops at the request of the King along the way. That's all I'm allowed to say."

"Are there other types of Blues?" Kolden asked, his curiosity burning like an itch that couldn't be scratched. His brother looked like he was trying to stab him with his glare.

"Yeah," said Delvan with a nod. "There are twelve different gifts." At least that question didn't seem to bother him.

"How does it work?" Kolden asked. His brother's glare remained, but he knew that Orne was as interested in this as he was. Knowing your enemy and all that.

"Do neither of you know this?" Delvan asked with a faint look of disbelief.

"We did not have the luxury of growing up in the city," replied Kolden. "Even the military academy we went to treats discussing any of you as taboo."

Delvan seemed startled by this.

*How are these high-society nobles always so ignorant?* Kolden wondered.

"With the sapphires," said the Blue, touching his chest, "we can draw from inanite as fuel for our gifts."

"I knew it!" exclaimed Kolden, "*That's* why you put muted inanite on the handles of darksteel weapons, so a Blue doesn't accidentally draw from the inanite in the metal while swinging it around."

He didn't actually *know* that, but had inferred it, and it was more complicated than that. Years of studying crafting techniques had required that the white mineral be used in hilt and handle construction of any darksteel weapon, and it had been the only logical conclusion. Affirmation of his assumptions was reassuring, though.

"Shut up, Kolden, you didn't fucking know that," Orne said. "What happens if someone else has your sapphire? Could I have the commander's strength if I was holding it?"

"No," replied Delvan, disappointing Orne as he finished another cup of ale. Kolden was going to need another pitcher. "They... change you. Physically. We're exposed to it our whole lives to become Blues, if you held one it would do nothing, except maybe get you on the wrong side of the King. Any Blue can use another's sapphire, though. It's sort of like they all give off the same... energy."

Kolden waved over a barmaid and ordered two more pitchers. He intended to keep this Blue talking. Years of inquiring at the academy, and he'd learned more in a few minutes than he'd managed in his entire enrollment. Laughter from across the tavern at the commander's table, however, reminded him of the present danger, a wolf lying in wait.

It persuaded him to keep looking over his shoulder, a habit he continued through the night.

The oil in the lanterns burned low, the night growing closer to morning than evening as the three sat and talked. Orne, being Orne, wanted to discuss fighting techniques, and went through—at length—which he and Delvan agreed or disagreed on. Orne even asked to duel the young Blue, which surprised Kolden given his earlier loss, but was told that their caravan was leaving in the morning.

*That answers that,* he thought. A sense of relief washed over him. After tomorrow morning he'd be free to decide what to do with the cadentite.

The commander and his group of apparent sycophants left after a time, and the three of them visibly relaxed. It was like a toxic gas had been cleared from the room. The topics they discussed became more varied and lighthearted, and he and Orne found themselves enjoying the company of the young Blue.

With the ale flowing steadily the three soon found themselves as the last patrons in the spacious tavern. Delvan seemed to shut down if his past were brought up, but otherwise he became more talkative as the night progressed. Their laughter shook the ceilings and the banter—drowned with cup after cup of the golden panacea—nearly drove the thought of the murder from Kolden's mind. What was he to do about it, anyway? The smart thing would be to ignore it and hope that his concerns left with the caravan the next morning.

Eventually the owner kicked all three of them out after allowing them to stay late thanks to their overzealous begging and Delvan's dignified status. As they walked into the crisp night air, Kolden took a deep breath, the chill cooling his ale-warmed blood.

He found walking difficult, especially on the icy path, but his brother still strode with a balance and grace that seemed to defy the pull of the earth itself. Delvan, however, was stumbling and only held himself upright with assistance from Orne. They had tried to ask Delvan if he was staying in the castle, as they would expect for a visiting noble, but in his few lucid moments he said that he was staying at the barracks. They walked there, or tried to, as a group, alone in the night.

About halfway along the short walk, Delvan muttered, "Thanks, Hil, just give me a minute to rest." He released his grip from Orne and collapsed in a snow drift that leaned against a building.

"What did he say?" asked Orne.

"I don't know," said Kolden with a slur. "Hey, what was up with him earlier, when he got all weird and quiet?"

"Battle shock, you dumb ass," replied Orne. "How can you call yourself a soldier and not recognize it? I've seen it in soldiers after bandit raids, they stare off into the distance like the shit's replaying in their minds over and over. Sometimes they take leave for a few months and then come back, sometimes they leave the army entirely. Always come out different than they started, though."

"Huh," said Kolden.

He remembered the words of the commander before he'd murdered the other man. The words had been a blur to him before, seeming irrelevant to his situation at the time. That, combined with his urgent fleeing, had put the last part of the conversation to the back of his mind.

Could they have been talking about Delvan? *Is he the cadet that the man named Magnar had said cut through his men and then had been involved in the supposed fire at the Merchants' Guild? Didn't he say that the other Blue had died?*

It would certainly explain Orne's diagnosis of "battle shock." He wished he'd realized the connection sooner, perhaps he could've talked more with him about the robbery. With them leaving tomorrow, however, that wasn't an opportunity he'd likely see.

*Do I want to tell him that Ferrand was involved in this other Blue's death? Would knowing that and traveling with the Knight Commander put him in danger?*

Kolden had taken a liking to the young Blue and didn't want to see him befall the same fate as the hooded man in the alley. Maybe he *should* say something?

He reached over to the collapsed figure of Delvan, his thick, blue cloak drawn over him like a blanket, and shook him. His body shifted limply, but eyes remained closed. Kolden looked closer.

"Is he… sleeping?" asked Kolden.

Orne peered down from his high shoulders, turning his head to look at Delvan more clearly.

"Yep."

Orne looked down at Delvan in the snow drift, a lake of blue in the white slope, and felt a swell of pity. His brother's ignorance to the boy's battle trauma was wholly unacceptable; the man had been on raids with Orne before, was he so self-centered that he hadn't noticed his own brothers-at-arms suffering the same affliction?

*Maybe if I beat some trauma into him, he'd finally understand.* It was a tempting thought, but the man could be petty, and Orne wanted his halberd back.

"You should probably get him out of that snowbank," said Kolden, who was swaying slightly.

"Fuck you," he replied. Kolden always liked to act as though he were a superior officer, even before they had enlisted. Orne made it a point to put him back in his place whenever he could.

"Well, *I* can't carry him," said Kolden. "And we can't just leave him here to freeze to death. Do *you* want to be responsible for the death of a Blue?"

He could feel his face tightening as his lips drew into a line. He looked down at his brother, who was much better at dueling with words than he was with a sword, and struggled to find an argument.

"You could fucking help me," he replied. He couldn't agree with his brother, if he did then it would just bloat his already inflated ego. Instead, he always had to perform this damn dance with his words. Even when his brother didn't have a weapon in his hand, he still found a way to challenge Orne.

*Maybe I should try going out on my own, find a traveling company that would take me on. Assuming the captain or the general don't hear about it.*

The thought shocked him with a pang of guilt and reminded him of the wager he'd made with Ferrand. As much as his brother could frustrate, demean, and gloat, he still had a hard time envisioning life without him. Kolden had, on more than one occasion, declined offers from mastersmiths and nobility alike to avoid their separation. Not that Orne hadn't made similar sacrifices, but he knew his brother would never have made that wager.

*Bastard,* he thought as his feelings contradicted his desires.

"He's taller than me," replied Kolden, "I can't carry him. And besides, you're basically a bull, I'm sure you can lift him easily."

"In all the ways that count," Orne said with a laugh that was more like a small grunt.

"Yes, we all know you eat and shit a lot. Let's go, it's freezing out here."

"Gods-damn it." There he went, twisting words again. "I meant my dick, you dumbass."

"I know what you meant, you—"

A sudden noise from a nearby alley caught Orne's attention. He froze, listening intently. It had been a sound of... pain, followed by something more sinister. He held a finger up to his brother's face to quickly silence him and walked a few cautious paces to the nearby alley. Squinting to see down the unlit passage—whose opposite end opened to another illuminated street—he saw the outline of a group of people standing in the narrow corridors center, perhaps three or four of them.

*Who is that?*

Kolden walked up beside him, maintaining the same silence as Orne. As the two of them stood there, Orne saw a shift from one of the figures, accompanied by a yelp—the sound that he'd heard a moment ago. It was followed by a laugh from the group. A whiny, pubescent snicker that pealed like a rusted iron hinge.

*I know that laugh.*

"Oh, those bastards," said Kolden.

A fire ignited inside of him. His fists clenched and the chill of the night evaporated as his whole body turned hot. He wasn't sure what it was—the ale, the loss of the duel, his anger at having been cheated—but he'd lost his patience.

With Kolden in tow he stomped down the alley, the frosted air carrying the metallic tang of blood and putrid stench of waste, until the group of young nobles—including the duke's son—came into clearer view. They looked disheveled, a nearly empty bottle of whiskey in one of their hands, probably stolen from the castle stores.

"Hey!" he shouted. "What do you think you're doing?"

They stood over what Orne could now see was a stray dog, its brown fur muddied and clumped together, panting and straining for breath as it whimpered on the ground. The kick he saw one of them throw a few seconds ago was obviously not the first, the snow around the animal bloody and mixed with its own defecation. Rage boiled over inside as Orne reached the adolescents. The duke's well-dressed son, who had been the one to kick the dog, looked at him with an arrogant smirk.

"None of your business, Lord Dipshit," said the boy. "Now why don't you piss off."

Orne was tired of this arrogant shit's belittlement and with these conceited egos who thought themselves elevated beyond the rest of civilization just because they were born with a title. His irk at the malicious nature of these children left him with muscles flexed so tight his tendons threatened to snap. He was witnessing the weakness of the lesser abusing power they didn't deserve, fueling their need for superiority.

And he was done with it. This despotic act would not go unpunished.

He took two large strides forward and grabbed the duke's son by the throat. There was a shock from his friends, and he hoarsely cried out as he grabbed at Orne's hand, but the teenager's weak, pampered fingers were incapable of prying apart Orne's grip as he gasped for air.

The boy then tried to grab the sword at his side, but Orne batted his hand away as though it were a pest, then drew the blade himself and tossed it onto the snow-covered cobbles. One of the other boys finally overcame their shock and pulled out a short knife, but Kolden, despite his current state, adeptly got his foot around the boy's ankle and shoved in a smooth motion, sending the boy to the ground before drawing an overly large dagger from his side and daring the others to try something.

As the two other cohorts backed away, Orne looked down at the dog, gasping for breath, each movement a source of pain, and his grip grew tighter. He lifted the boy from the ground by his throat and pressed him to the wall, his feet kicking and his hands feebly pulling at the thick, calloused fingers around his neck.

"I've had enough of you, you little worm. I should snap your neck for what you've done." Orne's words were colder than the icicles hanging from the roof above them, and the boy's eyes went wide.

Even in his rage, Orne knew that he couldn't kill the boy. But instilling a deep-seeded fear of consequences for his actions was clearly necessary, as it was a lesson obviously ignored in the child's privileged life.

Orne reached down with his free hand and scooped some of the soiled snow, the warm brown and red mixture wafting a pungent odor that reminded him of a battle's aftermath. He moved his hand up from the terrified boy's neck and squeezed the sides of his face to force his mouth open, his flailing hands doing little to stop Orne's muscled arms. His body writhed as he began to scream in an octave that revealed to Orne how much of a woman this boy was, but the screams did nothing to stop what was coming.

With a warm feeling of gratification, Orne shoved a handful of the soupy mixture into the boy's gaping mouth.

He left his hand there, engulfing the entire bottom half of the man-child's face, whose eyes were now so wide it seemed they would pop from his skull. The boy squirmed as he held him in place, pinned against the wall and smearing the foul blend of excrement over his face with each twitch of weak-willed resistance. Orne's enormous hand made breathing impossible for the boy as it covered his mouth and nose. Muffled screams made Orne's work easier, wasting energy and driving the instinct for a penalizing breath from the frantic captive.

With the wide eyes now squinting and tearing in misery, Orne finally felt the boy swallow out of the animalistic necessity for air. It was clear even in the dimly lit alley that the face he held was now turning a shade of green, like a rot that should be cut away.

He released his grip, the boy falling to all fours and immediately vomiting over the ground at Orne's feet. Orne stepped forward and pulled his leg back. He would demonstrate what it was like to feel helpless, something the trembling boy would forever remember.

"Orne!" shouted Kolden. "Stop!"

He looked at his brother, pent up rage now being directed with his scowl. "What?!" he questioned loudly.

"You've done enough! You'd kill him if you kicked him. And you," said Kolden, pointing his dagger at the cowering teen who looked up with his painted face and dripping nose, "leave. Leave now. If we see you again, I won't stop him from breaking you in two."

Orne stood there, fuming, and watched as the young teen scrambled away, dry heaving hard enough to curl his back. One of the others—the boy Kolden had tripped—helped him away, while the other two ran with consideration only for themselves, abandoning their slower friends. Orne watched as they reached the end of the alley and then turned to his brother.

"I *wasn't* going to kill him," Orne said.

"He got what he deserved, Orne, you made your point. I hate them too, but do you want to be like the commander? Murdering people in dark alleys?"

Orne seethed at that comparison, and his brother knew it. He *always* knew what to say to get under his skin. He stood quietly for a moment, the sounds of the warring emotions within deafening him. Hearing another whine from the dog, he finally spoke.

"Pick up the dog!" He hadn't intended to shout, but the pressure building inside of him needed to be released somehow.

For once, his brother didn't argue with him. He walked over and knelt, sliding his hands under the dog's fragile body.

"Careful!" exclaimed Orne.

His brother flashed a look that said: *I AM BEING CAREFUL!*

He knew that Kolden wouldn't hurt the animal, but he hated seeing the result of such abuse, and his anger needed an outlet. Once Kolden had the dog safely in his arms, they marched out of the alley, where Orne recovered Delvan by casually lifting and folding the Blue's body over his shoulder.

They trudged as quickly as they could towards the barracks, each of his feet landing heavily on the mixture of snow and ice with the burden of Delvan bearing on his shoulder. The short walk felt as though it were taking longer than it should, as if the street had stretched itself and were trying to delay their progress.

Fueled by an engine of ire, Orne stormed forward regardless.

After walking the eternal road, he and Kolden finally turned the last corner before the double storied, stone barracks. A few lights flickered in the narrow windows, dim light from hearths fighting to retain heat in the thick stone walls. Damn place was always cold as hell. In fact, hell might be a reprieve.

Orne threw the door open, and iron clashed against rock as it swung fully ajar. He walked through the mess hall and into one of the main sleeping quarters, again flinging open the door with disregard for the inhabitants.

Soldiers groaned and cursed as they rolled over in their bunks, Orne scanning them for one in particular.

He dropped Delvan on an empty bunk and then stalked through the room, his boots landing heavily on the thick wooden planks of the floor, creaking loudly with each step. Kolden still followed closely behind, the dog whimpering softly in his arms.

In the low, flickering light of the dying hearth at the center of the bunk-lined room, Orne managed to finally find the bed he was looking for. He ripped the blankets off and shook its occupant.

"What the hell... Orne?" said Nalhen groggily. "What time is it?"

"Grab your healer's kit," Orne said urgently. "I need you to look at something."

Nalhen reached under his bed and sat straight up. The man was a good soldier and was always ready to go at a moment's notice.

"What's wrong?" he asked, looking Orne up and down.

"I need you to help him," Orne said, pointing to Kolden.

"Kol, are you injured?" he asked, the faint flickers of fire making it difficult to see.

"Not Kolden, Nalhen, the dog," corrected Orne.

Nalhen's tense muscles loosened, and the sense of urgency seemed to dissipate. "You woke me up for a *dog*?" Nalhen asked.

"Yes!" said Orne, his voice rising and causing other blankets to stir. "Those little shits were out there beating it to death for *fun*, Nalhen. Help it, right the fuck now, and I'll forget about yesterday's wager."

"For fuck's sake, Orne," said Nalhen with a shake of his head. He sighed and unbuttoned his kit. "Put it near the fire and add some wood, I'll see what I can do."

Orne sat on a nearby bunk and watched as Nalhen went to work, the dog clinging to life. The fire grew to a hot blaze as Kolden rekindled it, washing heat over Orne's body. The longer he watched, the deeper the roots of his hatred for the young nobles grew. He put the rest of the day's events out of his mind as he sat there and waited.

If an owl showed up, he'd toss it into the fire.

# Chapter
# Thirty-Four

*The freedom of home, and the power of rule, are both now locked away. The latter would certainly destroy us, and the former may yet do the same, a punishment for the desolation of so many kin.*

Desnia sat on a crate at the bow of the ship, the country air gliding over and softly rustling her azure dress. She hated dresses. They were a necessity for some disguises, true, but overall, they flaunted her as a piece of meat to be stared at. She hadn't had many options, however, with her other clothes being ruined by the swim and smoke.

River water broke over the merchant ship's hull beside her and sprayed a rainbowed mist into the air, catching the afternoon sun with colorful refraction. The brilliant rays adorned the verdant slopes along the shore with an intensity that could only be brought by the clearest of days, a beauty waiting to be admired which seemed more resplendent here in the south.

Desnia hunched forward, oblivious to the landscape's splendor, staring at the bundle of cloth in her trembling hand.

It had been over two weeks since she bought her passage on this ship after being discovered as a stowaway, costing her almost half of the money she'd managed to grab from her stash. In that time, she'd attempted to remove the ring from inside the bundle of gray cloth on several occasions, but each time failed to overcome her fears and shoved it back into the hidden and ignorable depths of her bag.

The voice had come to her—while *awake.* It had come and, more frighteningly, guided her to this ring and then to her escape. She had always thought that it was just a figment of her dreams, something that could be ignored and written off as a terrorizer trapped behind closed eyes. But now it was *real*, a tangible sensation which she couldn't dismiss. It had told her to run.

And it probably saved her life by doing so.

Yet, here she was, falling back into the habit of ignoring her oppressor. Why was this ring—Masini—so important to her dream warden?

*I can't believe that I'm even considering a ring to be a* person, she thought, closing her eyes and shaking her head.

Desnia let out a reluctant sigh. She thankfully hadn't had another visit from the voice, escaping her to that plane of purple and white, but if it did, she *knew* it would try to command her to talk to Masini. It was better to face the pain now, rather than the unimaginable torture that she may have to endure should she go against the voice's wishes.

And she didn't know how much her mind could take.

Despite all of that, she looked over the side of the ship to the quiet river waves, a white-crested blue hiding depths that could stow this burden. She could just reach her arm over the railing and release her hand...

*No*, she thought, *I tried that. Somehow, I would be brought back to it.* There was an unvocalized assurance in her mind, as though an invisible hand laid on her shoulder and confirmed with rigid confidence that this was not a fate she could hide from.

With a slow, reluctant hand, her chest tight with anticipation, she unbound the cloth and began to carefully peel back the layers of fabric. She braced to hear—

*YOU SADIST!* came Masini's voice inside her mind, ringing like a shout in a cave. *You drown me and suffocate me in this damned cloth for weeks after a simple conversation! By the Greats, I swear the people of this ridiculous kingdom and time have no respect.*

Her muscles seized at the sound, her eyes flitting to see if anyone was nearby. Most of the deckhands were in the small galley eating their afternoon meal, so for the moment it was just her and the steersman at the opposite end of the ship.

Desnia turned, facing directly ahead along their course. Her mouth opened, but her throat constricted as her body tensed. "Am... Am I insane?" she asked in a strained whisper.

*That's the worst apology I've ever heard,* Masini said. *And we've been over this. No, you're not insane, but if you shove me back into that cloth, I swear I will make it my life's purpose to drive the sanity from you.*

Why was she asking a *ring* if she had lost her mind?

"How was I supposed to react to a *talking ring*?" she replied in a louder whisper. "You… said things. Things that you shouldn't have known, and I thought that maybe you were just something that my mind conjured to torture me."

*Hmm… Apology accepted,* replied Masini, a cheerier undertone emerging through his anger.

"What?" said Desnia, her eyes scrunching together in confusion. "I didn't apologize." Apologies were signs of weakness, and weaknesses got you killed.

*Well, given how stubborn you appear to be, I figured that was the closest thing I was going to get. So, apology accepted. Now, where in the Greats' names are we?*

Her tension was exchanged for teeth being snarled at the polished ring in her open palm, reflecting the light off its silvery finish. "You keep saying shit like that and I'll throw you overboard," she said, almost forgetting to keep her voice down.

*Do you always resort to violence?* asked Masini. *I mean, c'mon Desnia, it's clear that we're meant for each other. You don't hate me* that *much, after all, you came back for me. Must be my charismatic eloquence, I'm sure.*

She didn't respond. She remembered the feeling of relief of dropping Masini in the canal, the ease of putting him out of her mind to be ignored and forgotten. It was a custom she'd become adept at over the years, forcing her dreams from her mind to maintain the mask of normalcy.

Not that her life had ever felt all that normal.

*Eh, Desnia,* Masini said hesitantly, *the polite thing to do here would be to agree to my conceited self-image assessment.*

"I didn't go back for you because I wanted to…" she said. "The voice…" she trailed off as she struggled to speak, her own mouth betraying her mind, refusing to form the words into sounds. She forced out what she could, choking on each syllable, "Who is he?"

Silence.

The uncharacteristic muteness of Masini screamed louder than his voice. The one time she wanted—needed—him to talk, his proverbial mouth became sealed. Ideas began to swirl in her mind, a turbulent cacophony of doubts and fears which grew stronger with each passing second of painful silence.

"Well?!" she exclaimed, nearly shouting. She cringed, turning her head slightly to see if the helmsman had heard her.

*What? The last time I talked about this, you waterboarded me,* Masini replied. *I'm not exactly eager to discuss it further with you, considering we're surrounded by WATER. You missed your calling as a specialized inquisitor.*

"I won't throw you overboard," Desnia said. *Would I, though?* she wondered. She wanted to imagine herself as in control of her own life, the master of her will. But she'd given herself—willingly or not, she still couldn't be certain—to the guidance of the voice in her time of desperate need. It had brought her to Masini, and a part of her detested him for being a physical representation of her inability to control her own life, a subliminal urge driving her to reject him and regain her "free" will.

*Promise?* asked Masini.

"...Yes. I promise." Her voice lacked conviction, her subconscious still fighting to grasp a semblance of domination.

*Oath accepted,* said Masini. *If I could c-c-c-fucking-damn-it-all, do things, I would bind you to it, but instead I will have to trust that you won't betray your word and throw my imprisoned soul into the water.*

*'He,' like I said before, is a god. Sort of. At least as far as you're concerned. And for the first time in millennia, my goals and his happen to align. Partially, anyway. I need you to help me find him and free him to protect us, though he may try to kill me when he sees me. I know you think rather lowly of your own home, so think of it as ensuring you don't become some sort of slave.*

"You've already mentioned all of that," she said, frustrated. "I want *answers,* Masini. How does he speak to me in my dreams? And why would he try to kill you?"

The voice had guided her to Masini, and she'd assumed they were similar, or allies at the very least. Why would Masini be worried about this supposed god wanting to kill him?

*Well,* started Masini, sounding dramatic, *I mayyy have helped to imprison him. They can* really *hold a grudge, let me tell you. As for the rest, uhm, I can't tell you.*

Desnia shook her head in disbelief. "What do you mean, you can't tell me?!" There was fury cutting into her voice now. "This bastard has been haunting me almost my entire life, and you won't tell me anything about him?"

*Woah, just take a breath and calm down,* said Masini in a tone that she took to be condescending.

"I was nearly murdered, am wanted for being an accomplice to the death of a Blue, and have hardly enough money to survive past a few months. *Don't* tell me to calm down."

*Look,* there was a sound of desperation to his voice, *I want to tell you, but I can't. Not unless you want me stammering like a dyslexic child with a stutter trying to read an encyclopedia of the world's longest words. I just need you to trust me for now.*

Trust.

There was a word that she knew but remained foreign to her. Like a tale spun by some traveling merchant of creatures that live only in the desert, or strange animals native to the jungles of the southern continent. Exotic beings that she had been told were real but would remain forever distant.

*Look where trust has gotten me,* Desnia thought, looking out to the shoreline.

*I'm impressed,* said Masini, *you haven't thrown me overboard. I think you may be turning a new leaf, Desnia, I'm so proud.*

"Shut up," she said dismissively.

*Not sure that's ever going to happen,* he said. It was like she could hear him smiling. It made her shiver in the warm sun. *Do you maybe want to tell me why we're on the run, or why the royal guard thinks you had anything to do with the death of a Blue? Seems like it would be important to know, since we're stuck together. Speaking of which, do you want to put me on? I promise not to make any jokes about you being inside of me. Sitting on your palm like this makes me think that you're not entirely serious about your oath...*

"Gross," she said with a repulsive sneer. "That 'mouth' of yours is fouler than a pile of pig shit on a hot day."

*I will have you know that I have been described as 'Tastefully grotesque and charmingly crass, not unlike a unicorn's sphincter.'*

"What's a 'unicorn'?" Desnia asked, befuddled.

*You don't have them here, but just know that they are majestic creatures that spread euphoric joy and defecate rainbows. Huh, I'm actually surprised I can even say that. Unicorn. Huh, interesting loophole.*

Desnia rolled her eyes and let out an exasperated sigh.

*Alright, no insertion then, just put me on a necklace or something. Just not back in the cloth dungeon, please. Also, not to be pushy, but what exactly happened while I was being suffocated in a not-so-fun way? Did you rob the vault?*

Flashes of that night went through her mind like lightning in a storm—painful emotions and the tumultuous thunder that came with them. The grief of the Blue washed over her like the oncoming rain, her lip started to shake. Too much about that night—

"Wait," she said, her face exploding with shock. "I never... I never *told you* about the vault!" She sprang to her feet, the light dress flowing around her, and extended her arm over the side of the ship, curious eye of the helmsman be damned.

*WAIT! Waitwaitwait!* pleaded Masini. *I can explain! Please, please don't drop me!*

"Talk," she said, keeping her arm outreached, the light spray of breaking water misting her arm.

*I... I knew about the robbery, yes. But there was a very good reason!* He was speaking rapidly, an authenticity soaked through his frantic and voluble explanation. *The organization that I'm a part of, the Sr-Sr-Sra—fuck. Never mind, that part isn't important. We had heard that there was something of monumental importance inside that vault. Something the bastards who've systematically killed off my friends need.*

*You remember the door I talked about? The one that, if opened, brings all of our impending doom along with it? Well, every door needs a key, and the one that this door needs was supposedly nestled away inside that vault. So, my, uh, friends and I, hired a group of thieves to rob it, including yourself.*

She almost opened her hand right then, but her grip grew so tight that her fingernails dug into her palm.

"Those bastards tried to *kill me!*" she growled.

*They were definitely* not *supposed to do that! We gave them strict instructions that you were not to be harmed! I swear on the Greats and everyone I know that is still alive or dead, I did not intend for you to come under harm's way. Desnia, I told you that we needed you, and I meant it, we can't find that... god, without you.*

Was he telling the truth? Desnia thought back to Magnar, the sly smile that masked his rotten heart. She'd sensed something off about him from the moment she'd met him. He'd tried too hard to display the charismatic man pretending to be a noble. That feeling was strangely absent from Masini, despite everything else she thought about him. He was, if nothing else, apparently genuine.

*He still lied to me,* she thought.

"Why didn't you tell me this earlier?" Desnia asked, retracting her arm.

*Well, you didn't exactly give me an opportunity to, did you? I was just trying to introduce myself and then, whoosh, back in the black bag for Masini.*

"What did this key look like?" she asked, her voice filled with trepidation.

*Glowy, square, about the size of your fist. Has a bunch of markings on it.*

"The cadentite..." her voice drifted with the hint of salt on the breeze, remembering the mesmerizing glow of the cadentite block she'd seen before... everything.

*Yes! You must have seen it then? Does that mean you have it?*

"I... I don't know what happened to it," she said. The blow she'd taken to the head made parts of that night fuzzy, more of feelings than images. She remembered seeing the cadentite, Magnar threatening to kill her, Blues charging in, then it sort of blurred until she woke up with the Blue beside her, his partner dead in his arms. She had stabbed someone? Grunner, maybe?

She recounted what she could remember to Masini: the deaths, the fire, her escape. She kept on a hard face, but inside she ached, wanting nothing more than to huddle in a corner and hide from the world. Instead, she had to march forward. The world wouldn't stop for her, why should she stop for it?

Masini was quiet for what seemed an eternity. She noticed the sound of the lapping waves, having been ignorant to their rhythm earlier, and they seemed to grow louder and louder in an overbearing way.

Desnia finally broke the silence. "You... You there?"

*Obviously,* he retorted. *I was just thinking. I have no way of contacting anyone, and even if we had a carrier to send, I doubt anyone is going to be around to send something to. We have to assume that your accomplices weren't able to get the key, if any even survived. If that's the case, we need to get to the door and recruit some help to stop them from opening it before anything else.*

"What is this 'we'?" she asked. "I haven't agreed to anything. And besides, I don't work with others, especially after the last job where you almost got me killed."

*Did you hear the part about enslavement and torture? I could go into detail if you'd like. Lots of burns and puss, maybe sliding some slivers under your fingernails as they try to get you to—*

"Enough!" Desnia's voice almost broke above the hushed tone she was talking in. "Where is this gate, anyway?"

*The city you know as Brethefen,* said Masini. *Which is in, uhm, some direction from here. Where are we again?*

Brethefen *was* on the other side of the kingdom, far enough where no one would recognize her, and large enough that another girl from the east wouldn't raise too much suspicion. *Am I actually considering this?* she thought. *This is too large of a risk, the vault job nearly got me killed. I don't care what the voice tells me, I'm not risking my life again for someone else's cause.* Whatever was going on, Masini would have to get help from someone else.

"I'll see what I can do about getting us passage to Brethefen," she said. "But once we get there, I'm going to drop you with whatever friends you have and let you deal with this gate. I've already been nearly murdered for your cause and am not interested in getting myself killed."

*Desnia, this isn't really—* started Masini.

"No," she interrupted. "This is the best deal you're going to get. Take it, or I'll pawn you at the next port."

*When you put it that way... Fine. I can see you're being* extra *stubborn about this, so I'll just have to work some of my linguistic talents on the way there. You'll be jumping to help me like a soldier to a brothel before long, you'll see.*

"Keep talking and—"

"Irisi, my dear," a voice called out from behind Desnia.

She spun, her golden hair glimmering in the radiant daylight. The ship's captain, Claudion, was walking towards her, a small bowl of food in his hand. He was young for a captain, the dark colors of his clothing matching the deep olive tone of his skin. Aside from his ability to talk almost as much as Masini, Desnia hadn't found him to be particularly remarkable, but, being the merchant he was, he'd willingly taken payment from her for passage to the furthest port after catching her trying to stowaway in the hold. She was sure he charged her double what most others would, but she wasn't in a position to complain.

"I thought I would bring you some lunch," Claudion said, presenting a bowl of cold soup—a traditional southern dish, from what she'd been told. "This batch came out almost as good as my own mother's recipe, I tell you."

He smiled as he handed it to her, and she forced a smile back. She tried to tell herself that she was jaded, thinking of Magnar every time she saw that white, overly zealous grin that was the trademark of any successful merchant. Still, she'd found herself sleeping with a small knife she'd stolen from the kitchen under her pillow every night, each creak of the wooden vessel's skeleton waking her from her tense and shallow sleep.

"Thank you," she said, taking the bowl. In the motion, Masini must have caught the light and glinted, because Claudion's eyes seemed to light up with cupidity.

"My, that ring is exquisite!" he said.

*At least* someone *has good taste,* she heard Masini say. She needed to assume what he had said about people not hearing him as true. At least Claudion didn't react, though her stomach still knotted at the sound of Masini's voice in the presence of others.

"It's a cheap trinket," she quickly said. It was careless of her to have exposed it, but better for Claudion to presume it had no value in the event he would think that there was more money to be had from her.

*Wow, rude,* Masini said, sounding appalled.

"It does have some... sentimental value to me, however, and it doesn't fit my fingers. Do you happen to have a necklace chain I could purchase?"

"For you, Irisi," he said, calling her by the fake name she'd given, "I have just the thing, an elegant chain of silver, and I'll even give you a deal. Say, twenty moons."

*That price is nearly extortion,* she thought, trying to hide her distaste. Claudion seemed like a kind enough person most of the time, but he was always looking to make a profit.

"That's a little more than I can spare," she said, trying to force herself to be as polite as possible. She couldn't risk getting kicked off the ship for letting her mouth run with what she was thinking. "Do you instead have some string?" *You price gouging asshole.*

*A string?* asked Masini, sounding offended. *Am I the buttocks of some cow to be flossed to you? The lack of respect the youth show for your elders, so impudent.*

"Irisi, let's not be rash now," he said, holding that perfect smile. "That is too fine a ring, even for a fake, to be strung around some string! Alright, you force it from me, I will offer you the chain for twelve moons, but that is as low as I can go, I tell you!"

"Fine," Desnia replied. It was a low cost compared to the incessant whining she would need to tolerate from Masini if she went with the string. It was still probably double what he paid for it.

"Excellent, a brilliant choice from the beautiful lady," he replied. "I'll go fetch that for you. Oh, and I wanted to tell you, we're still on schedule to arrive in Aliova tomorrow morning. Wait until you see it! It's the most serene beauty you'll ever lay eyes on, aside from the mirror, of course."

He smiled at her again, and it was everything she could do to curl one corner of her lip in response. She wanted to punch him. *Damn this dress and the attraction it brings.* He walked away after a small bow of his head, leaving her with her meal and Masini.

*He seems… friendly,* Masini said. *Have you two, uh, been doing the midnight dance? Playing hide the weasel? Slipping the slithering snake down the den of delicacies?*

"What?!" she said with a grotesque disdain in her voice, matching the sneer on her face. "No! Gods, you're fucking disgusting, I should throw you overboard just for suggesting that."

*What?* he asked innocently. *Why not? Seems like a nice enough guy, might even get yourself a free charter out of it. Women have used sex to gain advantage since the beginning of time, I don't see why you should be so disgusted by it.*

"I am *not* having this conversation with you," she said firmly.

*Maybe you should give it some thought, might help trim the corners off that attitude of yours,* he said.

"Do you want to get wrapped back up in the cloth?"

*Alright, I'll leave it be. Greats, you need to relax a little,* he said. *So, Aliova then? Haven't been there in decades, though I recall there was this one street food vendor that made the* best *grape pie you'll ever eat. Oh, how I miss food. I never really appreciated it until, you know, the whole non-corporeal thing.*

"Yes, Aliova," she replied. The coastal city was the final destination of Claudion's before turning back to Calentine, and where she planned to disembark.

She had never been to the infamous seaport. As one of the largest commercial hubs in the kingdom, it held a certain notoriety, and she hoped that she was far enough ahead of her pursuers that she would be able to charter a ship before they caught up. Her funds were low, however, and she questioned how far she would be able to actually make it before thieving became a necessity again.

That was a problem for the future. She needed to focus on the now, which deemed obtaining passage to Brethefen as her next move.

# Chapter Thirty-Five

*My master has managed to contact me, though it greatly depleted my now scarce cadentite supply. It seems that there is, after all, a way home from this hellscape. It will defy the council, but I care only for the bosom of my mother land now...*

Flakes of snow drifted lazily past the glass behind the captain's grimacing visage. A lantern burned in the castle's stone walled quarters while his young chambermaid struggled to light a fire to warm them in the early morning hours. Orne and Kolden were both in the same clothes they'd worn the night before, Kolden having fallen fast asleep upon their return from the tavern, and Orne apparently having stayed up most of the night to watch over the dog they'd rescued.

Kolden tried to focus on the captain, doing his best to stand at attention despite his body wanting to lean and sway from the residual ale that lingered in his veins. The captain wore a heavy robe of fur, clearly having been woken almost as recently as Orne and he had been.

"Do you two," the captain started, his voice croaking and groggy but still cutting like a knife, "realize the fucking position that you've put me in?"

They both stood there, facing the captain sitting behind his desk, silent.

"I was pulled from my bed this morning by the *duke himself,* to inform me that you two fuck-wits had ASSAULTED his SON!" The chambermaid jumped with a start, her hands trembling as she tried to spark a flame in the cold hearth. "What in the hell were you thinking?! Are you even capable of thought?! After what happened was described to me, I don't think there is even half a brain between the both of you!"

Kolden winced at the man's screams, his brother holding firm and brow furrowing deeply.

*Please don't say anything stupid,* he thought, seeing his brother out of the corner of his eye. *He doesn't want to hear—*

"Sir," said Orne. Kolden's gut turned over, his hands clenching. "They were beating a dog to death, sir."

"I don't *CARE!*" the captain exclaimed. Kolden's lips drew into a tight line, and a cold sweat broke over his brow. This wasn't the first time they'd had a conversation like this. He should be accustomed to it, in fact, but attacking a lord was a new level of disaster, even for them.

"Do you know what the duke is demanding of me? He wants you two hanging from the ramparts—today! He wants to set an example, he doesn't give two shits that you two are lords. The man's been itching for a show of power since he arrived here, and you've just handed it to him in a golden chalice!"

The captain dug his face into his hands, letting out a frustrated sigh. He ran his hands through his thinning hair and leaned back, his face looking tormented. He glanced at the struggling chambermaid and in an outburst, screamed, "How hard is it to light a gods-damned fire?!"

The girl let out a startled yelp, and with a flurry of sparks from flint, finally managed to ignite a flame in the blackened fireplace. She hurriedly placed a few larger chunks of wood on the growing embers, and then—after a quick curtsey—quickly shuffled out of the room.

"I swear, you two are going to be the death of me," the captain said, leaning back and rubbing his head again. "I'm half tempted to hang you both for such idiotic insubordination, but I know that I'd end up on the wall right next to your rotting corpses once the general found out. And if I disobey the duke, the man who speaks on behalf of the *King*, then there's a good chance I end up there anyway." He sighed again.

Kolden stood there, tense, adrenaline forcing his body awake and alert, despite the lack of sleep. Orne remained unmoving, his face angry and betrayed. He knew that his brother felt what they'd done to be justified, and Kolden—in large part—agreed with him. But he was also aware that it had been foolish and moronic. He assumed there would be punishment for their actions, but never thought the duke would resort to hanging two lords. While he and Orne despised their title, it *had* been enough to keep them sheltered.

Until now.

*What is he going to do?* Kolden wondered. *Will he actually resort to hanging us? There must be a trial, court martial, something that would buy us time to have the general speak with the duke.*

The captain turned, facing out the window into the gray dawn, contemplation set deep into the wrinkles of his face. Kolden held his breath, waiting to hear the verdict. After a tense absence of sound between the three of them, the captain finally turned and looked at them, his shoulders slumping to the ground, and broke the silence.

"I'm going to grant your request, Sergeant," said the captain, tapping his fingers on the desk. The chill seemed to leave the room, or was that relief flushing through Kolden's body?

"Sir?" asked Orne.

"You're joining one of the caravans leaving this morning and getting a new stationing assignment. I'm going to send a letter to the general and explain the... situation and hope he can smooth things over with the duke."

"Sir. Thank you, sir," replied Orne.

Kolden sighed inside and refrained from rolling his eyes. Wasn't it obvious to his brother what the captain was doing?

"Shut the fuck up, Sergeant. I'm not doing this for you, I'm doing it to salvage whatever bit of my career and life I possibly can. The caravan leaves in an hour. I'll send word to the commanding officer and let him know of your arrival. Once you leave, I never want to see either of your faces again, understand me? Don't return to Drunt. Ever."

They both saluted. Kolden could see a hint of a smile creeping past his brother's scowl, and he let out a small sigh. Wasn't Orne aware of how close he'd gotten them to a trip to the gallows? How could he *possibly* be happy about this situation?

*It's because he got what he wanted,* Kolden realized. *He got his justice and transfer and is happy even though the duke may very well hang the captain.*

Orne probably wasn't considering that. He just saw this as *winning.* Idiot.

"Go, pack your things and report to the west gate. *Don't* let any of the castle staff see you. Now get the fuck out of my sight. Dismissed," said the captain, sounding more resigned than angry.

They each released their salute, Kolden's heart pounding as he realized how close this had brought them to not just consequences, but *capital* punishment. He could feel his knees shaking as he and Orne turned and left through the door, leaving the sulking figure of the captain in the flickering light of the now blazing fireplace. Orne's face tightened into a smile, or as close as he ever came to one, a sort of mixture between smugness, anger, and gloating all jumbled together.

"I can't believe we're finally getting out of this place," Orne said, proudly.

"You're lucky that we're walking away from this, gods was that fucking stupid," Kolden hissed, a small echo reverberating in the tapestry-lined hall.

"Those little shits had it coming," Orne said with defiant confidence, "I'd do it again."

"How dense do you have to be? We're barely getting out of this!"

"We get a new command *and* get to leave this place—permanently. This is great."

Kolden smacked his hand to his head. Conversing with a boulder would be easier than this.

"Let's hurry," Kolden said, "we only have an hour and I need to get my things from the shop and the barracks."

The cadentite worried him the most. He was going to have to hide it somewhere among his possessions, making sure to keep it and the dagger made from the same material hidden away until he could figure out what to do with it. It racked his already shaken nerves to think about, remembering the murder from the previous night.

"Good," said Orne, "while you're there, grab my halberd."

"Fuck you!" replied Kolden. "You're coming with me and getting it yourself, I have other shit to carry. You got us into this mess, the least you can do is help me carry some of my stuff."

Orne grumbled but didn't disagree. They picked up their pace and made the trek to the barracks, they didn't have much time.

Almost exactly an hour later, after enduring his brother's shouting to hurry—as if he wasn't in a rush himself—they approached the western gate. Orne had wiped Nalhen's debts clean in exchange for continuing to watch over the dog they'd saved, before each frantically packed up what few items they had and made their way to the forge. After hiking across half of town, the city limits were a welcome sight to Kolden.

There were fragments of stone wall here, the masons having not yet reached this portion for repair, and the gate was part of a fashioned palisade. The sharpened wooden poles speared the air, a walkway along the upper ledge occupied by one guard looking down to the forest beyond.

Kolden dragged his trunk through the snow, an overstuffed bag and crossbow hanging from his shoulders. He wore his custom archer's armor, fashioned of heavy leather and chainmail, and struggled to heave all his gear as they approached the caravan. Orne carried no less than five different weapons, his custom armor, and his trunk as though he were the human form of a pack mule, striding effortlessly through the snow.

As they came to the caravan a few squires thankfully came over and began helping them, as if the two were expected. Kolden stretched his sore muscles as the heavy items were taken from him, including the trunk which carried the cadentite dagger and block under a false bottom, wrapped thickly in inanite-dyed blankets.

He eyed the squires as they loaded it onto a carriage. The trunk was locked, but that didn't make him any less wary. His attention, however, was suddenly drawn by someone approaching them with an assertive stride. He turned to see who it was, and his face went pale, sweat becoming ice on his forehead as his insides lurched.

Stepping towards them was Knight Commander Ferrand, Orne's sword upon his back and its hilt rising above his head.

*This is* that *caravan?* he thought in a panic. It made perfect sense, Delvan had said they were leaving in the morning, but in his groggy stupor he hadn't put together that this was the commander that they would be reporting to.

Clearly his brother hadn't made the connection either, as he was distracted by yelling instructions at the squires on how to care for his weapons.

With jaw agape and body cold, verging on numb, Kolden tapped Orne's arm, his wide eyes fixed on the approaching commander. Orne tried to brush him off, eventually turning and following Kolden's perplexed stare. Kolden saw Orne's face flash in shock, then turn a deep red as he clenched his fists and ground his teeth at the approaching Blue.

"My, my, what do we have here," said the commander, his focus primarily on Orne. He gave the towering man a smile, digging into Orne's chagrined demeanor. It was all Kolden could do to hold the contents of his stomach, thinking of how this man killed someone with nothing but a punch the night before.

"When the captain said he was sending me two fuckups, I have to admit I didn't expect you to be among them," the commander said to Orne. "If I had known, I wouldn't have argued with him about the matter. Though I'm not sure what use you're going to be," he said, turning to Kolden.

Kolden wasn't angry, despite the fact that he should have been. He could feel the blood draining from his face, his hands trembling as he froze, petrified. He thought of the cadentite and was certain he was going to be sick. Would the Blue know it was there? What would he do to Kolden if he found it? His mouth went dry as he tried to listen to the commander.

"Roll call. Name and rank, boys," the commander ordered.

Instinct took over and overrode his paralysis. Kolden's body snapped to attention alongside his brother.

"Lord Orne du Traskor, sir. Sergeant."

"Lord Kolden du Traskor, sir. Sergeant," he replied with a shaky voice.

"Lords? You two are lords, and still only sergeants? That explains the armor and weapons, I guess. And *this* is your brother? Gods, am I glad I didn't take your original wager."

*What does he mean by that?* Kolden thought.

"Did your mother get all used up making the big one?" Ferrand asked, looking to Kolden and thumbing towards Orne. Kolden would normally have some snippy remarks, but kept his lips thinly pressed together.

"Either way, my name is Knight Commander Ferrand ce Lione. I don't tolerate fuck ups, so plan to make yourselves useful. And... Wait, did you say Traskor?"

The commander looked at them questioningly, gears turning in his mind. Out of the corner of Kolden's eye, he saw Delvan appear from behind a carriage, looking sickly and wiping his face free of what Kolden could only assume was vomit. As they caught each other's eyes, Delvan cocked his head to the side with a curious expression.

"Traskor..." repeated Ferrand. "Do you mean to tell me you two are the offspring of *General* Traskor?"

Kolden groaned, the first thing he'd been able to do since standing at attention.

"He's our father, sir, yes," replied Orne in his deep tone.

"By the gods! Gentlemen," Ferrand exclaimed, turning to the rest of the caravan and grabbing their attention, "we have here military *royalty*!"

Kolden could feel the rush of blood to his face as it flushed with rage. He wanted nothing more than to escape his father's shadow, but like smoke from a forge, it seemed to follow him and Orne wherever they went. He stood there quietly, remembering the cadentite hidden in his trunk.

"Well, boys, it's a pleasure to have your company, but don't expect special treatment. I can spare you a squire and two horses, but that's all your titles will get you out here on the road.

"I also hope you enjoyed your night of drinking. Our final destination is Brethefen and I intend to be stationed there for a considerable time, so it will be your last for a while."

"Sir," said Orne, a confused expression blending with the angry scowl, "what does drinking have to do with Brethefen?"

"The city is exceptionally devout, boy, and it's completely dry." He turned and walked away, a smug grin on his face. As he walked, he turned and saw Delvan, shaking his head and saying with a sharp distaste. "Look, the other fuck-up I have to deal with. You lot will make good company."

"What does he mean, dry?" asked Orne as Ferrand stomped away. "I know it's a desert, that doesn't have anything to do with ale, does it?"

"He means there's no *alcohol* there, dumbass," Kolden replied with a shake of his head.

"What?!" Orne's face turned to one of shock and therefore ire. He began spouting curses that would make a sailor blush while Kolden just watched the Blue walk away.

He'd hoped to avoid the bear in the forest, instead it would seem that he'd jumped right into its den.

# Chapter Thirty-Six

*There are some that recognize our intent. They wish to adhere to the orders of our distant council. They dare to declare me ignoble! All for want of returning. Do they not crave the same? Do they see themselves to be so detestably honorable?*

*And now these traitors have declared war upon us! Our own kind, fighting one another! Such blasphemy has not been seen by nigh our most significant elders! I will control the gate. I will rebuild. And I will see home again.*

Desnia found herself at the ship's bow once more, the morning light reflecting off the white, gravelly limestone that made up the river's steep banks to either side. Neat rows of vines covered every inch of the rocky slopes, which Claudion had proudly told her were plantings of grapes used to make Aliova's infamous wine. Masini now hung around her neck from a glinting silver chain, though having "him" touch her skin was an unnerving and almost nauseating sensation.

She'd tried to offer storing him in a pocket or her bag to save from buying the chain, but he'd insisted that he couldn't "see" if she did that. She wasn't sure if it was the truth, or him just being his typical, masculine, perverted self. When asked about how his "sight" worked, she'd been given the standard answer of, *'It's complicated.'*

Sleep had been fitful, at best. Thinking about how to proceed after reaching Aliova had been easy enough when the reality seemed a distant destination, but now that the journey was nearly to its end, she found her mind racing.

Even now, as she stared ahead down the river, the tapestry of blue-green water swirling around the hull giving off a faint smell of salt, her finger tapped on the railing's edge to the variable beat of impatience.

How was she going to get to Brethefen? How much would it cost? Would she have enough money to cover the journey, or would she be forced to turn to other means?

These questions and more encompassed her thoughts, drowning out the sound of the wind in the sails and the crew working the deck. Which is why, upon hearing Claudion's voice, she spun with a start.

"Irisi, my dear," he said in his overly charming way as he approached her. "I cannot wait for you to see this, I tell you." He went to put his hand on her arm, which she instinctively jerked away, her other hand reaching for the painfully absent dagger at her side.

*You have some, uh, serious issues,* Masini said.

Claudion ignored her reaction with a smile and pointed forward with his other hand as though nothing had occurred. "Around this next bend," he said with a passionate glean in his eyes, "is my home, the beautiful city of Aliova. I do not wish to spoil it for you, but it is unlike anything I think a Calentinian like yourself has ever seen.

"Perhaps, before you continue your travels, you would grace me with the opportunity to show you the lovely city as only a native can? I grew up among the city's leaders and nobility, I can show you the best it has to offer, I assure you."

*You should do it, you could use some socialization with someone who has an* actual *body,* Masini said.

Desnia suppressed the scowl that tugged at her face. She had forced herself to be—at least moderately—kind to Claudion as to prevent being forced off the ship before their destination. Clearly, he had misunderstood her insincerity for something else. *Damn this fucking dress.*

"Thanks, Claudion," she said with a feigned smile, "but I don't think I'll be able to. I need to find another charter as soon as possible."

*Are you always this boring?* came Masini's voice, sounding disappointed.

"If a charter is what you need," said Claudion as though she hadn't just rejected him, "then I must offer my assistance. While my crew and I unload at port today I will ask to see who is willing to board you for a journey. I know many of the traders personally, I could possibly even get a discount for you. One so lovely as yourself should never be forced to pay full price."

*Says the man who overcharged me,* she thought.

"Although," he continued, "most ships will not embark until the early morning hours. Come and see me at the docks this evening, I know of this wonderful little restaurant where we could discuss the matter over dinner."

*He certainly is persistent,* said Masini, *I like him. But if you don't accept his offer, I'm going to find a way to torture you. I know this one annoying song that I could sing loudly through the night, who needs sleep anyway?*

"I, uh," she said, trying to filter her own thoughts through the sound of Masini's voice.

*That,* Desnia thought, *is going to take some getting used to, assuming I don't throw him into the sea after a while.*

Masini's voice came again, *If you don't go for the company at least go for the discount, you're not exactly wealthy, in case you forgot, and we have a long way to travel.*

That sparked an idea in her mind. Masini's argument might have some potential validity. Not the socialization aspect, of course, the thought of eating a meal with anyone, let alone Claudion, repulsed her. But it did present an opportunity which she couldn't disregard.

"Alright," she finally replied to the ever-patient Claudion, "see what you can find for charters to the southern continent, and I'll plan to meet you at the ship this evening."

"Most excellent!" he exclaimed. "Your beauty and company brings light to my heart, Irisi. I shall see what I can find for passage to the south. It is a voyage for only the strongest of hearts, none of which compare to yours, of course. The expanse of the sea, the sunsets that fill the horizon with near-unmatched beauty, sailing around the edge of the darkened Perpetual, it's truly an event that stays with you for a lifetime, I tell you. Though I should mention that even with whatever discount I can procure, this will be an expensive voyage."

*Um,* she heard Masini say, *you realize that Brethefen is west of here, not south, right?* Desnia ignored him, unable to speak her plan aloud with the captain present.

"Ah," said Claudion, turning and looking ahead, "we're here!"

The ship crested the river's bend, and as they emerged from the planted slopes of the river's banks—which had become progressively taller since yesterday—Desnia found herself awestruck.

Aliova was positioned at the river's mouth, its amphitheater shape carved into the white slopes that reached hundreds of feet skyward. Its stage was its port, whose backdrop was the open vastness of the endless southern sea beyond, the turquoise water pressing its salted breeze against her fluttering dress, the sound of sea birds a strange but fitting ambiance. A massive break wall extended out into the distance, protecting the port at the city's heart from the distant and crashing ocean waves.

"I feel that same way each time I come home, I tell you," said Claudion, looking at the transfixed expression on Desnia's face. "I recommend heading to the upper rim for the day," he said, pointing to buildings at the farthest reaches of the semi-circular embankment.

Desnia had been utterly engrossed by the sheer *expanse* of the sea and had hardly noticed the city itself. She was stunned yet again as she turned to see where Claudion was pointing. The white limestone had been carved in steps, not too differently from Calentine. But instead of the monotone scheme of stone she was accustomed to, the buildings here were of vibrant reds, blues, and yellows, like an artist's brushstrokes of brilliantly colored flowers against white canvas.

"Why?" she asked in response to Claudion's recommendation. Her mind associated the high reaches of the city's escarpment with the Upper Tier back at Calentine, and the wealthy pretentiousness that came with it. What would be the benefit of climbing all that way if she were just going to be surrounded by the insufferable aristocracy?

"The lower part of the city is filled with sailors on shore leave, and sailors on dry land—me and my well-mannered crew excluded—tend to be, how do you say, uh, rowdy. On that ridge you'll find the finest view of a sunset you could imagine, and without the crowds of the docks."

"Thank you," she said as he bowed and stepped away to assist with berthing the ship at port. She didn't necessarily have an issue with a "rowdy" tavern, as Claudion put it. In fact, she would probably feel more at home there than the upper rim that he'd recommended. But more eyes meant more possible attention, and the last thing she wanted was for anyone to remember her.

*So, uh, did you decide to change our travel plans?* asked Masini.

"No," replied Desnia in a whisper. "I just don't want him knowing where we're going."

*Why agree to meet him then?*

"Because, you were right about not having much money. He's unloading today, which means he's going to be flush with enough suns for us to get anywhere we want comfortably."

*…You're going to rob him.* It was a statement, not a question, from the exasperated Masini. She could almost feel his "eyes" rolling while he said it.

"Why else would I get dinner with him? Or did you happen to forget why you hired me in the first place? And what's the fastest way to Brethefen from here?"

*You know, I feel like they could write a book about trust issues with you as the sole study subject,* said Masini, his tone more condescending than Desnia had patience for.

"Eat a dick," she replied tersely.

*Oh! Speaking of which, there's actually this one country on the southern continent that serves whale penis as a delicacy. They claim it to be the most powerful aphrodisiac in the world. Last time I was there—not that I needed any help in that area, obviously—I had to try it, just out of curiosity. Imagine my surprise when I woke up the next day, naked and surrounded by a dozen—*

"Stop!" she cursed. "Gods, you say there is something wrong with me… The fastest way to Brethefen, Masini, focus."

*By the Greats, you need to lighten up,* he replied. *Fine. If we can charter a ship to the western port of Tennefen we will be maybe two weeks' ride from the city. Otherwise, we will have to take the trader's road, which would be the better part of a five-month journey.*

*Let's avoid that,* she thought to herself.

The ship pulled into a dock, easing between a variety of other vessels ranging from triple-masted frigates, smaller galleons like Claudion's, and some cutters that were clearly meant only for the river. The masts rising from the water like reeds reminded her of Calentine's port, but that was where the similarities stopped. Everything moved here, but in a less hectic way. The people seemed calmer, as though the hot sun worked to sedate the clamoring merchants. They sauntered about, working, but with less urgency, even their shouting sounded tamer.

As she disembarked onto the stone pier, people smiled and waved, sounds of laughter could be heard in the distance. Everyone seemed... pleasant.

Desnia found the whole experience incredibly unsettling.

*Are we heading to the upper rim?* asked Masini as she cautiously eyed her surroundings.

"Yes," she whispered, "we can't set sail until the morning, and there's a clear view of the port from there. Plus, it'll be less crowded. But first, I need to make a stop."

As she left the small tailor shop, she heard Masini in her mind. His comments seemed to be endless.

*I don't know why you needed to buy a bunch of men's clothing. The dress you're wearing will get you much farther than dressing like a homeless teenager.*

"I don't *want* to draw attention, that's the whole point. I hate dresses."

*Then why are you wearing that one?*

"Because it was the cheapest article of clothing that Claudion had on his ship, and my other clothes were ruined. It was impossible to get that smoke scent or the charring out."

*Wow, he's a clever one.*

"Gods, all of you men are the same," she said with disdain.

*Exactly, which is why you should at least wear the dress until dinner. Your looks are an advantage, not a hindrance,* he said, trying to sound convincing. *If you learned to use them for your own gain, you'd make more money than you did as a thief, and the best part would be that people would give it to you, willingly!*

"Drop it, or I drop you." Desnia had no interest in seducing men for money, not that she had anything against prostitutes. She understood as well as they did that you had to do what was necessary to feed yourself, or even others. The thought of trying to do it herself, however, made her stomach turn.

Masini grumbled something as she walked the winding road that switchbacked up the city's incline. Each time she looked out at the sea she expected to see something in the distance, the elevation gain surely enough to reveal some distant land. Instead, the deep blue of the boundless sea met the lighter shade of sky at an impossibly distant horizon. How did people cross that unending plane, each direction the same unknown? Did they just go where the wind took them? Or were they confidently choosing a direction and announcing it as the correct path?

The question played in the back of her mind until she reached a small tavern at the top of the road, near the city's limits—what the locals seemed to consider a tavern, at least. It was more like a house, with a patio in the front covered with sparsely occupied tables. Further up the road she could see a stable, probably holding loaded stalls of horses for rent or purchase to take along the trader's road. As she approached the tavern, an older woman with olive skin and white hair—which a few strands of black defiantly fought against—smiled and walked up to her.

"Hello, dear," the woman said in a kind manner, "have a seat. What can I get for you?"

Desnia had spent weeks aboard Claudion's ship, mostly eating the same cold soup every day. She longed for a hot meal, some tastes from home coming to her mind.

"Would I be able to get meat pie and an ale?" she asked hopefully.

"Ah, a northerner I see. I'm sorry dear, I have a few soups available, but no meat pies. We do have some fried fish, fresh from the docks. Also, you won't find much ale in these parts, but I'll get you a glass of wine, you'll never go back to that northern swill again."

Her heart sank. She wasn't sure she could eat another bowl of soup for the rest of her life, and she'd always detested fish, eating it only when it was the only option to survive. The smell of it always reminded her of the foul stench of the Calentine Port. She thought of something Masini had said earlier.

"Do you have any grape pie?"

"Do I have grape pie?" the woman said, taken aback. "Dear, this is Aliova, there isn't an inn or house that doesn't have a grape pie sitting on the sill. I'll get you a slice."

Desnia sat on a nearby wooden chair, its fittings rusting slightly, and waited at the table until the old woman came back out with a slice of pie stuffed with a deep purple filling, and a tall glass of blood-red wine. She rested it on the table, smiling at Desnia and then leaving to sweep the patio.

*I hate you so much right now,* came Masini's voice, green with envy.

"You can't even eat," she said, picking up the wine and taking a sip. It was... different. Like an ale that had gone flat but also fruity. She tried it again and... it wasn't *terrible.* It wasn't ale, but it would do. She picked up the fork and took a bite of the pie. A sweetness exploded in her mouth, the rich flavor overpowering the wine and making her eyes go wide. It looked so unassuming, so simple, yet she had never eaten so much sugar in a single bite in all her life. The combination with the bit of tartness was unlike anything she'd ever eaten.

It was the most humble, yet hedonistic, food she'd ever consumed. And it was bliss.

*Maybe you could, you know, just dunk me in the wine a little,* Masini pleaded. *Then slather some of that pie filling on me, for old times' sake.*

She ignored him, and kept eating the pie, inhaling it until the slice was gone. She asked for another and indulged in bite after succulent bite of the incredible dessert. It was almost enough to make her forget about her pursuers and shed the oppressive burden of fear.

Eventually her stomach argued against her, forcing her to slow down. She eased back in the chair and stared out at the ocean. Despite some cramps from her stomach, her muscles loosened, and for the first time in longer than she could remember, she felt the faintest hint of ease. It was a rare reprieve from the worries of her existence.

*Is this how others go through life?* she wondered. *Are the privileged nobles endowed with the same lack of concerns or cares about the world?*

She wanted to spit vile hatred and venom at them, but as that fuel was added to the heaping ash within her, its sparks were smothered by the image of that Blue, crying over his deceased friend. She could still feel that pain, though it had faded, and it brought back memories.

Questions about that night, and how Masini was related to it, rattled inside her. There were some that she dared not ask, for she knew that the answers would do nothing but confirm her darkest fears and secrets. Secrets she intended to keep hidden. Part of her wanted to know everything, but her instincts fought against her. Why ask questions and become invested? It was better to follow the plan and part ways, knowing as little about her new companion as possible. Still, she couldn't help but ask *something*.

"Masini," she said, now alone on the patio, "why did you come here?"

*I'm, uh, going to assume you don't mean this patio?*

"This kingdom, my home. Why come to this place? These people you say want to come through this gate, I can understand that they want power, I've dealt with power hungry assholes my whole life. But what was here for you in the first place?"

He was quiet for a moment. Desnia wasn't sure if he'd even be able to answer her, but presumably these people would be pursuing her the same as the royal guard, and it was better to know your enemy than remain ignorant.

*Much of the same reasoning, I'm afraid to say,* he said solemnly. *My people aren't exactly known for our benevolence. We have a long history of seeking vi-vi-vi-ugh, let's say energy, and we use any means to acquire and control it. Having spent an era living here among you, I have grown a different perspective, but most of my people view anyone that is less powerful than they are as inferior, the way your people look at cows for slaughter. And I can tell you, with one exception, we have yet to meet any civilization that has been able to resist us.*

*We came here, as we do to so many distant lands, to claim, uh, certain resources. Things, uh, didn't go as planned. There was a catastrophe, one that cost us dearly. The door was closed, and we forbade anyone else from home from coming here. I remained, with others, to ensure such devastation could not occur again.*

*But now, thanks to the despicable machinations of a blinded and wounded pride, combined with the even more wretched, malleable bureaucracy that is politics, my people are trying to come back here and reclaim what some see as their given right.*

*Believe it or not, I have become rather fond of you all, and have fought an unseen war for a long, long time trying to prevent this exact scenario. I was here when the catastrophe occurred, I remember the horrors, the carnage. I refuse to let that happen again, to either side.*

*We've lost the fight—or nearly have, anyway. There are hardly any of us left here, except for those who wish to open the door and return home while ushering in your domination. That's why I'm here with you, probably the only person in the entire kingdom who could help me find the beings that so defiantly challenged my people, that sent them running, not to even consider returning for millennia.*

"So, you're saying," Desnia said, trying to process everything that Masini had told her, "that you want my help unleashing a god—that you helped imprison—so powerful that he challenged and terrified a previously unstoppable empire?"

*That about sums it up, yep,* he replied casually.

"Well, glad to know that between the two of us *I'm* not the insane one. You realize this sounds like a terrible idea?"

*As risky as taking a laxative and a sleeping aid at the same time, yes, I'm aware.*

"And, since you say we don't have time to find this supposed god now, how exactly do you propose stopping these people from opening the gate?"

*Is it* we *now?*

Shit, had she said "we?" Surely it was a slip of the tongue, or he'd misheard.

"Just answer the question," she snapped.

*I have no idea,* Masini replied.

*Great,* she thought. *So, I'm going to be walking into a pack of wolves with no weapons or plan.* She hated not having a plan. But why was she worried about this? She was going to hand Masini off to whoever he knew in Brethefen and let them deal with this gate, why should she jump to the whims of a being so willing to inflict pain in her dreams?

*Maybe I should throw him into the ocean and be done with it,* she thought.

*I have a question,* said Masini. *Actually, it's one I already asked, but you were kind enough to remind me of your imperious capabilities over me when I asked it.*

"What's that?" she asked hesitantly.

*What did he say to you? The, uh, god? Anything that might help?*

Did she dare answer? Face the truths of what she so actively avoided?

"He said... Well, I told you already. 'Stop the gate from opening.' Not that the asshole has done anything besides torment me and leave me broken morning after grueling morning. I don't know why he expects I'd do him any favors."

*Well, I know how much they hate me, but you, well, for you I bet he'd get all sentimental. Like a cat protecting her kittens. Except the cat is a tiger. And the kittens—that's you in this metaphor—are ants. Actually, no, that's a terrible analogy, let me rephrase. He—*

"Do you have a *point?*" she asked, annoyed.

*I'm* saying *that there is probably something in this for you, since, you know, you don't seem bothered by the whole 'enslavement and death' thing.*

There had been a promise made, she remembered. One to keep her mind from... what she'd always dreaded. The ever-present fear that she couldn't stop running from.

"I'll... think about it." It was as much as she was willing to concede. For right now, she just wanted to enjoy the brief, pleasant moment of her tiny sanctuary.

The sun began to touch the horizon, throwing an orange glow across the intermittent clouds and softening the ocean's dark waves to a lighter, comforting shade of blue. The sunset wasn't oppressive or difficult to stare at, as some she'd watched from the high cliffs of Calentine. It radiated a sense of tranquility that spread through her and in that moment, she felt a brief glimpse of an elusive peace.

And then, as the glowing mass inevitably dropped below the distant horizon, the feeling was gone. She was back in the semi-darkness of twilight, sulking in her fears and paranoias. A black flood of dread filled her chest as she realized it was time to go meet Claudion. She finished her glass of wine, paid her host, and began walking to the docks with her bag slung over her shoulder.

She tried focusing on her next task: robbing Claudion. She didn't intend to take *all* of his money, he had given her safe passage after all, but she had paid him for that service, doubly what he was due. What allegiance did she owe someone who had so willfully extorted her? One of the reasons she hated working with a team, as had happened with Magnar, was because there was *always* a risk of betrayal. Someone would stab you in the back for your cut, she was just going to beat this one to the punch.

The money would most likely be on the ship, in the captain's quarters. Though he was originally from Aliova, was there a chance he owned a home here? She would have to find out tonight, at dinner. She rarely shared a meal with anyone, but this was too lucrative an opportunity to turn down. She had performed half a dozen similar thefts before, but for some reason this one left her feeling nauseous, a bead of sweat rolling across her brow in the evening breeze.

*This will be good for you, Desnia,* chimed Masini. *Even if you are going under false pretenses.*

"I don't trust him," she replied, turning her face to whisper as she passed a pair of soldiers walking by.

*Well, if you only got together with people you trusted then you'd never go out. Hold on. You... you never go out, do you?*

"I'm a thief, not some Lady to be touted and displayed in front of people."

*By. The. Greats. We need to work on you, though I fear you're too far gone.*

"Oh would you—"

Desnia cut off as she passed another pair of soldiers. Were there more of them out tonight than when she'd arrived? Unlike Mixton's docks, these piers seemed to be run by the crown, but she didn't remember seeing nearly as many foot soldiers this morning. And had it smelled this bad when she'd arrived? The scent of rotting fish and taste of salty brine assaulted her. Was it low tide?

As she rounded the last bend in the road, bringing her to the entrance of the docks, she could see soldiers talking with dock workers and ship's crews, with others walking the length of ships. *Are these just inspections,* she wondered, *or are they looking for me?*

She hadn't seen any royal army ships arrive from her vantage high on the hill—she'd been worried about soldiers, or worse, Blues, following her from Calentine—but that didn't mean they hadn't sent a pigeon to warn about her.

She took a few cautious steps forward and felt a sickening pang as she saw Claudion standing and talking to two soldiers, waving his hands in his melodramatic way. She ducked behind some boxes, the unlit streetlamps and falling sun hiding her in shadow. She could barely make out what was being said in the distant conversation.

"...manifest and list of whoever you may have boarded on route, Captain," said the higher-ranking soldier.

"I am just a simple merchant, I tell you," said Claudion. "My manifest was given to the harbormaster when I arrived this morning. What is this all about? In all my years of living in Aliova I have not had my vessel searched like this!"

"Per order of the King, we are looking for a fugitive. A woman from Calentine, described as fair haired, maybe in her late teens, early twenties. Have you seen anyone like this? There's a hundred sun reward for anyone that provides information that leads to her capture."

*Oh fuck,* she thought, as her insides tried to force themselves through her throat. Claudion was going to sell her out, there was no doubt. Escape routes flourished in her mind. Could she make it onto one of the ships that had already been searched? She had no idea where any of them were going, but a direct route to Brethefen seemed less important now than her flight.

"What is this all about?" asked Claudion.

Was... Was he not going to turn her in? *No,* she thought, *he must be trying to barter for more money.* She wanted to run, her legs tense and ready to explode into a sprint if necessary. She couldn't help but listen, waiting to hear what he had to say.

*See,* came Masini's voice, *he* really *likes you, as I said. He won't turn you in, he's been staring at you in that dress for weeks.*

"Shh!" she hushed.

"There was an incident in Calentine," the soldier replied, speaking as though it had been recited a hundred times, "the local Merchants' Guild headquarters was destroyed, burnt to the ground. Lord Librun al Portaine's son was murdered during the event. The woman is wanted for her involvement in the crimes."

"Hilbrun is dead! You should have started with this, I tell you! I grew up with him, and you say this woman was involved in his death?!" There was pain in Claudion's voice, she could feel it emanating from him. She knew what would come next, before the words were spoken. "There was a woman like this, a stowaway on my ship that paid me for passage. She was due to meet me here a short while ago!"

*Shit.* Desnia's throat went tight, her heart pounding. Where could she run? She began scanning her surroundings more carefully, trying to find a path out.

*It would appear,* said Masini, *that I was, uh, wrong. Huh, that feels weird to say.*

"Tell the captain to lock down the port and keep an eye out," said the guard to his companion, who quickly trotted off to relay the command. "Sir, do you know where she said she was headed? She might have already tried to flee."

"Yes, to the southern continent!"

The guard turned to shout orders to another nearby minion, "I want guards posted on every ship heading south, then search them all again. Actually, post guards on *every* ship, we can't have her escaping. Move!"

Anger. That is what she *should* have been feeling. A righteous fury that would tear through those that betrayed her. Instead, there was just a crippling sense of... sadness? Disappointment? Had she been taking Masini's words about trust to heart? Had she *actually* considered opening herself, even a crack, to anyone else?

*Stupid,* she thought, *stupidstupidstupid. They're all the same. Why would I have thought one rat among many would be any different.*

Soldiers began hustling around the docks, a sense of urgency about them that she had not yet seen while in the port city. She tried to dispel the sinking sensation deep in her gut as she thought of her next move, ignoring the pounding of her heart in her ears.

*Uh, Desnia,* said Masini, *we should probably run now.*

A ship wasn't an option anymore. She instead kept to the shadows and crept from the docks, running up the street at the first chance she had. The dark blue of the dress helped her stay hidden in the landscape of patchwork darkness, but the sandals she wore made a horrifically loud clapping sound as she ran. She haphazardly ripped them off, then reached into her bag and pulled out a scarf she'd purchased, a bland colored square, and wrapped it around her hair. She wanted to change out of the damned dress, it was too obvious, but she didn't have time. She needed to get to the peak of the city's steps as fast as her legs would carry her.

"I *told you* we couldn't trust him," she said.

*You being proven right* one time *does not mean that there is no one you can trust,* retorted Masini.

How could he still be so optimistic? Wasn't it clear to him that people only ever served their own self-interest?

Sweating, legs burning, and feet blistered, she finally reached the stables at the top of the hillside. There weren't any soldiers here, not yet. She knew they wouldn't be far behind though. She saw the stable master shoveling hay in the stalls, unaware of Desnia nearby desperately trying to catch her breath. Outside, tied to a post and quietly chewing on a bag of feed was a black mare, saddled and waiting for its owner, likely the stable master himself.

Desnia couldn't risk being seen by the older man. Eventually the guards would figure out what she'd done or assume that maybe she had gone to the next port to sail south. But this would give her a head start, and with a few careful trades to get a horse less distinguishable, she could quickly blend into the countryside and become incognito.

Hopefully.

She untied the horse, mounted it, and with a few kicks at its side, she was off.

The trader's road was going to be a long and difficult journey, but that was nothing new to Desnia. Her whole life had been about overcoming challenges thrown at her, this was no different.

## END PART 2

# Interlude

The smell of fresh sawdust was almost enough to mask the acrid scent of the cooing pigeons. Pens for the birds lined the walls around a central desk where an elderly man wearing the official uniform of the Royal Mail service sat. His long, bent nose and lack of chin had the bemusing effect of making him look like he had a beak of his own. Or perhaps it was just the influence of the winged vermin surrounding him. He was looking down his spectacles at one of the silvery-gray birds held in his aged hands when the others all began to flutter inside their cages with fright.

Animals always seemed to react that way around The Hunter. Was it the way his boots scraped along the floor as he limped in? Was his aura visible to the simple, winged creatures somehow? Or was it the sixth sense of prey to flee from a predator?

He pondered the question as he hobbled over the worn and stained floorboards, approaching the aquiline mail room attendant who was putting the bird in his hands into a cage as it struggled upon seeing The Hunter. The attendant glanced at him in a cautious but curious manner, as though he were mimicking one of his flock.

*They are more similar to each other than they are to me,* he supposed.

He must have been an interesting sight, the wrappings around his face covering all but a narrow slit for his eyes, hiding the scarring that Protorus had inflicted upon him. The limp from an under-healed break in his leg made him unable to move at even a feeble pace, forcing him to use a makeshift cane. It had been weeks since their encounter, the old man had been stalwart to the end. Clever, clever Protorus.

It had been a long time since he'd come so close to dying.

And it was *thrilling.*

It was a shame that with Protorus gone, there remained no more High Realm mages among the ranks of the Sraddhana. Where would he find a challenge now?

*It won't matter once the gate is opened,* he thought. *I must discover where Protorus sent the key, otherwise I shall be trapped in this penitentiary of monotony for untold additional years.*

Protorus had proved to be an admirable foe in the end, and The Hunter respected him for that. Admired, in fact. What a *delight* for him to provide a new chase, a new prey. He'd almost been concerned about how mundane his return to Brethefen would have been should the old man have had the key on him. Hopefully there would be a message here for him regarding its possible whereabouts.

"King and His grace upon you," the attendant said as The Hunter reached the desk, closing the cage full of anxious pigeons and turning towards him.

He didn't respond to the greeting, he found it obnoxious that these mind-less livestock looked upon the luck of a single man as divine intervention. Yet when a *true* deity was in their presence, they ineptly showed reverence to someone who held a power they didn't comprehend.

"Looking to see if I have any messages in waiting," he responded in his hoarse and broken voice. His vocal cords still had not fully recovered from the damage of the vidut burst, and speaking was difficult. He gave the false name he was currently using and waited while the attendant looked through the wall of cubbies behind the desk full of miniature scrolls.

With an, "Ah," the man pulled a small scroll from one of the bins and looked it over, inspecting the unbroken wax seal on the outside. "This requires a code from you for receipt," the old man said in his shaky voice, squinting down his beaky nose to read through his polished glasses.

The Hunter recited the four-digit number that would be embedded in the wax for the man. A rudimentary precaution, but it was enough to keep most prying eyes from the content within.

Not that there would be much for them to find.

The old man extended his arm and placed the minuscule scroll in The Hunter's waiting, gloved hand. The old, wrinkled fingers had a tremor to them; not one of fear, but instead caused by the rapid decay of their frail bodies. A sign that this one's short lifespan was nearing its end.

*Pathetic.*

The attendant clearly tried and failed to avoid staring at him, glimpsing the wounds around his semi-lidless eyes. He shifted uncomfortably, turning to focus on other duties that would divert his wandering gaze.

The Hunter walked to a door that stood ajar nearby, a small room with a single table and lamp for writing messages within. He shut and locked the door behind him, sitting himself slowly into the creaking, antiquated chair that sat before the table dotted with spots of ink. There were no windows in the cramped space, only the lamp for light, to give privacy to those that required it.

He broke the wax seal on the scroll and unrolled it, placing two small paperweights on either end of the unfurled paper which, to most, would appear completely blank. There were some small risks with sending an encoded message such as this, but in matters related to the key it was warranted. These towns and outposts that he found himself in and sent messages to and from had no presence of the tainted warriors, though they wouldn't know what to do if they did discover the empty scroll.

He held his hand above the paper, palm facing the table with his fingers pointed downward. He placed his fingers at the correct intersection points and drew from his vidut reserves. Faint lines of purple light spread from his fingertips in seemingly random directions, until they coalesced into a repetitious pattern. The fractal spread out on a flat plane parallel to the table's surface, as though he were holding a wire disc of purple metal above the wooden desk's top. The repetitive lines created the symbol necessary to reveal the hidden message, creeping outward like ice crawling across the surface of pooling water.

As the last illuminating lines fell into place, glowing letters were written into existence upon the paper below as though being scribed before him, revealing the hidden message. He quickly read the note from his compatriots before dismissing the spell with a wave of his hand, releasing an exhausted sigh as he did so.

Healing himself had dwindled his reserves to almost nothing, and now casting something as simple as a revealing spell fatigued him. He'd been unable to move after the fight with Protorus for almost a week, being buried under snow while his body healed enough to allow him to function. Finding

Ptorous's horse after the ordeal had been another delaying endeavor, one that consumed time and coin alike. He was just glad he'd found it before the wolves did. Pesky competition.

Now, despite the draining fatigue, The Hunter sat and smiled.

*The tainted one who was present at the robbery travels west, apparently into our waiting arms,* he thought, mulling over the hidden note. *If he has the key, he may be able to hide it more easily once in the city. We should intercept before he has such an opportunity.*

This, of course, could be another one of Protorus's feints, the adroit plotter always had plans within plans. Their spies within Calentine had said the boy claimed one of the thieves escaped, and several of his brethren assumed this was where the key had gone in the ensuing chaos. It was certainly a possibility, but this was not something to be left to presumptions. All suspicions required confirmation. And there could still be much to glean from the tainted one, even if he didn't possess the key.

He shifted in his chair, trying to alleviate some of the pain that throbbed through the entirety of his being. Ideas and plans began to formulate in his mind as he tried to decide on his next course of action.

Others were searching for the missing thief, though he suspected it was as futile an effort as their search for the girl—the other survivor—had been thus far. It was probable that both were dead at the hands of the other Sraddhana already, it was what he would have done. At least this boy was still alive and his whereabouts known.

The Hunter wished that he could be the one to question the child, the tainted ones could be formidable opponents, the closest he would come to combating one of his own kin. But, alas, his wounds were still too grave to quickly close the distant gap from here to the distant west. The best he could hope for was capture during transit, then to have them brought to Brethefen under the careful eye of his associates. He could beat them to the city via ship, as it appeared they were taking the northern route on foot, where he may have the opportunity to speak with them himself.

Assuming they survived that long.

He drew a fresh scroll from the end of the table, along with ink and wax that he began to heat over a candle. He scrawled brief instructions on the thin strip of paper and, placing his hand above it as before, conjured another fractal to hide the message. He rolled it tight and dripped some of the hot wax onto it, using a stamp from his bag to seal the document with his code and crest.

As he placed the brass stamp back into the satchel at his side, his finger grazed the small chunk of inanite at the bottom beside the nearly muted cadentite gem beside it. He pulled the pitch-black stone from the secluded depths and rolled it between his fingers, thinking back to Protorus's final, ambitious effort.

These were all that remained of him now, this bead of tar-like rock and the other faceted stone, glinting even within the depths of his bag. This wasn't his typical trophy, but it felt... precious to him all the same. A prize well earned. The other stone would have to go towards completing the gate. A pity, but a necessary sacrifice.

He reverently placed it back into the bag before standing and hobbling into the next room. He handed the scroll to the attendant, painfully croaking instructions for its delivery. He paid the man and left the mail station, stepping back into the crisp, gray air of the condensed central street.

He needed to recharge before he could continue the healing process, preferably before his carriage left in the morning. Selection on the road was scarce, especially when encumbered by the eyes of a carriage driver. It was one of the many reasons he preferred traveling on his own, but his condition left him with little choice at present.

He hobbled down the covered porches that ran along the muddy street, horses mixing the wet earth into whatever snow landed on the path lined with the only buildings of this puny settlement. Their excrement mixed with the mud and produced a rank odor, even in the cold of coming winter. The Hunter crossed several storefronts of the adjacent buildings, stopping at the small tavern near the center.

Partaking in the swill of the locals had been an acquired taste. Abundant and plentiful as it was, each serving always felt... diluted. The wells of Calentine always provided a special, more concentrated flavor, a reason he'd lived in the metropolis for so long. But, on the road one could not abstain due to simple distaste. Needs must be met.

He entered through the heavy door of the tavern, the smell of stale ale, horse-infused dirt, and a sharp hint of mold assaulting him. Several locals turned to stare at him in a hushed manner, some whispers among them. They weren't completely unaccustomed to passersby, trade and communication brought foreigners in often enough, so they were all soon back into their conversations as The Hunter limped to a table near the warm and comfortable hearth.

He sat and waited, scanning his surroundings. He knew it wouldn't be long now. Why seek your quarry if they will come to you?

As expected, it was a short wait.

A young woman at the bar on the wall opposite stood and made her way directly to him. A forward and distinct action, a predator in her own right. He felt a pang of something... disconcerting. It was not the way of nature for hunters to target one another, though what was the fox to the wolf? If she could not recognize him for what he was, perhaps she was deserving of his needs.

She pulled out a chair and sat next to him, leaning forward to display the bust of her revealing dress, smiling at him as she folded her arms on the table. "Can I interest you in something to drink, dear?" she asked, her blue eyes reflecting the flickering fire. She stared directly into his, unflinching despite the grotesque scarring visible around them between the wrappings on his face.

The Hunter just shook his head. Speaking was difficult, and he would use words only when necessary.

"Ah, well maybe I can interest you in something else then? Something to warm you up?" she asked, running her hand along his forearm. She looked at him with the experienced gaze of intent, the implication of a look more communicative than words could ever be.

He grinned beneath the mask, elated at the ease of his pursuit. He nodded to her still smiling face, and he thought of the beauty he could paint on it, the expressions that could be displayed in instances of exposing the primal emotions of these primitives.

They both stood up, and she led him by the hand to the back of the tavern, down a long hall lined with doors. She walked slowly, accommodating his wounds. Such foolish kindness.

He longed for another great challenge, but that was coming. This would be a transfer of necessity, one that would help him reach Brethefen in a more capable state. He could feel it still, however, that eagerness of anticipation.

It was faint, this had been too easy, but he could sense his heartbeat slightly faster nonetheless.

He smiled under the mask as she closed the door. She would do.

For now.

# PART 3
## BROKEN

# CHAPTER THIRTY-SEVEN

*Your exasperation over the situation has been noted, but I implore you to put forth your best effort in bringing him to our side.*

Orne's side sword pointed directly at Delvan, his feet planted in a wide stance in the numbing snow. His teeth ground as his jaw clenched, a rage building in his eyes as his grip on the sword's hilt tightened. He planned his attack, and with a surge of motion launched forward at Delvan, whose short sword was held in a defensive posture, and swung a series of strikes at the Blue.

The blades clashed with a loud, but muffled *thud* as the thick, leather training bands along the sharpened edges beat against each other. Delvan adeptly countered each of Orne's strikes, but he hesitated at any opportunity to go on the offensive. Orne *knew* Delvan was a capable fighter. It was apparent in the way he moved, how his instincts took over and shifted his weapon before his mind had time to respond. Yet he seemed stuck, unable to do more than merely defend himself.

And it was driving Orne to madness.

*Attack, gods-damn it!* he thought as Delvan swiped Orne's longer sword to the side and drove its tip into the white-blanketed ground, presenting him with a perfect moment to "wound" Orne. But there was a pause, just a fraction of a second, and instead of striking, the Blue took a step back and fell into a defensive posture once more.

He knew he had to be patient, but it was so gods-damned *hard*. It had taken a week of constant pestering from him to convince Delvan to duel. He refused to fight Ferrand again, the man was a murderer, and a cheat. Delvan was an excellent fighter, one of the best Orne had dueled, but he lost to Orne time and time again, hesitating at every turn.

It was going to get him killed, and Orne was determined to get him past this battle shock.

It wasn't something that could be rushed. He had hoped that by dueling in a controlled environment, it would help Delvan overcome whatever trauma he'd experienced. But the truth was that no one had answers for how to rid someone of the disease that was spread by the carnage of battle. Theories abounded, but Orne had seen enough soldiers experience the effects to know that it depended more on the person than any supposed "treatment". It wasn't going to stop him from trying his own, however.

Orne adjusted his stance, adopting a more aggressive posture. He was growing tired of these small jousts of flourishes that ended with Delvan circling around him. Orne lifted his sword's hilt to his head, its point aiming directly at Delvan, watching as the Blue turned to a surprising stance, one meant for offensive striking.

He tried not to smile but felt a glimmer of elation from within. He lunged forward, thrusting the blade towards Delvan who smacked it away with skillful ease—just as Orne had intended. Delvan spun away from the deflected blade, bringing his sword with momentum at Orne's hulking frame.

*Finally,* he thought.

Orne was nimbler than people assumed, and they were often surprised—as Delvan soon was—at his maneuverability despite his towering frame. Regaining his balance before Delvan finished his whirling attack, Orne stepped in towards the young Blue, striking Delvan's wrist with his forearm, blocking the strike.

Delvan should have repositioned his feet, but he hesitated—again. Orne could see in his eyes that fear had gripped his opponent, or was it doubt? It didn't matter, either one got you killed.

He grabbed Delvan's frozen arm and with a hefty yank ripped him to the ground. Delvan landed with a grunt as his back impacted the snow, wincing. He opened his eyes to see Orne pointing his sword down at the defeated Blue.

"For the sake of the gods, give him a break, Orne," Kolden said from nearby. He was kneeling at an unlit fire, trying to spark it to life while squires erected their tents. The early sunset of winter was upon them, and the caravan had stopped for the day when Orne had convinced Delvan to participate in a few bouts. They were fighting in the gray glow of sunset, the body of Amenesol having settled for sleep behind the canopy of trees.

He reached an arm down and helped Delvan stand. "You had three opportunities to beat me," he said sternly. "Stop avoiding me, and *attack*." Delvan looked away and drew in his shoulders. Orne was left with the impression that he might have been too overbearing, but maybe that's what the Blue needed.

"As annoying as he is, he's probably right about that, Del," said Kolden as he struggled to ignite the pile of tinder. How did he work in a forge all day and not know how to properly get a fire started? "He may not have many talents but picking apart your fighting style and telling you what you did wrong is a specialty of his, even if he sounds like a dick while doing it."

"At least I know how to start a fire," he retorted.

"This wood is soaked, asshole. I'm trying. Hey, Del, do you think you could, uh, you know, give a hand?"

Kolden had clearly become more comfortable around the Blue, but Orne saw asking him to cast fire as a boundary not even he would cross. That his brother would even ask after how Delvan had reacted the first time a display of his "gift"—as Delvan described it—had been requested just went to show how naive and selfish his brother could be.

Surely enough, when he looked at Delvan, he saw the wide eyes, trembling hands, shallow breaths, and pale skin that seemed to infect the Blue at times.

*Gods, he's such an idiot,* Orne thought, glaring at his brother.

Kolden looked back at him with an expression that just said: *What?*

Orne shook his head with a growl. "Ignore him," he said to Delvan. "C'mon, let's go a few more rounds. I want to see what you can *actually* do."

Delvan took a few shaky breaths, short and rapid at first, then longer and more drawn out. He rested his hands on his knees, sweat dripping down his brow. He managed to shake his head, which Orne took as a pass to his request.

It was fine, he'd gotten more out of him today than he'd been able to all week. With some more time to get back to his old self, Orne hoped to get Delvan out of whatever rut he was stuck in. The road to Brethefen was a long one, but it wasn't without danger.

"Alright," replied Orne, "let's get some chairs then, hopefully Kolden can remember how to light a fire before we get back."

Kolden pretended to ignore him, but did a terrible job, sneering and muttering under his breath.

"The squires," Delvan said with a wobbly voice, "should be bringing them once they're done with the tents."

"You can swing a sword but can't carry a chair?" Orne asked. Delvan looked at him, his head slightly tilted, a confused look on his face. "C'mon, let's grab them so we can sit, the squires have enough to do."

*Damned lords,* Orne thought with a shake of his head.

Delvan followed him—the same confused expression on his face—the roughly hundred feet to the rest of the caravan. Orne pulled chairs for the three of them from the back of a carriage and handed one to Delvan, who took it in hand with that same, dumbfounded look.

*He's probably never had to do a day of labor in his entire life,* realized Orne. Well, that could change. Some humility might do the noble good.

They walked back to their camp, separated from the rest of the group as though they were lepers to be quarantined. Orne didn't care, of course, he'd rather be away from the cheat of a commander. He and Kolden had started having their camp set up alongside Delvan's after the first night, once they realized he'd been shunned beyond the outskirts of the rest of the troop.

Delvan hadn't explained why he was being treated with such disrespect, considering his station. Other soldiers in the caravan whispered during the march, but silenced themselves around Orne and Kolden, as though whatever had infected the Blue had spread to them as well through mere association.

*Fuck 'em,* Orne thought.

He and Delvan drudged through the snow back to where Kolden had managed to finally light the fire, smoke billowing from it in an opaque stream. Night was fully settling in, the last vestiges of dim light vanishing, leaving them with the black, clouded sky, hiding the glimmer of the stars.

Fires cropped up in the distance as the rest of the camp settled for the evening, casting wavering licks of light against the trunks of trees like fireflies in a field of grass. Orne could hear the other soldiers' indistinguishable chatter in the distance, a soft noise against the harsh, frozen air.

The three of them sat for a few hours, chatting about nothing of importance. Delvan was quiet, as he normally was—a surprise to Orne at first, given how conversive he'd been the night they met. The first few fires went out as people began to settle in for the night, and Orne noticed Kolden eyeing the distant camp, as though he were looking for something, or waiting.

Kolden stood up during a moment of quiet between the three of them and walked into his tent, emerging a minute later with something that caught Orne's eye.

A bottle of whiskey.

"Where did you get that?!" Orne said, his voice projecting loudly.

"Would you keep your fucking voice down?" hissed Kolden. "I stole it from the smith when we were packing up the shop. It's probably terrible, but I figured we had a long road ahead and it's better than nothing."

"And you're just telling us about it now?" Orne asked, his brow furrowed and eyes wide.

"I'm not going to let your thirsty ass drink it all on the first night, this needs to last us a while."

Orne wanted to smack him upside the head, but he *had* brought whiskey. He'd been furious the first night of travel when he discovered that the only alcohol in the caravan was reserved for the King's emissary, without even an allotment for the lords.

He held his hand in place as he eagerly said, "Well, open it!"

Kolden pulled the cork from the glass bottle using his teeth and took a long swig with a cringing face before handing it to Orne. He smelled it, a fiery burn pungently filling his nostrils. This was indeed no better than lamp oil, but it would still get the job done. He pressed the bottle to his lips and tilted his head back, taking three large gulps.

"Hey!" said Kolden with a judgmental tone. "Save some for Del, damn it. This needs to last, you oaf."

"Fuck off," he replied as he passed the bottle to Delvan, who looked at it with an eagerness that spoke more of craving than it did of desire, a glean that didn't dissipate after the Blue took a long swig of the caramel-colored liquid and passed it back to Kolden. Orne noticed the young Blue's eyes tracking the whiskey with desperate intensity as Kolden replaced the cork and shoved the bottle into the snow beside him.

"I can't believe that there's nothing to drink in Brethefen," Orne said, the burn of alcohol on his breath still fresh.

"We got out of Drunt, didn't we?" asked Kolden in his condescending tone. Orne wondered if his brother even realized how arrogant he sounded most of the time.

"Yes, but couldn't we have been assigned to a troop going literally anywhere else?"

"Well maybe if you hadn't shoved shit down that kid's throat, we would have more leeway to pick our destination," replied Kolden.

"You…" Delvan said, suddenly attentive to the conversation. "You did what?"

Orne and Kolden hadn't discussed why they'd been assigned to the caravan, and Delvan hadn't asked. Orne hadn't wanted to talk about it, anger building in his chest like steam, threatening to explode at just the thought of that boy's petulant arrogance. His brother avoided the topic as well, clearly holding a grudge, though it was waning.

*He has no right to judge, considering how many times we've gotten transferred because of his own stupidity,* Orne thought. *That's why he hasn't brought it up to argue about, he has no sure footing.*

"After we left the tavern with you," Kolden said, "we may have come across the duke's teenage son and his sycophants beating a dog for fun. Orne may have also taken that personally and forced the little shit to… consume some of his handiwork."

Orne let out a satisfied grunt, a hint of a smile tugging at one corner of his mouth.

Delvan turned and looked at Orne with a horrified expression, clearly he wasn't accustomed to such acts. Most people with his upbringing wouldn't be, he supposed. Delvan's mortification faded and molded itself into contemplative thought. "What happened to the dog?" Delvan asked, looking legitimately concerned.

"Left it with the company's medic," Orne said in his deep, low tone. "He owed me more wagers than Kolden can count to, he'll care for it."

He didn't have to look at Kolden to know what his expression was saying: *Asshole.*

"Oh," said Delvan with a nod, "well that's good. I'm surprised that you weren't court martialed though, assaulting another lord is a serious offense. I'd expect at least *some* punishment."

"What do you mean?" asked Kolden. "We are being punished—we're here, reporting directly to that mu—uhh, the commander."

Orne glared at his brother with a look that would have sent an enemy platoon running. He needed to watch his mouth, not that he didn't trust Delvan, but what Kolden had seen wasn't information that should be shared lightly.

Delvan's face turned hard, a sneer of contempt flexing his lip. Orne could see the hatred burning in the young Blue's eyes, a fire that he could not ably manifest outside of him but raged in his soul. What could prompt such disdain from the Blue? Orne and Kolden had avoided asking about his situation, thinking it likely had something to do with his condition, but he'd agreed to sparring, so maybe he would be willing to discuss it?

Kolden seemed to have a similar thought, and glanced at Orne as he started talking, "Orne and I have, uh, noticed how the commander treats you. I know he's a dick, but you're a Blue for fuck's sake, why does he treat you like a rabid dog?"

*Mhm, well put.*

There was an extended silence from Delvan, his eyes staring out to an impossible distance. They lacked the panic that Orne had seen from him time and time again, it was instead exchanged for an intensity that turned his face to stone. The crackling of the fire was the only sound for a while, until Delvan finally spoke.

"He knows that I know his secret," Delvan said in a quiet voice.

Orne saw his brother's eyes widen. How could Delvan know about the murder that Kolden witnessed? Orne had seen him at the tavern when Kolden had witnessed the commander in the alley, hadn't he?

"How do you know about that?" Orne said in a hushed tone, his brow digging deeply between his eyes.

Now it was Kolden that glared at *him*. The meaning was clear: *What the fuck are you doing?!*

Orne returned with a defiant: *What?*

Delvan turned and stared at them, his face shifting from stern to confused. "What are you talking about?" he asked.

Kolden went from looking annoyed to *outraged*.

"Ignore my idiot brother," Kolden said hastily, "explain what you mean."

Delvan's eyes shifted between the two of them before he continued, his voice sounding apprehensive, "I... I think, no, I *know* he had a hand in my friend's death, back in Calentine." He looked at the fire with his face solemn, eyes glazed in recollection.

"What happened?" Kolden asked, almost immediately. His brother's curiosity was tenacious.

Hadn't Kolden said that the commander mentioned something about another Blue dying when he saw him in the alley? He must have meant Delvan, didn't he? Orne racked his brain trying to remember, but he didn't always pay the closest attention when Kolden spoke.

"May I have another drink?" Delvan asked, nodding to the whiskey.

Kolden pulled the frosted bottle from the snow and handed it to him. After a long swig of the cheap liquor, Delvan began speaking. He started slowly, struggling to communicate through what was clearly pain and grief. The clouds shifted in the sky as he spun a tale, full of people and groups that went by strange names that Orne had difficulty keeping track of. But then he spoke of his friend's death, the fire, and how his father had banished him to the other side of the kingdom.

Everything circled the commander, including, it would appear, the death of two merchants. Orne decided that this just proved how corrupted the bastard was. *Something* needed to be done about him. Looking at the sullen Blue, he noticed how much of the bottle he'd managed to consume during his recital. Less than a quarter of the auburn liquid now remained.

He reached over and gently grabbed the whiskey, pulling it as Delvan's fingers resisted him at first, then eventually let go. He didn't think that Delvan needed more of the indulgence; plus, he wanted to make sure he had some for later.

"I have no proof that Ferrand was involved in the robbery," Delvan continued, "but I know he had to be. I can *feel* it."

Orne saw Kolden shifting uncomfortably in his seat.

*He looks like he's about to say something stupid,* Orne thought.

"Del," Kolden said hesitantly, "there's something you should probably know."

*Yep. Stupid.* Orne didn't like the idea of sharing what Kolden had seen with anyone, it seemed too risky. Yet, despite him looking at his brother and saying, "*Kolden!*" with a snarl, his brother began to speak.

Orne begrudgingly sat there as his brother leaned forward and whispered quietly enough that it was almost difficult to hear him over the pops and cracks of the wet firewood.

"The night we met you in the tavern, I saw the commander meeting with someone in an alley. I think he's the thief that went missing on you: dressed in all black, big scar on his face—which I'm assuming you were kind enough to give him.

"He and the commander talked about that night, and let me tell you, Ferrand was *not* happy. Said he'd hired him to be in and out quietly, was furious that your partner was dead, though the other guy seemed to shrug it off. Said he was a, uh... uh, *Magridi* or something?"

Orne didn't remember Kolden sharing all of these details with him, had he not told him? He sifted through his memory trying to replay the conversation that night, looking over at Delvan in the middle of his recollection.

The Blue's fists were clenched. He was leaning forward and listening with a concentrated intensity, his face a mask of anger and pain. Was there... *steam* rising from him?

"You heard this?" Delvan asked. "You heard the commander admit that he hired the thieves to rob the merchants' vault?"

"Yeah, and there's more," responded Kolden. "They talked about the girl you mentioned, the one that you said helped you and then escaped. Apparently, this guy was *not* supposed to harm her, Ferrand was even more upset about that than he was about your friend getting killed."

Orne saw the words crack Delvan's facade, the light of the fire casting shadows of misery and remembrance over the Blue's mask. Orne thought it was stupid for Delvan to have saved the girl. She was probably part of Ferrand's schemes by the sound of it, and likely helped Delvan just to save her own skin. And now she was out on the loose because of it.

Delvan was clearly thinking behind the emotions splashed on his visage. After a moment of considering Kolden's words he said, "We need to talk to this man you saw Ferrand speaking with. Maybe with his testimony and ours we could do something about the commander." Orne heard a lack of conviction behind those words, as though Delvan was trying to convince himself more than he was the two of them. Orne agreed with him, but his brother had thought it a ridiculous idea to try and turn the commander in. Clearly, they should have said something if he was responsible for everything that Delvan had mentioned. *I told him so.*

"Did he say what he was after in the vault? And do you know anyone in Drunt that we could reach out to find and question him, someone you trust? That medic you mentioned maybe?" Delvan said eagerly.

Orne and Kolden shared a look. Kolden hadn't told him everything yet, and he appeared to be intentionally leaving out the information about his precious glowing rock.

*About time he did something smart,* Orne thought.

"Del," Kolden said, "we can't question him. At the end of their conversation, Ferrand killed him. Punched him so hard that he snapped his neck and spun his head the wrong way round. Once I saw that I got out of there as quick as I could. He said he was after some kind of key, though, if that helps"

Delvan's head drooped as though he had been defeated. It lasted only for a moment, however, as he snapped it back up with a realization. "The girl then," he said. "We have to find her, ask her about that night. Maybe she knows something we can use."

"How are we going to do that?" asked Kolden. "You said she vanished in Calentine, with half the guard out looking for her. *If* she's still even there, they're going to find her. And if she's not, well, it's a big fucking kingdom. How are we going to find one person when the entire royal army is keeping an eye out for them?

"I think when we get to Brethefen we get as far from that fucker as we can. Keep our heads low and request a transfer."

Delvan stared into the fire, flakes of snow falling from the tree above melting in the air around his armor. His face snarled as he laced his fingers together, brandishing a spiteful stare.

"I'm not going to drag you two into this," Delvan said, still gazing into the distance through the fire's heart, "but I can't just let this go. I'm going to do something about what he did, no matter what it takes. I don't believe he was remorseful for Hil's death, he was probably upset about drawing attention to himself more than anything. Even if he *was*, I don't care. It's still his fault. This is all his fault."

Shit. He was going to do something stupid. Orne had enough experience with Kolden's idiotic plans to recognize when someone was plotting something disastrous, and Delvan's words strummed a beat of lunacy.

Orne took another long, long drink of what was left of the bottle, finishing it off. He didn't care about what Kolden had to say. His life was about to start tumbling like a raft through rapids, which was a sight more than he'd asked for. Except that instead of the danger being presented as bandits in the night, or enemy soldiers approaching in rank and file, he was at risk from his own people.

*Might as well enjoy the peace while it lasts,* he thought as the last drop of whiskey passed over his lips.

# Chapter Thirty-Eight

*A gift as rare as his cannot be wasted, nor ignored.*

Oversized awnings covered much of the crowded street in cooling shade, vendors of the outdoor bazaar calling to Nerio and those around him for attention, fishing for potential buyers of their various goods. Crates and tables piled high with spices and fabrics created a maze of pathways and claustrophobic passages, with scents of exotic foods and seasonings blending with the familiar wafts of local cuisine giving the moisture deprived air a distinct identity.

When Nerio started coming here regularly a few weeks ago, he'd wondered if being tightly condensed among a swath of people—similar to one of the nearby stacks of carpets—would help to make him feel less solitary. Could this community hub help him to break down the walls erected around his mind, the ones that made others seem so distant even when close? It had helped him escape Jerdine, perhaps it would help him to break out of this mental isolation.

*Perhaps I want for too much,* he thought.

After maneuvering the labyrinth of organized chaos, he reached the location of his favored morning ritual: a small tea stand. A wrinkled elderly woman behind the haphazardly constructed stall smiled at him with narrow, milky eyes, standing out against her dark skin. He read through the list of teas as though he didn't already know what he would order—a strange but comforting habit of familiarity. The different strains of tea were written out, their names mostly derived from old trethish, which he doubted many aside from himself would realize.

The ancient language pervaded much of the culture in Brethefen and the surrounding area, even the suffix "fen" was the ancient term to indicate a large town or city. Something about the tenacious nature of history, the way certain parts of various cultures could persist through time—like the language of a long-forgotten people—bothered him, despite his own fascination with the subject.

*Is it because my own past still endeavors to consume my present?* he thought.

The idea wrought a nauseous feeling inside of him, nearly strong enough to dissuade him from his morning tea. But no, he needed this sense of familiarity, this repeated act in a space that was safe, hidden. This was one of the few places he could truly relax. The freedom from constant worry, even if for a brief moment, was worth clinging to with desperate fervor. A stray thought was not enough to prevent his single daily reprieve.

Nerio ordered a cup of tea, the hot liquid producing wisps of steam that quickly dissipated into the air. He sat down at a makeshift table in front of the stall, his seat nothing more than an overturned vegetable crate made of aging, grayed wood. It was simple, as was the tea, but there was a serenity to sitting there, sipping the fragrant and delicious drink, watching the crowd from above the ceramic lip of his teacup.

It was pleasant to sit and stare at the people moving by, walls of sunlight breaking through the thin gaps of the awnings above flashing against the wanderers of the shifting group. He gazed absently, his mind comfortably quiet among the chattering static of merchant-filled streets.

His fingers found their way to his sash, fiddling with the broken fragment of blood-stained ceramic that he kept within. All these months later, and even on his day off, he still couldn't force himself to be rid of the painful memory or its token. It was a sobering moment, one which shattered his illusion of tranquility.

He sighed, putting down his cup on the rough, weathered table. The smells seemed to dull, and the white of his robe dimmed as though a cloud had passed overhead. Was this self-inflicted torment brought to him by the gods as some kind of penance? He closed his eyes and sagged his head as he pondered.

The scripture stated, '*The gods do not bestow more than one has deserved.*' Nerio always found that this verse, more than most, was interpreted in a multitude of fashions. The wealthy used it to proclaim their fortune as divine intervention, the farmer saw it as an expression of their worth upon a bountiful harvest, but some few, such as Nerio, deciphered the meaning differently.

*I am not deserving of happiness.*

With a deep and resigned breath, he opened his eyes, the bustle of his surroundings feeling distant and mundane. A flash as someone passed through a patch of sunlight caught his eye, a lighthouse in the hazy fog snagging and guiding his attention.

His eyes followed the source unconsciously, his mind having slowed to a crawl as it processed his turmoil. Baggy, torn clothing adorned a thin frame, the filthy fabric making Nerio think the teenage boy was homeless. A patched hood obscured the face, which he guessed would be equally unwashed. Why would one live in such a way within Brethefen? It was heresy, and unnecessary.

There was a way the boy moved, a conformity to his surroundings that allowed him to blend and go unnoticed. Merchants ignored the vagabond, focusing instead on those they thought would pay, not registering the boy as worthy of note. Which was an unfortunate mistake on their part, as Nerio watched the sleuth pick a few figs from an unobserved crate and slip them into the bag at his hip, the merchant continuing to discuss pricing with another customer, appearing none-the-wiser.

It took Nerio a moment to realize what had happened. His head drew back, he should feel aghast, but instead found himself shifting his eyes, looking for any guards. Not because he wished to call them to the thief, but because he thought there was a better way.

Part of him—one which felt as though he were tied to the box he sat upon, and it was made of stone—wanted to let the thief continue about their day. It fought against his basic instincts, demanding he remain and leave the situation to its own outcomes. Another part, however, rebelled against this, alleviating that weight and pushing him to move, to act. It was an instinct that still drove him, one that would not allow someone so impoverished to go without aid.

Nerio took one last sip of his cooled tea and stood—a simple task that felt as though a monumental feat. He watched and followed as the thief masterfully navigated the ebbs and flow of the crowd, gracefully slipping between people with what appeared to be casual ease. Nerio, however, struggled to keep up despite his knowledge of the area. More than once, he lost sight of the boy, only catching up when they stopped at different food stalls to palm what Nerio thought would only amount to a meager meal.

As he turned another bend, the hungry thief having eluded him again, he got a view down a rare, long straightaway. His eyes squinted as he strained to see through the foggy shade, a nearby tobacco parlor filling the air with pungent and sweet smoke. They searched through the haze, the darting stopping as he spotted the thief, standing at the entrance to an alley, the obscured face beneath the hood staring directly at him.

His stomach synched tightly. It was a confusing reaction, he wasn't the one being chased after all, but he didn't have time to process the thought.

He'd been discovered, and with a blur of motion the thief vanished down the alley.

Nerio ran as fast as his sandaled feet would allow, his narrow shoulders bumping into others as he made his way to the alley. He half turned and frantically apologized as he bounced off the bodies of the throng, keeping his feet constantly moving towards where the thief had slipped away.

When he finally reached the narrow corridor, he caught a glimpse of a foot disappearing around a distant corner. He took off in a sprint between the buildings, his sandals clapping against the brick pavers. He wasn't sure what made him want to chase this person in such a desperate way, yet he continued, even as the sun poured through the uncovered gape above, forcing sweat from his pores.

He slowed as he reached the corner, the sound of his feet echoing off the adobe walls. He went around the turn as fast as he could, perhaps he could catch up at the next street. Maybe there was something he could—

A hand—small but deathly firm—grabbed his shoulder and used his momentum to plant him face-first into the wall. The tight grip pinned him, and before he could resist, he felt a cold chill of sharpened steel against his neck.

"Why are you following me?" a feminine voice asked. Where had a woman come from? He tried turning his head to see who was holding him more clearly but was met with a push against his shoulder and more pressure from the blade at his throat. Had he mistaken the thief for a man?

"Answer!" his captor asked.

"I saw you stealing food," he responded. His voice did not quiver in terror, as he would have guessed. Rather, he felt a strange sense of relief, a patient acceptance. His heart raced, but it felt more like eager anticipation than fear for his life. It was the most alive he'd felt in months, yet it made him realize how mote his life truly was. How unexpected, yet unsurprising.

"You trying to turn me in? 'Cause it isn't going to fucking happen, understand?" the voice stated with a cold, confident anger. "I'm going to leave now, and if I catch you trying to come after me, this blade is going to quickly find its way between your ribs."

"Wait!" Nerio said hastily. "I'm not trying to turn you in, I want to help you."

"Bullshit," she said, pressing the knife so hard that he expected the edge to slice the skin.

"I swear," he said calmly, "if you're hungry, I can get you lodgings with daily meals, no need to steal."

There was a brief pause. He found his heart racing, whether it was in anticipation of her answer or next act, he couldn't say.

"What's in it for you? What do you want from me?"

"For me? Nothing, other than wanting you to get a meal that doesn't involve petty theft," he responded in a level tone. "You can join the Holy Hands, you'll be expected to work for the church during the day, but we'll house and feed you in exchange."

There was another quiet moment, silence somehow ringing in his ears. Finally, the blade and tight grip were removed in a swift motion, and Nerio slowly turned to see the captor two steps behind him, knife still held with the point squarely facing him.

He was surprised. The person whom he'd pursued stood before him, but who he had assumed to be a young, teenage boy was clearly anything but. An attractive, feminine face with bright blue eyes stared back at him, a few strands of blonde hair slipping down past the bandanna around her head. Her clothes were beaten, worn, and fringing as though held together by the grime ground into them. They spoke of hardship, which her hardened face seemed to be carved from. It was also covered in filth, she stank of horse, and the dirt was smeared and cut by streaks of sweat. He felt as though he needed to hold his breath. There was no excuse for being so unclean in Brethefen.

"Why are you trying to help me?" she asked, caution in her eyes as she looked him up and down.

"I'm a priest, helping people is sort of what I do." He felt a little guilty about that particular phrasing, thinking of Jerdine, but the point remained true.

"I've known plenty of priests who could give a shit less about someone on the streets."

He held back a cringe. *Not inaccurate, unfortunately.* He recognized her accent; she was definitely from Calentine—he'd met enough travelers coming to the Devapuram to pick it out—maybe she hadn't been here long enough to know how things worked in Brethefen? And was that a silver chain around her neck? Seemed out of place.

"Brethefen is a large city," he said. "We are mostly run by the clergy—though there is still a duke—and the city functions a little differently than what you are perhaps accustomed to. The Holy Hands are volunteers, exchanging labor for food and housing. It's mostly menial tasks, mind you, and you'll have to probably do your fair share of cleaning and taking orders, but it's one guaranteed meal a day and a bed."

She went quiet and turned her head slightly to the side, as though her ears had caught a sound. Nerio tried to hear what she was listening for to no avail, but someone so on edge must hear danger around every turn. Hopefully he could help her change that.

She looked back at him and lowered the blade, her grip loosening and posture becoming straighter.

"You know," she said, still maintaining her cautious air, "you're awfully calm for someone with a knife to his throat."

"I merely trust in the will of the gods," he said with a faint smile. It wasn't entirely untrue, but it may not have been as honest as it could have been. "Their knowledge is infinite and plans precise, and we must trust that our meeting was part of their design. Whatever happens is merely my destiny."

"Or maybe they're fumbling around like the rest of us, hoping to get lucky."

Nerio's eyes went wide, and he gasped. What was this blasphemy? How could one so nonchalantly accuse the gods of thinking like mortal men? His shock must have been apparent, because the woman *rolled her eyes* before she spoke again.

"I'll take you up on that offer," she said, "but if you try anything, or if it seems off, I'm *out*."

"There's no obligation," he said, shaking off her sacrilegious words and forcing a smile. He had to take this one step at a time. Working with the Hands would help rid her of such unholy thoughts, he was certain. "I'm Brother Nerio, by the way."

Her lips became thin as she pressed them together, mirroring her narrowing eyes. Nerio resisted the urge to shift uncomfortably under the judgmental stare.

"Delphini," she finally said.

"It's a pleasure to meet you, Delphini. Follow me. And since you seem to be new to Brethefen, I can take you to a few places along the way and show you around, if you'd like."

She looked at him and slowly nodded after a moment, motioning with a tilt of her head for him to lead the way. As they walked, he tried talking to her. Working in the Asylum didn't leave him with many opportunities to have conversations with people that weren't... afflicted.

"So, what brings you to Brethefen?" he asked.

"What's it matter to you?" she asked defensively.

"Just curious," he said, looking back at her. She kept him in front of her at all times, and the closest she came to walking at his side was still a full step back from him. He suspected she still had the knife in her hand, hidden up her sleeve somewhere.

"How'd you know I was new to the city?" she finally asked as they walked along the sun-beaten road.

"Your accent is a bit of a giveaway," he said. "And then, well..." How did he phrase this to not be rude? "Well let's say there are not many who do not take advantage of the Holy Hands when in a similar position to yourself."

He thought he saw her glance at him with narrowed, thoughtful eyes, but it was difficult to say with her a step behind him.

"Here is one of the many communal bathhouses," he said as they came to the broad, low structure. He shuddered a little, remembering the last time he was at this particular one. He had stopped and abruptly turned toward Delphini to speak to her. She responded suddenly with a step backward and raised her arm. There was a glint of light from the steel reflecting in her hand, and she looked ready to pounce, like a fanged dog forced into a corner.

Nerio raised his hands beside his face, taking a step back himself. She looked around, seeing the concerned glances from a few people walking past, and lowered the knife back to her side.

"Sorry," Nerio said, "I assure you I don't have ill intentions."

"What do you mean, *communal?* Anyone can use it?" she asked after some of the rigidity left her posture. She finally stood at his side, albeit beyond arm's reach.

*Ah, right, foreigners always seem so confused by this,* he realized.

"There are shared baths in the main hall inside. All residents have access, though they pay a small fee. It's waived if you are a priest or Hand, of course."

"Is there a different entrance for women?" she asked, seeing a man walk inside the door.

"Why would there be?" he asked. "All of the baths are in the same central hall." Why was that concept so strange to travelers?

The woman's face looked mortified. Her raised brow fell sharply after a moment, as though she'd had a thought or realization, and uttered under her breath, "Gross."

*Well, that's rude.*

"I assure you that this is very normal here in Brethefen, and not considered 'gross'."

"No, I wasn't... I didn't... Never mind," she said, rubbing her eyes with her hands. "Are there private baths at this place you're taking me?"

"There are very few private baths in the city, I'm afraid. They waste far too much water, hence the communal ones here," he said. "Even most of the wealthy residents use the bathhouses. If you're perhaps insecure about—"

"I'm going to need you to stop talking right the fuck now," Delphini said, glaring at him. It was a look that could convince stone to chisel itself, and he quickly closed his gaping mouth. She rubbed her eyes again and while pinching the bridge of her nose said, "When is this place the least occupied?"

"Probably during morning prayers," he replied, trying to ignore her brash language. "I suppose you could go to them early and then come here or pray privately at a church or the Devapuram afterward."

She let out a snort, but otherwise refrained from further profanity.

They continued their walk through the city, the monolithic white dome rising like a cloud above the nearby rooftops. Nerio still always found himself in awe of the atmosphere of the city: the bright pallet of paint, the monuments of faith and ingenuity, the reverence. But he noticed that while they walked, Delphini didn't spend her time taking in its unique beauty. Rather, her eyes darted from side to side, her hands hidden and concealing the blade she'd recently threatened him with. This was someone born into adversity, untrusting of all.

*And I somehow deign my life unfortunate,* he thought.

The four spires of the Grand Clergy House finally came into view, their stained-glass windows reflecting the sunlight. Rising nearly as tall as the crest of the Devapuram itself, they grew like spikes from each corner of the city's primary residence of the clergy, the space between filled with several floors of living quarters for priests and members of the Holy Hands. The exterior was ornamented with statues and carvings of great religious figures and scenes from scripture. To Nerio it was as impressive as even the Devapuram, a testament to the city's piety.

Delphini seemed less impressed.

"So, this is the clergy house?" she asked, sounding indifferent.

"Yes," he confirmed. "The main one, anyway. In here we can get you registered with the Hands."

"Mhm," she said. "You still haven't told me what you want yet, in exchange for doing this."

"Why must I want something? Is it not enough to desire to help others?"

She looked at him with that curious, thoughtful glance. "Is this where you live?" she asked.

"I did, until recently." She stared at him. Was she looking for an explanation? "I relocated to another, smaller clergy house, closer to where I work."

She nodded. Nerio lingered outside the building, still expecting Delphini to admire the architectural marvel jutting into the air before her. But her eyes didn't focus on the white masonry; they flicked from side to side, watching people and ignoring the sights.

"You know, I could take you to the library before we go into the clergy house. It's quite the sight, the most complete in the western half of the kingdom," he offered.

"Not interested," she said.

*No need to be so terse about it,* he grumbled in his mind.

Not bothering to argue in an attempt to change her mind, Nerio continued into the enormous building, quickly finding the office for Sister Gruthga. As he neared the arched, wooden door framed in stone, he began giving some guidance to Delphini.

"Inside is Sister Gruthga," he said. "She manages the intake and arrangements for the Hands and will be getting you settled. Once you've been given a robe and directed to your quarters, you're free to use whatever facilities are available to the Hands or priests. Sister Gruthga will provide you with more details."

Delphini's roaming eyes turned and fixed on Nerio. "You mean I can basically go wherever I want? Whenever I want?" she asked, looking surprised.

*That's an odd question,* he thought. "Yes, except for the restricted areas."

"Why are they restricted?"

"Well, several reasons. The upper towers are the private quarters of the four principles, and they do not wish for people to be entering their offices unsupervised. Reasons for other locations may vary, but as long as you follow the sister's instructions, you should be fine."

Delphini didn't respond with anything beyond a simple nod, turning her attention to the door that Nerio was opening into the cramped office. Inside the cluttered room was an older woman, whose stern features could possibly rival Delphini's angry glares. She looked up from the mess of documents strewn across the simple table, glancing at Nerio over the rim of her spectacles and then at Delphini.

"King and His grace upon you, Brother. Who is this you've brought?" Gruthga asked, standing straight with the posture of youth, despite her silver hair.

"This is Delphini, Sister," he replied. "She is new to Brethefen and wishes to enroll with the Hands."

"I assumed as much, based on the stench," the older woman said, looking Delphini up and down. Nerio noticed Delphini's hands clench, and her eyes turn fierce. He raised his hand and smiled before she had a chance to speak, talking to Gruthga instead. She was always so... blunt.

"Sister, Delphini was unaware of our customs, and has assured me that she intends to bathe as soon as she is able." That drew a look from Delphini, but she remained quiet. "She is willing to work and has graciously accepted my offer to join your humble servants. Perhaps you can register her and provide her with a room and robe?"

Gruthga's frown was a fixture, the creases on her face accentuating her perpetual annoyance. But she eventually nodded to Nerio before pulling a book as thick as Nerio's palm from a shelf, dropping it onto the table with a dusty *thud* that shook the towers of parchment to either side.

While she flipped to an empty page, Nerio turned to Delphini, who still glared at Gruthga with her own wrinkled brow.

"I must be on my way," he said. He had been invited to the library—again—and was going to listen to the head librarian offer him a position for the hundredth time. He did not intend to accept the job, but declining the old man's invitation was rude, and he always was willing to help Nerio when he had requests.

"Sister Gruthga can be a little... abrasive," he said in a quiet whisper, facing away from the priestess, "but she is quite capable. You only have to converse with her today, afterward you'll receive your assignments from others."

Delphini looked at him, her anger shifting to a shaken head of confusion, "You're leaving? Just like that?"

"Yes, I am already late for my appointment. Good luck to you." He gave her a smile and low bow of his head, and before she could respond he was out the door.

His sandals scuffed along the stone as he walked down the arched hall. He knew that he'd done a good thing, the *right* thing, in helping that girl. Yet, he still felt... the same.

What was it going to take?

# CHAPTER THIRTY-NINE

*If our spies' intelligence is accurate, then we must act with haste, as the enemy is doing the same in anticipation of our designs and he could be a powerful ally.*

Delvan rubbed the bruise on his forearm as his horse trotted through the thinning snow. Orne was by far the most... aggressive sparring partner he'd ever had and had recently taken to fighting him with a wooden training sword. Whether it was because he wanted to embarrass him or be free to strike with the force of a battering ram, rather than the comparatively dainty strikes with training bands, Delvan couldn't say. He suspected it was a combination of both.

Despite the regular daily beatings, Delvan was glad for the distraction. Having an outlet, a way to exhaust himself, seemed to lessen how frequently he felt the shadowy grip in his chest. He still struggled, however, to force himself to strike at Orne.

Each time he crossed blades with the domineering man he was brought back to that night. The heat of the flames, the sounds of death, an arrow protruding from Hilbrun's chest... It was a vivid, living memory, one that consumed him and held back his hand as he clashed with Orne. He'd tried to overcome the invisible resistance, but it was as though his wrists were cuffed by chains of iron.

*Could I have done better? Was there a way that I could have saved him?* he wondered. *Maybe I'm not worthy of carrying this sword, or even this gem.*

Orne probably thought he was helping Delvan, and in a way he was. He'd spent months on the road being shunned and ignored, feeling emotionally destitute. That was until he'd met Orne and Kolden. They bickered constantly, but for the first time in ages Delvan caught himself smiling on occasion, amused by the strange dichotomy of the brothers' personalities.

Unfortunately, it was overshadowed by a deep, seething abhorrence for the man who Delvan could see at the distant front of their caravan.

Knight Commander Ferrand.

Just thinking his name churned bile within him. Kolden's revelation the other night had only bolstered his detestation of the man. It *was* his fault that Hilbrun was dead, hiring the thieves that were responsible for his murder, covering his tracks by killing the one who'd escaped.

*He wasn't the* only *one to escape,* thought Delvan.

He'd wondered about the girl a few times, something about her seeming... off. His mind over the past few months had been a muddy lake, he a swimming fish hiding from its lurking predators. But as the murky waters began to clear, questions about that night began shining in like light from the surface.

Delvan hated admitting anything about what his father had said to be correct, but thinking about it, the girl *must* have been part of the thieves' crew, likely betrayed when they were done with her. *Was she the one responsible for opening the safe?* he wondered. It would make sense, though she could have also been a guide through the sewers. They'd turned out to be an impossible maze, with several guards getting lost in the aftermath of the attack looking for the lone thief's escape route.

But where had she gone?

Delvan thought back to the robbery, trying to think of what Ferrand's motives could've been to steal from one of the most powerful guilds in the kingdom. There was the obvious answer: sapphires. Delvan remembered sensing them, there must have been a dozen in that vault, yet none were found at the scene. The guild could have hidden them quickly, he supposed, and what would the commander need with additional sapphires? They were valuable, true, but he was a wealthy man from a prestigious house. He would have no need for such lucre.

Besides, based on what Hilbrun had told him, and what he'd seen during their original investigation, the man had but one, single-minded focus: cadentite. *Was there any in the vault?* he thought, trying to recall the brief glimpse he'd gotten of the darkened repository. He remembered *something,* more a feeling than a vision. It had been masked by the warm radiance of the sapphires, but it had been there. And there *had* been that strange glow.

Too bad there was now one less person to ask about the commander's intentions. He doubted he'd ever see the girl again, which only left the commander himself.

*In time,* he thought, *I will deal with him. He'll get his due.*

It had been a difficult conclusion to draw, one that anguished him and fought the doctrine he'd been raised by. Blues didn't turn against one another—it was a morality that was sown into their blood, something he had to consciously fight each time the thought formed in his mind. But what he'd done to Hilbrun...

*I don't care if he feels remorse for his death,* thought Delvan as he ground his teeth, *he deserves retribution.*

Water dripped from the melting snow on branches above. Despite the cover of clouds, the days had been progressively growing warmer, the snowfall less. Delvan didn't mind the cold, he was able to tolerate it more than most. Being perpetually wet from this humid, foggy air, however, was beginning to wear on him. Combine that with the constant chafe of riding in a saddle, and he was very much ready to reach anywhere he could stretch his legs.

He pushed his soggy hair to the side, trying to focus back on his question. What was the commander after? And *why* was he relocating to Brethefen? A thought struck him like a droplet of water from above.

*There* was *someone else who overheard the commander's plans.*

He tugged the reins of his horse, falling even further back from the caravan until he came beside Kolden and Orne, who were currently arguing over the correct grind angle for a sword's edge from atop their mounts. He tried getting Kolden's attention, but he was heated enough that Delvan thought *he* might start steaming.

"...and that's why it *can't* be too blunt! *How* are you supposed to make—"

"Kolden!" Delvan hissed, smacking him on the shoulder with a reach.

"Huh? Oh, what's going on, Del?" he said calmly. It was like these two had an on and off switch.

"I need to ask you about something," he said quietly, leaning over while trying to keep their horses from colliding.

"Um, alright," he replied with a raised eyebrow.

Delvan glanced at the caravan, hopefully they were far enough back that no one would hear them. He whispered, "The night you saw the commander, did he say anything else? Did he talk about *why* he wanted the vault robbed? What he was after?"

Kolden's face went pale, his head sinking into his shoulders. "Uhh, I don't think it's a good idea to talk about this right now," Kolden said, his eyes shifting towards the front of the caravan.

"Tell me!" Delvan said in a hushed voice. "Kolden, I *need* to know."

He saw Orne glaring at them with his permanent scowl, he seemed to smile less than even Delvan did. Of course, this meant that Delvan had no idea if the man was *actually* bothered by this conversation or not, but he didn't care.

"He, uh, might have mentioned something," said Kolden hesitantly. "But Del, I really can't go into details. I can tell you more when we get somewhere safe," he said with another glance at the forward caravan, "but now is *not* the time."

"Just tell me," Delvan said, nearly pleading, "did it have anything to do with cadentite?"

Kolden's head spun to face him, his eyes wide and lips agape. The man was speechless, something Delvan had yet to witness.

"I *knew* it," Delvan said as he tightly clenched his fists around his horse's reins, his muscles tightening. Kolden's expression confirmed what he'd suspected, but now other questions sprouted into being.

"Did they steal it?" Delvan asked before Kolden had been able to find his missing tongue. "Is that why we're going to Brethefen?"

Kolden, surprisingly, looked to his brother, who was just shaking his head. He then stared off, through his horse and the ground beyond before wiping his hand down his face.

"He... He doesn't have it," Kolden finally said, Orne grunting in annoyance as he glowered at Kolden.

Delvan felt an internal sigh of relief. Any failure of the commander felt like a small success.

"Where is it?" Delvan asked.

"Kolden," growled Orne, "don't you—"

"I have it," Kolden said quickly. "And shut up Orne, it's not like we can't trust him."

"How did you get it?" Delvan asked.

"They tried to hide it, but I saw the thief burying it and took it," he said, leaning closer to Delvan and speaking in a barely audible whisper.

Thoughts bloomed in Delvan's head. Ferrand probably thought he'd succeeded, that he'd won in getting what he wanted. This gave Delvan an advantage, but how could he utilize it? What outcome did he want, exactly? He'd originally considered gathering evidence and using it to strip the commander of his rank, title, and sapphire, but that was a fool's folly. Ferrand could confess and he'd still likely live out his days in peace and leisure. He was too familiar with the noble class to expect any different.

He'd resigned himself to punishing the Blue, despite his reservations and instincts screaming against it, but now that he had the leverage he required he struggled at the specifics. He wanted him to hurt, to share his pain, take from him to repay him in kind. But how?

*What would Hilbrun have done?* he thought.

An idea began to formulate. He wasn't sure if he could take on the commander himself, Jacks were notoriously deadly in combat, but with resources and aid the man could be subdued. And there was one group, trusted by Hilbrun, that likely sought revenge nearly as much as Delvan did.

The Merchants' Guild.

Could he exchange the stolen cadentite for their favor? Hilbrun, through legacy, had been a member, and his father was a powerful political figure. Surely he must want to avenge his son's death? And the other guild leaders would assuredly be furious over the destruction of their headquarters, it seemed unlikely that they would turn away from an opportunity to aid in the demise of the person who planned it.

*Yes, this could work.*

When they reached Brethefen, Delvan would find the local Merchants' Guild and offer them a trade: their cadentite for help capturing the snake, so that Delvan could remove its head.

# Chapter Forty

*We agreed that Brethefen was the most strategic assignment, for current and future plans, as I'm sure you remember.*

Desnia stood outside the white, two-story building in the mid-morning heat, wondering why it had windows that made it look like a prison. It was unmarked, unadorned, and poorly maintained, paint flaking from the mud walls in sporadic patches and gnarled weeds withering around its foundation. Was this really where the priest worked every day?

It had taken her weeks of inquiry to find out where the illusive priest spent his days. She'd wanted to go back to the market and attempt to find him there, but with spending her days scrubbing floors and collecting offerings from the Devapuram—the sheer volume of which astonished her—she hadn't the time to spend at the market.

She'd waited, expecting him to come and tell her that he needed a favor, or that she owed him some measure of debt for his aid. They always did, after all. Days passed into weeks, and nearly a month later she still had yet to discover him seeking some form of payment.

*This place looks depressing,* Masini said into her mind. *Why are we here again?*

"Because someone *lied* when they said they had friends in Brethefen," she accused, "and now I'm stuck helping you with no idea where anything is in this fucking city."

She denied speaking her true motives aloud to Masini, but the promise made to her, keeping her mind... whole, was more appealing than she cared to admit. She could only imagine what she'd have to provide in return, but if anyone could do something to prevent her from ending up like *them*, it would be this supposed god that was causing it.

Since she'd left Calentine she'd had no torturous visits in her sleep, and she knew without being told that it was because of her helping Masini. She did wonder about the results of her aid in finding this gate and whether it would bring her more harm than the mind-splitting voice. But, having seen what she could become, the benefits outweighed the risk.

*I never* technically *said I had friends in Brethefen, you just assumed I did,* he said. *Oh, and don't forget about the people that would kill us on sight.*

His ring—or body, more accurately, which still sent a confused chill up her spine—hung from the chain around her neck, atop her white Hands robe. She'd hidden him away for much of her journey here, the ring appeared valuable, and she had to constantly avoid would-be thieves enough as it was. Now that she had joined the Holy Hands, however, people left her alone, as though she were invisible, and it had made her comfortable enough to give into Masini's begging to be able to "see." She also had access to most places in the city.

It was a thief's dream come true.

*How has no one used this system to rob people blind?* she wondered.

"You've had plenty of time to tell me, asshole," she said. "And since you won't tell me who these people are, we need someone who knows the area. Otherwise, we're being sent to mine an empty lode. If we have as little time as you say, we're going to need help."

*Hmm,* Masini said, *I think that's about as honest as a husband in a whore house.*

"What? That doesn't even..." she sighed and shook her head. "What do you mean?"

*You* hate *working with others. I'm pretty sure 'collaboration' isn't even a part of your vocabulary. I'm amazed you've even put up with me this long, not to mention that you're* actually *helping me, which can only be explained as intervention by the Greats themselves. Wait, is my influence helping to make you a better team player? No. No, I'm amazing but even my greatness has limits, unless... ohhh.*

"What?"

*You tried to stab him, so now you want him to repay the favor? An old 'meat-stick joust' as they used to say.*

"No! Gods, do you ever stop? Fucking disgusting," she responded with a grimace.

The part about sleeping with the priest aside, Masini did have a point. There was this burning curiosity regarding the priest, something that nudged her forward she couldn't quite explain. Her argument to see the priest again was logical but fought every shred of instinct within her.

Why was she so determined to see him again then?

She dismissed the suppressed instincts with effort and walked into the building. The all-encompassing white of the interior felt not only disorienting, but it seemed to deaden the air, as though it were hands covering her ears. The priest in the entry room looked up from his writings in a thick book and smiled.

*Why do so many people do that here?* she wondered.

"King and His grace upon you," he greeted. "We weren't expecting another Hand today, are you here to relieve someone?"

"No," she replied, "I'm actually looking for somebody, I was told I could find him here. Brother Nerio."

The priest seemed surprised. "Are you not with the other fellow? The disciple? He just arrived not two minutes ago, also looking for Nerio."

*Popular guy*, said Masini, his voice somewhat muffled.

"No, I'm not with him. He helped me a few weeks ago, and I wanted to give him my thanks."

"Hmm," said the attendant, "well that's a strange coincidence, I've never seen one person searching for Nerio, let alone two in a day. Can't say that I'm surprised about him helping you though, don't think that boy is capable of doing otherwise. I keep telling him to take the librarian position, but instead he wastes his time here on these lost souls.

"Ah, but I'm just a rambling old man. Never mind me. He's going to be around here somewhere, the building is larger than it seems, so try not to get lost and don't open any of the cell doors without a priest present. Oh, and please make sure you remove any inanite you may have on your person before entering."

"Thanks," she replied. *No inanite? That's an odd request.* She didn't have any on her, though it was tempting to keep around to threaten Masini with.

She walked past the priest, through a vacant waiting room, and into a hallway beyond. It bewildered her how easy access to the entire city had become just for being a member of the Hands. It was a pity that such a program didn't exist in Calentine, she would've been rich.

The hall had a single, sleeping guard sitting in a chair against the wall, snoring loudly. The viewing ports on the doors revealed people within, the same omnipresent white dyed into their simple clothes. Some slept, others mumbled to themselves with distant stares, dribble secreting from the corners of their mouths. One ominously stood in the center of their room, head hung low, eerily unmoving.

"What *is* this place?" she muttered.

Desnia walked further down the rows of halls, failing to find anyone but the uncanny residents in the strange maze. It had seemed like such a simple structure from the exterior, but the layout inside was almost as confusing as its contents.

Normally her sense of direction was quite astute, but twice she found herself crossing an intersection of hallways which she had already passed. Her legs nearly stomped in frustration, until at last she turned a corner and saw the young priest emerge from one of the occupant's quarters, carrying a jug of something and locking the door behind him.

Her shoulders slumped as she sighed in relief. But then she tensed, now that she'd found him, what was she going to say? The question left her frozen in place, transfixed in the middle of a hallway until Nerio turned and locked eyes with her. He tilted his head with a curious expression, his voice snapping her out of the stupor.

"Delphini?" he asked. "What are you doing here?"

She composed herself. This shouldn't be too hard, she just needed some assistance in aiding a trapped god, a priest would obviously want to help with that, right?

*I sound insane,* she thought with a grimace.

"Hey," she replied as he walked towards her, "you're a hard man to find, you know that?"

He gave her a smile, but his eyes winced. "What brings you here? It looks like life with the Hands is treating you well."

*See? He's obviously infatuated with you, give in and have some fun for a change,* said Masini. She ignored him and a strange grumble from the person in the room to her side.

"Sister Gruthga is a bit much," Desnia said, "but it's hard to complain about a roof and food. I, uh, wouldn't have, well, made it far without your, uh, well you know." The words felt forced, like a deep-rooted flower being pulled from the earth, her ingrained biases gripping it tightly.

*Wow, you're truly incapable of saying 'thank you,' aren't you?* said Masini.

"Of course," he said with a smile, one that seemed more genuine. "And, not to say that I'm not pleased to see you, but I'm curious, how exactly did you find me?"

"The other Hands spend more time gossiping than they do working," she said. "I asked around. Took a while but I found a couple people that knew who you were and where you volunteered. They all seemed to have kind words about you."

"Were you... expecting differently?"

*Yes.* "No," she said. "I just thought you should know. What is this place, by the way?" she asked, quickly changing the topic.

"It doesn't have an official name, most just call it, *'The Asylum'.*"

*Maybe you should, uh, get a room here,* Masini said.

Her lip twitched with contempt as she forced herself not to chide him, instead tightly clutching his ring as though to strangle him. She turned her head at another grumble from the man beyond the door to her right, now pacing and mumbling.

"You needn't worry about them," said Nerio as if to calm her. "They're mostly harmless, at least to others." His voice faded at the last words, his normally bright face becoming a cloud of gloom. He shook the expression quickly.

"What's wrong with them?" she asked, still watching the man between the narrow bars in the viewing port of the door.

"They hear voices, mostly, some claim to have visions. It's a strange affliction, one of the mind. We don't know how to cure it, unfortunately, so we treat them with medicine that helps to quiet the voices," he said, motioning to the pitcher in his hand. "Some go so far as to say they hear the gods, as if they are the King Himself. We try not to too harshly judge their blasphemies, given their ailment. The most we can do is make them comfortable."

Desnia's stomach turned as her throat tightened and face turned pallid. She squeezed her hand to stop it from trembling. Her eyes went to the "medicine" that Nerio held in his hands, the murky white mixture was familiar as spring rain to her. This *was* a prison, and she had brought herself within its walls.

*It can't be,* she thought as her eyes grew wider.

*Wow,* said Masini, *you're in good company it would appear. Could you imagine if they could all hear me too? Gods, the pranks I could pull. I AM AMENESOL, YOU'RE GOD! BOW BEFORE ME! Hehe.* The way he laughed at his own "joke" sickened her further, but she was too petrified to respond at the moment.

The deranged man in the room suddenly dropped to his knees and prostrated himself, crying out, "Lord! Forgive me! Tell me your will!"

*Wait, did he just hear me?* quietly asked Masini. *Ohhh.*

Nerio spun his head and walked to the door, his eyes narrowing with concern. He looked to Desnia, who remained still as a stone, and asked, "You don't have any inanite on you, do you?"

Masini's words had stolen her focus, and as she gripped the ring tighter, she mumbled, "Shut up."

"What? It was a simple question," said Nerio, his head drawn back in offense.

She shook her head, realizing what she'd done, her heart sinking to the floor. "No! Sorry!" she exclaimed. "Not you, I just... It wasn't... I was just startled is all." It was the best lie she could conjure at the moment. Curses at Masini flew through her mind, maybe she *would* find some black cloth later.

"Oh," Nerio said, his eyes glancing at the floor and then avoiding her own.

"Who are these people, *really*?" she asked. She wasn't sure why she posed the question. She knew the answer, but that distant force seemed to nudge it from her, like a hand pushing her from a cliff.

His mouth opened to answer, but he hesitated, his head turning from side to side. After a moment he slowly responded. "They're nobles, sent to us for care by their families. They were all Blues, once in their lives. A specific sect: you would probably know them as Seers."

She stumbled a step backward, her knees buckling and Nerio stepping to her side as if to catch her. She waved her hand to dismiss him; even if he were as altruistic as he appeared, she still didn't want him touching her. She leaned her back against the wall to stop the visceral trembling, taking quick gasps of breath as she attempted to prevent her stomach from forcing its contents out in projectile fashion. Why did she ask?

"Delphini, are you alright?!"

"You just... just lock them away? How long do they stay here?" she asked, still trying to calm herself.

"They..." Nerio started, looking solemn. "They don't leave. We keep them here because no one else will take them. The Court calls them a threat, they say the King wants them banished. Even here, I'm one of the only ones who cares for them, they're forgotten about even by the clergy..."

*Locked away, forever alone and forgotten...* She shivered at the thought. *And they're left to scream at the walls, praying to whatever god they can think of to free them from this place. How DARE these assholes!*

"What's *wrong* with you?!" Spit flew and her face turned red as she exploded from quiet disbelief into a slighted rage. "These are *people*! You lock them away and toss the key because they're different? They can't help what's happened to them, who are you to be their judge and punisher?"

Nerio hung his head, a tear rolling down his cheek. Gods, he *actually* cared about these people.

*It's not his fault, Des,* said Masini.

Her breathing slowed and jaw loosened, her eyes stubbornly refusing to change from their hard glare. Masini was right, this boy was merely helping them, it wasn't in his power to do anything more than that. She wanted to open every door, send them out into the streets and away from this shambled hell. She realized that she couldn't expect Nerio to react like that, he seemed too timid to be so brazen. Her hands stopped shaking and her breathing became more regular as she looked at the priest with his head hung low.

*Why does he do it?* she wondered. *What drives him to be such a* good *person?* He'd done more for these people than most would, that was certain. The isolation they all must feel, the pain and torment of being alone with nothing but their shattered minds, day in and day out. At least he was here to offer some form of company in the dark plane of their existence.

Maybe he was someone whom she could trust, to a limited extent, anyway. Although she would have to be careful about what she said around him, lest he discover some of her secrets. As the thrumming in her nerves began to dissipate, she thought back to why she'd come here in the first place. She should probably ask him—

"Brother Nerio," a voice called out from down the hall. Both their heads turned to see another young priest, hardly into his teens, with a blue sash around his waist approaching them. "Brother Nerio," he repeated as he reached them, "I've been looking all over for you, every turn in this place looks the same. Kept getting turned around."

Desnia saw Nerio quickly wipe the tear from his eye, turning to address the young boy. She was fairly certain the blue sashes meant he was an Almedia disciple, it was hard to keep them all straight. Cordism here was elevated beyond even what she saw in Calentine.

She noticed that Nerio's shoulders seemed to pull upward, his lips becoming tight. She raised an eyebrow at his tense figure as the boy continued.

"Brother, I've been asked by Principle Jerdine to accompany you to his spire. He said that you've missed several appointments with him."

Nerio's dark skin paled, sweat dewing on his forehead. Were his hands shaking?

"I'm sorry," Nerio responded with a slight tremor to his voice, "but there are no other priests on duty here today, I must remain here until the next shift to care for these people. Surely the principle does not wish for these people to be unattended?"

"He expected such an answer and has sent for another healer to take your place. They should be arriving within the next quarter hour. I was strictly instructed to personally bring you to his chambers."

The boy's face seemed stiff with the callus of age, completely devoid of the naivety of youth. It was a look that many had on the streets. Desnia recognized it as the portrait of someone who had fought through the hell of survival, but she never expected to see it upon such a young priest.

He and Nerio stared at each other with what she could only describe as mirrored sorrow. Nerio's ghostly face betrayed a resigned fear, the wide eyes and tight lips giving her a sense that he was deathly terrified of this Jerdine. What evil was he expecting to face?

Nerio slowly nodded, and turned to her, speaking barely above a whisper, his voice quavering. "I must go. Goodbye, Delphini."

He forced a smile. It felt like a stab to the gut that twisted, becoming worse as Desnia watched him turn and trail behind the young disciple, his feet shuffling as though made of lead. He looked utterly defeated, like a convict approaching the gallows. As they turned a corner, leaving her standing there alone among the forsaken prisoners, the pain became worse, carving at her like an axe. It brought her back to that night, the Blue's grief flowing into her in a flood of empathy.

She had fled then, leaving behind the person who'd come to her rescue. At the time it had seemed the right—the only—option. There was still the part of her that wanted to avoid danger, keeping her head low and living to see tomorrow. But a shadow masked that urge, bringing into the light the realization that she couldn't do that again, not to yet another person who had come in her time of need. And she hated owing debts.

She'd been betrayed time and time again, but this was different, *he* seemed different. She could justify her actions before, thinking the Blue would have arrested her given the chance, that he could blame her for his friend's death. She'd been part of the crew that killed him, after all. Who was to say he wouldn't seek retribution after grieving? She owed him but had every reason to not repay the debt. Not like she would ever see him again, hopefully. She doubted his attitude would be a welcoming one should their path's cross again.

But there was no excuse now. And furthermore, she needed him.

She took a deep breath and then strode down the hall with conviction, shedding the fear that had recently consumed her. She was going to follow Nerio, and then see what she could do to help him.

She owed him that much.

# Chapter Forty-One

*If, however, you determine success an impossibility in this endeavor, then kill the boy.*

The soft orchestra of chirping birds fell on Delvan's ears as the caravan slowly moved forward ahead of him, the overcast afternoon bringing a brisk wind to chill the melting snow. The forest was still thick, the tall pines and heavy underbrush dusted with the ankle-deep snow that surrounded them even as the brutal winter of Drunt lay further and further behind.

After leaving the snow-covered city six weeks ago, they'd still only managed to cover half the distance between it and Brethefen, leaving Delvan feeling antsy. He desperately desired to reach the distant city, longing for the day he could walk into a Merchants' Guild and seek his revenge. His impatience brought about even more sleepless nights, his chest tightening and jaw numbing at the simple thought of the commander. But he would fight through it, for Hilbrun.

Orne and Kolden were arguing—it being their most fluent dialect—about something next to him. He mostly tuned them out, listening to the calming sounds from the trees, the *clops* of horses' hoofs. He still hadn't discussed with Kolden his plan to turn the cadentite over to the guild, but that conversation could wait. He didn't want to argue about it while still traveling.

Orne was berating his brother, and a bit of their conversation caught Delvan's attention.

"...I'm telling you, she's never going to let him sign off on it! We have to get transferred *outside* his chain of command, otherwise we're going to see denial after denial like we did in Drunt," Orne said.

"The southern war though? Why do you want to go *there*, of all places? It's fucking hot down there, I hear," replied Kolden.

"We're literally going to a fucking *desert*, Kolden, how much worse could it be? And I don't care *where* we go, just as long as there's combat. I refuse to accept promotions based on *father's* title and rank, I want *my* name to be the one people know, not just his."

"What are you two going on about?" asked Delvan, leaning forward in his saddle to look at them.

"We're trying to figure out how to get a command transfer once we reach Brethefen," replied Kolden. "One that gets us away from you-know-who and also doesn't result in us being on guard duty in the middle of nowhere."

"But…" said Delvan, confused, "your father is a general, he's *the* General Traskor, you should be able to get transferred to whatever station you want, no?"

"Our father isn't the problem," said Kolden with a roll of his eyes, "it's our *mother* that's the issue."

Delvan's head drew back in surprise. "What? How's your mother the problem?"

Kolden let out an extended sigh. "Ma lost three of her brothers in the first southern war. *Hates* that we joined the military, despite that our father desperately wanted us to take up the family mantle. Once our father got his title and fame, though, she kind of realized that she didn't have a choice. We both wanted to join anyway. I think it's the only compromise that our father's ever been able to reach with her, come to think of it. Love her to death, but that woman is…"

"Fucking terrifying," interjected Orne.

"Mhm," said Kolden with a nod, "well said. Anyway, every time we request a transfer, she either tells our father to deny us, or grant a transfer, but to wherever would be the safest. Which means that I'm stuck with drunken shams for smiths, and Orne is assigned wall duty or guarding some stuck up, noble shithead. No offense."

"So, you mean to tell me that one of the most powerful military leaders in the kingdom constantly bends to the whims of his *wife*?" said an aghast Delvan.

"Basically," said Kolden. "But, I mean, it's not like he takes her on the battlefield or anything like that, but when it comes to us, he doesn't argue with her. Pretty sure she'd murder him if he put us in harm's way."

"More likely cut his dick off," grumbled Orne.

*Well, that's a disturbing thought.*

"Why didn't she get you guys sapphires?" asked Delvan, the thought just occurring to him. "Blue's tend to be in the back of battle, directing it, or performing diplomatic duties. Probably safer than you fighting bandits and guarding from would-be assassins. Your father must surely be able to afford it."

"Eh," said Kolden with a shrug, "I think they looked into it, but we were already too old when our dad was promoted and given a title. We just have to get through life without awesome gifts."

Orne grunted again. It was almost like he spoke a language with the inflections of the non-vocal tones, and Delvan could swear that he was saying more than just an agreement with his brother.

Extreme parental oversight was something Delvan could empathize with and didn't push the issue further. Maybe he could use some of the Merchants' Guild's influence to help get them the transfer they wanted? Kolden and Orne might be more easily convinced to give the cadentite back to the guild if that were the case. He'd have to present that as part of his request later.

He shifted himself around in the saddle, trying to get more comfortable. Riding every day for months on end had left him sore and wishing for the comforts of home. He closed his eyes, thinking of a soft bed, a warm tavern, the beauty of a pretty girl's eyes. He tried to ignore the surrounding sounds as he pictured himself dancing with someone in a fine, silk dress, kissing their supple lips at the end of the night, laughing on the walk home.

Instead, his concentration was broken by the turning of spoked wheels, his horse's shoes crunching the icy snow underfoot, and the argumentative brothers once again delving into discord. He sighed, trying to focus on a more pleasant sound, but it was oddly absent.

Where had the birds gone?

A whistling noise broke the eerie silence, a *thud* and gurgle following it. Delvan's eyes snapped open, and before him he saw one of the company's soldiers pressing his hand to his blood-soaked neck, an arrow driven deeply into it.

Delvan suddenly wasn't able to breathe, the specter's hand once again coming and tightly squeezing his heart. His jaw felt numb, his arm spiked with pain, and his face turned a snowy white as he stared with wide eyes at the dying soldier ahead of him. He wanted to shout, to react, anything other than freeze in place, but all he could do was sit there in gawking silence.

The soldier fell from his saddle, the snow turning red from the seeping blood. Then came a volley from both sides of the road, the missiles cutting through the air without discretion.

"We're under attack!" shouted Orne as he spurred his horse forward. The caravan became a wild storm of chaos, soldiers frenziedly trying to take cover from the ambush to either side. Some ducked behind the carriages, others tried to pull shields out of them for protection, with many falling to bolts piercing their backs. The company archers tried to return fire, but the dense forest to either side obscured and hid their assailers well.

Kolden jumped down from his horse and smacked its hind, sending it fleeing back down the road before diving between a small boulder and a fallen tree for cover. He unslung the crossbow from his back and fired into the thicket, ducking down to reload before peeking back up and launching another missile downrange.

Delvan held the reins of his horse—his mouth hanging open, body unable to function—while the animal neighed and reared its head. The mare was well trained, but it was no destrier, and it shuffled uneasily in the onslaught of death, screams, and gore.

The arrows pelted the carriages and soldiers like rain against glass. Soldiers collapsed to the ground, some crying out loudly, others without a word. The barrage of arrows slowed to an eventual stop, everyone huddled and silent save the wails of pain from the wounded. A scream grew in the distance to either side, a low cry that grew into a roar as a flood of attackers came charging at the caravan, swarming both their flanks from the trees.

Delvan watched, his heart pumping furiously with beat after agonizing beat, as the band of enemies crashed into the line of carriages like an ocean wave over pebbles. They threw themselves at the remaining members of the company, their bodies clashing with the heavily armored soldiers and creating a field of mayhem.

They dressed like bandits, wearing makeshift leather armor or plain civilian's clothes and armed with mostly axes, spears, and a few swords. But what they lacked in equipment they made up for in sheer numbers. The caravan was being overrun, outnumbered at least three to one, and still all Delvan could do was sit atop his horse, desperately trying to breathe.

The screams of his fellow soldiers filled his head with visions of that night. His long-healed rib ached as it recalled snapping against stone, his face was flush with the heat of flames, and the arrows... the arrows were everywhere. The body of each soldier that had been pierced by the small, winged spears wore the same face. *His* face. The friend he'd been helpless to save.

And now he was helpless again.

Three people swarmed Delvan's horse, who reared and kicked at the few who came too close. Something heavy and blunt struck him in the back, forcing what little air there was from his lungs. He hunched over in pain, losing his balance as his horse reared again, sliding off the saddle and falling to the snow below.

They ignored the horse once he had been forcefully dismounted—they were too valuable to risk injuring—and instead focused on Delvan. A spear and two axes were now pointed at him at the periphery of his blurred vision. His back lay flat in the snow, head pounding, and sounds muffled, indistinguishable to his ears, but through the ringing he heard one of the three above him yell out.

"We've got him here!" he thought the man said.

Delvan squinted to see the man, who suddenly keeled forward, a fletched bolt jutting from his chest. Another arrow. Another flash of Hilbrun's face. Delvan felt sick.

Then he felt something else: vibrations, the gallop of a horse. There was a blur of motion above him, the man holding a spear to him losing his head with a spurt of blood. The last of the three was struck by the breast of the steed, launching backward and getting trampled under the swift, iron shoes.

There came another shadow, looming and eclipsing the gray sky above. It shouted down to him, booming and threatening. Delvan was still paralyzed, his muscles unable to so much as twitch. He hadn't even drawn his sword.

The monolith above him reached down and grabbed the collar of his armor, hauling him to his feet. His eyes were glazed, a fog filling them, unable to see or comprehend what was happening around him. The shouting continued, but his eyes gazed blankly into the distance, all he could see was Hilbrun's shocked face before crumbling to the ground, as if asking: *Why? Why didn't you save me?*

There was a loud crack as his head whipped to the side, an intense stinging sensation emanating from his reddened cheek.

Did someone just... slap him?

He shook his head, his vision clearing as the surprise of the open-handed strike snapped him from his stupor. With refocused eyes he found himself staring at Orne, holding him up by his collar, pulling a bloody sword from the ground with the other hand.

"Delvan!" shouted Orne with a red face, spit flying from his mouth. "Pull yourself fucking together!"

Delvan stumbled a little as Orne released his grip. He looked from side to side, carnage rampaging around him like a stampede over grass. He suppressed the urge to vomit, pain again gripping his heart, squeezing for all its worth.

"Hey!" snapped Orne, grabbing Delvan's chin and locking their eyes. "Fucking get ahold of yourself, man! Now is *not* the time for you to feel sorry for yourself. I know this is hard, but if you don't help, we're going to die here, you understand?! Is that what your friend would have wanted? For you to die before you can do anything to avenge him? Huh?!"

Delvan set his jaw and clenched his fists. Orne was right, he couldn't fall while the commander walked free, untried for his crimes. He saw Kolden, a few yards away desperately shooting arrows into the battle, drawing his knife and stabbing a bandit who dared draw too close.

*I can't just do this for Hil,* he thought, *I... I can't lose these two either.* It was an epiphany that twisted his insides, a mixture of elation and terror.

Orne and Kolden's friendship had seemed a figment of the otherwise consumed background of his mind. How had he not stopped to consider how much he valued their bond, how they'd remained his companions despite his being ostracized? He'd been too focused on his loss, his revenge, to realize what he'd gained. And now their lives were at risk, just as Hilbrun's had been.

He drew the sword from his side, taking a deep breath and nodding to Orne.

"'Bout fucking time," said Orne. The behemoth of a man sheathed his sword and ran to his horse nearby, removing a covered shaft from a sling at its side. He pulled the protective hood off the head and gripped the handle of his halberd tightly, his face stern but eyes smiling.

A man with a cudgel charged at Delvan, raising it above his head and attempting to slam it down on him. He stepped to the side with the grace of experience, and as the heavy weapon parted the empty air and collided with the ground where Delvan had stood, he gave a thrust of his short sword, piercing the man's throat with a spray of crimson.

Orne charged forward to reinforce Kolden, running the spear end of his polearm through the gut of a nearby axe-wielder. He shouted for Kolden to focus on the remaining bowmen in the woods while spinning the halberd above his head and masterfully connecting its hammer with the skull of an opponent, dropping him to the ground and coating the black metal in a mist of blood.

Delvan moved to help as three more ran at Orne, but they underestimated his prowess with the deadly weapon. He held it upright, then dropped the axe-head deep into the shoulder of a man who stupidly thought himself beyond its reach. He yanked it from the cleaved body and spun it to force the others away from him. One charged, but Orne deflected his sword and pierced his chest. He jabbed one behind him with the butt of the weapon and then kicked him in the face as he fell gasping for air.

One after another met their end in a whirlwind of death as Orne wielded the halberd like it was an extension of his own body. Even the shaft was deadly, Orne deflecting the swing of a sword to the ground, thrusting the section of wood between his hands into the man's exposed throat, crushing his windpipe.

Delvan was awed. Watching the majestic brutality, he couldn't help but wonder if perhaps Orne had been holding back in their sparring sessions.

Orne clearly having the fight in hand, Delvan moved to help the others. He crossed swords with a snarling man that looked to finish off a wounded soldier, blocking his blow and then slicing him across the gut, dropping his entrails upon his boots.

Enemy after enemy succumbed to Delvan's blade. He hadn't forgotten these skills, these instincts ground into him since childhood. They may have been dormant for a time, hidden behind a wall of grief and loathing, but they were here now, released back into the world with renewed purpose.

His sword gleaned between streams of blood, cutting as his arm willed it. Orne had made his way to Delvan's side, the two leaving a trail of corpses in their wake, Kolden spiking those out of their reach with arrows.

They approached the center of the caravan, the orange coated carriage a few yards ahead of them. Out of it came two of the bandits, dragging a kicking and screaming emissary between them. One raised an axe above his head. He was going to cut down the King's emissary, killing the unarmed man.

He was too far to reach, Delvan only had one option. He held his hand to his side, palm facing upward, focusing with all his might. He could picture the ball of flame, imagining it floating above his hand as he conjured it into existence. He *had* to do this, he couldn't let anyone else die because of his inadequacy.

But as he tried, gritting his teeth, he felt the heat of the flames again, the smell of burning flesh. It nauseated him, turning his stomach and denying him the flame he so urgently needed. Morose anguish consumed him as not even a spark formed above his palm. He screamed as the axe fell, digging deeply into the chest of the emissary, abruptly stilling his flailing limbs.

An arrow flew from Kolden and struck the man down, but it was too late. Delvan gripped the handle of his sword tightly, his eyes squeezing shut as he let out a roar of defeated rage. He couldn't do it. He couldn't bring himself to cast fire again, the memories blocking him like a dam against a river.

He opened his eyes between wrinkled features of disdain, a deep well of self-loathing trying to drag him back into the murky, opaque depths. His chest heaved as he fought it, swimming against its current. As he looked down at the blood-stained robes of the emissary, another man emerged from the ornate carriage, a gold, filigreed box under his arm. He looked around frantically as he started to sprint into the forest, and Delvan's face went cold with realization.

*The sapphires.*

There were still a few undelivered sapphires, and although Delvan couldn't sense them through the muted inanite-lined box, he knew without question they were inside. He turned, wanting to shout for Kolden to shoot him, but he'd vanished from his position to their rear. Delvan started sprinting after him, shouting to Orne to stop him.

Orne looked over from where he had driven the axe of his halberd into someone's forehead, seeing the man fleeing the battle with the treasure beneath his arm. He jerked the polearm free, lifting it above his shoulder and launching it like a javelin. It flew through the air and found its target true, spearing the man through the side, the box breaking open on the ground and scattering the sapphires.

Delvan felt the warmth of the radiating gems cover him like a thick blanket and sprinted over to protect them. Orne recovered his halberd and together they faced the onslaught of assailers, all coming for the precious stones, falling to the ground among a sea of red as they were struck down.

There was a raucous exchange to Delvan's side, men fleeing in all directions from a scream that cut the dew-filled air like a banshee. He turned, seeing Ferrand swinging his enormous sword and severing a man's torso from his legs with a single, sweeping strike. As the two halves fell to the ground, the commander locked eyes with Delvan, his face splattered with blood.

Delvan held his gaze, and for a fleeting moment, he considered lunging at the commander, running him through in the madness of battle. He could almost feel an ember growing in his hand, the fuel of hatred burning down the barriers within. His brow furrowed as his knees bent, legs ready to thrust him forward at the commander.

Ferrand took a step forward and bent down in a seamless, rapid motion. When he was quickly upright again, he held a stone—no larger than an apple—in his hand, and with a continuation of the same, fluid motion, threw it towards Delvan at the speed of a meteor.

There was no time to dodge, the stone rocketing at him like an arrow. His only thought was that the commander had come to the same conclusion he had: end him in the heat of battle, and no one would be the wiser. If only he'd acted sooner.

But the stone missed, the air it moved weaving through Delvan's mess of hair as it shot past him. He spun his head, looking behind him, had the commander really been so off with his throw?

A bandit lay on the ground behind him, half his face ripped off from the impact of the rock. Delvan turned back to the commander, his eyes wide with shock and breathing quickly as sweat poured down his face. Did the commander just *save* him?

"Stay with the sapphires!" Ferrand ordered, pointing at Delvan and Orne. He marched off, cutting through men as if he were a scythe slicing grass.

"Well, *that* was unexpected," said Orne as he dropped the axe of his halberd into the collarbone of yet another foolish bandit.

Delvan couldn't help but agree. It didn't change anything, though. There must be a reason he didn't want Delvan dead yet, he just wasn't sure what it was. But he was going to find out.

A horn bellowed in the forest, and the bandits who hadn't already fled ran into the trees, leaving their injured brethren lying in pain on the ground. Delvan kept his sword up, poised in case the enemy were regrouping. But, as time passed, it became clear that they had left for good, and he eventually wiped off the blade and sheathed it.

The road had become a river of scarlet, the clean white snow transforming into a torrent of blood and mangled remains. Delvan placed the sapphires back into their box and set it by the former emissary's carriage. Royal soldiers and bandits alike covered the ground, the rank smell of death hanging in the air like a morning fog. Delvan saw only a handful of their soldiers still standing, many rushing to those still alive to tend to wounds.

"There you are," said Kolden as he appeared from around a carriage.

"Where the fuck did you run off to?" asked Orne.

"I had shit to check on, you were fine. But you guys should come with me, quick," he said, ushering them with a wave of his hand. "The commander captured one of the bandit leaders alive, he's questioning him. C'mon!"

Delvan followed closely behind Kolden as they stepped over the jumbled corpses and made their way to the front of the caravan. There they found Ferrand, as Kolden had stated, interrogating a man who sat on the ground, his back against the spokes of a wheel. He wore more expensive armor than the other bandits had, and a darksteel sword lay out of reach at his side. The expensive blade had done little to protect him, however, as there was an arrow protruding from his thigh, the nock coming up almost to his eye.

"How many of you were there?" asked Ferrand, his enormous sword held in a hand to his side. He seemed to ignore Delvan and the brothers' presence.

The man tilted his head forward and spit bloody phlegm on the ground at Ferrand's feet, a defiant sneer on his face.

"Alright, asshole, I'll ask again," said Ferrand as he grabbed the end of the arrow sticking from the man's leg and began to twist it. His scream exploded like shrapnel, his hands grasping onto his thigh as Ferrand roved in the tissue with the arrow's tip.

"Two! Two hun-hundred!" the man cried.

"See, that wasn't so fucking hard, now was it," said Ferrand. "Captain, do you have a preliminary casualty count?"

"My Lord, we're still checking the wounded, but we believe there to be over one hundred and fifty attackers dead or mortally injured, with over seventy of our own dead from the caravan."

*Seventy?* Delvan thought dismally. *That's nearly two thirds of us.*

"Looks like you should have brought more men," said Ferrand with derision to the captive.

"It's only a matter of time, Sraddhana scum. You can't hide it forever, we'll—"

With a flash of silvery black, Ferrand's blade swept from the side and removed the man's head. Delvan looked from the commander to the executed captive and back in rapid succession, his mouth open, wanting to scream. But all he could do was stand there, looking dumbfounded as Ferrand wiped the man's blood from his blade.

*No...* he thought. *No! I needed to hear what he had to say! Bastard!*

"Give no quarter," the commander said as a general order to everyone in earshot. "If any of these bandits are still alive, end them. No one is to speak with them, under any circumstances. If they do I will execute them myself. Tend to the wounded and gather the horses, we bury our men tonight and burn theirs. Post guards on shifts, I want to be prepared if these fuckers regroup and try again. We leave in the morning, consolidate what you can into a few carriages and leave behind what we don't need. We need to quicken our pace. We're being hunted."

# Chapter
# Forty-Two


*He cannot be allowed to turn against us.*

Nerio walked along the brick-paved road, the breeze touching his face with its sandy, abrasive hand. The colors of the surrounding buildings seemed dim, despite the bright sunlight, and he felt cold even in the afternoon's fiery radiance. He'd fought for so long to avoid this moment, but he supposed it was only a matter of time. He'd done what he could.

And failed. Again.

The blue-sashed disciple led him through familiar streets, along a well-treaded path, towards memories that he wished for nothing more than to forget. He didn't blame the boy. Denying him would have displaced Nerio's fate onto him. Jerdine was not one to go without and would supplement his needs with whomever was most readily available. Nerio couldn't bring himself to knowingly consign this child to that, so he instead followed, his feet heavy and insides hollow.

He wanted to think of a way to escape, a way to run and slip out from under the thumb of Jerdine, but he couldn't conceive of a means in which the preying malefactor didn't destroy the life of someone else in his stead. How had all of the others escaped? The friends that fled in the night and weren't seen again? They'd found a way to remove the short leash connecting them to Jerdine. Nerio wasn't upset that they'd left him behind, he'd merely wished any of them could have taken him with them.

Time was lost on him, whether he'd walked ten steps or a thousand, he couldn't say. When he found himself walking through the carved, arched doors of the Grand Clergy House, he wasn't surprised, as it felt like he'd taken both only a moment, and an eternity to arrive. They walked to the stairs of Jerdine's spire, twisting up the center of the tower like the bone of a limb. His legs struggle to lift themselves onto the smooth stone steps, glowing yellow in the light of the lanterns lining the wall.

The disciple unlocked the door which provided access to the section of tower that rose above the lower levels. Nerio knew this passage well. They would continue to climb, passing rooms of studious disciples, private libraries of the principle, quarters for the principle's closest aides, and finally the top. The dreaded destination.

They walked through the door, the young disciple closing it and turning the heavy iron key with a final, metallic *click*.

They began the arduous climb, Nerio counting the steps in his head.

*Seventy-eight, seventy-seven, seventy-six...*

Desnia watched as Nerio and the disciple disappeared behind the arched door, hearing the lock turn behind them.

"Shit," she muttered.

*Um, mind telling me what we're doing?* asked Masini.

"Not now!" she hissed under her breath.

*Des, we shouldn't be here, this is dangerous—*

"Quiet! I need to think."

She looked around frantically, ideas furiously racing through her mind. She could go back to her quarters and get the lock picking tools still stashed away in her bag. But no, there were too many people up and active in the clergy house during the day, she'd surely be caught, no matter how discreet.

She *needed* keys, not only that, but a way to disguise herself as to not draw attention. Who had keys? Principles. That wasn't an option. High ranking priests, maybe? But she didn't have time to not only find one but steal their keys unknowingly, assuming they even *had* the right keys. Disciples. Yes, all the Almedia disciples would have a key to this door, but the ones who weren't currently in the tower would be off doing other duties. There might be some in the library, or maybe at the Devapuram. She could lift the keys and hope to return quickly, but it could be a half hour before she was able to return. Too long, too long. Where else would she find them? Where would—

The bathhouse.

These idiots always left their personal possessions in the changing rooms, like they were *asking* for them to be stolen. Was this place so picturesque and perfect that it didn't have any crime? It baffled her.

There wasn't time to ponder the curious nature of Brethefen's crime rates, however, and she turned to sprint back down the stairs. The bathhouse was nearby, and she could return in a few minutes if she hurried. She just hoped that it would be fast enough.

Desnia wasn't sure what it was that Nerio was facing in that tower, and as she skipped stairs two at a time, she hoped that it wasn't what she thought. There was a sense of urgency in her, as though his fear lingered within her, and she knew there was no time to spare.

She burst through the entrance of the clergy house, nearly running into a group of soldiers accompanying a very important looking military man, a general, she guessed. They seemed startled, but otherwise dismissive of her. She ran around them, ignoring the tingling sensation at the back of her neck, still amazed at people's disregard for anyone in a Hands or priest's garbs. If she'd run like this in Calentine and a guard had seen her, she'd be chased through the streets.

She didn't look back as she sprinted to the bathhouse, the arid heat stealing away her sweat. She slowed to a walk as she crossed the threshold into the changing room of the enormous building. Men and women alike were there in varying forms of undress, as though it were the most normal thing in the world.

*What is with these people and nudity?* she thought with a sneer.

Her own distastes needed to be pushed aside, and Desnia instead focused on the task at hand. Her eyes darted along the walls, looking for the telltale blue sash she was seeking. Trying not to seem rushed or in the hurry that she was, she forced herself to saunter about within the humid room, brushing shoulders with bathers as she walked along the walls.

At last, her eyes caught sight of a blue sash, hanging from a hook on the wall. She sighed a breath of relief. No one paid attention to her as she walked up to the hanging clothing, still ignoring her existence as she reached under the robe and found a ring, a single iron key hanging from it.

She wrapped the sash around her waist, tucking the key into it. She rolled up her sleeves to hide the white rings banded around the cuffs, and then walked back to the entrance of the bath house. Her breathing had finally returned to normal after the sprint, but it quickly became rapid as she exited the stuffy bathhouse and broke into another run.

People watched and gasped as she flew past them, gawking at the sight of someone bounding through the streets. She didn't care. She should have, drawing this much attention was dangerous, but she knew there wasn't much time.

As she reached the entrance to the clergy house, she found the group of soldiers still present, the important looking man at the center of them barking at some priest in front of the door. She slowed as one of the guards around him finally seemed to deem her worthy of their attention, eyes following from within an unmoving helm.

She kept her head tilted to the side, trying not to act suspiciously as she attempted to skate around the band of soldiers, the man at their center raging at the priest before him.

"...I *DEMAND* to see him. Now!" proclaimed the man. He wasn't quite screaming, but he spoke with the firmness of authority, like a noble who was accustomed to getting what he wanted.

*Arrogant bastards.*

"Deepest apologies, my Lord General," the priest said, "but Principle Jerdine has left strict instructions that he's not to be disturbed."

"I don't *care* what he wants!" the general said in a way that was both powerful but level at the same time. "You will either bring me to him, *immediately*, or I shall have my men break the doors down."

*Gods-damn it,* she thought. Now she didn't just have to get to Jerdine without being caught, but she had to beat a *general* to him. Unless...

"Sire, I apologize, but—" started the priest.

Desnia stepped towards the general, ignoring the priest to her side. "I can take you, my Lord." The words came out in loud blurt. She hadn't even thought about it, her body had just... taken control. Her throat went tight, and stomach sank to her knees as she finally got a full look of the man who she'd addressed. Tall, with thin and aging features cutting a distinctly noble air into his visage, he wore a military uniform and a strange, hooked sword at his side. Most notable of all, however, was the massive sapphire sitting atop his breast, the bear-headed chain presenting it glinting in the white of the sun.

The general turned to look at her, the priest to her side looking shocked and taken aback. He was nearly as speechless as Desnia was.

"Sister," the priest said, his words filled with bile, "we cannot go against the wishes of the principle, as a disciple you of all people—"

"Silence!" the general demanded. He looked at Desnia, a chill running through her frozen figure. "Please, Sister, lead the way, and thank you for your assistance, unlike that of your brethren."

The look of disdain he gave the glowering priest would have shriveled most men into the tiniest grain of sand, but the priest stood quietly firm. Desnia had to admit she was impressed. She turned away from the furious priest and began walking with the general following closely behind her. Her heart pounded with a force that threatened to propel it out of her chest, the sound of it ringing in her ears. She could do this. She *had* to do this.

She just hoped that she'd make it in time.

Nerio's feet were planted to the polished stone floor, his body facing the blue-painted door arching to a peak above his head. He knew this door. It was buried in the deepest recesses of his memories, locked away, forcefully forgotten, but the sight of it turned a key and allowed the torment to rampage through his heart once more.

The young disciple stood beside him with hands clasped. Neither had moved for a time, how long he wasn't certain. The pause couldn't last forever, they both knew it, but it would appear that he nor the boy were looking to hasten what came next.

Fear and pain ran amok in the chasm of his chest, his core long ago hollowed out. It had kept him numb for a while, but it seemed that the cavern allowed these emotions to create havoc, inflating to fully inhabit their enlarged surroundings.

The disciple at long last reached past Nerio and knocked on the door. Nodding to him while refusing eye contact before walking away, the sounds of his footfalls upon the stairs echoing through the hall Nerio stood in.

The door swung open. Jerdine, adorned in his blue robe with rings climbing from his wrist to his shoulders, appeared before him. His teeth reflected the drape of blue light upon him as he smiled, the late afternoon sun streaming through the stained windows.

"Nerio," Jerdine said, "how good of you to come. Please, come in, no need to just stand in the hall."

He wanted to resist, to scream or run, but he couldn't. He shuffled in through the door, Jerdine closing it behind him. Not much had changed in the richly ornamented room—the principle had always been rather set in his ways. Ancient books that Nerio had always been forbidden to touch, despite his many visits here, filled a case on a far wall. A small patio lay beyond two double doors opposite him, and a collection of strange and valuable objects decorated the walls.

The clergy were supposed to live meager lives, lacking in finery or objects of lavish lifestyles. Jerdine only ascribed to certain parts of doctrine, ones that befit his own desires. It was just everyone else that was expected to follow the way of his preachings, as was evident by the glass of Aliovan wine in his hand.

"Sit," said Jerdine, motioning to the plush couch. Nerio did as he asked, while the principle refilled his crystal glass. "I wanted to tell you in person," he said, putting a cork back into the bottle, "that I've ordained for you to take the librarian position. It's where you belong, Nerio, an aptitude such as yours should not be wasted."

His face fell, heart sinking impossibly lower. "Sir, I-I am still needed at the Asylum. I cannot just abandon my duties."

"Bah, don't worry about them, they're tainted, their minds lost. There is no helping them. Besides, I assumed you'd say as much, so I have contracted someone as your replacement. They will be starting immediately. You'll be able to move back here, where you belong."

*And in your domain,* he thought.

A strange conflict stirred inside of him, a voice that accepted what he was told. An invader of his soul which said, yes, the librarian position *is* where I belong. It fought his urge to run, a clash like the rain against the mountains. Where were these feelings coming from?

Jerdine took a sip of wine and sat beside him, his thick thigh touching Nerio's. Nerio shrank inward, wishing to become so small he could vanish, his palms clammy and face numb. Jerdine rested his arm on the couch back behind Nerio, leaning in closer. He thought he was going to be sick, but his muscles froze, unable to move.

"I've missed you, Nerio," Jerdine said, his breath hot against Nerio's cheek. "You should be pleased, in all my long years, of the many, many disciples, you were my favorite. So intelligent, so... supple. I've tried to give you space, as much as it pains my heart to do so, being certain that you'd make it back to your proper place eventually. But you've impressed me yet again, child. Few, so very few, can resist my... influence. Yet years later and you still insist on remaining sympathetic to those weak-minded fools. Your will is strong, something so rare among the common pestilence. A fruit among the weeds, making it all the sweeter..."

He took another sip of his wine and placed it on the low table before them. The same hand found its way to Nerio's thigh. It made his soul tremble, but his body stayed still, as if it were held in place by invisible chains. There was a chill that entered his leg from the touch, an ice that paralyzed. His mind screamed, begged, sobbed, and yet his face and muscles stayed still. There was no running from this.

Nerio closed his eyes, staring into the black. In that moment he wanted for nothing more than that darkness to take him, submerge him into the depths of the immortal emptiness, trapped forever in the blank sanctuary. He felt sick, tasting bile in the back of his throat, repulsed by the situation and his own inadequacy to change it. He prayed. He reached out to the gods, the saints, the great figures of old, anyone that might listen as he'd done so many times before. They had never answered.

*Why? Why have you all forsaken me?* he wondered.

There was a sudden, thundering clash of metal against stone, so loud it nearly disoriented Nerio. His eyes opened with a start to see the door to Jerdine's chambers kicked open, the wood around the door's lock splintered and broken. A man in a military uniform strode in, his stiff posture supporting eyes full of ire.

Jerdine stood up with surprising quickness, his face turning red with rage. "What is the meaning of this?! How *dare* you intrude without permission! You have no right—"

"I am a member of the Sapphiric Court, general of the western armies, and report directly to the King," the man said firmly. "I have *every* right. You and I are to have a discussion about your infringements into my command. You *dare* to order my men around? Removing them from their stations at the bath and clergy house? Attempting to do so at the Devapuram as well? You might have reign over members of the clergy, but do not mistake your influence to be so absolute as to be able to command soldiers of *my* military."

The general turned his attention to Nerio, still huddled on the couch, and a flicker of contempt flashed over his face as he looked back at the principle, whose fists were clenched and jaw tight.

"Son," he said to Nerio, "you rightfully don't look as though you desire to remain here. Leave us."

Nerio moved to stand, but Jerdine pointed a finger down at him and shouted, "You stay, Nerio, the general will be taking his leave."

"Leave, son," the general repeated, his eyes fixed on Jerdine. "There are a dozen soldiers outside that door, principle, but don't think for a second that I need any one of them to snap you in half like a reed. The boy will leave, or we will be continuing this conversation with you behind iron in the dungeons."

Jerdine's fists were shaking. Nerio had never seen the principle so enraged. Nonetheless, he wasn't about to waste this opportunity, and with a quick motion stood and nearly ran for the door. Shouts of the principle trailed behind him, but words fell upon his ears like an unknown tongue. He moved between a tight mess of reflective armor outside Jerdine's quarters, hearing sounds that his mind couldn't interpret. He had to leave, had to escape.

*How long can I run?* he thought.

He hurried past disciples gathering in the stairs, forcing his way through with abandon. His feet were a blur of motion as they clamored down tread after tread, the railing in his hand the only security against a downward tumble. He reached the base of the spire, sweating, out of breath after rushing through the echoing cacophony of the spiraled steps. His feet forced him into a run, his body fleeing with reckless disregard for those around him.

There was a high priest at the entrance to the clergy house who pointed in his direction and started shouting. Nerio wasn't sure what he was saying—he didn't care. As he passed his wrath-spewing brother, the man walked past Nerio, pointing and screaming at someone behind him. Nerio was unphased, if the man had been directing his anger at him, he would have kept running.

The setting sun cast a red glow over the city, the sky a blaze of color. He knew where he was going, an unspoken thought coming to his mind, a decision made. He couldn't handle the thought of this happening again, it was apparent that there was nowhere to hide, nowhere to run where that monster wouldn't find him.

He reached the base of his belltower, the peals of other bells tolling through the air as the hour reached its summit. He was out of breath, but it didn't slow his ascent. Droplets of sweat rained upon the worn wooden stairs as he climbed, the sound of bells drowning out the creaks of boards under his feet. These steps didn't require counting, they didn't lead to his demise, but to his salvation, and the anxious dread had left him.

Ignoring the heavy, dangling rope that so ritualistically required his attention, he climbed the short ladder to the platform above, emerging in the basking red light of sunset. The bell hung there, motionless, its siblings ringing loudly in the distance as Nerio put it to his back and took a step towards the ledge.

His fingers found their way, as they often did, to the broken ceramic in his sash. He pulled the stained shard out and felt it between his fingers, remembering Lord Grundan and the prejudice with which he'd judged his actions. He felt none of that now, and where those thoughts used to be, came an epiphany of understanding. The man had needed an escape and Nerio, of all people, could understand that. Empathize with it. Now more than ever.

He reverently placed the shard on the ledge's lip beside him, standing straight and taking a deep breath with closed eyes as he shuffled forward until his toes hung in the air above the belltower's edge. He welcomed the blackness, the nothing hidden behind closed eyes.

As the distant bells stopped tolling, their rings fading away, Nerio raised his foot and stepped forward into the empty air beyond the bell's platform.

He would embrace the dark.

Desnia moved as swiftly as her legs could carry her, tearing through the bustling street like a leaf caught in a storm. She'd tried to catch Nerio's attention as he'd shot out of Jerdine's office, but between the guards and crowd of disciples that had collected as she'd led the general up the spire, her attempts had fallen on deaf ears. He'd moved down the stairs and through the clergy house like a bludgeon, forceful and unyielding as he fled, and it was everything she could do to keep pace.

None of this had been made any easier with Masini worked up into a panic by her actions. He'd been subdued, oddly quiet even, since she'd left the principle's spire. She'd have to ask him about it later.

Then that bastard at the front entrance had seen her, obstructing her way to berate her for allowing the general access. Avoiding him through another entrance had cost her time, and now she sprinted to find where Nerio had gone.

The warm breeze did little to cool her sweating skin, causing her golden hair to stick to her brow. She brushed it to the side in a quick motion as she looked around, spinning her head in search of Nerio, wondering where he had run to.

Desnia had *felt* his panic, the pain, the loneliness as he'd fled from the principle's chambers. It reminded her of that night, many months ago now—although fresh in her mind—with the grieving Blue. The feeling lingered, that insurmountable agony that weighed down on her like the sky itself were upon her shoulders.

Nerio had seemed so pleasant, helping and smiling when others wouldn't. He couldn't possibly have lived with this pain for long, could he? She felt a stab of guilt for how she'd treated him at first, threatening him as though he wanted to use her. It was clear to her now that he'd wanted anything but. This turmoil was that of one who'd suffered, she knew it in her soul.

But now she feared what he would do.

It was another feeling, a push within her to find the priest, and with haste. There was a sickening fear, a morbid anticipation that forced her heart into her throat. She *had* to find him, it was as guttural an instinct as her own survival, though she couldn't explain its origins.

There came the sound of shocked annoyance from someone nearby, then another, and another. Desnia turned to see a distant figure in white forcing themselves through the street-goers like a bull through wheat, ignorant of those around them.

*That must be him,* she thought.

She took off running, gaining on the blunt instrument which was Nerio's body as it hammered its way through anyone in its path. She called out to him to no avail; he either didn't hear her or ignored her altogether. The wind whipped her hair as she ran along the paved street, ignoring people and donkeys alike as she ducked around the large animals and pushed bystanders to the side.

Nerio eventually reached the base of a belltower, rushing inside. She slowed and took a few deep breaths, wiping her forehead with her hand before following suit.

*What is he doing?* she wondered as she sprang through the door, hearing the pounding of inelegant feet climbing the stairs. Her lungs strained as she flew up the treads two at a time, her legs burning and chest pounding. She tried calling out to him again, but the other, distant bells began ringing, drowning her voice in their chiming tolls. Arms pulling her forward via the adjacent railing, Desnia propelled herself ever upward, desperate to gain ground.

*Does this staircase ever fucking end?* she thought, exhausted and panting.

She arrived at the top at last but was met with only a vacant room containing a thick, frayed rope hanging from the ceiling in the center. Chest heaving, she looked around frantically, looking for any sign of—

A ladder, near the opposite wall. There was nowhere else for him to go. She ran over and climbed the narrow and aged rungs through a small opening above, emerging onto a platform mostly filled with a massive, bronze bell.

Heights were nothing new to her, she'd climbed the cliffs of Calentine since she was a young girl, but even she was surprised to see just how high the belltower truly was. The city was splayed out before her, drenched in the red of the evening sun, the breeze starting to carry a cooler air. She could almost see a pattern in the layout of the streets, all forming around the Devapuram at the city's center.

Desnia turned, her heart dropping and eyes becoming wide at the sight of Nerio standing on the platform's precipice, his back to her. She took a step forward and Nerio, as though mirroring her, took a step of his own.

"No!" she cried as she reached out. Her arm extended as far as it was able, her fingertips skimming along the folds of fabric along his back. They searched for purchase as they cruised between his shoulder blades, then along his spine, until at last catching the sash around his waist.

With the strong grip of a climber, Desnia latched onto the band of linen. Her body was leaning forward awkwardly, but with all the strength her muscles could muster, she heaved on Nerio's sash.

She nearly fell forward past the lip's edge herself, but managed to balance as Nerio came flying towards her, colliding with her narrow frame. They both stumbled backward, striking the huge bell with a *clang*, a low-pitched hum resonating afterward.

Nerio fell to his knees as Desnia's body slumped down, sliding along the face of the bell until she sat on the platform, her legs extended out before her. Nerio turned his lowered head, looking at Desnia from the corner of his reddened, tear-filled eyes. His body began to shake as he broke into a sob, and Desnia felt a well of pity growing for him from within her.

She sat there quietly as the sun sank below the mountains to the west, pulling them and the city into darkness. Nerio was a deluge of emotions, bursting from the seams in a continuous outpour. Desnia felt that he was shedding himself of years of pent-up agony, for he went on longer than she'd ever expected, trembling while streams burst from his eyes. Lamps along the streets were being lit before he had calmed, his face soaked from the rivers of tears. She sat there and waited. For all the pain she could feel, she honestly had no idea what to do to console it.

The air was cooler and darker before he finally spoke. "You should have let me go," he said in a quiet, broken voice.

"I'm sorry," she said sorrowfully, "but I couldn't let you do that."

"You don't know what it's like," he said, still avoiding her gaze, "this pain, this fear. I've run from it for so long, but it always finds me, I just can't take it anymore."

She didn't dare make the claim that she'd felt his pain, that it had penetrated her very being. She searched for something to say but couldn't think of what. Her whole life she'd sheltered herself away, never sharing with any-one, never trusting that she could present her true self out of fear that it would be used against her. It had left her dissociated from human connections; safe, but distant.

Nerio didn't need the lesson of hardship taught on the streets, like what she'd endured. He needed something real, something honest. She didn't know if she could *be* honest, a lifetime of survival beating it out of her. Seeing this vulnerable, shattered person before her opened something, a part of her soul that had been locked away for so long it'd been forgotten. She stopped trying to think of what to say, and just let the words flow from her.

"I've been running my whole life," Desnia said. "Hiding from the things that scare me the most, avoiding connections at every level, trying to fight my way through life's challenges by myself. Never being able to trust any-one because if they knew the *real* you, you'd end up in a prison cell, or worse. It's... lonely. Safe, or I should say *safer*, but painfully lonely."

Nerio finally looked at her, his face and eyes red, wiping his dribbling nose on his sleeve. "I'm sorry," he said.

"You have nothing to be sorry for, I'm the one who's sorry for you. Jerdine, he's the one who's made you like this? He's why you're up here?"

He nodded his head, a fresh tear forming in the corner of his eye.

"He's a demon," Nerio said, "no one stands up to him. He holds all the power and suffers none of the consequences. I've spent years trying to avoid him, though I think he had just... lost interest for a while. This entire city is under his thumb, he knows everything that happens within its limits."

"I'll help you," she said. "I've spent my life hiding, I can help keep you safe. It's the least I can do after what you did for me."

He shook his head, "I merely guided you. You seem smart, you would've found your way to the Hands eventually. I don't want you to think you owe me a debt."

"You're far too good for this cruel world, Nerio," Desnia said with a sigh, tilting her head back to rest on the cool metal of the bell.

"The gods would seem to disagree," he said. "They bring this torment on me, and for the life of me, I can't seem to figure out why. What have I done to anger them?"

"We must bear the pain of burden to be free of its weight..." she said, thinking back to words once said to her. "When the world, the gods, whoever you think is directing your life, comes down on you, what choice do you have but to push forward? You think that this is the way to go? By your own beliefs you'd be committing your afterlife to an eternity of imprisonment. Have you thought about those in this life that would be pained by you leaving?"

He sniveled, "No one is going to care."

"*I* care," she said. It was honest, she could feel it. She didn't know why, but she realized at that moment that she would care if he were gone. "And what about all those people at the Asylum? The ones that no one else will take care of? Just because they hear a voice doesn't mean they won't remember or miss you. I'll take on all the tortures of my life before I willingly walk into death's talons."

He was quiet, his head still hung low. He didn't seem convinced.

"I almost died a few months ago," she said. "Some greedy shitbags in the crew I was working with wanted to kill me and take a larger share for themselves. They had me, I didn't have an escape, and I can remember that fear, the panic as I thought about what they were going to do to me, my body, hoping that they would at least have the decency to kill me first. As if they were even *capable* of decency. I can remember that look in the fucker's eyes, the cold, reptilian stare. I wouldn't wish that fate on anyone.

"But then I was saved, by someone I would never have expected, someone who on any other day would have arrested me and carried me to the gallows. A Blue and his partner. They came charging in and not only saved my life, but pulled me from the fire. It cost one of them their lives, and I *felt* the other's pain, his grief at his loss. What you're feeling is terrible, awful, and I'll happily stab that priest in his fucking sleep for it. But the pain of loss? It's equally crippling.

"I've never told that to anyone," Desnia said quietly. "It was so many months ago now, and yet it feels like it was yesterday. There's an image that haunts me: the sight of the Blue, grieving over his friend's dead body, flames burning in the background. My own phantom, the punishment of my own guilt.

"I may not completely empathize with your situation, Nerio, but I assure you that I have known pain in my life. I understand it's not the same, but I want you to know that you don't have to do this alone. You saved me from starving in the streets; admittedly, at the time, I assumed you had other motives, but my entire life I've never found any reason to put my trust or faith into anything. Everyone I've ever known has left me, hurt me, or betrayed me. But you, I see now that what you did was truly altruistic, a trait so rare I thought it was more legend than real. So, I wanted to say: thank you."

They were quiet again, night beginning to fully envelope them, the metal of the bell feeling cool on her back.

"It sounds like the gods intervened to save you," he said. "It seems that you're a part of their plans."

Desnia thought about the implications of that statement: the voice in her dreams, its instruction to come here, commanding her to take Masini. It all came tumbling down on her, realizing that despite all her beliefs—or lack thereof—Nerio might be right. She let out a chuckle. It was an odd response, but after years of ignoring her own sanity, lying to herself in saying that the voice wasn't real, she'd allowed it to guide her, she'd even listened to Masini for months now without a second thought.

Her chuckle grew into an uproar, a boisterous laughter that carried itself over the city below as if it were coming from the bell to her back.

"What's so funny?" he asked, looking at her confused.

"It's just, I think you might actually be onto something there," she said, calming herself and wiping a tear from her own eye.

He raised an eyebrow at her. "You're rather strange, aren't you, Delphini?"

Hearing that fake name was a sobering thought, wiping the joy from her face. Now it was her head that hung, looking at the weathered boards beneath her.

"Nerio," she said, "my name, it's not Delphini. I'm sorry I lied to you but trust has never been a strong suit of mine. There are dangerous people in this city that might be looking for me, and I couldn't risk telling it to you."

Nerio turned his head to the side, he looked hurt, betrayed even. It stabbed a knife in her chest seeing him react like that. But after a pause, he nodded and said, "I understand. I realize that you are trying to stay safe, I can relate to that. You don't have to tell me your name."

"Desnia," she said without hesitation, looking at him.

His fiddling hands suddenly stopped, his whole body going rigid. She felt a twist in her gut, had she made a mistake in telling him?

"What... What did you say?" he said, looking up at her with wide eyes.

"Uh, Desnia. That's my name."

He nearly fell backward from his kneel, his hand covering his chest, then reaching for his sash. She tensed, reaching for her own waist, her hand hovering there, waiting. Would she need the knife tucked away there? He patted at his waist, then spun his head from side to side, reaching for something at the ledge. Desnia pulled her knees closer to her, ready to pounce at a moment's notice.

Nerio grabbed a small, broken piece of something, holding it in his palms, staring at it. Desnia allowed herself to relax, leaning forward to see what it was he cradled.

"Do you know what your name means? What it's shortened from in old trethish?" he asked, looking at her with eyes now eager.

"Uhh," she said.

*I* tried *to tell you, but* someone *couldn't be bothered with a history lesson,* came Masini's voice. She nearly jumped to her feet in a start upon hearing him, forgetting he was there all this time. Had he been listening to all of that?

"It's shortened," said Nerio, "from *Niallai oc Deste.* Meaning *Night Daughter of the Eighth.* I... I think this is part of the gods' plans. Desnia, I think I was *meant* to find you."

**END PART 3**

irty water flowed over Floran's pruned, aching fingers as he pressed the thin appendages against the pebble of faintly glowing cadentite, digging its faceted edges into the steel grindstone. His back was still bleeding from the most recent lashing, a more acute reminder of his master's will than the sore-covered skin under the ankle bracelet chained to the wall.

He wanted to cry, he wanted to yell out in agony at the crack of the whip, but he couldn't. Those who did were seen as weak, and those who were weak went into the cages. There he would find a worse fate than a broken body, and the thought of it kept him hunched there, doing as he was instructed.

*I can't let them see me slow or falter. I must keep going.*

The glow of the cadentite flecks—spread on the bottom of the water-filled catch basin beneath his wheel—cast shadows on his face and the damp walls of the cavern. The musty smell of his surroundings was mixed with the taste of metal as the grinding wore down the steel wheel as much as the stone in his hands. He'd become accustomed to it, ignoring it, pumping his foot to perpetually keep the wheel spinning, reminding himself with each new split in his skin: *It's not the cages.*

He heard screaming from around the nearby corner, where a continuous hum of purple light emanated from the larger cavern beyond. It was the only illumination in the dripping cave, aside from the cadentite in his hands. He didn't want to seem like he was listening—those who did ended up in the glowing cavern—but it was hard to ignore the ravings.

"*How* did they escape?!" came the enraged voice of his eldest captor. At least it wasn't produced by another like Floran; those screams weren't angry, but entreating, and still carried the clarity of youth. "We *need* to know where that bastard sent the key! How did we ever let this happen?! Do you realize what your incompetence has cost us?"

"But, sir," came another voice—younger, but not youthful enough. Floran let himself sigh a small, internal breath of relief. "We did as we were instructed! We ambushed them, outnumbered them, but they fought like demons. The Blues cut down more men than I could count, and even some of the common soldiers fought with the skill of an army! We caught them by surprise and had double their number!"

"You know *nothing* of demons, you insolent fool. I told you what to expect and you still failed. Do you know how difficult it will be to find the key if they bring it here! It could be under our noses for a century if it's hidden well enough, and I will not be forced to remain in this parched wasteland any longer!"

"Sir," the other man said. Now Floran could hear the pleading in his voice over the constant grating of stone against steel. "I can fix this, I can still be of service to you. Let me gather more men and go back, they are weakened, we can strike anew and claim the prize you seek."

"You barely beat them back here yourself," the elder said condescendingly. "No, I have another, more proficient friend who I will be assigning this task. *He* I have faith in, unlike you. But don't fret, you can still be of use."

"Thank you, sir. I won't fail you, I... Wait, no. No! Please, I-I-ahhh!"

The screams faded into a familiar choking sound, and the steady glow from the other room grew a little brighter, a nearly imperceptible shift in luminosity.

Floran kept grinding, his eyes fixed on his task. He fought back the tears, he couldn't show weakness, he couldn't let them take him to the cages. Even as the sound of shuffling feet came from the other room and he heard them stop and turn towards him, he kept working, pressing the stone even harder, spinning the wheel faster.

Feet approached him, a looming figure coming to his side. Still, he kept his gaze set upon his work, unflinching, strong, determined. He gripped the stone tighter to stop his hands from shaking, sweat dripping down his brow despite the damp cool of the caves.

His work must have been satisfactory, for the feet turned from him and walked away. He didn't allow himself to relax, to slow the pace of his effort, however. If he did, he might be next.

He pressed harder.

# PART 4
## TRUTHS

# Chapter
# Forty-Three



*Fire, angry and swift*
*A wake of death, cleansing, untamed*
*Life birthed from ashes*

The desert heat flowed over Delvan like a blazing furnace, the midday sun unrelenting in its dry ferocity—well beyond anything he'd ever experienced while growing up in Calentine. Riding the horse next to his was Kolden, with Orne at the helm of a nearby wagon, which was better suited to bear his weight than one of the overexerted steeds. The sweltering heat had forced them to abandon wearing their armor weeks ago, getting drenched through in sweat before noon each day. The danger of another ambush lurked ever over them, but fighting while dizzy with dehydration was more dangerous than their exposed skin.

Less than half of their original caravan now rolled over the dusty, stone-paved road. Carriages had been abandoned, men buried, and urgency stirred as they lightened their load and pushed the horses and men alike to their limits. Much had been lost in the attack, but Delvan had been able to find his blue-gray mare wandering the nearby forest—possibly the singular positive outcome of the ambush's aftermath.

*I wish I'd been able to ask that man some questions,* he thought, remembering back to the beheaded bandit. *What other secrets does Ferrand have that we don't know?*

Delvan glared towards the front of the line of carriages and wagons at the rider in blue leading it. In the time since the battle other questions had floated to the surface, things that came to mind once his blood had cooled and mind calmed. Why had the commander saved his life? And although the memory was clouded, he still could have sworn that one of the bandits had been seeking him out specifically.

As he rotated through their possible motives, sleep became even more fleeting for him. He was convinced the attack had something to do with Ferrand, but the man wouldn't have his own caravan attacked and then spare Delvan. His reasoning went in circles as he dismissed one conclusion after another.

*I'll find out soon enough,* he thought.

The last several weeks of travel had hauled them beyond the limits of the snow laden forest, then over great plains of grass that soon thinned and became more sand and gravel than vegetation. As they journeyed on, the small shrubs and trees became fewer, and those they found often had only sparsely leafed branches. The heat had grown oppressive, and water had been a constant struggle to obtain—over the past week especially. They rode in near silence, the thirst consuming their minds, hoping to find a creek bed or pond that had not run dry or become rancid.

The trek had been difficult for all of them since the ambush. Guards were posted in shifts every night, a rotation through the remaining company allotted reprieve for no one except the wounded. Concerns over another attack were as omnipresent as the blaring sun, and Delvan knew he wasn't the only one who slept uneasily in the warm nights. The paranoia began to fade, however, as their cracked lips begged for water.

Whether the trick of a mirage or a credit to their fortune, the near-lifeless desert began to fill with tilled fields of barley and orchards. They happened upon a farmer guiding his donkey—heavy saddle baskets on its sides—and the caravan slowed to a near stop as the commander spoke with the man, everyone listening anxiously with parched lips and hoarse breath.

To their elation, not only did the old man proffer a basket of reaped fruit, but with a tanned and wrinkled smile he offered to guide them to a nearby irrigation well. Delvan knew that, legally, the man was obliged to supply soldiers with their needs, but nevertheless, the whole of the caravan expressed their enormous gratitude with bowing of heads and coins from their pockets.

After drinking their fill and snacking on the ripe and delicious fruit, they turned their minds to other matters, asking the farmer how far they were from their destination—the grand city of Brethefen. To their immense relief, the city gates were only a half day's march, and beyond the next rolling knoll the city itself would come into view. The old man laughed and said that if they missed it, they were more blind than his elderly donkey.

Much to the man's point, as they crested the next hill the sprawling city emerged from behind its veil, the waves of heated air distorting it slightly, but doing little to hide its vast size. Its walls, which blended with the dirt it was partially constructed of, were drastically offset by the vibrant colors they encircled, with the great dome at the center dwarfing all in the vicinity. Although it was marginally less populated than Calentine, its breadth seemed a strange inverse to the compacted valleys and cliffs of the mountain capital.

"Finally!" said Orne with relief, "I never thought I'd be so damn happy to see a place with no taverns."

"And I never thought I'd be so fucking happy for you to take a bath," said Kolden. "I don't know what smells worse, you or the horse." His steed neighed, sounding disgruntled. Patting the animal's neck, he said, "Sorry. You're right, you could never smell as bad as that, apologies."

"Fuck you," retorted Orne.

The two continued to bicker, their vigor rejuvenated by the quenching water, until the caravan reached the city gates. As they crossed through the ancient stone fortification, a silence of awe came over them, their mouths gaping as they trotted down the brick paved roads. Calentine had been a beautiful—though monotone—metropolis of carved stone, with crisp lines and carved masonry, but this was more imperfect, a culture spoken through the texture of adobe walls and bright pastel colors.

Delvan allowed his attention to be drawn away from the burden of animosity he held, taking in the smells and sounds as people stopped to stare at the line of foreign soldiers arriving in their home. Many of the residents—men and women alike—wore robes, as if it were normal to adorn a nightgown in public.

*Some are made of silk!* he thought, perplexed as a wealthy man walked past wearing an ornate garb. *What a strange place.*

His mind wasn't entirely consumed by the intake of this odd culture; part of it was searching, planning. Where was the Merchants' Guild located in Brethefen? He couldn't risk asking while still with the caravan, but he hoped for a sign or indication of its whereabouts. He had thought about what he would say, who he would demand to speak with, but something bothered him.

It wasn't that he was thinking about backing down from his plan, he was still committed. He just had this strange feeling of... doubt? Perhaps confusion? A plethora of questions were unanswered, and while Hilbrun had clearly trusted the guild, Delvan wasn't sure to what extent he could do the same. Afterall, they'd been hoarding sapphires—something that Hilbrun had seemingly been willing to ignore. Delvan wasn't so passive.

However he handled the situation, he'd need to be careful. Choosing the lesser malefactor did not acquit them of wrongdoings, nor the ability to commit said acts. He couldn't go charging in—a life lesson he wasn't soon to forget—despite how he ached to enact his revenge.

Delvan continued to consider his best approach until they arrived at the garrison's barracks. While the exterior was constructed of similar materials to the surrounding structures, there was a familiarity to it. The narrow windows, the plainness that spoke to defensible design and utilitarianism. If the military was anything, it was consistent.

What appeared to be the barrack's captain emerged from the building and started speaking to the commander. Delvan had difficulty discerning the topic of their discussion over the sounds of hooves and wheels against brick, and beyond the initial greeting he strained to make out anything of importance. He did, however, sigh a breath of relief as nearly two dozen junior soldiers marched out of the barracks behind the captain, each approaching the wagons and carriages to begin unloading.

*Finally,* Delvan thought, *I've had to break my own camp for weeks, at least now we have some proper aid.*

He'd grumbled about the laborious task once when in earshot of Orne and Kolden, to which they'd responded by mocking him for being lazy for the next *two weeks*. He'd kept his mouth shut after that. After knowing them for months, he was still constantly surprised by how ignoble the two lords acted. They were of a well-respected—albeit new—house and should act according to their station. They were obviously educated and were no doubt aware of Court standards. He also knew, however, that there was a better chance of convincing a rock that it was a fish, and he let it lie.

"My Lords," came a young voice from his side. The three of them looked down from their perches at the young infantryman, wearing the standard non-combat uniform of the army.

*Glad to see something else is the same,* he thought looking at the orange trimmed uniform of deep blue.

"I've been ordered to show you to your quarters," the young man continued. *He must be a fresh recruit.* "If you would follow me."

Delvan unsaddled himself from his horse, petting her on the neck. "You're probably as happy to be rid of this saddle as I am," he said to her quietly before handing the reins to a nearby soldier.

"We need to unload first," said Kolden.

"We'll take care of your belongings and equipment, my Lord," said the man. "No need to exert yourselves."

"Who told them we were lords?" grumbled Orne as he stepped down from the wagon.

"I don't want anyone touching my gear," said Kolden protectively.

*He's probably worried about the cadentite,* thought Delvan. *Which I still need to discuss with him.*

"I assure you, my Lord, that we will treat it with the utmost care. Please, if you'll follow me."

Kolden reluctantly hopped down from his horse, warily looking towards the wagon with his gear. "Fine," he said after a brief hesitation, and the three of them followed the young soldier into the barracks. Before they entered, however, Delvan caught sight of the commander being led by the captain to a building across the street. It was clean and well kept, and Delvan assumed it to be apartments for officers.

*At least we're not in the same building,* thought Delvan.

They were led up a flight of stairs to the second floor, the interior the pristine clean that was a standard of the army. They were presented to three separate rooms adjacent to one another, allocated for each of them. It wasn't as spacious as the quarters he'd had in Calentine, but the furnishings were adequate, and compared to the tent he'd spent the last six months in, it was a castle. He nodded, contented, but noticed there was no bath or cleaning area.

Kolden let out a whistle as he walked to his door. "Wow," he said, "we don't even have to share a room? Maybe I could get used to this."

"Mhm," grunted Orne satisfactorily.

"Why are there no baths?" asked Delvan, desperately needing to be rid of the stink of horse and sweat.

"There is a bathhouse one street north," said their guide.

They looked at him, confused. Bathhouses weren't uncommon by any means, but Delvan had always found them to be patriarchal social clubs more than anything else, and he wished for nothing other than quiet time to think.

"Oh, right," said the soldier. "I've heard things are different in the west, although I can't imagine having personal baths in your home. What a waste of water."

He proceeded to explain the workings of the bathhouses to the gaping trio. This surely couldn't be the truth, could it? Was this some form of hazing set up by the local garrison for the newly arrived soldiers?

The first trunks of their gear were brought in while they listened, Kolden's scrupulous and untrusting eyes watching all the while. They were provided with fresh uniforms—Delvan's a sky blue compared to Orne and Kolden's deeper shade—their filthy armor and gear being taken by a squire for a thorough wash. It seemed an uncomfortable concept for the brothers, Orne especially protective of his equipment. Delvan was flushed with relief, a few amenities would give him the freedom he required.

The young soldier offered to guide them to the bathhouse, which Delvan still assumed would be prepared with some sort of ritualistic prank. *Men and women bathing together? Surely he's joking.* But much to all their surprise, it became quickly apparent that their host had been truthful in his explanation, and in the bathhouse, they found men and women alike bathing and casually chatting as if it were a mundane experience.

*These people are so* strange, he thought.

Orne strutted like a plumed bird as he walked down the aisle, turning heads as they walked to a much-needed bath. Kolden was quite the opposite, fidgeting in visible discomfort as they walked between the massive, steaming tubs. Delvan's eyes caught a small group of attractive women nearby, his attention drawn by seeing them in a state of undress. It wasn't that he wanted to stare in some perverted sense, but rather he found himself looking at them with prejudices abandoned. Their hair was lush and wavy, their eyes large and dark, and he didn't for a moment stop to consider what house they were born into, what status their parents or siblings held, what the gossip might be if he were seen with them. He only cared, in that sliver of time, that they were beautiful.

It was... freeing.

He smiled at them as he walked by, doing his best to maintain polite eye contact. But instead of returning his gesture, they gawked themselves. Not at him, but at the large sapphire hanging from his neck, their faces a mixture of curiosity, wonderment, and what he could only describe as fear.

Delvan's shoulders and head sank like a deflating water bladder. In Calentine—most of the kingdom for that matter—the sight of a sapphire would be met with veneration. Here he was stared at as if a walking legend, something from stories to keep children in line lest they misbehave.

*Have they so little experience with Blues? I wonder how many are even in the city?* he thought. To his dismay, he sensed no other Blues within the confines of the bathhouse, and aside from the commander, he recalled the barracks feeling as desolate as the arid land beyond.

The bath, despite the strangeness of the experience, was pure luxury. They soaked until their fingers and toes pruned, and then soaked some more, adding handfuls of the dried soaps to the deep tub. Orne complained about the fragrance, but Delvan ignored him, taking in the first pleasant experience he'd had in months as the bliss that it was.

He felt the thick humidity upon his skin, the weightlessness of floating providing buoyancy for his body and concerns. The narrow skylights kept the space comfortably dim, and his thoughts wandered like a boat upon a river, the estuary finally becoming straight and wide after a long journey of twists and confusing branches. He wished the sensation to last forever, but alas, one could only hide away for a time.

Eventually they left the bathhouse and returned to their quarters, the day having shifted to evening. Bells tolled in a grand synchrony, and the masses flooded the streets. They seemed to be heading to speaks, but Delvan wasn't inclined to the same reverence, not now anyway. The removal of the grime and stench which had become a daily part of his life these past months cleansed not only his flesh, but his mind. He was approaching his upcoming conundrum with fresh eyes and ideas and began to concoct an approach to his bargaining with the guild. They were, after all, businessmen, and what did businessmen do more often than negotiate?

He settled back into his quarters, his armor now cleaned and polished upon a rack in the corner. He sat at the small writing desk in another corner of his room, pulling a piece of parchment from the nearby tray and mixing some ink. He held the quill above the blank page, feeling apprehensive as he considered his wording.

There was an internal urge against such drastic measures. But his anger, the betrayal, the loss, burned hotter and deeper than the cold reasoning. Nonetheless, perhaps cautious discretion would be prudent.

In the dwindling light, he began to scribe the anonymous letter.

# Chapter Forty-Four



The attic space of the church was beginning to become stifling, the stagnant air hanging like an invisible cloud. Soft light filtered through the thin linen shades, the faint beams of light highlighting the dust floating in the air. It shined through the single, circular window, centered in the wall beneath the peak of the vaulted roof above. Desnia sat on a small, worn cot, her back against the short wall beneath the ceiling's rafters, waiting quietly while Nerio knelt.

He, like so many others in the devout city, insisted on praying twice a day for some ridiculous reason. As if the gods were going to respond to them because of their superfluous piety. She knew better than most, if a god wanted something of you, you'd know it.

Nerio had been appalled at her lack of reverence, but saving his life had earned her significant leeway, and while he made a few off-hand comments, he mostly left the subject alone. She'd assured him she prayed in her own way, which was *technically* true, but it was a stretch, even by her standards. Masini had gotten a laugh out of that.

"Are you sure that Jerdine isn't going to find you up here?" she asked, shifting uncomfortably and feeling a glob of sweat crawl down her back.

Nerio peeked from the corner of his eye, but kept his head bowed. "I was a disciple with the brother of this church's head priest, both of us under the principle. It is known that he detests Jerdine, for reasons similar to my own, hence his assignment to the decrepit church on the outskirts of town. I do not believe he will willingly expose my location to him."

Nerio stood up and tied his white sash around his waist after he finished praying. "What are you doing?" asked Desnia.

"I am going to the Asylum," he said. "Their need of me has not lessened, despite recent... events."

*Wow,* said Masini, *he's almost as stubborn as you are.*

"Sit down," said Desnia. "You're not going anywhere, not for at least a few days anyway."

"I must—"

"No! They know you're going to go back there. If you want to avoid Jerdine, that means avoiding the Asylum and anywhere else he might expect to find you. Now sit!"

He shuffled to the cot on the other wall, sitting on it with his head hung low. She felt like she'd just kicked a stray. Communicating well with others—for an extended period at least—was not her strong suit. She was still amazed she'd managed as long as she had with Claudion.

"Look," she said, "you said yourself that Jerdine was going to have someone else there to replace you, right? They should be fine. We have other things to worry about."

*Impending desolation is a bit of a concern,* said Masini.

"I can't just leave them there," he said, sullen, his eyes on the floor.

She squeezed her eyes shut and tilted her head back until it hit the wall behind her. She took a deep breath of the dusty air, letting it out with a resigned sigh. He needed something to console his fears, but how far was she willing to go for the priest?

"I'd go if I could," she said, her eyes opening and staring at the ceiling's rafters. "But I have to go to the Devapuram in the mornings, otherwise Gruthga will pull my rations. And then I have cleaning duty, which is going to be as miserable as this heat. But you can't risk going anywhere that you're expected, hell even I'm taking a risk after what I did with the general."

It was the truth, but she was glad for the excuse to not go. She detested that place. It was a living testimony to the numb hatred that men held against that which they didn't understand, a culmination of her worst fears. A part of her worried she'd enter and never leave, becoming a resident among the misunderstood tenants. But the light that shone in Nerio's eyes, the eagerness to help, and pain that he couldn't, ripped at her guts.

*Damn him.*

"I… I understand," he said with eyes welling with tears that were larger than the globs of sweat on his forehead. "But I can't stay here forever, either. I hate to ask more of you, you've done so much, but I am at a loss as to what to do next."

*You and me both,* she thought, lolling her head to the side.

There was a discussion to be had regarding that topic, one she had been yet to broach. Each time she tried to bring it up, her tongue became tied, her wits failing her. How was she supposed to ask about finding this gate without saying, "The voices in my head told me to."

*I sound insane…*

There was—at least as Masini put it—little time left. She had to ask soon. She closed her eyes again, squeezing them tightly in wrinkled bunches, the stuffy attic causing sweat to drip down her face. How was she to ask something of Nerio? He had been through an ordeal that she hated to imagine, one she herself had feared succumbing to and seen committed by the atrocious pigs in power, like Jerdine. But she couldn't sit stagnant forever.

"I'm going to help you Nerio," she said. She winced as she continued, "But I need help myself, and you're the only person I know that I think can."

*Because you know so many people,* cracked Masini.

*He is* not *helping,* she thought.

"Anything!" Nerio said eagerly. How innocently loyal he seemed to be. "Whatever you ask, Desnia, I will do my utmost to help. I am in your debt."

"Would you please shut up about that," she rubbed her slick forehead as regret struck her before the words finished leaving her tongue. "Sorry, I'm just not used to people… being like this. I'm looking for something, or, well, more accurately I'm looking for how to reach something."

Masini had explained to her, in his stuttering, roundabout way, that the gate had previously been where the city's center now was. After spending a few hours attempting to explain this, all while he was blabbering like a toddler learning to speak, she'd come to the conclusion that the gate was likely near the Devapuram or clergy house. After weeks of searching, however, she'd found nothing.

*What am I supposed to do when I get in there?* she wondered. *I don't know anything about how to stop this thing from opening, or whatever it does.* She would worry about that later, it wouldn't matter if she couldn't figure out how to reach the damn place. One thought kept her moving forward, one sparkle of hope: *Maybe, if I do this, I can get this 'god' to stop the pain, to ensure I don't end up like... them.*

"Part of the reason that I ran to Brethefen was, uh, something I'd heard," she said, delicately selecting her words. "That something was hidden away in the heart of the city. Something of incredible value. I'm trying to figure out how to find it."

"There are many items of value in the city's center, what do you mean exactly?" he asked.

"It would be hidden, something that a group of very dangerous people would want to keep away from prying eyes." Desnia's eyes roved as she thought about what she would do to hide something like this gate. "Maybe even in a basement, or under the Devapuram somehow."

"Beneath the Devapuram?" asked Nerio with a tilt of his head. "I'm not aware of anything beneath the sanctum. If there is something there, I've never heard of it."

"It's there," she reassured, confident now that she thought about it. Too many people had access to all parts of the city. The entrance would need to be close, somewhere they could keep an eye on it at all times. Though she still wasn't certain who *they* were. Masini had yet to be forthcoming with that information. "Are there any underground tunnels, deep basements, or sewers beneath the city? Anything like that?" She thought back to the Calentine sewers, shuddering.

*It was most definitely* above *ground, last I saw it,* said Masini. She ignored him for now, she'd looked everywhere he'd recommended to no avail.

"Sewers, yes, but not anything that you can access, not that I'm aware of. And our basements are not dug overly deep, since there is a shelf of shallow stone a few feet down. I'm sorry, but if something was built underground to house this treasure, it has been lost. I suppose I could check the library, if you needed."

"No," she said, shaking her head and sighing again. "You shouldn't go there, and besides, I doubt anything about this is written down anywhere."

*What am I doing?* she wondered. *How am I supposed to find something hidden away centuries ago?*

"Can you tell me more about what it is that you're looking for?" he asked.

"Not really," she said. "I've heard it was called a 'gate', but other than that I don't know much."

*Sorry about that,* said Masini. He wasn't one to apologize often, but they both knew if he could speak to the subject this would be a lot easier. Whoever the man was that gave him to her clearly hadn't thought through what a hindrance a restriction like his would be. Could he not have removed the inlaid pattern? She'd have to ask later, but she suspected it was unlikely.

"Please, tell me whatever you can," pleaded Nerio. "The gods themselves wanted me to find you, this must be the reason why. I have to believe that, otherwise a man's last words are just meaningless ravings, a waste of a good man and life. I can't accept that, he must have heard instructions, a last command for me to find you."

"He heard something..." she mumbled.

*He raises a good point, actually,* said Masini. *Your dreaming dialoguer wouldn't have told that Seer Nerio found dead to practice his penmanship just to give the priest a waste of a message. He must know something or be able to help you in some way.*

Masini was probably right. The voice was often ambiguous, but always spoke to a purpose, at least in her experience. Fortunately, it was one she hadn't endured for some time now. She still wasn't sure why that was, but she wasn't about to complain.

"Desnia," Nerio asked, his fingers threaded and thumbs fiddling, "can I ask you something?"

"I don't see why not," she said.

"I... I didn't want to ask before, but you said something, on the belltower. Something about the Seers in the Asylum. I didn't want to press the matter, but you're foreign, and I don't know how you could possibly—"

"What are you asking?" she said through narrowed eyes.

"You said they heard *a* voice."

Her insides felt like they'd been wrung, her head lifting from the wall and staring at him with wider eyes, breaths through her nose becoming rapid.

"Isn't that what people say? That they hear voices?" she asked, feigning ignorance.

"Well, yes, but something less known—that even most of the clergy doesn't know—is that, at least based on what I've heard in my years there, they only hear *one*. A singular voice that speaks to them, telling them things that get repeated. People who've never met come in and recite quotes word for word with others who've long since passed away. Jerdine has us keep records of it, but I don't know where they go, they're not in the library. He's never explained why, either.

"I've wondered who it is they're hearing, how such a thing can be possible, and my mind is filled with blasphemous thoughts."

Desnia had pulled her knees to her chest, wrapping her arms around them—a natural and unconscious reaction. *Does he know?*

"It's said," continued Nerio, "that only the King can commune with the gods. The principles, who're the King's chosen, attempt to hear them through the use of iguan, but I understand that even this is muddled and unclear for them.

"I wonder: what if there are others, like the King? Ones who can speak with the gods, or perhaps just one of them? But this goes against everything I've been taught, combatting the core doctrine of the church. I pray for forgiveness each time one of these thoughts intrudes upon me, begging for the gods to absolve me of my ignorance. But you knew. How?"

*He's got you caught with your dick in a goat on this one,* said Masini.

She tried to still the trembling in her core, taking a deep breath to calm her wavering lungs. She didn't want to lie to him, he didn't deserve that. But she couldn't tell him the truth. Despite everything that had happened to her over the last few months, she still found her throat choking if she tried to discuss it out loud.

"I'd... rather not talk about it," she said, quietly, only a faint quiver in her voice.

Nerio opened his mouth to speak, but thankfully stopped himself and nodded, his head hanging low again. It hurt to see him abashed, his emotions still raw like an exposed wound, but she couldn't do it. She couldn't say the words. They sat there in silence, and it occurred to her that she would have to leave soon to make it to the Devapuram for—

Her head jerked upright with a realization. "Nerio," she said energetically, "you said 'anything *built*'."

"What?" he asked.

"You said you didn't know of anything *built* underground," she said, now leaning forward on her cot. "Is there something else, under the city?"

"Of course," he said, "the caverns that serve as the city's reservoirs. Pumps in all the bathhouses and wells are connected to them, but I've never heard of anyone managing to go down *into* them. There are no entrances."

"Huh," she said, "strange that the one who told me about this thing I'm looking for never mentioned that."

*Hey!* said Masini. *I only came through the thing once, and visited once more later and there was nothing above or around it, alright? I don't remember seeing any caverns. Also, this was more years ago than you probably know how to count to. I'd like to see you remember every detail of your adolescence after a few thousand inebriated summers.*

"But like I said," replied Nerio, "I don't know how to access them. I didn't even think you could."

Desnia sighed. It was something. A useless something, but more information than she'd had, nonetheless. *Now what?* she wondered.

"Thanks anyway," she said, standing and tying the white sash around her waist. She made for the door after saying goodbye, it was a long walk to the Devapuram and she was already going to be late. The trek would serve as a good time to get some other questions answered though.

"Masini," she said as she strode through the church's front doors into the hard shadows of the searing morning. The air was carried by a slight breeze, and despite the heat it felt like a respite compared to the stuffy attic. "This isn't working. We're never going to find an entrance to these caverns unless by dumb fucking luck. I haven't seen a single open well since arriving here, they're all hand pumps, and I can't exactly fit down a pipe."

*Hmm,* he said.

"What?"

*Huh? Oh, nothing, I just feel like there was a really good joke in there somewhere, but I was coming up blank.*

"Gods-damn it!" she said a little too loudly, a few nearby heads turning and glaring with blasphemous ire. "Damn it, Masini," she said more quietly, "I need ideas, not fucking jokes."

*We just need to keep looking, I'm sure we'll find an entrance.*

"No, not good enough. You say we're in a rush, but we've been searching for weeks and finding *nothing*. We need a different approach."

The streets were packed with people leaving the various churches, heading to their different jobs and responsibilities. Their robes were nearly as colorful as the buildings, the mud-brick pavers seemingly the only earthen tone the eye could see. That was, at least, until you saw her white robe, or that of a pair of priests that walked past her, reminding her of a question.

"Tell me about Jerdine," she said, trying to keep her voice low in the crowd.

*What?* Masini asked.

"Jerdine. You freaked out when we went near his office trying to help Nerio. Why?"

*I don't know if I'd say, 'freaked out,' more just a precautionary—*

"Horse shit," she interrupted. "You know him. You're *scared* of him. Why?"

There was a vacuum of silence, filled by the chatter of the surrounding crowd. Not even a retort came from the normally verbose ring.

"Masini, what aren't you—"

*He's like me,* he finally responded.

"What? You mean, like, from… wherever it is you came from? The other side of the gate?"

*Yes,* he said tersely. *Used to go by Ree-Ree-Ree.. ugh, a different name. But we were both sent here on the same assignment.*

"And *why* am I just hearing this now? Do you realize how useful this information is? We can follow him, break into his office, he's surely going to be able to lead us—"

*No!* It was as much a scream as she'd ever heard from him. *No, Desnia, under no circumstances are you to go near him. We will find another way.*

There was a tremor to his voice, a tone of vile disgust and hatred. She could tell that this was something he was vehement about, a finality in his voice.

"Masini," she said, "there *is* no other way. I can only imagine what he's capable of, knowing what he did to Nerio, and I'm not sure what has you so scared of him, but you recruited me to help you. Do you think I *wanted* to accept that a fucking ring was talking to me? Do you think that I robbed that vault because I thought it was simple and safe? Nothing worth doing is ever easy, Masini, and you need to accept that we don't have a choice in this."

*You don't understand,* he said, his voice dark and low, *he's the one who's leading the charge to get my people home. He sends his pet to hunt us, but he pulls the strings, the dark puppeteer of our demise. He's consigned many of my friends to fates worse than death, with a lucky few finding a quick end, and he won't hesitate to do the same to you.*

"All the more reason to follow him!" exclaimed Desnia. "We could probably have found the entrance by now!"

*No! He'd know. I assure you, Des, that he would know. The things he could do... You can't imagine, you don't want to imagine. He's a sick, twisted, putrid waste of air. He's driven by dark ambition and jaded by this r-r-r-ugh, place. I don't care how talented you are, Des, if you try to steal from him, or follow him, he will catch you. We're the only hope for this... place, I can't let you throw this chance away.*

"*What* are you so scared of?" she asked, frustrated.

*Death!* blurted Masini. *Death, alright! I've almost died once, Des, and it is* not *an experience I want to endure a second time. I want to help, but not... not if it involves* him...

She stopped, her sandals scuffing against the sandy brick. She'd never heard such candor from Masini, and to an extent she knew his pain. Empathized with it. But now it was clear that it was her turn to convince him.

"Will any of that matter if he opens the gate?" she asked.

*No,* he said slowly. *No, it won't.*

"If we don't do this, and they come through, they're going to find you anyway, right? Along with me?"

*Highly probable, yes.*

"Then I'm going to follow him. There's no other way, unless you have any other information that you'd like to share."

*Fine,* he said after a pause. *But, Des, you have to be careful. He can do more damage with one finger than an army led to conquer.*

"I bet, as a ring, that gets you rather excited."

*Did... Did you just make a joke? he asked, astonished. I don't believe my silvery ears. Alright, I suppose I can die now, Desnia has cracked a joke, the stars have aligned, and the world is going to end anyways. But in all seriousness, if I still had a body I'd have a raging erection right now.*

She rolled her eyes as she began walking again, turning and weaving through the crowd. At least now there was something she could plan. It was a ludicrous plan, but those tended to be her specialty.

# Chapter
# Forty-Five


*Unity through bonds*
*Violence through separation*
*The chaos of life*
*Havoc and gravitation*

*A*re all *of these people going to morning speaks?* thought Delvan as he, Orne, and Kolden flowed with the dense crowd, pressed together in the organized madness with everyone who walked along the street. Even the confined streets of Calentine were barely more crowded than this sprawling city's, and he again found himself baffled by the strange culture.

They broke from the river of people into the welcoming frontage of a small tea stand, the awning above shielding them from the onslaught of the sun's brutal presence. They weren't in a hurry to reach their destination, and Delvan had other concerns, so it was a welcomed stop to their little excursion.

None of them had heard of most of the teas available, deciding to order whatever the elderly man recommended with his wrinkled smile. They sat on backless chairs, waiting in hopes that the packed street would thin before they set back out.

"Who the hell drinks hot liquid in the desert?" asked Orne with a raised eyebrow and sneer, looking at the small cup in his gigantic hand.

"I think it's pretty good," replied Kolden, sipping his with a slurp.

"Says the guy who stands in front of a blazing forge all day," grumbled Orne.

Delvan sipped his own and found himself agreeing with Orne, but to prevent an hour-long argument, kept his preferences to himself.

After being given a few days of leave, the trio had decided to visit the wonder that was the Devapuram but had only made it halfway to the domed sanctum, spending most of the time working their way through overly crowded streets. It was considered one of the greatest monuments in the kingdom, and freedom to rejoin civilian life for a brief respite presented an opportunity to experience it firsthand. The congested traffic of people made the walk slow, but after months spent on horseback Delvan was enjoying getting use out of his legs again. He wasn't certain if they'd be able to take horses down the packed thoroughfare anyway, and now that he thought about it, he was fairly certain he'd only seen donkeys on the street.

The clear sunlight gave the paints of the walls around them a radiant shimmer, so bright that Delvan nearly had to squint as he watched the people walk by. His eyes followed them, still trying to adjust to their strange garbs as he sipped on the florally fragranced drink. His watching soon slowed, and gaze looked toward the horizon as if he were able to see through the mud-brick building before him.

His focus gravitated to the letter in his pocket, the unsigned request for a mutually beneficial exchange folded and sealed within. He wasn't sure if the Merchants' Guild would see it the same way he did, they might say it was extortion. They did deals like this countless times per day, surely they would come to see it as the negotiation that it was.

Or so he hoped.

There was one matter that still needed to be resolved.

Delvan put his tea on the table, "Kolden, I wanted to ask you something."

"What's that?" Kolden asked, slurping his tea again.

"It's about," he said, leaning forward and speaking in a whisper, "the cadentite."

The slurping stopped, Kolden's eyes flicking to Delvan and then his surroundings. Orne sat straighter, also suspiciously glancing around from atop the chair that he made seem to be sized for a child. Delvan understood their vigilance, his instincts were afire with caution, constantly looking over his shoulder as a tingling sensation skittered along his neck. No one had stuck out as following them, but in this crowd, it would be impossible to tell.

They were being watched, he was certain of it. And it would seem the brothers were of the same opinion.

"I don't know if this is the place to talk about it…" said Kolden, keeping his eyes darting among the crowd.

"There's no other time," whispered Delvan, "we can't discuss it at the barracks, and I need to talk to you. I have a plan."

"A *plan*?" said Kolden. "Del, I appreciate it, but I'm sure I can figure out something to do with it."

"Shut up, Kolden," said Orne. "Let's hear what he has to say."

Kolden shook his head and rolled his eyes but didn't comment further.

"I think I have something that gets us all what we want," said Delvan. "If we take the stone to the Merchants' Guild, we can exchange it for—"

"The *guild*?" said Kolden, his head snapping towards Delvan. "If we take it to them, they're going to think *we* stole it. The only thing they'll give us as payment is a realigned neck."

"Guild's a bad idea," said Orne, his brow deeply furrowed.

"Just hear me out," said Delvan raising his hands placatingly. "I have a letter, anonymous and ready to send, which explains that we have it and approximately how it came into our possession. I left out the major details that might allude to who we are, but it should be enough to absolve us and incriminate the commander.

"We get them to agree to meet us, in a location of our choosing that allows us to ensure they come alone, and give them the cadentite for what we want."

"And what, exactly, is that?" asked Kolden.

"For you? Use of their influence to get you transferred to whatever station you want."

"And you?" asked Orne.

Delvan hesitated, biting his tongue. He knew how they were going to respond, but he was going to be honest with them. As much as he dared, anyway. "Their assistance… with capturing and interrogating the commander," he said.

Kolden nearly spit out a mouthful of tea. "Are you *insane*?!" he hissed. "Del, that's treason! Fuck, this *discussion* is treason. The man is a bastard, a murderer—"

"A cheat," interjected Orne.

"—and more. But Del, if he's going to pay for his crimes, it needs to be through the Court. We can't vigilante this, no matter how well connected the guild might be."

"He needs to pay," said Delvan, his eyes hard and resolve sound. The Court wouldn't do anything about it, he was certain of it, and there was no one else that could hold someone of his station accountable.

"Yes, but..." said Kolden. "Listen, even if we convince them that we didn't steal the stone, and they don't betray us out of spite for extorting them for *their* property, and *then* we persuade them to help you, you *still* have to somehow capture and question another Blue! Then what? Huh?"

Despite the wafting heat, Delvan felt ice chill his heart. He didn't look at Kolden, but again adorned the distant stare, his thoughts consumed by the hatred he felt. His grip became tight around the small teacup, his jaw flexing tightly.

"The guild will want to deal with him, I assume," he replied. The frozen heart within him wanted more, desired to make the traitor's end more personal, but that wasn't a discussion to have with the brothers.

"This is a bad idea," said Orne, shaking his head. "We should bury it in a hole and be done with it."

"Think about it," said Delvan, "it's too valuable to not use for our own gain. This thing is worth more than entire duchies, the guild will laud us for returning it. They'll be so deeply indebted to us for its return that they will be obliged to acquiesce. Beyond that, Hil was a legacy to one of their most senior members. If I tell them that I have testimony and proof of who was responsible for his death, I have no doubt that they would help me."

Kolden and Orne shifted uncomfortably in their seats, the wooden joints creaking. Orne had a scowl on his face, which was common and unreadable, but it did appear deeper and more roughly cut than normal. Kolden held his chin, staring at the ground.

"Look," continued Delvan, "I'll be the only one communicating with them. I won't even tell them you're involved. Once I have their assurances and favor, I'll ask for your transfer. You'll be kept out of all of it."

"You think that your friend's father can protect us if we do this?" asked Kolden.

"This is a stupid fucking idea," repeated Orne.

"Hil spoke highly of him, that's all the assurance that I need." Delvan tried not to let the doubt seep into his voice. *This will work. It has to work.* If it didn't, then what was Hilbrun's death but a callous waste of life?

"You're just going to do this anyway if we say no, aren't you?" asked Kolden.

Delvan didn't respond. He just stared at Kolden, feeling the ice crawl from his chest into his eyes. Kolden sighed, digging his hand into his face. He groaned through a sweat covered palm.

"There's nothing in it that describes who we are, just a time and place to meet tomorrow," said Delvan.

"How were you going to get it to them?" asked Kolden.

"What do you mean?" asked Delvan, confused. "I was going to give it to a carrier."

Kolden smacked his head and Orne's glare intensified.

"Del, for someone so fucking smart, you sometimes say really stupid shit," said Kolden.

"What?" he asked, his arms splaying out.

"Seriously?" asked Orne. "You're a fucking Blue, Del. You stand out like piss in snow. If you give it to a carrier, all the guild has to do is ask who sent it to them and they'll immediately identify you. Gods, are you sure you've thought this through? Fuck. Let's just bury the damn thing."

*Damn, they have a point. How had I not thought about that?* he wondered. He had never been one who stood out, being a Blue drew attention, true, but among the nobles of the Upper Tier, it wasn't uncommon. Given the apparent scarcity of Blues in Brethefen, he could see how he'd be memorable.

"If you're set on doing this, then give me the letter," Kolden said, holding out his hand. "I'll go pay a street kid to deliver it, they're less noticeable and probably not in the pocket of the guild. Probably."

"I still think this is a terrible fucking idea. I know he was your friend, Del, but this is suicide."

"I'm doing this, with or without your help," he said, the ice in his voice now. Cadentite or not, he was going to make Ferrand pay.

Kolden looked at his brother for a moment, then snatched the sealed envelope from Delvan's hand. "I'll be back," he said as he stood and walked away, leaving Delvan holding his tea, where tiny bubbles had begun forming.

An hour later they were walking up the white stairs to the pillars of the Devapuram. The walk through the bustling streets as they approached the massive building had been absent a word from any of them. Delvan knew they were upset with him, concerned for him even, but this wasn't something he could let go. He wanted answers, he wanted to bring Ferrand pain that was so severe it would erase his own from his mind.

It was in the hands of the guild now. He had no choice but to wait and hope that eventually the brothers would come to understand his decision. He checked over his shoulder again, getting that same strange sensation along his neck. He searched for faces that might have been there since they left the tea stand, but in a crowd with so many journeying in the same direction, it was impossible to discern.

*Someone* was following them, he just couldn't pick them from the crowd.

*Probably one of Ferrand's lackeys,* he thought.

His inquisitive gaze scanned the crowds, but it was hard to keep it from the Devapuram. It had seemed large from a distance, but up close it was beyond what he could have imagined. Only the King's Tower was impressive enough an engineering feat to compare, and having grown up around the great spire made him indifferent to it, never mesmerizing quite like this.

People were removing offerings from the bases of the forest of pillars, a small army of aides laboring to return the polished stone floors to their lustrous splendor. Priests projected their voices in prayer, small crowds gathered around them.

"This is fucking impressive," said Orne as he and Kolden craned their necks to the curved, muraled ceiling.

They meandered as they gazed, the normally blinding sun reflecting off the smooth white pillars with a peaceful radiance. Eventually they found themselves at the heart of the garden of columns, entering the tall cylindrical room that stretched to the ceiling. The smell of incense pungently hung in the hazy air, and yet again the trio were left breathless by the sight of the five carved figures within.

The brothers joked about the indecency of the statues, much to the condemnation of priests and worshippers alike. While their voices echoed off the curved walls, Delvan stood in silence. He stared at the figure of Almedia, a replicate sapphire held in her outstretched hand.

He touched his hand to his chest, feeling the hard gem beneath his shirt, basking in its warm embrace. His heart was torn, he knew it, ignoring it for months, but it remained all the same. In a way he was glad for the contempt held in it, it numbed the pain, drove him to move forward. Beneath the ocean of abhorrence, his soul screamed, drowned and begged him to give it breath.

He couldn't. Not yet. Not while the man responsible for Hilbrun's death roamed free. Forcing him to face the repercussions of his actions would drain the hatred from him. It had to.

He closed his eyes and felt the world move around him, hearing the shuffling of feet, the crackling of dried herbs being set alight. There was something, not a scream of his own pain or his deference to it, but an urge, like an invisible hand resting on his shoulder, comforting, consoling. The hair on the back of his neck rose again. What *was* that...

There was something else—faint, as though distant, but recognizable.

*Could that... No, he wouldn't be so brazen. Who is it then?*

His eyes snapped open, and he turned, jogging out of the circular room. He passed two priests on either side of the intricate doors and spun his head from side to side, searching between the endless pattern of pillars. He squeezed his eyes shut and concentrated, reaching, sensing.

*There.*

He turned to his right, weaving between the carved columns and through beams of light that speared the narrow gaps in their many layers. His boots chirped against the polished floor as he sharply banked left or right, dodging surprised parishioners, seeking the flicker in the distance. He couldn't explain why he was rushing, other than the feeling that the consoling hand now propelled him with, an urgency that he surrendered to.

Shouts came from behind—probably Orne and Kolden trying to call to him or the people he rushed past—but he ignored it, his all-consuming purpose to find what lay on the fringes of his senses. He rounded a pillar, a glimpse of someone fleeing behind another catching the corner of his eye, the light reflecting off them like a beacon. He ran. Ran as fast as his legs could be willed to move, the falling of his feet echoing strangely among the stone supports.

Around the perimeter of the dome's roots he gave chase, avoiding supplicants and orators alike as he twisted his body and tried to maintain balance. He gasped for breath, his lungs on fire as he sprinted around the endless curve between pillars.

White streaked past him in blurs of motion, his vision tunneling as he darted between the crowds and pillars. His hard landing feet echoed strangely off the smooth stone, though he hardly heard it over the wind rushing over his ears. They were there, just beyond the edges of his sight, like a dream freshly forgotten that he longed to recall.

A scream came from ahead, clear and piercing. Delvan skidded to a stop as he came upon Orne standing there, Kolden panting heavily with his hands on his knees, and someone kicking and flailing as they tried to escape the clamp of Ornes oversized arm pressing them against his side.

Golden locks of hair tossed in a flurry, and there was a glint of silvery metal as the woman pulled something from the sash of her white robe. Delvan tried to shout, his hand reaching forward and eyes wide. Panic struck him as he thought the small blade would find its way to Orne's gut, but the man grabbed her wrist in an impressive display of reactive quickness, squeezing it and shaking until the knife clattered to the floor, his face unphased.

"What... the hell... Del..." said Kolden between breaths.

"Why were you chasing this girl?" asked Orne. "Was she the one following us?"

He didn't have an answer for Orne, because he didn't know himself. With deep, rapid breaths he walked forward towards the girl, who was frantically kicking and punching at Orne at awkward angles. She screamed, "It wasn't me! Let me go you fucking giant! I won't let you take me back there, I'll fucking die first you—"

Delvan stopped mid stride, his muscles freezing and face going pale as the girl's head whipped back, tossing her hair from her face. Blue eyes stared back at him like glistening jewels, their wide glare dragging his specter from the ground and strangling his heart. Pain shot through his arm, neck, and jaw as his body began to forget how to function, his already racing heart breathing faster as he struggled for air.

*It can't be*, he thought as memories of that night coursed through him, his mind reliving the fires, the expression on Hilbrun's face as he fell. His emotional dam burst, threatening to overwhelm him with tidal force, destroying everything in its path. Here, on the other side of the kingdom, among nearly a million people, he'd found something he thought lost.

"You..." he said to the equally frozen girl, their eyes locked together in shock. Time seemed to stand still, the warm air as unmoving as the stone around them. His mind struggled to accept what it was seeing.

"You mind telling us what's going on?" asked Kolden, looking between the two of them, their mouths open.

"This," Delvan rasped as he struggled to breath, his body crying out that it was dying, "is the, uh, girl from the vault. The one that was there when Hil..."

He couldn't finish the sentence, his vision beginning to blur from the pain and heart attempting to burst from his chest. He reached a shaking hand out and leaned against a nearby column, his eyes never breaking from the silent woman. *This must be someone else, it's impossible.* But he knew. Her hair was longer now, her skin tanner and red from the sun, but it was her.

"Del, you alright?" asked Kolden, walking over to him.

He took a deep, trembling breath and nodded. He wanted to close his eyes and just breathe, but he couldn't take them off the deep wells of sky blue looking back at him. Her eyes were wide, but her face was pained, a vague mirror of his own. He didn't sense anger in her gaze, but there was *something* about her, strange and unfamiliar. Where had he felt that before?

"Pu-Put her down, Orne," he said, quivering atop shaking legs.

"You sure?" Orne asked.

Delvan nodded as he leaned his back against the cool stone of the column, his knees struggling to keep him upright. Orne removed his arm from around the girl's stomach and she tore herself away, reaching down in a smooth and fluid motion to grab her fallen blade—which looked to be little more than a sharpened eating utensil. She took two steps and turned, pointing the knife with an outstretched arm at Orne and Kolden. Delvan noticed she never pointed it at him, and a fraction of his pain faded.

*She's not running away.*

"I wouldn't recommend that," said Kolden, nodding at the blade held tightly towards him and Orne.

"Fuck you," she said.

Orne grunted with a mildly impressed, "Hmm." He didn't bother reaching for the sword at his side, his arms crossed.

"How did you find me?" she asked, keeping the knife forward but turning her head to Delvan.

"I didn't-I didn't mean to," said Delvan through shallow breaths. "I got assigned here af-after..." His jaw seized.

"You here to arrest me? To throw me in some cage to be displayed in the square while I'm tortured? Those bastards tried to kill me too, you know," she said, a harshness to her voice.

Delvan finally managed to draw breath into the bottom of his lungs, letting it out slowly and as evenly as he could. "I'm not interested in punishing the person who saved my life," he said. *Punishing another though...*

Her muscles relaxed, her posture less stiff, but she still kept the blade directed at the brothers. "You the one who dragged me out of there?" she said, her hand touching the back of her head.

Delvan nodded.

"Why'd you chase me then, huh?" she asked.

*She's an untrusting one, isn't she?* he thought. *A good mindset to have, I suppose.*

"I don't know," he said, honestly. He felt like he could be honest with her, regardless of her defensiveness. Maybe it was remembering her saving his life by taking another's during the blaze, a bond of blood. Or perhaps it was this persistent sense within him that he just *should*.

"I... I felt something," he said, "earlier, inside. I can't really explain it, it was like someone guided me, urging me forward."

Her eyes squeezed together as she grimaced. She muttered, "That bastard," under her breath before returning her wary eyes back on the brothers.

"What?" asked Delvan, wondering why she'd cursed at him.

"Nothing," she said with a shake of her head, "I didn't mean you, I... Never mind."

He saw Kolden raise a suspicious eyebrow but remain quiet.

"Were you the one following us?" asked Orne, mistrust set deeply into his eyes.

"Do I look fucking stupid to you?" she asked him with a sneer. "I don't follow people who could arrest me or might hold a grudge, *especially* when they're Blues. Not that it would be hard to follow *you*, you giant troll."

Orne glowered, his face turning a faint shade of red.

"You can put the knife down," Delvan said, "we're not going to hurt you. You're free to go, if you wish, but I'd be in your debt if you stayed." Here was an opportunity he never thought he'd see, a chance to glean more damning evidence against the commander—assuming he didn't pass out. He wiped cold sweat from his brow.

She hesitantly lowered the blade, taking another half step back. The area behind her was unobstructed, a clear lane to turn and sprint if she needed to. *She's careful.*

"How about you tell me what you want and, depending on what it is, I might consider us even," she said tersely.

"The ni-the night in the va-" his throat choked.

"What about it," she said with the same terse tone, looking him up and down as he grappled with the pain in the side of his body and chest, stabbing tingles running down his arm and thoughts bouncing through his head like lightning in a bottle.

He tried to steady his shaky breathing again, slowly inhaling. "Who hired you? Do you know anything about a knight that might have planned the robbery?"

She tilted her head, looking confused. "A knight? As in a Blue? No. Like I said, I typically avoid them, kind of a job haz—" she cut herself off, her eyes flicking down and to the side. After a moment she returned her beady gaze back to Delvan, and he saw Kolden's eyes narrow. "We were hired by someone I only met once, but I didn't even know he was our employer until later. I met him in an iguan den and never saw him again."

*An Iguan den?* he thought, remembering back to the man he chased, the strange encounter still confusing to him. She must have misunderstood the pondering expression on his face.

"I wasn't there to smoke it, asshole," she spat. "I was dropping something off after a job."

"What? No," said Delvan with a shake of his head, "I didn't think that. I was just remembering something."

*If it was the same iguan den as the one we raided,* thought Delvan, *then that would connect the man I chased and the commander as co-conspirators in the heist. But that would also mean...*

"Are... Are you the one we chased the night before, in the slum?"

"That *slum* was my home, privileged dickhead."

Orne let out an amused snort.

"Sorry," he said, his face turning an uncomfortable flush. If only it could just feel calm and normal. "I didn't mean... Is there anything else you can tell me? Please?"

"Not really. Sorry," she said, the corner of her lip tugging down in an almost remorseful expression. "I'd never worked with that crew before, I only met them a few days prior. Not sure it's the information you're looking for, but I don't think it was the money in that vault they were after. There were... more valuable treasures in there."

Orne and Kolden shared a glance, not one unnoticed by the blonde-locked woman.

"We're... aware," said Delvan. "That's all you know?"

"Yes. You happen to know if any of the backstabbing bastards got out of there? Wouldn't mind repaying them an overdue favor later, if any of the assholes are still alive."

"They're not," said Kolden confidently.

She looked at Kolden with a curious glance. "Good riddance to them, then. Now, if that's all you wanted, I'll be leaving. Don't take this the wrong way, but I hope I never have to see you again." She paused for a moment, biting her lip as if trying to stop herself from speaking. Finally, she said, "For what it's worth, I'm sorry about your friend."

Delvan rested his head against the pillar at his back as she spun on a heel and turned. Tears began to well in his eyes, a lump growing in his throat. He forced the emotions down, wiping his eyes dry.

Thinking back to what she'd said, he'd hoped for more information, but he'd at least learned something. Delvan felt his heart sink with an odd sense of regret as she stepped away, he wasn't quite sure why. Was it that she gave him some distant connection to Hilbrun? Or her sympathy when few others seemed to care?

His heart skipped a beat, however, when she came to a stop a few strides away, her back to them. She just stood there, and Delvan thought he could hear whispering. It was impossible to tell in the midst of the strange acoustics of the Devapuram.

She rubbed her forehead, hand on her hip. Eventually she let out a long sigh and turned around, walking back towards the trio.

"I... have something I want to ask of you," she said, now struggling to maintain eye contact with Delvan.

"I... I'll do what I can," said Delvan.

"I can't talk about it here," she said in a hushed tone. "Can you..." she seemed to struggle to speak, as though talking through a locked jaw. "Can you meet me later, alone?"

Both Orne and Kolden looked at him with an angry expression. He wasn't fluent in their unspoken dialect, but their directed ire could only mean one thing: *Don't you fucking dare.*

"Yes," he said with a nod. He saw Orne shake his head and Kolden roll his eyes. "Where?"

"There's an old church, near the north gate. Come before evening bells and we can talk then."

He nodded, and she turned, shaking her head. Why did she seem so upset?

"Wait!" he said as she walked away. She spun but remained a distance from him. "I never got your name," he said.

"Des," she said in her brusque way before turning and leaving, vanishing behind a pillar.

Delvan closed his eyes and realized that the pain in his arm and chest were gone, his mind having become calm. His nerves were frayed, but he breathed normally, and his face had lost its pallid tone.

When had that happened?

# CHAPTER
# FORTY-SIX



*See, that wasn't so hard, was it?* asked Masini as Desnia walked away from the Devapuram.

"I don't know if we can trust him," she said.

*The kid saved your life. Twice. And you're still unsure about his character?* asked Masini. *This is the greatest stroke of luck I've ever witnessed! I could have used some fortune like this one time in this Trethefen gambling parlor, speaking of stroking. I lost everything because the waitresses would crawl under the table and—*

"I don't think this is luck," she interrupted—it was best not to let him regale. "I think *he* had something to do with it."

This couldn't be a coincidence. It reeked of the voice's influence. It was bad enough when he plagued her dreams, sending her along this path with Masini, using her like an indentured servant. Now there was a Blue involved? When would the manipulations end?

*He'd better not be fucking lying to me,* she thought. What she wouldn't do to be free of the torturous agony endured during their encounters, and the potential results of too many of them.

*In that case,* said Masini, *all the better! If anyone is going to be able to stand against Jerdine—which I think is a terrible false name, by the way, yours are much better—it's one of the fi-fi-fi-fuck, a Blue like him. Together we might actually stand a chance, albeit a small one. Like an ant against a boot.*

She stopped in the middle of the street, the person behind her nearly bumping into her back. The boiling sun shadowed her eyes under a lowered brow of concern, heat rising along her legs from the warm bricks beneath her feet.

"You mean to say that a *Blue* would hardly stand a chance against Jerdine? The guy can spew literal *fire*. What is he going to do against that?"

*Well,* he said in a drawn-out way, *that sort of depends. Mostly on how many glowy rocks he has. And I'm not saying your friend's not powerful, quite the contrary considering his particular pair of abilities, but I think you're still underestimating Jerdine. Blues are full of extreme potential, it's just underdeveloped and somewhat unwieldy. We've had millennia to perfect our abilities, and eons of experience to reference and learn from. It's like a sword master challenging a toddler. And the toddler only has a stick. Actually, a stick might be generous.*

The assessment made Desnia feel like she'd just been punched in the gut. Masini had said how dangerous Jerdine was, but she'd taken his ravings as exaggerated tales. If he thought that a Blue—capable of destruction she was all too familiar with—wouldn't stand a chance against him, what hope did she have? Her breath left her, and shoulders sank as she stood in the street, contemplating.

She began walking again, her legs shuffling slowly under the weight of melancholy. She ignored the sounds of street vendors calling out, the chattering of passersby. *How am I going to do this?* she wondered. The plan for the afternoon had been to tail Jerdine, start to look for patterns in his movements and schedule.

But now that all felt moot.

*You, uh, there?* Masini asked.

"Why am I even *doing* this?!" she nearly shouted. It had been more a question for herself than Masini, an existential inquiry. Why had all of this fallen to *her*? Her life was difficult enough on its own, and she had allowed herself to be roped into a clash of all powerful beings? She was a *thief*, not a hero. Was some veiled promise leveraging her deepest fear enough to keep her here?

*Maybe,* she thought, *I could just get Nerio and myself out of here. Run away from this damned city and its obligations.*

But then, what would happen to Masini? To that Blue? To Nerio even? If Masini was right, then there wouldn't be anywhere to hide. Could she even save herself? Recent events contradicted the idea that she could, as much as her pride wanted to believe it were the case. How long could she stay on the run? Would it be better to live in constant fear, a state she'd experience perpetually her entire life, or to risk the danger now for the bliss of freedom and safety later?

Desnia sighed as she ran her fingers through her hair, the strands hot from the exposure to the sun. Masini didn't respond to her outburst in a rare respect for her frustration. She headed north, towards the church, her gait short and languid.

*Um,* said Masini after an extended quiet, *where are we going?*

"Back to the church," she said, her voice as sluggish as her feet. "I need time to think. I still need to figure out what it is that I'm going to tell that Blue to convince him to help us. Although it sounds like it's not going to matter much..."

*I have faith in you,* said Masini. *You do, after all, have my incredible wit on your side. Oh, and a demigod, I suppose. That's* almost *as impressive.*

"Some help that's been," she grumbled, a small pang of fear striking her as she wondered if the voice's speaker could somehow hear her.

*We just need to approach this in the way that you know best: Stealth,* he said. *You were the best thief in Calentine, trust me, we checked. If anyone can sneak into wherever the g-g-g-door is, it's you. And now with the help and protection of a Blue, there's a real chance of success.*

"Spoken like we never had a chance to begin with. Nice," she replied sardonically.

There were no good options, she knew. Finding the gate was her only path; moreover—though this wasn't a deciding factor—it was the path to what she *needed.* In her experience, however, the ones who always tried to do the extraordinary typically ended up dead. Surviving was about picking what was best for you, regardless of the potential payout. Living had always been the priority.

*And now there are people I have to consider aside from myself. Damn it all,* she thought as she walked.

Eventually, she ambled her way to the church, the white paint flaking and adobe chipping away at the corners to reveal the mud brick beneath. Passing through the creaking doors, she entered into the pew-lined sanctuary, vacant save for Nerio at the far end of a distant bench. She walked down the aisle and sat next to him, light from a cracked stained-glass window filtering in the afternoon light.

"What're you doing down here?" she asked.

"The attic is so hot I thought I was going to have a stroke," he said. There was a chuckle from Masini.

"I... I think I found someone who can help both of us," she said, ignoring Masini.

"What do you mean?" he asked.

She chronicled the encounter with the Blue at the Devapuram, Nerio listening with the calm patience that priests seemed to somehow always maintain. He just sat there and listened, an understanding expression on his face, holding any questions until she finished. The effect of such a respectful peace was like a fishing line that lured information from her, and she caught herself almost giving away too much.

"So, this is the same Blue who was there at the fire, the one you told me about? Are you... *alright?*" he asked once she finished.

Of course his first instinct was to ask about her. How was he so damn caring? Part of her was repulsed by the altruism, but she was also thankful for it and tried to snuff out the instinct of distrusting his nature.

"I'm... fine," she replied. "But I think he can help me. Help us. He's a noble, a powerful and influential one. If anyone is going to be able to get you somewhere safe from Jerdine, it'll be him."

Nerio considered and nodded to her words. "What do *you* need his help with?"

"Finding this gate. I think that Jerdine knows where it is, but he's dangerous and I need help." Admitting that put a foul taste in her mouth, like the strange, spicy food that was found everywhere in this city.

"I... I could—"

"No," she said defiantly. "You don't need to put yourself in danger on my behalf. You've been hurt by Jerdine enough, and I'm not going to let him do more to you."

He turned his head and nodded solemnly. "Why are you so desperate to find this gate? What is it to you?"

*That's the question of the day, isn't it?* she thought.

# CHAPTER
# FORTY-SEVEN

*Sailing the celestial sea*
*Exploring where desires lead*
*Whether by hidden eye, or presence of body*
*Unconfined by any boundary*

Delvan watched as a stray cat prowled and then pounced atop a rat, digging its claws into the squealing creature and silencing it with a firm bite to the back of its neck. Trophy in hand, the orange feline strutted away down a nearby alley as the mountains were beginning to cover the city in curtains of shadow.

He walked along the street with Kolden and Orne, his exhausted brain moving through thoughts at a crawl. The buildings and roads still clung to the warmth of the day, radiating a gentle heat, a welcome relief from the blaring sun which helped to relax him a little.

The letter they'd sent to the guild had dominated over all other thoughts, and he wished he'd made the meeting time earlier than tomorrow. His finger tapped his thigh from inside his pocket as he walked, wondering what the guild's reaction would be.

Like an oracle, he'd gone over the futures and possibilities innumerable times, sifting through the worst, the best, and all scenarios in between like a peruser among a hall of portraits. But there was nothing more he could do for now, and he tried to put it out of his mind.

They reached a fork in the road, one branch heading north, towards the church the girl, Des, had designated as a meeting location, the other east, to the barracks. He looked north along the sparsely crowded street, appearing a more desolate world before the bells were tolled. The possibilities of what lay down that path became the new art along the hall of his mind, fervent brush strokes forming new images.

Feeling that crawling along his neck, he snuck another sly glance over his shoulder, trying to see if he recognized anyone among the semi-crowded street. Yet again it lacked any memorable faces.

"You actually going to go meet this girl?" asked Kolden.

"Yeah," he replied, pulling his focus back to the conversation. It was still difficult to explain why. Seeing her poignantly brought him back to that night, but it also, in a curious way, reminded him of Hilbrun. The good times and the bad. Did he need more reason than that? "I'm not sure I'll be able to help her, but it can't hurt to find out what she wants. Besides, maybe there's more she hasn't told me about the commander."

"I don't think you should go alone," said Orne. Delvan tilted his head back from below the behemoth's shoulders to look at him.

"Too risky. If you come, she might get spooked and take off. I'll be careful, don't worry. Head back to the barracks, I'll see you tonight," he said.

"You were careful last time you ran to her aid, too, you know," said Kolden, crossing his arms.

*That was a low blow,* he thought as his face turned cold and throat tightened. He wanted to rebuke Kolden, to tell him that he was wrong, but words didn't form, his mind and his mouth absent a valid argument.

He wanted to believe that she lacked ill intentions, but how well did he know her? Despite the harrowing pain he'd felt upon seeing her earlier, there was this odd connection, not unlike what he felt with other Blues. Was this strange tether enough to absolve her of potential mischief? It certainly wasn't for the commander.

The most glaring question of all, however, was why would she, a thief, request the help of a Blue? Was she involved in something dangerous again? Did it stem from the incident in Calentine? He'd spent his entire day either thinking about the guild letter or recuperating his battered senses after their chance encounter, and he hadn't stopped to consider the implications of her request.

Last time his overzealousness had cost him dearly. He shouldn't be brash and repeat the mistake.

"Fine," he finally said. "One of you going to come with me then?"

"Take Orne," volunteered Kolden. "I need to go back to the barracks anyway. I've been thinking about where I've got... well, you know, stashed. It's been bothering me all day and I want to do something about it. I'm sure you two will be able to handle whatever the damsel needs."

Orne rested his hand on the pommel of his sword like an enormous sentry, grunting in agreement. Delvan debated trying to convince Kolden to come, he'd been the one to witness the commander's murderous act, after all. But keeping the cadentite safe for the time being was more important.

After a silent farewell, Kolden went east and he and Orne veered north, walking along the road as the bells began ringing throughout the city. It wasn't quite like Calentine, there were no cliff walls of the mountain here for the sounds to reverberate off, but what the city lacked in acoustics it supplemented with quantity. The surfeit of bronze created a tumultuous cacophony that deafened, the vibrations shaking their bones. It still managed, however, to remind him of the great bells in the King's Tower.

*Too many things remind me of home lately,* he thought.

Fewer people than he'd expected filed onto the street as they moved further north, the commoners and buildings alike looking worn and uncared for. Beggars, the first he'd seen since arriving, sat along the street's edge, returning him to his time in the Lower Valley. At least the arid breeze didn't carry the same stench.

After a time, he and Orne came upon the north gate, then the nearby church, its white steepled roof standing out among the blocky, colorful buildings. As they stalked forward from down the street, holding tightly to the side of the road, their eyes darted, looking for any sign of an ambush.

*She definitely chose somewhere secluded...* he thought.

The dusty street appeared abandoned, the mild breeze twisting small cyclones of sand and debris before them. It looked like a place abandoned to time, the crumbling veneers a stark contrast to the city's meticulously cared for heart.

Delvan reached the church's wall, peering through a small chip in the pane of stained glass. Inside looked a sight better than out: candles burning, the floors and pews clean and polished, but completely empty. An uncanny sight in the pious city.

If there was an ambush planned, he couldn't find any sign of it. No crowns of archers' heads from the roofs nearby, the building and alleys barren. Orne scanned the street, his eyes hard and concentrating intensely. He turned to Delvan with a shrug and a small shake of his head.

"I thought I asked you to come alone?" came a voice to his side, causing him to nearly jump out of his skin. He turned to see Des in her white robe, somehow hidden in a shadow at the building's corner. *How long was she watching us?*

"Did you really expect for just me to come?" Delvan asked, collecting himself after being flustered. He looked at Des, her arms crossed and face dark, and noticed the absence of his specter digging its nails into his chest. He'd dreaded it after their earlier confrontation, but while there was tension, there was a distinct lack of pain and despair. "I trust Orne with my life, I think that should speak for itself."

She stared at the two of them with annoyed, but thoughtful eyes. "I expected you to at least be on time. Come this way, we're not using the front entrance."

Relieved she didn't argue further, they followed her down the paint-chipped side of the building and through a weathered door that she unlocked with a key from her waist. Stepping down half a flight of stairs led them into what appeared to be a shallow basement, which Delvan guessed was underneath the main dais of the gathering space above.

A smell of stagnant, dusty air filled the cluttered, windowless room, which was lit by two lamps, illuminating storage shelves that were falling apart. They wove between crates and stacks of junk, the ceiling low enough that Orne's head and neck were forced to tilt to the side to avoid the joists above.

Des led them to the back of the room. A small area had been cleared, a few crates acting as makeshift chairs with one in the center like a table, all as dilapidated looking at the church's exterior. Sitting there was a young priest, scrawny with heavy bags under his eyes, making him appear older beyond his years.

"Who's this?" asked Orne in his deep voice, ducking his head under another beam.

"Someone I trust with my life, that should speak for itself," she retorted as she sat and leaned against a wall—the one that let her see the exit.

*Fair enough,* thought Delvan.

Delvan followed suit, carefully easing onto the crate. Orne seemed reluctant, but being unable to straighten his neck must have worn him down. He pulled the last crate a little further away from the table than the rest of them before sitting down cautiously.

"King and His grace upon you," said the young priest with a tired smile. "Thank you for coming, I know your help means a lot to Desnia. I'm Nerio."

Desnia flashed a subtle glare at Nerio, but quickly turned it away, as if ashamed.

"And you," replied Delvan, Orne remaining stoic. "I'm Delvan, this is Orne. Most people just call me Del."

"What do they call him?" asked Desnia with a nod to Orne. "Giant?"

"Only the ones trying to piss me off. And can't we talk upstairs?" asked Orne. "Cramped as fuck in here."

*And with only one exit,* thought Delvan, knowing that was likely Orne's larger concern.

"We don't dare risk being seen," said the priest, shifting uncomfortably. "And this is more accommodating than the attic, I assure you."

"Is whatever you're hiding from the reason that you asked us here?" asked Delvan.

Desnia and Nerio shared a glance of discomfort. Desnia remained leaning back against the wall with arms folded as she began to speak. "Partially. It's... a long story. Nerio's avoiding someone, so we're laying low until he can get out of the city."

*Is smuggling a priest really why she asked us here?* "I'm not sure how much help we're going to be with getting you away from here," said Delvan. "Since the... night in Calentine, I haven't been in the best standing with my family, and Orne's doesn't even want him here."

The tension in his chest grew a little tighter, and his breathing more rapid at his mention of that night. Some sweat trickled down his temple as images of Hilbrun's face flash in his head, but he managed to dissuade the stabbing of his heart, doing what he could to remain calm. He could get through a conversation about that night, he had to.

The face of the priest sank upon hearing Delvan's familial situation, but Desnia just shook her head. "We would... *appreciate* any help you could give.

We're..." she struggled with speaking the words, like they had their own claws dug into her and she was forcefully ripping them from her throat. "Frankly, we're broke. The clergy doesn't exactly pay either of us much, at least not enough for, say, a bribe. If we could pay off a small caravan or buy some fake documents, getting out of town becomes a lot easier. And if you could also use your influence to convince them to take us, it would go a long way to avoiding suspicion..." her voice trailed away. She couldn't look Delvan in the eyes, her face a mixture of shame and disdain.

Money wasn't a concern for him, it was mostly his father's anyway. The man may have been a terrible parent, but Delvan was still a Saffstar and appearances must be maintained. His access to funds had never been revoked. His father probably thought it would help to stop him from complaining. A visit to a bank in Brethefen would provide him with whatever was needed.

"Money's not an issue," said Delvan, removing a coin purse from his pocket and tossing it on the crate between the four of them. "There're a couple suns in there, should be enough to get you through a few days. I can get you more tomorrow for your bribes."

Desnia's eyes went wide and Nerio's head pulled back, his jaw dropping. "We couldn't possibly—"

"Yes, we could," cut off Desnia as she quickly leaned forward and snatched up the jingling pouch. She looked at Delvan and turned her head away. "Thanks."

*She wouldn't have brought us to the edge of the city just to ask for money.* "What else do you need?" he asked.

Desnia practically writhed in her seat as her lips went into a tight line. "I'm... searching for something hidden here, in the city. But the people guarding it, including the fat fucker that Nerio is hiding from, are dangerous. It's... I need..." she stammered, grasping for words.

"I don't like where this is going, Del," said Orne.

"Let me start from the beginning." She finally looked into Delvan's eyes with glistening blue orbs that pleaded for him to listen. "There was more to the robbery at the guild, things you probably don't know."

Delvan leaned forward, his pulse pounding with anticipation. He'd hoped for this, praying that he'd finally get an explanation, one that he could trust.

He planned to pry one from the commander, eventually, but now he would be able to compare—and punish any lies.

"There was something in the vault, a priceless object held for safekeeping by the guild for a powerful group that operates out of Brethefen. Since that night I've learned that we were hired to steal it specifically."

"What was it?" asked Delvan.

"A solid, massive piece of cadentite, the largest I've ever seen. Maybe a few inches square," she replied.

*That aligns with what Kolden heard the commander tell the man in the alley,* thought Delvan.

"A lot of that night is blank for me," Desnia said, rubbing the back of her head. "We've been working under the assumption that it never left the guild's possession, and they're sending it here. I hope that someone managed to get out amidst the chaos with it. But given how things went that night, I doubt that happened..."

"Who's *we*?" asked Delvan, noticing the phrasing. Surely she wasn't referring to the priest, he hadn't been in Calentine during the robbery.

"Huh?" she asked with panicked eyes. "Did I say *we*? I meant... never mind."

*She's... odd,* he thought. And why did she seem so nervous about the cadentite coming to Brethefen? The commander didn't want it here either, he tried to hide it. *Their goals can't possibly be aligned, let alone well intended, could they? Why the opposition?*

"Look," she continued, rubbing her forehead, painstakingly selecting each word, "the cadentite is part of something bigger. *That's* the thing I'm looking for. If the guild or this group brings them together then... Ugh, how do I say this?!" She frustratingly dug her face into her hands. "It's a door, a barrier, and the cadentite is the key. On the other side is, uh, well I don't know how else to say this: an army. *That's* what I need your help with. Stopping them before it's too late and destroying this door."

Delvan stared at her, perplexed, face frozen in confusion. "Do... Do you mean, like, an army from Trethefen? A way for them to avoid the blocked mountain passes? Have they tunneled into the city?"

"No. Well... It's hard to explain. Listen, all that's important is that if they open this door, then the force that follows will come to conquer, and nothing you or I can do will be able to stop them."

*Maybe she isn't just odd, but insane*, he thought. *An unknown army, attacking from inside the city? And a cadentite key? It's a glowing rock that is used to make drugs, I hardly think it could be used to open some kind of door.* Even the priest seemed surprised by all of this.

"How do you know about this?" Delvan asked.

"I... I met someone in my travels here. Someone who helped plan the heist, they... they told me..." she said reluctantly.

*Is... is she willingly working with those bastards?* he thought with a flare that ignited a fire in his gut. His face slowly changed from calm to contorted with rage as the small ember grew into an inferno. *She has the gall to ask me to aid the people that are responsible for Hilbrun's murder?! How dare she?!*

The furnace blazed within him, building pressure and threatening to rupture in a violent explosion of rage. The pain in his chest was gone, extinguished by the enveloping ire that now flowed through him. His teeth gritted together under pressure that was on the brink of shattering them, his face a red mask.

"Where are they?!" Delvan demanded, rising to his feet. "I'm going to make them answer for Hilbrun's death!" If the informant she spoke of had been before him right then, he would have struck them down with satisfaction, free of remorse or guilt.

Nerio shied away. Desnia clutched her necklace, leaning back but not turning her eyes from him, despite the flickers of fear the crystalline blue betrayed.

"They're gone," she said. "Their soul removed from their body."

*Why can't she speak like a normal person?!* he thought, still in a rage. *They're dead, then. Gods-damn it!* There didn't seem to be a lie in her eyes. She was clearly ignorant of her employer's methods and machinations, and he realized his anger wasn't directed at Desnia, but the ones manipulating her. His temper cooled, but he remained standing, his head only a few inches below the ceiling.

He took a few deep breaths, his face slowly reverting back to its normal state. Desnia needed to know who these people were, the scheming of which they were capable.

"The people who hired you," said Delvan, "are liars and murderers. You can't trust them. I know of one alone who is responsible for four murders that I'm aware of, including Hilbrun's. If they want you to find this doorway, I suggest you do the opposite. This supposed *army* is probably just a fabrication as well."

"You don't understand—" she started.

"No, *you* don't seem to understand. I don't blame you for Hil's death, honestly," said Delvan. "You saved my life in that fight, so you've earned my trust in that. But if you think for a *second* that I am going to find and destroy this thing because those bastards are asking for it, think again. I want them dead, choking on their own blood!"

Spit flew with the last words. Hearing the unfiltered thoughts of wrath speak what he'd avoided admitting in his own mind was shocking. Was that honestly what he wanted? Anger and grief had grown inside of him for these past months, and now it was breaking through the cracks like weeds between bricks, heaving the hardened path into a fractured jumble. Now that he was walking it, he wasn't sure where to step.

The stale air cooled his tongue as he took deep breaths to calm himself, closing his reddened eyes as he tried to think. He'd come here for information, but discovering that the bastards responsible for Hilbrun's death were still trying to accomplish their goals was beyond anything he'd expected. Especially not from Desnia, who he still found himself compelled to trust.

"Why are you even helping these people?" asked Delvan, breaking the silent aftermath of his outburst. "They nearly *killed* you. What in the King's name makes you think helping them now is a good idea?"

"That job dug the pits," she said with a scowl. "That fucker, Magnar, got greedy and wanted to kill me for a bigger cut. They were under strict instructions to not harm anyone, me included, which they clearly ignored."

"And you *believe* this?" asked Delvan with a wave of his hands.

"Kolden did say that the commander was furious at that guy for killing a Blue, same with attempting to harm her," cut in Orne, ending his quiet audience.

Delvan glared at him. He didn't want to share too much information, especially if Desnia was working for these people, misguided or not. Orne was unphased by his glare, however, looking at him with his unmoving stare.

"What?" asked Desnia, sitting upright and looking inquisitively at Orne. "What *guy*? Do you mean you saw Magnar? Is that what you meant at the Devapuram when you said you knew they were all dead? What happened?"

Delvan spoke before Orne had a chance to reply, wanting to be careful with what they said next. "Kolden, the other one who was with us, saw him have a clandestine meeting with someone in an alley back in Drunt, right before he was murdered. They apparently talked about the heist."

"*And?*" she asked, leaning forward in her seat. Nerio was still watching the conversation unfold, looking lost.

"This *Magnar* hid your key there, in the city," Delvan said. *At least if she or the people she works for go looking for it there it'll be a fruitless endeavor.* "The man he met with seemed to be tying up loose ends."

Desnia leaned back and let out a long sigh, closing her eyes. The tension visibly left her body, her arms drooping to her side.

"That's a relief," she finally said. "I hope the fucker at least hid it well, gods know he wasn't one who liked to get his hands dirty. Still wish I could have been there to see him get what he deserved."

Nerio looked at her, mouth open, aghast. She pointedly ignored him.

"Why is that a relief?" asked Orne.

"Because," she said, "I was told that these people who want the key are ruthless. Given what's been described to me as their way of operating, and how desperately they're seeking it, I don't think it would be beyond them to slaughter the entire city and burn it to the ground to find it."

"That's a bit of an extreme exaggeration, don't you think?" asked Delvan. Hilbrun would never have knowingly been involved with a group capable of such genocide. They were merchants, not ruthless zealots. This was clearly more brainwashing.

"It wouldn't be the first time they've done it, or so I hear. In fact, I think that having it hidden there merely buys me some time. They *will* find it and will painfully torture and kill anyone who has it, even if they need to desolate a city looking for it," Desnia said, some of the stress returning to her muscles, her face wrinkling with concern.

Delvan and Orne shared a glance. There was worry on Orne's face, an uneasiness in his eyes. Delvan immediately understood his concern: Kolden had the key, and if these people were oriented solely towards its recovery, then he'd be in extreme danger.

And they'd left him alone.

Delvan didn't want to believe Desnia, his faith in Hilbrun holding steadfast. A trickle of doubt managed to creep in as he wondered, *What if Hilbrun didn't know about their brutality?* History was filled with people who have done worse for less... *But he wouldn't have knowingly followed them if that were the case. He was a critical thinker, someone who asked questions of the motives around him. He couldn't have been so blind, could he?*

Orne wasn't going to leave his brother's fate to chance, clearly disregarding Delvan's opinion as he stood up, almost colliding with the ceiling above. He looked down at Delvan with a deepened grimace of urgency, one that told him he wouldn't wait for long.

"We have to go," said Delvan to Desnia, trying to cover the faint worry in his voice. "I'll help pay for the bribes to get you out of here, but only if you leave by tomorrow. Don't go looking for this door, or whatever it is that these people want you to find, Des, you can't trust them."

Desnia and Nerio both looked at them, confused as to the abrupt end of the conversation. "Where are you going?" Desnia asked. "What aren't you telling me?"

"Find us at the barracks tomorrow," said Delvan as he and Orne turned and strode towards the stairs. "We have something we need to take care of."

They left the pair dumbfounded by their sudden abandonment and strode out into the street, the breezy air of nightfall rushing past them as Delvan hurried to keep up with Orne's overly long legs. He was nearly in a jog as he tried to talk with the mountain of a man.

"I'm sure Kolden's fine," he said, reassuring not only Orne but himself. "No one knows we have the key. And even if they suspected, it's not like they're going to come at us in the barracks with a garrison of soldiers."

Orne stopped and spun to face Delvan, his boots grinding the sand into brick. "You don't know that!" he said, glowering down at him. "Did you hear what she said about what these people would do for that fucking rock?! They don't know where it is, but there are *two* fucking people still alive who they *know* saw it last. That girl, and *you*, Del. And *she* didn't just write a *FUCKING LETTER* to them saying she has it!"

Delvan swallowed hard with a dry throat. He'd never seen Orne in such a furious and frightened state. Convincing him that Hilbrun hadn't been a murderer, or a member of a homicidal cabal, might be the only viable way to calm his boiling fury. Afterall, it was Ferrand and the people that *he* worked for that had an ever-increasing body count, not the other way around.

"Do you really think a bunch of *merchants* are going to come after us, Orne?" asked Delvan, finding his voice again. "Des has been completely misguided. The group that hired her killed multiple people to steal this cadentite, why wouldn't they lie about the guild? If *anyone* is going to be looking for the stone, it's the man who stole it in the first place: *Ferrand*. The guild is going to get it from me tomorrow, with the only cost one they are probably more than happy to pay. *Why* would they try to take it now instead?"

Orne's brow dug deeper into his nose, his eyes holding Delvan's while he thought. His face was carved as though from stone, painted red and coated in wrath. "Bah!," he finally spat. "I don't like any of this. I *told you* we should have just buried the thing and been done with it. You and Kolden are both so *fucking* stupid!" He shook his head, still angry, but Delvan had managed to deflect a significant portion of his rage. "Let's go! Clearly a lot of people are looking for this damn thing, and I don't want to take any chances."

He took off with his expansive gait, forcing Delvan back into his slow jog. Before long, they were out of the thinly populated slum and into the cleaner, well maintained eastern quarter. The barracks was situated not far from the eastern gate, and the empty streets allowed for an unobstructed stride. Lamps were beginning to be lit, and lights showered through the stained glass of several churches they passed, pews filled and preachers casting their voice over the crowd of lowered heads.

With sore feet and burning legs, the duo marched on. On the surface, Delvan convinced himself that this was ridiculous, that Orne was overreacting. He was certain that the guild wouldn't come for them, but another thought kept him from complaining about the pain of each hastened step.

All day they'd suspected someone was following them. It was assuredly the commander sending someone to keep his ever-watchful eye affixed. Delvan had rarely been out of his sight in six months, and for whatever reason the man intended to maintain his surveillance. What if whoever he sent to tail them had seen Kolden hand off the letter, and intercepted it?

*Gods-damn it,* he thought, *I knew I should have delivered that myself. At least then he'd only know I went to the guild, and not what the content of the letter was.*

Their brisk march brought them to barracks in a time that could have rivaled one of their horses. The door burst open with a *clang* as Orne pushed through it with the force of a battering ram. Through an empty mess hall and up the stairs they stormed, until reaching the hall with their rooms. Everywhere Delvan looked, rooms were vacant, only passing a single guard on duty during their charge.

*Is everyone at a speak right now?* he wondered, still shocked at how devout the city's populus seemed to be.

"Kolden!" Orne's voice boomed as they approached his door. It was ajar, which wasn't uncommon if he were inside. Orne turned and walked through the opening, ducking his head, Delvan close behind. As he reached the door's threshold and looked into the room, his feet froze in place, and his insides tumbled into knots.

Clothes were strewn all around, the drawers they had resided in tossed about, and a chair and table knocked over to the room's side. Tools, knives, and other random objects covered the floor, including Kolden's oversized dagger he'd been wearing earlier. His travel chest—where the cadentite had been hidden under a false bottom—had been smashed, splinters scattered in all directions. Delvan didn't see any blood, but his heart beat through prongs of sharp pain all the same, his lungs deflating as his face went numb.

Kolden was gone.

# Chapter
# Forty-Eight

*Behold, the change*
*Heart to stone, soul to earth*
*Ever constant*

*Wow, you're* really *bad at asking for help,* mocked Masini.

Desnia scowled and shook her head, unable to curse him out in front of Nerio. The stagnant, dusty air of the basement was still settling after the expedient departure of Delvan and Orne, leaving Desnia standing there, confused and angry at her inability to obtain their help. How was she to convince them of something that sounded insane even to her?

"Desnia," said Nerio with reproach, "did you mean what you said to them earlier? How could you wish such harm unto a person?"

"How can you *not*?" she said, spinning to address him, her own chagrin saturating her tone. His body retracted from the harsh words, his gaze falling away. She groaned and ran her fingers over her scalp, now even more irritated.

"I know your past has been a troubled one," he said sheepishly, "but that does not mean it must continue. 'One who seeks the destruction of another, ultimately finds their own'."

She rolled her eyes. Now was not the time for his benevolence or quotes from scripture. She began pacing, kicking up more of the fine dust from the basement floor, her robe swishing just above it. That entire conversation had gone miserably, and now it seemed that the Blue was more against her than ever.

"Why did they take off so suddenly?" she asked as though thinking out loud, covering for her communication with Masini.

*Probably has something to do with your excellent interpersonal skills,* said a sardonic Masini.

"The things you said," came Nerio's quiet voice, "why did you not tell me of this before? I knew that Jerdine was dangerous but, Desnia, what you claimed him capable of... What can we hope to achieve against such evil? We can't possibly—"

"Would you *please*—" she cut off her raised voice with tight lips. "Sorry, I can't take both... Just please let me think for a minute."

Nerio hung his head low, avoiding her gaze. She felt a stab of guilt. He'd been through so much misery, he didn't deserve to be berated by her. Yet here she was, snapping at him like a petulant child.

*You're such a people person,* said Masini.

"Grr..." she growled. Nerio shied away even further, thinking her animosity was directed at him.

*The priest does have a point, actually,* continued Masini. *They took off as soon as you brought up the whole maniacal genocide thing.*

"I don't think they left in a hurry because I scared them off," she said, speaking to the ceiling with a craned neck and closed eyes.

*They knew more than they were telling, that was clear,* assessed Masini. *I wonder if the commander they mentioned was... No, it couldn't be, he's stationed in Calentine. Though I don't know who else it could be...*

"Desnia," said Nerio. How was she supposed to think with two people talking to her at once? "About Jerdine—"

"Not right now," she said, waving a dismissive hand. *I can't focus on helping him escape Jerdine and finding the gate at the same time. He's going to have to wait.* "Who could this commander the big fucker mentioned be?" she said.

*In Calentine there was a knight commander that worked closely with us,* said Masini. *Name was Ferrand, I think. He helped us plan the initial robbery, run interference with the guild, that sort of thing. He would have known this Magnar fellow that you're so well acquainted with, since he would've been the one who hired him.*

*But he should never have been the one to collect the k-k-k-gah, glowy rock. Smaller pieces, yes, but one as important as this? No, my friend would have been there himself. Something is wrong here, very wrong...*

"Could that mean the commander is here then?" Desnia asked to the air again.

*Seems probable. We should find him if he is. I want to find out why he's here, and if nothing else he'd be a much-needed ally. I should warn you though, he's about as pleasant as a snake biting your taint on a hot summer's day.*

"Great..." she mumbled.

Desnia rubbed her forehead, feeling overwhelmed. A deep breath followed by a prolonged sigh helped calm her nerves, but there was this ever-present weight bearing down on her shoulders. A pressing load that filled her with urgency and dread.

*And I still don't know why those two just up and left,* she thought. At least now there was potentially another Blue that could help her, although if Masini was saying that the man was an ass, she could only imagine—

"Desnia," piped Nerio again. "I really think there's something you should know."

"What?" she asked with a resigned sigh. She tried to remove her grimace of annoyance as she turned to face him. Her discontent shouldn't be brought upon him, but her foot tapped the floor anxiously as she waited for him to speak all the same.

"This group, the one that wants to open this door, you said that Jerdine is a member, correct?" he asked, repositioning himself in an uncomfortable shuffle.

"Probably the bastard running it, yes. Why?" she asked.

"So he would know where this thing you're looking for is?"

"*Yes,* Nerio, what's your point?" she said, agitated.

"I... I think that you might have been wrong about its location not being written down..."

Delvan's visage was one shaped from ice. Cold and ragged, the only movement upon it the beads of sweat that flowed down through its ridges and valleys. He crawled forward like a glacier, shuffling slowly into Kolden's room while Orne kicked a drawer against a wall, screaming as it shattered against the brick.

"I'll kill them all!" Orne cried as Delvan took in the scene in his daze. The cadentite was clearly gone, and Kolden along with it, but how could this have happened? He'd been certain, confident that no one else knew of the treasure they held in their possession.

"I told you!" shouted Orne, pointing a finger at Delvan with a deranged look on his face. "Why'd you both have to be so *fucking* stupid?! Now someone's taken him! Where's the guard?!"

Orne stormed out of the room, brushing past Delvan and nearly knocking him to the ground. Pain pulsed through his side, further paralyzing him as he looked at the destruction in the room. He tried to breathe, but his lungs refused air. He couldn't lose someone else. Not again.

They had to find Kolden.

There was another angry shout from down the hall. Delvan heard Orne berating the lone guard, his screams resonating through the corridors with clarity. Words like incompetent, lazy, and inept shook the narrow windows, threatening to crack and shatter them. Delvan heard Orne's thunderous footsteps coming back down the hall long before he reentered the room.

"He didn't see a fucking thing," exclaimed Orne. "Fucking *idiot*. And there aren't even enough guards here to be stationed at all the doors. Where the fuck is everyone?!"

Delvan knew they were all likely at a speak but sensed that Orne's question was more rhetorical than inquisitive. It *was* strange that the place seemed abandoned, despite it being the hour of prayer, but it didn't matter now. The only thing that mattered was that Kolden and the cadentite were missing.

Orne's feet *thudded* against the wooden floorboards as he paced in the room, fists clenched at his side. His head leaned forward, his jaw tight, as if he were about to charge headfirst at something like a bull.

"I *knew* writing that letter was a dumb fucking idea," he shouted, still pacing.

"No…" muttered Delvan, beginning to regain his senses. He had to fight this pain, this unseen hand that marionetted his life. If not for his own sake, then for Kolden's. His hands shook as he managed a few half-breaths and wiped the cold moisture from his face.

"No," he repeated. "This wasn't the guild. This was Ferrand, it had to be. He realized that Kolden found the key in Drunt and came to take it back. Maybe Kolden walked in on him moving it and they struggled."

He couldn't think straight, he was seeing Hilbrun's face flashing through his mind, but it kept being replaced with that of Kolden's. In the visions, he fell, over and over, surrounded by fire with desperate anguish on his face. Delvan was going to lose both of them.

He shook his head, forcing the image of Kolden's slain corpse from his mind as much as he was able, trying to focus on the now. He hadn't been able to save Hilbrun, but maybe there was still time to rescue Kolden.

There had to be time.

"You keep saying that, but how the fuck do you know, huh?" asked Orne, his face red and flecks of spit raining down on Delvan. "Gah! Fuck this, we don't have time to argue." He stomped past Delvan again and went to his own quarters. Delvan followed, standing at the threshold.

"What're you doing?" he asked, his voice still shaky.

Orne pulled his freshly polished armor from the rack, the mixture of mail and interlocking plates rattling against the hardened leather padding as he began to strap it on. "I'm going to find the commander, then I'm going to beat him within an inch of his fucking life until he tells me where Kolden is. And if *he* doesn't know, then I'm going to the guild to break every bone in their bodies until *they* tell me."

Delvan stood there, Orne quickly tying the straps of his armor together with a skilled and purposeful hand. Orne was wrong about the guild, he had to be. If he wasn't then that would mean that Hilbrun…

*No, I refuse to accept that,* Delvan thought. *Orne will see, the commander will confess, and I'll be there when he does.*

"I'm coming with you," Delvan pronounced.

"No shit," spat Orne. "Well? Why the fuck are you standing there?! Go! Get your fucking armor on!"

Delvan ran with vigor into his room, strapping on his own armor. The blue-dyed leather covered in darksteel was never intended to be turned against another of its bearers. Delvan still, despite everything, had to fight through his own reservations at harming another Blue. He swallowed with difficulty. He could do this.

He was ready.

"You're telling me," Desnia said, with a renewed interest in what Nerio had to say, "that Jerdine has a library in his private office that no one is allowed access to?"

The revelation by Nerio created a whole new list of possibilities. What if she didn't have to follow Jerdine for days or weeks, and just needed to get to his chambers instead? Would he have the gate's location written down? It would have been stupidly arrogant to retain such documentation, but he struck her to be as conceited as they came.

As if to confirm her postulation, Masini chimed in. *I bet they're his personal journals, he was always a vain bastard. Thought that he'd have a cou-cou-cou—ugh, a very high position among my people. Probably kept records of everything thinking his supplicants would want to learn from his 'greatness.' Man's more sour than anal leakage.*

"Even when I was working in the library it was well known that of all the principles, he was the only one so exclusionary with loaning from his personal library," said Nerio. "They're kept in his chambers, behind lock and key, I was never allowed to touch them, even after..." he shuddered. "He would become very angry if I ever asked."

Nerio's visceral reaction helped reinforce her already rooted hatred for this man. It made her look forward to robbing the bastard. She rested her chin in her hand as she paced again, considering her next move as she strode between the cramped crates.

"I think," she finally said, "that we should try to find this commander that the ogre mentioned first. If he was one of the ones who planned the robbery, then he could be willing to help us. Assuming we can convince him, we then plan a break into Jerdine's quarters, and steal the books we need." *And maybe smash a few things for good measure.*

*Just a warning,* said Masini, *he's probably got more protection on them than just a lock and key.*

That didn't sound promising, but it was the closest thing resembling a plan she'd had since arriving. Finally, she didn't feel like she was running around aimlessly, a fish endlessly swimming in a pond searching for air. A plan meant she could take action, hopefully before it was too late.

"Do you think this commander will be at the barracks?" Desnia asked Nerio.

"I believe there are officer's quarters in a building nearby," he said, scratching his head. "But I haven't spent too much time there."

"It's a start," she said. "Stay here and keep low, I'll come find you after I find the commander. Assuming he's even here..."

She didn't want to wait until the morning. The Blue had said that the key was safely hidden in Drunt, but could she trust that to be true? They were hiding other information, why not something about the key's whereabouts? Then there was that sense of panicked fear that she'd felt as they left...

A voice in the back of her mind whispered doubt about their words and insisted on urgency. An instinct that drove her to continue believing she was low on time. What if someone had found it since its concealment? What if the Blue had unwittingly told someone of its whereabouts? Too many things could go wrong for her to rely on the word of someone else.

As she turned to leave, her sandals twisting on the dust-covered floor, Nerio spoke. "Wait! I'm coming with you."

*Why?* she thought as she closed her eyes and lolled her head back.

"I'll be fine," she said, half turning to speak with him.

"The gods commanded that I find you, help you. Sitting here does none of that."

*Of course, can't risk upsetting the gods.* "You *have* helped, Nerio. But there's nothing for you to do tonight. I'm just trying to find the commander and talk to them, it's not even that dangerous."

Nerio stood up and walked towards her. "If it's not that dangerous, then it shouldn't be an issue if I come along."

*Wow,* said Masini, *you're oh-for-two tonight. Quite the streak.*

She sighed and her shoulders sagged. There was going to be no dissuading Nerio, though she supposed she could force him to stay. Was it necessary? Finding the commander might be easier with him, he knew the city better than she did. It felt risky nonetheless, but she didn't have time to waste searching for the commander's residence, and the locals were more lenient towards priests than even Hands. After a moment she made her decision.

"Fine. But keep up, I plan on making good time."

Delvan and Orne marched out of the barracks, darksteel gleaming as it reflected the dull gray of the ebony moon and nearby street streetlamps like stars against the black night. The metal *clinked* in a quick rhythm with each drumming step, beating a march into battle.

They made directly for the officer's housing nearby, lights from a few windows illuminating the street ahead with a dim yellow glow, many more remaining dun.

"What should we be expecting in a fight?" asked Orne, his words grating the air.

"Jack's have strength like you can't imagine," said Delvan as they stomped along the dark street, "and can take a hit. They can still be hurt from a punch or kick, but not as badly as you're expecting. Steel should work just fine."

Orne grunted at that.

"Best to use the element of surprise if we can, and we can't have him bleeding out before he tells us where Kolden is, so only use your sword as a last resort," he continued. "We're going to be in tight with him here, and in close combat he's going to be the most dangerous."

"If things go bad, torch the fucker," said Orne.

Delvan's pace slowed for a second, long enough for Orne to get a stride ahead. He jogged a few steps forward to close the distance, but the statement weighed heavily on him. He hadn't cast fire since that night, images of death walling in front of him like a barrier against conjuring the flames. He remembered the attempt during the ambush and felt a sickening wrench of his stomach.

"I... I don't know if I can," he said honestly. "Let's try to subdue him before it comes to that."

"How are we going to hold him once we do?" Orne asked, his combat instincts seeming to speak through his rage.

"He'll have a pouch on him like this one. Get it away from him and keep him away from any inanite. If we can do that, he shouldn't be able to use his gift."

"Surprise him, remove pouch, and then proceed to beat where Kolden is out of him. Got it."

A lone guard stood outside of the building's entrance. He raised a hand to Delvan and Orne, a look of sternness deeply set into his eyes. He opened his mouth but stopped as the pale light of the street revealed Delvan's Blue armor, giving the guard pause.

"My Lord," he said, "I'm sorry... but only officers are allowed inside uninvited, Sire."

Delvan remembered back to advice that Hilbrun had once given him. He wasn't an officer, but he was a Blue all the same. A power that most men didn't understand, and with that came fear. Quieting his own—trying to remove the tremble in his voice, the ache in his jaw—he spoke at the guard.

"Do you think I come here at leisure, in armor, soldier?" He tried to project authority, but he could feel his muscles quivering. Unseen, thorned vines wrapping around his chest and arm. "I'm here under orders, which you are currently obstructing. Now stand down and get out of our way."

Delvan tried to keep his face hard, but he could feel it faltering, twitching and fighting to reveal his own internal trepidation. The guard paused as he considered what to do, a brief moment that dragged on endlessly for Delvan.

"Yes, my Lord," the soldier finally said. Delvan felt a release of tension from his neck, one that he hadn't noticed until the overly taught muscles finally relaxed. He let out a long sigh after he passed the soldier returning to his post at the door.

Inside, he and Orne made their way to the stairs. The radiant warmth of another sapphire washed down on him from above, his own wrapped in a cloth dyed with muted inanite, smothering it to the senses of another Blue. They climbed, treading as silently as they were able, a steady creep that kept their armor from clattering.

At the third flood Delvan motioned to Orne: Ferrand was here. They stepped carefully down the wide, opulent passage, reaching the lone door with a bar of lantern light glowing from underneath. He nodded to Orne, pulling the sapphire from under his chest plate and prepared to rip the cloth off as Orne kicked down the door.

He didn't pray. He didn't expect the gods to accept what it was that he was about to do. He did hope. Hope that on the other side of this door he would find the vengeance he had sought for all these months. The answers to all the questions, including the most important one.

Why?

With a nod, Orne raised his long, muscular leg and kicked the door open with a crash of wood and metal. Delvan tore off the fabric from his gem and followed behind Orne as he stormed through the splintered frame.

Inside they found Ferrand, who had been sitting at a writing desk. The chair toppled to the floor behind him as he stood up, a confused scorn cut into his face. "What in the hell are you two doing?!" he shouted. "You fuckwits dare to break into my rooms? I'll have you court-martialed you little—"

Orne took four long strides forward—ignoring the rantings—and with steel covered knuckles brought all of his weight and strength to the commander's face with a herculean punch. Ferrand's head twisted to the side, his body fixed like a tree. Slowly, he turned his head back towards Orne, his face red and fists clenched, the smallest trickle of violet blood dribbling from his nose. Veins bulging on his temple and neck, he glared at Orne with a rage that seemed to dwarf the enormous man before him.

Orne reached for Ferrand's inanite pouch at his waist, his arm moving like a spring. But the commander swatted it away like a fly. With a scream he flung both hands forward and shoved Orne. Ferrand's feet slipped on the smooth wooden floor as they fought for purchase to move the mountainous man. They caught, and gave him leverage, sending Orne flying and landing on his back with a groan at the door, his armor scraping across the polished boards.

The commander turned to Delvan, his face alight with fury. "So, it finally comes to this, does it? I wondered if that southern shit-stain of a cadet ever got to you, pulled you under his influence. What did he tell you? Huh?"

"Don't you *dare* talk about him," said Delvan, tears in his eyes, lip shaking. "He's dead because of *you*, and I refuse to allow you to do it again!"

Delvan lunged forward, ducking under a punch from the commander and reaching for his waist. His fingers extended out, brushing against the leather pouch. It was nearly in his grasp. The commander twisted out of the way, pulling his precious inanite beyond Delvan's outstretched arm, leaving him stumbling forward towards the wall.

Delvan caught himself and spun, facing the commander who stood there staring at him, a mixture of curiosity and anger on his face. "Six months and you don't try a thing. To think, I was actually beginning to believe your father, seems that the infallible bastard *can* be wrong. What made you grow the balls now, boy? Huh?"

"You know *damn well* why," he said through gritted teeth. Delvan drew his sword, the steel sliding against its sheath with a menacing hiss. Ferrand raised an eyebrow at him, his eyes flicking to his massive sword leaning against the nearby wall.

*He won't use that in here,* thought Delvan, *there's not enough space to recover after a swing. He's going to have to improvise.*

Delvan still hesitated to approach the unarmed Jack. To them, everything was a weapon, and he couldn't afford a duel that resulted in the commander dead. Not yet.

With bent knees he took a defensive posture, stepping side to side as the commander leaned left or right. His hands were trembling, the light's reflection on his blade shimmering. The commander gave him a haughty smile, a smug expression that nursed the ire inside of Delvan. His jaw clenched tighter, he couldn't wait any longer, he *had* to act.

An outline appeared behind the commander like an oversized shadow, and from high in the air Delvan saw Orne bring down a chair on top of the commander's head. It exploded into fragments, chunks of wood scattering over the floor, leaving Orne standing there with the splintered stubs of a leg in each hand.

Ferrand staggered forward a step, putting a hand on the corner of his desk as he clutched the bleeding wound at the crown of his skull. His eyes went wide at the sight of the violet blood on his hand as he pulled it from his head, a mad wrath building behind them like a coming storm, his teeth flashing in a snarl.

Orne drew his sword, and again sprang forward to reach for the pouch. Delvan found his own courage in the company of his brother-at-arms and lunged forward as well. Ferrand was wounded and dazed, this was their opportunity, it must be seized.

But a predator is most vicious when cornered, and Ferrand was as animalistic as they came. He grabbed the leg of his man-length desk and twisted his body, the desk's legs leaving the ground as it spun through the air like a cudgel, a bludgeoning mass rotating and keeping Delvan at bay.

The carved wooden corner whirled only a few inches from Delvan's face as he teetered backward, the furniture-made-weapon continuing to rotate around until it reached Orne, who had been too close to Ferrand to avoid the full length of the wooden mass. He raised his plated forearms as it came at him in a blur, the edge of the desk striking them and sandwiching him against the wall. Chips of wood burst like shrapnel as he and the desk collided and slumped to the floor, his body limp.

Delvan cried out at the sight, a tear rolling down his face. He couldn't lose them both. His heart wanted to jump through his throat, his vision wavy as tears clouded his eyes and began to flow like a river. Instincts and grief moved him, raising his sword and slashing downward as he leapt forward.

The commander was dazed, but not immobile. With the grace of a lifelong fighter, he sidestepped, Delvan's blade whistling through nothing but air. With speed that could only come from the power of the sapphire around his neck, he grabbed Delvan's sword wrist, the other hand latching onto his throat.

Delvan felt the fingers squeezing, pressure building in his head that felt like it were being filled by a bellow. His vision went red as his feet left the ground, Ferrand raising him into the air. Orne was on the ground, still unmoving, and the crimson fringes of his vision brought back flashes of the fire, Hilbrun's face a mirage before him. Kolden was gone, and everything rested on him now as he was choking, dying, failing.

Not again.

He raised his left palm a few inches in front of the commander's face. Warmth began to radiate there, a distant feeling. The barricaded fire within him began to fight for freedom, a singeing heat emanating from him as his vision began transitioning from red to black.

"You actually going to be able to do it? Huh?" said Ferrand with derision. "No, you're weak, an ignorant fool, like your friend."

He grunted, it felt like the blood in his face was about to split his skin. His vision became blacker. He couldn't feel his arm any longer, the fire held at bay as the limb wavered and swayed. Hilbrun's face flashed before him once more, but it was not the torturous expression of death upon it. It was something worse.

Disappointment.

Desnia and Nerio moved at a brisk pace. The empty streets at the hour of speaks made movement quick, the sunset concealing them in darkness. Nerio did his best to keep up, but she could hear him panting with heavy breaths. Credit was owed, however, as he hadn't complained once.

As they approached the barracks, she pondered the question that had been bothering her the entire trip: Why had the Blue and his friend left earlier? What had she said to derive such urgency? It must have been in regard to the danger posed to the people in Drunt, but why leave so abruptly if that were the case. Unless they thought the danger was closer...

*Hey,* chirped Masini, *isn't that the Blue and his disproportionate friend?*

Her head shook from the cloud of her thoughts, focusing on the road ahead. As Masini had pointed out, she saw the two walking down the street, the tall one unmistakable even in the dim light. *Are they... wearing armor?* she thought as glints of light reflected off their shoulders and back.

A nauseous feeling churned in her stomach, her instincts telling her that something was wrong. Where were they going like that? And right after they'd hurried off?

"Nerio," she said, "where're the apartments for officers?"

"A few buildings ahead, on the left—" he cut off, squinting his eyes. "Is that... Lord Delvan and Orne?"

"I think so," she replied as the two spoke with the guard at the door before entering the building. "This can't be a coincidence..."

She wanted to rush, her legs full of tense anxiety, sensing that she didn't have much time. With a great deal of learned restraint, she walked at a more casual pace, not wanting to alert the guard as they strolled up to the building a minute later.

The soldier raised his hand—looking far too serious about his job—stopping them in the street. Desnia had to admit she was impressed, but also embittered. Most people wouldn't think twice about a Hand and a priest coming and going, she was normally invisible. What had the Blue said to get through?

"This building is only accessible by invite or while accompanied by an officer," the man said sternly.

*Or fully armored soldiers, apparently,* she thought.

Her mouth opened to speak, wanting to rebuke the man for not stopping the other two, but Nerio cut her off. "We're here to perform a private speak," he said politely. "We were requested by a Lord..." his eyes flicked to Desnia.

"Ferrand," she said quickly.

"Yes, that's it," confirmed Nerio. "Lord Ferrand has requested us, do you really wish to keep him waiting?"

*You should take him with you more often,* said Masini, *he's much better at this than you are.*

Her eye twitched as she resisted retorting him, waiting as the soldier looked at both of them. He sighed, "No one ever tells me anything," he said. "Fine, go on, the commander doesn't strike me as the patient type."

She forced a smile and nodded to him as they walked through the door. As they entered the building's anteroom, she looked around, hoping for information as to the commander's whereabouts. Frustratingly, the walls were bare save for the lavish paintings and superfluous ornaments.

"Where do you suppose he is?" asked Nerio.

"Not sure," she replied. "We might have to look around, maybe we can find—"

A distant crash from the stairwell caught her attention. Loud enough that it spoke to extreme force, but quiet enough that the guard past the closed door behind them didn't notice. *Must have been a few floors up,* she thought.

*Looks like we found him,* said Masini.

"Come on!" she said to Nerio as she sprinted for the stairs, jumping two at a time and pulling herself forward with the railing. The commotion continued, cries becoming clearer and clamoring louder as she flew up the stairwell. As she reached the third floor the noise settled, no longer guiding her way. But she knew they were on this floor, she could feel it, a chill running down her spine.

Their sandals smacked against the polished wooden floor, her hair whipping behind her as they sprinted at the lone open door that spilled light into the hall, a glowing marker of their destination. She skidded to a halt, perspiration soaking her hair as she gasped for breath.

Orne lay against a wall, a shattered desk atop of him, and a short man with gray streaks of hair held Delvan by the throat, his feet dangling above the floor.

"Stop!" she shouted as Nerio arrived behind her.

The man turned his attention to Desnia, his face twisted in angry bewilderment, Delvan's gurgling throat still in his hand. "Who the fuck are you?"

Shit. What was she supposed to say?

*Damn, looks like we're late to the party,* said Masini.

His voice triggered a response from her, a statement that she could only hope would tranquilize the situation. "Masini sent me," she said, her eyes wide and frantic.

*Uhh, Des,* came Masini's voice, *I'm pretty sure he thinks I'm dead. Might have forgotten to mention that...*

Shit.

The man—who she could only assume was Ferrand—narrowed his eyes, lowering Delvan so his toes almost touched the floor. The wreckage splintered across the room, combined with the man's controlled demeanor, made her knees feel weak. The blood trickling down the side of his face further imbued a sense of panic, wondering what he was contemplating doing to her.

"Prove it," said Ferrand tersely.

*Oh, uh, tell him 'When wolves meet lions,'* said Masini. *Also, that his hair makes him look like a rabid badger. That's important.*

"He, uh," she stammered, "said to tell you, 'When wolves meet lions'." Ferrand's expression revealed a glimpse of surprise through the intense inquisition, but he remained quiet while glaring at her with a terrifyingly cool rage. *Do I really have to say the last part? Gods-damn it, Masini.* If he had a body, she would've given him a swift knee to the crotch. "He also said… ugh, he also said that your hair made you look… like a rabid badger…"

She flinched as she said the words, turning her head away and watching the commander from the corner of her eye, waiting with nervous anticipation.

"So, the annoying fucker *is* alive. Here I was thinking I'd been blessed with never having to hear his voice again," said Ferrand.

*Well, that's just rude,* said Masini, sounding offended. Desnia wasn't sure why, it seemed like a common enough opinion.

"Are these two with you then?" he asked, motioning with his head to Delvan and Orne.

"Um, no? Kind of?" she said hesitantly.

"Well, which fucking one is it?" he asked.

"It's… a long story. Just, don't kill them, please," she said.

"Kill them?" the commander asked, now looking offended himself. He released Delvan's throat, his body collapsing on the floor as he coughed and wheezed while Ferrand pulled the sword from his hand. "I never intended to kill them, just give them a long overdue lesson."

With the tension broken, Nerio rushed past Desnia and knelt beside Orne, who finally began to move, groaning loudly as he pushed the desk's remnants off him. He shoved Nerio away as he rubbed his head, a scowl affixed to his face.

"What's with the priest?" asked Ferrand as Nerio abandoned Orne to check on Delvan, who was still hacking on the floor.

"Long story," she said.

"Desnia," said Nerio, his voice sounding fraught, "Lord Delvan is already bruising on his neck, there may be internal damage. We should get some herbs, I can—"

"He'll be fine," said Ferrand dismissively. "He's a Blue, the bruises will be gone by the morning on their own." He turned and looked at Desnia, his head tilting and eyes roving, as if digging through her. "Desnia? Why is that name so familiar?" His hand rubbed the top of his bloody head, his eyes suddenly lighting up. "Desnia, as in the *thief?* From Calentine? What the fuck are you doing out here?"

"Uhh," she said. She could talk to him about all of this, right? He knew Masini, who'd said that he was familiar with much of their operation. Did he know about the gate? *Here goes nothing.* "Looking for the gate."

A sharp breath pulled into Ferrand's nose as he looked her up and down. "Protorus didn't mention he was sending you out here too," he said. "Suppose it wouldn't hurt to have the help. Though I thought he implied that you were going to be doing something else."

A sigh of relief left her lips. Finally, someone who didn't reject her as sounding insane. A physical someone, anyway.

*Oh!* said Masini excitedly. *Him, the person he just said, P-P-P-damn it! That's my friend, the one you met at the iguan den. Find out where he is, why he didn't come himself.*

There were plenty of questions that she wanted answers to, but it was clear that Masini cared about this person. She was his voice, and this didn't seem the time to play games with him. Ignoring the low-toned screech of the desk across the floor as Orne kicked it away, she repeated Masini's question.

"After the robbery," Ferrand said, seeming unphased by the pair writhing on the ground, "which this idiot and his Magridi senior managed to epically fuck up, we drew a lot of *unwanted* attention. Protorus thought we were being hunted, as he put it, and drew them east, while I went west to the planned meeting spot, then here."

"Have you heard from him?" Desnia asked at Masini's request.

He shook his head. "Nothing for five months. And he's too punctual to not send me something. I think those fuckers got to him, which is all the more worrisome."

Desnia suddenly felt hollow, her heart ripped from her chest and tears forming in her eyes. Her body felt heavy, a weighted darkness that pulled down on her and attempted to collapse her to the floor. Masini was quiet, but his emotions pierced her like an arrow. She hadn't known this man, Protorus, but Masini had known him for longer than she could comprehend. This loss that flooded her... it was his.

It took a deep breath to calm the feeling, but it remained like a cloak over her shoulders. She pulled herself up, standing straight, debating what question to ask next as Nerio attempted to dress the commander's head wound. He waved him away and used a cloth to wipe the violet blood from his face, and Desnia's hand unconsciously felt at the scar on her forearm from what seemed a lifetime ago.

There was a loud cough that pulled her from the trance, Delvan rolling to his side, propping his body up with his arm.

"Where—" Delvan's voice was hoarse, and coughing came in fits. "Where is he? Bastard."

"This conversation doesn't concern you, cadet," said Ferrand. "I'll deal with you two later."

Orne pulled himself to his feet and, even hunched over, holding his head, Desnia still stood below his chest. His eyes were pinched tightly closed as he groaned, holding the wall for support. "Kolden, you fucking asshole. Where's Kolden?!" Desnia took a step away as the man spoke the words as though he were spitting fire and took a threatening step towards the commander.

"Your rodent brother? How the fuck should I know? Is *that* what brought you up here? Uh-uh, don't try it," he said, pointing Delvan's sword to Orne's throat as he reached down to grab his blade off the floor.

Orne stood up, peering down from his distant, vertical perch. There was only anger in his eyes, but Desnia could sense the worry, the concern burning within him. The fury was a mask, a thick plaster covering his distraught heart.

"He's missing, taken," said Delvan, still on the floor, his face slowly returning to its normal color as he wheezed.

"And you presumed *I* did it?" asked the commander. "I knew you two were dumber than jesters at a funeral, but this is a whole new level of stupid."

"He and your precious key are gone," said Orne, his face glowing scarlet. "We know you killed the last guy to keep it hidden, so don't even try to tell me you don't know what happened to Kolden. Now where is he?!"

"Orne!" exclaimed Delvan from the nearby floor.

*Did he just say, 'key?'* thought Masini and Desnia in unison.

Another pit opened in Desnia's stomach. That was the answer, the reason the pair had run off from her earlier meeting. The third one had *the* key, the one they had explained to be safely hidden in Drunt. Which meant that it was here, in Brethefen, and now it was missing.

*Oh fuck,* she thought.

"Shut up!" Ferrand snapped at Delvan, turning back at Orne and pressing the point of the sword against his throat. "Explain to me *exactly* what you meant by 'key'," he said, punctuating each word.

"You know damn well, asshole," said Orne, his face and voice rich with the same unwavering wrath. "The fucking rock that was hidden in Drunt, the one stolen from Calentine. Kolden found it, and now he and it are missing, and his room's been torn to shreds."

Desnia saw the commander's eyes flicker wide open before his brow furrowed and darkened them in rage. His loud breaths were audible, his grip on the sword's hilt tight enough to make the leather wrapping creak. He let out a slow, guttural growl that erupted into a scream of unadulterated, deafening ire.

"You *WHAT?!*" he bellowed.

*This is bad. Very, very bad,* said Masini, his voice sunken and lacking his chipper demeanor.

The commander stomped away from Orne, not caring that his back was to him, and kicked the desk that now laid on its side with a force that sent it rocketing at the wall. It exploded with a tumultuous crash, the wood bursting into minuscule debris and the plaster wall cracking to reveal broken bricks beneath.

Desnia shied back, her instincts telling her to run as she put a hand against the warm wall. Emotions ran wild through her, a stampede of anger, fear, betrayal, and dread flattening all in its path. She took a deep breath, looking around the room, Orne standing firm, Nerio with his back to a wall, and Delvan on his side, white as a sheet.

"Do you realize what you two dipshits have done?!" Ferrand screamed. "You've signed our death warrants! Us and the rest of the kingdom, the *world*. You've killed us all…" His shoulders slumped as he paced back and forth, his head low as he pulled on his graying hair. "When was he taken? From where?" he asked Orne, his voice still pealing through the room.

Orne glared down at him with narrowed eyes, arms crossed, lips drawn into a straight line. Ferrand leaned forward with growing impatience as seconds passed, Orne still silent. Finally, the towering man spoke in his deep resonance, "In the past two hours. From the barracks."

"Then pick up that sword, you're going to need it," said Ferrand as he went to the tall cabinet against the wall, opening it to reveal his armor within.

No.

This wasn't happening. Delvan watched from the floor—his throat aching and head still dizzy—as Ferrand yelled and lashed out, thinking that it all must be an act, that he was hiding the despicable fact that he'd taken Kolden.

But his thoughts were betrayed by his body, by the unseen hand that now gripped his heart harder than ever before. Paralysis took him, pain pulsated throughout, and his face turned cold as he tried to scream, rebel, fight against it and say something. All he managed was to open his throbbing jaw ever so slightly. A monumental effort for such little gain.

Ferrand was spitting lies, and now the girl, Desnia, was here too. Had she been working with him this entire time? They seemed acquainted, but he hadn't heard the start of the conversation. Not that it mattered. She was here now, and he was spewing the same sort of nonsense that she had been.

Had they planned Kolden's kidnapping together? A spike of pain and gasping lungs struck him at the thought. He couldn't allow them to hurt him, no matter the cost.

"No," he croaked, his voice weak and hoarse as he forced the word out from his position on the ground.

Orne seemed to be letting the commander order him around, or at least he was wasting opportunities to strike. Had the man truly been convinced that Ferrand was innocent? Was he believing his ravings and denials? Ferrand *had* to be responsible. If he wasn't...

The other explanation would be that Hilbrun was who Ferrand and Desnia claimed him to be, an agent of forces that slaughtered with disregard and sought utter destruction. The thought split cracks in his already weak facade, the dam of denial faltering and its leaks streaming from Delvan's eyes.

Desnia heard his faint words, turning to look at him with those same, empathetic eyes he'd seen once before. They were difficult to distrust, an honesty beaming from them, but no, he couldn't accept her sympathy without accepting that her logic may be of merit. And she was wrong. Misguided though she may be, she couldn't be right.

If the commander had heard him, then he'd been ignored. He bolstered himself, tightening his muscles despite the pain, forcing out the word louder through his cracked voice and bruised neck, "No!"

The commander stopped pulling his armor from the cabinet and turned to him, taking two strides forward and looking down at Delvan's crumpled figure.

"What the hell are you saying, boy?" he asked.

"I-I don't believe you," Delvan said through the stabbing agony in his throat. "You've done something with Kolden, you must have."

"You're fucking dense, you know that?" Ferrand asked with a shake of his head. "Listen, dunce, you think that I'd still be in the city if I had the key? No. I'd be halfway to the sea right now, going to throw it in the deepest fucking crevasse I could find. The Magridi have Kolden, they've probably been following you since you arrived in the city and somehow figured out that you had the key."

The last comment drew a glower from Orne, directed at Delvan. He tried to ignore it, he'd prove the truth to Orne.

"The fact that Kolden wasn't dead in his rooms," continued Ferrand, "means that he might still be alive. But if it's the person I suspect that has him, then he'll be alive for a while, but soon he's going to wish he wasn't…"

"I don't believe you," said Delvan. "Hilbrun's dead because of you, what's to stop you from hurting Kolden to get what you want?"

The commander's face shifted, the bright fire of anger darkening to a duller, grim shade. He actually looked remorseful, as if pained by the death of Hilbrun. *This is all an act,* Delvan reminded himself, *he's putting on a show for the others.* But it felt raw, real. Doubt began trickling through, eroding more of his internal barricade.

"I didn't want your senior dead, Cadet. He was Magridi, a southerner," Ferrand said, spitting on the floor, "but he was still a Blue. You two were the ones who went charging into that fucking place, no support, nothing. It was a catastrophic fuck up, yes, but I dealt with the bastard responsible, and you, as I understand it, killed the rest of the lot—present company excluded.

"You think your friend so high and noble, but tell me, Cadet, what was the guild, which he and his father were members of, doing with a half dozen sapphires? Hmm? Have you thought about that? Or did you just ignored that little bit of information because it didn't fit *your* stupid fucking narrative?"

Delvan looked away, searching for an answer. He remembered the sapphires, their radiance unmistakable to him, but he'd never understood why they had been there. The strictest laws in the kingdom revolved around the King's gems, and no one—outside of a bearer—was permitted to own them. If they were not being worn, they were stored and guarded by the crown.

And yet, there had been several in that vault.

Maybe... Maybe he'd been wrong? He didn't believe that, but what other argument could be made? "My father said they didn't find any sapphires in the wreckage," Delvan said, unable to say it while looking at the commander. "I must have been wrong."

A voice from behind Ferrand came, softer and full of sorrow. "You weren't," said Desnia. "I saw them, they were there."

"Your father," said Ferrand, "said what he had to in front of the rest of the Court. It's difficult enough to deal with those fucking merchants having half the nobility in their pocket, accusing them of treason without evidence would never have gotten anywhere."

Delvan suppressed the urge to vomit, his hands and face becoming clammier than they already had been. His whole body began to tremble, the room's lanterns blinding him. For months, images of that night, the fire, the pain, had haunted him, replaying in his head and hindering his life, crippling him. But now he thought back to the events leading to what happened.

Hilbrun was a member of the guild, there was no disputing that. Delvan remembered being outside the vault, Hilbrun taking his side as he... as he argued that he could sense sapphires in the vault. Hilbrun had known, there had been no surprise in his eyes. Did that make him guilty of everything else they claimed about these *Magridi*?

The feeling in his stomach compounded tenfold, and there was no resisting the bile that forced its way from his stomach to the floor, splattering across polished wood and splintered refuse. Every fiber of his body shook and trembled as he collapsed further onto the floor, grief, anger, betrayal all washing over him like waves across a hull. He'd sought retribution for months, grief masked by hatred helping to drive him forward. What was there now? If… If that is who Hilbrun was, could he justify becoming the same?

"We get it, the guild are assholes," came Orne's booming voice. "Now tell me where the fuck they took Kolden before I go back to beating it out of you."

"Aren't you fucking tenacious. If he had the key," said Ferrand, "there's only one place *to* take him: the gate."

Kolden. Delvan lay there on the floor, tormented by the spirit of his lost friend, forgetting that another was in danger. Hilbrun was dead, but there was a chance that Kolden was still alive. If he did nothing, then what chance did Kolden have? Doubts flourished within him: What if he was wrong? What if he made a mistake? Would it cost Kolden his life too? Would he be able to live with that? He wanted to act, but his body felt like a stone, resisting him.

"Then why the fuck are we standing around here?!" boomed Orne. "Let's go!"

"I don't know for certain where it is," said Ferrand walking back to his armor. "That's part of the reason I came here, to find it and go on the offensive while there were still any of us left alive. Thief girl, is Masini anywhere nearby? I might need to gag the annoying shit, but we could use his help. I don't know what we can do against however many mages are in the city."

"Uh," Desnia said, "he's… not available to help, no. But Nerio and I—"

"Figures," interrupted the commander. "Alright, we'll just have to do this the old-fashioned way. Find some people and beat the information out of them. *Maybe* we reach the gate before they can activate it."

"Mhmm," grunted Orne satisfactorily.

Delvan listened to all of this as though a spectator in the high seats of a theater. His world spun around him, collapsing into the eye of the storm within. His longing for vengeance waned. It had held back his grieving, damming it to protect him from its constant flow, but now it had failed, and he was flooded with pain. He began to sob, alone on the floor. He was helpless to save Kolden. How could he hope to rescue him when he hadn't even been able to protect his friend?

Not only that, but now he'd failed to avenge Hilbrun. Everything had seemed easier when Ferrand was the villain he'd constructed in his head, the mastermind behind Hilbrun's death and agent of the enemy. But now everything was muddled, as obscure as his vision through his clouded eyes.

It ripped him apart to admit that Ferrand hadn't kidnapped Kolden, because it diverted the blame for all of this. Discovering the plot that led him and Hilbrun to the guild, and now the letter that he'd written which preceded Kolden's abduction. The person to blame, the introspective understanding that he'd avoided all this time, was none other than… He couldn't say it, even in his own mind.

And that crushed him.

A gentle hand rested on his shoulder. He opened his blood-shot eyes, pained and blurred, to see the priest, Nerio, kneeling beside him, a look of understanding on his face. His eyes seemed old beyond his years, aged by his own internal conflict, and as much as it hurt, Delvan knew he wasn't alone.

He sat up and embraced the priest, his face burying into his robe and soaking it with the torrent of tears spilling from him. His ears heard the world moving around him, the others continuing their conversations while he held Nerio, but in their shared pain the world stopped for a moment, the floodgates of his self-loathing opening wide.

# Chapter Forty-Nine

*Water falls*
*On wind blown*
*Seas rage*
*Among storms sown*
*Blossoms bloom*
*By its will, grown*

*What is this pain in my head,* thought Kolden as he rolled onto his side, the cold rock beneath him rough and damp.

His eyes gradually opened, trying to blink away the translucent haze. The room glowed a steady purple, the distant periphery a deep shade bordering black, like a starless night sky. As his vision cleared, he realized that he was inside of a cage, the bars thick and heavily rusted, too low for him to stand completely up in. The rods of iron were set directly into the stone he laid upon, a heavy lock on the top lip.

He groaned as he grabbed the back of his head, feeling slick blood in his hair. *What happened?* he thought as he tried to remember while his head throbbed in pain. He'd gotten to the barracks, started digging through his trunk to find the cadentite, then a sound from behind him before everything went black.

He sat up from the wet rock, his clothes damp and clinging uncomfortably to his skin, hearing water dripping somewhere in the distance as each drop echoed off the cavern's rough, dome-shaped surface. It was gigantic, the ceiling reaching high enough that the dim light struggled to reach it, and doubly as wide. At the center, the floor *glowed*, as if dim sunlight were beaming upwards through stained glass, casting dark shadows all around the expansive, circular perimeter of the chamber. He couldn't get himself tall enough to see what the source of the strange light was, but it captured his curiosity.

*Where am I?* he wondered.

A soft whimper caught him by surprise, twisting his head to find its source and wincing, his teeth flashing at the sharp pain shooting through his neck. Rubbing it he realized that the blood had flowed down past his shirt. *That would explain the lightheadedness,* he thought. Kolden opened his eyes again to find that his was not the only cage in the room.

Several of the barred prisons lined the far wall alongside him, some vacant, others with curled bodies that lay still. The cage adjacent to his held what he thought to be a young boy, maybe thirteen years old. It was difficult to tell with his hollow face and thin, frail limbs garbed in a filthy and tattered robe. His knees were held tightly to his chest, and he was shaking as he cried.

"Hey," Kolden tried to say in a calming whisper that came out as a haggard groan. "Hey, where are we?" he said as he shuffled to the edge of the cramped box of iron rods and leaned on the coarse metal, getting as close as he could to the boy.

The boy just shook his head, keeping his eyes fixed on his knees. He rocked slightly as he avoided Kolden's question. *C'mon,* he thought, *I need to figure out where I am and how to get out of here.* The abused child was obviously terrified—not that Kolden could blame the kid—but he *needed* information. He decided to try a different approach.

"Hey," he said again, whispering just loud enough for the boy to hear. "My name's Kolden, what's yours?"

"Shh," the boy hushed. "Be quiet, or you'll make them angry." He spared Kolden a half second glance before turning his eyes back to his knees.

"C'mon," Kolden whispered, "I just want to know your name."

There was a pause as the boy's gaze drifted, the odd glowing light casting deep shadows over his starved face. After a few moments he responded with his weak voice, "Floran."

"Alright, Floran," Kolden said before sucking air through his teeth at a flare of pain in his head. It eventually passed, dulling back to the agonizing pressure that filled his skull. "I'm going to get us out of here, Floran, but I need your help. Can you tell me where we are?"

"Under… Underground," he said with a tremor.

*I realized that much,* thought Kolden, *I need specifics.* "Do you know where? Or how they got us down here?"

"There's tunnels," the boy said quietly enough that Kolden strained to hear from even a few feet away. "All around. I don't know where they lead exactly."

Kolden rubbed his face before realizing he was smearing his blood all over it. He sighed, wiping it with his sleeve. It wasn't a lot of information, but it was something. As he posed another question, he began carefully testing the bars for any that might be loose. "Did you see who brought me down here?"

Floran nodded. "It was the new one, I haven't seen him before. They're all scared of him though."

*Well, that's reassuring.* He tried not to show his concern as he jiggled another bar. *This is all because of that gods-damned cadentite. If only I'd just left it buried in the wall back in Drunt.* The bars were grouted into the floor, none seeming to budge. He tested another, feeling a slight give in the corroded metal.

"How long have you been down here?" Kolden asked, trying to divert his focus from the frightened thoughts in his mind.

Floran shrugged. "Not sure, it's hard to keep track of time here. Months, maybe?"

*He looks like this after a few* months? *What are these bastards doing?*

Kolden pulled harder on the metal bar, hearing it creak and pop, but it refused to release. Questions swam in his mind as he tried pressing on the bar instead of pulling it. Had the others noticed he was missing? How long had he been unconscious? Could he hope for Orne or Delvan to find him?

"Do you know why we're in cages?" he asked Floran.

The boy's eyes went wide, a horrified expression from the gaping sockets, his gaunt face drawing back. Floran just shook his head as he began to rock back and forth more vigorously. Kolden sensed that the boy knew the answer, but whatever it was petrified him.

"Why, so you don't escape, of course," came a voice that slithered through the cavern. Kolden spun, putting the bar he'd been prying at to his back, his head splitting at the sudden movement. A man walked towards them, a slight limp to his gait. His face was heavily scarred, and despite his young appearing features, more white hair than black flowed from his head. He looked at Kolden with a smile on his lips that his eyes did not reciprocate, a dangerous falseness betrayed by the look.

In one of his hands was the cadentite key, pitting his features in ominous shadow from its purple luster, and in the other hand was something that Kolden recognized.

"I must admit," the man said with his slow, unnerving voice, "I had hoped that you'd make finding this more difficult. I'd heard that your party held their own so valiantly along the road from Drunt that I presumed I'd be able to enjoy some of the fun myself once I arrived. And I don't really appreciate the amount of scrubbing I had to do to clean the black paint off of this, clever though it may have been."

He walked closer to Kolden's cage, squatting down to put the two of them at a similar level, rotating the hand that held the key as if to display its masterfully carved grace. Kolden stared back at him with a chiseled anger, thinking about what more this man could want from him. He saw Floran huddling in a corner, making himself small and trembling.

"But then," the man continued, "you surprised me; a difficult feat, I assure you. Finding this inside your footlocker made you so much more..." he took a deep breath through his nose, a strange, sickly smile came to his face. It seemed genuine, in a revolting sort of way. "Interesting."

He slid the key into his pocket—pinpricks of light filtering through the fabric—and held up the item in his other hand. With a brief hiss of metal sliding against metal, he drew the knife that Kolden had forged using the cadentite dust—among a concoction of other things. It still fluoresced with the same purple hue that filled the cavern, albeit much fainter, and it seemed to pronounce the scarring on his captor's face as he held it up and stared at it with reverence.

"I'd thought all the vi-blades in this realm to be muted or destroyed," the man said. "Tell me, where did you get this? It is not from the High Realm. Was it forged here?"

*What the hell is this freak talking about?* thought Kolden. He kept his lips tightly pressed together, answering this man didn't seem the wisest choice. He had no reason to keep Kolden alive now that he had what he wanted, did he? Were this man's questions of Kolden keeping blood in his veins, or was there another sinister purpose?

"A quiet one, most excellent," he said with another haunting smile. "You're going to give me a challenge after all, how considerate of you. It will provide me with a distraction while we finish preparing, and then I can be on to new, exciting prey.

"Tell me, Kolden, was it? Did the person who gave this to you explain what it was capable of? No? I assumed not, there are so few of us that still remember, after all. I could explain it, I suppose, but I've always found demonstrations to be the most effective teaching tool. Although it's unfortunate that it lacks runes. The instrument that it could be..." The strange man trailed off, spending most of the one-sided conversation staring at the luminous blade with a distant awe.

Kolden's curiosity itched at him, wondering what it was that this deviant meant by his confusing admiration. He kept his mouth shut, however, trying frantically to think of a means to escape. *I need to buy time,* he thought.

"Normally," the man said as he stood, "I like to take my time, enjoy the artistry of the process. But vi-blades don't function properly if such recreational pleasures are indulged." He took a step away from Kolden, to Floran's cage. With a key from his pocket he unlocked the cell, pulling on the cage's top and pivoting it on groaning hinges, removing the roof of the small prison.

*What is he doing?* thought Kolden as his heart began to race in a panic, nearly forgetting about the pain in his head. The man reached into the cage, grabbing Floran by his stick-like arm and hauling him out while he whimpered and feebly tried to resist. A smile curved from eye to eye of the disturbed man as he looked down at the pleading child.

"Wait!" cried Kolden, but he was ignored. "I'll tell you what you want! Just let him go, and I'll tell you whatever you want to know!"

"I know you will, in time," said the man as he began to raise the knife up high.

"Stop!" cried Kolden. He stood as tall as he could, pressing the bars on the roof of his cage to his back. He pushed with all his might, grunting as his legs exerted every pound of force they could. But it did little more than rattle the unmoving iron. He tried slamming upward, battering himself against the bars to no avail. He fell to the floor, ready to start kicking the bars in front of him with his bare feet when he saw the knife plunge down, the full length of the blade disappearing into Floran's chest.

The boy's fearful eyes went even wider, his body becoming tense and rigid. The malevolent creature that held him tilted his head back with a euphoric smile, as if the experience were giving him a high. Kolden's jaw fell open, his heart dropping to the floor as Floran's body went limp.

*Why?* Kolden thought with disbelief. *What kind of a monster is this... thing?*

With a quick breath through his nose and steady exhale, the abomination before him let Floran's corpse fall to the floor, withdrawing Kolden's blood-soaked blade from his chest. It glistened and shimmered through its crimson coating, and despite the thick layer of dripping blood, Kolden saw that the blade had grown brighter. It was still soft on the eyes, but bright enough now to clearly display his captor's scarred face.

"Beautiful, isn't it?" asked the man as he wiped the blade clean on Floran's grimy clothes, then holding it up like a trophy. "If only most of you Samrans weren't so weak, perhaps this could burn with its true potential, rather than this paltry essence. It is a start though."

Kolden was still sitting there, motionless, feeling like his insides had been ripped out. Floran's body remained a crumpled heap on the floor, blood spreading outward on the smoothly textured floor of stone. All of this had been... for what? A demonstration, as the man had put it? A life taken for another's amusement. The depravity...

The man pulled the key from his pocket, holding it in his palm, the surrounding fingers pointed directly upward. To Kolden's astonishment, thin lines of light formed around the man's digits, just above the stone, transforming into a glowing pattern of purple-like ink on an invisible piece of parchment.

With careful precision he dipped the point of the blade down through the center of the illuminated disc of repetitive light and touched the blade's point to the key. Like a lantern being dimmed, the light faded from the knife, the radiance within the key becoming a nearly imperceptible shade brighter, its gently wavering luster a tranquil shine that veiled the horror of its new contents.

As the blade's own gleam faded to just brighter than where it had originally been, the man pulled it away, the bizarre pattern of light disappearing.

"Thank you," said the murderous sociopath, "this will make things so much faster for us."

*Us?*

"Hunter," came a commanding voice that resounded through the cavern, as if to answer Kolden's question. As the other man strode in, Kolden tried to pull himself from the shocked grief to see where he had come from. *Is that the cave entrance out of this place over there?* he wondered looking at one of the many gaps in the wall nearby.

This one was older, rotund, and balding, with lush blue robes that made him easily identifiable as the principal for Almedia. He walked to the man before Kolden without reproach nor regard for the remains of the young boy at his side.

"Yes?" Hunter asked with his serpentine draw.

"You've found it? Excellent, well done." The principle smiled with a mad grin, taking the key from Hunter. "It's nearly muted, what were those merchants doing while it was in storage? It's going to take weeks to harvest enough energy to fully open the gate."

Kolden watched the pair, debating which of them was the more insane. A pit grew in his chest for the boy, but he couldn't focus on that now. He had to figure out how to escape these lunatics before he became the next supplier of this *vi-blade* he'd unwittingly created.

"Not with this," said Hunter, presenting Kolden's craftsmanship to his partner. "It was with the key."

"Well, well. You've truly outdone yourself, we may see home sooner than expected. It's not one of ours though, where'd it come from?" the principle asked, inspecting the blade.

"I was just inquiring about that as you arrived, actually," said Hunter.

"Ah, so this was the key's keeper," the principle said, turning his attention to Kolden. He walked over to the cage, Kolden glaring at him while he looked down through the bars with contemptuous apathy, as though Kolden were a violent dog to be put down. "I'm most curious to hear your findings," he said, addressing Hunter. "If there is someone of this realm who is capable of forging a vi-blade, we should eliminate them before they can teach others.

"I do suppose it will be the problem of the next governor... Maybe it would be best if we avoided the subject once the arrival begins."

"Of course. I can have the answer soon enough, I'm sure," said Hunter with a look to Kolden that made his insides turn. "If you weren't already aware, this one arrived with two tainted ones."

"I'd heard that," replied the principle. "I'd considered it too great a risk, but with a vi-blade... We could charge the key well beyond minimum levels. Yes, excellent thinking, Hunter. Can you deal with them tonight? I'm sure this one can wait."

"Been a while since I've killed a tainted one. Should be fun."

*Oh fuck, Del,* thought Kolden. *And they might be looking for me... They'd be walking into a trap.*

The principle turned from Kolden as if he were little more than a penned animal and began walking towards the center of the cavern, admiring the glowing stone that shimmered like a star in his hand. Kolden watched as he walked over the source of the room's illumination, the floor throwing long streaks of black over his clothing and face.

Kolden had to warn Delvan. His palms sweat and heart pounded as he tried to plot a method of escape. He cautiously moved his hand over his pockets, wondering if they left anything on him. Dishearteningly he found them empty, and aside from his boots, his belt had also been removed. His lips downturned into a grimace, wanting for nothing more than to jump from the cage and stab Hunter in the heart.

He looked to Floran's body again, pity welling within him. *How many people have they done this to?* he thought. *And to just a kid? What kind of heinous, twisted people would do this?* He looked to the other cages, the fragile, weak bodies of others laying there, too exhausted to move. None of them appeared large enough to be a grown man, and Kolden's stomach somersaulted once more.

"Our appointment will have to wait, it seems," came the chilling voice of Hunter again as he looked at Kolden. "Don't worry, I'll save some energy for you."

Kolden shifted uneasily on the cool floor, trying to avoid those dead, glossy eyes that didn't seem to blink. He watched the principle reach the center of the cavern's floor, where he stopped and inspected the key once more, as if he were admiring it, before kneeling down and resting it on the floor.

Kolden craned his neck, trying to see what he was doing, but his low angle made it impossible. Hunter watched with quiet reverence, as if this moment were a holy ritual. Kolden heard the cadentite touch against the rock of the floor, but strained to get a better—

The area around the principle flared with a massive burst of light. Where once the cavern's distant walls had been draped by shadow, their every nook and surface now came into clear view. Kolden had to shield his eyes from the glare as they painfully adjusted to the now nearly white radiance, its outer reaches a lustrous purple. He squinted as he pulled his hand away, seeing both Hunter and the principle with malicious smiles.

It was as though they had captured the power of the sun itself. Kolden's eyes eased back open with sickening horror. Whatever this was, it being controlled by these two left no doubt that it was intended for nefarious acts, and Kolden's hands began to tremble as he wondered at the power before him.

The principle looked to Hunter with that unnerving smile, and with his voice echoing over the walls said, "There might only be enough for one or two right now, with the—"

He cut off and looked down with confused anger as the light flickered, the floor's radiance reverting back to the comparatively dull glow from when Kolden had awoken. A moment later it flashed back to its intense illumination for but a fraction of a second, then repeated the sequence intermittently, creating a dizzying strobe effect that hurt Kolden's eyes.

The principle reached down and pulled the key back up from the floor, the room graciously staying the same dull shade as Kolden tried to repress the nausea that the flashing had induced. Even as his eyes adjusted back to the dark, he could plainly see a scowl on the principle's face as he held the radiant stone a few inches from it, his eyes observing its every detail.

"Someone has ground away one of the corners!" the principle shouted.

Kolden's heart began beating harder and he could feel his neck pulsating as it pumped fear through his veins. He remembered back to the days he'd spent grinding enough material to create the knife that Hunter villainously adored, his nausea returning stronger than ever.

"Who did this?!" the principle screamed as he stormed back over, the faceted stone waving in his hand. "Who dared defile this in such a way?"

He looked at Kolden as he asked, apparently now expecting him to speak. Kolden shuffled to the back of the cage, keeping his mouth shut. He suspected there wasn't an answer he could give that would calm the man's fury.

"Can it be fixed?" asked Hunter.

"Can it-Can it be *fixed*?" stammered the principle. "There probably isn't a piece of cadentite in this entire *realm* this size. We're going to have to modify the seat... It could restrict how many could come through, or at what rate! Damn it!" He waved his arms as his cries reverberated across the smooth walls.

*Well, at least something good came out of all that effort,* Kolden thought, trying to claim whatever victory he could from his cramped cell, even if it were a small one.

"But a new one could be made, once enough supplies were brought through, no?" asked Hunter.

"Yes! But... Gah! It's going to delay everything. She'll be furious!" The principle's voice was now almost as panicked as it was angry. He was pacing, running his hand through his hair.

"She's waited millennia," said Hunter in that eerily calm voice, "a short while won't change anything. She will have her prize, and us ours."

The principle's pace slowed as he considered the words. His lips remained in a tight line, but he nodded slowly. "Yes, yes we can fix this. I will make a modification to the key's seat. In the meantime, deal with our unwanted guests."

"Yes," Hunter said with a slight bow, "of course—"

Someone ran through what Kolden decided *must* be an exit on the wall nearby, and for a moment his heart jumped with hope. A soldier trotted in, calling out in a frenzy. *Yes,* thought Kolden as he waited for more reinforcements to come.

But his heart sank back into his bowels as the soldier began addressing the principle and Hunter directly. "My Lords," he said, using a title that wouldn't normally be appropriate for a member of the clergy, "something has happened, you must come."

"I *told you*, no interruptions!" screamed the principle.

The soldier flinched but continued. "I know but, my Lord, it's an emergency."

"And what," said Hunter, "is so urgent you felt it warranted our disturbance?"

"Sire," the soldier said, addressing the principle. "It's... better if you come see for yourself."

# Chapter Fifty

*The mind's sight*
*Infinite within, endless without*
*Borne by others' wills*
*Sailing into shadow*

W ould you all just stop and shut up for one *fucking* second?!" screamed Desnia.

She couldn't handle the storm of their emotions raging within her, tearing her one direction then another, from grief to anger, from despondent to anxious. She tried to drag and suffocate them under her normally stern and callous surface, but the effects of everything in the disheveled room caused her to lose control, breaking as her fuse reached its end.

Nerio only responded to her outburst with a glance and was still consoling Delvan on the floor, but the heads of Orne and Ferrand turned to her with their tenable scowls. They understandably wanted to hurry and find the key and Kolden, but rushing off aimlessly wasn't going to get them anywhere. Not in time.

"You can't just go fighting your way to the gate," she said, "Nerio and I—"

"We absolutely fucking can," said Ferrand, Orne nodding in agreement, "and that's what—"

"Interrupt me again and I'll stab you in the dick while you're sleeping," spat Desnia, her brow furrowed deeply into her eyes.

Ferrand's brow raised itself high, silently surprised by her outburst, while Orne just looked at her, seeming impressed.

*Nicely done,* said Masini, who still lacked his upbeat tone. *I don't think I've ever seen him gawk before.*

"Nerio and I have a plan, one that *doesn't* involve killing anyone *and* gets us a potential map to the gate," Desnia finally managed to say.

"Why didn't you just fucking say so?" asked Ferrand in a condescending voice.

She looked at him, her eyes colder than the steel blades they threw. "Stabbing... Dick..."

"What's this 'plan'?" asked Orne.

"We think that Principle Jerdine might have—" she started.

"Jerdine?" retorted the commander. "You want to go after a High Realm mage? Are you insa—"

"I swear to the fucking gods, if you don't shut that waste of air you call a mouth, I am going to do so much worse than just stab you in your sleep," she said, exasperated. "You talk about Masini, but I'd take him over your intolerable ass any day."

*Aw,* said Masini, *you say the sweetest things.*

She could feel her face turning red, the tumult of emotions twisting together to become rage towards this insolent prick of a Blue. They glared at each other, both refusing to back down from the other's stare, her hands clenched tightly into balls.

"We don't have time for your pissing contest," boomed Orne. "Speak."

Desnia ground her teeth, finally pulling her eyes from the commander to look at Orne, his face stricken with worry layered with wrath. Delvan had pulled himself from Nerio's embrace, looking at her with eyes like red coals, face drenched in tears as he and Nerio sat side by side on the floor.

"Principle Jerdine," she continued, with a cold glance to the commander, "is one of the people trying to open the gate, he has been for a... long time. Nerio has been in the principle's chambers, and we know that he has a small library kept behind lock and key. We suspect that one of these books contains the location of the gate."

"And what?" asked the commander. *At least he didn't interrupt me this time.* "You plan on just going up there and asking for it? Because I don't know that, even *if* that worthless waste of armor," he said, pointing at Delvan, "was with me and Orne here, if we'd be able to take him on."

"What?" said Orne, looking confused. "How could some old fucking priest be so dangerous? We can absolutely take him."

Desnia knew that Orne didn't understand. Hell, *she* didn't even fully understand. Masini had never been able to describe much about the people like him or his friend, Protorus, and she'd been left to make assumptions based on his vague and ominous descriptions.

"You two dipshits couldn't even take *me* by surprise," snapped Ferrand. "Him and the other mages are ancient. Masters of power unlike anything even a sapphire can imbue, and they see us as fucking *livestock*. If we charge into his chambers *maybe* we stand a chance, but not all of us are making it out. We'd lose too many of our already limited resources before we'd found the gods-damned gate."

*Does this ass see everything as a fight?* she wondered. The streets had taught her that painful lesson early. Run, and you live. Fight only as a last resort. The bold could occasionally battle their way to the top, but most died along the way. The most successful were smart, making others fight for them, or using other tactics altogether...

"We're not going to fight him," Desnia said, "we're going to rob him."

Orne grunted. Was he... upset? The man was a difficult read. Ferrand thankfully shut his mouth, his hands resting on his hips as he looked at her with thin eyes. She could feel him judging her, as men were wont to do, trying to find holes in her plan. It made her seethe.

"Isn't the tower also his sleeping quarters?" Ferrand finally asked. "You just going to try and break in while he's home?"

"Jerdine gives the evening speak at the Devapuram tonight," said Nerio's humble voice as he stood. "He goes to the bathhouse afterward for an hour. Always."

Desnia and Nerio had discussed the plan on the walk here. She'd hoped to do this tomorrow or the day after, giving her more time to prepare, but the circumstances dictated otherwise. Nerio knew the principle's schedule well, and they were confident she'd be able to work without intrusion.

Assuming everything else went as expected.

"If he's not there, let's just use the front door!" exclaimed Ferrand. "Why bother with this sneaking around when we can get in and out in no time?"

"There's at least a hundred disciples in that tower," she said, remembering her climb up the stairs, the looks from each of them as she led the soldiers upward. "If even *one* of them recognizes any of us and goes and tells Jerdine what we've done, he'll come for us. No, this is the best way."

"Gods-damn it," said Ferrand with a resigned sigh, as if he were incapable of admitting someone else was right. It made her nails dig into her palm. "That barely gives us over an hour. Can you get in and out that quickly?"

"If we hurry, yes," she said, a sense of urgency building. "I hid my tools in my old room at the clergy house, I can grab them and then..." She hesitated, this was the part that was daunting.

"Then what?" asked Orne, stopping forward.

"I... I'll need to climb in from the balcony," she said, her guts twisting. It wasn't the heights that concerned her, but their lack of time. Getting a few hundred feet into the air by scaling the tower was no small feat, even for someone with her expertise. She would still need time to get through the lock and escape—another hole in her plan currently.

"We can talk about this on the way there," said Ferrand, buckling the last piece of his armor on and strapping the sword that was taller than him to his back. "Dumbass, you coming? You're probably going to be useless, but we need everyone," he said to Delvan.

*He's fucking insufferable,* she thought as she curiously wondered why Ferrand was willing to quickly forgive the person who'd just attacked him. Was he just looking for resources, help in finding the gate? Or was there more to it?

Delvan hung his head low, and Desnia felt that stab of guilt and loathing again. She could feel her eyes beginning to water and fought it off. He slowly pulled himself up, the lantern light reflecting off his dark, polished armor, giving him the appearance of a wraith—a husk of a person. He looked at Ferrand with his raw, red eyes, haunted by grief and torment.

"I don't forgive you for Hilbrun's death," he said, his hoarse voice like ice.

"For fuck's sake," said Ferrand, tossing up his hands. "Get a hold of yourself, dipshit. Do you know how many people have died in the millennia that these fuckers have been warring? Do you think that you're the only one to lose friends? The lives of everyone in the kingdom, anyone you've *ever known*, are at stake here.

"You want to have it out with me? Fine. You want to report me to the Court? It's a waste of fucking time but go ahead. Do what you want. Just do it *after* we get the key—"

"And Kolden," said Orne.

"—and the rodent, back."

Delvan stood there, motionless, hand on the hilt of his sword that he'd picked back up. He looked too tired to be angry, a sense of defeat set into the sockets that stared at the commander. He turned his gaze to Desnia, then to Orne before sheathing the blade and running both his hands through his hair, sighing.

"I'm coming for Kolden," said Delvan, drawing out the words. "But when this is over, I swear by the gods, I'm going to—"

"Yeah, yeah. Complain on the way, let's go!" said Ferrand as he stormed out the door, brushing past Desnia.

*Ah yes,* said Masini, *as pleasurable as I remember.*

Desnia turned, looking at Delvan's chagrined visage once more in the full light of the destroyed room's lanterns before walking into the much dimmer hallway. She followed the commander, Orne's feet landing heavily enough behind her to make the floor bounce slightly. With a quick glance backward as she reached the stairs, she saw Nerio and Delvan hurrying behind.

There was a sense of relief seeing the Blue, though it was difficult to say why. His help could be the difference between life or death for them, but that wasn't the reason she wanted him here. There was more that she couldn't explain, like she was staring at the glimmer of a distant fire in the night—apparent but shrouded in mystery.

She rushed down the stairs as fast as her legs could pedal as she attempted to keep up with Ferrand. They stormed out of the front door, ignoring the confused guard beside it. The clergy house wasn't too far, assuming they got there before most of the speaks finished. Still, the worry of time hung in the back of her mind.

As they marched down the street Orne's stride faded. After a moment she looked back to see him running to rejoin them, the chain on his armor rattling. She listed to the side of the road to put a gap between her and the others, whispering under her breath, "I'm sorry about your friend."

*Thanks,* said Masini. *He'd tell me to focus on the task at hand or some logical nonsense, but, uh, it's harder than it seems.*

"Sounds like he did this to buy us time," she said. "Seems he did a lot to try and protect you. Must have been close."

*As close as cohabitation can make someone. We were very different people, as you can imagine, but we shared the same ideal. The important one anyway. Can you believe he never accepted my invitation to an orgy? Not once. I had sworn to get him to one eventually, then the bastard went and pulled this self-sacrificing ridiculousness.*

There was a pain that cut through the jokes, a mourning that dragged everything down with it. Her pace slowed for a second as they walked down the lamp-lit street, falling even further behind the inhumanly quick trot of the commander.

"Well, let's make it worth something," she said. "We can end this. Tonight. What were you saying about Jerdine having protections on the library?"

*Yes, um,* he said with a wounded voice. *Yes, he's definitely going to have more than a lock and key. I'm guessing a few sp-sp-sp-ugh, things that are meant to deter theft.*

"Such as?" It was a claim she often heard, one that she took pride in ignoring. But she knew this wouldn't be like anything that she'd encountered before.

*Oh, you know, like boils covering your body if you touch it, sudden combustion of the book—which would probably scorch your hands—and other minor things like that.*

She nearly tripped over her own dragging feet as she listened to Masini's descriptors. "Why didn't you mention this *before*?!" she hissed.

*Hey, you're not allowed to be angry at the grieving inanimate object with speech issues. By the Greats, you're so inconsiderate,* he said, a hint of amusement returning to his voice. She was glad to hear his change in mood but her blood boiled all the same. *Those are somewhat avoidable anyway. If he has a concealing sp-sp-sp-grrr. If he hid the contents, we're in even more trouble. Oh, and bring a cloth or blanket dyed with inanite with you, too."*

"Why?" she asked. "You volunteering to get put in solitary confinement again?"

*Ha-ha,* he said sarcastically. *No, his... protections work off the same energy my ring does. The inanite will let you handle the books without becoming a leper. Probably...*

She almost stopped in her tracks. "*Probably*?!" She caught Orne giving her a look from the corner of her eye.

*If it makes you feel better, it's not exactly safe for me either,* Masini said. *He probably has specific protections for other m-m-m-damn it! That is so annoying. Anyway, it could be interesting, considering I don't have a 'body.'*

His voice made an attempt at sounding confident, but Desnia could tell that he was nervous. What risk was he taking by accompanying her?

"I could leave you with Nerio," she whispered.

*I knew it, you do care,* he said. *Wait, you don't love me just because of my shiny, lustrous body, do you?*

With rolling eyes she shook her head, not bothering to deign his comment with a response. He was insufferable when praised.

*Or not. Anyways, I appreciate the offer but you're going to need me there. I won't be able to give you specifics, but if there's anything I recognize, I can give you a warning.*

"I have to get in there first..." she said, thinking about the climb. She hated rushing a job. Haste led to poor judgment, which led to mistakes. Even from a few stories, a fall would be fatal, let alone one from well over the ten floors she'd have to climb to the balcony.

"You shouldn't trust him," said Delvan's voice from her side, causing her to spin with a start. *Was he listening to me talking with Masini?* she worried as she moved her hand from the small blade at her waist.

"Who says I do?" she asked, trying to keep her voice from reaching Ferrand. "But you should probably put less faith in your old friend." He winced at the words, and she felt a pang of guilt. "Listen," she continued, "I appreciate what you two did for me, but did you ever think that maybe he didn't know the full scope of what these people were planning? What he was helping them to achieve?"

"I... yes," said Delvan.

"We'll get your friend back *and* stop them from opening the gate. But we need to work together." Those words put an acrid taste in her mouth and a shiver down her spine. "And you need to put your past behind you, at least for tonight. If you don't trust him, trust me. We can't let them succeed."

"As long as we get Kolden back, I don't care," said Orne. Where had he gotten a halberd?

"You'll care if they start coming through," said Desnia.

"I still don't get how you say an army can come through this thing. If you're that worried about it, why not bring the garrison with us?" said Orne.

She frowned at him. It would've been helpful if people had made suggestions *beforehand*. As much as she wanted to rebuke him, he had a point. He seemed arrogant enough without her concession, and she stayed quiet.

"Because," came the commander's voice. *Gods, can't I have a* single *conversation without everyone eavesdropping?* "Most of the soldiers stationed here are locals, and we don't know the extent of the Magridi's influence. Can't risk having them turn against us. They also would serve as little more than fodder if the gate *were* to open."

"What? There's no way," said Orne. "Even a group of Blues can fall to overwhelming numbers, it's happened before. Hell, it happened not far from here."

People began trickling onto the street, joining them in the warm air of the lamp-lit dark. *The speaks must be starting to end,* she thought. There wasn't much time now, but her burning legs had almost carried her to their destination.

"If we run into a single High Realm mage, we're in deep shit," said Ferrand, careful with his volume as people passed them. "If the gate opens, they'll send their warrior mages. Legions of them with a singular purpose: conquering."

"That doesn't make any sense," said Delvan, whose skepticism had apparently exceeded his hatred of Ferrand. "Where are they coming from? I'd never heard of this 'High Realm' until today. How could we not know about an entire other kingdom?"

"Because it's not a *kingdom*, dumbass," Ferrand said. "It's a *realm*. As in you cannot get there from here without the use of magic so powerful it makes our sapphires look like children's toys by comparison."

*Hmm, not really accurate,* chimed Masini.

They all quieted as the street grew clamorous with the chatting and shuffling feet of worshipers walking home for the night. They worked their way through the throng, several people fearfully giving the Blues a wide berth. They had traveled most of the distance before the crowd became too thick, and the spires of the clergy house thrust into view above the roofline, unmoving sentinels overseeing all.

The streetlights flung long, dark shadows, creating refuge for the group as they pulled away to the street side a block away from the imposing structure. Desnia eyed the rising spire, debating the best route to scale its peak.

"Desnia," said Nerio from behind. He'd been quiet the entire walk here, aside from his panting breath. "Let me come with you," he said. "I know the principle's chambers well, and—"

"No," Desnia said, "I'm sorry Nerio, but it's too dangerous. I said I was going to help you, remember? Climbing on the outside of a tower in the night would be the exact opposite of that."

His face bowed low in disappointment. "I'm meant to help you Des, I know there's more for me to do. Please..."

"I'm sorry, Nerio, it's too risky. I'll be faster on my own," she said.

His shoulders slumped. If she could take him, she would, but this was going to be a difficult ascent in the little time she had as it was. She couldn't afford to help an inexperienced climber along the way.

"You really going to climb up *that*?" asked Delvan.

She looked at the effigy covered facade of the tower that rose like a dagger's point into the black of the night sky. The slight slope would make things easier, and there were plenty of footholds, but it would just take a single loose stone to send her plummeting to her death.

"I'm going to go up the first five floors inside, then climb out a window and climb the outside to avoid the disciples," she said. "I don't have long, so wait here."

"Hurry up," said Orne, Ferrand fidgeting impatiently next to him.

She threw her hand up in a vulgar gesture as she walked away from the group, leaving them at the nearby intersection. Hopefully she didn't come back to them at each other's throats... again.

Ducking her head to the side to avoid a few Almedia disciples, she walked through the front doors of the grand building. The arched corridors echoed with the prattle of hundreds of feet walking their tiled halls, the white stone brightly reflecting the lanterns burning along their length.

After a brief—and thankfully uneventful—walk, she reached her room, appearing exactly as she'd left it a few days prior. The cramped space didn't have much—a bed, chair, and desk—but that's all she'd ever needed. Pulling the fabric back from the end of her meager mattress revealed the slit she'd cut in it previously. She reached her hand in and pulled out her bag of tools, the lockpicks rattling inside as she threw it over her shoulder.

She left the room in a hurry, her head low as she strode through the long halls. Now that she was away from the others she could finally think straight, methodically going through each aspect of what she was about to do.

The brisk pace made her stand out from the lethargic mass as she twisted and pushed her way between people. The stairs were the most painful experience. The wide steps felt claustrophobic among the tightly packed crowd, and she took a deep breath of relief as she emerged on the top floor of the main building.

The passageway was nearly empty by comparison, and as she began to stride down the corridor she passed a window with curtains drawn. She stopped, cocking her head as she inspected the fabric—dyed black to block the sun's scalding rays during the day. With a contented shrug she yanked on the curtain, ripping it down and stuffing it into her bag.

*Alright, that's taken care of,* she thought, *now I just need to find an open window near Jerdine's spire and—*

"Hey! You there!" came an irrationally angry voice from behind her. She turned to see a bald man stomping towards her, a high-level priest that she didn't recognize. Why was he—

*Oh, shit...*

She *did* recognize him. It was the priest who'd been denying the general entry to Jerdine's tower. The one she'd promptly pissed off by ignoring and taking the general to the principle herself. *Time to go,* she thought, her sandals squealing on the polished floor as she spun and started running.

"Hey! Come back here!" the priest shouted as he rushed after her.

*I don't think he likes you,* said Masini as she shoved a bystander out of her way, throwing them to the floor as she sprinted down the hall. She approached an intersection, quickly orienting herself to which direction the spire lay, and then launched herself down the correct hallway, towards Jerdine's tower.

The priest nearly fell as he skidded and lost his footing trying to take the turn, giving her precious distance. Adrenaline propelled her legs forward, helping the muscles forget about the burning ache from traversing half the city in the past few hours. The priest was struggling, luckily, his breathing almost as loud as his weighty footsteps.

The corridor she ran down now was short, the last window before the tower open at its end. She skidded to a stop at the pane-less portal, narrow and tall, looking to the street below. She climbed onto the sill, not bothering to see what precipice might lie beyond, and squeezed through the tight opening, her robe chafing against her skin as the stone pressed it tight against her.

The window released its grip as she pulled herself through, yanking her bag between the opening behind her. With a pivot she spun herself to the window's side, pulling her body tight to the exterior wall.

Her heart pounded as she heard the clapping of sandaled feet running down the hall. Winded breaths echoed from inside the window as the foot-falls came to a standstill, and she did her best to ease her own panting. With bated breath she waited, avoiding looking down to the street several stories below.

A curse came from inside. The sound of a few doors opening could be heard before the feet trailed off into the distance. Desnia let out a long breath and looked up, the spire only a few feet away and touching the sky above.

*They always look so much taller up close,* she thought as she carefully shuf-fled along the stone molding beneath her feet, her heart still pounding. She pulled herself up by the fangs of a stone face, a snarling monster with demonic eyes looking down upon the city. The climb was steady and went faster than she'd expected as the many figures of demons and deities pro-vided easy handholds. Smooth stone walls and tight connections spoke to master masonry she'd not seen outside of Calentine, making the smooth surface between statues treacherous for her sandaled feet.

*What I wouldn't give for my old boots right now,* she thought as her foot fought for purchase.

Part of her wanted to turn and look for the group below, wondering what their expressions might be as they watched her carefully hoist herself ever upward. But that would just distract her. Taking a deep breath, she jumped from the head of some saint and grabbed onto the pedestal base of another statue above, her fingers aching and starting to bleed.

The peak was growing near, and the spacing between the spire's radial ridges were close enough for her to carefully stretch out a leg above the abyssal emptiness below and find another landing. She precariously made her way around until the edge of the principle's balcony was only a few feet away, elevated just above her head. The next effigy was too high for her to easily reach. There was only one option.

She'd have to jump.

She shook her hands, eyeing the balcony's edge like a cat looking to pounce. If she missed, there was nothing below to stop her from falling onto the street. They might not be able to find the gate in time. And what about Nerio? And the Blue's friend?

*Can't think about that now.*

With a deep breath she bent her knees before lurching upward with as much thrust as she could muster towards the elevated balcony. She soared through the air, a warm breeze flowing over her, making everything seem to slow as her body was gripped by fear.

Her fingers grabbed the balcony's edge, but pain seared through her left hand as the carved stone cut into her fingers. She gasped as her hand slipped, her heart jumping into her throat as she suddenly dangled by one arm, a dizzying fall beneath her.

Desnia tightened her grip with determination, getting the free hand back onto the balcony and ignoring the pulsing pain. Through acute throbs and straining muscles, she persevered, ignoring the burning in her arms as much as she was able. With a great heave, she hauled herself up using the stone balusters before finally rolling over the railing and laying on the stone floor, feeling her heart race as she slowly recovered from the near fall.

*I thought for sure that we were going down there for a second,* said Masini. *I mean, uh,... Well done, I never doubted you.*

"Fuck off," she said between breaths.

She sat up, composing herself. There wasn't a lot of time, and none of it was to be wasted. Pulling herself to her feet, Desnia walked through the open balcony door and into the opulent chamber. It was lavishly decorated with fine carpets, paintings, and furniture that would have been the envy of any nobility. Even in the dim moonlight it felt ostentatious.

"What a hypocrite," she muttered.

*The biggest,* said Masini. *This room feels like it's buzzing, my ears are ringing.*

"Was that supposed to be a pun?" she asked, looking around the dark room.

*What? I... I mean, ahem, yes, don't you know how clever I am?*

She actually chortled as she made directly for the lone bookcase. Wire mesh framed by locked wood served as the door protecting the roughly two dozen tomes within. The lock looked old, a foundational classic that inspired designs for decades after. It'd been a while since she'd seen one. She selected the picks she needed but hesitated before putting them into the keyhole.

"Is this safe? This hardly seems like it would keep anyone out if they were motivated," she said.

*I don't recognize anything around the lock, I think you're good,* he said, his voice sounding quiet. *Inside might be a different story.*

With slow, cautious hands, she slid the picks inside the lock, the faint movements of pins and springs vibrating through the thin metal and into her experienced fingertips. She pushed the lingering pain of the climb from her mind. She'd done this hundreds of times, but never with such stakes, the sound of her heart pounding in her ears betraying the statuesque calm she attempted to portray.

The picks worked their way backwards with urged patience, Desnia trying not to focus too much on how much time had elapsed. She toiled away, the only light what filtered in from the street and moon through the tinted windows and balcony door.

As the pick reached the last pin and pressed upward, she felt the sweet release of the lock as it spun and turned the bolt. Her shoulders fell as the tension in her neck released, slowly letting out a sigh. As she grabbed the handle, she creaked the door open with her face turned and eyes cringing, bracing for something unexpected, Masini's descriptions still fresh in her mind.

The door swung open uneventfully, and her face became quizzical. "Huh, I thought there would've been... more."

*Me too, actually,* said Masini.

"So, which of these do you think we need? I can't exactly sneak them all out of here," she said as she pulled the black curtain from her bag and unfurled it on the floor. None of the strange markings on the spines made sense to her.

*Uh, let's see. Looks like there's some dates on these ones. Some are labeled as journals, accountings... I don't know, Des, you sure we can't take all of these? I think they're partially what's causing the buzzing I feel, but I can't tell which one. And I don't think we have time to sort through them.*

"Walking out of here with these slung over my shoulder won't exactly be discrete..." she said, feeling resigned. "But... Actually, I know what I can do," she said with a grin.

*What's that?* he asked.

"I'm going to make us a distraction. You'll see."

Desnia fidgeted with nervous energy. Time constraints were normal for her, hell, she'd even robbed places where the owners were in the same building. But more was at stake here, more than she'd ever asked for. And for some gods-damned reason it all became her burden to bear. She needed to move fast, there wasn't time, it couldn't be long before Jerdine was back. The thoughts of what he could do to her twisting her guts in knots.

She hurriedly reached out and grabbed the spine of the first book. A jolt shot through her arm, a spike of pain that reached into her chest and flung her hand away. She gripped it tightly, groaning loudly as she tried not to scream with a red face and bulging veins. The cuts on her hand were now cauterized, the smell of singed flesh fowling her nostrils and throbs of residual pain pulsing up her arm and into her chest like a thousand bee stings at once.

*Well, that was dumb,* said Masini.

She grunted vociferously, taking a ragged, gasping breath as she tried to ignore the radiating agony. "You could've said *something*, fucking asshole," she said, the words strained.

*I did warn you they'd be protected, don't blame me for your hastiness. Use the curtain like a glove, that should stop any further barbequing.*

"Is there anything *else* I should know beforehand?" she asked, still bent over in pain.

*Not immediately,* said Masini. *It looks like he's just got some basic protections on these. I can feel something, but I think because I don't have a 'normal' body, whatever he did isn't affecting me the way it should. I'm a little concerned though, he might have something that activates if you open them. Hard to say without knowing how much ca-ca-ca-aghh. Just, don't open them and let's go.*

"Fine," she said as she wrapped one end of the curtain around her uninjured hand and—with the utmost care—grabbed at the same book, her heart skipping a beat as the protected fingers touched the binding. There was no pain, no shock or searing as she pulled it gently from the shelf and set it in the center of the laid-out curtain.

One by one, the rest of the books were set on the cloth, creating two stacks about a foot and half tall. Desnia brought the four fabric corners together and tied them, forming a makeshift sack around the tomes.

"Alright," she said, looking around, "now we just need that distraction." Her arm was still dully pulsating in pain.

It only took a few strides to find what she needed: a wall of bottles, displayed as if to flaunt Jerdine's own dissidence. She pulled the cork from one of them, the smell of whiskey fuming from within. *This will do*, she thought. She pulled the cork from another and began pouring the liquor over the carpets and furniture.

*Seems like such a waste,* said Masini.

"You can't even drink it," she said as the alcohol splashed on the floor.

*But I have an imagination, damn it! Ugh, that's probably twenty-year aged whiskey. Say what you want about the man, but he has impeccable taste.*

As the fifth bottle emptied and Desnia tossed it to the ground, she looked back at the wall of liquor, spotting something on it. "Alright, maybe we shouldn't waste *all* of it," she said as she took a bottle of Aliovan wine from the shelf.

*Girl after my own heart,* said Masini, *I knew you'd come around.*

"Still would prefer ale," she said as she lit a candle at the ornate desk in the corner.

*I can fix you, with time,* he said.

She rolled her eyes as she slipped the bottle into her bag, putting the straps back over her shoulders before heaving the bulky sack that was once a curtain onto her back. She walked to the door, unlocking and opening it before tossing the candle onto the whiskey-soaked carpet. A fire sprang up from the floor and spread wildly through the room, engulfing it in smoke and flame.

She watched with a satisfied smirk, letting the black smoke billow into the hall before she started towards the stairs.

She reached the stairwell and spiraled downward as fast as she could, screaming before she reached the first door, "Fire! Fire! Save what you can!"

A disciple popped his head out of the door as Desnia flung herself past it, pointing backward and screaming in her most panicked voice. "Fire in the principle's chambers! Run!" Smoke trailed behind her as she ran down the steps, more and more people walking into the wide stairwell, their eyes becoming wide with panic at the smell of smoke.

Chaos followed her like the moon chasing the sun, the entire tower turning into a frenzy as people ran. Some flew down the stairs at her side, others headed up in what she couldn't decide to be either a courageous or idiotic act. No one paid attention to her, the raving messenger. They all only cared about the greater danger above.

She made it into the main building, still screaming and shouting into the halls she passed while running down the stairs. As she got closer to the ground floor, she became quiet, letting the others around her cry out in hysteria. Bells rang and people scurried all around as she reached the stairs' end. They called out in alarm and ran past, oblivious to her and the large black sack over her shoulder.

Desnia strolled through the front gates, those around her ignorant to the theft committed, and walked into the street brightly lit by the flames raging atop the spire hundreds of feet above, glowing like a torch high in the sky.

It was one of the most beautiful things she'd ever seen.

# Chapter Fifty-One


*Deals bartered, set in stone*
*Truths spoken, naught unknown*
*If broken, flesh from bone*

A bit much, don't you think?" asked Ferrand as the group walked along the side of the library. Behind them the spire still roared with yellow and orange flames—a portent of its occupant's machinations for the city and all beyond.

*Is he capable of giving a compliment?* she wondered as they passed under the tall stained-glass windows. Nerio was leading the group, his face pale with the horror of the destruction that Desnia had wrought. Orne carried the makeshift bag containing the books, a grin on his normally scowled face. Delvan looked back at the fire, his face deep in thought.

"I thought the whole point of this was to *not* attract attention," continued Ferrand as Nerio reached a small, wooden door in the center of the great breadth of the stone wall.

Crowds were gathering in the street, staring at the fiery blaze with wide eyes that gleamed with the reflection of the blaring inferno. They passed thousands in the streets just in their short walk here, not a single one paying them any mind. The distraction had worked better than she could ever have hoped.

*And yet this fucker is still complaining,* she thought.

"I didn't want to attract attention to *us*," she said. "Jerdine might assume that this was retaliation for taking Kolden and the key, but by the time he asks the disciples what happened and puts that together, we should hopefully have found the gate. If nothing else it buys us more time than just running in there, swords drawn."

Nerio unlocked the door with a metallic click, opening the small passage. They filed into the dark room, a doorway in the distance shining with the glow from the library's grand hall, providing them just enough light to avoid stepping on each other.

"Come, this way," said Nerio as they turned down a nearby hallway, even darker than the one they'd just left. At the first door, Nerio gave a push, opening it against creaking hinges. Silently, they waited while he lit a candle, and then a lamp, bringing light to the cluttered room.

A long table littered with books and parchment stood in the center, shelving and more cluttered surfaces lining the walls. It was a mess of scribbled ink, disorganized scrolls, and dust, just large enough for all of them to collect around the table where Orne dropped the black bag with a rattling *thud*.

"This is a study room," said Nerio. "No one should bother us here, most of these are empty at night. But don't raise your voices too loud, just in case there is anyone still in the main hall."

A flare like stinging needles stabbed Desnia's fingers in a painful reminder of her daring leap and reckless haste. Air rushed through her clenched teeth as she looked down at it, parts of the skin red and blistered. Nerio took notice of her contorted face and walked over, his eyes filled with concern upon seeing the burns.

"What happened?" he asked. "Were you burnt in the fire?"

"No," she said. *But something equally stupid.*

"I think there are some ointments in a room down the hall," he said with an air of urgency. "I'll be right back."

Before she could say that she was fine, he was out the door. This wasn't the worst injury she'd ever had, it would heal, but apparently Nerio wouldn't accept that for an answer. She shook her head as she turned her attention back to the bag that Orne was untying.

The cloth peeled away, revealing the two small stacks of books within. It seemed such an effort for something that she didn't even know would contain the answers they needed. Then there was the other issue: how were they going to open them without frying their skin?

"Doesn't seem like much," said Ferrand, taking a step closer to the table, his hands resting dangerously close to the leather and vellum covers. His eyes squinted as he inspected the bindings, his hand lifting from the table.

"I wou—" started Desnia.

*Wait, wait, wait,* said Masini. *Let's just see what happens.*

The commander grabbed at one of the spines, immediately dropping it with a cry and recoiling his arm. He gripped his hand tightly, back arched in pain. Desnia flexed her own fingers, remembering that recent agony, and found herself suppressing a small smile.

Masini was laughing uproariously, making it difficult for her to hear the curses that the commander was spouting. Orne and Delvan looked confused, taking a step back from the cursed tomes. Their situation was dire, and they shouldn't be joking, she knew. But it was hard to stop the tugging at her lip's corner as Masini filled her head with his infectious laughter.

"They're protected," Desnia said, Ferrand glaring at her from his low angle as his knees bent, trying to keep him standing. She held up her own hand for him to see, the pink and white blisters shining. "You can handle them as long as you're using something with inanite to block it. But we-uh… I'm worried about something happening if we open any of them."

"Then what the hell was the point of stealing these?" asked Orne with a wave of his arms. "We're wasting time!"

Nerio hustled back into the room, a small jar with some cream-colored ointment inside. He came to Desnia's side, opening the jar and gently taking her hand. Old habits kicked in, her hand snapping backward from his touch. It was a foreign sensation, the hands of another, and normally one that was met by threats or the sharp edge of a blade. She knew Nerio bore no ill intent, but it was still with great reluctance that she extended her hand back out into his.

Orne paced back land forth while Nerio applied the salve, a cooling sensation coming immediately. Desnia released a sigh of relief, not realizing just how much pain her hand had been in.

"Are you alright, my Lord?" asked Nerio as he turned from Desnia to Ferrand, approaching him with concern.

"I'm fine," he snapped, standing back up straight. *His loss.*

"Orne's right," said Delvan, "we can't just sit around. This was a good idea, but—"

"We'll figure this out," interrupted Desnia, "this is still the best—"

"This is a waste of time!" bellowed Orne as he swept his arm across a nearby desk, scattering the documents to the floor in a flurry of crinkled parchment.

The room exploded with shouting, Orne pointing to Ferrand and Desnia in a rage, Delvan desperately trying to talk him down. The deep bass of the over-sized man was met with Desnia's pitched soprano, the escalating baritones of Ferrand and Delvan creating a violent orchestra of irate hollering.

Frustration ran rampant, anger flowing through her and amplifying with each shout that was thrown in the small room. She didn't care if anyone heard in the main hall, she only cared about the moment, becoming enraged as she was told her efforts were a waste of time, that anything else could have been done. Her singular focus was the reddened faces spewing vile curses, trying and failing to once again convince them that she'd been right.

Why couldn't they just stop and think? What was so difficult about accepting that results might come in other forms than broken doors and battered faces. Everything had gone as it should have to this point, but one obstruction appears, and everyone turns against her? Could they—

Between shifting her steeled eyes from Orne to Ferrand on the opposite side of the table, she caught sight of Nerio between them. He was quiet, his head bowed low, invisible to everyone else. And he was holding an open book in his unprotected hand.

"Wait!" Desnia screamed so loud it threatened to tear her throat. She reached out her arm, and all other heads turned towards the table, eyes going wide and lips falling dramatically silent as they gapingly stared at Nerio.

"Hmm?" Nerio asked, looking up and turning his confused face to the suddenly quiet group staring at him in wonder. "What?"

"How... How are you..." Desnia stuttered.

*Huh, I... Ohh, that poor, poor child...* Masini said, his voice trailing.

"How the hell can you hold that?" asked Ferrand, taking a cautious step closer to Nerio.

"What do you mean?" ask Nerio, open book in hand. He appeared bewildered, spinning and turning his body towards each of them as he began to awkwardly shrink from the attention.

"Maybe it only affects certain people?" asked Delvan, who slowly stretched out his arm, tapping the corner of a book with a single finger. "*Fuck!*" he screamed as his arm flew back and he keeled over in pain.

"Hurts like a bitch, doesn't it?" asked Ferrand smugly.

*I think I know what's happening,* said Masini. *The books recognize Nerio as Jerdine. I always knew he was a sick bastard, but this...*

"I don't understand..." said Desnia, her jaw still slack.

*The buzzing I felt when we were in Jerdine's chambers, it wasn't the protections on the books. I think he had down a perpetual love, uh, thing. Like what P-P-P-ugh, my friend did to you when you grabbed me. But to this extent, it's heinous. And I can't even imagine the amount of, uh, glowy rocks and recharging he would need to keep it up. They're meant for small doses, like parties and events if you want to take someone home—*

"Disgusting," she said in a barely audible whisper.

*—it's not like... yes, fine, but morality aside, prolonged exposure can have strange effects on people. After a* ridiculous *amount of exposure, it can start to physically alter your bodies, uh, energy... markers? I guess. I've seen it done before, back home, some of the returning soldiers would bring conquered slaves back with them, and, well, you can imagine the rest. It has not only the immediate effect of lowering his will to fend for himself, but after a while Jerdine would be able to sense him if he were close.*

"How often?" she whispered.

*...Years worth. Repetitively. It must have altered him so much that the book's protections recognize him as Jerdine and aren't affecting him. Honestly, I'm impressed he didn't try to step off that bell tower sooner.*

Desnia's throat became tight, tears welling in her eyes. What Nerio must have endured—what he must still be enduring by even helping them—was beyond anything she'd ever experienced. There had been times in her life she wished to permanently forget. Deplorable acts committed by the malevolent scum of the city's underbelly as they took advantage of the lone street girl. The evil glint in their eyes, the insecurity in their grip as they held her. But this...

Burning down the man's home wasn't enough. He needed to pay, to die a slow, torturous death until he begged for mercy again and again.

"Who cares why he can touch it," said Orne in the first intelligent statement she'd heard from him. "If the priest can read them, then let's have him go through and figure out where Kolden is!"

"Well, I would but," said Nerio, flipping through several pages, "these pages are all blank."

Desnia's heart fell as though dropped from the spire. Blank? Surely there was a mistake? She took a few steps closer as Nerio cracked another book and thumbed through more blank pages. They were all leaning on the table now, watching as Nerio flipped through each book to find more of the books blank. Desnia began sweating. This plan *had* to work. The only alternative would be to face Jerdine head on, at the risk of all their lives.

*Hmm,* said Masini, *have him wipe his hand along the pages.*

"Uh," she said, "Nerio, can you, um, wipe your hand along the page?"

"What?" Nerio asked as he turned his head towards Desnia along with everyone else.

"Just, try it," she said.

Nerio shrugged and ran his hand down the page like he was dusting it off. Ink began scrawling across the empty sheet, as if he had blown away sand from carved stone. The pages filled with diagrams as well as letters and words in a language that Desnia didn't recognize. Every subsequent page became covered in the scratchy symbols, and Nerio turned to her in shocked curiosity.

"How did you know to do that?" asked Delvan.

"Uh, lucky guess?" she said, trying to sound convincing.

Delvan stared at her, doubt cast over his eyes as Nerio opened all the other books and began wiping his hands across their pages. Desnia turned away from Delvan's questioning brown eyes and back to the books that Nerio was laying out.

"These are all written in old trethish," said Nerio, placing the last book on the table. "Many are ancient, I think some are even complete texts about the Ones Before... Unbelievable." His jaw slacked slightly as if he were staring at the greatest treasure horde of all time.

*'The Ones Before.' Pfft. I always hated being called that,* said Masini.

"Can you read it?" asked Ferrand.

*I can!* exclaimed Masini. *But it's going to take a while to go through all of—*

"Yes," said Nerio, "I can. What are we looking for?"

*Wait*, said Masini, *really? This kid can read these? Huh, impressive.*

"I can read it too," said Desnia. She turned everyone's head again, disbelief on each of their faces.

"You... can?" asked Nerio.

"Well, aren't you full of fucking surprises," said Ferrand. "Alright, get fucking too it then, time is not our friend right now. We need information about the gate, anything not related to it can be set aside. Entrances, the way it was built, anything that may be relevant."

Desnia cut away a corner of the inanite curtain, using it to flip through pages for Masini to "see." She intentionally kept her gaze away from Delvan, whose inquisitive eyes hadn't been taken off her. As she scanned the pages, Orne paced back and forth, grumbling and tapping his finger on the pommel of his sword. Ferrand wasn't much better, standing behind them, tapping his foot while he peeked his head between Desnia and Nerio's shoulders to look at the strange text.

Nerio leaned over to her, his voice low. "I told you this was the gods' plan. I don't know why they selected me for this task, but clearly I have been gifted this talent to help you. Thank you, Desnia, for bringing me and allowing me to aid you."

Her mouth opened, quickly shutting again. She didn't have the heart to tell him, to explain why he was able to do this. Instead, she just smiled and went back to the books.

"And, if you don't mind me asking," he said in the same hushed tone, "where did you learn to read old trethish?"

"Masini," she answered with another forced smile. She left it at that and dug further into the book in front of her.

The minutes slipped by like sand through their fingers until an hour passed. She tried turning pages faster, but Masini would snap at her if he didn't have time to finish reading. The tension in the air was palpable as an hour turned into two, several of the books still remaining untouched on the table.

The next page of her current tome displayed a strange diagram, a repetitive pattern that resembled twisting flower petals. It seemed familiar for some reason, though she couldn't say why.

*Stop!* chirped Masini. *This is it, the fr-fr-fr-gah! The damned squiggles that make up the door.*

Her head leaned closer, the chain that Masini hung from dangling from her neck as she closely inspected the drawing. There was a tiny square at its center, everything spiraling outward from it. For something as dangerous as Masini described, it was oddly beautiful.

*Next page,* he said.

To the next page she went, more diagrams and drawings covering it, including one that detailed the key, colored by rich, heavy ink. Each was meticulously drawn, seemingly by a different hand than the one that'd drafted the other bound pages.

*Mhm, yes, next,* said Masini.

With a crinkling sound she turned the page, covered by twelve rows starting with a strange, demonic face and different patterns in the following columns. *What is that?* she wondered.

"I have something!" cried Nerio. She turned her attention to what he was looking at, the others quickly gathering around the table. "Look, these are maps and construction designs. It looks like, well I don't completely understand it but this seems to say that they *formed* caves around this gate you're looking for, raising the whole center of the city."

*By the Greats, that must have taken him decades,* said Masini. *He probably used most of the, uh, energy he had to make it.*

"So it's underground," said Orne. "How do we get to it?"

Nerio narrowed his eyes as he looked closer at the drawings, dragging his finger along the page looking for details. "There are a few entrances, but this map is ancient, I don't recognize most of these buildings. But there's something mentioned at each of them, a pattern or something that I don't recognize."

Desnia leaned closer, trying to get a better vantage. Repetitive patterns—similar to the floral design in her book—were where Nerio had pointed. Each was identical, a mass of swirling, thin lines that were labeled with the strange writing.

*They're en-en-en-oh c'mon! They're, uh, things, that, uh, only let other certain things through. Ha! That make sense?* Masini asked.

"They're barriers," she said. "They only let certain objects through."

*Ha! I knew you'd get me.*

"How can you know that?" asked Delvan with that same, deconstructive stare.

"I, uh, spent a little too much time with Masini," she said, turning her eyes away.

"Is he the one that planned the robbery?" asked Delvan.

She felt her face go pale, her gaze unmoving from the book before Nerio. Did she dare answer that? He still seemed set on avenging his friend somehow, would he start to think he could do that through her? Was he already thinking that?

"Give it a fucking rest," said Ferrand. "What do these barriers block?"

*Uh, they block anything they don't recognize. Like people or objects,* said Masini.

"They stop anyone or anything unknown from entering," she said.

"Damn it!" yelled Orne. "So, we're back to where we started!? This was a waste!" His fist slammed on the table as he spoke, causing it to quake. "Why don't we just get hammers and break the damn thing down?"

"You touch one of those books and tell me that's a good fucking idea," said Ferrand pointedly. Orne grumbled, and Desnia could see his eyes beginning to become bloodshot, but he didn't speak further.

The room went quiet again as they pulled their hair or hung their heads. Pressure mounted, putting them all on edge. How were they supposed to find solutions when they hardly understood what they were going against?

"Huh." Nerio leaned in even closer to the book, his face only a few inches away from the miniscule writing. "I think I know where one of these entrances is."

"Where?" said Orne.

"In the bathhouse, the large one near the Devapuram." Nerio picked up the book and flipped through a few more pages, holding it near his chest. "There're a couple private rooms in the rear of the building, it looks to be in one of those."

"Then let's go!" Orne boomed, spinning and grabbing his halberd from its resting spot on the wall before stepping towards the door.

"Wait!" said Desnia. "We don't have a way to get through these barriers, and I can't exactly pick the lock."

*Yeah,* said Masini, *that's going to be tricky. Can't be having any of you start melting.*

There was an image that made her shudder. If the pain associated with protecting a simple book was that severe, she could only imagine what these protections might be like. She hoped Masini was joking but didn't dare to ask.

Delvan pointed to Nerio. "What about him?"

Nerio looked up, that same confused innocence on his face. "Me?"

"He's the only one who can touch these books," said Delvan, "maybe he can do something with the barriers."

*Ohh,* said Masini. *That could actually work. If he stood in them while you walked through, it could recognize him as Jerdine, and let you all in unscathed. Probably. I would bet it's how he gets others down there when he needs to.*

*Reassurances abound,* she thought. If Masini was wrong, it would cost them dearly. Then again, if they did nothing, it probably wouldn't matter anyway. Her eyes scrunched as she rubbed her forehead.

"That could work," she said. "Do you think you could help us again, Nerio."

Nerio bowed his head. "I believe it is my purpose. Yes, I will come."

Her insides turned upside down. He *had* been chosen, just not by who he thought. The vile tastes of a hedonistic deviant combined with the needs of the supposed god that spoke to her had happened to align. This hadn't been planned for him. The fact that his life—and similarly, her own—were being manipulated for the gains of others, denying them the ability to choose, was a far greater crime than any she'd ever committed.

Perhaps if Nerio better understood what it was he worshiped, he'd have a different opinion about faith.

"Let's fucking go, then," said Orne as he stormed out the door, not waiting to see if anyone followed. Nerio snapped the book shut and tucked it under his arm, walking behind Orne with Ferrand and Delvan at his heels. Desnia ran her fingers along her scalp, pulling at her hair again as she took a deep breath.

This is what it came down to. A lifetime of torment, skills acquired, and her guided fate all led to this. It was overwhelming. But there was hope. Hope that, if she made it through this, she'd could go and get what she wanted most.

Desnia turned and walked out the door, taking the steps ordained for her.

# Chapter Fifty-Two



*To glimpse the shimmer of life*
*Which surrounds us all*
*Is to know its strife*
*Guide its path homeward*
*Or doom it to fall*

The steady dripping of water that echoed off the cavern walls was drowned out by Kolden's heavy grunting as he pulled on a bar of his prison. With both feet pressed against the iron rods on either side of the one in his grasp, he heaved with all his strength, the metal groaning as it resisted him from its stone setting.

Sweat poured down his dimly lit face, the cavern back to its dull purple glow now that Hunter and the principle had left with the key. Witnessing the man fly into a rage upon hearing that his spire was being incinerated had both frightened and delighted Kolden. He doubted it was a coincidence that it had turned into a blazing beacon just after he'd gone missing. He wasn't sure how Orne and Delvan had put together who'd taken him, but he was glad of it all the same.

*They better be careful,* thought Kolden. *The look in that one's eye when talking about killing Del... It takes a stupid or dangerous man to speak casually about killing a Blue, and he doesn't strike me as daft.*

He couldn't say how long they'd been gone. Maybe an hour? Two at most? In that time he'd worked at the bar in the back of his cell, leveraging it in every direction, trying to fatigue the corroded metal. It was starting to give, the hairline fractures where metal met stone beginning to loosen and move with his efforts.

Kolden just hoped it would come free in time.

Floran's body lay on the ground not far from him, discarded by the monster who'd stabbed him. He tried not to look at it, avoiding the memory of his gaunt face pleading for mercy. They'd treated him like an animal, as though killing him was no more difficult than butchering a fowl. He thought about the remaining people in the adjacent cages, his gut wrenching knowing there was nothing he could do for them right now.

*If I don't get out of here, they'll do the same to me,* he thought. There wasn't time to pity the dead and dying. He had to focus on his own escape.

He pulled harder, his wet clothing stretching over his arched back as his face twisted and darkened. The rusted bars beneath his bare feet dug into his skin, the pitted, corroded remnants of what was once iron cutting and chewing away at the thick soles with rusty edges. But the bar cracked more, sending faint *pings* that vibrated through to his strained hands. It wasn't free though, not yet, but any moment now...

A sound came from one of the nearby cave entrances, feet slapping against stone in the distance. They sounded rushed, it wouldn't be long before they emerged into the cavern.

*I'm out of time,* he thought as he braced himself, giving the bar another pull. He could feel his shoulders stretching, the muscles of his back and legs burning and screaming. Pain stabbed at his feet and calloused fingers as he grunted through locked teeth. The footsteps came closer, each hurried step matching the thunderous beats of his heart. It sounded like two pairs and flooded him with the strength of panic as he imagined Hunter and the principle rushing down the cave. He needed—

With a loud *creak* and sharp *ting* the iron bar broke, sending Kolden flat on his back. He coughed, ignoring the new pain along his spine and skull that now accompanied the rest of his aches. Adrenaline and relief surged within him, giving him the strength to pull himself up. The bar hinged inward from the top, still connected to the flat plate above, but the base was free.

Kolden grabbed the sheared end of the rod and with all his remaining strength leveraged it back and forth, the sound of grinding metal resonating in the domed cavern until it finally broke away, leaving a small gap between the bars where his feet had been propped.

For once, he was thankful for his diminutive stature as he wriggled his body between the bars. He twisted his head to fit as his chest scraped along the rusted metal, the abrasive texture stabbing through his shirt and digging into his raw skin. The metal scraped along his torso, cutting lines of red down his flesh as he pulled himself through, releasing their vice-grip as his legs reached the gap and his body collapsed outside his former prison.

Reaching back into the cage, Kolden grabbed the iron bar he'd broken free. He held it close as he crouched low and made his way to a nearby cave entrance on the outskirts of the cavern, passing the unfortunate souls still trapped in their respective cages. He could just hear the drips of water over his heavy breathing, his bloody feet leaving a trail behind him.

*Fuck,* he thought, *I'm going to lead the bastards right to me.*

He continued creeping away but realized that the sound of running feet had stopped. No one had entered the cavern, had they? He looked over his shoulder as he ducked behind the entrance to a nearby tunnel, pressing his back to stone. He hadn't seen anyone, maybe he'd gotten away unnoticed? He ripped off the sleeves of his shirt and began tightly wrapping them around his feet, hoping to conceal his steps as he fled. It hurt to acknowledge, but there was nothing he could do for those remaining, he had to escape and hope to bring back help in time.

The sound of footsteps fell upon his ears once more. A single pair this time, walking steadily at a quick pace, not the frantic sprint he'd heard before.

There was a glimmer of hope, a small spark in his heart that whoever this mystery third person was would be Orne or Delvan. He waited, pain throbbing through his body as he finished bandaging his feet and stood. He peeked his head around the corner and looked into the purple tinted cavern, his heart nearly beating out of his chest, his breathing rapid and deep.

His hand touched the stone as he peered around it, a familiar texture under his fingers. He'd been so busy trying to free himself from his cage that he only now noticed that the stone beneath his hand—and that of the entire cavern—was solid inanite.

*Of course,* he thought, *that how they hid—*

His mental analysis was thrown to the wayside as a figure entered the large chamber from the cave he'd seen the two men leave from earlier. Kolden's heart sank and grip on the iron bar tightened as he saw the disgustingly familiar form of the principle strut in, blue robe shifting around his bulging frame.

Thoughts of beating the man's face in with the rusty bar filled Kolden's head as he crouched there, watching the man walk towards the center of the room. His eyes went wide as they caught sight of what was in the principle's grasp, his hands shaking as his mouth went dry, mind racing through the implications of what he was seeing.

Throwing dark shadows across the principle's face and the rest of the gigantic cavern was the cadentite key, its radiance piercing the gaps between his fingers.

And unlike when he'd left, it was glowing as brightly as the sun itself.

## Chapter
## Fifty-Three



When we get there, Nerio will open the entrance and have to stand in or under the barrier as we all pass through," shouted Desnia over the pounding of their feet on the brick as they ran.

*How does she know all of this?* Delvan wondered from the back of the group. Something was off about this girl. Ferrand had spent who knows how many years among the ranks of these Sraddhana, and yet his knowledge seemed insignificant compared to Desnia's. How could she know such a great deal about the intricacies and methods of the mysterious people they were facing?

A part of him wondered if she herself was one of these High Realm mages the commander seemed terrified of. Where would her allegiances lie if that were the case? She seemed to be helping them, but would they be able to tell if she was using them to her own ends?

His instincts wanted to trust her, and at his core, he did, but there were too many unknowns. He shook his head as they ran, trying to clear his mind. Could he judge who this girl was or what her intentions were with the little he knew or understood? He didn't know, nothing made sense anymore.

His entire world had been flipped upside-down this evening. The singular driver of his life these past months revealed to be a falsity, a polished image fractured to reveal the hidden, grimy interior. He'd forced himself into thinking that Ferrand had *wanted* Hilbrun dead, that any information contrary to that was merely another ploy. But that wasn't the case, it was clear to see now.

He had to admit that there was a high likelihood his friend worked for some terrible people, and that the perception he'd bestowed unto Delvan was, similarly, a misrepresentation. But, even if Hilbrun hadn't been everything that he'd constructed and idolized in his mind, he *knew* there was good in his fallen friend. He needed to believe that much of his judgment had been correct.

And if Hilbrun had been able to be misguided, who was to say that Desnia and the commander weren't as well?

That he found himself sprinting behind the man he'd sworn to kill to avenge Hilbrun was a poignant reminder of how ignorant he was of the world. If he couldn't trust his own intuition, what—or who—could he put his faith in? He felt alone, a ship lost at sea without the stars to guide him.

For now, he would just have to maintain the same wary approach with Desnia as he was with Ferrand: until they got Kolden back, he'd help, but his hand would never be too far from his sword.

They forced their way through the crowds that were still gathered in the streets, some of the people turning and fleeing alongside them. It seemed the entire city had flocked to the wide roads and narrow side streets, the normally calm roadways turbulent with boiling chaos.

*What is going on?* he wondered.

The sky was lit a pale gray, as if the sun had started rising from the wrong direction beyond the buildings to their side. They turned a corner and slowed as a sight of unchained destruction came into view, taking their breath away in horror.

The clergy house had become engulfed in flame, the fire's insatiable reach touching the buildings around it and setting them ablaze, spreading like a plague. Its roar rivaled the crowd of a stadium, the heat pressing uncomfortably against even Delvan's skin from several streets away. He almost forgot about Kolden, about their imperative quest as he gaped at the flames devouring the building and clawing at the sky above.

"What... what have we done?" asked an aghast Nerio. Desnia held her hand to her mouth, the rest of them watching as people cried out, running for their lives—or to save that of another's. The fire before him blended with his memories of the one in Calentine, flashes of that night appearing before his eyes with each flicker of the inferno. His face became cold despite the heat.

Pain once again pulsing through him, setting him to teeter on the precipice of inaction, that shadowy, crippling grip on his heart only a stray thought away.

Why did destruction and death follow him wherever he went?

"We have to help them!" cried Nerio, as he ran forward, directly towards the indiscriminate flames.

"Wait, no!" said Desnia. But Ferrand was already ahead of her, grabbing Nerio by the arm and dragging him away.

"No! We have to help them," cried Nerio desperately, pulling in a feeble effort against Ferrand's grip. "They're going to die!"

"A fuck of a lot more will die if we don't do our jobs," said Ferrand with a hard tone. "We need you to get to the gate. You're coming with us."

Delvan's lips drew into a line. He wanted to rebuke Ferrand, to go and help, but Kolden might be running out of time. Hatred flowed through him as he tore himself away, directed at himself as much as any of the others. *Why does it feel so wrong to make the right decision?*

He glanced back as he started to follow the others, stopping as he saw Desnia still standing in the intersection, people running past her motionless body, wide eyes reflecting the rampant destruction of her doing. "Des!" he called out. Her head turned slowly towards him, remorseful horror portrayed across her face.

With another look back at the fire, a long void of a shadow stretching out behind her, she took a deep breath and then turned and jogged towards him, her head hung low. "I... I never meant for this."

*We never do,* he thought. "C'mon, worry about that later. We have other concerns." He tried to sound strong, but by the gods he didn't feel it. There was solace in that they shared something now: the realization that a simple act rippled with consequences. He empathized with her, but he was also intimately acquainted with how crippling that mounting guilt could be, and there was much yet to do.

Her shoulders sank, but she nodded, joining him as they ran to close the distance between them and the others, passing a building that plunged them back into the shadow of the dim night air, now cold without the fire's heat against their bodies.

They reached the bathhouse sweating and out of breath, the street swarming with pandemonium as the glow in the sky became brighter, shielding away the stars and covering the city in a twilight gray. They charged through the doors into the nearly empty changing room, the last few bathers frantically grabbing their possessions before running past them out the door.

As they marched into the bath chamber, Delvan saw a young boy run past, his clothes dirtied by ground in muck, his face marked with grime. *That's odd.* He turned his attention away and back to the group ahead as they reached the back of the humid room, the scented bath air sticking to his skin.

"It should be here, in this room." Nerio held the open book in his hand, head turning from it to the small door that led to a private bath area. Inside seemed bare, aside from some benches and a single tub at its center. *Where did they hide a secret tunnel in here?* he wondered.

Desnia grabbed Nerio's arm, pulling him into the room. "Nerio, let's see if we can find—"

"My, my," came a voice with a long draw that echoed through the vaulted stone room. Delvan spun, hand on his sword, to see a thin man dressed in black standing a few yards behind them. Scars covered more of his face than his natural skin, and he favored his right leg as he took a few short steps forward.

He, Orne, and Ferrand stepped together in a line, Nerio and Desnia behind them. Delvan heard Desnia gasp, walking behind them and whispering, "Careful, apparently this one is a sick fuck. He's called 'The Hunter'."

"Why?" asked Delvan, looking the strange man up and down. *How did we not see him when we came in?*

"He's a mage, like Jerdine. He tracks and kills other mages that stand against opening the gate."

The question of how she knew this itched at Delvan, but he put aside his curiosity, focusing on the danger before him.

"I've heard of this twisted shithead," growled Ferrand. "Gets off by killing, turned against his own kind merely for the challenge."

The Hunter held a palm to his chest, a poorly imitated expression of offense on his face.

"You and Nerio go and try to get the door open," Delvan said to Desnia, "we'll handle this."

"Watch yourself," she whispered before hurrying into the room with Nerio close behind.

"Mhm," said The Hunter, tongue licking part of his lip. "It's always so much more… gratifying when they put up a fight. Your friends won't be able to open the door, but no matter."

Delvan's eyes flitted around the room, seeing if the gimp had any other reinforcements. But the grand, bath lined space was empty. He and Ferrand drew their swords, Orne's grip tightening on the shaft of his halberd as the sickly-looking man took a limping step forward.

"I had hoped," The Hunter said, "that finding you would take more effort. I must admit, however, that destroying the commander's room did throw me off, and I'm still trying to piece together what happened there. But *shh*! Don't tell me, it'd ruin the satisfaction."

Orne took a few steps to Delvan's left, and Ferrand went a few to his right as they cautiously moved to encircle the rambling mage. Delvan didn't know what to expect, but he remembered back to the alley in Calentine, his foot becoming fixed to the ground and the shot to the rib. What could he do to prevent something like that again?

The thought made his heart begin to race, a tingling sensation running down his arm. Despite outnumbering the unnerving creature before them, he felt at a disadvantage. What strange tools of combat did this man have hidden away? And why did he seem so… calm?

"Quite the chaos you've caused out there. A good cover, I must admit. I'll have to remember that one," The Hunter said with twisted admiration.

"Where's Kolden?!" asked Orne with a guttural ire seeping into his voice.

"Hmm? Oh, yes, the short one. Don't worry about him, you can be reunited soon enough. Perhaps he'd be more inclined to tell me where he got this if I tortured one of you instead? Do you think him the voyeuristic type?" The Hunter pulled a short knife from the sheath at his side, the blade giving off a faint, steady purple light. Delvan felt the slightest bit of a strange sensation, like cold water down his throat on a hot day, one he'd not experienced since the fire at the vault.

The man was completely unarmed otherwise, as far as Delvan could tell. His grip on the handle of his short sword became tighter, taking another precarious step closer to The Hunter, who appeared unconcerned as to the blades surrounding him.

The Hunter smiled, sharpened edges of darksteel all around him. His eyes grew unnaturally wide, more white showing than color. "Let's not dally, shall we? I would so like you all for myself, I even sent the guards off to help with the fire so that we are not disturbed." Delvan's eyes caught what he could only describe as thin lines of light forming around The Hunter's free hand at his side. They swirled into the shape of a flat disc, the repetitive stems branching out from his clustered fingers. He blinked, wondering if his eyes were playing tricks on him.

"Don't let him cast!" screamed Ferrand as he lurched forward. He thrust his lengthy sword's point at The Hunter, but it fell short. Delvan looked over, seeing the commander struggle to move his right foot, a faint and familiar symbol glowing from the stone around it.

Orne was unafflicted and raised his halberd high, dropping the axe down at The Hunter, who remained calmly in his place, that uncanny smile tugging the corner of his lips. He raised his hand at Orne, the thin pattern of light around his fingers growing brightly as a force exploded from it with a flash, aimed directly at the giant man. Orne and his halberd were flung backward by an impact. Delvan held his shielded arm to his face, his feet bracing as a shock wave punched against him, ringing his ears and turning the fringes of his vision white.

With breath held and eyes wide in fear, Delvan looked to Orne as the dizzying effects of the concussive force faded. The hulking man groaned as he rolled over, trying to push himself up while a trail of smoke rose from his armor's chest plate. Delvan let out a short breath, his furrowed eyes turning back to The Hunter, whose lips were still held in that thin smile.

Ferrand plunged the tip of his sword into the soft marble floor at his feet, directly into one of the glowing lines surrounding it. There was a crackling noise as the glowing pattern vanished, his foot moving freely once more. "Break the fractals if you get caught in one!" said Ferrand as he pulled the darksteel blade out of the floor.

"Ah!" said The Hunter excitedly. "This should be fun indeed! It's so rare to find anyone familiar with High magic. It's... thrilling."

Ferrand charged forward, Delvan doing the same as they pincered him between them. The commander's sword sang as it swung through the air with impossible speed. The Hunter twirled away and dodged the enormous blade, putting him face to face with Delvan, who slashed with his own weapon, the man's horrendously scarred face uncomfortably close to his own.

With speed that would rival Ferrand's, and accuracy which spoke to an acuity of experience and talent, The Hunter swept with his small, radiant knife, catching the edge of Delvan's sword and deflecting it to the side. It was a bold maneuver—insane to try—and yet it was executed with such ease and grace, as if he were an artist drawing a line.

The motion twisted both their bodies to the side, Delvan's instincts reacting and ripping his elbow backward, directly into that vile, twisted grin. The Hunter staggered a step back, pink blood that almost fluoresced dribbling down from his nose. He wiped it away with a sneer, ducking just as Ferrand's sword came whistling through the air again, narrowly missing him.

Any limp Delvan had seen was gone, though he couldn't explain how. The Hunter's movements were blurring streaks of black as he dodged and deflected each swing from the sapphire bearing pair. Sweat streamed down Delvan's brow and into his eyes as he wondered how long their opponent could keep going like this. Was he similar to Blues in that he needed inanite to fuel these strange powers? Or was there something else?

Orne had pulled himself to his feet and began marching back to join them, a black scar across his chest plate. The Hunter had been defensively postured this entire time, dodging and deflecting blows, rarely seeking an opportunity to strike. It wasn't how one fought—it made no tactical sense. The smile on his disfigured face grew wilder as Orne joined back into the fight, thrusting forward the spear point of his halberd, nicking The Hunter's side.

A few drops of his strange colored blood fell to the tiled floor. The Hunter looked at it, then back at them with chilling eagerness in his eyes. Delvan sensed he *wanted* this, to have all of them attacking at once. They needed every advantage. He couldn't stay idle any longer.

Delvan raised his hand, palm facing The Hunter. He could feel it, the power beneath the surface, feeding all this time from his anger, resentment, and fear. It churned inside of him, a wild animal beating against its cage, desperate for release.

"Ah, yes, show me, First born. Show me your breath!" came the maniacal touts of The Hunter.

Desnia ran into the room with Nerio, looking over the blank stone walls, spinning every which way to search for clues in the small room.

*This is bad. Very, very bad,* said Masini. He'd been mortified since The Hunter appeared, hardly able to speak in a quiet first.

"Focus! We need to find the door," she exclaimed.

"I'm not sure where it is, it's not described in here," said Nerio, thumbing through the book in his hands.

"No, not... Never mind," she said with a shake of her head.

A deluge of panic filled her as she heard metal clashing in the main bathing chamber. It was almost enough to suppress the thoughts of the spreading fire beyond these walls, the inferno that was raping and ravaging the city. A catastrophe caused entirely by her. *How many people have I killed tonight?*

*Yes,* said Masini, *yes, the door. Need that door. Um, it won't look like a door, obviously, that would be dumb. It's probably part of one of the walls, but you won't find any seams. Do you see any stones that are too clean? No moisture or film from the bath on them?*

Desnia began running her hands across the walls, fumbling around as if she understood what it was she was searching for. The smooth masonry was indistinguishable from one stone to the next, the white blocks all appearing equally clean and polished.

"They all look the same!" she said, pounding her fist against the stone. "Doesn't that book say *anything* about where this door is or how to open it?"

Nerio stepped closer to a nearby lamp and held the pages almost to his nose, his eyes darting as he shook his head. "I'm sorry, I don't see anything here."

The sound of an explosion from the main hall cracked the air and vibrated the floor beneath her feet. Desnia covered her ears as Masini began his jittered rambling once more. *This is bad, we need to go, we need to go!*

She removed her hands from her ringing ears, looking at the walls around her. She could do this. Afterall, finding things people wanted to keep hidden was her specialty. *There's an adjacent room,* she thought, *so it's probably not on that wall.* Could it be through the tub somehow? *No, that would be a pain if he came here every day. The building's exterior is that wall, so that just leaves one...*

"How is it activated?" she asked as the sounds of grunting and clashing metal resumed out beyond the door.

"Again, it doesn't say," said Nerio, sounding exacerbated as the pressure of the fight outside seemed to be affecting him as well.

*Touch, most likely,* said Masini. *He doesn't have the, uh, amount of glowy rock he needs to do anything more complicated. It's probably an il-il-il-fuck it, just have Nerio touch all the stones!*

There wasn't time for Nerio to come in contact with every piece of masonry in the room. Desnia decided to go with the wall that made the most sense, hoping that she was right and there wasn't some other form of strange magic that could hide this door in one of the others.

"Nerio, drop the book and come to the back wall here. Run your hands over the different stones, quickly! It's going to recognize you, just like the books. Hurry!"

Nerio had rushed over and was now rubbing his palms along the wall as if he were scrubbing it with a sponge. Desnia stood behind him, anxiously looking back at the doorway leading to the main hall, expecting that scarred, disfigured sneer to come walking through at any moment.

*They can do this,* she thought, *they can hold him.*

She stood to the side, feeling helpless. She was trapped, trying to break through a lock she couldn't comprehend, waiting for impending doom while trying to simultaneously prevent it. She fidgeted, drying her sweating palms on her robe. Never had she been this nervous during a job, but, then again, the stakes had never been quite this high. What would she—

A sudden glow from the corner of her eye pulled her gaze away from the rear door. Nerio was standing with his hand pressed against a stone near waist height, the area around it glowing with tiny, faint lines in a weird triangular pattern. To his side, a tall rectangle of lights began to hum on the wall, patterns and shapes of a strange writing took form to create the perimeter of the entry-shaped square. Then, in a phenomenon that was difficult for her mind to comprehend, the stones within their boundary faded like mist in the sun, until they simply *vanished.*

*What the fuck...* she wondered in awe.

A small landing lay beyond, a passage of inky shadow looming behind it as stairs led down into the ominous darkness. It felt as though she was staring at a door to the prisons of the underworld itself, the pitch-black hiding dark secrets beneath the surface.

*That's it!* cried Masini. *Have the priest stand under it, if it glows a little brighter, we're all set! Let's put as much distance between us and that feline-fuck as we can!*

"Nerio, can you stand in the door for a moment?" she said, hoping it was safe, picturing what Masini could have meant by "melting."

He closed his gaping jaw as he turned to her. "Um, yes, yes of course." With a loud swallow and two steps forward, he was atop the threshold, the faint purple lines glowing with the tiniest increase in their luminance. Nerio felt at the freshly appeared stone faces of the door's frame, his jaw becoming slack once more.

*I have to tell the others,* she thought, hearing more steel *clanging* outside the entrance. *Maybe they can get away from the fight and join us. I need to give them a chance, I need to help them.*

Desnia ran to the door, hoping that this would mend the mistakes of the night, that she could save the lives of these three and the rest of the kingdom. Maybe that would help to offset the tragedy she'd set ablaze outside, the one taking the homes and lives of so many.

Her instincts wisely told her that she might have to leave them behind, that the gate was more important than any of them or anyone in the city. The destruction was horrific, but it would all be for naught if she stayed and tried to help the others fight The Hunter. But for once, she didn't *want* to. For the first time in more years than she could remember, she'd found *trust*. Some measure of it, at least.

As she reached the doorway, she hoped, prayed, that she wouldn't have to abandon it.

A voice called out from behind Delvan, a resonance that manifested the spectral hand and the debilitating pain that came with it. Desnia was shouting, her cries manifesting a recollection that drenched him like rain, smothering the flames within as that night flashed before him once more. All night he'd been on edge, balancing his ability to function against the upheaval of his life he'd undergone in the past few hours, as well as the raging inferno outside, reminding him of that night... He'd been barely holding himself together. Now, in the heat of a battle that stressed him to his limits, that familiar tone was the feather that collapsed his world. His face went cold, his hand trembling as her voice fell upon his ears.

"We have it open! Come on!" she shouted.

"Well, now isn't that interesting?" said The Hunter with a tilt of his head. "I *do* love surprises, what a delight you've all been!"

"Go!" shouted Ferrand. "Leave us and get to the gate!"

Delvan looked over his shoulder, locking eyes with Desnia for the briefest of moments. She didn't need convincing to follow Ferrand's order. Unlike some, she wouldn't wait and fret over them, it was as clear to Delvan as her sky-blue eyes. That miniscule lock of their gaze told him everything: how she would do what was necessary, regardless of her own feelings or theirs, and despite the pain in her eyes she would make the hard decision. There was no hesitation. She was strong, stronger than Delvan ever had been.

He wished for a bit of that strength now.

With a blur of gold, she broke their connection as she twisted and ran, vanishing beyond the distant door.

Delvan turned back to The Hunter, hands absent his wielded flames like a torch underwater. The maniacal face turned to a frown, cantankerous disappointment written upon it. "Alas, we can't be having your friends scamper unsupervised, can we? Seems our time has run short, then." He lifted a pattern encircled hand, its ink-line, purple shape illuminating his face and dragging shadows across his scars. It outstretched it towards Ferrand, who had his sword raised and ready to slice down in a broad strike.

The Jack suddenly slowed, grunting and face turning red as he strained, his body moving as if he were underwater. Delvan knew these effects, but it couldn't be coming from The Hunter, could it? Ferrand moved his sword at a speed that resembled a child attempting to swing a massive war-hammer, his movements bulky and weighty.

Delvan shook himself from his bout of triggered trauma, overcoming the confused daze. Gripping his sword tightly and setting his jaw, he charged forward, Orne taking the opportunity to run at his side and join his attack. He raised his sword and Orne his halberd, preparing to strike.

In a smooth, adept motion, The Hunter sheathed the knife and waved his now free hand towards them. A different pattern drew itself into existence around his waving fingers, aimed directly at them. Delvan's face lit up as he saw a glow begin to brighten, emanating from the outstretched hand. In a futile effort, he tried jumping to the side, Orne attempting to duck as he too recognized what was coming.

But it was all too slow. There was a bright flash, a burst of light following and punching into Delvan's chest like a ram, tossing him backward.

The room shook through his white, dotted vision, his ears ringing as he looked up at the ceiling. He turned his head, seeing Orne with eyes clenched in pain on the floor next to him, another scorch mark on his chest. Delvan winced, a stabbing pain piercing his chest, turning each breath into a gasping struggle. He did his best to push through it as he painfully sat up from the floor he'd been thrown to, smoke burning his eyes as it rose from his darksteel chest plate. They blinked rapidly to clear the fog from his vision, and as he squinted, he saw the shape of The Hunter walking towards him, glowing blade in hand.

Adrenaline surged through him, eradicating the pain and leaving only panic as he tried scrambling backward. But his body wouldn't move. It felt as though his backside were fused to the stone beneath him, and as he looked down, he found the edges of a glowing symbol peeking out along the tile from underneath him. Just like in the alley all those months ago, he'd become immovable. He reached for his sword a few feet away as The Hunter walked closer with this calm, limping gait. The sword was too far, resting well beyond his overextended arm.

He tried to pull the small darksteel dagger from its sheath at his side, but that menacing grin of perverse pleasure was already standing above him looking down with glee, the wide eyes displaying the white of excitement. Orne groaned and rolled, coughing blood onto the floor not far from Delvan. Ferrand still waded towards them from behind, The Hunter's outstretched arm slowing his pace.

"I'm sorry we didn't have more time," said The Hunter. "I had hoped that this encounter would last longer, but duty calls, I'm afraid."

Delvan felt like he was being choked by the tightness in his throat as The Hunter raised his knife into the air. He was frozen, paralyzed and held in place by his own fear as much as the symbol under him. The shadowy grip was finally going to achieve its goal, the herald of his death, and he was helpless to stop it, as he had always been.

In that moment he *wanted* to be better. All that time, wasted on his petty vendetta. Sulking and feeling sorry for himself while he plotted against Ferrand for retribution, which he now wasn't entirely certain the man deserved. His ignorance had birthed a hatred. What could he have accomplished should he have directed that energy elsewhere?

None of that mattered now, the end coming at him with a dull radiance and sharpened edge.

There was a cry, a scream that tore through the air. The Hunter spun, looking towards Ferrand as a long, black streak came spinning through the air directly at him. He lurched to the side just as Ferrand's massive sword tumbled through where he'd been standing. The returned limp seemed to slow him, and the sword's tip managed to slice him across the back before clattering on the floor in the distance.

The Hunter staggered forward as he arched his back, and his face writhed. The glee had gone from it, leaving little more than agony with a hint of the smile that had once been there.

"Come and fight me, coward," said Ferrand as he stepped forward, fighting the Reach of The Hunter, his body moving as though ten times heavier than it actually was.

*No*, thought Delvan. *What is he doing?*

Delvan saw the oozing, pinkish blood of The Hunter soaking his back as the man turned and limped towards Ferrand as quickly as his hobbled stride could carry him. The commander threw a punch, one that was sluggish and easily dodged by his assailer. Ferrand's body twisted as his fist went harmlessly past the mage before him, exposing his unprotected flank. The Hunter raised the glowing blade high, and with a smooth, obstructed motion, plunged it into Ferrand's neck.

Violet blood poured out from the puncture, and with a choking sound it flooded from his mouth and over his lips. A gurgling sound followed as the light left Ferrand's eyes and they became distant and empty. He crumpled to the floor as The Hunter ripped the blade from his throat, now glowing brightly enough to appear white, filling the entire room with the brilliance of a thousand torches.

Delvan lay there, mouth gaping as Ferrand's blood pooled on the floor. Confusing emotions battled within him. He'd dreamed of this event, day after day for months on end. The person he'd considered most responsible for Hilbrun's death, laying there lifeless on the floor. And yet, there was no sense of fulfillment, justice, honor or any other manner of gratification. Nothing. Merely the same well of sorrow, grief, and loathing that had carved away at him. It was then he knew that the person he blamed most for Hilbrun's death wasn't Ferrand. It wasn't the strange groups that worked in the shadows, or even the man who'd fired the bolt. It was the one who had led Hilbrun into that situation, who had failed to stop the danger.

It was himself.

Tears streamed down his dirtied cheeks as the last of the life left Ferrand. He didn't want the man dead, he knew that now. Now, when it was too late. Despite his abrasive, abusive, and belittling nature, he'd given everything to save Delvan. And now he was gone, taken by the heinous aberration standing above him.

The hot white of the blade in The Hunter's hands drenched the massive, tub lined hall in swaths of purple light. It gave his visage an eerie glow as he grinned and took a deep breath of satisfaction before turning to face the stunned Delvan and Orne, knotting Delvan's stomach with fear.

The sound of a door opening echoed through the hall. Delvan went to move his arm, but The Hunter's Reach shifted its twisted eye of patterned lines—now barely visible against the knife's radiance—to Delvan. His body stiffened, his arm moving less than an inch when he commanded it to his belt as he fought an unseen force. This was a weak Reach, but Delvan knew he wasn't going to be able to do anything fast enough to fend off his captor.

From the end of the hall, footsteps approached. Delvan craned his neck as The Hunter stepped to the side, revealing a principle—who Delvan assumed to be Jerdine—approaching, his robe swaying in the breeze of his hastened walk.

"Well done, Hunter." Jerdine came to a stop at The Hunter's side. "Thank you for sending for me, I see you have this well in hand. Your messenger said that you believed these to be the ones responsible for the fire that burned my spire to the ground? Damned vermin. I just came from there, half the city is ablaze now!"

"Yes, indeed. They are searching for the one we captured earlier, as well as the gate," said The Hunter.

*Captured,* thought Delvan, *does that mean he's still alive?*

"How interesting, though I suppose that explains why your friend had this." Jerdine pulled the cadentite key from his pocket, the dull, faint glow that had once captivated and mystified with its endless depth from within now drowned by the blinding brilliance of the knife. "I'm not certain which of you had the audacity to alter this most precious of artifacts but know that you will come to regret your decision. You thought something so disgustingly pedestrian as reshaping the key would stop me? I helped to *build* its lock, you fools! And I for one shall not waste any more of my life away on this stagnant, uncivilized, inert pile of stone and rubble you call a realm!

"And yet, despite your horrid transgression, you ineptly delivered it directly to me, you disgusting, tainted imbecile. When the boy said that letter had been given to him by your friend, well... You made it easy."

The Hunter handed the knife to Jerdine, who held it pointed down towards the stone in his other hand. "I'm almost tempted to linger and watch The Hunter practice his art for a time, perhaps your screams would quench this rage I feel for your defiling of my personal sanctum."

As he spoke, light drained from the blade, like a fire falling away into the distance. The key began to glow brighter, its shifting resplendence shining out as if from waters that had unreachable bottoms.

"You should be aware, there were two that escaped down into the tunnel," said The Hunter as the blade dimmed above the swirling pattern around Jerdine's fingers. "A woman and a young priest. They arrived with these three."

"What?!" spat Jerdine, turning his scowl to The Hunter. "How did they gain entry?"

"I was wondering the same," The Hunter responded.

Delvan's hand had slowly been getting closer to the dagger at his belt, moving only a few inches in the time that Jerdine had been speaking. His eyes flitted over to Orne, who rolled onto his side with a groan. His insides turned over themselves. *C'mon, Orne,* he thought, *don't die on me, I can't lose you too.*

Here he was, statically held in place while his friends' lives were in danger, unable to do anything for them.

From the ashes of the guild fire he'd gained a new life, full of new people. Strangers that were willing to hold him when his life fell apart, take him under their wing as one of their own, and trust him when he denied the same conviction to them.

Now it was all at risk once more.

The realization made him resist the Reach more fiercely, his muscles exerting every ounce of strength they possessed, pushing his hand slightly closer to the hilt of his dagger. He wouldn't freeze again, he *wouldn't* lose anyone again. He would fight, and they would all reap their demise, the spectral hand be damned.

"Damn it all. I've already contacted her, they'll be waiting for us to open the gate and we *can't* afford any more delays. Here." Jerdine handed the knife back to The Hunter, its glow so faint it was no longer visible against the flood of light now beaming from the key like the sun at midday. "I will deal with the two in the tunnel. Do with these two as you wish, but do not linger. I intend to have the gate open shortly, once I mend the lock, and you should be present once they arrive."

"Mhm, I will do my best to keep it brief," The Hunter replied with that sinister sneer.

"And use whatever you draw from the boy to close those wounds as much as you can. Don't plan to greet our guests while still bleeding," said Jerdine as he walked past them and into the room Desnia had fled through, the sounds of his footsteps trailing into the distance. His departure left the room feeling dark in the timid light of the torches, the resplendent key taken with him.

Delvan saw Orne's eyes open as he groaned and cursed, spitting blood onto the polished floor, his face covered in black soot from the smoldering scar on his armor. He pulled himself to one foot, then the other, picking up his Halberd from the floor with gritted teeth.

The Hunter's lips smiled, but his eyes glinted with death—steeled and unmoving like a predator's. Delvan tried even more desperately to reach for his dagger, his arm barely moving as he fought the Reach. He couldn't let Orne fight this monster alone, he had to help, or else this would all be on him once again. He groaned as he tried to speak, but his cries came out merely as tongueless syllables.

Orne stood, hunched with the spearpoint of his polearm aiming at The Hunter, whose free hand still held Delvan from a distance, his blood dripping to the floor from his back and side. "It has been a pleasure, gentlemen," said The Hunter, "but I'm afraid—"

A thrust came from Orne, the spearpoint shooting forward. It was smart, Delvan knew, not to wait to attack. One could become accustomed to the rules of engagement in tournaments, duels and the like, but the reality of battle, of combat, was bloody—and unfair. The only rule was survival, there was no such thing as cheating.

The Hunter was off guard, but even in his injured state he still had the reflexes of a seasoned warrior. To Delvan's dismay, he leaned himself backward, his face flinching from the pain as his gimp leg stepped back to support his dodge. Delvan's heart sank. Orne had taken his shot and missed.

The spear's tip, however, did something that Delvan hadn't anticipated, nor had The Hunter, it would seem. As he leaned to avoid the weapon, the acute point of sharpened darksteel penetrated the lines of the glowing pattern around The Hunter's hand, grazing the fingers with a small nick.

*He wasn't aiming for The Hunter,* Delvan realized. *He* wanted *him to dodge, all so he could pierce the fractal.* In the single most elegant maneuver Delvan had ever seen, Orne had manipulated his opponent with near clairvoyant precision, and as the spearpoint broke a single line of the casting around The Hunter's hand, the entire array of repeating lines crackled and burst away into nothingness.

Delvan's hand slapped against his dagger's hilt. He drew it, stabbing its point into the line protruding from under his backside along the cold marble floor. There was an immediate release, and he felt his body shift and slide slightly along the polished stone. He sprang to his feet, ignoring the sword on the floor.

He wouldn't need it.

Delvan raised both his hands forward as The Hunter staggered back, grabbing his knee to hold himself steady. He looked at Delvan, eye's wide but lips thin and pale as they drew back and curved to his eyes. Delvan had a new life to fight for, new friends to fill it with. He wasn't about to allow anyone, no matter how ancient or powerful, to take that from him again.

With a flicker before his outward palms, light flared into existence. Orange flames gushed forward from him in a torrent of blazing destruction that sprayed out at The Hunter while Delvan let out a scream that soured the air with abhorrence for the man before him. The cascade of heat and tendrils of flames spouted forth like geysers, charring the floor black as they reached out and sought the crazed deviant before them.

As the flames nearly reached their quarry, The Hunter threw both his own hands before him, dropping his knife to the ground. A hazy wall of purple materialized like a mist in front of him, suddenly snapping into a solid pane of purple. The flames collided with the shield and broke to the side like water over stone, but Delvan wasn't going to stop, he *couldn't* stop. The flames grew hotter and brighter as he pushed himself to his limits, pouring everything he could muster into the assault. Through the wall of flames and the tinted shield, Delvan could see The Hunter straining, his face twisting as he sweat and let out a hollow, drawn out laugh that reverberated through the hall even over the roar of the flames.

But Delvan wasn't alone.

Orne, standing to the side of the searing flames, spun his halberd over his head and used the full reach of its seven-foot length to whirl the axe-head through the stream of fire and slam it against the veil of light protecting The Hunter. The translucent barrier shattered like a pane of glass, dissipating into the air and exposing the mage behind it to Delvan's onslaught.

Flames of wrath leapt forward, unobstructed, engulfing The Hunter in their unforgiving fury. Cloth, leather, and hair erupted into flames, followed by skin and flesh as the fire consumed him with ravenous abandon. Smoke rose to the vaulted ceiling, and the scent of burning flesh enveloped them as Delvan released all his anguish in the flood that sprang from his hands, The Hunter continuing his haunting laugh until his body collapsed on the floor.

Delvan ceased the fountain of death, panting, with perspiration soaking his hair and face. There was no tremble in his hands, no ache in his heart or shortness of his breath. Inside of him wasn't the contemptuous loathing he'd felt for himself, nor the paralyzing grief of ones lost. For the first time in a long while, he felt... himself, cleansed by the fire. Remnants remained—he doubted he'd ever be truly free of them—but they were charred husks, figments of the power they once held. Not unlike the blackened, disfigured shape before him in the center of the scorched, tile floor.

Delvan approached what remained of The Hunter slowly, Orne taking a step forward with the spearpoint of his halberd at the ready. Skin had turned the color of tar, cracking and flaking like old paint on a sill, red flesh visible beneath the oozing landscape of burnt dermis. The Hunter lay flat on his back, and as Delvan stepped closer, the pungent, nauseating scent of smoldering tissue made him gag. He covered his mouth with his hand, lip pulling back in disgust as he crept forward, a strange sight emanating from the remnants of his chest.

It appeared to be *glowing*.

Thin lines of purple created a complex, overlapping pattern that re-sembled a tattoo embedded in The Hunter's skin which covered his entire torso. At an intersection of the pencil-thin lines, above his heart, was a fingernail-sized piece of faceted cadentite glowing dimly, nearly all of its luster gone.

*What is that?* wondered Delvan.

There was a low groan that came from the body on the floor, giving Delvan a start. Orne retracted the polearm at his side, bracing for a thrust to ensure the man was ended. "Orne, wait!" Delvan remembered something that Desnia had said. "With Nerio gone down the tunnel, we have no way of passing through. But, if this scum is still alive, maybe the protections will recognize him and let us pass. I don't think we can risk killing him yet."

Orne's face was one of disgusted hatred, but Kolden's life was above his own emotions and wants. With what must have been the full extent of his restraint, Orne held back his blow. There was a twitch of The Hunter's hand, a motion that set his and Orne's senses on high alert. How he was able to move—let alone still be alive—baffled Delvan. The bone-tipped ends of his fingers began to rise off the floor, arm shaky and lethargic and, to Delvan's shock, lines of light forming around the ashen stubs beyond his palm.

In a blur of motion which Delvan couldn't hope to react to or stifle, Orne had brought the head of his Halberd up and dropped the axe to the floor, the casting hand caught between edged steel and stone. It severed completely, the lines vanishing and The Hunter's body writhing in soundless screams as pinkish blood spurted from the stump and the charred hand flopped to the floor.

"Mhm," grunted Orne, contented.

"Bring him," said Delvan, "we don't have much time. Who knows what the principle is doing to the others right now, or what he's already done to Kolden."

Orne nodded, grabbing The Hunter's ankle and dragging him as they made their way to the nearby entry room. Delvan picked up his sword, dagger, and the small, glowing knife from the floor as they walked. A sound that could turn a butcher green came from the toted body as the charred skin on the back of The Hunter peeled away on the tile as if from a boiled vegetable, a smeared trail of oddly-colored blood following Orne on the floor as gasps left the mouth of the now convulsing madman. Orne disregarded the raspy sound, continuing to drag him by the leg without a second thought.

They trudged into the room where the others had run. Beyond the small tub of steaming bathwater was an opening that stood set into the stone wall, framed by more of the strange patterns and symbols, each faintly glowing.

*What? That wasn't here before,* thought Delvan. But it didn't matter, questions could be asked later. "Put him on the threshold, under those symbols," Delvan said. Orne was happy to oblige, dropping the limp leg to the floor and grabbing the half-dead man by the throat, picking him up by it as the last functioning ligaments caused the charred remains to squirm and wriggle in unimaginable agony.

Orne held the man out before him, his massive size having little issue holding the comparatively diminutive man, and slowly carried him forward until the gurgling remains were under the glowing patterns. They luminesced slightly brighter as Orne held him in place.

"I think that's it," said Delvan. He took a deep breath, the remnants of adrenaline still pumping through his veins protesting in a panicked frenzy at the daring action he was about to undertake. But this is what he had to do. He set his jaw and extended his hand forward into the opening alongside The Hunter's body, a pinprick tingle reminding him of the pain that had come from a mere touch of the book. It inched forward, slowly crossing the threshold as he held his breath and wrinkled his eyes in anticipation.

No pain came, no strange sensations coursed through his arm as it waved in the air of the doorway. *It's all or nothing, now.* He took a broad step, crossing the door into the tunnel beyond, a set of stairs before him leading into darkness below.

Orne followed suit, rotating around the suspended, limp remains in his hand until he passed through to join Delvan. Both let out a sigh of relief, Orne dropping The Hunter to the floor.

"What do we want to do with him?" asked Orne as the chest of the decrepit man still rose with tiny breaths.

They could need him, Delvan knew. If Nerio had fallen, and Jerdine escaped, they could be trapped in here. But that wasn't going to happen. He was going to make sure that all of them, Kolden included, were going to leave this place—unscathed.

"We don't need him," Delvan said, pulling the strange glowing knife from his waist and plunging it into the remnants of The Hunter's chest. "Enjoy the labors of hell, you bastard." The light in the tattoos and central stone dimmed, slowly fading and losing their brilliance until they eventually turned black, blending with the charred skin.

Delvan pulled the blade out, and it shined more brilliantly than any torch, as bright as after it had stabbed Ferrand. It hurt to look at, and Delvan shielded his eyes as he stabbed it into the sheath for his dagger, shoving the other knife into his belt.

Orne grunted, and without awaiting further orders or instruction, raised his halberd as much as the small space would allow, and dropped its axe-head on The Hunter's neck, cleanly removing his head from his body and sending it rolling down the shadowed, stone treads.

"No chances. Let's go," said Orne as he turned and ran down the stairs. Delvan lit a ball of flame for light and followed behind, their steps echoing down the rough stone walls as they descended into the unknown.

# CHAPTER
# FIFTY-FOUR



The uneven, curved walls of the tunnel wicked away the lantern's light as Desnia and Nerio ran down the winding passage, the gentle slope of the black stone leading them ever further down its throat. Their feet smacked against the smooth surface of the unlit corridor, light failing to reach more than a few feet in front of them, absorbed by the thirsty darkness of the stone. Desnia cursed under her breath.

She hated running into anything like this, the risks and uncertainties hovering over her head like vultures as possibilities ran through her mind. Nerio's heavy breathing was close behind her, another reminder that she had something else to consider on this sprint into the dark depths.

Worse than all that, her thoughts were tormented by what she'd left behind up above. Abandoning the others had been necessary, an instinct of survival, but it being the right choice didn't make it any easier to accept. The agony in Delvan's eyes… She'd thought her own deprecation terrible, the fire outside raging and costing the lives of an untold number. But those eyes, they spoke of an unseen torture that she had difficulty fathoming.

Desnia tried to put all of that out of her mind. Any job could go poorly if you lost yourself in distracting thoughts, and this was no exception. Years of experience helped her to bury the guilt of leaving them in a place more unnerving than this musty tunnel, her full attention turning to what lay at the end of their path.

As Desnia was beginning to wonder if the twisting cave had an end, the eerie hue of a purple glow became visible at the distance. Desnia raised her hand, causing Nerio to slow just behind her, shoveling the moist, dank air in and out of his lungs with great heaves. She blew out the lantern, quietly puffing the flame out of existence. She moved to the tunnel's side, hugging the wall as she moved forward, Nerio close behind.

The glow became brighter, pouring into the chamber that they entered from a roughly shaped opening further along the wall. The space was filled with what appeared to be workstations, grinding stones and benches spread throughout. Desnia's heart dropped as she noticed something far more disconcerting—chains mounted to the wall, grimy, dirtied cuffs at their end.

*What has that bastard been doing down here?* she wondered.

She moved past the stations of indentured servitude, crouching low and footsteps softly, silently landing on the hard stone—greatly offset by the blatant and audible stride of her companion. She turned to Nerio and held a finger to her lips, his face looking apologetic. He was trying, but trying could still get you caught—and killed.

She poked her head around the corner of the opening that the strange colored radiance was pouring through. Her eyes fell upon a massive cavern, a few steps down from the entrance at which she crouched. Light filled the room, emanating from a massive, circular pattern of illuminated lines set into the black stone, its diameter a hundred yards or more. They lit up the domed cavern with their steady hue of purple, and revealed cages lining the otherwise barren, potholed outer ring of the room.

Which appeared to contain *people*.

"What... What is this place?" gasped Nerio.

*Oh, fuck,* said Masini. *Des, that's the g-g-g-cock-monger! That's the doorway thing. And, well, it looks complete. I don't know how he did it... Those lines used to be thick engravings filled with, uh, glowy rock, but a long, long time ago they were, uh, how do I say this without sounding like an idiot? Sucked dryer than a sailor at a brothel. It was essentially destroyed, which means he's had to get more, uh, glowy rock to rebuild it. But I didn't think this much existed in the entire kingdom...*

"He's been at this a long time," Desnia muttered.

*Indeed, but still, it's an incredible feat. And it looks ready, which is a bigger problem. If they lock the stone the others stole into its center, it's over.*

"How do we destroy it?" she whispered.

"What?" asked a confused Nerio. "I... I'm not sure," he said, opening the book under his arm and thumbing through the pages.

*If you break any of the lines, then it should render it inoperable, but unless you have any inanite or darksteel, I'm not sure how we're going to be able to do that. There is another option, but... no, no I don't think it's an option for you right now. We need to get closer, see what we're working with.*

"I don't see anyone else in there. We should go help those people, by the gods, what has Jerdine done?" said Nerio. It was hard to deny him, given how empty the space was aside from the cages and mosaic floor. She was still wary, just because you couldn't see the danger, didn't mean it didn't lurk nearby. She put her arm out in front of him as he went to charge into the cavern.

"We need to be careful, we don't even know whether Jerdine ever went to the clergy house. Maybe he just sent his pet up to investigate." Desnia pointed away from the door, ignoring the disappointed look on Nerio's face. "Those tunnels look like they circle around the main cavern. Let's make our way, *slowly*, around and see if we can find anything that we can use."

*And hopefully,* she thought, *the others can manage with that freak in the bathhouse and come to join us.* Her insides tumbled at the thought, making her heart race even faster. It was a strange feeling, one she wasn't accustomed to.

"But Desnia, look at them. They're—"

"*Shh,*" she said with a finger to her lips. Hair stood up on her arms, the weird, radiating sensation that she'd been feeling since coming near the cavern suddenly had become more acute. She spun her head, looking back down the tunnel they'd come from, her neck throbbing from the beating in her chest. She waited in tense silence, hoping that her instincts were wrong.

After a few seconds, she began to think that she'd been mistaken, that her intuition had been wrong. That was until a glow began shimmering in the distance, a light that brightened even the thirsty walls of black as it approached.

"*Go!*" she hissed to Nerio, scrambling further down the tunnel as it curved around the large room. They passed a few more small openings, their outlines cutting streaked shadows across the floor and walls. She held her hand up, stopping and crouching down near one of the openings. She peered into the domed cavern, looking for the source of the incoming light, hoping against reason that it was one of the others, emerging victorious and rushing to her aid.

*When did I become so dependent?* she wondered.

The air left her lungs and was replaced by chagrin as Jerdine sauntered into the cavern from the opening they'd just abandoned. A glow like a thousand fires beamed from his hand, a shining symbol representing the futility of their efforts.

*No...* said Masini. *No, no, no. Desnia, he has the k-k-k-the glowy rock! Stop him, now! If he locks it into the center, it's over! It's radiating enough energy to pull through a small army!*

"Fuck," she whispered, her heart somehow beating faster and threatening to burst. "If you're going to send some help, now is the time," she whispered, so quietly that Masini didn't even hear.

It had come to this, then. Her, armed with nothing more than a tiny, crude knife in her sash, her only aid the scared priest behind her. She didn't fault Nerio, he had every right to be terrified, gods knew she was. But he didn't have the experience of being under the type of pressure that could lead to your arrest, torture, death... worse. She was here, alone, like she had been her entire life, and now everything came down to her. If the voice in her head *truly* was a god, she'd like to ask why the cruel bastard had chosen her for this.

Desnia took a deep breath, pulling the blade from her side. *Here goes nothing,* she thought. She'd wait until his back was turned, then leave Nerio behind and creep up on Jerdine. Maybe, *maybe,* she could get a single blow in before—

Jerdine came to a sudden stop about a quarter of the way across the massive floor, his head turning with a puzzled expression on his face. Desnia's knees bent back down, pulling her further back behind the rough opening into the chamber, shying away from the light.

"Ahh," let out Jerdine in a drawn-out way, "Nerio, my boy. I see now how you were able to get past the protections. What a rare oversight on my part, although I can't say I suspected you'd find this place on your own. You should know, I never intended this ending for you. I tried to protect you, to keep you from this fate. You are, after all, so very *special.*"

*Protecting him my ass,* she thought. *What twisted world does this power-hungry bastard live in if he thinks that he was protecting Nerio?* She looked to the nearby cages, the motionless lumps that were once people within making her want to vomit in disgust.

"This... this is where they went," whispered Nerio in quiet horror. "I'd thought they'd escaped, but he took them here. To do... *this* to them. By the gods..."

The sight of a deathly still figure outside a cage caught her attention, dark liquid pooled around him. *What* are *they doing?*

"Come Nerio," continued Jerdine, "there's no need to hide in the shadows. Join me, help me usher in the new regime. Stand by my side and watch as this realm is forever changed once more. I can open your eyes to things you never thought possible, just come out here."

*You should send him out there,* said Masini. *He can distract Jerdine while you go after the stone.*

"*What*?!" she said with an edge like a knife. "The hell is wrong with you?"

To her wide-eyed disbelief, Nerio stood up beside her and began walking forward. It took her a moment to react, the utter shock seizing her thoughts in incredulity. Grabbing his arm, she thrust him against the wall, his eyes distant and glazed.

"*What* do you think you're doing?" she asked with eyes full of disappointed fury.

"I... I must. He knows I'm here, and there is no hiding from destiny," he said. "There is a reason for this, I'm certain. The gods have a plan."

"*Fuck* your gods," she cursed with curled fingers. Nerio didn't seem phased by her blasphemy, merely turning his head to meet her angry gaze. "They don't *care* about you, Nerio. They are using you, using *us*, to do their bidding. That man out there, he's no different than those fucking gods you pray to. They torture us, defile us, manipulate us, all to their own ends without thinking of us as more than replaceable fodder. The *only* difference between them and that sick fuck is that *he* can hurt you, right here, right now. So don't you *dare* go to him."

Nerio gave her the most calming, heartwarming smile she'd ever seen. She fought to keep her eyes full of ire, resenting how he was disarming her. "I know what you're doing," Nerio said, holding that damned smile, "but you cannot talk me out of this, Desnia. I must go. I appreciate your heart in this, that you are willing to say such things to protect me, but this is what I was meant to do, I can feel it. If I do not go to him, then he will come to us, and you have a gate to destroy. Thank you, for everything."

Her lip quivered, a tear forming in her eye. She had no excuse now, nothing and no one to blame for the sadness pooling inside of her. Masini—damn him to the labors of hell—was right. Sending in Nerio was her best chance. But she knew—felt—that this would be disastrous. *Why, why you abusive bastard, did you put someone in my life, only to take them from me so soon? Damn you!*

Nerio touched her shoulder, and for the first time in longer than she could remember, she didn't flinch away. There was a warmth to it, a comfort that washed away her resentment and anger. It didn't make it easier, but it diluted the pain.

"Fuck you," she whispered.

Nerio smiled. "Good luck." He walked past her and strode with a slow, resigned cadence into the cavern and towards the outstretched arms of Jerdine. Her nails burrowed into skin as her fists balled up tightly. She'd see that smile removed from that fat, smug face, and it would be a slow, agonizing death for him.

"*Psst.*"

*What the hell?* she thought, looking around, pulling her eyes from Nerio as he nearly reached Jerdine.

"*Psst.* Over here," came a low whisper.

She squinted her eyes, straining to see past the empty dark of the tunnel nearby. The faintest of outlines was visible, a short man hunched down low in a dark corner. She crept over, her hand resting cautiously on the blade in her waistband, feet quietly falling heel to toe.

As she got near to the hidden figure, their face came into view in the residual glow from the cavern. She recognized the narrow, lean features as those belonging to the man she'd seen with Delvan and Orne at the Devapuram. "Kolden?" she asked.

His head cocked to the side. "You know my—Wait! Fucking hell, you're that girl from the Devapuram! Did Delvan and Orne find you? Are they here?"

"They're... up above. They were fighting someone along with that other Blue, Ferrand. They told me to run, so I—"

"Ferrand?! That fucker, I knew he'd turn against us eventually." Kolden flashed his teeth, the metal rod beating into his empty palm menacingly.

"What? No, he's fighting *with* Delvan and Orne."

His eyebrow went up and jaw dropped as he stared at her, silent as he processed the information. "I... I don't know what to say to that, I guess I'll have to take your word for it. Why'd they send you down here? Are they alright?"

*If you let me finish, asshole, I'd tell you.* "They were alive when I saw them last. I came down here to find *that*." She turned and pointed through the arched, moist stone entry at the gate glowing beyond. "We *have* to stop Jerdine from putting the key into the center of the gate, if he does, he'll bring an army of mages from another realm and desolate us."

Kolden's eyes narrowed. She doubted he'd believe her, but she didn't have time to go through the drawn-out explanations to convince him. That approach hadn't worked anyway. Nerio was nearly to Jerdine, and in a few more steps she was going to be out of time.

"You know, a few hours ago I would've called you insane, but I'm fairly certain I saw some crazy bastard steal the soul of some poor kid and use it to make a rock fucking glow brighter. So, I'm inclined to believe you."

"Wait, what did you say?" she said.

*Desnia*, said Masini, *you need to focus on Jerdine, he's almost there!*

Something didn't make sense. The key hadn't been glowing that brightly the last time she'd seen it. Had Jerdine done what Kolden had said? If so, whose soul had been used to brighten the key?

"Delvan..." she whispered. "Masini, what aren't you telling me?"

"Who the fuck is Masini?" asked Kolden. She ignored him.

*Uhh*, said Masini hesitantly, *there isn't really a good way to say this, but the, uh, glowy rock is about as bright as it can be. It would take thousands of souls to get it to that level, or...*

"Or?" she muttered.

*Or someone more... potent. Say a person who wields powerful, uh, energy. Like... Like a Blue...*

She almost fell to a knee, bracing her hand against a wall. It couldn't be true, could it? Was she going to lose everyone today then?

"Hey, get it together, what the hell is wrong with you?" Kolden asked.

"I... I don't think the others are coming," Desnia said through a tight throat. "We need to do something. Now."

Kolden looked her up and down. "You can believe what you want, but there is nothing getting between Orne and what he wants. They'll come. But if what you say is true, we might not have a lot of time to wait for them. Good news is: That fuckers precious 'key' doesn't fit."

*What did he say?* asked Masini.

"What do you mean 'doesn't fit'?" Desnia asked skeptically.

"I *may* have grinded down one of the corners," said Kolden with a sarcastic tone, "and now it doesn't fit. Or at least that's what he was screaming about when he tried it earlier. It made the floor blink really brightly a bunch of times, hurt my damn eyes to look at. Seemed *really* unhappy about it. Thought I was done for, until he found out that you guys lit his spire on fire. Also, another question, what's up with the priest?"

Desnia turned her head and looked out towards the chamber, seeing Nerio reach Jerdine and the old bastard putting his arm around him. It made her skin crawl.

"It's... a long story. He went out to provide us with a distraction," Desnia replied.

"Well, that seems fucking stupid, but if he wants to become entombed in a rock, so be it. How do we destroy this thing anyway?"

"If we break any of the lines on the floor—"

*Or the glowing stone,* chimed Masini.

"—or the key, it'll stop it from working."

"Right, well, I'm assuming that the key is more precious to them, given how that principle reacted when he noticed what I'd done. That should be our main target. Here, rip off your sleeves," Kolden said with an outstretched hand.

"What? My *sleeves*?" she asked, looking at his own sleeveless arms.

"I'm running out of fabric and need it if I'm going to help, so yes, give me your fucking sleeves."

She begrudgingly looked at him, then her garments. She didn't have time to ask what he needed it for or why, and with a cringe at the noise of tearing linen, she ripped off each sleeve and handed it to him. Kolden quickly got to work, biting the fabric with his teeth and pulling it into long, thin strips he tied together at the ends. With each long rip, she looked back towards the chamber, thinking at any moment Jerdine would hear them and come searching.

The principle was completely consumed with his task at hand, however, and as Kolden began picking up and looking through rocks on the ground around them, Jerdine reached the center of the cavern. His and Nerio's faces were lit up in the drenching purple glow as he muttered something inaudible into Nerio's ear.

Jerdine reached down, setting the vibrant key into its place, which looked to be a shallow socket in a mirror image to the stone carved into the floor. The dim lines surrounding Jerdine and Nerio suddenly burst with light, becoming a hot white and nearly blinding her. She looked between fingers of an outstretched hand as outlines and shadows began to phase into existence in an awesome sight, a terror filling Desnia as she watched misty specters take form across the entire surface of the strange, glowing floor.

Thousands upon thousands of them.

*Des,* said Masini in a frantic voice, *we have to get in there, NOW! It's almost—*

The lights winked back down to the original hue that had been present when they arrived, the only bright glow remaining was the key at the center with Jerdine and Nerio, casting their towering shadows on the cavern walls. Desnia let out a sigh of relief, but her muscles still held themselves tightly in nervous fear.

*By the Greats,* said Masini, *that was too close, but we can't delay. He might still be able to get a few people through, and they could bring whatever he needs to fix the damage. This has only bought us a few minutes, maybe more but I doubt it.*

The lights of the floor started to flicker and strobe as Nerio knelt down beside Jerdine, putting his hand on the accursed key and fidgeting with it while Jerdine pointed and wrapped his arm around him. Her eyes ached looking at the blinding, flashing lights. She turned her squinting eyes away and back to Kolden, who was using her sleeves to tie three pieces of inanite to the end of his metal rod, the one sandwiched in the middle having a sharp point at the end.

"What're you doing?" she asked.

"The fuck's it look like I'm doing?" Gods-damn it this asshole was condescending. "I'm making a hammer. These caves are solid inanite, which, as it so happens, is probably the only thing harder than fucking cadentite. If you can go around and distract them, I'll sneak up from the other side. The key is the priority, but if I can't get there, I'll use this to smash the lines instead."

*He has to break the line completely, he can't leave it partially connected,* said Masini.

"Alright," said Desnia, "but if you go after a line, make sure you completely sever it, it has to be a clean break. I'll go around the other side but be careful. Ferrand said that Jerdine was powerful enough that he could easily take on a couple of Blues."

Kolden gave her a blank stare, blinking with his mouth open. "Wow, I, uh, wish you hadn't fucking told me that."

She shook her head, then turned and made her way in the other direction. She carefully peered around each of the openings she passed, checking to make sure that Jerdine's attention was otherwise occupied. It made the going slow. The lights continued to flicker, the shadows appearing and vanishing each time.

Desnia had no idea how she could distract Jerdine. Would he kill her on sight? Was there something she needed that he didn't have? Normally her goal was to distract away from herself, then run in the other direction. That wasn't an option here. It was just her, and Kolden was relying on whatever she did to get near enough to the key.

*I don't like this, Des,* said Masini. *He's going to have this patched soon, and if we go charging in there, he'll flay you alive.*

Her stomach turned again. There *was* something that Jerdine would want, or at least want to know. The very thought made her ill, but with the world at stake, did she have an option?

She crouched low as she reached one of the cave entrances facing Jerdine's back as he stood over a fidgeting Nerio. She took a deep breath, hoping that it wouldn't be one of her last. Rounding the corner in her quiet haunch, she crept forward, walking over the black stone floor and reaching the edge of the illuminated lines in the room's center.

*He used powder!* said an astonished Masini. *He used cadentite powder to go over the original lines! If I wasn't so terrified, I'd be impressed by the clever bastard. He must have it on some adhesive, like a resin. You might be able to scrape some of it away!*

*Good to know,* she thought, distracted by Jerdine and what she was about to do. She needed to give Kolden a chance, first and foremost. A scraped line Jerdine could fix, but a shattered key? That was the best solution, and she knew it. She took Masini's chain and slipped it under her robe, trying not to think about *him* touching her skin.

*Uh, what're you doing?* asked Masini.

"I, uh, heard you were looking for the person who torched your place?" she yelled out, standing up a few dozen yards from Nerio and Jerdine.

Both of their heads spun, Nerio's painted with shock and Jerdine's with anger. The furious principle took a step away from Nerio towards her, his disgusting eyes looking her up and down. She swallowed hard, trying to keep her body from trembling.

"And what, you've come to confess? Or do you intend to oust them in exchange for something? Do I look a fool? Or that petty?" asked the principle with another step forward. *Yes, you do, actually,* she thought. "How did you get down here? Or... Oh, my dear boy," Jerdine said, starting to turn to look at the terrified Nerio behind him, hands still on the glowing jewel at the center.

Desnia saw Kolden creeping out of an opening on the far side. He'd be right in Jerdine's line of sight if he turned around. She needed to act, now.

The floor blinking brightly again, she called out with squinted eyes. "Masini's still alive!"

*Wait, what the fuck are you doing?! Desnia, don't!*

Jerdine stopped in his tracks, slowly turning back to her with an eyebrow raised. Desnia resisted the urge to look over at Kolden as he stalked across the floor towards them, holding Jerdine's gaze with shaking hands.

"You say this, but The Hunter rarely fails in his assignments," Jerdine said with narrowed eyes. "And if he is, what of it? He and his ridiculous loyalists are finished."

"He's here, in the city. He's the one that set your spire ablaze. Also, he's who sabotaged that chunk of cadentite. You let Nerio go, and I'll tell you where he is," she said, holding her trembling hands open and to the side.

*What the hell? Desnia, what are you doing?!* said a fervently panicked Masini.

Jerdine's eyes lowered as he glared at her, his own hands moving with a slight tremor, face noticeably red even through the blinking light from the floor. Nerio was fiddling with the rock, his fingers straining as it appeared he was trying to pull the key from its seat to no avail. Kolden was nearly halfway to the key, wrapped feet carrying him quietly over the illuminated floor.

Jerdine's hand lifted from his side, a glowing pattern forming around the fist pointed directly at her. Desnia suddenly found herself restrained, an unseen force holding her as she pulled at her arm, barely moving it. She pulled again, moving a few inches, the force against her feeling as though she were trying to pull an anchor from a deep, silty lake.

"You think to blackmail *me*?" asked Jerdine with the rage still in his eye. "I have killed for less, you vapid waste of breath, and I will not indulge such delusions. If Masini is alive, then it won't be for long, he thinks to interfere, yet he's allowed the key directly into my hands. Once again, that drunken dote has shown his lack of foresight and planning. The fact he managed to elude us so long was a matter of dumb luck.

"And what are you? Some messenger girl? Does he have some other, rudimentary plan then? That vulgar whoremonger didn't even have the conviction to appear before me himself. Well, he shall bear witness to the consequences of his own inaction, and you shall be the prize displayed for him to remember his weakness by. Once I am done with you, I doubt even your own kin would recognize you beyond the mutilations. Nerio, stop fiddling with that, I have an alternative solution."

Desnia struggled to move her hand closer to her waist, sweat beginning to soak her robe as she resisted with exhausting effort. Jerdine had taken a few steps closer, his back still to Nerio. Kolden was only a few steps away. Maybe she could get the blade from her waist and have at Jerdine as a last distraction, but the knife might as well have been on the other side of the cavern. Kolden was upon the key in a few moments, Jerdine close enough to her to smell his rank breath. Nerio stepped to the side. Kolden raised the hammer above his head, the flickering floor drawing shadows along his body from below.

Nerio's foot made the faintest scraping sound, and Jerdine spun his head, his other fist outstretching at Kolden who froze with the hammer cresting above his head. *Damn it all! How did he even hear that?* she thought through the quiet groans she was releasing as she fought the strange, unseen bindings. The resistance against Desnia lessened as Kolden came under Jerdine's utter control, but she hardly noticed as her heart sank, soul crushed upon seeing Kolden so near to success, only to fail. What hope remained for them? Jerdine was going to tear them apart, all while he ushered in a season of darkness and death.

"*Tsk, tsk,* Nerio," said Jerdine, arms extended in either direction. "I expected better of you. Now, step aside."

Nerio looked at Desnia with saddened eyes, defeat set heavily into them once more. It ate away at her to see that expression on his face again. She wanted to scream for him to do something, to defy the manipulative master and ignore his bidding. If he could fight, maybe they'd stand a chance.

Despite her hopes, Nerio hung his head low and took a step to the side, shielding his eyes from the blinding flashes of light. The unnatural power that Jerdine held over Nerio was more than the tormented priest had the ability to resist. It was difficult to tell who was more distraught by his inaction, herself, or Nerio.

Jerdine flicked the wrist aimed at Desnia and she went flying backward, landing with a hard grunt as she collided with stone. He did the same to Kolden, the makeshift hammer skidding across the floor. Jerdine pulled a small blade from his pocket and dug the point of his finger into the blade's tip. Desnia watched—rolled over on her side in aching pain—as a small amount of strange colored blood began to drip from his finger. He leaned down, holding the bleeding tip to the corner of the faceted stone in the shallow setting, squeezing it to let more blood from his hand. The blinking faltered, the painfully bright light holding steady. Only minor flickers occurred, noticeable only because it took the pain from her eyes for the fraction of a second that they happened.

Desnia's heart was pounding. It felt like her arm was broken from the impact with the floor as she agonizingly pulled the small knife from her sash. With the light now unwavering, the shadows began to appear once more, their shimmering bodies becoming darker and tangible. The shape of a fit man in black, scaled armor fully materialized beside Jerdine, a cape hanging from his shoulders, a large, heavy bag in one hand and sword in the other. It was as though he'd been mist that suddenly magnetized together, solidifying into a solid being with a snap.

The others around her began to go through the same process, the people nearest the key forming faster than the outskirts. Desnia's gut wrenched. She had to do something. Their success was unallowable, everyone's death was not an option.

She was going to ensure they survived.

Desnia gripped her crude blade with both hands, Jerdine's back still to her, and the warrior at his side turning his head as he gained his bearings. Rolling to put all of her meager weight on the knife's point, she dug the tip into the edge of one of the glowing lines crisscrossing beneath her, only a few inches wide, and dragged the point across it with a toe-curling, high-pitched scrape.

She collapsed, a hairline mark now cut through the line from side to side, a tiny mass of glowing cadentite dust mixed with a hardened resin on the tip of her blade. The shimmering mirages around her suddenly evaporated out of existence, despite the floor holding its brilliant shine.

*By the Greats! Desnia, you did it! You did it! I can almost forgive you for selling me out,* exclaimed Masini.

Jerdine's head and the singular warrior in black both turned their heads to her. The newly arrived man, his hair dark and features more so, started speaking brashly in some language she didn't understand. No interpretation was needed, his meaning was clear as he pointed his sword—glowing as brightly as the key and covered with similar markings—directly at Desnia.

*Well, fuck,* she thought.

He strode towards her, dropping his bag to the floor with a heavy *thud*. She heard Nerio cry out but couldn't take her eyes off the petrifying sight approaching her. His armor moved like fluid over his body, the masterfully formed scales like the skin of a black snake, etched with strange runes all over. The man's face and hands—the only visible skin on his body—were covered in tattoos that were similar to the great pattern on the floor. Some spiraled inward, some were more geometric, but they all were repetitive flowers of strange lines—each glowing with the same purple hue as the floor.

She heard Nerio's voice muffle. Jerdine must have done something. She couldn't look, her eyes transfixed as the man walked closer, his armor barely rattling with each step. Her heart pounded its way into her throat, tears flowing from her eyes over a shaking lip. Death approached her, draped in black and from the underworld itself.

And she was terrified, paralyzed by her fear.

*Des, run! RUN!* screamed Masini.

She tried to scramble away, but the black knight held out a hand and held her in place. Her reaper's feet stopped before her, pulling back his sword and with a furious, hardened face, thrust the blade's point at her chest. She didn't look at it, her eyes locked with his, she braced for the stab, her muscles tighter than she'd ever known them to be.

She was surprised. She thought it would have hurt more, but she felt... nothing.

Perhaps this was the feeling of final moments. The screams she'd always heard when others fell merely reactions to the incoming passage to the underworld. She still didn't dare look at the glowing steel in her chest, the long broadsword stabbed directly into her heart. Maybe that's why they screamed? Because they saw their wounds? Did it inject a fear she couldn't comprehend? She didn't know how it could be greater than the one she felt now.

The strange man's head tilted to the side as he retracted his blade, his face breaking from the stoney visage of death to one that seemed more... curious. Desnia continued holding his eyes. Witnessing her own death was something she'd hoped to avoid her entire life. If this were to be her final moments, she would know the face of her killer. At least that much courage still flowed through her body.

The man's grip on the vibrant blade's hilt tightened, and some of the symbols on the blade grew a hot white, visible even through the surrounding glow. He thrust the sword's point forward again, why she didn't know, one stab would have—

Pain.

Her body shook with it as it spread from her chest to the distal extremities. A flood of it emanating from the pointed, unbearable searing that burned in her sternum. Breath left her lungs, mouth and eyes wide as her hands clawed at the blade and then the gaping wound as the sword was pulled from her body. She rolled onto her back, body writhing as blood fountained through the fingers held above the pierced flesh.

She heard shouting but couldn't tell who it was. Masini maybe, or perhaps Nerio. She didn't care. The world started to go black, shading even the blinding light of the room around her. Fear without a beating heart was a strange sensation, it reminded her of dreaming that she was falling through the sky, the land below rushing towards her.

Perhaps she'd be free of those dreams now.

Delvan and Orne burst through the cave opening, armor clinking with each step of their run, glistening in the light of the ball of flame above Delvan's open palm. The light it emanated was scant, however, in comparison to the bright fluorescence of the enormous, domed cavern they found themselves in, which illuminated the horrifying scene of tribulation before them.

Delvan's attention wasn't drawn to the pattern on the floor, the cages on the walls, or the sheer massiveness of the space. It registered but ignored Kolden lying on the floor in the distance, and neither did it turn to Jerdine standing near the room's center.

Instead, it was on the man in black, his vibrantly glowing sword thrust into Desnia's chest.

He skidded to a stop, heart pounding as it sank into the depths of his chest. His eyes went wide, the flame in his hand dissipating as he gaped at what his eyes beheld. This couldn't be happening, not again. They'd come too far. *He'd* come too far. He saw Desnia wriggle on the floor as the dark warrior pulled his glowing blade from her chest with a spurt of blood. The man turned his tattooed face to them as Delvan let out a scream that filled the cavern like a flood of water, his face turning red and burning with pain as he emptied his lungs, sweat and tears alike streaming down his face.

He coalesced a ball of flame above his hand and flung it at the scale-clad warrior. Then he threw another. And another. Orne charged forward, halberd in hand, but as he reached the edge of the floor's glowing pattern, Jerdine held up a glowing fist and held him in place with a Reach.

Delvan continued marching forward, lobbing shot after shot with flared teeth and brow dug deeply down over his eyes. He wouldn't lose someone again, and the stilling body of Desnia drove him even further off the edge, a rage exploding inside of him. This girl, despite his doubts and curiosities to her nature, had saved his life once, and he her's. There was a bond shared between them, one of blood, one that he knew well. He refused to allow this to be her end, but it would be that of her assailer's.

The black-armored man threw forward a palm, a disc of glowing lines around it. Before him came a colored mist, snapping together to form a pane of purple-tinted glass that stood like a wall in front of him. Delvan's spheres of flames burst and sprayed against the barrier like water, the glowing pane growing bright and crackling with each collision.

Jerdine then extended his other arm to Delvan, the same Reach directed at him. But it was distant and weakened by his hold on Orne, who was motionless as stone. Delvan screamed as he raised his arm as though pulling it through molasses, slowly bringing it forth while his teeth gritted together. He forced the other palm up and forward, Jerdine's pathetic Reach be damned.

He spewed forth narrow streams of flames from his outstretched arms, one directed at Jerdine, the other towards Desnia's attacker. The twisting, orange flames stretched over the distance from the floor's patterned edge to their target's location at the center. Jerdine was forced to release his Reach and threw up a similar barrier as the man to his side.

The tall, purple sheets flickered brightly, nearly as white as the floor, as the flames pounded against them. Delvan marched forward, unrelenting in his assault of fire and death, an inferno spiraling forth all the while. He could feel the inanite surrounding him, drawing on it as he took each step, the stone beneath his feet turning a stark white. He drew from the black stone more copiously than he ever had before, fire blazing from him like hot breath on a cold winter's day.

Orne—his body released from the Reach—sprinted forward, running alongside the torrent of flames. Delvan stopped his onslaught of fire as Orne reached the twin barriers, and stabbed his halberd forward, shattering Jerdine's pane with a pierce of the darksteel spear point.

The principle raised his hand towards Orne, but Delvan wasn't about to allow him to attack as he had with The Hunter. Protection would come for those he was able to provide it to, another of his friends wasn't going to fall to the floor as long as he drew breath. He hurled another orange ball of flames at the balding man. It burst as it found its mark and struck his ornate silk robes, sending him to his knees screaming and feverishly flailing his arms to extinguish the flames crawling up his body.

Delvan now sprinted forward himself, nearing Orne as the mountainous man moved past the wails of Jerdine and went to destroy the barrier of the black warrior. But as Orne thrust his polearm at the protective pane, the man released it with a puff like smoke and swatted at the head of Orne's halberd with his glowing broadsword, the *clang* of metal striking metal ringing through the cavern.

The expression of the black warrior changed, his tattoos contorting into a confused visage, as though he'd been surprised by the outcome of his sword's deflection of Orne's weapon. It rapidly turned back to a chillingly calm anger as he turned to Delvan, who was now alongside Orne, his short sword drawn.

He raised a tattooed hand towards the two of them, but Orne adeptly rolled to his side, and Delvan raised a hand in turn, spouting flames before the man could attack. Their foe's hand dropped as he too rolled away to evade Delvan's assault, his armor scraping along the floor and marring it.

As the man turned over and onto his feet, Delvan charged forward, sword raised and slashing down as Desnia's attacker tried to stand. His blade was deflected by the glowing sword, the strange symbols on it humming in a bright, foreign pattern. They continued to cross blades, metal clashing together as Delvan let out a guttural cry of anger and agony. When the man attempted to raise his hand, patterns swirling around his fingers, Delvan raised his own, forcing each of them to dodge away before their swords found one another again.

Orne recovered himself to his feet and charged forward to join Delvan, swinging his halberd and attempting to land a blow on their opponent. The tattooed menace fought them both, ducking to avoid Orne's swings and rolling to avoid his downward axe strikes, all while parrying Delvan's flurry of slashes and jabs as his black hair flourished in the air.

The three fought in a combat of ferocity and skill unlike any Delvan had ever experienced. His blows were as accurate and deft as any he'd ever made, Orne maneuvering his polearm as though it were an extension of himself. Yet no steel found its mark as the armored warrior fought them with skill that would have rivaled that of the gods' greatest, as though he were the embodiment of a song of ancient warriors come to life.

Sweat beaded down from Delvan's eyebrows, stinging his eyes as the three struck at each other. Each time Delvan raised his hand to throw fire his target would dodge, finding himself between Orne and Delvan, forcing him to hold back the flames for risk of setting Orne alight as well. Conversely, any time one of his tattooed hands raised itself, it was targeted by Orne's spear point or Delvan's own hand and forced back to his side or the hilt of his sword.

Delvan's heart pounded as neither he, Orne, nor their foe showed any sign of relenting or fatigue. There were no mistakes, no errors or miscalculations from either party. That one fighter could fend off both he and Orne spoke to a mastery he doubted any of his instructors could compare too. Was this only *one* of the fighters Ferrand and Desnia had spoken of? He'd expected more combat like that of The Hunter, but this wasn't the arrogant boasting of one who'd become complacent or preyed on the weak. This was a fighter who'd honed their skills through uncountable trials. A champion among the greatest.

Or so Delvan hoped.

If all of the High Realm warrior mages fought like this, then what Desnia had said was true. They were doomed.

A loud *crack* turned the heads of all three combatants. The light of the floor flickered and dimmed, leaving bright lines in Delvan's vision as he looked back to the center of the room they had shifted away from.

Standing above the key was Kolden, a rudimentary hammer in his hands, the pointed head dug into the now shattered cadentite key in the floor's center. There was a loud, thunderous cry of rage and anguish that resonated from Jerdine, who had managed himself to his knees, the fire extinguished and a large portion of his chest and shoulders black and red from the scalding flames, fabric and flesh alike melted away.

Delvan and Orne's heads snapped back to the warrior between them, who quickly turned his head, glancing at the two of them. Delvan moved to attack but saw some of the lines drawn across their opponent's face begin to brighten and become white compared to their purple counterparts. Beneath him, the glowing portion of the floor began to dim, the lines that burned the brightest forming a pattern over the black warrior's eyes and mouth. Delvan raised his hand, and Orne his halberd to strike in unison. But before either of them could attack, a pulse of energy was released from the warrior between them, its shockwave of purple translucence battering them and tossing them backward like dust in the wind.

It radiated outward, throwing Kolden back to the ground, as well as Nerio, who'd been kneeling over Desnia's body, oblivious to the fighting as he held his blood-covered hands to Desnia's chest. Delvan hit the stone floor with an impact that knocked the wind from him. He gasped for breath as he rolled over and propped himself on an elbow, his ears ringing, and vision dizzy.

He saw the black warrior stand, sheath his sword—which Delvan swore now looked dimmer than when they'd entered—and raise his hands. The floor flickered once more, the majority of its radiance diminishing to a barely luminescent hue as a lined pattern formed before the man, circular and taller than he was. Its overlapping lines began to spin and, with a flash that pained Delvan's vision, became a solid circle filled with light that illuminated the space.

Delvan tried to stand, to charge the several yards that now stood between him and the mysterious warrior. But before he could even bring himself to his feet, the scale-clad man picked up the large sack he'd dropped to the floor and grabbed Jerdine by the seared arm, his screams raising the hair on Delvan's neck. With a few steps forward, he walked into the blinding disc of light with his full hands and vanished along with Jerdine.

Then, like a sun eclipsed, the window of light went black and crackled out of existence, leaving them alone in the massive cavern. The once brilliant fractal pattern on the floor was now too faint to cast light to the ceiling, and the one source of illumination—the shattered key in the center—was greatly diminished, throwing long, sorrowful shadows across each of them as they struggled off the floor.

Delvan coughed as he pulled himself to his feet, a sharp pain in his abdomen accompanying it. He wiped his face, finding blood on his hand. He cradled his side as he trudged forward, making his way with leaden footsteps towards the remains of Desnia on the floor. He heard Orne getting up and calling out to his brother, ignoring whatever it was that Kolden responded with as he approached the too-still Desnia.

His throat choked, chin pushing upward as he walked what felt like a thousand miles to reach Desnia's side. He collapsed to his knees next to her, the pain in his ribs disappearing—a mild annoyance compared to the stabbing in his chest, the aching that flooded his body and threatened to burst from his skin. He couldn't go through this again: The pain, the loss, the regret.

*I'm sorry... This isn't what I'd ever intended,* he thought solemnly. *If I'd been better, stronger, like you, maybe I could have prevented this.*

He put his arm under her head and lifted her to his chest, cradling her lifeless body in his arms, her chest soaked in the darkness of blood in the dim light. He rocked back and forth as he held her, crying tears into her hair, thinking of the fire, their meeting at the Devapuram, their lives as intertwined as the glowing lines beneath his knees.

*This shouldn't be the end, I shouldn't be allowed to go on while others around me fall.* He'd been so skeptical, even after all her warnings, and she still put faith in him. *Whether it was out of necessity, or trust, I can't say, though I'm not certain it matters. I fumbled that trust, and you paid the price. You were right, about everything.*

He felt the chill in his heart again, his other senses fading to the background of his grief. Nerio had come and knelt beside him, tears flowing from his reddened eyes and over his dark skin. Kolden limped over with Orne, peering at the fallen Desnia from over Delvan's shoulders.

They all seemed so far away from his tiny world. An island of agony and torment, trapping him as its only occupant.

# CHAPTER
# FIFTY-FIVE

*Hands across an empty face*
*Pass a gap long since forgotten*
*By those who could recall*
*The one that filled and bonded*

Y ou've got to be shitting me," said Desnia.

Was this death? *Really?*

Her gut turned with disappointment as much as fear. She found herself standing in another cavern, similar to the one she'd just been in, except this had the strange, repetitive patterns of cadentite set into white stone on not only the floor, but the entirety of the domed walls and ceiling as well. It released a gentle hue that gave the empty room a warm, purple glow that subtly reflected off the white surroundings. And something about it felt... familiar.

She looked down at her sleeveless robe, the white garment unstained by blood, her chest noticeably lacking a gaping sword wound. She patted her sternum in a panic, feeling to see if it was intact. It felt solid, free of the agonizing pain she'd just experienced, making her let out the breath she'd been holding.

As her palm rubbed her chest, her stomach knotted as she realized what was missing: Masini. She instinctually patted at her waist, feeling her neck absent the chain normally around it. Her head spun as she frantically looked to the floor for the missing ring and chain. Her heart raced. Where had she lost him? Surely he hadn't been taken by the bastard who'd stabbed her, or even worse, Jerdine, had he?

"Do not fret, the mage did not travel with you," came a soft, feminine voice from behind Desnia. Did she know that voice?

She spun with a twirl of her golden hair to find a woman standing behind her, not four feet from where her heels were planted on the illuminated floor. *She was definitely* not *there before,* Desnia thought. Long black hair flowed over a white, silken robe that shimmered in the light which highlighted her attractive face and curves. Desnia squinted under a furrowed brow as she tried to remember where she'd seen this woman before.

*The Iguan den*, she realized with a start.

"You... How are you here?" asked Desnia with wide eyes and a step backward.

"I am not the woman you knew. I have merely borrowed her image for this conversation since I thought you would find it more suitable to speak with. My natural form is more... difficult to acquaint oneself with," she said, turning her lips up into one of those damned, disarming smiles. *I'd forgotten about that fucking smile,* she thought begrudgingly.

"Did you hurt her?" Desnia asked, her tone turning angry.

"I did not. Unfortunately, however, she has passed beyond this plane, but I assure you I had no hand in it."

Desnia felt her face go pale. She wanted to vomit, grief pumping through her, though she wasn't sure why, she'd hardly known the girl. Desnia tried to put it out of her mind, but seeing her stand there made it difficult.

"I realize this is upsetting to you, but I'm also aware that you are of a disposition that would prefer to be informed of such matters. I can, however, take on a different image if you'd prefer," she said in a voice that seemed to sing.

"No," blurted Desnia. "I... no, this is fine." She looked away, thinking now about the question that consumed her, the one that she already knew the answer to, but didn't want to accept. Her initial instinct was now being smothered by her own doubt and denial, but she had to know. She took a deep, angered breath, finding it more difficult to pose the question than she'd anticipated. "I'm dead, aren't I?"

She braced herself, the itch of the question unbearable, burning at her core. Why did she even ask? She knew the answer. Was it because there was some trace of hope left in her? Did the charm of this face give that to her?

"Yes," came her answer in her soft tone, the words inversely cutting the air like a knife.

The simple response hit her harder than she'd expected. Desnia sank to her knees, jaw open and hands to her side. She'd fought her entire life against this, struggling every day to merely make it to the next. And now it was over. Although she'd never been devout, even spiritual, she'd hoped deep down that perhaps she'd been wrong, and bliss would come once her heart had stopped beating.

Turns out the life after wasn't much different than the world she'd left.

"And who are you, then?" Desnia asked through the shock.

"I have had many names, some forgotten, others new. Though you yourself have mostly called me by one vulgarity or another, for which I do not fault you. I know our conversations take a tremendous toll and leave you greatly distressed. You may call me Asta."

Desnia felt a chill run down her spine and along her skin. "You're... You're the voice. From my dreams."

"I am."

Desnia groaned and pulled at her hair, the finality of her fate settling in. Realizing where her fate had brought her stabbed deeper than the blade that had pierced her chest. "Is there no escaping you?!" she screamed. "Didn't I do what you asked? I gave my *life* trying to destroy the gate, and now you bring me back here? To this... this cave of torture?! All you've ever done is bring me pain! Pain and fear that I'd end up like all the others! Can you imagine what it's like, to think yourself insane? To go to sleep every night wondering if you were going to be tormented by your own mind and the voice lying dormant inside of it?"

She'd sacrificed *everything* to avoid the snapping of her mind by whatever it was that stood before her. Desnia tried to tell herself that, despite the voice now being produced by the ample lips of a calming face, it still held the same intentions it always had. She held her glare to the soft eyes of Asta before her, that subtle smile dousing her anger and smothering it to smolders. Damn her. Damn her to the prisons of hell—assuming they weren't already there.

"I apologize for that, but you are, as the mage put it, a very specific child of circumstance," said Asta. "One that I have been waiting for longer than you can imagine. I needed you, Daughter, for you were the only one who could listen and still walk a normal life."

"You *used* me, like a pawn in your games."

"Those that must sacrifice often despise their obligations. Yet we harrow forward all the same."

"Fuck your obligations! Look where they've gotten me," said Desnia with outstretched hands. "I wanted a life that was my *own*, damn it! Yet you set me on this journey because it benefits *you* and strung me along with promises that mean *nothing* now. I did this all to get rid of *you*," she said with a point of her finger. "And now in death I find out that I still can't be free of your torment? What was this all even fucking for?!"

She was angry, furious at the situation. Her hands shook at her side, face pin-pricked with pain as she locked eyes with Asta. Even the placating smile was beginning to lose its hold over her. If she'd known that her version of the pains of hell would include her tormentor, she'd have left Masini in the water all those months ago.

"You've stopped an invasion of the realm, a feat not performed—"

Desnia couldn't stand that self-righteous voice anymore. "*WHY ME?!*" She was panting now, looking up from her knees as she fueled her rage with each breath. It wasn't fair, the life she'd been given, the trials she'd overcome. "Why couldn't you have picked anyone else?"

"There was no one else. Tell me, where were you before you began this journey? Alone, Daughter. Alone against the world, fighting every day to merely survive, so far below your potential that you might as well have been swimming along the bed of the sea. And what do you have now? Even as we speak, several surround you in mourning. People who have cared for you and brought out the best of your life. You wanted a life of your own, and you have it."

Desnia thought of the others. Nerio may not be able to contend with her death, and the thought of his end due to her own tore her apart. She already found herself missing Masini, despite his rude or obscene comments, and the thought of actually abandoning him in the waters of Calentine clawed at her insides. Even the thought of the Blue, Delvan, who'd been there to save her when no one else would, pained her.

"I gained all that," she said, hanging her head, "all so it could be taken away. I finally knew connection so that, what, it could be stolen for nothing but *your* ends? You're a cruel bitch of a god, you know that?"

"Cruel would be what the High Realm would be doing should they have succeeded. I have seen the possibilities, stared into the Astral Plane, and if it could have been done a different way, I assure you I would have. But even now, our world is not safe, for they have brought the means to attempt their invasion yet again. There is more to be done."

"Looks like you'll need someone else to torture then," Desnia said bitterly. "Guess I died for nothing."

"Your sacrifice was not in vain, for it has saved countless lives, my own included. For this I am eternally grateful and extend my offer to not only you, but those you've surrounded yourself with, if they aid you further."

"Your... *offer*? Ha! What the hell does that matter now?! I'm *dead*," said Desnia with a flop of her arms. "What are you going to ask me to do, go and *haunt* someone?"

"Find me."

Desnia looked into those brown eyes with disbelief. Find her? What the hell did she mean by that? She held both her arms forward. "Looks to me like you're right here."

"In the mountains, to the west, find me. The mage knows where. For what you've done, and your aid in the future, I will bestow you and the others a gift that will realize desires both deep-seeded and not yet awakened. For you, my promise remains: reign over your own life, and protection of your mind from the breaking it will inevitably endure. We will always share a bond, there is nothing that can change shared blood, but our connection does not need to be the one of torment that you have been forced through. For the others, they will know power that will challenge the High Realm and their mightiest, bring them to the pages of legends, and give them the strength to change the world and those in it."

Desnia gawked at her, dumbstruck. She was dead, what miracle was she expecting from her?

"What do you want?" asked Desnia. No offer like this was made of pure philanthropy. Desnia knew a barter when she heard one, though in her current state, she wasn't sure she'd even be able to help. Or if she wanted to. Her mind would remain sound after death, right?

*Wouldn't that be a bitch...*

The smile on Asta's face turned down slightly, a sadness and ache in her own eyes. "As you're aware, I'm currently imprisoned, and this," she said with a wave of her hands, "is my cell. I wish to be free, something I expect you can empathize with. Help release me from the High Realm's entombment, and I shall be indebted to you. With me in here, everyone in the realm is in danger. Ambitions are at work that you cannot understand. Following them will be the destruction of you and your kind, along with my own."

"And if I refuse?" Desnia asked. She was so tired. Tired of running, looking over her shoulder, marching to the crack of someone else's whip.

"Then you, and the others, will die." Asta's voice was calm. She didn't hold resentment in her tone, or anger, just a factual statement of what would be.

"A bit late for that, don't you think?" Desnia asked.

The smile returned, softening Desnia's hardened exterior. "I have seen many fates for you, Daughter, and all of them are full of hardships, but such is life. The one I offer you now will not deviate from that, but it will give you a life you cannot imagine, full of wonder, and love, and pain, and power, and most importantly, freedom. Do not idle. You have succeeded today, but more attempts will come. Hurry."

With that, Asta and the surrounding room began to fade into blackness.

Delvan knelt there in the quiet, dim chamber, Desnia's body still warm in his arms. He hated life, the indiscriminate nature of it, how one soul could be taken as easily as any other. There was no hierarchy to it, no order to the madness. A monster like Jerdine could escape with his own, while one far more deserving lay expired on the floor.

He'd thought it all through in his mind as though time itself had slowed, hundreds of scenarios and calculated changes to their actions that night processing in his mind. What if he'd just gone with her when she first asked? He'd been so stubbornly set on believing Ferrand to be his enemy that he missed the truth right in front of him.

Now Ferrand was dead, and he wasn't even sure how to feel about it. His heart felt as though it were shrinking, crumbling under the weight being pressed upon it. Was that the loss of Desnia weighing on him? The fate of the commander? Both?

Everything was jumbled, his chest becoming an empty cavern as its contents burrowed themselves away to hide from the agony stomping down on them. He felt a hand on his shoulder, Orne's broad palm and fingers gripping it.

"She's gone, Del," he said in his low voice.

Delvan barely turned his head, not wanting to accept the words coming from Orne, despite the evidence held in his arms. He put one of his hands over the wound, pushing the ring hanging around Desnia's neck to the side, trying to put the bloody stab out of sight as he pictured her still alive.

He felt his grief begin to churn, transforming itself as it dragged him from the dark depths that blocked his sight into the daylight above. A spark of anger showered him, igniting the tinder of rage. He wanted to find the black-armored warrior and use Jerdine as a pyre, watching them scream the last of their life away. The air wavered around him as it heated, his body ready to combust into an inferno of retribution. Orne retracted his hand, air sucking through his teeth. He ignored him, scowling as he fantasized about the slow, painful deaths of those responsible.

But Delvan had felt this before. It'd driven him to the edge of madness, able to cripple him with a single thought as it simultaneously drove him forward. It had blinded him, tortured him, followed everywhere he went and threatened him to dare deviate from his path. It had led him directly here, with someone that he should have trusted in his arms, and another that—while maybe not deserving of friendship—he'd misjudged.

The air cooled, and Delvan tried to not focus on the radiating inanite around them. He turned his senses away from channeling it, the sapphire on his neck feeling heavier than ever as it pressed against his chest. He could still feel that cooling contrast, the one that spread an iced chill through his chest. He closed his eyes, growing that sensation within him, fanning it and losing himself in the odd coolness. It spread downward to his legs, creeping into his arms and extremities. It was an opposite to the fires of rage that'd become a natural part of him, a more calming presence, but with as much a desire to spread and grow.

And that's what he let it do.

There was a small gasp, and Delvan opened his eyes. Around him a green aurora shimmered, growing brighter as the floor dimmed. He watched it in awe, eyes reflecting the dancing waves of light that fluttered like curtains in the breeze. Where had they come from? Delvan and the others gazed around, their jaws hanging low as they took in the ethereal sight.

The floor grew dimmer and dimmer, the remains of the cadentite key fading until their luminance extinguished like embers to ash. The short knife in his belt lost its luster, fading like a sunset until it too went black as night. The only illumination was now the captivating streaks of green that surrounded and wove between them, playfully raveling through the air.

The light was slow and gentle, its movements mesmerizing and tranquil, but as they all watched in awe it began to gain a faster cadence, swirling and twisting through the cavern as if trailing unseen birds that darted around. It became a blur, forming what Delvan could only describe as a haze of color that surrounded and enveloped them until it blocked the domed walls from sight.

Then, suddenly, it drew into them.

It was as though the light were air and their bodies lungs, each of them expanding and pulling the light into them through the entire surface of their being, plunging the room into pitch black. Delvan felt a surge of relief in his side, forgetting about the rib that had likely been broken until now that it no longer afflicted him with each stabbing breath. Orne and Kolden were cursing in confusion behind him, though he could not see his hand before his face, let alone their wounds to judge their state. Coughing and groans came from the far wall, sounding as though the occupants of the cages were rustling in the distance.

*What... What was that?* thought a confused Delvan, the sensation in his chest dissipated.

He removed his hand from Desnia's chest and lit a ball of flame above it, the light blinding compared to the otherwise devoid cavern. He looked around, trying to get bearings of those around him. They should probably check on the people in the—

A groan came from his arm. His head whirled, finding Desnia's head lolling to the side, eyes wrinkled together. She let out another groan as her eyes blinked open. Delvan's eyes blinked as well, disbelief filling them as they scanned Desnia's body. Her chest, while still surrounded and coated in blood, was otherwise composed of smooth skin visible through the sliced cloth at her sternum. His mouth gaped as he struggled to speak, questions racing through his mind.

The stab wound had completely vanished.

Desnia's eyes blinked again, going wider as she took in Delvan's face, her head spun as she sat herself up and out of Delvan's grasp, looking to him and then the others in confusion.

"What... What just happened?" she said, feeling at her chest.

"By the gods..." muttered Nerio. "Desnia, you have risen from the dead. It's a *miracle*." He knelt down beside her and embraced her, Delvan watching while she squirmed uncomfortably.

"Glad to see you too, Nerio, but whatever just happened hasn't changed my opinion on being hugged, if you don't mind," she said, lightly pushing him back.

"Yes, of course, whatever you say," Nerio said before prostrating himself on the floor, arms extended reverently towards her. "This was the bidding of the gods, and I now realize I was sent to aid and bear witness to your rebirth. Bless them in their infinite wisdom, for they guided me to you—"

"Oh, get up," she said with a shake of her head. "Don't you dare start to fucking worship me."

"How the *fuck* are you alive?" asked Kolden, standing next to Orne, both of them looking dumbstruck. Delvan's eyes remained fixed on Desnia, wondering the same thing.

She rubbed her head silently for a moment, her eyes pressed tightly closed. Delvan waited, desperate for an explanation. *I beat myself down, but now she's here, alive. It's like the gods have given me another chance.*

"You should ask him," Desnia said after a long silence, pointing to Delvan. *Me?* "But it sounds like we did it? The gate is destroyed?" She looked around, feeling at the floor, her hands running over the now black streaks that were glowing until a minute ago.

Orne let out a grunt that sounded disappointed.

"What's your problem?" asked Kolden.

"Now all the songs people sing about today are going to be about the girl who came back to life," replied Orne, sounding petulant. "The rest of us are just going to be footnotes. Gods-damn it, I thought for sure this would be what got us out from father's shadow."

"*What?*" asked Kolden. "You mean you came down here for fucking glory and not to save me, your *brother*?!"

"No, dumbass, of course I came down here for you," Orne said, looking annoyed. "It would have, you know, just been a nice perk."

"Ignore my idiot brother," said Kolden to Desnia. "Whatever they were trying to do, it seems we stopped it, yes. Though two of them—"

"Escaped. Yeah, I know," Desnia said. She lifted herself up, getting to her feet while Delvan just stared. "Oh, I really hate that bitch right now..." she mumbled.

"I don't understand..." said Delvan.

She extended a hand to him. He took it and came to his feet with her aid, their eyes locked together.

"I'll explain what I can in a bit, but first, let's help the people trapped down here, yeah?"

He composed himself and nodded, extending his arm with the sphere of flame burning above it, lighting the way forward.

# Epilogue

*Changed by blood*
*Mistakes will falter*
*Powers will bud*
*Worlds to alter*


Desnia pulled the cork with her teeth, a loud *thunk* sounding as the bottle released its grip and freed it. She spat it away, letting it roll down the white stone steps of the Devapuram, tainted with gray ash from the smoldering ruins around her. Smoke filled the morning sky, patches of the first break of sunlight struggling to penetrate the thick billows as people shuffled through the dirty streets among what buildings remained.

Desnia took a long swig directly from the bottle, savoring the wine she'd stolen from Jerdine's office as she looked upon the destruction she'd wrought. From what she could tell, close to half the eastern quadrant and a portion of the central square had been reduced to rubble. Homes to tens of thousands, gone.

*You know you're supposed to drink that out of a glass, right?* asked Masini. *So uncivilized.*

Part of her was glad to hear his voice, the other was mostly annoyed. "How many people do you think are dead because of me?" she asked, staring out across the ruins from her seat on the top of the stairs.

*A lot less than would've died if you hadn't managed to close the door,* he said with a sigh. *Don't beat yourself up over it, you couldn't have known what was going to happen. You stopped, uh, my people from coming through, and that's what's important.*

"For now…" she grumbled.

*You, uh, going to talk to me about it?* Masini asked. She'd mentioned her visit with Asta but hadn't been able to discuss it with Masini yet. With another head tilt she downed a second swig. Asta's offer had been weighing heavily on her, the added death toll before her not making things easier.

"She said the same thing you did, more or less. Free her, save the realm, and she'll grant us 'gifts.' Whatever that means," she replied. "Basically said that if I didn't, my mind would snap, and I'd end up as insane as… well, you get the idea. But she thought that the one who managed to get through the gate brought means to attempt creating another one, or at least something that would allow them to bring people here. Said there wasn't a lot of time." She felt a little of the weight shedding as she drank another gulp. "Do you know who that was? The one that stabbed me?"

*Not sure,* said Masini, *I didn't recognize him. Based on the sigil that was on his banner, I have an idea, but regardless, he's bad, bad news. The first through a g-g-g-guh… door, are normally commanders and generals. And ours is not a culture that promotes the weak. You can bet that he'll be working to get more of our kind here, and fast.*

"Joy."

*So, you going to take Asta up on their offer?* asked Masini.

"Considering the alternative, I'd say I'm giving it serious consideration, yeah." *Nothing like feeling like your hand is forced,* she thought. "What can you tell me about her? This *Asta.*"

*Probably has a serious grudge against me. Can't understand why that's such a theme. Weird. But other than that, 'she' has an interesting pair of abilities. She can see into the a-a-a-fuck. Uh, she can do two things really, really well. I'll try to think of ways to explain them that don't have me stuttering like a virgin in a whorehouse. Why?*

"She called me 'Daughter'," said Desnia, thinking back to the conversation. "I thought it was just the translation of my name, like Nerio had said, but I don't know. It sounded… maternal, I guess?"

*Ahh, yes, they always were somewhat possessive. It's, uh, complicated.*

"I swear, Masini, if you say that again I'm going to—"

"Hey," said a voice from behind her. She turned, finding Delvan approaching, his face dirtied with soot and sweat, still wearing his Blue armor. He sat down next to her, closer than she'd have normally preferred, but she was oddly comfortable with it.

"Hey," she replied. "Seems I owe you a few times over." She took a swig of wine, then offered the bottle to Delvan.

"Um, no, thank you," he said with a gesture of his hand and a polite but forced smile.

"Suit yourself," she said with a shrug and another drink.

"And I don't know about you owing me, not even sure what I did."

"You channeled cadentite to heal," she said, repeating what Masini had stammered out after she'd woken up, jabbering like a squirrel that had drank too much tea. She'd needed to fill in several blanks in his rapid-fire wording, but she'd gotten the gist. "Pyros, specifically, can do it, luckily for me. Not exactly a lot of cadentite around, so almost no one knows about it, not surprising you didn't either."

She took another drink. Where had the other half of the bottle gone?

"How can you *know* that?" asked Delvan incredulously. "I believe you, you're clearly alive, but I was trained and schooled by the most knowledgeable masters in the kingdom, each with access to hundreds or thousands of years of experience. How can you know what they didn't? Did this mage you talked about tell you?"

How much should she tell him? One admission could snowball into several, and to be honest, she was too tired to want to explain everything right now. She looked into Delvan's curious eyes and then back to the gray scar across the face of the city before her.

"Yes," she said. "He told me. I have a... way to speak with him. It's... complicated."

*Hypocrite,* chimed Masini.

"Does it have something to do with that?" he asked with a glance and nod towards the blood-stains in her robe, now dry and beginning to flake.

*Damn, I really need a change of clothes,* she thought. "I'm going to need a *lot* more wine if I'm going to answer that question." This wasn't a topic that she felt like explaining, not when she had so much else that she needed to discuss. Changing the subject, she asked, "Where'd the other two go?"

"Helping the rest of the garrison sort through the rubble," he replied, thankfully not pressing his question. "Everyone has been called to active duty to help manage any remnants of the fire. They were both feeling fine, but I think they would've gone to help even if they weren't. What about the priest?"

"Nerio? I think he's tending to the others we pulled from the cages still. And if everyone's on active duty, what're you doing here?"

"Waiting," he replied. "I sent for the general, not a lot of other people I trust with handling a dead Blue." He nodded towards the nearby bathhouse, one of the few buildings unscathed by the fire, guards posted at the door. "There's a lot to go over, not sure how I'm going to explain all of it. It's taking a while to find him though, he's probably busy with the fire and all."

"Mhm," she said with a nod and mouthful of wine. "Have fun with that."

He let out a short snort and slight smile as he shook his head. "Oh, before I forget," he said, reaching to his waist. "Kolden said to give you this." He extended his arm, a small, darksteel blade in his hand, the milky black metal reflecting the scant sunlight from its polished surface.

She took it, looking it up and down, feeling the sharpened edge of the blade. "Huh, here I was thinking that short asshole hated me."

"Ha!" Delvan laughed. "No, he's just like that. Kind of abrasive but shows that he cares in different ways. He made that, you know."

"Well, that's generous of him but, uh, why is he giving me this? What's he want in exchange? Thing's worth more than some jewels I've stolen."

"It's the blade that The Hunter used to, uh, well, you know. I certainly don't want anything to do with it. And I think that most of what I channeled to do, well, heal you I guess, came from that. Thought it was only appropriate that you have it. Sightly better than the other one you're carrying."

"Ah!" she pretended to gasp. "You *dare* insult my weaponry? I thought you knights were supposed to be all noble and shit?" He laughed again. When was the last time she'd not taken herself seriously and joked like that? She couldn't remember. "Well, tell him I said thanks, I guess."

*You're terrible at this,* said Masini.

"The last time I saw this," she said, turning the knife over in her hands, "it was glowing. What happened?"

"Not entirely sure," said Delvan with a shrug. "Kolden grabbed the smashed bits of the key as we were leaving, think he wanted to test it a bit more. But when we got to look at it in the daylight, it was black. Far as we can tell, it's solid inanite now. To say that he was disappointed would be an understatement, and he thinks the same thing happened to the blade."

"Weird," she said.

*Not really,* chirped Masini. *Pull all the 'energy' from the, uh, glowy rock and it turns black. Basically useless at that point, unless you're a Blue. Haven't I told you this?*

Desnia rubbed her eyes as she shook her head. *That would've been helpful to know. Ass,* she thought. As she looked back out at the carnage before her, she took another drink, feeling some more of the guilt peel away. She hated that this had happened, and she wondered if it could be justified by the good she'd done. As though devastation like this could ever be offset by good deeds. Having Delvan next to her seemed to help, for whatever reason. Or perhaps it was the wine?

*Better drink more, just to be sure,* she thought with another swig.

"So," said Delvan, "what're your plans now?"

Now she was the one who snorted. "Aside from getting drunk? Was thinking about hiking into the mountains to find and free an imprisoned god." Desnia turned and looked into his narrowed, inquisitive eyes staring at her between locks of brown hair. "Care to join?"

# Afterword

Thank you for taking the time to read this book. An immense amount of effort went into creating it, and after countless hours of planning, editing, and writing, I'm thrilled that it's made it into your hands. If you've enjoyed reading this epic tome, a review from you could be the catalyst that gets it into someone else's hands, and as an indie author I don't have the visibility that large publishing houses do. Help spread the word! Also, if you are looking for more updates on current or future works, or are looking for book recommendations, head to my website: lambertsbooks.com. Subscribe to my newsletter if you want to get periodic updates on the status of the series, or are looking for some sample chapters or sneak peeks.

This book is the first planned in a series, titled Borne by Blood—for reasons that will become clear in future installments. The inspiration, oddly enough, was seeing my breath mist in my car on a cold, winter's day. I had a long drive and no heat, and after a long, long Rube Goldberg effect, I ended up with this story. I truly hope that you enjoyed it enough to be interested in reading what the future has in store for the likes of Desnia, Delvan, and the rest of the crew. I can't wait to write it.

www.ingramcontent.com/pod-product-compliance
Lightning Source LLC
Chambersburg PA
CBHW022358110726

47903CB00004B/1043